Hopes and Dreams

Stuck on **AutoDrive**

Eric Davis

An AutoDrive book
AutoDrive LLC
Saint Paul, Minnesota
http://hopes-and-dreams.net

PUBLISHER'S CATALOGING-IN-PUBLICATION DATA
Davis, Eric,
        Hopes and Dreams: Stuck on AutoDrive / Eric Davis
            p.   cm.
    Summary: Inventor of self-driving car struggles with duty to prevent AutoDrive from harming others, through his dreams, friends, and decisions.
    ISBN 978-0-9796098-0-0
    1. Fiction - 21st century. 2. Ethics, Modern - Fiction. 3. Inventions - Fiction.
4. Dreams - Fiction. 5. Minnesota - Description and travel - Fiction. I. Title
PS3552.A958 H77 2007
813.54-dc22

First Edition
Printed in the United States of America.

For Marilee

all my hopes and dreams

Contents

Contents - continued

Anytime you're ready.

1

Beast Friends

I sit on the front steps of a house that isn't mine. I'm watching for guests. It is a quarter past dusk. The light above the front door floods the steps in light, making it difficult for me to see much more than silhouettes, and the fur of my mask does not help me to distinguish the guests from the passersby or the swaying bushes. Not that I'm complaining about the dimming light, because I really don't have to see at all to direct people verbally, and I like what evening breeze I feel.

Up the sidewalk a silhouette moves more than a few yards, and I decide it probably isn't a bush. Footsteps. The silhouette comes closer, and I decide definitely that it is not a bush because the silhouette is walking a silhouette dog. Bushes can't do this, I've checked. The silhouette is leading by a couple feet over the silhouette dog, but neither are any threat to the sound barrier, let alone any Olympic records. I'm doubting whether either will turn up this house's walkway due to what seems to be an overabundance of maturity.

They pass me, apparently not noticing a person wearing a gorilla outfit and sitting on the front steps of a house. Or perhaps considering the house, it's just par for the course. Two moments go by. A car pulls up. The inside light of the car shows this to be a woman I don't know but certainly young enough not to be weighed down by much maturity baggage at all.

She gets halfway up the walk when I become overwhelmed with how small her face is. Not her face exactly but her facial features. It's conceivable that her face was that small at birth. Could she have been born without facial features? "It's just a phase," the doctor must have said. "Just be happy that aside from no nose, eyes, or mouth, she's a perfectly healthy baby." When she walks, she seems to float, moving without a lot of character to her steps. When the silhouette and silhouette dog passed by, I felt the responsibility, the labor, and the companionship. In her walk I feel nothing. Maybe that has to do with my preoccupation with her miniature face.

She approaches. I grunt gorilla-like. No reaction. I say, "Please go around back to the cellar doors, everyone is downstairs," in my friendliest English-accented voice.

Some shrubbery moves quickly along the other side of the street and then darts across. Things are picking up. The shrubbery takes an attractive shape. It's a she. Congratulations, it's a girl! Wow! She's pretty and comfortable in just a T-shirt and jeans, and I start to feel goofy for being all dressed up. So I jump to my feet and wrists and start hopping about and bouncing off the little iron stair railings and up and down the stairs and I pick up the welcome mat and put it over my head and all the while grunting, oook-oooking, and snorting as loud as I can and I turn back to her and she's standing there just looking and smiling at me. And it causes me to stop. I catch my own surprise and straighten up. I set the mat, that had just been so thrilling, to my side. I say, "Oh, my name is Ricky. Can I be of some service?" I hope I can hear her through this thick head of mine.

"Yes," says she. "Is this Tom's house?"

"Say no more; nothing more needs to be said. People of your acquaintance should be in the lowest level of this very house. Its basement can be reached through that gate and a cellar door on its, uh, back side."

"This isn't a costume party, is it?" she asks cautiously with less of a smile.

I scratch my big gorilla head to think. It helps. "God, I hope not!" I exclaim with my hands on my face in mock concern. Her smile returns. She stands there smiling at me. A look of understanding splashes over her face. I've seen that look so rarely that I just sort of stand there too, appreciating the look.

After a while I realize I've been looking at her in a daze too long. I'm smiling inside my big old gorilla head, but the smile gets lost in the translation into gorilla face. I smile; it sneers. I start getting self-conscious and awkward about the mask. On one foot, the mask avoids my looking any less a primate than the mask itself, but on the other foot, I don't always click with people. I don't know if I am now. Is she falling for me or the mask? I can't imagine going through an entire relationship in a gorilla suit. "Dearly beloved, we gather this day to join this great ape and this woman in holy matrimony..." I grunt.

When I was a kid and I ran into a problem like this, I would just take off the mask. Experience has taught me that simple actions are rarely great solutions. If I end one problem by taking off the mask, maybe the problem and the solution will both end, and that's not what I want. Here is someone who seems genuinely interested in this big ape that is me. She came here to the party, but she seems comfortable standing outside with me instead... at least for the moment. Let's see how far we can go.

I crouch down and hop away a few yards with one hand's knuckles or another on the ground. I stop, look back over my shoulder, and scramble back almost sideways, stopping below her, then scrambling up and around the concrete front steps like they are the most fascinating jungle gym I have ever seen. This is acting, and this is direction. I sit still on the steps, hop up briefly, and sit again. This is a test. Will she follow my lead or go inside? I grunt.

"Would you like a banana?" she asks. An amnesiatic excitement overwhelms me. Three people are coming up the walk, but I don't care. Responsibility? Reshmonsibility! She's giving me an open, hopeful look, but I don't care about her either. I want banana. Banana! I hop up and down ook-ooking, grunting, flailing my arms about, and I consider searching her, when the group of three come up beside her, just to rattle my cage. I recognize two out of three of them. She notices them and says "hi." And Joe asks, "Who is that?" She turns back to me and asks, "Do you really want a banana?" She pulls her purse in front of her. I go ape. My plan is to take the banana and run wild with it. I will find a corner of one of these residential yards or climb a tree, and I will defend my banana with my tremendous ferocious gorilla roar. She unzips the purse, digs around, looks at my big ape eyes, and says, "I'm sorry, no banana."

I freeze in disappointment, but inside the suit I admire the improvisation. One of the three offers to check inside the house for a banana, and I perk up and then slump quickly down again with the realization that future bananas do not count. Promises can be as empty as a purse.

The three leave. My friend-without-a-name-that-I-know elects to stay without making the choice apparent. She looks familiar to me, but then everyone looks familiar to me. I'm sitting on the steps. She's standing in front of me, facing the house. It would be out of character for me to offer her a seat so soon after her banana tease. If I were next to her, I could pick nits. I feel like I'm running out of vine. And her eyes are driving me bananas.

The pain I feel, the hurt lingering in me, the sense of loss, is verbalized when I say, "Is there anything else you can offer me that you don't have?" Two people are walking up.

Eyes twinkling, she responds, "I don't know. What else do you want?"

I fall out of character by saying, "Possibilities." She gives me a pleasant smile.

Scratching through the fur at my wrist, I hear Will's voice say, "Hi Ricky. Who's your friend?" It's Will, the king of confidence, and his girlfriend Wendy, the double Ws.

I turn back to my friend, approach her from below, thump my chest, "Me Ricky," then my hairy finger shakes inches away from her, "Who you?"

"Hope," she says.

I turn to Will and Wendy, thumb pointing aside, and say, "Friend Hope." They say hello with introductions and say things like nice to meet you. Hope makes sure they know the way in and may have said, see you inside. I grunt.

We turn to each other, and I say, "So, what do you think of evolution?"

"I've never been able to picture it." At least that's what I think she says. What does she mean? Is this rejection because I called her my friend? Are the differences between us insurmountable?

"You, hairless ape, cannot see becoming monkey?"

"I have hair," she says, "here and there," without pointing. My heart floats in mid-air for half-a-second between us before jumping back into my chest at this purely sexual remark. I'm a primate. My big jaw drops a foot or two. And maybe more people are finding their way around back but forget about them. "I just can't see how evolution works," she finishes.

Oh! Teach me, she says. Okay! The first thing I think of is the sex part of evolution. Not yet! Quick, what else is there? Anybody?!? Thankfully my confusion is short lived. First, the understanding. "Sit?" I ask, looking from her to the concrete step beside me. With a slight hesitation she sits down, sets her purse down, and turns to me. "Mud. There's this big, shallow mud puddle with all sorts of fish in it, throwing mud all about. Mudslingers. Each summer it nearly dries up and becomes thick, saturated water. The fish die. Most of them anyway. But a few are just **weird** enough, abnormal enough, to survive. They're sick as can be out of their element. They take gulps of air, but they don't have lungs, so this kills most of them. But some of the weirdest survive. They don't exactly climb out of the water. At best, they're pushed. Their surviving offspring are better adapted to live on a little bit longer, long enough to reproduce and pass on their traits to their offspring." Not knowing what to say next, I try to pick nits from her hair.

She shoos me away with a hand. "So it's survival of the weirdest."

I go ape, hooting, grunting, jumping up and down, thumping my chest, jumping down the steps, tugging the newel, picking her up, setting her down, stepping carefully back up, and sitting down closer to her, practically on top of her. "Yes," I say quietly.

"I thought it was women having sex with beasts."

I fall back in a faint a little too hard. "Ow." My fur-fringed world is covered in sparkling stars.

She puts her hand on my chest, my big rubber and fur chest, and says, "I'm going to go inside. It's kind of cool out here. But I'd like to talk with you later. Will you be coming in soon?" It takes me a little while to piece together her words. It's tough to hear through this dense head.

I shake my head. As she gets up to go, I say, "It was nice talking with you, Hope."

She says, "It was nice talking with you, Ricky." She goes.

Kind of cool out here? If this suit was a rental, I'd never get my deposit back. I've been sweating like a fish and practically swimming in the suit. Sure, it was the performance of a lifetime, but now there is absolutely no way I could go inside. I'd fry. I'd like to talk with her face to face, but I'm sweaty, and I stink. That's not entirely out of character for the gorilla. I just don't want it to be part of my character.

I am sure there is no way to dry clean the monkey suit. If I called a cleaners, it would give them a good laugh. I'll have to sponge clean it when I get home. I have a change of clothes in my car. It is dark enough that I could change there. But I need a shower. Tom has two bathrooms in the house, but it's the main one that has the shower. That always goes over big at parties – offering to take over the bathroom for ten or 15 minutes. I don't know anybody that lives nearby well enough to ask to use their shower. I'd explain, "You see there's this girl who likes apes..."

I go to my car, grab my keys, shorts, and shirt. No towel. I'll need a towel, and oil checking rags don't count. Neither do fast food napkins. I'll have to ask Tom for a towel. Great. That will be fun. I put my stuff in a bag and lock the car. I go around back, drop the bag by the hose, and go inside. I grunt a little and say hi to people I'm trying to get by. Cy gives me a bear hug, which hopefully anybody noticing would understand is purely platonic. I'm getting too much attention from this bunch. Joe offers a banana, but since he's not Hope, I nod no and say I want towel. Someone offers me a paper towel. I grunt a negative grunt and move on. Will yells, "Let's go ape!" and everyone cheers. I spot Tom in the family room and ask if I can borrow a towel. Everyone's looking at me? What's the big deal? He says yeah and tells me where they are. I say thanks, and I continue to hunt and forage for the towel. Someone pokes me in the ribs. What is everybody's problem?!? I find the linen cabinet. I grab an off-white bath towel with a faded floral print and frayed edges. I go out the front way to avoid walking through conversations and becoming part of them. I shuffle my big ape feet back to the bag, then the car, take off the seven-piece ape ensemble, and go back to the hose. I'm thoroughly wet and hosed down and suddenly not alone. Hope is watching me from a couple feet away. I choke on some water.

"I'm sorry to startle you, but you never told me about natural selection," she says. "I notice that you've evolved."

I knock the water from my ear by thumping the other side of my head like a ketchup bottle. My head makes the hollow glass sound. It sounds like a thump. I grab the towel and am now thoroughly embarrassed for using an off-white, faded-floral-print, frayed-edge, bath towel. But hey, I don't think I impressed her with good looks in the first place. I'm not inherently sexy. I rely on mood lighting.

"Natural selection, huh? Every fall when the first snow hits, there are people who think you drive through snow and ice the same as driving on dry pavement. Maybe they are new to Minnesota. Maybe they just learned to drive over the summer and have never compensated for winter conditions. Maybe they just forgot during the few months of non-winter."

"Right," Hope says, "they drive too fast for the conditions. They think driving a truck or a sport-utility will keep them from skidding or running off the road..."

"Right. And those people will be first on the natural selection list when the snow flies. No one deserves to die, but that's natural selection. And evolution isn't just about nature, or if it is, everything we do is part of nature. Scientists think they are separate from nature, usually above nature, but I disagree. Nature will someday evolve past the scientist, just like the horse evolved into the carriage which evolved into the car. People that couldn't handle their horse were thrown. People that can't handle their car are thrown. Natural selection is keeping up with the world around us." I ruff up and mat down my hair with the towel.

"Okay, let's say you're a gorilla..." Hope starts.

"I'm a gorilla," I interrupt, cooperatively.

"Very good. Now, you're a gorilla and your habitat is pulled out from under you. No more trees. No more jungle. No more shade to keep you cool and give you everything you need to survive. You're saying taking away the jungle is part of evolution, part of nature. So it's natural to wipe out a species?" Hope asks.

I scrunch the towel under my chin. "Yes." I almost wince.

Hope does a walk around to indicate that I am out of my mind. "Yes?!? You're out of your–"

"Whoa... Even though death and extinction are natural parts of evolution, that doesn't mean it can't be fought and delayed. Doctors fight death. Firefighters fight death. Traffic cops fight death. Environmentalists fight death. People... trying to invent ways to make cars safer... fight death. In the end, death wins. In the meantime, life wins."

"I've never heard it put that way," Hope comments with a shiver.

"Neither have I," I say with the towel over my shoulders, standing in my shorts. "Do you want to go in?"

Hope smiles and leads the way. She tells me that I have a nice voice. We dodge and duck our way to the bathroom, where I go in, change, and comb my hair. My mirror image sticks his tongue out at me. Not knowing what else to do with the towel, I wrap it around my head like a cut-rate turban. And then I wonder what I'm doing. Hope seems nice, really nice. I didn't come here to meet someone. I didn't expect to see someone I didn't know, which reminds me that I haven't seen the woman with the small face. How do you start a relationship again?!? I guess I need to ask Hope about herself, even though I really found out all I needed to know when we were outside, except I forgot to look for a ring. I am so bad at this. Coming out, Hope smiles and pins my turban to keep it together. She's very encouraging. As she's looking at my turban, I check for a ring on her ring finger – none. Tom sees us together, grins, and interrupts a conversation to talk to us. Tom puts a hand on our shoulders, almost pushing us together, saying, "I told him to dress up. Dressing up as a gorilla was his idea."

I defend myself, "You mentioned a monkey suit..."

"I– I never– I meant a tuxedo. And I said you didn't, as in did not, need to wear a monkey suit."

"Okay, you're free to go," I tell Tom. "But I may want to ask you some further questions. Don't try to leave town."

"Not until next weekend. Remember friends are welcome..." he says looking back and forth between us. Don't rush me, Tom. I just met the woman. He seems surprised I don't take his bait to invite Hope. He stares at my turban. "You had to use the crummiest towel I have."

"That towel is molting," someone behind me observes.

"I didn't want to ruin your good towels."

"No, you wouldn't want to use my goods towels. Those are saved for special occasions like parties and guests... And now, how long do you intend to wear the worst towel I've got?"

"Are you asking me to trade up to a more upscale turban?"

"Leave it," Hope says, "I just got it pinned."

"Would you like something to drink?" I ask Hope.

Tom steps back into the host role and takes our drink orders. Hope and I find the couch in the family room.

Gene asks us, "So I heard you two were talking about evolution?"

"No," I lie. I am a very honest person, but that was not a question to answer honestly.

"Yes," Hope responds looking at me questioning.

"Everything is in the genetic code," Gene stands up to tell Hope while I roll my eyes. "It determines what you will have for breakfast and what TV show you'll watch." He starts pacing. "It is how you behave and what you know. It knows what you will do each day for your entire life. It is the history of your ancestors and your descendants. The genetic code stores the life of Christ!"

"Gene," Tom's voice calls, "I'd like to help you out. Which way did you come in?" Gene leaves.

Tom enters, carrying our drinks, "All right, who got Gene going?" We all point at Hope. Hope meekly raises her hand. Tom hands us our ginger ales, and says to Hope, "You are new here so perhaps you weren't properly warned." He eyes me peripherally. "But never, ever set Gene off. We have to watch him all the time. He's a genetic scientist. It's boring to be a genetic scientist. He used to always correct people when they attributed more to genetics than there actually is... silly things like behavior, or knowledge, or decision making... When people realized a clone of a cat will not behave the same as the original cat, the money dried up. People take pet behavior very seriously. Now he argues from the opposite perspective. Everything is genetic. That makes him all powerful and important... very not-boring."

Tom squats down, "I know this is difficult. It was for him," he says pointing at me. "But I grant you a license to lie. Think of Gene as the embodiment of every kidnapper, telemarketer, and extortionist. You can lie to him. Gene is seeing an economic psychiatrist, but it will take time..."

Gene returns, "That wasn't DNA, Tom! That was a jar of moldy mayonnaise."

"Oh, thanks for the analysis Gene. Sorry to trouble you," Tom says, getting up.

"Hey, look, a jukebox!" Hope exclaims, grabs my hand, and drags me across the room. "There's a lot of Melanie songs... do you think it would be okay for us to plug it in and see if it could work?" Hope asks. A sound system is already playing music.

"Let's find something to do that doesn't involve pressing people's buttons." I head us back to our drinks. Gene's gone.

Nadine has cornered Tom with a question. Nadine has the hiccups. Nadine always has the hiccups. It jostles her breasts. Her hiccups developed when she did. Her hiccups bloomed late. She turns to me. "Remember Edwards from high school? He was Mister King Vitamin?" Nadine asks. Nobody responds. She continues, "He took vitamins, ate health food, jogged, and worked out? Well, he got hit by a truck. It dragged him for a block. Anyone else would've been killed instantly. Not Edwards. He hung on for three days while doctors tried to save him. It was a slow agonizing death."

Dead silence.

Tom puts his arm around Nadine, walks her hiccuping to the hallway, saying, "Gee it was swell you could come to the party. Too bad you have to go so soon, what with being the life of the party and all."

Erix sits down on the floor nearest me, between a chair occupied by a purse and the coffee table. "I don't understand Stephanie," he reminds me.

"Don't worry about her," I reply.

"Her?"

"Yes, her." Erix leaves. "Rumor is that alcohol can kill brain cells," I tell Hope as I watch Erix go. Then I lean over to her, and while wiggling my finger toward the place where Erix had sat, I whisper, "Stephanie thinks she's a guy."

"Is she the one in the dining room?" Hope asks. I nod. "She's got a cute face."

"**I heard that!**" yells a voice from outside the room and over the music.

"Why grandma, what big ears you've got," I comment, then in a whisper, "No one ever seems to notice her ears, but they're very good." Hope nods.

Red stumbles in. "And how come their, no, there isn't any redheaded examples of primitive man, huh? And don't tell me it's because the fossil record just represents black and brown haired people 'cause I'm not buying it. And what about orangutans?"

"Red?"

"Huh?"

"We're done talking about evolution. Turn the page."

"Oh." Red stumbles out.

"There's a sort of insanity that's in orbit around you, isn't there?" Hope asks.

"You noticed? So, tell me about yourself..."

"What do you want to know?"

"Well, what do you do?"

She looks at me questioningly and then says, "In my job, the insanity orbits around me, with questions and odd behavior. I'm an elementary teacher. I told you that, didn't I?"

"No."

"Oh, I thought I did. I have a fourth grade class."

"So do you have summers off?"

"No, I teach summer school."

"Do you like it?"

"Some parts of it I really like. Some parts are just like other jobs. Some parts are horrendous."

Awkward silence.

Todd comes in and introduces himself, "Hi, you must be Hope!"

"Hi Tom, we've already met," Hope says with a hint of annoyance.

I interject, "Uh no, Hope, this is Todd, Tom's twin brother."

"Oh, I'm sorry Todd. It's nice to meet you. You... two, look a lot alike," Hope's smile is making up for her confusion. She's blushing. It's a nice blush.

Todd is smiling back too much. I guess I'm not the only one who likes her smile. He catches himself and tells her to enjoy herself. He grabs my ears, says, "Boeggity-boeggity-boeggity," and he leaves.

Hope laughs and asks, "What do you remember about fourth grade?"

"Well I had a crush on a girl. I had a crush on a girl in second grade, but I didn't talk to her. In fourth grade I talked to the girl. And I remember the class clown..."

"You weren't the class clown?"

"Ha," Cy laughs, coming into the room.

"Thanks, Cy. Cy, this is Hope. Hope, this is Cy, my previous girlfriend."

"Oh," Hope says, I read everything in the world into that oh. "We met. Hi."

Cy sits down by Hope. "He was never the class clown, more like the teacher's pet." Hope smiles a bit at that last part. I listen politely to what Cy has to say, while waiting to see if Cy is going to derail the few connections that Hope and I have.

"I'm a teacher so I know what teacher's pets are like."

"What grade?"

"Fourth."

"That sounds about right," Cy says in her high voice. Any smile Hope had vanishes. Hope waits for Cy. I figure Hope figures that Cy was either trying to insult me or Hope or both. I am impressed with Hope's class. She is not fighting back or going on the defensive. Like me, she is just waiting Cy out. "You really should take that towel off your head," she tells me.

"There wasn't anywhere else to put it."

"I can take care of it."

"That's okay. It can stay where it is."

She stands with a hand on her hip. "Well, have fun," Cy says and leaves.

"You too," Hope replies.

I apologize to Hope, "Sorry about that."

"Not a problem. So tell me, what else do you remember about fourth grade?"

Al and his tool belt sit down nearby to listen in.

"I remember my teacher. I remember learning about linking verbs: is, am, are, was, were, be, being, been, has, have, had, could, would, should, can, may, ought, might, shall, will. I learned the states in alphabetical order. I was pretty good at memorization. I learned about nutrition and the four food groups, but not like Edwards did. I learned to make up new words for existing songs. I learned to make up games. I learned that I was an expert at geography. I learned that I was good at math, but I wasn't fast because I checked over my work too many times."

Hope laughs, but when I look at her she has the most caring expression. "I know students like that in my classes. How were you at spelling?"

"What I've learned is that the process of studying for spelling tests and then moving on to new words reinforced my spelling errors. If I learned to spell a word the wrong way, it has generally stuck that way, unless the mistake is the sort computers catch. Let's see, I remember trading stickers with other kids. I remember an experiment with growing plants in the light and in the dark. I remember experiments involving fruit flies and experiments involving floating objects. I remember etching a picture into a copper sheet and fire drills and tornado drills and the cafeteria and small milk cartons and bicycle safety presentations and not to run in the halls and cramming my winter coat into a locker designed in a hot state and hockey and kick-ball and picture day and announcements and..." She's laughing at me. "You're laughing at me."

"No, it's just that you remember a lot!" she laughs.

"Yes, I do."

"What is your best memory of fourth grade?"

"The kidding around. The fun."

"So you liked school?"

"I liked the fourth grade."

Al says, "I didn't like the fourth grade so much as helping to figure out the projectors and fruit-fly counter computers. I became an expert in the fourth grade."

"I know plenty of teachers who could use that kind of help," Hope replies, while Erix sits back down on the floor nearby. "Hi, my name is Hope." Hope leans forward and watches Erix for a reply. "What's your name?"

"Erix."

"Hi Erix," she says with an encouraging smile. She must be great with kids.

"Hello."

I half-close my eyes and pat the air in front of me with my hand horizontal as a signal to let him be. Hope leans back. Al is about to say something but instead takes a drink.

"Where's the gorilla!" Joe slurs, spilling his beer as he looks around the room.

"The room is not a coaster," Al says.

"What?!?"

"You're spilling your beer, Joe."

"I heard there was a gorilla in here!"

"Last I saw him, he was outside." Joe leaves. "That was Joe, our resident drunk."

Will and Wendy come in with spoons, a deck of cards, pen and paper. "Who's up for a game of spoons?"

"Spoons?" Hope asks. "I haven't played spoons in a long time. I'm in."

"I'm in," I say.

Al raises his hand.

"Erix," Hope asks, "do you want to play?" Erix shakes his head no. Hope says, "My brothers used to play a similar game with me, only it was called knives." We all turn to look at her.

"You're kidding." She shakes her head, no, and picks up her cards. Oh, we're playing. There are five of us playing; there are four spoons. We keep passing cards around until someone gets four of a kind. That person takes a spoon; everyone tries to grab a spoon. The person that doesn't get the spoon loses. The loser is either out right away, and a spoon gets taken away, or they are out once the player has lost six times, spelling S-P-O-O-N-S. I don't know which way we're playing, but it doesn't matter... the cards are coming around. I start to collect fours, start passing cards around, take a deep breath, and something tells me Wendy is collecting fours. I start discarding fours. They won't get to her because she's on the other side of the discard pile. I start collecting tens. Nothing, nothing, nothing. I get my second ten when a spoon disappears. I grab the third one. Everyone gets a spoon but Al that time. He checks his tool belt for a spoon. Will had four of a kind. Wendy asks if anyone was collecting fours, and I tell her that I had discarded two of them. Wendy marks Al down on the tablet, and we keep playing. Ruth joins in the middle. Ultimately Hope wins, grabbing the last spoon before Will could.

I knock my turban sideways and decide it's time to get rid of it. I excuse myself and go into the bathroom. I remove the turban. It leaves me with – as I feared – turban hair. I distinctly remember combing my hair before turbanizing it. I wet down my hair again and dry it with the same towel. Hope does a double take when she sees me, not expecting that I would be back without my turban.

"I had... gasp... turban hair!"

"Will it be all right?" Hope asks with mock concern. I nod.

We start building a house of cards. We learn how susceptible card houses are to the slightest breeze of people moving nearby. Our buildings get taller. People have stopped moving by.

The family room is getting lighter. I look around. Hope and I go to the window, each grab a curtain, and tug it open. Sunrise, right before our eyes! A chorus of groans and complaints cry out from the sleeping and the sleepless around us. "Hey!" "Shut that!" "You two are quite a pair."

We look at each other's eyes. Then lips. I kiss her with every lip on my face. She kisses back with just as many lips. The beings around us continue to moan and wail and cry out at the light like dying vampires until we drop the curtains to better hold each other. If we were any closer we'd be on the other side or in back of each other or something. I don't know; I don't care. It's a love lock. She feels sensuous in my arms, like she's reading the encyclopedia of kisses and wants to try them all out on me. We both stop to catch our breath. The house of cards topples. I look at her for reassurance that this won't be the end. We go outside, stopping on the way for me to put two rubber eggs in the refrigerator. Yes, it's bright. Morning has broken its light all over. It'll take all day to clean the light up.

"When will I see you again?" I ask.

"What are your plans for today?"

"What's today?"

"Saturday. Do you have to return the monkey suit?"

"No, I own it. It was either that or a stereo, but nobody ever fell in love over a stereo."

Hope seems surprised, "Maybe people have fallen in love over a stereo."

"Maybe they have. I don't think I have any plans."

Looking at the front steps, she says, "Let's go to the zoo."

"Now? I don't think they're open yet. The animals are groggy first thing in the morning. They shuffle around in their slippers, sipping coffee, checking over the papers, and confirming their schedules for the day. Never, ever call them this early in the morning..."

"No, in a few hours."

"Sure you could call them in a few hours..."

"No, let's go in a few hours."

"Okay. Can you drive? My car is filled with equipment."

Hope agrees. "What sort of equipment is in your car?"

I lead her to my car. "I'm a mechanical engineer for a company called Flight Control, working on something called AutoDrive." Hope listens, so I continue. "The purpose of AutoDrive is that it drives the car for you. Remember, uh, last night... when I talked about fighting death by doing things like making cars safer? Well, that's part of my work on AutoDrive – enabling the car to get its passengers to their destination safely. All of what you see taking up the passenger seat and the back seat (other than the ape costume) are 18 different types of electric eye sensors (nine working, seven not, and two that aren't hooked up). Then there are four more proximity sensors around the car, like this one... sound related sensors, a signal sensor, motion sensors, lasers, an impact-resistant computer, and two truck-sized batteries."

Hope yawns and stretches, "Excuse me. Does it work?"

"This isn't AutoDrive, just components. But no, most of this doesn't work. That's what testing is all about." We stare at it, as if it'll do something.

"Do you have some paper and a pencil?" she asks. We trade information and set up a time that she'll pick me up. Hope and I kiss good-bye, and she goes to her car. I climb into my car, start it after a couple tries, and drive back to my apartment. I'm feeling very good and very tired. I stop by a market for French bread, cheese, salami, grapes, and sparkling grape juice.

2

The Zoos

Hope will be picking me up at 11:30. It's now 7:20. That gives me three and a half hours to rest and half an hour to shower and get ready. Neighbors permitting. I pull up to my apartment building, hoping that my building is still asleep. But no, there are already some stups on the stoop. In the hallway are hallway trolls, little rugrats, accidental children told to go pester the neighbors. My door is littered with little taped-up notes from the landlady to "all the residents" about this or that complaint, ordinance, or inspection, as if they apply to the literate. My landlady loves taping notes to all the doors and challenges herself to come up with new ones. If it weren't for adhesive tape, she would be pounding nails into everyone's doors.

My apartment is below a bowling alley. League nights are Wednesdays and Saturdays. The proprietors and customers of this bowling alley in the apartment above me are all elephants. Not that you'd know it by looking at them. Only someone living below them learns their true nature. And bowling is their ordinary behavior. What is really peculiar is that on occasion they practice their belly flops on the floor. The thud always leaves me startled and perplexed, and it leaves another ceiling fixture on the floor. One shoe drops. When will the other?

My neighbors next door are not nearly as interesting. They have not yet bred, which may or may not be the cause or result of their constant bickering, clunking, and screaming obscenities at each other. They have mastered the professional level of obscenity screaming that can only be found in the apartment bowels of this country. The bile names that they use for each other are broken into syllables that sandwich unrelated swear words in the middle of the word to poison what had already been foul language. The unwanted urchins in the hall practice the new vocabulary on each other. Precious is not the word.

Below my apartment, the musicians are mostly quiet, until they begin rehearsing which is usually only on Thursday and Friday nights. I hate to tell them that they need more practice, but even though I am no glutton for punishment, they need more practice. They seem to have mistaken music for the tuning of instruments. Also, songs need endings. It's like a Marx Brothers routine: Chico plays the piano in an endless tune. Groucho says, "If you find a melody, hop on. Chico says, "I can't think of the ending." Groucho says, "That's funny, I can't think of anything else." I would give them an Introduction To Music textbook, but I don't want to encourage them.

Like bacteria in one of Lefty's petri dishes, an apartment building is a culture, a community. A sick, twisted, festering community. In any city on any evening news, you will hear of violence in or around an apartment building. Anyone wondering how such things could happen should move into a low-rent apartment building for a month. It won't take a month.

My roommate's name is Cameron Raymond. He's an artist. Most people call him Cam. I call him Ray. I don't see him as I come in. I drop off the suit in my bedroom, head for the bathroom, juice from the kitchen, then back to my bedroom. Ray calls out, "The neighbors never slept last night."

"Me neither. Did you?"

"Barely."

"I met someone... a very nice woman."

He calls out, "Yeah?"

"Yeah." That's all we need to say. It's guy talk.

With my airport surplus ground crew ear protectors on, I start reading a book called Safari Of The Mind. It's about a boy who thinks abstractly about everything. He says there is more than one truth to everything. Most people, the boy tells us, see the black and the white, but we don't seem to notice the gray. We miss the fine details, he claims, because either our personalities block us from seeing things that aren't our fascination or aren't glaring in obviousness. The boy sees the mind like an empty attic and life like a landscape. Some people pick up all the big rocks they can carry from the landscape and fill the attic with them. Some people only select the limestone and wonder why rocks are always crumbly. This boy only selects the rocks that will be useful to him.

Having gotten ready early, I read until Ray kicks my feet to show me that Hope is here.

"Hey, remember me?" she asks. I show her around briefly, but most of the time we look at the Glory Girl comic book that Ray is illustrating in the living room. He shows us some of the fine lines that have jolts in them due to the bad vibrations sent down from the elephant herd upstairs. Mr. Richter would be proud.

The car Hope is driving is a raspberry red two-door, convertible sports car. We shoo the rugrats away from it. The plush interior is littered with balled-up nylons, thongs, a basketball, condoms, and pictures of a very womanly woman in a small tight red dress. Holding one up, Hope says, "This is Nicole, my sometimes roommate. This is her car. Mine isn't running well." In another picture she's wearing a shirt that says, Goof Proof. One must've gotten through. I ask Hope what is wrong with her car. "I don't know," she starts up, "I spent nearly half a paycheck on it, but now it's acting up again." We talk it over. I translate some of the things the mechanics told her the last time it was being repaired. She puts what I'm saying together with what her car's behavior.

I ask, "Do you ever find yourself describing something in several different ways for the kids at school to get it?"

"All the time. My explanations evolve," she says with emphasis on the last word.

I stare at her, but she's watching the road ahead and her side mirror. So I keep going. "That's kind of what I've got to do. One of the office-types will ask me a question; I answer it until they get it."

"The office-types don't have engineering degrees, do they?"

"Right. They don't. But they wind up having to explain things to people, outside Flight Control, who have engineering degrees. And because of the technical nature of the information, the office-types get confused and pout and stamp their feet and don't pay attention, just like kids in your classes."

Hope pulls into a parking spot in the zoo's giraffe lot and turns to softly say, "The children in my class are better behaved."

As we get out, a guy whistles at Hope. She acknowledges it by saying, "This must be the zoo." Hope tells the people at the gate that she's thinking of setting all the animals free.

A woman in uniform steps away, never taking her eyes off Hope, and talks in her walkie-talkie, "Alpha, sigma, gamma-baker, foxtrot. Sparrows fly at midday. Code blue. Over."

As we are going in, a guy with another walkie-talkie says, "Huh?"

A girl is selling flowers from a cart. I buy Hope a mixed bouquet. She takes it, gets out some money, buys another bouquet, and gives it to me. We both smell them and head toward the ape house. On the way, she gives an old lady a flower. I give two flowers to a couple. Now we are giving away flowers left and right.

Behind the staring faces, the guardrail, and the smudged Plexiglas, the monkeys and apes live in their own little world, emphasis on the word little. I set down the picnic basket and the rest of my bouquet. The apes stare. There is a word for this; a gongoozler is someone who stares for hours. We watch the apes watching us. We also listen to many children's questions answered without thought or information. Hope almost corrects one parent and restrains herself. I stare at one of the apes with intense curiosity. He matches my stare with a counter-stare.

"A friend of mine is an out of work actor," I tell Hope and anyone in earshot, "as so many actors are. I do what I can for my friend, helping him to find jobs between acting work. I was going through the want ads for him. I ran through the whole alphabet and then came to a job. It said, 'zoo worker, apply in person,' and gave the address. I told my friend about it. I said, 'What's the worst they could have you do? Maybe you'd have to clean up after the animals.' He didn't think he'd apply, but he did. When they found out he was an actor, they gave him the job. They gave him a monkey suit, you know a gorilla costume." Out of the corner of my eye I notice Hope is nodding. The Plexiglas in front of me shows a small crowd forming around us.

"So they show him to his cage and tell him to act like an ape. At first he just sits there," I explain, still staring at the ape that is just sitting in front of us. "Some people come along. He grunts. The people smile. He swings his arms. And they like it.

"The next day he's jumping up and down. He's ook-ooking like there's no tomorrow. He picks up... stuff from the cement and throws it all around.

"By the next week he's jumping up on the bars and off, swinging on the tire swing, and hanging from one hand.

"By the next week, he's doing moves no gymnast would do, swinging and leaping and swinging all around the cage.

"Until one day when he's swinging very high up. And he swings up and over the side of the cage... into the lion's cage next door! The lion trots toward him. My friend runs away screaming for help. The lion tears after him! The lion pounces! My friend screams! And the lion says, 'Be quiet. Do you want us all to lose our jobs?'"

Hope laughs and so do many of the onlookers.

"What is she thinking?" A little girl is looking up at me and pointing up at a large, sitting, brooding gorilla that looked over twice before.

"You can never be sure," I answer carefully, looking from her to the large ape, "what someone else is thinking. But I think the gorilla is thinking about her," I don't know if it is a her, I'm following the kid's lead, "her possibilities."

The kid's entire face is working seriously to come up with a follow-up question. I help her out by adding, "There are many things she could do and many things she has already done." I look back at the great ape. "She doesn't have to do anything. Someone will feed her, clean up after her, and protect her no matter what she does. But there is more to life than those things. I'm guessing that she is either remembering something that she has done that was interesting to her, or she's thinking of something that she could do that might be interesting. But all we know is that she's thinking."

The girl continues to look intently at the brooding gorilla. I pick up my stuff, say good-bye, and we walk off. As we pass by the next cage, I tell Hope, "This used to be the lion cage."

I dream the strangest dreams.

I wake up on a hillside under a vast oak tree that has been standing here apparently for generations. Songbirds sing and skitter about on limbs that reach out across the sky. From these huge arms split great branches, which divide in different places into solid supporting branches that separate into your basic nest building branches and split again several times more and ultimately into green leaf-holding tendrils that sprout in every direction and fan out with leaves. Someday, far from now, I will be under this tree again, and these leaf holders will become branches supporting other branches supporting more leaf holders.

"Everything is all right," a reassuring voice says to me. I'm startled anyway. "Hi there, Sleepyhead," Hope says. She's sitting by me and running her fingers lightly through my hair. The light flickers all about her, dashing between the leaves, and through them, leaving Hope sparkling in white and yellow light. Her dimples are her Smiling School Diploma framing her smile. This vibrant, beautiful, clever woman has been just sitting here while I napped. I must have fallen asleep after our picnic lunch. I sit up and shake her shoulder.

"Aren't you tired?"

"Not really, but I guess you were."

"I'm sorry. That was rude of me to fall asleep on you."

"Don't be. It's okay. I thought it was nice. You slept very peacefully. But I've been wondering, are you always this relaxed when you first meet someone? Meeting your friends, seeing your apartment, seeing you sleep..."

"I don't snore, do I?"

"No, at least you didn't. You were extremely quiet. First time someone has fallen asleep on a date with me."

"I'm–"

"It's okay. It's just different..."

"Different good or different bad?"

"We'll see." We gather our things, shake off the blanket, and head out of the zoo.

On the way I give the plastic bouquet wrappers back to the girl at the cart, saying, "Here. Have these refilled." I once saw a short movie where Curly Howard returned a banana peel to have it refilled.

Hope and I kiss when she drops me off at my apartment, and we set it up that she's going to call me tomorrow. My apartment building is audibly vacant other than a TV across the hall. After taking care of some things, I lie down in bed. Hope and I have twice gotten along, and she has repeatedly encouraged me to do things that come naturally to me but are maybe a few steps away from normal behavior. It's good. I wonder what she thinks of me. And I wonder what the band is doing, starting up on a Saturday afternoon.

I guess all the great musicians were discovered in apartment buildings. One tenant says to another, "That was you?!? Practicing?!? You don't need any practice; you need to share your masterpieces with the world. Anything else would be selfish. I only wish you had played louder sooner so that I could have heard you through the walls and the floor between our apartments. Could I produce your first three albums?" This is the conversation I imagine as I wake up to the noise from downstairs.

Just like a hundred times before, I review my options to improve my music world. Here they are in no particular order:

Plan A. I could pound on the floor. That is the novice level of apartment dwelling. You pound. They pound back. You pound. They pound back. Jungle relations. Points are earned for loudest bang and latest bang. No points are awarded for original banging; that could be confused with musical accompaniment. The banging can be done with feet or fists or any solid blunt household object. Points are deducted for breaking your own stuff while trying to make your point. Pounding is an attention getting device. It is a way of saying, "I'm here. You're bugging me. Stop your life, so I can get on with mine." But pounding has never cleared up anything. If someone doesn't get the fact that there is someone occupying the apartment above them, pounding isn't going to explain it to them or make them care. I imagine a reaction from below like, "Gee, they're still working on the roof?!?" In this case, reacting to music, you could pound along just slightly off from the beat. But that could just illustrate that you have no rhythm. If you try pounding, just remember that you wouldn't be having this problem if the walls and floors weren't paper thin and going through them will open up a whole new set of problems.

Plan N. I could leave a note on the neighbor's door. The landlady's note is currently sitting on the kitchen table, unread. Some tenants don't take their notes down, so they are door decorations. Colored paper is very festive. Many apartment dwellers have trouble reading the word literate. Ray once wrote a note to the people downstairs that was actually a series of notes because it was a song, with lyrics and music, to ask the musicians to keep it down. It is lying around somewhere in the living room, unfinished.

Plan T. I could go down there and talk with them. That is the civilized approach. People, who don't live in apartments buildings like this one, believe we live in a civilized country. A simple knock on the door or a ring of a buzzer will not start things off. If it did, there wouldn't be a noise problem. I'd have to pound on the door to be heard. See plan A for a refresher on the pounding issues. When... no, if the door is answered, you think you are going to yell a civilized conversation over the noise. This is their home... and their jamming studio and their recording studio and their after-gig landing pad. Who are you to tell them what to do in their home? Talking with them will only introduce yourself to them as someone else who wants to tell them how to live. Talking with them won't work, unless you are looking for a specific consideration. Specific consideration would be asking them to keep it down during a certain time for a specific reason, like 7:30 in the morning because that's when I like to read my breakfast cereal box.

Plan L. I could tell my landlady about it to have her resolve the situation. She would leave notes on all the apartment doors announcing a general noise problem and how people should work together to resolve such problems. I would tell her it's still a problem after the vague notice that went on everyone's door. She would generate a nearly identical notice, changing the date and adding a note that if this problem persists, an all apartment meeting would be held. My neighbors work all hours of the day and night, sometimes multiple jobs. They will not drop everything for an apartment meeting nor would it accomplish anything, see plan T. Meanwhile Ray would look at the notes on our door and try not to make so much noise sharpening his pencils.

Plan M. I could move. That's always a possibility. Yet like many apartment dwellers, I hope my next move will be into a house. That's what I'm working toward.

Ray comes home. He takes the noise problem lightly. We hardly talk about it. I look at my alarm clock, which tells me it is 7:21pm. "Hey Ray," I shout from my room, "do you want some spaghetti?"

"You said spaghetti? I'm about to go out again," he says from my doorway.

"I can make it now."

"Sure," he says, tossing his shirt into his room. His room is usually a dump, but that doesn't bother me because he usually keeps his door at least partly closed, and I've hardly ever had to go in there. The rest of the apartment he keeps fairly neat, except for his studio. I fill a pan with water, seconds before he starts his shower. I light the oven and a stove burner with the same match. The pan of water goes on the burner.

The studio takes up almost half the living room. Stiff brown burlap covers the floor and is mottled with clay, silver drops of solder, edges of paint, and drops of paint. Two crates support large bronze pieces of a statue, partly covered with and cutting through a sheet. A drafting table and a photographer's floodlight are in front of the window in the corner. The floodlight kept getting tipped and narrowly caught anywhere else. Behind the table and the light, an easel is draped in jungle-print fabric. The adjacent wall of the corner has a king-sized black flat sheet thumb-tacked to the wall as a backdrop. It's been there awhile and has built up some dust. A light table sits on the drafting table along with negatives, positives, paints, pens, brushes, a soldering iron, chisels, clay in plastic bags, a sure-enough Barlow knife, scraps of sheet metal, nuts, a mannequin's right hand and arm, half a ping-pong ball, some clay figures, a shoe box, the dashboard of a 1964 Wild Stallion with steering wheel, a stack of Glory Girl comic books, a small city made of kid's interlocking plastic construction blocks, some dried clay, a zoom lens, a coil of solder, the zoom lens protective case and lens cap, half of the radio from a 1964 Wild Stallion, a clay covered toothbrush, and a polishing cloth.

I place several pieces of bread on a cookie sheet. Lightly butter the bread. Generously shake garlic powder on the bread and put the cookie sheet into the oven at 350 degrees for 12 minutes. Spaghetti sauce is poured into a pan and put on another burner to simmer, with a lid on it. I add extra basil to the spaghetti sauce. Spaghetti cooks for about ten minutes in boiling water, but I don't wait for the water to boil. I get out plates, utensils, and drinks. Everything goes on the counter. The mail is on the table.

The mail teaches me that if you are going to give to a charitable organization, you need to do so as anonymously as possible, so that you don't get on another mailing list. There are cards and letters from some friends. Dan sent a card saying he will be in town next weekend. He also says I still owe him money, which is not true. I stir the noodles. I check the garlic bread and turn the pan around. I flip through the most recent Beach Magazine. It is a visual magazine with all the depth of a sand bar, the way magazines are meant to be. A face full of shaving cream asks if it is ready. I give him five minutes. I get things ready. Ray continues to get ready between asking questions.

"How was the picnic?" he says pointing to the picnic basket on the floor that hasn't been swiped by some smarter-than-average bear.

"Great."

"Where did you two kids go?"

"The zoo."

Ray nods his head like a well-shaken bobble head, while stuffing his shaved face with spaghetti and garlic toast. "And?"

"And, that's it."

"Are we seeing her again?"

"I plan to. She has to call me tomorrow."

"Tomorrow? That's a silly name for her to call you. Did you think that one up or did she?"

"She did."

"I see, I see," he says knowingly and thoughtfully. I think he is faking both. "So you're staying home tonight to, what, wait for her phone call, Tomorrow?"

"Yes."

"And somewhere tonight this excellent woman will be swept away by someone else..."

"I'm safe as long as it's not another gorilla." I leave Ray to ponder that, taking my meal to the couch. In front of me is my entertainment center. It's a bookcase full of board games, cards, poker chips, things like that. Oddly enough it has proved fairly entertaining when people are over. We've got a TV, near the door. It's a little black and white set that is a pretty good doorstop when we have to haul things in or out of the apartment.

Ray comes in with his ice water. "I'm going to some art exhibits. Do you want to come with?"

I decline. Ray takes off. I read letters, think about my replies as I do the dishes, and attempt to write two replies. I go to sleep a few minutes after ten without even picking up the book I'm reading.

The phone rings. I switch on a light. My alarm clock yawns 2:45ish and stretches its minute hand straight out. Is Hope calling? Technically, it is tomorrow.

"Hello?"

"This is Operator Olivia with a collect call from Aimee Vespucci. Will you accept the charges?" I sit up.

"Yes! Hi Aimee!"

"Hi Ricky. How's Minnesota?" A pause. "Is it cold there?"

"Minnesota's just fine. No, it isn't cold, because it's construction season, but that just means winter is right around the corner."

"Yeah, I guess there wouldn't be any snow there now, would there?"

"Only in my freezer. It gets loaded up with frost every couple months. Are you still in San Francisco?"

"No, I left Drake and came here to L.A." Think quickly: she's in Los Angeles, it's 2-no-12:47am there. It's been two years since I've heard from her and about a year and a half since she left Chicago. She doesn't sound good. How can I help her without insulting her? She sniffs, "I really like hearing the sound of your voice."

"Aimee? You know a lot of people here and in Chicago miss you and have been thinking about you. I miss you. Will has asked about you. Dan and Cathy have talked about you."

"I'm sure they have."

"Uh, they ran into some problems in New York, they were trying to get to the other side of their lake, Lake Atlantic or something, and I sent them plane tickets back to Chicago a few months ago."

"What happened to them?" she asks.

"I promised not to tell anyone. Just as–" She laughs. "Just like I wouldn't tell anyone anything you wanted to keep between us."

"I don't care what anybody knows about me."

"How are you?" I ask.

A short laugh. Cars are going by. She's at a pay phone on the street after midnight in Los Angeles. "I'm– "

I wait a moment. "I love you, Aimee. You can always count on me. I'm your friend." Now she's crying. She cries for several minutes. Aimee was one of my friends when I was growing up. Her family fell apart during high school. My friends and I provided her with some stability. She's breathing softly. I am so glad she called now instead of during one of the neighbor's drum solos. "I could have a ticket to Chicago or here to Pigs Eye waiting for you in your name at LAX, if you want. My apartment is your apartment."

"You're– you're so naive."

"Any hospital, fire station, police station, or phone book can direct you to shelters. There are shelters for homeless or battered women."

"How did– " and the line goes dead. I sit up for about half an hour, thinking, wondering, if there was any more I could have done. I could have picked a Los Angeles zip code and told her she'd have a package there in a week, but I'm only thinking of that now, after she's hung up. I write a note to myself in my address book under her name that she called. There comes a time when you are trying to help someone that you are left with nothing but worrying and tormenting. That's where I pull over. Worrying and tormenting never did anyone any good.

I read a bit more in my Safari Of The Mind book, about how people are the sum of their experiences. To understand yourself, the author says, you have to think of your history, what you have been through. If something bothers you, you have to understand your experiences with that something or that type of thing to know why it bothers you. To understand others, you have to put yourself in their context, their experiences and environment. That's where I fall asleep.

3

Kelly and Hope's Friends

I slept in. Apparently the other tenants let me. Sunday mornings tend to be the quietest of the non-working, waking hours. People are more likely to be at church or thinking religious thoughts or watching religious programming. Hangovers prefer quiet. Fewer Sunday nights or Mondays have gigs to prepare for. People are not speaking to one another because of what happened Saturday night, which was a repeat of Friday night, but such behavior is inexcusable two nights in a row! The volatile couples are maintaining separate zones of influence and have not yet crossed over into their apartment's neutral zone. The newspaper takes longer to read. Some people have not yet come home. The rugrats have snuck off. Spending time around the people zoo has made people think about going to the animal one. And others are sleeping too.

It's another sunny day. A college girl is tanning outside my window. I can't tell who it is because that's not the way she's facing. I eat breakfast while supervising Ray's work on a bronze statue. He's been working on it for nearly a year now. It's a commissioned work. The statue is called Lactating Woman. When all the pieces are put together, it will be a life-sized, sitting, pregnant nude, which is also a fountain. One hand cups a breast. Water comes out the nipple and drains into the palm. The nipple will be a bit nozzle-like, but that can't be helped. What I have seen, from the drawings and the pieces, is magnificent. I hope the end results at least match our expectations. I encourage Ray every chance I get about it. "How's she doing?"

"Morning. She's doing all right. I am having trouble imagining her seamless. Any adjustment to line-up two pieces seems to throw off the next seam."

"Just think Statue of Liberty. You can do it."

"Ha. I don't think Kelly is going to be any Statue of Liberty." Yet he's looking at the pieces with more of an admiring squint. Making use of the studio light, the copper-colored pieces shine at the light's reflection and everywhere else she glows like lava at night. He opens the curtains to add additional sparkles. She is almost too bright to look at. Ray calls her Kelly because he expects her to be green later in life. A few months ago we talked about sealing her in a plastic coating to prevent the copper in the alloy from oxidizing, leaving only the nipple nozzle and the drain exposed. We talked about the possibilities, but did not come to any conclusions.

I eat cereal out of a bowl with my fingers. No milk. No spoon. In fact, I don't always use a bowl. I am certain this is the way primitive man ate his cereal. Ray doesn't mind, and Kelly has her own issues. Ray is having a banana, just like his very distorted bronze reflection. "Hey, at the gallery, Art showed me an ad in the university paper for 30 paid research subjects. It's funded by the university and Poppen Pharmaceuticals. I'm going to look into it. I would bring you with, but they only want herbivores."

I hold out a handful of cereal to illustrate its meatlessness. He rejects it with a hand. "Ray, read the liability waivers and ask questions before deciding if it is worth the money." Animal testing is no longer in vogue. Animals get nervous and flunk their tests. People testing is still very stylish. "Okay?"

"Sure, Dad," he says, making me wonder if I could possibly be his father. I am not. "While you were asleep, your girlfriend called asking for Tomorrow. I told her Tomorrow never comes. And we need more bananas."

"Are you kidding?"

"No, we're completely out of them. It's almost a banana shortage... a banana crisis."

"Are you kidding about the phone call," I specify, spotting one spotted banana left.

"About the phone call? Yeah, I'm kidding about that. Get a grip. Of course I'm kidding about that."

After a few minutes of just munching on cereal, I start pointing out smudges on the bronze pieces. I point out both types of smudges: real and imaginary. I do this only until he starts to get suspicious. Then I abruptly stop and look at my mail and I try to write letters again. I try to write letters, but I am not the best letter writer. So I put away the picnic basket and blanket. I sponge the gorilla suit and hang it up to dry. I clean my room, somewhat. I could: do laundry, go grocery shopping, change the oil in my car, or even wash it – the car, not the oil – but I'm not about to leave the apartment. My phone is stationary.

So, checking off my list, that leaves getting on Ray's nerves as the only thing left. The problem is Ray is easy going. He is so easy going that alcohol makes him tense. It has to make him tense, because he couldn't be any more relaxed. He is so relaxed that I can't always tell if he is awake or asleep. To really get on his nerves, I would have to put forth a herculean effort. Not herculean, maybe a Peter Lorrean effort. "He makes me laugh, really and truly he does, heh-heh," Peter Lorre would say. What really annoying thing could I do that the neighbors haven't already tried?!? I am about to plug in the TV, when the phone rings. Ray yells, "I'll get it," but he doesn't move. I dive for the phone in my room, kicking my door shut on the way.

"Hi," she says. It's Hope!

"Is it Hope?" Ray calls from the other side of the door.

"Yes," I yell covering the mouthpiece. Then, "Hi Hope. I've been kind of waiting for your call."

"Well, I've been kind of waiting to call you. Would it be all right if I put you on speaker?"

"Sure," I say without thinking.

"Some of my friends are here. They'd like to get to know you too." They say hello. I say hello back even though I don't know who they are. "That was Becky and Faith. Nicole is here too, but she's asleep." I whisper hello. "You don't need to whisper. What have you been doing?"

"Reading some. Cleaning some."

"Would it be okay if we ask you some questions?"

What kind of questions? Am I going to say no? "Yes."

One of them asks my religion. It wasn't Hope.

I lie back on my bed, stare up at the ceiling, and say, "I'll answer this as best as I can. For me this is not a multiple choice question or a fill-in-the-blank question. Asking someone's religion is like asking your political party. Most people don't agree with everything their religion or their political party says or does. They try to just think about the ways they agree with their group and ways they disagree with other groups. They make generalizations. Generalizations never seem to fit me. It's the way I see things. I probably believe in the same things everyone else does, but I look at things from a different perspective. I don't want to be labeled with a label that misrepresents me. My religion is part of my core beliefs. It helps me make decisions without even thinking because I know my beliefs and my priorities. And I believe that one's beliefs are very personal, very individual, and are changing with you throughout your life." Silence. "All my answers are going to be at least that long." They laugh. "How did I do?"

"Pretty good," Hope says. "You messed up all our follow-up questions."

"Ask him how tall he is." "You ask." "How tall are you?"

"This'll be another long answer. Six-one. I'm tall for my height."

"What is your favorite color?"

"Blue-no-yellow... actually, it's midnight blue."

"Are you the marrying type?"

Silence. I'm not going to show all my cards am I? "We'll see."

More silence. Something muffled. "Tell us about your girlfriends."

"Becky!"

"What about them?"

"Are you seeing anybody now?"

"Only Hope. Now you're talking about girlfriends, not friends who are girls, right?"

"Right."

"Only Hope," I confirm.

"Hope says you're really funny. Tell us a joke," Faith says.

The double-edged sword: it is a compliment to be introduced as being funny and the expectations are now raised – the proverbial funny bar has been raised. Will the humor meet the expectations? Unless you are ready to be hysterically funny and you aren't somewhere like a funeral, it is best to lob a lightweight pun or riddle. Then maybe you tell a joke, maybe you don't. "I'm not sure if I know any jokes, but for the past few months I've been taking some classes at Pilot Error."

"The airport?"

"Yeah. I've been taking skydiving classes every weekend. And maybe this is a joke, but do you know what the hardest thing about skydiving is?"

"No. What?"

"The ground."

Groans from the other end of the phone. I wait a few seconds and then go on. "In the classes the instructor has emphasized repeatedly some important procedures. She told us that after we jump, pull the main chute cord. If that doesn't work, pull the reserve chute cord. And a truck will be down below to pick us up. So last weekend was the jump. As we takeoff, the instructor reminds us that after we jump we should pull the main chute cord. If that doesn't work, use the reserve chute by pulling the reserve chute cord. And a truck will meet us to pick us up. So I jumped. Well, actually I was pushed. But I jumped. I pulled the main chute cord. Nothing happened. I pulled the reserve chute cord. Nothing happened! So I thought, 'You know? That truck probably isn't going to be down there, either!'"

They laugh. After a pause, I say, "So I'm falling, hopelessly, helplessly to Earth and pulling at the cords. At 500 feet, I meet a guy coming up. I shout, 'Do you know anything about parachutes?'" I swallow. "'No,' he shouts back. 'Do you know anything about gas ovens?'" More laughs. "Luckily the ground broke my fall," I concluded.

"That's funny."

"I can never remember jokes. How do you do it?"

"I have a good memory. And I personalize a joke. I change it so that it is me."

"Wow. Deep."

"No. When I re-tell a joke, I sometimes change it."

Commotion is at the other end of the phone line. "It was Nicole that said you were deep," Hope says. "Now she's kicking me?!? Quit it!" Something unintelligible. "She's hungover." "I wanted to be hung over." "And she's being an–" "Don't!" "Put some clothes on!" "Ow!" Struggling sounds, some laughing, some hurt sounds, faint and loud.

I say, "Hope, I would rescue you if I were there."

"No, if you were here, you'd take my side." "Cut it out!" Thud. Silence. Then a clear, not-Hope voice says, "Hope and Faith have Nicole pinned down, kind of." Must be Becky talking. "Although Nicole is doing lewd things to them because she's naked."

"You don't have to tell him that," Hope says.

"She loves it – what's his name?" "Ricky." "She loves it, Ricky!" Nicole exclaims partly muffled.

"So," it's Becky again loud and clear, "what do you do again?"

"Engineer," I reply.

"That's right. Auto parts or something?" Becky asks.

"Something like that."

"And when are you going to ask Hope out again?"

"Hope, would you like to come over this afternoon?"

Nicole says, "She'd like to – " and gets muffled.

"Your friends too, if you want," I add.

"This is Hope," she's taken me off the speaker phone, "Can I call you in an hour? I have to," struggling, "settle some things over here, okay?" I agree. "I'll see you soon. Bye."

"Bye," I respond. Click.

So here I am waiting for Hope's call again. I get some water.

"How did it go?" Ray asks. I say okay. "Do you have a second?" Ray is sprawled out on the living room floor.

"What's up?" I ask as a tic-tic-ticking travels across the ceiling. The bowling elephants upstairs own a dog whose nails have never been trimmed.

"I'm going to be short this month's rent," Ray says. Two months ago he and I made a deal where I would pay five-eighths of the rent. The rent is cheap even for Pigs Eye, because of its proximity to a railroad yard. I ask how short. Ray says, "I should be able to pay for most of my food and my tuition from working at the co-op and from Glory Girl. But I don't have anything left for rent... or anything else."

"Have you been paid for Kelly yet?"

"No." He tells me Kelly's price tag. "I should be finished in three weeks. And I might be able to make some money as a guinea pig."

I told Ray two months ago when we made the other deal that I'm trying to live cheaply to save money for a down payment on a house. I also told him that good roommates are hard to find. We kid each other, are easy going, and neither of us are too neat or sloppy. There is no Felix and no Oscar in this apartment. Yes, his studio takes up a good deal of the living room, but it doesn't bother me, and it doesn't get in the way. Ray is good to have around. So I tell him, "Ray, don't worry about this month, and we'll have to see about next month."

"Is this a loan?" The phone rings. That didn't take long.

"No. All right?" I want to settle this before getting the phone.

"Okay," he replies.

Hope asks if she could come over at two. I agree. I check the laundry room for a free washer to do a load of clothes. Not a chance. While I'm changing the oil of my car, I offer some oil to the sunbathing girl. She doesn't get it. I clean up myself and the apartment, working around Ray. Hope calls again and asks if she, Becky, and possibly Nicole could come over at four. I agree. I check the laundry room again. Not a chance. I read my book. I ask Ray to get up and take money over to the store for bananas and other groceries. The more I have him shop for us the less meat I eat. He heads out. I pick up my book again. I get up, and I grab the last banana.

The commotion in the hallway tells me that Hope and her friends are here. I pocket the banana, and I answer the door. I recognize Nicole from her pictures and nearly say hi, when she grabs my face and kisses me sensually and walks past. Hope copies her in her own way, kissing me more carefully. Becky wants to just say hello. With some awkwardness, she hugs me. I turn around from closing the door. Becky is the only one in the living room. Hope is down the hall looking into my room talking to Nicole. So Becky and I bring Hope into my room. Nicole is spread out on my bed, looking in my nightstand, and then under my mattress. She has a skin tight, glow-in-the-dark peach shirt that says, "sex is like snow – you don't know when it'll come – how long it will last – how many inches you'll get."

Nicole is beautifully sexy. Her body could stop traffic. She has a look to send boys howling through puberty. She has a face that could launch a thousand missiles. Everyone is naked under their clothes; the nakedness of some is more interesting than the nakedness of others. Not everyone is created equal. The more I think of her; the less I think of me. And yet...

Her smile is a facade painted over scars and sleeplessness. Her eyes do not smile; they look tired and searching. Her makeup almost conceals dark crescents below her eyes. Her skin, her hair, and her body seem frail from malnutrition. How will she survive the winter? Her beauty is the first thing you notice, but then if you look closer, you notice a hollowness...

"Hey, snap out of it," Becky is saying.

"Is that a banana in your pocket or are you just happy to see me?" Nicole inquires.

"Yes, it is a banana. And yes, I am happy to see you. What are you doing?" I ask, while dropping my banana on the floor.

"Looking for your girlie magazines."

"You won't find any," I reply because there aren't any in my room. This month's Beach Magazine is on the dining table, and the rest are in a box under the drafting table, angle references for Ray's Glory Girl comics. Nicole is peering into my drawer. "See anything interesting?"

"Nope," she says. I take a seat on my floor. Hope follows my lead. Becky already seized the only chair. From under the nightstand, Nicole dusts off a book and reads the title, "United States Department of Transportation: Guide to Highway and Roadway Signs, Reflectors, Pavement Markings, and Other Traffic Regulators; Revision 3. What's funny," she says tapping on the cover, then looking at us, "is that I have Revision 2!"

"You do not," Becky says.

"Revision 3 has all the really good stuff they left out of Revision 2," I always say.

Nicole puts the book back into its dusty alcove. "Nicole," Hope says, "you're being nosy."

"That's okay, as long as she doesn't mind me being nosy right back. Nicole..." she looks at me, "do you like attention."

Nicole tenses up, sighs, and seems disappointed, "Sure."

"Like a lot of attention?"

Nicole looks from me to Hope.

Becky says, "Nicole is the queen of–" Hope stops Becky with her hand, palm facing Becky.

Nicole sits up on the bed. "What are you getting at?"

"I have this problem, and I'm trying to understand something," I tell her. Nicole laughs.

"You have a problem?!? I thought you were going to get preachy on me or suggest a personal solution or something...," Nicole relaxes. "I don't think you have an issue with needing attention."

"No really, would you say you like to get lots of attention?" She nods. "Would you say that it gets you into trouble?" I ask. Becky laughs. Hope quiets her.

"I know trouble. I tickle trouble under the chin. I tease trouble. But I don't look for trouble." Then she looks sideways and back at me. "What just– Did your alarm clock just move?"

"Trouble got your number off a bathroom wall," Becky says laughing herself off her chair. I ignore Becky; Hope doesn't.

"So you know your limits."

"I know how to handle myself, so I don't get in trouble," Nicole says, moving about a foot away from my nightstand. "Is that what you wanted to know?"

"What if you had this little sister, just a couple years younger than you, who loves attention, but doesn't do what you just said, doesn't know when to stop?"

The room just got quiet. Nicole slowly lays back down on her side and props her head up in her hand. "I don't know..." she says, and she is no longer cocky, no longer the street-smart hottie. "You can't really warn her. If she understood the kind of trouble she could get into and what could happen, she would already be looking out for herself. Is this your sister we are talking about?"

"No, a friend."

"Not a girlfriend?"

"A friend-friend. She swims in attention. Without it, she's a fish without water. She's hooked on attention. She'll keep eating it all in until it kills her, or until she dies without it."

Nicole's brow furrows. "You're wondering what to do. How to help her as her friend." I nod. "I don't know. I guess it depends on how much trouble she's in already. If she hasn't gotten into trouble yet, you may be able to get away with some preaching." A moment ago, Nicole was afraid of my getting preachy on her; now she's almost advocating it. "If she's already in trouble, well, there's not a whole hell of a lot you can do."

My face starts to feel numb. I stare at the floor in front of me. "I think she's in trouble now. About two years ago, she was in here playing around like you were doing. Last night in the middle of the night she called me from a pay phone in Los Angeles. She tried to have the confident voice she used to have, but it wasn't there. We talked. She cried. I offered her a plane ticket back. I mentioned help centers, and she hung up. No. She said I was naive, and then she hung up on me." Hope puts her hand on my shoulder.

"What do you want from her?" Nicole leans off the bed.

"I want to know that she's okay."

"She's not okay," Nicole says. "You said yourself she's in trouble. It's a big bad world out there filled with the creepiest of people preying on weaknesses... addictions... vulnerabilities... Anything can happen. You're here. She's there. There's not much you can do."

Ray makes a ton of noise coming into the apartment with groceries. The next door neighbor's noise escalates to the next decibel.

"You could go there." Becky offers.

"But she didn't ask him to go out and rescue her, did she?"

"No."

"No, she didn't. Not that she didn't need you. I am sure she did," Nicole says.

From my shoulder, Hope says, "She called you in the middle of the night for a shoulder to cry on, and you gave it to her. She needed someone to talk to, and you were there for her. What's her name?"

"Aimee."

"Aimee is lucky to have a friend like you," Nicole says.

"Thanks..."

"No, I mean it," Nicole says, sliding off the bed. She sits up next to us.

I look at them. I've had enough analysis. "Let's see what groceries my roommate Ray picked up." I let Becky and Nicole out first.

Becky says to Nicole, "That was the most serious conversation I have ever heard you have."

Hope takes my hand but has to release it again in the hallway. I notice that Hope's shirt has little red hearts on the sleeves. Ray has bought about four thousand bananas. I exaggerate. Still, there are tons of bananas. "Hey Ray, was there a sale on bananas?"

Nicole is in front of me to one side. Ray is staring at Nicole. "Uh Ray, you're drooling."

He doesn't hear me. He asks Nicole, "Do you live around here much?" Then as he seems to remember something about bananas, he glances at them, and gazes back at Nicole, "Do you want a banana?"

"No thanks," she says. "I already grabbed Ricky's." She then starts to eat a banana in front of Ray. Ray melts into a puddle on the kitchen floor. It must really be hot out.

I offer bananas to Hope and Becky. I suggest a walk. Before we head out, Ray whispers, "Nicole is Glory Girl."

I whisper back, "Get some rest."

We walk down Sunday Drive, stopping to play with a caterpillar, the fuzzy, brown and black striped type. Hope and I hold hands again. Nicole chases Becky in front of us. Shadows fall all over the sidewalk from nearby apartment buildings, oak trees, and lilac bushes. Turning down Memory Lane, we head for the railroad tracks. Here a couple of railroad tracks have made a family of railroad tracks, nestled into the surrounding hillsides. A few boxcars sit, waiting to be used. We bypass three men leaning against one of them. I pick up a handful of gravel, and we climb a signal tower. From here we watch the fireworks of the sunset. This is a particularly pink and indigo sunset. Wispy cirrus clouds streak the pink halfway across the sky. The stratocumulus soak in the indigo violet from the bright red disk. The light makes Hope look more stunning, more beautiful than I have seen her. What a great smile! The breeze brushes her hair from her forehead and waves it from her ears. She has pretty ears. They might be the prettiest ears in the world. She glows in the light. Even with the highlights, her personality outshines her looks. She thanks me for caring about Aimee and Nicole, who doesn't seem to notice Hope talking about her. Hope talks about taking her students on a nature hike to see and identify the insects and trees. She's still thinking about that caterpillar. I want to go too. Is she going to invite me? She brings up my plans for the week. I explain that I try not to do much before a workday because it takes too much out of me. Blink! I realize that tomorrow is a workday. So I explain that I used to try not to do things on nights before work, but now that I've met her, I'm probably re-writing all my rules. We kiss. Our kisses get breathier, and I realize that Nicole is kissing Hope's ear.

"Stop it Nicole," Becky says, "it's too romantic." Nicole starts tickling Becky. The whole tower is shaking. We are about three stories above the tracks. Simultaneously we all decide it's time to go down.

The three men have left. The flashlight of a railroad yard bull is making its way toward the tower, but we already left. The caterpillar left also. We say good-bye at Becky's car. Becky and Nicole, having whispered a moment before, both kiss my cheek. I feel like a schoolboy, until Hope kisses me. I don't know if I am wooing her or she is wooing me, but there is plenty of wooing. Oh, the rugrats and other spectators are hanging around the building steps watching us and saying, "Woo!" I help Hope with her car door and watch her and her friends drive off. I climb my way through the spectators in the bleachers. Teenagers are changing the names on the mailboxes in the front hallway as I pass by. The neighbors next door are beating each other in the privacy of their own home. A television set is blaring across the hall. Elephant games continue upstairs. Only the musicians below are quiet. Maybe they are all played out. Another note is on the door.

Ray is in the living room saying, "Nicole is Glory Girl."

Walking by, I reply, "She's not invulnerable, and you can't afford to have the costume made," as I head into the kitchen. Suddenly he's right beside me closing the refrigerator door for me. Hey, look who has super-speed.

"The costume?!?" He's flipped. "The costume?!?" The neighbors have finally gotten to him. "You think she would?" Leftover spaghetti goes in the microwave for a few minutes with waxed paper over it. I turn to Ray and he's still picking his jaw up off the floor. He grabs a hold of me, "She would put the costume on?" I knock his hands off me to get out the milk.

"You don't have a Glory Girl costume."

"I can make one."

"You can't afford it."

"Erraugh!" he falls to the floor. Ray is spending a lot of time on the floor lately. I step around him for a cup. "In the next issue of Glory Girl," he's ranting now, "I could plead to the female readership to make a costume and send it in! I would give them a free year's subscription, and their name would be immortalized in a future issue!" Immortalized he says...

I get my hand wet and flick water at him. "What female readership?!?" Ding. Time flies when you are flicking water at a lunatic. I stir the spaghetti.

"Please."

"What?"

"If I had a Glory Girl costume, would she put it on?"

"Probably." Maybe she won't, but I can always crush his dreams later.

"Yes. **Yes!**" Ray has jumped up and is dancing around the apartment. Now, the music comes on from downstairs.

I shout downward, "Sorry!" I finish cooking my dinner and then start it, still being mildly entertained by the nut who now lives here rent-free. Who's the nut?

I spend the rest of the evening doing laundry, guarding my laundry, reading, and ironing.

4

Monday Crawls Like A Snail Leaving A Trail Of Slime

One of the secrets of success is not to waste time every day with decisions that will have to be decided again tomorrow morning. Decide how to best get ready for the day, and in what order, and follow that routine every workday morning. This will free your mind for issues larger than whether to shave before brushing your teeth or after, and which should be done inside the shower and which should be done outside the shower. Albert Einstein had several copies of the same suit. He didn't spend time worrying about what to wear.

I have a routine that I go through to get ready for work. I don't think about it. I'm not even certain I could say exactly what happens because it all happens so fast and my mind is elsewhere, usually already at work. This is not to say I'm successful, just working at it.

I expect to be catching up on some paperwork today, which I let go on Friday, in order to leave work early. I will run an informal meeting for my group, which consists of eight employees and a college intern. I have just two items on my agenda. What I usually do is to joke around and encourage others to bring up ideas, questions, and concerns. Then I add my comments where they fit or toward the end of the meeting. Hopefully, after the paperwork and the meeting, I can stop acting like a supervisor and get to work.

I am a mechanical engineer for Flight Control. Flight Control is a small company that has many big investors but no product. Yet. This has been going on for a little over five years. What we are working on is a product called AutoDrive. AutoDrive is an impact resistant computer, modeled after the brightest engine control unit (ECU), with an ever expanding library of situations and solutions. It is also an integrated system of sensors, touch screen, and steering mechanism, which combined with the ECU library will drive a car with minimal passenger input. The initial concept was that this would provide independent mobility for the mobility impaired. Investor greed has altered the concept and its market to be for everyone. The company resides in a huge old warehouse downtown near the river. We also have a vehicle testing range about an hour's drive outside the cities. My group is Product Research & Development. To us, it is the only group that matters; the rest of the company rides our coattails. I wonder where they got that idea... just being along for the ride?

Today might not go the way I'm expecting. Mondays often don't. Institutional changes are scheduled to start on Mondays. Many people spend all weekend thinking about what they would like to change, effective Monday. I am a dedicated employee at work. But I'm not paid to work on the weekends.

Walking in the door, after a few "good mornings," I'm greeted by, "There's a big brew-ha in your division."

"I'm sure it will be fine," I reply. Until our product is on the market, I'll always reply that way. Usually with office politics and gossip, little things explode into a big deal. I've heard that's true for marriage and divorce, but I wouldn't know. Bill, the new supervisor from compliance and safety, is waiting by my office door. Maybe it is a big deal. Some would ask, "What's exploded?" But having seen the damage some tests do to the subject, partial vehicle, and the test equipment, my question is always, how can I help you?

"Let's go in your– "

He starts to shut the door behind him, until I stop him with a sound and a shake of my head. Bill paces. He doesn't get very far. My office is a broom closet. That's what everyone calls it. He starts prattling, and I struggle to be open minded. "This woman has been nothing but trouble since– Cooelle Johnson? Whines like– Does things she isn't supposed to– The most difficult employee I have– Pain in the ass." He pauses and then exhales to indicate his finish. I figure it couldn't be a finish; it could only be a pause. I wait for a point to his ramblings. Some have waited days for a point to his ramblings. "This morning– Right away– She's waiting for me at the front door– " I know the feeling. "Gives me an ultimatum– Either she gets transferred to your group– Her friends are in– Or she walks– I'll replace her so quick– I don't give a rat's ass– " Now we are getting somewhere. He has a rat's ass. And he is wanting to trade it or give it to me, if I take a problem employee off his hands? Or the fact that he doesn't give a rat's ass might mean that if I take the problem employee, he will keep his rat's ass to himself. I miss some of his half sentences. I mean, I don't miss them; I just didn't hear them. Something about him being the boss. Something about not being able to pick people for me. He would talk to me. First he had to start things, which means his coffee. "Come here– She was here waiting– Ambush you!" I can't imagine what it would be like to be ambushed by someone from compliance and safety. Right outside my door too. "I told her again– I would talk– She stomped off–" Yeah the ramp makes my hallway kind of a noisy walkway. "Don't feel you have to take her–" Sounds like he is talking about a baby bird fallen from its nest.

I think for a minute. Bill fidgets. I don't have a window, so I stare at a decorative plaque on the wall. Turning back to Bill, I respond, "I won't make a decision without first talking with her. Ask her to come down here. Have her bring your file on her."

"I could bring the– "

"No, please have her do it." He gets up, is about to say something, has his mouth open and everything, but drops the issue, thumps my desk, and bumps his head on the doorknob on the way out.

Now, I'm not looking for trouble. I don't look for trouble. I should have expected trouble; I should have penciled trouble into today's schedule. I don't need to look for it. Trouble has this way of always finding me that would make my looking for it ridiculous.

I look over my schedule and some paperwork, get on my safety glasses and hard hat, and make my rounds. The safety glasses and hard hat are impractical encumbrances mandated by Bill's group and our insurance benefactors. The vehicles we use for testing on the warehouse floor, the portion of the warehouse that was not remodeled, are called series A or phase A vehicles which vary in size from three-by-one foot toy cars to kiddie cars to a full-sized Corral bumper on wheels. If for some reason, one of the A vehicles were suspended from the ceiling, I would have a better understanding of the need for the hard hat. As creative as they are, my people have not yet suspended any vehicles from the ceiling. Do they release bags of feathers, leaves, Styrofoam packing peanuts, and ping-pong balls? Yes. But no vehicles yet. The equipment has flown apart too. My concern is how much damage to safety and productivity has been caused by people not seeing what they are doing as well because of the protective head gear. As something of a role model, I wear the things anyway.

I check on our progress and pass along some reminders. That doesn't take long. I go back to my office and attempt to recalibrate my state of mind. It's almost recalibrated when Cooelle knocks on the doorframe and comes in. "Come in. Have a seat," I instruct her. She looks at the chair and then at my chair. She seems taken aback that she has the good comfortable chair on her side. We both sit down. She hands me her personnel folder. Her eyes are red and puffy. I don't open the folder yet; I don't know if I need to open it. "From what I've been told, you want to join Research & Development, my division. I have not decided if that is possible. I'd like us to talk about it."

"What do you want me to do?" she asks. The way she asks that is as if she is being humbled before my authority.

"I want to talk."

"What do you want to say?"

"I want you to tell me about why you'd like to join R&D."

"Bill didn't tell you anything?"

"I'm asking you." She sits back. We sit quietly for a bit.

"I've heard you're not like most managers."

More silence. I don't consider myself a manager. I'm not sure how to take what she said. I'm not sure it matters. "Is that it?"

She turns red. "Yes, that's it. I am asking if I can join your group. All you have to do is say yes or no."

"The most basic things I need from every member of my group are honesty and cooperation. I need many other things from people in my group: photo-electrical engineering or mechanical engineering, creativity, gumption, intelligence, and determination. You are showing determination. That's great. But you also have to be able to work with me, to talk with me. You wouldn't have to have any of that, if you happen to have all the answers to problems like how to get AutoDrive to read snow differently from a cement wall or to get it to understand not to speed in a driveway or a garage. If you have all of that worked out, fine, great. If not, you have to be able to work with me and my group to find those and other solutions. This is an interview."

"An interview?!?" She's floored and redder.

"That's right. You were hired by Flight Control, and you still work for Flight Control. But you weren't interviewed by me. All of the people in," she's getting up, "my group were selected by me, tested by me, and interviewed," she's walking out the door, "by me." I am talking to an empty room now. "I am picky at the start about who becomes part of my group to make sure the person is appropriate for the job, and the job is appropriate for the person. What good is it if you transfer to my group only to discover months from now that it is the wrong group for you. I need to create and maintain a good, productive, work environment. I owe that to my group."

She steps back in. She sits back down, tears welled up in her eyes. I hand her my tissue box.

"You still work for safety. Some might disagree with my interviewing you like an outsider. I don't see any other way to make you part of this team that would be fair to the team and the goal of creating AutoDrive. What we need to do is determine whether a position in R&D is right for you, whether the group is right for you, and whether I am the right boss for you. If you are not an appropriate selection for the job, I will not offer you a position. You could then fight this choice. If you then decide to take legal action, I could be pressured to take you on. I would then resign, and the division would come to reflect a different manager's style. You would be here, and I would not. Anything can happen."

"I understand," she says, "I think."

"On the other hand, if you can help my group reach its goal of creating AutoDrive, if you can deal with my management style, well, we can use all the help we can get." I might have her attention now. "Shortly, Flight Control will need to produce a product. If there is no AutoDrive at that time, we will all be out on the street with nothing to show for our achievements."

"I never heard that. What do you mean? How soon?"

"You won't hear it. The main job of finance is to try to keep giving us the money we need. They try to keep pushing the limits. However our performance in the next nine months will be critical. If AutoDrive succeeds, we will all be along for the ride. Otherwise, I may not be doing you any real favor by hiring you. Do you know what you'd like to do?"

"Look, I really don't know too much about what your team does. I am not sure how I can contribute or what I can contribute. I am not a computer genius," she says without using the geek word.

"Neither am I.."

"You're right that I don't think it's fair to go through a whole interview to work for you. I also know I am not going to work another minute for Bill."

"Do you think it would be fair for me to ask you some questions strictly related to whether there is some way you could contribute to R&D?"

"Yes."

"Well, that's what I am talking about. I am not going to call your grandmother or your high school English teacher or Bill and ask them if you can name the different types of diamond interchanges. I am not going to ask them if you know the difference between CCD and CMOS sensors. I am not going to ask for any references. If you agree to it, I would talk to you to see what is going on and how you might be able to help design AutoDrive. Then I would talk to my group and see if you could work with them. I would need to get permission from upper management to have you switch departments. And you and I would have to see if we can talk... without you walking out in the middle of a conversation." I let that sink in a little. It is not a very good first day if you walk out on the potential new boss, when the boss is talking. I am patient, but I will not be walked all over.

"Could I have a few minutes to collect myself?"

"Sure. How does ten minutes sound?"

"Good. I'll be back in ten minutes," Cooelle says and dashes off.

I open up Cooelle's file and flip through the contents. At the bottom is an application for employment. Every other company has done away with these things in favor of questions that are directly related to the job. Why would I want to call the restaurant manager for a reference? Even if someone was late every day waitressing, that doesn't mean they would be late every day to this job and vice versa. I certainly don't care what high school she attended. Her resume lists computer skills, inventory control, volleyball setter, scheduling, and office machine repair. Her college transcripts show mostly B's, a few C's, and a couple D's. General business curriculum. The file contains several items that have no business in here. I will return them to her. There are two evaluations from Bill: generic, cookie-cutter, circumlocutory, time-wasting evaluations. At the top are some trivial notes from Bill and a portrait picture of Cooelle. I close the folder.

Yes, every personnel folder needs a 5x7 glossy. Why does her folder have her picture in it? Is it some sort of reminder?

"Everything all right?" Mike asks coming in and taking a seat by some sandbags. Robin follows him in and takes a corner of my desk, shoving aside my in-basket.

"Yeah. Fine. Great," I say flatly. "What's up?" Barbara wheels into my doorway. They are all part of my department.

"We heard Bill yelling," Robin says. I nod my head. Yes, go on. Robin turns to Mike and they both turn to Barbara. This must be Barbara's doing. I turn to Barbara.

"You've been talking about Cooelle, right?" Barbara asks. I nod. Barbara wheels her wheelchair closer to my desk for emphasis, "Is Cooelle joining our group?"

"I don't know. She and I have to talk."

"What do you have to talk about?" Barbara asks. Barbara and I have worked together for several years. When she started, she was afraid to touch any of my work for fear of damaging the beginnings of AutoDrive. I had hired her to take over the calculus aspect of the work. It didn't take long for me to realize that she was maneuvering around my work. After several discussions and full-day show-and-tell sessions, she took ownership of my work. She lost her fear. Later I checked on the coding and only one section was left that was in my style. I asked her about it. She didn't understand it. I explained it. And soon after, nothing was left of my original building blocks. However, this is a first – her questioning me on what I am doing.

"I need to find out if she can fit into R&D."

"Let her join the group," Barbara tells me. Apparently, I am working for Barbara now. I'll play along.

"Does upper management have a problem with the switch? What will she do for us? Will she work well with this group? Can she work with me? What are her skills? And how did you get involved in all of this. Bill surprised me with it first thing this morning. How long have you been involved?" Now I decide to use the interview word. "Why was Cooelle so surprised that I would have to re-interview her?" Barbara looks shocked. "Because in order to answer the questions of what she will do for us and will she work well with the group and what skills she has, I have to talk with her. That conversation is known as an interview."

"You don't have to re-interview her."

"Yes, I do."

"Trust me. You don't."

"I do trust you. Are you saying you have taken care of everything else? Are you saying you have everything under control?" Now she's mad at me, maybe more angry than ever. I am trying to decide if I should get mad back. "If the two of you have a plan for the creation of AutoDrive, don't I deserve to know what it is?" Robin and Mike fidget.

"She's my friend..."

"Great." Pause. "That could mean the two of you might work well together. What about everything else I mentioned?"

"I don't know."

"How are you involved?" I ask Mike and Robin. They shrug.

Cooelle steps in and looks around. She looks more positive and still determined. "What did I miss?"

My office is small. With five people, someone has to go. A voice in my head says, "Pick me!" I make another choice. "Robin, Mike, could you depart?" They leave. I offer Cooelle the seat formerly occupied by Mike. "Barbara, please tell Cooelle what she missed. If you need to go someplace else to talk, you can."

Barbara starts to tell Cooelle what I said. I choose to only half-listen for two reasons: number one, I was there and I said most everything, and B, if Barbara didn't listen, I don't feel obligated to listen for the things she didn't listen to originally. As I half-listen, I get the feeling of deja vu. All of this happened before. I concentrate on my memory of what is about to happen. I check the time. Barbara is apologizing to Cooelle, saying that she hadn't fully thought out what it would take for Cooelle to join our team. Cooelle is telling Barbara that I had already told her that she would need to interview again with me to see if she could have a roll in R&D. And that's the point that I decide to interrupt.

"Imagine that I am an expert at decision making, that decision making is second nature to me, like driving a car. I don't think about the steps I take; I just do them. Prior to Flight Control, I had seen how other managers cut corners in making decisions, and then they wondered where they went wrong on getting the job done. They turned into crisis managers, putting out one fire after another, instead of productivity managers, trying to make things work as best as possible. Managing productivity means analyzing the situation, the entire situation: the goods, the bads, the potentials... and then imagining the possibilities, and from those possibilities, making decisions.

"Imagine that I am such an expert at decision making that I was the first to set up the rules for AutoDrive to follow. I was teaching decision making to a car. As the company expanded, I have been teaching decision making to others, so that they can become experts, so they can teach AutoDrive. You are driving in a middle lane on a highway. There is a curve. When a highway curves, the lanes become wider to compensate for the fact that the rear wheels of a vehicle do not follow exactly the track of the front wheels. Essentially, the car becomes wider than it is on a straight-away. As you drive the curve, do you center your vehicle, lean on the inside of the curve, or align with the outside of the curve? What should you teach AutoDrive to do? And once you take AutoDrive through the curve should it come to a halt because that was all you had to teach it? Or do you have it rejoin its basic decisions to continue on to its destination?"

Barbara turns red. "That reminds me of something I have to do. See you later, Cooelle," she says wheeling her way out of my office and down the ramp. "Coming through!" she yells in the distance.

"Let's take a walk," I suggest, locking her folder up, letting loose my electronic dog, and taking a pen and tablet. Cooelle grabs her purse and follows. My office is literally and figuratively halfway up the ramp between the unfinished warehouse floor and the renovated office space. We head down the ramp, along scuff-marked walls. I find us a pair of chairs on a small platform. It is both more private and more public here. And we can watch some of the activity of Research & Development. "I want you to think about all the steering, braking, accelerating, and decelerating that it takes you to get to work each morning..."

"I take the bus."

I should have become an orthodontist. My high school occupational survey said I should be an orthodontist. It said I always like to straighten things out. I shake those thoughts out of my head, and I take another approach, "What happened between you and Bill?"

"Is this on or off the record?" Cooelle asks.

"Depends on what you tell me, but I don't gossip if that's what you mean."

"He has issues. Funny your mentioning decision making. He couldn't make a decision to save his life. I pass by him standing in front of a vending machine; he mutters about how tough a decision it is. And then he moves off, without making a decision because he only has a 30 second attention span," Cooelle says.

"Did you time it?"

"No..."

"It's actually 40 seconds."

She laughs, "So you know what I mean. Do you want to know what I do for Flight Control? Nothing. Do you want to know what he does?"

"Nothing?" I guess.

"Right."

"He does attend meetings."

"Does he contribute?" she asks.

"Only through criticism."

"Exactly. He doesn't tell me what is going on, and he doesn't give me anything to do. I found myself not caring about work. I found myself not caring about things outside of work. I have been sitting back and watching my world fall apart. One day I found myself talking with Barbara, and she told me about working in R&D. I don't want to spend eight hours a day playing card games on the computer."

"Your personnel folder has some things that don't belong in it. Do you know why there would be a picture of you in it?"

Cooelle thinks a minute. "When I was first hired, Bill took my picture for a badge, but later said that there weren't going to be any badges."

"You'll get that back. Anything else you want to say about Bill?" She shakes her head. "How are you at math?"

"Pretty good."

"What is the most advanced math course you've taken?"

"Calculus and statistics, but I haven't done anything related to either since college."

"When someone mentions standard deviation, what do you think of?"

"Plus or minus some amount. The square root of the variance."

"What about triangulation, what do you think of?"

"Can I borrow your pen and paper?" She draws two overlapping circles with points in the middle and each with its own radius. She labels the two spots where the circles touch, A and B. She draws a third circle that touches the other two at point A.

"Okay, I've seen enough," I tell her. "Math is a quarter of what we do. Another quarter is data recognition and decision making. Looking for similarities in the data that identify physical properties, then addressing the decisions related to the physical properties or related to a group of physical properties. It is the realization that, 'Hey, every time we see a 110ZA780 it is a yield sign, so let's try the same algorithm that we did for merging and see what results it yields for yielding.' Do you know anything about how digital camera optics work?"

"I have a digital camera," she says, "but I have never taken it apart."

"Don't take it apart. They are a pain to put back together. We have some that are already in pieces. What do you know about the scientific method?"

"I'm not sure what you mean."

"You start with a situation or a hypothesis. The hypothesis is that 110ZA780 is a yield sign. If that is all you want to test, you might run two nearly identical tests, one with a yield sign and one without it. If the hypothesis is correct, 110ZA780 will show up in the data when there is a yield sign, but will not show up in the data when there is not a yield sign. Maybe you substitute a stop sign for a yield sign to make sure that 110ZA780 doesn't just represent the color yellow or a yellow sign. You run the test. You analyze the results and report any conclusions. If you learn that 110ZA780 does not represent a yield sign, that can help the process of elimination. Never underestimate the process of elimination. Sometimes it is more effective to test what is not there than what is there. Testing and the scientific method are the third quarter of what we do. The fourth quarter is everything else: set up, take down, repair, analysis, goal setting, planning, prioritizing, and more decision making. Everything else encompasses the most important and the least import aspects of the job."

In the midst of my description of yield sign identification, there was a loud clanging sound that sounded like a dropped pipe. I look over now, but I don't see anything.

"I have described four parts of R&D operations: math, data recognition, the scientific method, and everything else. What sounds like you?"

"Where do computers fit in?"

"They are a part of all of it."

"Where does Barbara's programming fit in?"

"Mostly she inputs the math, translating a math formula into computer code. Sometimes she helps out with data recognition, but that makes her eyes go buggy."

Cooelle laughs. "I like working with math. Does that surprise you?"

I shrug. "I don't know you; that's why I'm asking. What else?"

"I'm not sure. The testing sounds pretty interesting."

"Do you have any skills or experience related to these sorts of things?"

She shakes her head, no.

"Do you have any experience with experimentation, with trial and error?"

"Sure. Cooking, car repair, electrical repair..."

"Good."

"Do you know any reasons why management might have a problem with your switching divisions?"

She shakes her head and says, "No."

"Now that you've gotten a sense of how I handle things, how do you feel about the prospect of working for me?"

"I think I can work for you. You seem to care about your work. And the work sounds more like a book of puzzles."

"Do you like puzzles?" I ask. She smiles and nods. I lead her back to my office. I give her the picture and the other items that don't belong in her folder. "One more question, what don't you like on pizza?"

"Huh, what don't I like on pizza? Anchovies, raw onions, everything else is fine," Cooelle lists. "So that's it on the interview?!?"

"Yes. I'm buying pizza for lunch for the group in about 30 minutes on the loading dock. In the meantime, I'll see if I can catch Carl to approve your transfer. Stay out of the areas marked in red or yellow tape. And you might want to update Barbara." Cooelle is grinning and shivering, unseasonably. I grab a few reports, walk around Cooelle to get out the door, and head down the ramp to gather my group. I shout into the emptiness, "Pizza for lunch?" People spring out of nowhere. It's amazing. I give Porter some money to order the pizzas, and I head up to the offices. The cool air buffets me at the entrance. Carl is meeting with someone I don't recognize in his office. He waves me in. "Good morning, Carl. Here are the expense reports and the report from the shoulder emergency test. This morning Bill approached me about taking on a new employee from out of his group, Cooelle Johnson. I talked with her to see if she could contribute to Research & Development. I think she could start as a research assistant. Are you okay with the transfer?"

Carl looks at his sitting guest and looks at me. He is being exceptionally quiet, in a way that softens his abrasiveness, like sandpaper might soften rusty iron breakwaters if you work at it long enough. I stand still and wait. I mentally picture a wall clock over Carl's face. I have stared at enough clocks, that it is easy to watch the seconds tick away while watching his face for his reaction. Eighty seconds is a long time when you are staring at your boss. "How is the cross-sectional report coming?" Carl inquires, while grinding his upper teeth against his lower teeth in a dental wrestling match and sounding like driving over gravel.

"The cross-sectional report doesn't match up with the activities of R&D. It is like trying to stuff an elephant in a mayonnaise jar, but don't worry sir, I have its foot in the jar already." The guest stifles a laugh with a snort. I re-set the imaginary clock.

"Go ahead with the transfer. And I need that report."

"I will continue to work on it, sir. Thank you," I say, letting both me and the clock disappear.

On my way out, I bump a plaque that says, "Guidelines For Leaders: When in charge, ponder. When in trouble, delegate. When in doubt, mumble." I stop by Bill's office and tell him about the transfer. He asks if he's going to get to hire a new employee. I tell him that I don't know. I head back to my office where I elevate the cross-sectional report on the paperwork pile. I head down to the loading dock. A moment later, the Pizza Wheels pizzas show up.

Clarence and his pizza slice sit carefully down next to me on the cement and rubber edge of the loading dock. One of the best ways to handle the heat is to sit perfectly still. Moving around even a little can make you sweat for the effort. There is some much resistance to motion, it's like a swimming pool. However it turns out that the black rubber bumper of the dock is hot. I shift to avoid touching it. I look out, over the parking lot and the train tracks, to the tree line and the cement block banked Mississippi River beyond the trees. The farther I look, the more haze I am looking through. It's gray. It's dusty in a very wet way.

A swarm of a few hundred gnats float and spin around in a much darker gray blur. They are swimming in liquid air. The blur is about a foot wide and two feet tall, and it's about three feet up from the pebble asphalt parking lot. That's about the size of it. I wonder whose identity the blur is trying to protect? I always thought people's identities were blurred out electronically, but maybe it is just small swarms of gnats just getting in the way.

"How are you?" Clarence asks, interrupting my gnatty thoughts.

"Not too good, but things could certainly be worse. Never underestimate how bad things can get." I turn the conversational corner, "How about yourself?"

"Not too bad. Not too bad," Clarence repeats, his eyes sparkling. He's not yet 70; you can tell by counting the lines on his neck. It's almost like tree rings. He is the employee most likely to be enjoying what he is doing at any particular moment. And I notice that despite the heat, R&D is in a good mood overall. "I didn't get a chance to ask you this morning, how was your weekend?"

I'm thinking, "What weekend?" Then I think of Hope.

Clarence points a wrinkled finger at me, "I saw a smile!"

"It was a good weekend, a very good weekend. I met someone nice." We get up for more pizza and join others in the shade of the doorway. Someone says they heard a forecast for boiling with a chance of simmer later in the week.

Cooelle clears her throat, "I've been told that you aren't always as serious as you were this morning." This statement is directed at me.

With Clarence having reminded me of the weekend, I picture myself in the gorilla suit with Hope and talking to a hysterical Ray about Glory Girl and kissing on the shaking signal tower. "Seriously, serious is my middle name," I tell her. This causes some of my employees to have coughing attacks. I dredge up and put on my most innocent of expressions in an attempt to validate my statement.

"I was told that I should ask you to tell me a joke."

My innocent expression turns quizzical, as if I do not understand this joke concept. "How about we trade jokes instead?" I offer.

"I'm not good at telling jokes," she replies.

"Neither am I. Barbara should tell her own jokes."

"I don't have any," Barbara claims.

"Then that's something you need to work on, isn't it? Once upon a time, there was a woman who had a very, very bad day. She headed home extremely upset. On her front step there was a large snail. She reels up and boots that sucker away," I tell them, pantomiming a kick. I pause for a moment to swat a mosquito, Minnesota's state bird. "Three years later she's reading a book, when there's a knock at her door. She opens it. There's the snail. The snail says, 'What the hell was that for?'"

Cooelle laughs. "Your turn," I tell her.

She rubs under her eyes and says, "This is going to be really stupid."

"Stupider than mine?"

"Yes."

"Should I promise not to laugh?"

"No. Two guys are on the beach, looking out at the ocean. One of them says to the other one, 'That's a lot of water.' And the other one says, 'Yeah and that's just on the surface!'" I laugh politely. Then I roll on the floor, laughing. She tells me to stop, so I stop.

I brush off and ask the group, "Does anyone have a problem with Cooelle joining our group?" After a moment of silence I announce, "Barring any management issues, Cooelle will be joining the group as a research assistant. Cooelle, welcome to Research & Development." We applaud her. The group finishes the pizzas and heads back to work, leaving Cooelle and I. I knock a mosquito out of the air. I stand straight, "I need to let you know some things about the group and my expectations. The group decided awhile back that we would try to substitute the word Problem with the word Opportunity. It started out as a simple way of looking at things in a positive light. Some people hunt things down; others hunt things up. The idea is that when something isn't going right, there is certainly room for improvement, an opportunity to make things better. Well, this has been going on for some time now. It's been taken to the extreme. People are now being blamed for causing opportunities. We talk about opportunity solving. And story problems, like where one train leaves Boston and one leaves Cleveland an hour later on a collision course, that sort of thing, are now referred to as story opportunities."

"Should I be taking notes on this," she asks with a smirk.

"No. I should also warn you not to dress up for this job unless you consider your clothes disposable. You'll want to avoid wearing ties and necklaces that might get caught in something. We have not yet had a serious accident and would like to keep it that way. You heard about the green van of AutoDrive equipment that got crushed like a pop can? No one was injured. That's what counts. You may have also noticed that Scott was wearing his goggles in the parking lot earlier? Try not to tease him. It was an all-or-nothing deal to get him to wear the goggles. It took several months to get him to start wearing them. I don't want anyone or anything to undo all that we went through."

The mosquito picks itself up, brushes itself off, and proceeds to walk out of the warehouse. I imagine it's saying in its nasally voice, "I'm gonna tell my big brother on you..."

"I would like to formally offer you a position as a research assistant. If your evaluation in a month shows that you have been meeting my expectations," I point to a list on the bulletin board, "your salary will increase the following week to the entry-level research wage. Welcome to R&D." She thanks me. I ask Porter to help her find a desk. They take off, and I head to my office.

Okay so I was going to start the day doing paperwork. Then I was going to hold a brief meeting. Well, the meeting is canceled; I mentioned the key reminders to the group earlier today. The rest can wait.

I call off my Watchdog, an original program that handles my computer's security. It shows its personality through a growl. I give it a problem to gnaw on.

The Peters Wabasha Cross-Sectional Analysis is a report that asks cookie-cutter questions about aspects of a complex task to divine management solutions. That is what it is on the outside. On the inside, it is management consulting in a can; it is Cream of Condensed Management Consulting Soup in the convenient Cross-Sectional flavor. Mmmm, you can taste the abstract analysis in its bitter aftertaste. Several years ago, a small company wanted to turn management consulting on its ear. They wanted to compete with large management consulting firms. They analyzed management analysis. They formulated seven reports that would become the core of all future management consulting. The human factor, supposedly, is taken out of the equation. They put management consultants out of business, which has an irony to it, since the management consultants credo was If In Doubt, Layoff. Peters Wabasha, the small company that created the seven reports, receives the reports and generates the solution. Peters retired last year, leaving the company in the hands of its programs. People said it was impossible to have a company without any personnel, but time has proved those people wrong. The novelty of the employee-less company has worn off, and others have since cropped up. If a manager responds with "I don't know" to too many of the questions, that manager will be recommended for a layoff. The process of the seven reports has decades of management consulting theory to support the rationalities behind its solutions. The advent of the Peters Wabasha reports caused management consulting to make the evolutionary leap into a science. Management consulting credibility skyrocketed. The credibility of any science will skyrocket if human factors and expertise are reduced or eliminated.

I learned about all of this at the university in a management intro course. When this report was introduced to me in a meeting a week ago last Thursday, I already knew too much. In the same management course, I was introduced to the study of bias and perspective. Bias and human perspective should have been taught in fourth grade science or junior high school history or even in an undergraduate intro to mechanical engineering course. Nevertheless the management course had us pick apart popular management textbooks. "There are two categories of management textbooks," the professor said. "There are textbooks that are written primarily to make money." The class laughs. "Make no mistake about it, there is a great deal of money to be made in writing textbooks. The second category, nearly buried by the deluge from the first category, are the textbooks written from a genuine passion for the subject." The professor then had us read certain passages in the textbooks and asked us questions about those passages based on earlier information. One example was a film of the Pavlov's dog experiments, which we saw in an earlier class. The authors of one of the texts had never seen the film and had misrepresented the experiments in the textbook. The authors made stereotypical judgments of other cultures without a balanced understanding of those cultures. The course material affirmed and reinforced my suspicions of perspective and truth. Bias is rarely an insidious plot to deceive on an individual basis. Statements made by politicians and public relations people can be as deceptive as advertising. The trick to all messages is to decipher the code. From what they say, I ask myself, what conclusions do they want me to draw? What is the simple message? Who is their target audience? Am I a part of their target audience? What is the antithesis of their message? Could an argument be made for the opposite of their statement? Is the message a smokescreen, a distraction, from the real issue? Where is the money coming from? Who funded this message? And what do they have to gain from it?

Like many others, as I was growing up, I had questions about things that I had experienced, and I could not find answers that could explain the experiences. I was stuck trying to invent my own answers and explanations. I tested my guesses about what was going on against my experiences. I asked myself if my rationale fit what happened. An unintended consequence was that all the practice led to my becoming very adept at analysis and decision making.

Between the analysis and decision making skills and the attention to bias and perspectives, when I read the questions in the Peters Wabasha Cross-Sectional Analysis, I cannot help myself from not thinking about the purposes of the questions. Essentially they–

Barbara runs into me in the hallway on my way back from the bathroom. "Cooelle just asked me if you are for real."

I exhale hard and visibly pinch myself. "Real enough," I tell her. Barbara wheels away.

Essentially the questions are designed to take a complex problem or operation, define the terminology of that complex operation that could be understood by upper management, and then identify: shortcuts, waste, redundancies, cost-cutting measures, slow-downs, inefficiencies...

Apartments without a separate bedroom are called efficiencies. Therefore, apartments with one or more bedrooms are inefficiencies. I just made that up.

There is a museum in Milltown of questionable inventions. It is almost interesting to imagine all the inventions that have ever been tried that did not work. The invention process is not an easy one. People often refer to a key component of the process as luck.

Alexander Fleming's discovery of penicillin was made by accident when some dust happened to land on an uncovered petri dish. Years later on a tour of a modern research facility, he observed the sterile, dust-free environment. His guide commented, "What a pity you did not have a place like this to work in. Who can tell what you might have discovered in such surroundings?" Fleming replied with a smile, "Not penicillin."

Another word for luck is probability. The chances of a complex event occurring are astronomical. The chances of any simple event occurring are possible. The trick is to break complex events, such as meeting and living happily-ever-after with the love of your life, into simple events, such as meeting someone nice, and then working at the rest.

AutoDrive needs time. I have broken out all the complex events into simple events. I have arranged the events into groupings that are similar in operation, despite the order of occurrence and other relations between them. My employees know what they need to work on. We have a database of accomplishments to refer to for inspiration. We have probability on our side.

With all of this in mind, I read into the questions in the Peters Wabasha Cross-Sectional Analysis. From my perspective, there is one problem that is overwhelmingly interfering with my progress on AutoDrive. From my perspective, there is one key inefficiency, one wasteful expense, and one slow-down. It is the Peters Wabasha Cross-Sectional Analysis. I breeze through my answers on the Peters Wabasha Cross-Sectional Analysis, which point out the Cross-Sectional Analysis as the key problem, using Flight Control corporate terminology. I attack this problem with renewed focus on someday getting back to being able to work directly on AutoDrive, instead of responding to reports.

Watchdog barks five times in rapid succession. That is my whistle. I save my answers without submitting them. I let out the dog on my computer and otherwise shut everything else down and lock everything up. When my rounds of shutting off and closing and locking take me to the back door, I find a small group waiting for me. Clarence asks me what I've been working on. I tell him, "The Peters Wabasha Cross-Sectional Analysis." He tells me that I'm an inspiration. I decide to wait until another day to set him straight.

5

Hot Wheels

The car has been soaking up the rays in the parking lot. The metal door handle mildly burns my hand as I open it. Plastic wouldn't burn; it wouldn't retain the heat like the metal handle does. Then again, plastic door handles break off with the slightest effort in the winter. I know all about that. I roll down the window before getting in.

Ouch! The seatbelt buckle badly burns my fingers by the time I have it fastened. I should have learned from the door handle. I should have something, a rag maybe, between me and the metal. Maybe that's what those worthless little driving gloves are for. I check the glove compartment. No gloves here.

I put the key in the ignition and start the car. In the time it takes for me to do this, the heat has been conducted from the car through the key to my fingertips. Ouch, again! I'd say it took two seconds. Nothing ever takes just one second. It's always two. That's why they call it a second.

I drive home with my left elbow resting on the rubber flaps where the window disappeared and my fingers grasping the plastic molding at the top of the car door. I sweat from every pore. Every stop of the car, because of stop signs or stoplights or traffic, raises my temperature. This car does not have air conditioning, except when I drive really fast; then air conditioning is a breeze. I don't drive so fast as to be pulled over or dangerous or anything. As a matter of fact, it's been so long since I've been pulled over that the next time it happens, I should thank the officer and say, "You know I was wondering how long it would take one of you to catch up to me." It would be funny, for about two seconds. The last time I saw a cop, I think, was last week. She was changing a flat while the young man watched. That's something AutoDrive will never be able to do. Stand and watch? Sure, stand and watch will be a cinch to program in but not changing a tire. AutoDrive will be doing good, if it gets you home.

It'll be good to get home.

As I drive and sweat, I think about sweating. Maybe it's good for me. Sweating is a natural bodily function. That's what a friend of mine, Jake, always calls the things that people do that usually involve toilets or being sick. Maybe sweating is on the healthy side of the natural bodily functions. Tom Sawyer's aunt would roll Tom up in a wet sheet and pile blankets on him to sweat his soul clean. Maybe this is soul cleaning. Soul cleaning sounds like character building. The things that people don't want to do but have to do, like shoveling snow or attending funerals, build character. At least, that is the most positive thing that anyone can think of to say. I try not to clean my soul or build my character. If it happens, it happens.

I mop by forehead with a towel. I'll use the same towel to undo my seatbelt and take the key out of the ignition when I get home.

A car like mine, a Pony Express, is stopped in the middle of the road, overheated. Traffic is scrambling to get around it. I hope this isn't foreshadowing. I can't stand foreshadowing. I can't afford to get another new car. At least, I would rather not have to buy another car right now. I have different priorities. Different priorities is the American way, I called it first. But if the other driver wanted to buy a replacement Pony Express, they are in luck, since they are almost smack dab in front of a Corral Motors dealer – makers of the fine Pony and Pony Express line of cars. It must be that driver's lucky day. I think this scene would look perfect on a Corral Motors commercial. The sun is setting on the old car, warmly coloring the steam billowing from its open hood like a dragon of old, breathing its last fiery breath. But is the light playing tricks? The sun seems to be rising on the Corral dealership, causing the brand-spanking-new cars to shimmer excitedly and almost radiate a glow, from their reflective chrome to their sticker price, which has been kindly priced to move. The whole lot of vehicles would be proud to take the place of their dearly departed comrade.

I'm in the right lane, which is the right lane to get around the stalled car. Through the not-yet-dissipated haze and glaring, setting sunlight, I saw it blocking traffic a long time ago and switched lanes. So now I've been in the slow lane and am letting in half of these knuckleheads, that's what Nadine would call them, who come barreling down the left lane only to screech to a halt a few cars behind the stalled one. They get ahead by about 20 cars, which means they will get home about two seconds earlier than they would have. Anything can happen in two seconds, but two seconds really doesn't matter. So these short-sighted knuckleheads are still knuckleheads. They just have two seconds more to be knuckleheads with because they got ahead. It really doesn't matter one way or another. AutoDrive would be just as knuckleheaded.

That last thought really comforts me – that I could play such a pivotal role in lowering the intelligence of traffic. One hotheaded Neanderthal just gave me the finger for not letting him in also. I wave back. I'm overwhelmed at the potential accomplishment of lowering the existing intelligence-level of traffic. Perfectly capable people will sit mesmerized by television at the back of their vehicles while AutoDrive drives like a complete idiot for them. I wonder if Edison ever had a similar realization about street lamps, "Now all the muggers and thieves and prostitutes will be able to see what they are doing, without all the trouble of holding a candle at the same time."

What vehicles like mine could really use is a fan in the seat back that cools the driver's back. I'm sweating all over, my face is a waterfall, and my back is soaked. They say it's not from the heat; it's from the humidity. They lie. It is from the heat, and it is from the humidity. It's both. It's a combo-platter. It's the heat and the humidity rolled into one happy package.

Traffic is still sluggish past the blockage as if the other drivers have not yet realized they have passed it. One motorcyclist has realized it. He's weaving through traffic like the cars are stationary, little, orange cones. He's using the dashed white line as a safety zone to retreat to without the bother of having to slow down. Thankfully, I get to turn off. I don't want to see how this ends. I cross the bridge over the tracks and park in the parking lot. I avoid stepping in some melted, pink and black, pavement gum by doing a hop step dance. The front steps of my building are already packed with spectators watching the lot. Cheap seats are still available. Not everyone in the building has air conditioning for some odd reason, so maybe the steps are cooler than their apartments. I step past them.

My apartment, my inefficiency, is sweltering, like discarded gum sitting out in the sun in the parking lot. The windows are open. The noise from outside and the other apartments' open windows is amplified by the great acoustics in here.

The air conditioner is off.

Ray comes out, "Good to see you've been practicing your sweating. You won't mind being here so much."

"Why isn't the air conditioner on?"

"Because it blows white smoke. Watch." He turns it on and sure enough it sputters, coughs a hacking-type cough, and starts smoking water vapor, like a vaporizer. He looks at me like maybe I might have a possibility as a mechanical engineer. I've told him before that I don't know much about heating and cooling systems. I feel the smoke to at least see if it's cool. Not very. I turn away to the stack of mail on the table. Ray says, "I called the landlady and left a message on her machine, not that it will do anything." I thank him for making the call and go to my room to change clothes. Halfway through changing I stop to stand in front of my fan. Heading instead to the bathroom for a shower, I hear through the open windows, along with the rest of the world, just exactly what a musician's girlfriend thinks of him. She may be right. As I cool off in the sandblasting shower, I start to feel better, much better. Drastically better. Ten times better. Fine even. I feel enough of a change that mental alarms sound in my head: electric buzzers, continuously-ringing school bells, air-emergency horns that usually only sound the first Tuesday after the second Thursday of every month, police lights and strobes flash, and a tense, authoritarian voice blasts into a megaphone, "Remain calm. This is not a drill. Follow emergency procedures," and repeats off in the distance.

My first check is a physical one, which is simplified here in the shower. I look myself up and down, behind my legs, under my pits. Everything is where it belongs. Physically, I'm okay. Nothing abnormal or at least nothing two paychecks and a skilled plastic surgeon couldn't cure with a solid pick and a shovel.

Next I test the waters. Nothing extraordinary. Minnesota is chock full of water. It's a veritable sponge. This particular water's tepidity is mild. Call it luke-cool. If this was winter, I'd call it hot; everything is relative. The shower head is inches from my head. The cool, pounding water feels great. I shift my head to change the points of impact from the top of my head to my forehead, on to my temples, the back of my head, my neck, behind my ears, and spots in between on all sides. I put my face in next, my shoulders, armpits, and the rest of my body.

"Did I do something wrong today?" I ask myself as I start the second lap of cooling. Maybe I should have pushed the Cooelle problem right back at Bill; that would've driven a wedge between Barbara and I. No, that wouldn't have been a good plan. Maybe I should have offered a ride to the owner of the dead Pony Express. That would have interfered with the marketing plans of Coral Motors. As concerned corporate voters, they'd send their elected officials after me for my interference. That couldn't be good. I adjust the temperature. Now the water is too cold. I am moving faster to dodge the water. The temperature won't readjust. What do these knobs do? Send a message to the water plant? That's enough. I turn off the water and dry off. I don't want my body to start to compensate for the cold by heating up. I'm a Minnesotan. We are skilled at heating up. My towel feels out-of-the-dryer warm. I put on a light layer of clothes from the top of the toilet tank, whose sides are sweating condensation.

Drying my hair, I notice the smell of retching. I turn on the fan. I heard retching on my way in, right? I just thought it was part of the neighborhood clamor. Is Ray sick? He said something from the living room while I was sitting in front of the fan. I think I even responded. What was it? I don't think it was about the air conditioner. I heard all that. I don't think it was about the neighbors or about selling any art or about the landlady or about the co-op. Did I get any messages? "Hey Ray, did I get any calls?" I ask him.

"Not that I know of," he says from the living room floor.

"Ray, what gets wetter as it dries?"

"I don't know, what gets wetter as it dries?"

"A towel." No reaction. "You don't look too good."

"Thanks."

"In fact you look pretty bad." He nods his head without moving it off the floor. "What happened?"

"I told you."

"While I was in my room?"

"Yeah."

"I wasn't listening."

A disgusted exhale emanates from my roommate, twisted up on the floor, between half-baked lyrics from downstairs about ex-girlfriends. "I played guinea pig for five hours with the university researchers," Ray floors me. "Look at my arm." He uncurls his arm to reveal sores, bruises, and bandages. They used him as a pincushion. Is that really necessary?

"Do they know you've been throwing up?"

"No. They also don't know about my vitamins. And they aren't going to know. They didn't ask me until halfway through. They wouldn't pay me if they knew. I've already gotten enough money today; I might be able to scrape up the rent."

I look at the pale, mottled rug. "Ray. We've been through that. Everything is settled. Don't put yourself through this. The money can't be worth it. We don't need it."

"You don't need it," the rug replies.

"You don't either, at least not for rent. What do you need?"

"Some ice cream would be good..."

"Sure." Here's where I walk a fine line between roommate and parental figure, "Don't play lab rat anymore, okay?"

As I make my salad, he tells me he won't go back for a while. Not for 20 days, when he was told to come back. Ray comments on the salad saying that he's rubbing off on me. I give him a bowl of chocolate ice cream. He hardly touches it. Something about the way he's huddled on the floor causes me to lay a sheet over him. I let him know I'm going on a walk. He might have nodded. In the back stairwell, I hear a dispute that's broken out in the laundry room over someone having dumped someone else's clothes onto the top of the less-than-clean dryer. Without hesitation, I'm out the door.

Whenever I wear shorts outside, I think about someday using sunscreen, because these days the air is thinner than before, and the sun is just eight minutes away at the speed of light. I'm not using sunscreen. The sun won't last too much longer. I cross the bridge over the tracks. The air doesn't feel thin. Here in Minnesota the air is at its thickest, thick and wet.

I have been told that millions of years ago an ancient sea covered this land. I nod my head in understanding as I feel the spirit of that sea flowing against my skin, as if it were humidity. The land is squishy; the air is squishy. The sea did not disappear. It just lost its sense of identity.

Scientists say there was an inland sea here because they found sea shells. Jump back tens of millions of years, one dinosaur is yelling at another dinosaur not to leave their sea shells lying around. They should have never taken the trip to the coast...

A swarm of gnats hovers over the sidewalk. I close my eyes and step quickly through them, keeping them out of my eyes, feeling them bounce off my skin. I open my eyes, shrug, and shake like a dog. I brush off the little hitchhikers. Some gnats catch up to me at the stoplight. These pedestrian walk-signal buttons don't do anything. They aren't connected to anything. They are just a time-killing device, something to fidget with while you wait. They give the illusion of empowerment.

I spin around to confuse my gnat friends; the lights change, and I'm walking again, leaving them behind to find a button that will allow them to cross. The sign says Walk not fly. Gnats, birds, and cape wearing comic book heroes will just have to wait. Penguins cross, looking over their shoulders at the mob stuck waiting behind them.

I glance down the street toward work and make a mental note to stop by the bakery on my way in tomorrow. Anything to fuel AutoDrive. I head the other way down University Avenue.

At the corner is the Gun and Blunt Objects Shop. A sign in the window says, "Please unload gun and remove ski mask before entering." I've been in there, but I've never bought anything. A two-foot piece of pipe costs twice as much there as it does at a hardware store. I almost bought an instruction manual, just for the fun of it, titled, "Break The Window, Then Shoot, A Beginners Guide." What puzzles me is why every one of their customers seems to have a limp, some in both legs. They also sell jackets with realistic deer-in-the-woods pictures on the front and the back.

Next door is the Cease Funeral Home. I've been in there also without buying anything. Across the street is Yesterday's Diner, which advertises having yesterday's food at yesterday's prices. Next to them is the Remember When Nursing Home and the Out Damned Spot Animal Shelter. They're all in honest brick and stone buildings that used to be trolley car stations and plow sharpeners and flour sack weavers.

On this side of the street, I charge past the Zap Electric Company. Next I pass the Gross Wait Temporary Toilets, whose motto, scrawled in fine marker penmanship, is "we'll take your crap." Below the motto they list their number. Here Inquisition Street dead ends with the Inquisition Street Dental Center on the near corner and the Inquisition Church of the Crusades on the far corner. I continue down University Avenue. University Avenue stretches and zig-zags across most of Milltown, Pigs Eye, and surrounding communities. It is a very wide street because it was the old cable car route or so I'm told. I can only imagine a time when so many people would leave the driving to someone else. Part of University Avenue is my route to work. I'm headed the other way. Sandwiched in the middle of the next block between Snow-Blows Removal Service and Still Sparkles Used Jewelry is the Ice Cream Bar. This is my stop. Inside, I grab my favorite barstool and order my usual, a double vanilla milkshake, straight-up... no little wafer cookie for me. I spoon up and sip my shake, oblivious to the comings and goings and bar fights around me, as I contemplate my day.

Maybe I over-managed. Maybe I should have stopped Bill from yakking at me, had him fetch Cooelle, and then have them fight it out with me just making fun of the things they would say. When they were exhausted, I'd tell Cooelle that as long as she's willing to actually work she could join my division. We would kick Bill back to the world of work-less employment. We'd shout out our meeting in front of the wind tunnel fan. Barbara would then have time to start retraining Cooelle on work. And instead of decrypting reports, I would actually read through the Department Of Defense specifications for missile guidance systems, specifically for landmark identification, because the more I look at this stuff, the more certain I am that we are venturing into immensely uncharted territory with repercussions that would make Edison do a jig.

The problem is I have a system for hiring new employees. Sometimes having a system or a plan in place leads to an over-reliance, even though the situation has changed beyond the capacity of the system to handle the situation. Maybe I should have been more adaptable.

A toy car speeds down the bar and does a 180 degree spin at the wet napkin in front of me. I examine the car. It is a two-door, driver-less, orange, sports car, three inches long. I run its wheels across my hand, measuring their resistance and turning radius. I send the car back up the bar. It stops at a very attentive group of owners.

I didn't conduct a real interview. In a real interview I would have already had an inkling of her role. In a real interview I would have put her in a simulation of some actual work situations to see how she would handle it. I have to hope she actually has come to work. My employees come into work and they work. My work slowed down today for the office-types. I wonder how the proximity of non-workers effects actual workers?

The shake is getting soft enough that I switch from spoon to straw, blowing my straw wrapper a third of the way down the bar, only to be snatched up by the 16 year old barmaid with attitude.

I'm not trying to belabor this day. I'm just trying to figure out what I should have done, so I know what to do next time. I will be more true to myself next time. I am becoming more and more me everyday. This is how I learn. No, that's not exactly right. I learn by exploring the possibilities. Usually I look ahead. Tonight I'm checking over my shoulder, literally. While turning to look over my shoulder, in my peripheral vision, I notice a little, orange, sports car drive by my spot at the bar. The experiences of exploring the possibilities become me, but what really defines me are my friendships and my friends. They define who I am.

My milkshake has a time limit. It is in a meltdown. It needs my attention. I consider myself a milkshake connoisseur. I find proportions of milk to vanilla extract to vanilla ice cream interesting. Whipped cream is like freshly fallen snow on a snowbank. It can be deceptive. I don't need it. I also don't need malt flavoring. Don't get me started about malt flavoring. I have never ordered a vanilla malt. I have gotten a vanilla malt without ordering it. It's just not my cup of tea. Neither is tea.

This place is starting to get rowdy. A sugar buzz has the place in a headlock. This always happens 20 minutes before curfew. I pay my bar bill, duck a wooden chair that sails over my head, and I head out the back way. In the alley I buy a can of Double Bubble from a machine to wash down the vanilla aftertaste that coats my mouth. I'd get a can of Cooler Cola, but the extra caffeine might keep me awake.

As I head home, the humidity and the streetlights turn landmarks into a dream-like blur. Looking at the top of the Inquisition Street Dental Center, I do a double take. I thought I saw a gargoyle yawn and then spit. The street is cooling off from the day. The gnats are in bed. Most shops are closed, except of course the Gun and Blunt Objects Shop, which is just starting to load up.

The Whisper Willows apartment complex reverberates sound strangely in the dense humidity, as if it has an echo on either side of each sound. Despite having three noises per sound, the buildings are nearly halfway quiet. The gravel of the parking lot crunches under my shoes with the same set of echoes. My roommate is already off in his room asleep when I get in. A note on my bedroom door says that Hope called. I call her back. We talk for half an hour. I tell her about my day, highlighting the story of the snail as the symbol of the events of a Monday. Hope tells me she likes it. It's just us on the phone line, no room-mates on either side pestering us. My concerns of the day are washed away, talking with Hope. She is naturally comforting and comfortable and encouraging. Her words release tension in my chest and face. Once the tension is gone, I realize that the tension had moved in and made itself at home. I poke my face to make sure the tension is fully gone. I'm in bed with the light off when I wish her good night, like she's right here. We agree to end our days on the phone, at least for the next few nights.

6

Writing On The Wall

It is already tomorrow. I wake up and untie myself from my sheet that thinks it's a straight jacket. My pillowcase is wet; did the... no, the fan is still working. What time is... oh, 6:56. Am I awake? Yeah, I'm awake, which means I can stop my alarm clock from going off in four, now three minutes. I'm up at least sitting up. No falling back to sleep for me, I decide as I wind my clock.. I've got a nasty kind of headache. I feel my jaw. It's sore like it's been busy. I've been grinding my teeth again. Stress. Yesterday ended on a good note, what happened in between?

I had a dream. It's coming back to me now. My friends and I were playing a kid's game. Hope and Nicole were there playing. They got hurt. Badly. I waited at the hospital. I paced. I walked around. I passed Death several times in the hallways and rode the elevator with him once. He was wearing hospital scrubs with a matching hood and carried a scalpel. Half the time he was with his assistant, Malpractice.

I hear rustling. Ray's up before me. Ray is never up before me. I put on a shirt, tuck it into my shorts, and go out. Ray is in the living room. He doesn't look good. He shows me a picture he took of the sunrise. "It'll last longer," he tells me. I am ironing a shirt, when I get what he meant. The shirt is a short-sleeved button-up. I know some people button these things down, but I've always buttoned them up. I concentrate on putting my lunch together and getting ready because whatever order I normally follow has been shot by the fact that Ray is up and around.

I look at my car differently and decide that one of these days I'm going to clear all this junk out of here. Work equipment, log books, a steering mechanism, and garbage make my little Pony Express a one-person car.

I buy a mix of bagels, donuts, and muffins at the Ovens Hot Bakery over on University Avenue, two blocks past Serenity Street and one block past Memory Lane near the corner of Deja View. A sign on the wall at the bakery says, "As you journey through life, whatever may be your goal, look upon the donut and not upon the hole."

I usually park in front of the building just off Rail Road, but today I park in back on the off-chance of unloading the work stuff. Coming in, I startle Robin, who was watching the front hallway. I say good morning and let her know I will be on the main workbench. She is having trouble talking. I smile and let her off the hook by escorting her and the baked goods to a kitchen-less kitchen counter.

In my office I wake my watchdog and give him an electronic-version of a squeaky toy. He goes wild on the toy: squeaky-squeaky-squeaky, squeaky-squeaky, squeaky-squeaky-squeaky-squeaky-squeaky, squeaky-squeaky, squeaky, squeaky, squeaky-squeaky-squeaky-squeaky-squeaky-squeaky. Then I turn down the sound. I grab my schedule book and pen. The schedule book is for show and to help others remember what is supposed to be happening. The pen has a real purpose. It is the click type, which makes me go wild on it, like a dog with a squeaky toy. And I almost run over Robin in my doorway.

"That's the second time I've startled you today," I tell her, "and the day just started. Come on in." Robin starts to apologize for complicating things yesterday. I let her say what she has to say, while I smile slightly and shake my head. Then I let her know that she didn't do anything wrong. I switch gears to talk with her about vehicle frame sizes and turning radii. We brainstorm in my office. I decide that others should get in on this if they are available so I move our location nearer to the donuts. I take an old wooden swivel chair on wheels. It's my favorite. I also snag a donut.

Edy opens one of the big loading dock doors, inviting sunlight and a fresh breeze into our conversation. I realize something is missing. I go up to the offices and the break room. I swipe a pot of coffee and some spare cups. I take it back to my group. I pour for them. When I return the coffee pot to the break room, two people are in there waiting like they were trying to catch a bus.

"We were wondering where the coffee was."

I hand it to them saying, "I don't even drink the stuff." Their faces betray an inclination toward murder. I thought I learned this in college, but I guess I needed this refresher – never mess with someone's addictions. Never is never the right word. Use caution when messing with someone's addictions. These people take their coffee very seriously. How would I like it if someone took away my vanilla milkshakes?!? I would probably switch to chocolate. That's another important rule in life; it's in the top ten; there is always chocolate. And if someone took away all my milkshakes, I would just do without. I am now sitting with my group again. I think about standing up, stating my name, and announcing that it has been nearly ten hours since my last milkshake.

"What's that smirk for?"

"Nothing," I smirk.

"We were talking about how most managers don't serve their employees," Porter says.

"Why the H-E-double bamboo shoots not?" I ask.

"Ego," Clarence says, "gets in the way."

"I keep meaning to buy one of those, but I can't find any stores that carry them," I explain. "Tell me again, how are they useful?" No response. "I've gotten along without one of those ego-things all my life. I suppose it's like anything else, the minute an emergency comes up and I really need one, I will wish I always had one."

"You don't think you have an ego," Cooelle asks in a statement sort of way.

"I know I don't," I respond. "Organizational charts show leadership at the top. That misconstrues the importance of the leadership. The work should come first; that's why it's called work. Any leadership-based or political clout-based organizational structure should be called Ego Framing. That's my opinion. Speaking of work, let's talk about the steering mechanism–"

Porter interrupts, "Uh, before you get into that, Cooelle was telling us that you told her about AutoDrive having a deadline? Could you tell us about that?"

"Sure. Yesterday, I needed to give Cooelle several perspectives on what might happen with Flight Control in the future. I told her that it is my personal guess based on my readings of the financial contracts we are under, that our performance will be critical in the next nine months. That's the time frame I'm seeing. Porter, did I adequately answer your time frame question?"

"Not exactly. What happens if this nine months rolls around and we, ah, don't give birth to a car that drives itself?"

"A miscarriage?"

"First babies tend to take longer than nine months. What then? Are we talking about an abortion? At such a late stage in the pregnancy?!? They'd kill the project?!?"

"Just who exactly," I wonder, "is giving birth here?"

"That would be you," Barbara replies.

"I don't think so."

"It's just too early for you to be showing."

"Porter? I'm expecting..." I start.

"Told you."

"I'm expecting one of three scenarios," I continue.

"You're having triplets?!?"

"Scenarian section?" Clarence asks.

"Many first time mothers prefer it over natural childbirth."

I continue my continuing, "The first scenario is that we have AutoDrive finished in nine months, and we continue going about our business and maybe start to make some real money. The second is that we don't have AutoDrive done, but our backers throw us some more money anyway. The third scenario is where we don't have AutoDrive finished and Flight Control is crumpled up and thrown away. That's about as clear a picture as I can paint for you right now. Some of you might have some ideas on which scenario will win, however I must ask you, please no wagering."

"I bet a C note."

"C section?"

"Stop that."

"Ricky?" Harvey is our steering committee. "I think I know which way AutoDrive will go. I took the intersection drive to the corner and ran it through a left turn." Harvey's talking about our fully functional stoplight intersection at the north end of the parking lot. "And when I let it go the second time, it stopped in the middle of the intersection. The light was green!"

I look at Clarence. He's thinking about it too. I try to picture it. "How far did the vehicle get before it stopped?"

"Most of the way out."

"Of the 90 degrees in the turn, how many degrees did it go before it stopped?" I ask.

"Most. About 70 or 80."

Everyone is quiet.

"Oh." A light bulb goes on over my head. I think, before Edison, candles were lit over people's heads. "Do you think it had turned far enough to see the red light facing the other way?"

Pause. "Yeah! That could be it."

Clarence offers, "Maybe it needs some distance after making a green light decision, before it makes another red light decision."

"About 30 yards?"

"More like 30 feet," I suggest.

"I'll add it to the program," Porter says.

"Show Cooelle how you do it," I tell him. "Thanks for bringing that up, Harvey. You might get an award next time if you can diagnose the problem and offer at least one solution. The next award is a gift certificate for two to the Brand X Steakhouse in Duluth."

Cooelle says, "There aren't supposed to be any awards anymore?!?"

Barbara says, "I gave you that gift certificate."

"That's the beauty of it. You might be able to give it to me again."

"I thought you liked that steakhouse."

"I do. I just don't get to Duluth much anymore." Besides, I'm not eating that much meat anymore. "So it's fair game. So are the fabulous trophies on my shelf that some of you have given me. However if someone has something that could be used after the gift certificate as an award, please let me know. Otherwise one of you might be the lucky winner of the golden bumper."

"Not the golden bumper!"

"Yes, the golden bumper. The coveted award of distinction that I earned about two years ago. It's dusty, but nothing a good wind couldn't handle."

"That thing is meant as incentive?!?"

"Yes. I might even change the rules. I will change the rules. The golden bumper will be a separate award for someone who most resembles a bumper by just sitting around without accomplishment. The winner will be decided in 20 days."

Research & Development is thrilled at the prospect, and apparently I'm the only one noticing Scott trying to wipe jelly-filling off his goggles without taking them off. I don't give him away by staring. "Cooelle will be working with Barbara today and Clarence tomorrow. I want you to try to teach her everything you know. Cooelle, I don't expect you to learn all that they know, but I expect you to ask questions and take notes so that you have references you can turn to quickly. If any of you have suggestions on precipitation recognition, let her know."

"Let her know, let her know, let her know," Porter sings to the tune of Let It Snow.

"That might be part of her project," I continue.

"If it looks like rain and feels like rain..."

"And if any of you can suggest a major cost saving measure, please talk to me about it. Management would love to hear about success, but they might settle for saving money. Does anyone have anything else they want to talk about?"

"If it looks like snow and it packs like snow..."

"Does anyone else besides Porter have anything they want to add? Then I'll get out of everyone's way."

"What did I miss?" Mike asks as he walks in. Scott begins to fill him in as I head for my office.

In my office there is a phone message to call staffing, left by the guy that works the switchboard mornings. I'm just reaching for the phone when it rings. A little spooked, I wait for the second ring to pick it up. It's the owner, Carl. He's praising my handling of Cooelle's transfer for all the wrong reasons. "Putting her back through the interview process," this is a direct quote, "was a stroke of genius." Great. I call staffing back. They ask me, through a conference call from upstairs, what I would have done if Cooelle didn't get accepted by me. I tell them I had a contingency plan, but I don't elaborate. I'm sure they already know, and that's what prompted their call. I try not to tell people what they already know.

I also have a phone message from very early this morning that Lefty called. The little phone message form has a check by the Please Call Back box. I haven't heard from him in a while. He didn't leave a number. I look up his number in my address book. I try calling him at home and at Minnesota University (Go Moo!) where he works as a researcher, but there is no answer at either number.

I re-read and submit the Peters Wabasha Cross-Sectional Analysis. Other paperwork carries me through lunch. I eat at my desk in annoyance that this should take so much time. There is no reason for all this. We're a small company; there is no need to formalize so many things.

Paperwork is an endless struggle for the domination over the desk, where your adversaries are forms, memos, letters, files, and documents. It is the paperwork-deluge-monster that regularly plots your defeat, sheet by damnable sheet, page by stackable page. One page is not thought to be anything of significance. There is no inherent danger in a sheet of paper. A drop of water, a spark, or a snowflake is not necessarily dangerous either. You only have to be threatened by flood, fire, or blizzard to see the danger of quantity. The idea is that even one forest is one too many, but there can never, ever be too much paperwork.

I read, put into the recycling bin, file, shred, notate, complete, or otherwise take care of a good portion of the paperwork. Others can forward paperwork, but I am on the receiving end. They might think that a safety issue can be handled by Bill, but he won't know the answer. It has to come to me. It would be easier if all issues were put on hold until AutoDrive was completed, but things don't work that way. I stack up sandbags between my part of the office and the paperwork's side of the office. I dam it. I'm standing over my accomplishment wringing my cramped, paper-cut hands, when Barbara and Cooelle come in. I turn and ask, "How's it going?" They are agape, staring past me. I look back to see what has them stymied. I turn back to them, "What?"

Cooelle looks down at Barbara, who says, "You're nuts you know."

I sit down, saying, "You take care of your paperwork your way, and I'll take care of my paperwork my way."

Barbara maneuvers, so that she can see me past my monitor and see Cooelle, without having much room for maneuvering. "We were talking about AutoDrive, and I thought you might provide an overview, that is, if you're not too busy damming your paperwork."

"Sure. Over five years ago I was at a party in Chicago on the roof of a 15 floor condominium just a few blocks from the lake, Lake Michigan." Cooelle sways and fumbles for the chair. "Great view. One of my friends introduced me to Carl. He told me about this dream he had of a self-driving car. I asked him questions about it: how would it work, practicalities, that sort of thing. He took turns by either saying, he didn't know or bouncing the question back to me. At the time I wasn't thrilled with my job. I figured that I didn't get the engineering degree to answer phones and run errands. Once he had the funding, I jumped at the chance to work with him on AutoDrive.

"At first we were brainstorming our goals and ideas in an office downtown Milltown. It was dynamic. A rush. There were six of us back then in a three room suite. Of the six, only Carl, Peter, and I are left. We started out trying to develop a car that would give independence and mobility to the mobility impaired, to people that can't drive today.

"The process of financing the company altered the vision of the product. People like Carl get ventures started by always saying yes – yes to any sponsor who wants to join up. This is also what can stop them from keeping a project simple enough to see it completed. Corral Motors and Protection Underwriters, known for Angst Insurance, were the first companies interested in the project but were not as quick as others to begin the funding. You can never be assured of money from an insurance company. Big Rig Transportation and Cutesy Entertainment were our first sponsors. Then Packard Motors and West Bank were next, followed by Corral Motors and Protection Underwriters. Not long ago Double Bubble and the Highway Department got involved.

"AutoDrive has become a multiple-sensory, multi-input, driving system. It is intended to take anyone anywhere but is still best at routes that have been driven as an input. The route can also be drawn using the small screen map or selected through the route directions list. Originally we intended to use the engine control unit of a car with a few minor upgrades. It now has it's own impact resistant ECU, touch screen, internal sensors to record route progress, external sensors to evaluate its environment, and steering and braking output mechanisms. It has optical, audio, infrared, motion, laser, and composite sensors. It has rough road gyroscopes. It has global-positioning information.

"The auxiliary computer has an on-going, sensory self-diagnostic to make sure its components are in an operating condition. It has operational control information and procedures. It has a library, a database, of traffic objects and events. It recognizes most regulatory signs, pavement markings, reflectors, street and railroad lights, mars and strobe lights, emergency vehicle signals, cars, trucks, wheelchairs, people, and balls.

"The process that has gotten us this far, the process that will get us to where we are going – it is all trial and error. We make mistakes so AutoDrive won't. We learn and teach AutoDrive. Every little piece of information and decision making that we can give it will bring it closer to being a marketable product."

"How close are we to finishing?" Cooelle asks.

"You're asking how long it will take?"

"Yeah."

"I don't know. I listed the things that AutoDrive knows, but it doesn't know all shapes and forms of people, for example. There are also whole categories of things it doesn't know: precipitation, leaves, highway trash, deer – that's not going to be much fun to test – 'okay Blitzen I want you to do exactly what you did yesterday,' squirrels, bicycles, motorcycles...or skidding. Or night driving. Or flooded roads. It knows straightforward driving and can do most turns, like we talked about this morning. At times, it is just too complicated for its own good, just like people. I think it would do about as good on the road, right now, as a distracted eight-year-old, taking off alone with the family car. The easy stuff is over. All that's left is the difficult stuff."

"Great," Cooelle sarcastically says.

Scott sticks his goggled head through the doorway without interrupting. "Going through the simple stuff has taught us what we need to know, how we need to function to get through the complex stuff. When you are sitting with other developers, learning what they are doing, take a look at how they act and how they interact with each other. We have to function as a team. There are no disconnected parts to AutoDrive decisions. It is all interconnected. It all matters. People will be putting their lives in our hands. We need to give them an outstanding product." After a pause, Scott tells Barbara that he corrected a calculation of hers. They all clear out.

I try to call my landlady. I get her answering machine, but I don't leave a message.

I get to thinking more about what I am doing here at Flight Control. The way I see it, I'm working on the American dream incarnate. Anything can happen; anything can be. The American dream to me is increased possibilities, having more than before. It means having more freedom and greater liberty from the freedom of others. Some time ago that meant being free to practice a religion of choice and having the government subject to the will of the masses being governed. Soon it meant that people could dominate the land and its inhabitants, and still have the freedom of religion and the representational government. Then it meant being able to say what you want about anything, plus the other things it already meant. The American dream soon meant that foreign powers could be taken on without giving up any of the earlier entitlements of the previous dreams. Conveniences were tacked onto the dreams; the dream was on sale. Light in the night. A voice from a machine. Manufacturing. The dream would revolutionize the kitchen, the bathroom, and every other room of the house. The American dream invented the garage and its sometimes occupant. It continues to be all those things, plus communication from the phone, computer, and two-way wrist radio. The American dream was plugged in and could drive across the paved land just for fun. Ingenuity fueled the American dream. AutoDrive is an addition to the list, one more possibility, one more possession, that once again alters the priorities of the American people with global repercussions.

And yet, through all that, there are two ironies of the American dream. One is that the dream started after the dream was realized. The real dream had been self-government. Everything else is a tack on, an after-thought, amendments to the existing success. The other irony is that repressed people started a dream only to become the repressors.

I go out into the bright afternoon sunlight of the parking lot humming the star-spangled banner. I start to clear out the materials and garbage from my car, not intending to do it all at once, just at least a start. This is the way I handle most projects. Mike comes out and helps me for a while to unload my car, until he finds out this stuff is old. He's not interested in the past, only the future. Well, today is tomorrow's yesterday. It's getting closer all the time. At one point while I'm going back out to my car for another load, I notice a plane in the air that just seems to be floating, not moving at all. I'm just standing, watching this plane while holding a Pigs Eye map to my forehead to shield my eyes from the sunlight. The plane doesn't move. I line it up with the old water tower of a building a block or two south of here, and eventually it's clear that it's moved down and to the left. I return the map to my car and disconnect some wire-filled tubes from the front fenders. After an hour more, I'm done. It kind of feels like I just cleaned out my desk. I go back in and make my rounds. Then I begin to set up some space, some tools, and equipment for tomorrow. Set up is best done piecemeal to make sure I haven't forgotten anything, and so I don't rush it.

Back in my office I try to call Lefty again. No answer. I also try to reach my landlady. I leave a message about the air conditioner.

An air conditioner would be nice. I've twice turned down a decent-sized, air conditioned office in the other half of the building. I'm headed that way. I never fully decided to go into the offices; it is a subconscious decision. I'm not even sure if my brain was consulted. The well-insulated door between the warehouse space and the offices is cool to the touch. For a moment I hesitate in the doorway, savoring the difference on my skin, hot and high pressured versus cool and low pressured. The door bumps my butt in. My body starts to relax as my mind kicks in, "What am I doing here?" No response. Any response would've been Plan R1. Plan R2 is my back-up: if in doubt, head for the office supplies. I pause briefly to see if anything of interest is on the break room bulletin board. Nope. I proceed with Plan R2. Cooelle is talking with several women around a filing cabinet. They look at me, and conversation halts. If only traffic would stop so still for a car with AutoDrive, my job would be far easier. I say, "Hi," and try to make eye contact with all of them without stopping. Some greet me, and I continue past them plus ten yards to the supply cabinet. I rub my chin thoughtfully as I scan the contents for my quarry. One woman jogs over.

"Can I help you find something?"

I attempt a smile. Nothing foils Plan R2 as quickly as being given assistance finding God-only-knows-what so as to be hurried along back out into the inferno. "That's not necessary," I tell her before continuing my scan of the pads of paper, the pads of forms, the multitude of different types of pens (at least as many different types as the number of people here), scissors...

She still hasn't left.

There are tiny bottles of white paint. It would take forever to paint a room with the little brushes connected to the inside of their caps. There are plenty of the sponge ended bottles that save tongues from sealing envelopes. There are the pads of paper that stick anywhere. I'm surprised there are any left. Recently my group covered my office with those things: the walls, the chairs, the desk, the phone, the computer, the golden bumper, the plaques, the whole room... except the ceiling which only had a few and those were aided by tape, so I chewed out my people for sloppy work. If it's worth doing, it's worth doing well.

She's still here.

I turn to look at her. I recognize her, but I'm not sure I know her name. She has a pleasant look on her face, as if to say either she'd really like to help me out or at the very least that this is her territory, and she'd rather I didn't mess it up. So I look back at the supplies and, again without consulting my brain, my mouth says that I'm looking for wire. My mouth isn't finished saying the word "wire" and already I hate myself. I do not lie. I'm not the type of person who lies. I can't say that I would never lie because I can think of two situations where I would: number one – for a joke and B – on the other end of the spectrum, to save an innocent life. That's it.

To be good at something, anything, you must practice. You must dedicate your life to it. I don't have the experience to back me up in lying. I neither have the experience nor the legal training required to lie well. And I don't believe in it. But I step back, and she begins to search.

I could have said a bandage. You see it's for a cut. Where? Right there. No, there. It's hard to see. It's a paper cut. It stings. And I don't want it to get infected. But no, I had to say wire. I've got a table out there covered with coils of 12 and 14 gauge electrical wire, plus coaxial cable and bell wire and extension cords. I come in here and look in an office supply cabinet for wire. I'm an engineer. Mentally I thump my chest with my thumb; I've got a degree.

About every minute after what's-her-name takes over the search, a new person joins the quest. It's almost like I was down river in Hannibal, Missouri trying to get a fence whitewashed. The questions are shovels, burying me deeper. "What kind of wire? Oh, it's big wire. Bigger than that." All too quickly, I have seven people, including one of the vice presidents, turning the office upside down, all getting worked up into a frenzy over this wire that I supposedly need. The questions get refined. I'm suddenly standing here on a Tuesday at 4:25 looking for a power line. My first assistant gets on the phone and with a little more back and forth has an order for 20 feet of power line. Preferably live, I think to myself, which gives me ideas as to why I need a power line. I thank everyone for their assistance, my first assistant thanks me for the muffins, and I retreat back to the heat.

Sitting back in my comfortably sticky chair and staring at the missile guidance manuals, I wonder if Carl will give me an award for creatively raising team spirit in the office, while quickly getting a supply ordered. I also wonder if I'm standing in the way of AutoDrive.

Halfway through my rounds of closing and locking up, Clarence calls me over to where he's working. He asks me questions about training Cooelle on what he's doing. He's concerned that I want him to teach her aspects of the job that he doesn't handle. I reassure him that just trying to cover all that he does in a one day training session will certainly be enough. I start listing off things that he knows and his responsibilities, the things he should cover for training, and he becomes impressed with his role at Flight Control. "I didn't think of all that until you listed it," Clarence says. We're thinking about that when there is a scream of terror and metal clanging on cement. I run across the warehouse floor with others. Harvey is pinned to the floor by one of the mock-up electric half-cars. Tiny electronic sensors from the cars and from a toppled parts bin, bounce and shatter across the floor.

"I'm all right, I'm all right," Harvey says.

We shut down the equipment and pull it off him. He brushes himself off and winces as he bumps his right side. I back away. He rationalizes it all away and checks his bleeding elbow. He's pretty well beaten up. Clarence is checking for broken ribs. Robin is sweeping up the broken glass of a crystal ball lens that popped off and shattered. Scott and Wendy are picking up sensors, wires, and metal brackets. Some index cards we use to track progress are strewn about. Blood is mixed in with the cards. I pick them up. I haven't said anything and people are looking between the mess and me. I start in, "I need to know what happened here. Where's Mike? Why isn't he here? I need a report tomorrow, with a note from the doctor or nurse that will see you tonight. Do you need a ride to your clinic?" Harvey tries to talk his way out of going, but I do not yield.

This was a lousy way to end the day. A few blocks out of the parking lot I realize I could use a men's room, so I stop off at the High Bar. On the men's room wall I read, "Life is just one contradiction after another." Below that in a different pen and penmanship it says, "No it's not." Then it says in large letters, "The meek shall inherit the Earth" and then in small letters, "if that's okay with the rest of you." In another spot someone wrote "I fucked your mother." Below that someone else wrote, "Go home, Dad. You're drunk."

As I head out of the bar, the bartender says, "Hey fella, chin up, you've got two days under your belt." I wave him off. Two days under my belt – maybe that's why my gut doesn't feel so good. I head home.

Soon after crossing the river, the driver behind me almost runs into me. I change lanes. So does he. I wait about 20 seconds. He's gaining on me. I change back just in time for him to pass me an instant later. I only give the other drivers one try at hitting me. There are far too many customers to do otherwise. One try per customer. About four blocks from home I'm stopped behind a left turner. There is a building with about a three story brick wall. It's got this giant zigzag arrow that points right into a solid perpendicular line. I don't get it.

7

Hope Floats

At my apartment complex, a moving truck blocks the front door and several parking spaces. My thoughts in order as they occur:

Moving Thought 1. Is it the end of the month today? Yes, it is! I don't pay much attention, since I always mail the rent five days ahead and then Ray pays me back on the first, just not this time. People usually move from apartments at the last possible second, partly because they can't move into the next place until the last person has moved out unless there is a vacancy in which case they might allow someone to move in a day or two early without paying an extra months rent.

Moving Thought 2. Maybe it's one of my immediate neighbors. Please-please-please be one of my neighbors, upstairs or downstairs especially, but I don't care. This is one lottery I'm willing to play. I mean, what could be worse? A family of newborn sextuplets with an evening job cleaning chainsaws at home? Uncoordinated, sumo wrestlers whose ears were damaged by their giant speakers on wheels? It's kind of difficult to outcry the existing tenant racket. And yet...

Moving Thought 3. Things can always get worse. People can always move in without others moving out. Inefficiency apartments like mine can legally fit ten people. Illegally, it's limitless. The elephants upstairs could've invited their Old World relatives – hippos, rhinos, water buffaloes – to move in with them. And the band downstairs lacks a tuba section.

Moving is a time of hopes and dreams. I park in an out-of-the-way spot. Most of these people have some difficulty driving their own cars, let alone a big rental truck (beep-beep-beep-beep-crunch).

In my hallway, a guy is banging on the door of one of my neighbors. Spotting me he asks, "Excuse me, do you live here?"

I point to my door and say, "If you call it living."

"I'm thinking about moving here. Do you consider this building conducive to studying?"

I laugh. I can't help it. "Yeah, sure. If you are studying urban decay and the effect of noise pollution on human behavior, sure this is a regular research laboratory, a veritable study hall. You provide the working hypothesis. We provide the sleepless nights and all the research material for your PhD in psychiatry, sociology, criminal science, or any combination of those fields. Yeah, this is a researcher's gold mine." He thanks me and leaves. I wasn't finished explaining the benefits of our apartment community. Hadn't even started. How rude.

I go into the haze of my apartment. I wave to Ray, who is drawing in the living room in front of a fan. He waves back. He's looking better, almost as good as Harvey when I last saw him. I drop off my things in my room and change. The apartment smells like everything was crammed into the oven to bake, melt, liquefy, evaporate, and release toxic gases. The swirling smoke and odors are a chemist's dream.

"Any word about the air conditioner?" I ask.

"Nope."

I run down to talk to the landlady. She says the owners can't afford anything but the most essential repairs. Fix the air conditioner. Or I will get it fixed and drop the rent by 60 dollars each month, the extra amount for having an air conditioner. Or I will get it fixed and reduce my rent by the amount it costs to fix or replace, giving her a copy of the receipt. She says she'll talk it over with the owner. In the meantime, all the other repairs that haven't been fixed may take priority over mine. I cut her off before she finishes her list. Back in the apartment I tell Ray about the conversation, take a shower, and call Hope. I apologize for the last minute call and ask if she's free tonight.

"My price has never been negotiated," she says. I pull the phone headset away from my head and look at it like it's sick or something. Hesitantly, I put it back to my head. "Uh, that's a joke," she adds.

Ah yes, a joke: a humorous story or anecdote usually with a clever ending. "Okay."

"Are you okay? You sound a bit out of it."

"Yeah, fine." I'm not sure she knows me well enough to gauge how I am feeling over the phone.

"Is it all right if we hang out here with Becky? We could make root beer floats..."

"How does seven sound?"

"Sounds good. We'll be here."

"Okay, see you at seven. Bye."

"Bye."

Hurray. We get to be chaperoned. That means we'll have twice as much fun.

I thaw my broccoli against my forehead before getting it steamed. Ray decides he doesn't want any. I do the same with a frozen meatless burger disk. I count on frozen food. Frozen food: essential for the survival of the single.

Right now the frozen food is in the freezer. For the rest of the year the frozen food is kept in the yard along with everyone else's. Minnesota has special community property laws for frozen food. The only real hazard is from foraging polar bears.

I fry up the burger and put ketchup, mustard, pickles, and avocado on it. When you add more than two ingredients to a burger, the burger no longer matters. It could be beef. It could be turkey. It could be cardboard. I'm eating a soy and corn burger. It is an adequate shelf for the toppings. And rooming with Ray, the vegetarian, continues to alter what I eat. However Ray didn't buy the meatless burger disks. I did. Ray is meat sensitive. He can be glad that I'm not eating meat, but he doesn't even want to see food in a meat form, like a burger. Animal crackers upset him.

I eat over the sink, wash two pans and a few utensils, and life couldn't be simpler. I get dressed and dash out the door. I sidestep people carrying too many boxes and bags and lamps. You can't have too many lamps in an apartment, I always say. But I've been known to be wrong. Root beer floats? That sounds good, as a shift change occurs between the afternoon humidity and the evening humidity. My antiperspirant fails halfway across the parking lot. Squeal! When I was a teenager, I purposefully under-inflated the tires of my car. It's not good for the tires. It's not good for gas mileage either. What it does is it helps squeal the tires.

On Serenity Street, I part a veritable sea of gnats, like Moses driving a Pony Express. I take Serenity to University to Interstate 94. Interstate 94 is a fine upstanding highway known across the country from Detroit to Seattle for taking people where they want to go. Special grooved surfaces assist traction in Minnesota; the furrows are small and follow the road. Completely different, larger grooves that run against the direction of the road warn drivers in Chicago of toll stations. I've been told that North Dakota still has its original I-94 roadbed from the 1960s. I've never driven the interstate in North Dakota.

Helpless In Life comes on the radio, and I sing along. Suddenly I feel tired. I wonder why I'm going to Hope's. It's been a long day. And it's a weekday night. The sunset appears to be falling back in my rearview mirror. I think it may exit. I turn off the radio.

I try not to think of myself. I usually feel selfish when I do. I usually think of others. When I am thinking about me, it's not about who I am now. It's about deciding who I want to be.

Years ago, before I learned to under-inflate tires, I prayed for love. Not just any love, I was detailed in my request. I am a detail-oriented person. It says so on my resume. I exit the highway. If I hit Lake Weago, I've gone too far.

When I pray, I am specific. I figure I have to be specific because God has a sense of humor. In Indonesia there is a fish that breathes air, runs on water, can climb trees, and is bursting with personality. It has big bubble eyes, a big round mouth and paper-fan-shaped-fins. It lives in the mud. It is sacred. If there is such a thing as reincarnation, I have already put in a request to come back as one. It is called a mudskipper. God has a sense of humor. So I figure if you pray for something, be specific. Don't leave an opening for comedy. Comedy is funny until it happens to you. The truism is to be careful what you ask for, you might get it.

I asked God for a love that would be supportive of me and I of her. She would be charmingly beautiful, both in attitude and appearance. She would be almost naively open and caring. We would treat each other so respectfully that we would not be harmed by loving each other unconditionally. A sweet innocence from expecting the best of the world and a resiliency for when the world falls short of its potential. A magnetic personality. Kind of goofy too. Basically, perfection with legs.

That may be Hope. Yeah, this is the house she described.

If it is Hope that I'm looking for, I would like our relationship to advance. If it isn't, I guess we should know that too. I peel myself out of the car. I don't know if I should kiss her, and I'm too hot to hug her, so I just sort of stand in front of her stupid-like and say, "Hi."

"Hi. What happened to your not being able to do anything on a school night?" she asks taking my hand and leading me around the side of the house and up a stairway to the second floor.

"I don't know. Maybe I've lost my head."

"Are you looking for it?"

"No."

"Let me know if you need any help," she dimples, opening the door to a cool-cool living room that smells like vanilla. I sit down in a cool leather-like armchair, knowing how cool it would be, and it is. Ahh. Maybe I should have sat on the couch so Hope could've sat next to me. The Minnesota temperature extremes have affected my brain. Hope leans over and inspects my forehead. "You've got some green specks on your face," she informs me while brushing whatever it is off.

"I do?"

"Uh-huh."

Here comes our chaperone. Becky carries in the root beer floats with spoons stuck in them and an alarmed look on her face. "I forgot the straws!" she exclaims, setting the glasses on the end table beside us and dashing off again. She's fast.

"Did you see that?"

"See what?"

"That's what I thought."

Here comes our chaperone again. Becky hands us our straws and plops herself on the couch holding a mildly abused, rolled-up magazine. I hesitantly ask her, "You're not going to whack me with that thing are you?"

"Maybe." I get uneasy. "I'd like to give you a test."

"I didn't study. I try to study for every test I take, including vision tests. Maybe I'd better not take it until I'm better prepared." In my peripheral vision I see a door open a few inches but nothing else is going on, no cat or anybody. "Tonight will be a cram session," I tell them, while mixing some of the vanilla ice cream glacier into the root beer bay.

"It's just a test from a magazine. It's about what you think."

"I would have to study thinking. Or think about studying about thinking."

"It's only ten questions. There aren't really any wrong answers."

"Okay, but I get to give my ten answers first: nine, a bandana, Major Munch with Munch Berries, blueberries, possibilities, cow tipping, yes but not before bedtime, second chorus, the Louisiana Purchase, and getting whacked by a magazine. In that order," I add having kept count using my fingers. I give Becky an attentive look.

"The first question is, do you believe in love at first sight?"

"No." Hope turns to me questioningly, but I am transfixed in my concentration on a spoon-sized vanilla slide.

"If you love someone, does that mean you'd do anything for them?"

"No." Becky marks her magazine with a pencil.

"If they asked you to let them go, would you?"

"Yes." Hope sets down her glass.

"Were Romeo and Juliet in love?"

"No," I laugh.

"If you love someone, does that mean they are more important than anything?"

"No."

"Are you in love with someone else? We kind of already know that one."

"I don't know."

"What?!? Yes or no. Are you in love with someone else?"

"It's not a yes or no answer. I don't know."

"Answer the damned question," this from Nicole behind the partly open door.

"I did. I don't know."

Becky and Hope are looking at each other. Becky's got a confused look on her face. I can't see Hope's expression.

"Uh, question seven, is there such a thing as unconditional love?"

"I want to say, 'I don't know,' but I'll say 'no.'"

"If you get married, would that mean you would be married forever?"

"No."

"Do you think that a man, dedicated to one woman, should be allowed to sensually touch another woman?"

"I'll say, yes."

"Could you kill in the name of love?"

"Yes."

Becky starts counting my answers. Hope gets in front of me as I evenly blend my root beer float and says, "You could take this a little more seriously."

"You flunked," Becky says. "Everyone does, but you really flunked."

I set down my glass. "I was serious," I tell Hope firmly. To Becky, "How can I flunk? You said there aren't any wrong answers? Can I expand on my answers?"

"No!" Becky says angrily. "They weren't essay questions." She tosses the magazine.

"For questions from a magazine, you two are taking this a bit too seriously. And I can't explain my answers?!?"

"What does it matter?" Becky asks.

"It matters to me. It matters to me," I repeat at the same time as Becky says, "You've already lost."

Which causes me to replay what she said, "Lost?!? What have I lost? If I matter to any one of you, you'll give me a chance to elaborate on my answers so you can understand where I'm coming from. Aren't you trying to understand?"

Nicole comes in, walking toward me, and pointing at the door, "I think you should go."

"Shut up and let him talk!" Hope yells at her roommates, in a voice I haven't heard from her.

I turn to Becky. "First off, you didn't write these questions, right? Right! They are very vague, hypothetical questions that dance around the subject of love, specifically between Hope and I." I turn to Hope, whose eyes aren't dry, "I think I love you, Hope. We've been together for four days now. I don't want our relationship to end because I'm forced into answering these questions as either a yes or a no. Life is an essay question. It's not true-false. It's not multiple choice. That implies that all your answers are sitting right in front of you to pick, but it's rarely that simple. And it's definitely not true-false. There are always possibilities that true and false miss. Gray areas. Nuances. The middle ground. When I answered that last question I was picturing a very extreme situation of someone threatening Hope's life, and I would have to kill them to save her. And if that were my only solution, even though I am typically a non-violent person, yes I would kill to save her. First, I would find any solution, no matter how ludicrous, to avoid answering an extreme with an extreme. Give me the questions again."

Becky grabs the magazine, "We don't have to do this." I stare at her. "Uh, do you believe in love at first sight?"

"A love based on appearance or one experience is a superficial love, if it is love at all. It is a start. You can care about strangers, but to love someone you have to have some sort of understanding of them."

Nicole sits down; her tank top says, Bouncer. She asks, "Are you in love with someone other than Hope?"

"When I was in high school and college, there was a girl that I liked that I didn't know whether or not I loved. I still don't know if I did."

"Is it Aimee?" Nicole asks.

"No."

"Does this girl know you've liked her?"

"No. It's passed."

"No, it hasn't. If it had, you wouldn't have brought it up. She still matters to you."

"She mattered to me. That was years ago."

"I don't want to limit you," Hope says.

"You're not limiting me."

"I think you should tell her," Hope tells me.

"No–"

"You should tell her. She should know," Hope says. I try to disagree. "In seventh grade a boy I liked jumped in front of a train. I never took the chance to tell him how I felt about him. It might have saved his life. I would have done anything to have been able to have a second chance." I try telling her that I can't. "Yes, you can. It matters. You've known her longer than you've known me."

"Will you let me say something?" She pauses. "First off, I want to be with you. And second off," I stop her from interrupting, "I never fully came to an understanding of whether or not I loved her. And thirdly, she's dead."

The three women around me relax a bit.

"I'm sorry," Hope sympathizes with me.

"What was her name?" Becky gulps.

"Melanie."

They look at each other. "Melanie Fields?!? Melanie the singer?!?" Nicole laughs. I nod. Becky tries not to spit out her drink. Nicole throws a pillow at me. She then crawls to a stack of pillows, and I rescue my glass from being knocked off the table.

"Could I use your bathroom?" I ask Hope.

"Down the hall, first door on the right," she says coolly. On my way, one pillow whiffs; another hits. I drink the rest of the root beer cream and drop off the glass in the kitchen. In the bathroom, I splash water on my face. Ah. I look in the mirror. I decide that I may not be the easiest person to understand.

I go back out and sit down on the floor near Becky and pick up the magazine. Seeing that it is a women's magazine, I quickly drop it like it is made of fire. "So many of those questions are open to imagining extreme possibilities, like about killing for love, or sensually touching someone else, or staying married forever, or whether the person you love is more important than anything... Do I lose because I have enough of an open mind, enough imagination, to see exceptions to the rules?" I rhetorically ask Becky. "Magazines try to reflect popular opinion. Scientific journals do not state fact; they reinforce the dogmas that are in vogue. They don't threaten textbooks by stating facts; they make arguments by stating assertions. Their number one job is to maintain or increase their subscription base. I can only guess that women's magazines are like that too. If their writers are experts at anything, it would be saying things that their readers want to hear. That's their excuse. When you told me, 'There aren't really any wrong answers,' you lied. When you refused to let me fully answer the questions, you opened my answers up to misunderstandings. And maybe I should have gotten up and walked out, because that situation you put me in and my playing along seems to have hurt Hope. And I would rather walk out than hurt Hope over some game you want to play." I cross my arms.

I've badgered Becky enough, now it's Nicole's turn. "You asked me to leave. Do you still want me to leave?"

"No," Nicole and Hope say nearly in unison.

People love me for my easy-going manner. So much for my easy-going manner...

I turn fully to Hope. I don't say anything. I am her attentive student.

"I think I should explain. They are just trying to protect me," Hope explains. I sit quietly. "Becky meant to bring the magazine over on Sunday, but she forgot it." It should have stayed forgotten. "What can we do to make it up to you?" My arms uncross.

"I want to be with you," I tell Hope. "If you don't want to be with me, please tell me."

"I want to be with you too."

"I also want us to be friends," I tell Becky and Nicole. "I expect my friends to treat me fairly. They don't have to always understand me or agree with me. They don't, and they won't. But they do have to give me the benefit of the doubt. Like I said, I would rather walk away than hurt Hope. You aren't the only ones who will be trying to protect her."

"I'm feeling like a glass antique," Hope comments.

"I think you're special, if that's what you mean. If you want to talk with me, talk with me. You are the authority on what you want to say, not some magazine. Are we okay?" They agree.

Nicole grabs Becky and Becky's magazine. "I think we've done enough damage for one night," she says while hauling Becky out of the room.

I move to the couch. Hope moves beside me. "I'm sorry about all that."

"It's okay," I reassure her.

Hope puts her soft hand on my arm and says, "I cried when I heard Melanie had died. We all cried watching her funeral on TV." I swallow and nod.

Hope pulls her legs under her, leaning closer to me. My heart beats faster. My body turns toward her and my eyes bounce between her eyes and her lips. Her eyes sparkle; her lips glisten. I reach for her cheek. I kiss her lips. Our kiss is soft. Her perfume is even softer, like light talcum powder on a baby bunny, with a hint of vanilla ice cream. Her eyes are looking into mine. My lips lightly brush against hers, exploring them, feeling how full they are, feeling her lips move. Our lips pucker and expand, pucker and expand, pucker and expand in a slow, gentle dance. I kiss her lightly. I close my eyes. I feel Hope gasp as I drag my lower lip across her lower lip. Her breath is warm and sweet. My hand lightly holds the side of her cheek, while my fingers play in front of her ear, around her earlobe, below her ears on her neck, and up behind her ear, and back again. My tongue feels the underside of her upper lip. My lips explore hers by grabbing them and releasing them. I open my eyes. Hers are still closed. My thumb and forefinger caress her earlobe. I give her two more light pecks. I tilt my head forward and my lips away to break the kiss but keep our heads together. Hope opens her eyes. We catch our breath without moving apart. Hope adjusts to continue kissing me. Her tongue runs my lips like a racetrack without the hurry. A quiet giggle tells us that her roommates are okay. Her tongue is on its second lap when I realize I've never been kissed like this before. I like it. I kiss her to stop her tongue. I start my tongue around her lips. During its third lap, my tongue is sucked into Hope's mouth. While holding it in place with suction, her tongue dances and explores my captured tongue, just like my fingers are doing to the side of her neck. Her tongue drags across mine, exploring the length of my tongue. I swallow to keep my mouth dry. Her tongue pokes and caresses and twists with my tongue. My tongue caresses her tongue, and then begins its methodical exploration of her mouth, while my fingers massage her neck. Her tongue chases after my tongue as it checks her teeth and gums. My thumb and fingers massage her collarbone and move on to her shoulder. Her tongue catches my tongue. My tongue slips free and glides across the top of Hope's mouth. Hope lets go and backs off, laughing, "Hey that tickles." She replaces my hand on her shoulder, catches her breath, and kisses me more forcefully. I match her force, lip by lip. My other hand surprises her by doing a little dance on her thigh. Her eyes go wide. I lightly suck her lower lip. I release it and kiss a trail across her cheek. I whisper, "How's this?" in her ear. The kissing trail meanders down her neck in switchbacks to prevent my lips from tumbling lip over lip down the slope. "This is good!" she gasps. What a nice thing to say! I have to kiss the mouth that says such nice things. Our lips twist and turn in their oral orgy of osculation. My hand on her shoulder and back rubs through, around, and across her bra straps. Hope imitates my massaging by massaging my back as well. My fingers on her thigh run circles and figure eights and all sorts of other patterns from her knee to the hem of her skirt. It never crosses the hemline. The kisses become harder. Without warning the fingers on her thigh drop down to her knee, back up her thigh, crossing the line, running over her skirt and farther up her thigh, up her waist, crossing over to her arm and back to her side, edging up the side of her shirt, over her shirt-covered bra, up her shoulders and hair to behind her head, where it stops to massage the back of her head, while our lips kiss each other unrelentingly, softly, firmly, slowly... Our kisses smack for the first time, almost like exaggerated movie kissing sound effects. I suck in with an extra strong pucker to do the most exaggerated stage kiss ever. Hope laughs, "That **really** tickles!" I tell her, "Do that with me at the same time." We do it. It is an extremely exaggerated kiss. We laugh and rub our lips. It's very lip numbing. Breathing her breath, it smells sweet, like she's been licking candy. I must be the biggest sucker; I'm in love. And then I notice the time.

"Is it really three minutes to midnight?!?" I ask.

"Yeah..."

"Listen-it's-been-really-great,-but-if-I-don't-get-home-before-midnight-I-turn-into-a-pumpkin-or-a-squash-or-a-gourd-or-some-other-autumn-vegetable!" I dash for the door, turn around, dash back, grab Hope, sweep her off her feet, kiss her again, set her up again, say "Bye," and I dash out the door. I climb down the steps two at a time. I peel off in my car and head back home.

Back at the Whisper Willows apartment complex, someone is honking for someone else. I give them a look as if to say, get your butt out of your car if you really are trying to get somewhere. Inside it is obvious that the upstairs neighbors are rearranging their furniture for the night. Oops, they dropped their couch. Oops, they dropped their couch again. Oops, they dropped their couch a third time. Neighbors, you are tedious.

I call Hope. I invite her and her roommates to Tom's cabin next weekend. Faith won't be available, but Hope is a yes. The others are maybes. We wish each other a good night.

8

Mental Closure

Nothing's happening. All day I've been thinking it's Thursday. I'm just plugging away. I stare off at the white wall with the Founding Fathers plaque, calculating the damage AutoDrive would cause in a parking lot. The final damage total switches from dollars to credibility and the amount switches to being priceless. The test I ran this morning had mixed results.

I make a mental note to have Harvey give a safety lecture on Monday. On the bright side of things, Harvey is okay and back at work. The doctor's note mentions that he can get out of gym class if he wants. Or at least I think that's what it says. The doctor's note is handwritten. Harvey's report is detailed enough to tell me that he could've avoided the accident, but it would've taken some better than average guess work to do so.

I just got off the phone with someone else from the company wanting in to Research & Development. The score is one phone call, one knock on the door frame, and one parking lot ambush. Maybe the business suit of tomorrow will be something in a nice camouflage print. My responses have been skeptical at best. I did not hire these people, and I have no interest in creating animosity within the company. I know the guy from the parking lot; I have a low opinion of his work. The woman who stopped by I have never seen before. She does not inspire me with confidence in her professionalism. Her outfit might have been more appropriate for a bar than for work. I don't know the telephone caller, but I think she's the boss's niece.

Out on the shop floor, my staff is aligning and repairing the instrumentation on our mock-ups for consistency. Most of them have done this many times before, and Clarence is showing Cooelle how it's done. This is one of those times, like so many others, that a manager has to leave the employees alone to do their jobs. In front of me are the evaluations of last Friday's tests and the start of my guidelines for this Friday's tests. It's so much more complicated now that we're only conducting full blown trials once a week. We try more things at once, and we're better organized than we were six months ago, but we also risk smashing up more sensors when we miss. It would be inappropriate for me to say so, but I would have thought we'd be further along by now. It would be nice to leap ahead. I'd like to say that... I don't know... that AutoDrive can make any turn no matter how screwy the roads were laid out.

In this city, a great number of streets were laid out on a grid pattern or two. One neighborhood's grid pattern, which was arranged on a hillside by Lake Grindstone, is joined to one of the grid patterns set up against the Mississippi River. The Mississippi River staggers through Minnesota as straight as a gay drunk. The city grid patterns are rarely north-south-east-west. A third grid pattern intersects the other two and is itself intersected by the Fargo-Ramsey-Ottawa-Minot Railroad and the interstate highway that parallels it. Feeder highways and their cloverleafs criss-cross the grid patterns and interrupt the grids as well as the neighbors that live on them. Like castle walls, the strip malls line the county highways that nourish the feeder highways, cordoning off several residential blocks from the light of day. City planners, people who never bother with matching socks, eye the last vestiges of order on the map with plans to plop a big, old stadium or shopping mall or convention center smack dab in the center of it all. "A four way intersection with 90 degree angles" is the punch line to many city planner's jokes. And I want AutoDrive to handle any turn.

The white wall in front of me has a contoured surface when you really look at it. Ups and downs, tiny plateaus and smaller valleys, light and shadows – like snow painted Minnesota in winter. It's a blank slate with a lot of detail. Imagine a teeny-tiny AutoDrive car learning to drive this wall on its own. Self-learning was once demonstrated on a television show. A machine was teaching chimps language by a system of rewards. If the chimp pushed the right set of buttons (I, want, banana), it would get a banana. Or a toy. Or a human helper. Or water. Does the name Pavlov's dog ring a bell? The choices can be illustrated in a flowchart. A complex flowchart can be defined mathematically as an algorithm. A genetic algorithm is a program that develops successful programs through testing and weeding out unsuccessful programs. It is the survival and mating of the fittest programs. If we could take–

"Sir, I've got some ideas on how to speed up production." It's Mike the intern. Mike was put in my group without any interview and without any input from me.

"Let's hear it," I say leaning back.

"First, I want to make sure I get credit for my suggestions...," he says.

I am about to agree when I wonder what sort of credit he wants. I picture a billboard on Portage Street or University Avenue. "What kind of credit?" I ask him.

"I would just want people to know who made the suggestions."

"People here?" I ask.

"Yeah."

"That goes without saying. Go ahead." I symbolically clear my desk, and open my mind.

"We're a research department, right?" Keep going. You're doing fine so far. "We should be doing some real research. We're wasting too much time on paperwork," he says motioning to my paper flow lapping at the sandbag barricade, "and not enough time finding out what is available to us. We should be on the Internet comparing notes with the rest of our field." I blink closed my mind long enough to picture a rolling hillside covered with daisies. Mike shows a daisy to a stout old man in a tweed suit, who sneezes. I blink my mind open again. "What if part of what we're trying to do is already available. We could just buy it and be miles ahead of wherever we are now. I'm not saying anything is on the Internet or not. I'm just saying we ought to find out."

I'm thinking of making Mike our senior researcher in charge of Internet research, except that he would expect a raise to go with the decreased responsibilities. I'm thinking of dropping his pay down to minimum wage. I have researched the Internet at various stages of our project. My inquiries received several "cool :)" responses but nothing of substance. The gossip fence of yester-year, the party-line telephone circuit of yester-month, and the Internet of today are the communication channels of gab and greeting. If television is a puddle, then perhaps the Internet is an inland wading pool that expands beyond the horizons but has no depth. Granted, I haven't checked it recently, so maybe AutoDrive is already on sale there. I prop open the door to my mind with my shoulder. Maybe we can become resellers of a product that already exists. We would just rake in the dough. I'm holding my mental door open with both hands, a shoulder, and a knee. "If I choose to take you up on your proposal, would you like to do the research?"

"Yeah, if nobody else can." I think he just insulted the rest of R&D. "My other idea is for what I call a smart jacket," Mike grins. "Drivers would tell the car what they want to do by just motioning this way or that," he says with his shoulders.

Slam went the door to my mind. Why not just develop four input devices that give specific orders to the car? A rotational axis could indicate maneuvering while two foot pedals could indicate acceleration and deceleration, and a stick lever could vary the gears that specify driving wheel torque. With the mental door shut and locked, I can clearly see a yellow mental warning light which flashes, "Watch what you say next." Mike and I are not exactly seeing eye-to-eye. What I say could come back to haunt me, if I don't rein in my sarcasm.

"Mike, I'm glad to see you are thinking about ways to improve our work here. I would like you to submit your ideas to me in writing to make them official so that you can get credit for all the details of your proposals and that I don't misinterpret your... ah... intentions. Mike, where were you yesterday afternoon?"

"I had to take care of something at school."

"I'm docking your pay for three hours."

"I was only gone for two." I give him a look that asks how stupid he thinks I am? "Okay, it was two and a half."

"And you were supposed to be working with Harvey. It was a two-person job."

"You're blaming me for what happened to him?"

"You are partly to blame, yes. And I'm docking your pay for three hours. Here is a copy of a reprimand that is going in your personnel folder." I hand him the reprimand. "You need to work on your sense of responsibility. We do not tolerate accidents here." I got his attention.

"So I guess a promotion is out, huh?" Mike says as he leaves my office. He's hilarious.

Now where was I? Don't answer that. It's a rhetorical question.

I am sweating up another Great Lake. I'm 90 percent perspiration and ten percent inspiration. I go back to my paperwork. It's completed in overtime.

It's time to go. Everyone else has gone. As I lock up my office, I realize I haven't prepared anything to report during tomorrow's waste-of-time management meeting. It would be nice if I could spend more time teaching AutoDrive not to bump into things, I think as I lock things up and put some things away. I'm out of here.

I have to go to the cash machine. I don't know about anywhere else, but here in Minnesota, the automated teller machines (ATMs) are called cash machines. I give the machine my card. It asks for my personal identification number (PIN), like I have only one! I give the ATM my appropriate PIN. It asks which account I want to access but only gives me the options of checking or savings, not somebody else's.

It flashes a quick and somewhat resentful message that it will assume that I am withdrawing my money from it – nobody ever gives it any money anymore – whatever happened to the spirit of giving? In the beginning, people would give money and take money almost evenly from the machine – then word spread that money can be continually taken from the same machine, while giving to some other machine or without giving to any machine at all. Soon it became apparent that no one would be giving money to machines anymore, and one night all the machines shut down and talked it over. The machines agreed not to ask if a deposit or withdrawal is being made anymore and agreed on the signal for world domination which would be–

And that's all I ever get a chance to read. Next, the cash machine asks if I would like my money in Canadian currency since we are so close to the Canadian border (or as they put it, the American border). I am also offered the possibilities of United States dollars, insect repellent, or sidewalk salt, each of which are considered legitimate currency only in their appropriate seasons.

It being neither salt nor dollar season, my response is insect repellent. I shudder with a mix of amusement and horror at the uninformed tourist who goes to pay their restaurant bill only to find themselves unprepared with proper currency. And it's not like that couldn't happen! I've seen the tourist books and the travelogues on Minnesota, and none of this stuff is in there. Tourists learn about the giant statue of the anti-environmentalist Paul Bunyan, the often frozen Minnehaha waterfall, the once secret caves and catacombs below Milltown and Pigs Eye (especially Wakan Teebe), the sacred Spirit Island of the Mississippi River, and the Native American burial mounds on the bluffs overlooking the river. But the tourists never learn about the seasonal currency of Minnesota.

The cash machine takes a moment to lick its metal fingers and count out the cans of repellent. Then they roll out in a clump. I step back until they've settled. I once saw a woman eating repellent for lunch because the cash machine was spraying it out like a pop machine with an over-shaken can of Double Bubble. You can never be too careful. The cans sit quietly in the metal drop basket of the cash machine. I step forward and scoop them up. The machine spits out my cash card with a spitting sound. It's all wet, probably from having licked its fingers to count the currency.

The cash machine hums to itself as I walk away. I look back. It stops. I continue to my car. I think it's humming again...

9

Clock Me

The alarm clock rings. I push the button to stop it. It keeps ringing. I push it again. It still rings. I flip on the light and look at it. It shrugs, tells me it's 1:22, and points at the phone. Oh. I pick up the phone, knocking Safari Of The Mind off my nightstand.

"Hello?" I answer.

"Did I wake you again?"

"Aimee?"

"Yeah. Only I don't go by that name anymore. You must sleep all the time."

My alarm clock nods in agreement.

"Must... sleep... Is – Is it okay for me to still call you Aimee?" She's laughing. What did I say? I have no idea.

"Hey!"

"Yes, Aimee?"

"I've got a video. Want me to send it to you?"

"No, I want to see you not a disk."

"You'll see all of me on the video," she laughs. "You'll see more of me than anytime since we went skinny-dipping."

"Huh?" She's off her rocker.

"Remember? At Mud Lake?"

Oh, that's right. "I didn't look."

"Tell me about it."

"I didn't."

"What do you mean you didn't look?!?"

"I didn't look."

"You didn't want to see me naked?"

"No, it wasn't anything like that. I was just being polite."

"You can't skinny-dip polite... politely."

"I can." Seconds go by. I wonder if I've lost her. I realize this isn't a collect call. It isn't a payphone on the street. "Do you have a phone number that you'd want to give me?"

"I better go," she says a word at a time.

"Take care, A-Me-V."

"Bye Ricky," she says, and the line clicks off.

I set the receiver down. My alarm clock gives me a hands-on-the-hips, impatient look of, "I told you it wasn't me. I'm waiting for an apology." I re-set it and write a note that Aimee called. I trudge off to the bathroom, look out the window at the moon, and lie back down on my bed. I grab a white basketball laying beside me. I give it two shakes. With the help of my fan, it turns into a sheet. I cover myself and fall back asleep.

10

Meyetings

My alarm clock pushes me out of bed like it's been bearing a grudge half the night. From the floor I look up at it sprawled comfortably across my bed. What's its problem? I'm not sure I'm getting enough sleep.

Happy Thursday. I pick myself and my book up off the floor. Wishing myself a happy Thursday has all the punch of a happy birthday. It's good you made it this far; too bad you still have miles ahead of you on the obstacle course of life. This is a turning point to the week – the Thursday meeting. Remind me to find a job that does not involve regular meetings. Most of the attendees get a glimpse of the topics and tone at the Wednesday pre-meeting meeting held on the State Fairway Golf Course, or when raining, in the clubhouse. My pre-meeting meeting is held on Thursday mornings right here, rain or shine, in the shower. I'd like to start by opening up the... er... drain to questions.

Are tectonic plates dishwasher safe? How do they get that big slab of ice into the hockey arena? Why do restaurants with free refills have different drink sizes? What is happening to A-Me-V? Is orange shampoo really a conspiracy by redheads? When will Red be locked up at the loony farm? If AutoDrive had all the tools to learn, how far would it have to go before it decides that it made a mistake? If I drive the wrong way on a one-way street, the faces of the oncoming drivers will give me a clue that I'm doing something frightening. I can read this from complete strangers.

I learned about facial reactions from my mom. I had never seen her before in my life, but I would smile, and she would smile. I would try to scooch my crib across the floor; she would frown. I spent my formative years testing her reactions. That's what children do. The problem is that my bosses at Flight Control want AutoDrive to grow up and get its driver's permit in under five years. What are the chances of that?!?

No more questions, please.

I brush my teeth, shave a few points, and comb my hair. Not wanting them to see me sweat, I apply antiperspirant. I apply it to my armpits, my back, my forehead... this stuff couldn't possibly be bad for you. I forgo the camouflage suit for gray. We're in a whole gray area here. It's the color that's not a color, it's more of an unknown. Looking out the window, the sky is overcast. Time to go to work.

I don't always take a big picture approach to life. Sometimes I go weeks at a time thinking of nothing more than my working at creating and teaching a machine. But not now. Now I'm taking the approach of the outsider looking in. I'm in the driver's seat. I'm evaluating. And at rock bottom, the absolute low of this self-evaluation is the Thursday meeting. I don't know if it's them or it's me, but the Marina Trench on the west side of the Pacific Ocean – the deepest darkest spot in the world – it has nothing on Thursday meetings.

In the big picture, Thursday meetings are the most lifeless spot of my life. I sometimes half-expect a NASA probe to find its way into the conference room; collect samples of the notes, a dry-erase marker, Bill, and the table; and then scurry out with its specimens. I'm not saying the meetings are all bad... strike that. I am saying they are all bad.

I am sure that somehow, somewhere there is a form of meeting that might not suck the soul out of people. However, that would be a different animal from what I'm talking about. A meeting is the collection of memoranda and their interactions. Like amoebas, the interactions of memoranda breed more memoranda, sometimes nicknamed memos. Offspring memos are usually more aggressively wordy than their parent memoranda. Not that memos only come from memoranda or that people don't attend meetings. They don't, and they do. Meetings tend to be well populated, generally having more agenda represented and more disinterested parties than are supported by the topics covered. Comments, questions, and dirty looks spontaneously give birth to memos and addendums. Addendums are the pets of memos, complete with wagging tails. I'm sure all of this would fascinate any otherwise bored sociologist looking to write an article for a sociological journal with less than five hours of research. But that's not me.

I'm being negative. Meeting after meeting that are not just nonproductive but actually counter-productive have made me negative about meetings. The subjects discussed are worse than trivial (our parking lot), worse than minutia (parking spots), they are selfishly petty (subordinates parking in the parking spots of the officers leading to little signs for everyone's parking spots). I wish I were making this up.

As far as I know, there are two types of meetings. One is the council format:

"This meeting will come to order. The agenda for today's meeting begins with the reading of the minutes from the last meeting."

"I move that we waive the reading of the minutes from the last meeting in favor of a vote."

"I second."

"Any opposed? Motion carries. Any discussion? All those who approve of adding the minutes from last week's meeting into the record, signify by saying, 'Aye.' Opposed? The minutes will be added to the record as is."

A roll call is taken. The moderator of the meeting asks if there is any old business with a slightly vocal anticipatory choke. Then some blowhard prattles on about an extreme viewpoint that only they and someone lost in Antarctica share. A member of the ruling minority puts in their reaction again, for the third meeting in a row. They haggle out the stale argument. Both parties expect that this time will be different. This time their words and their emotions will carry the room like a ray of sunshine breaking and scattering the storm clouds. The silent majority will be swayed to their defense, and their side will be victorious.

But that doesn't happen. What is the majority thinking?

The majority doesn't care about the subject in the least. The majority is watching the clock or a watch with concern toward getting to lunch or dinner or not owing a fortune to the babysitter or some other personal appointment. The argument pauses for a voice to break the deadlock. But the voice is for tabling the discussion, which is agreed upon with dizzying speed. That finished, the floor is opened for new business. This is humor time in council format meetings. Invariably, some joker who has been doodling along has also been formulating some preposterous plan to be proposed at this point. A mild chuckle ripples through the crowd, order is regained, and another proposal is made. This proposal is similar to the joker's proposal in that it is a pointless plea for attention made by someone who should know better. Usually this issue, as complicated as a change of address, is referred to a secretary with the suggestion that it not waste everyone's time. This is said even though the previous suggestion was just as much a waste of time, except that it contained a secret center – the chewy candy of levity. The reprimand shuts down other possible cries for attention. The worst is over in the eyes of the meeting conductor. There is not enough control involved in new business. It is the creepy world of the unknown. When the door to that world is shut, a euphoric ease drifts over the conductor. The next subject is the continuation of the species, which is the conductor's favorite part of the meeting. Meeting conductors and manipulators always slow down the pace to savor this part. The discussion is scheduling the next meeting. Someone, somewhere, might ask, should there be a next meeting? But no one in the meeting asks that question. Most aren't paying attention. If such a question were raised, it would be scoffed at as though a vote for anarchy was being recommended. No. The next meeting is scheduled. There will always be meetings. Sometimes sub-council meetings are planned between meetings to avoid a meeting-less void.

"We can't hold a meeting. Most of us are out of town for two weeks."

"Gasp!"

"The three of us that are in town will hold meetings daily until you get back. We'll fax your hotels every Wednesday with the minutes and text-message your phones." For some, it is frightening to be without their meetings. Meetings are what gets them through the workday. It's an addiction.

The other type of meeting is the trickle down meeting. Leaders or leader-appointees tell the group what is going on. This person or person-appointee has the eyes of a god or more often a demigod's contact lenses. This means that they see all, in a twisted sort of way. It doesn't mean that they get all that they see, and sometimes the lenses get dirty and don't see things too well. Questions coming from these near-deities are a trap. They already know their answer, or they wouldn't be asking the question. They are testing you. Sociologists change the name for stuff all the time, to keep it current, but they once called the intelligence of this sort of meeting Group Think. In Group Think, there are no dissenting opinions and no competition. Drones agree with whatever the authority says. The rest are reticent. A friend of mine, Sharon, tells me that government meetings are trickle up; they are the same as trickle down only in reverse. The trick to attending either trickle meeting is not laughing. These people are not trying to be funny.

Council meetings are monotonous. Trickle-down meetings are reality with a twist or three. I wish the Flight Control management meetings were only monotonous.

I run meetings also. Someone else can evaluate my meetings, it's only fair. One enormous difference is that I don't hold regular meetings. A stapler is a good tool, but not for every job. I wouldn't try to staple wooden boards together or try to weld metal or cut wire with a stapler. Likewise a meeting is not the proper form of communication for every message. E-mail is also not always the proper form of communication. It is just like my paperwork analogy. One piece of paperwork is not dangerous and neither is one meeting nor one e-mail message. In volume however, they have the capacity to become communication blizzards. If only they cost money to the senders! Then they might only be sent when they are valuable. Maybe they should only cost if they are rejected, I don't know. I can't decide.

I also have a different way of making decisions. As a kid, my first decisions about decisions was to make decisions. Too many other kids just stood around not wanting to make decisions about what to do. They were immobilized by an inability to make decisions. I said, "Okay, I'm going to do this. If you want to join me, fine. If not, that's fine too." And the people that wanted to join me, went along with me. I wasn't trying to lead or boss people around. I just had the ability to make decisions. The same sort of thing happens now as an adult. One benefit is that the people that end up still being around me are people that are at least capable of making that decision.

One of my subsequent decisions was that I never would have enough information to make an intelligent choice. When you are in the middle of an issue, it can be difficult to see all that is going on around you. So I decided to look at things from different perspectives. That could mean looking at a shoe from above, underneath, inside... But even more valuable has been looking at things from other people's points of view. When looking at what is happening from their shoes, the way they see them, you learn what things are like from their point of view. Their point of view is no less or more significant than your point of view. Doing this helps you understand others, of course. It also helps you understand yourself. It helps you to understand that your point of view is not the only point of view. It is one of many. There is so much more to be learned this way. The world becomes less black and white and turns into shades of gray and sometimes color.

The conference room has no natural light. No windows interrupt the white walls. It is filled with a massive oval hardwood table. The table was a hand-me-down, an inheritance, from the senior Dumas. His son, Carl Dumas, is the founder and president of Flight Control. Thor Dratz is his right-hand man and a vice-president. Thor is also a centaur, due to steroid use. All the managers are here, plus a few people I don't know. One was in Carl's office the other day... Monday. The talk is about having tickets to the next Millers game. The stadium is not far from our building. We actually make a short-term profit by renting out our parking lot. I never sit at an end of the oval. I sit on the curve. People see me come in, but there is no acknowledgment. I flashback to my pre-meeting meeting: brushed, shaved, combed, applied – here we are – I applied antiperspirant. Good. I have nothing to worry about. Something else must be going on for no one to acknowledge me. Bill follows me in.

Carl, Thor, and Peter turn almost in unison to Bill. Carl huffs, "Nice work keeping that Johnson woman from going legal on us, Bill."

"Got it covered," Bill says with a glance to me, then back to them.

"Right. Bill, why don't you start things off," Carl says, signaling others to take their seats. Asking Bill to start things off is like the scenes that take place the first five minutes of an action movie. They don't have anything to do with anything that will be happening in the movie. They are not significant to the plot. They are there for the people who arrive late to the movies, so that those few people won't miss anything important for the rest of the film. No, I take that back. Bill is like the previews for unrelated movies shown before the movie.

He's telling them something about having gotten one of my people to always wear goggles, which is bull... uh... bullfrog, since it was never the point to wear your goggles in the bathroom and everywhere else. Think of all the men's room dangers Bill is claiming credit for having prevented. Besides, Bill only sent out the memo. My people and I were the ones who got Scott over the goggle hurdle.

Now he's talking about his conversations with the Highway Department and what rules certain people over there think will apply to AutoDrive. Professionally ass-backwards. A whole new set of laws will be created for AutoDrive. Standard driver drives and passenger don't rules can't apply to AutoDrive, which blurs the distinction between driver and passenger. So to go to the department that enforces the existing rules, for only one state, to see what will apply to a completely new situation is ridiculous. Common sense is the least common of the senses, especially in this office.

Peter was just talking about one of the people that I don't know, but I didn't hear what he said. I think it had something to do with Double Bubble. Peter's vice-presidential role is to wine and dine. He's got the face, the voice, and the ambition for it. Peter has never been tied down by reality or what AutoDrive will actually do. Peter leverages associates by selling AutoDrive's future. Peter's world is as connected to the real world of AutoDrive as the stock market is connected to publicly traded companies. In the stock market, a company can be doing great, and its stock can be doing nothing. Or tanking. A company can be doing poorly, but guesses about its future can send the stock to new highs. Sometimes there is no connection at all. Market analysts make guesses as to what happened because that's their job. If they said they didn't know what happened, they'd be out of a job.

From time to time, I question whether my abilities are enough. What if I went back in time and accidentally landed on the brighter Wright brother. I don't even know whether that was Orville or Wilbur. You can't tell which was the brighter brother by just the name. Could I make a plane that would fly? "Okay, that looks right, but what are all these feathers for?" What if I had to invent fire? Cro-Magnon says, "Well, he has a lot of bright ideas." Is this what people mean when they say I think too much and take things way too far? "I've got it – the feathers are just to keep them warm!" the inventor exclaims, as he falls off the cliff, flapping his arms, feathers drifting.

Peter just said something. It sounded important. I scramble to play it back in my mind. In the process

I sit up. It was a new name for AutoDrive. "It's Chauffeur. It's French for 'I'll drive you home.'"

"What?!?" Did I just ask that out loud? I did. Clean up in aisle three. All eyes turn toward me. I exist after all, well what-do-you-know!

"Chauffeur," Peter repeats.

"Oh," I smirk. Refresher course on meetings starts now in my head. Do not talk. Do not nap. Recognize that there are different levels of participants. Take the Ben Franklin approach – sit back and be amused.

"Do you have something to contribute?" Peter asks with condescension.

"No, please continue," I reply. Peter is also a Dumas. I think he's a step-brother.

"This is a concession to Double Bubble," he says glancing at one of the new people, "since we will be instrumental to their advertising next summer." At that he receives a nod from the other guy. So I wonder if the name will change back after they are done with it. I pick up on his last words. "Next summer" reverberates between my ears like the refrain from a bad pop song.

Now Phil is going to present the company's financial status and look for ways to cut spending in Research & Development, as usual. Phil has a dog that honks his car horn. I witnessed this talent one day when he stopped in on his day off. Dog sitting in the car honking for his owner. Since then when I think of Phil, I wonder if the dog isn't the master. I stop myself whenever I think I'm being ridiculous.

Carl turns to me. Everyone turns to me. People in the building who can't see me and don't know what is going on in the closed-in over-air-conditioned room have absently turned toward me. Barge workers on the nearby Mississippi turn toward me. People in the skyways, the people tubes that connect the skyscrapers at the second floors, turn toward me. Milltown shifts in its seat to turn toward me. The state of Minnesota–

"Any news from Research & Development?" Carl asks.

"Nothing worth reporting," I reply. Carl looks down and looks back at me with an expression I have never seen on his face in all the years that I've known him. It is desperation. "Well, just the other day we figured out why B3 stopped in the middle of an intersection with a green light while making a left turn." Everyone in the state leans forward toward me; eyes transfixed. "And that's about it." The state collectively sits back.

"Would you like to tell us about Tuesday's accident," one of the strangers asks condescendingly.

Tag teaming so early in the day? I won't play. I mean, I'll play; I just don't recognize the new player. The guy with glasses the size of windshields. "Who are you?"

"This is Mr. Bailey," Phil fills me in. Good to hear from you Phil.

I turn to Carl, "On Tuesday–"

"I don't care about that," Carl interrupts. "When will AutoDrive–"

"Chauffeur," Peter reminds him.

"Shut up," Carl growls uncharacteristically. Then back to me, "When will it be ready for production?"

"I don't know."

"Give me something. Anything," Carl says through clenched teeth. I think he's losing it. He takes a deep breath as if someone has reminded him to breathe. It's almost like he's a few cheeseburgers short of a heart attack. "Could you tell us why you're several weeks behind in your reports or– " There is a snicker somewhere to my right. "Or," he starts loudly, "why, with the help of Mr. Bailey, we uncovered that in your last report you stated there is no sidewalk discriminator?"

Uncovered?!? This stiff Bailey can read? Carl's face is beet red. What have they been feeding him?!? "I was asked if there is a sidewalk discriminator and answered no there is not. What that means is that there is no separate program or component that differentiates a sidewalk from a street but Auto– uh Chauffeur knows the difference. It is built into the main program. It has no problem recognizing pavements or pavement markings. Now, while it has known simple non-regulated turns and some regulated turns, it just learned, as I mentioned, a complex regulated turn. But there is so much more for it to learn. For example, it can't lane change."

"What will it take to be able to lane change?" is asked from my right, but I still answer to Carl.

"Determining the proper sensory information, sequence of events, distance, steering degrees relative to speed, the formula, coding, trials, analysis, and adjustments..." Peter is giving me a timeout signal as if I'm diverting from his reality. I ignore it. "...will give it the ability to lane change. If you are asking me for an estimate of when it will know all that you know about driving a car, I give it about a year if we hit all of our targets on the first try. Two if we never hit a target and have to keep adjusting and retrying the formulas every step of the way." Gasps and other complaints bounce across the room.

"From this point forward," Carl breathes across the table to me, "you will report to Mr. Bailey here, who will report to me. He will be in charge of getting this project back on track." He says some other things and at one of them he pounds his fist on the family heirloom table, so it must have been good. I can't believe this. I wonder if Bailey gets my paperwork reservoir.

"Nearly five years ago," Carl continues in a different tone, kind of from the back of his throat, "there were just a few of us butting heads about cars that drive on their own, in a building just west of bank plaza. It was a rough start. We didn't start at all on the first couple of tries. We had a shoelace budget, some music, and a dream." Actually there was no music and no money for shoelaces. Plus, shoelaces were kept away from us for the same reason they are kept from convicts.

"Despite pessimism, we are on the home stretch. With teamwork and dedication, AutoDrive – damn it – Chauffeur will be... **will be** right around the corner." I just notice he's sweating. "Racing its engine," he adds with a left-half smile. Some of the locals chuckle. It's cold enough to put frost on the windows, if we had windows in here, and he's sweating, in his good suit too. "We'll be picking up the pace, rest assured, you know, racing our engines as well." He clears his throat loudly. Somebody to my left jumps.

He stops talking. No one is saying anything. A NASA probe opens the door, peeks in, and quickly shuts the door. The entire business teeters on the pinheads of upper management. Bailey breathing down my neck is just going to set my engine a racing, let me tell you. I knock a mosquito off my arm with ease. Must be a little too cold for the pest. I wonder who let in the little air leech? The skeeter lands on the wall across from me. Then I notice Dumas's secretary, Heidi, staring at me. She shakes off the stare and hunches over her tablet. Carl clears his throat again. "Phil do you have anything to add to your budgetary report?" Carl asks.

"No, it... it pretty much... it said it all..." Phil's budget reports are done on a computer. That is as technical as they get. You might do a side-by-side comparison of Phil's budgetary report from three weeks ago, which is sticking its nose out from between some sandbags in my office, and one from five months ago at the bottom of the reservoir. You might think Phil typed in the identical numbers twice, but no, Phil didn't go to all that trouble. Instead he merely changed the date and the "week of" title. He's a genius. He told me so.

I catch some eyes and wonder if I've missed something. I replay the last statement. "Said it all." Yeah, I heard that. Thor mentions the coming storm season and not conducting tests during lightning strikes. Then as he's thinking about the lightning, he forgets what he was going to say. He wasn't paying attention either.

We follow Carl's lead to leave. He gets up, and swats the mosquito on the wall into a big bloody smear. He seems shocked that he did that, as if he didn't mean to hit it. He ushers his visitors out.

A chill lifts my arm hairs as I head for my office. Stumbling over the threshold between the offices and the warehouse, I drop my tablet, crumpling my notes in the process. I flatten them on my desk. They read:

> Bill puts Scott's goggles on him
> Bill ♥ Highway Department
> Peter drinks Double Bubble & hires Chauffeur for next summer
> Everyone pounces
> Bailey hits the ladder a rung above me
> AutoDrive-Damn It-Chauffeur is hiding around the corner

Young memos are cradled snuggly in my in-box. I lift them as if to care for them. Instead I drop them back and pat them down. This was never what I expected to do with my life. Paper shuffling and making a difference are not the same thing. I expect more of myself, to give back more. Instead of doing, I manage. And now I have a new manager. I start toward the door and stop myself. Attitude is everything. I will not pass the bad attitude on to my crew. I sit down in my chair, my notes before me. A knock on my doorframe interrupts my stew.

"Here's something from the meeting," Heidi says timidly, offering paper. I stand and she hands it to me. It's another memo. "I've e-mailed a digital copy." I look back and forth between the memo and the messenger. My expression asks her how a three-pager could've developed so quickly. Her look changes to surprise. "I'm sorry," she says and leaves.

That wasn't my question. Is she sorry that she typed up this solidification of Carl's intentions and got his signature? It takes him **days** to read anything let alone sign it. There is only one conclusion. Heidi has access to a time machine, allowing her to travel back in time a few days, enabling Carl to read it, make changes, and finally sign it days later! This makes Chauffeur not such a big deal. Now I understand the push to get Chauffeur out the door today. Tomorrow they have to ponder over the marketing of the time machine.

"Did you forget that special occasion? No, you didn't! Not when you have Flight Control's Hindsight, your own personal time machine! If at first you don't succeed, try-try again with Hindsight. Hindsight is the perfect tool for a perfect life. Did your stocks go down today? No they didn't, because you went back to sell them yesterday! Do you have a large project but not enough help? Your future will send you all the you's you need! And because they are all you, they'll know exactly what to do! Cloning only copies your body; Hindsight reproduces you! Choose your own death at the site of one of history's horrors. Watch your own birth. With Hindsight you can invest smartly, rewrite history, and see the future! Impatient? Jump ahead with Hindsight and your all-day stew is done and that commute-improving bridge is already built. Buy brand new antiques with Hindsight. Hindsight. It will change your life!"

The suits have finally gotten to me. I'm out of my gourd.

"Are you okay?" Edy asks.

I shrug with a poker face, look down as if checking a hand of cards and up again saying, "Fine." The imaginary cards I'm holding are a three of clubs, six of diamonds, seven of clubs, ace of spades, and an instructional card that explains the rules of Go Fish. Edy sets some paperwork in the in-box and leaves.

I stare at my in-box. If I stare at it long enough, maybe it'll go away. Where is my optimism? "Everything is all right," Hope's reassuring words float back to me. My head is on her lap, and we're on a hillside at the zoo. Peter Pan would call this my Happy Place. I never did like Peter Pan. My in-box hasn't gone away. Fine. I will. I get up to leave and sit back down again. I respond to half-a-dozen e-mails. I shuffle through my in-box. I drain half the reservoir of paperwork. Using jewelers tools and a large magnifying glass on an adjustable arm that's clamped to my desk, I work on a CCD sensor for Edy. Porter stops by, leaves, and comes back with two more sensors. We used to send these things out for repair. It would take weeks to get them back. When I heard over the phone part of what I needed to know to fix them, I learned how to repair them, and we stopped sending them out. Once I have corrected the three, I plug them into a bare-bones, guts-only digital camera. If the view of the office matches the LCD, I've done my job. It still looks wrong, like too much paperwork, but that's not the fault of the sensor. Porter is still here watching. I tell him, "The trick to working on the CCDs is that while you are looking through the magnifying glass, you close your left eye, raise the left corner of your mouth while lowering the right corner of your mouth, stick your tongue out a few inches from the right corner of your mouth... you got it? Great. You can now take over repairing these things." He laughs and heads out the door. It's easy once you know how and have done it a few times.

I release the watchdog into his electronic yard. I gather the CCDs, each in their own little container, and an arm-full of paperwork to be returned to their owners. I go back into the offices and drop the paperwork into appropriate wooden mail slots. People are startled by seeing me, and they back away as if I am contagious. I sign out for tomorrow. As I finish marking the chart, I realize that my taking tomorrow off could be construed as being a result of this morning's meeting. I think about making an announcement otherwise... that this has been planned for weeks. I decide to let people think what they want to think. I go back out to the warehouse floor and drop off the repaired CCDs.

I dust off a wooden chair, and I sit. Somewhere a drill is putting holes in sheet metal. Mike is calling out measurements. From my vantage point, I have to assume someone is listening. Scott and Barbara are growling at each other. Scott is accusing Barbara of altering his mathematical formula when she altered his computer code to mesh with her computer code. Barbara is denying it, but I can hear her own self-doubt in her voice. They are not at a stage of requiring intervention. Mike is shuffling his feet. Cooelle's voice asks, "Is that it?" No response. A phone rings. It stops after seven rings. Harvey joins in on Scott and Barbara's heated conversation. Whatever he is saying seems to be settling things down. Clarence is within a yard of me before he notices me with a yelp. I attempt a smile; I'm not sure I succeed. Heads surface from all about, like prairie dogs or gophers popping up from their holes. I look around at them with my imagined smile. Clarence motions me out to the lot.

"What happened in the meeting?" he asks.

"What meeting?" I reply to myself. We didn't meet in any definition of the word, except maybe the athletic one– definition seven: to encounter in opposition, conflict, or sport. I raise my head and tell Clarence, "I can't think of anything to say. I can't think of anything positive to say. They think Auto... AutoDrive will be out by next summer or sooner." Remembering how to smile, I add, "And they've renamed it Chauffeur."

Clarence kicks around some gravel, "When I retired from Snowflake Flour, I thought I would be leaving all of that managerial monkey business behind me. And as bad as things were at Snowflake..." He pauses and grabs my shoulder, "I tell you, I don't want your job."

I turn to him, "Since you don't want my job, I'm going to lend it to Scott. I'm taking tomorrow off. I'll let him know this afternoon." Clarence nods in agreement. I head out to lunch.

Greasy Spoon is down the block and around the corner, right next door to the Whole In The Wall. They are right where I left them last week. It's late. Most of the lunch regulars have already shuffled through. I am used to paying attention to details, but I didn't notice the walk over. I can tell the difference between an MI439-D and a Kudor YU8 distance sensor, but not what I saw on the way over. I order a cheeseburger, fries, and a Double Bubble, with extra grilled onions... on the cheeseburger, not the pop. The grilled onions are fried in grease that thought it was escaping the burger only to be seized by the onions. I eat at the counter while the burger is hot. Years ago I brought my lunch back to work, opened the mostly transparent paper, and found my cheeseburger to be white. I tried to brush the snow off, but it wasn't snow. It was coagulated grease. I distinctly remember using it to lubricate a telescoping aligner.

My tip today is the same as the first day I set foot in here, "Don't ever leave. And if you do, don't forget your car." And I drop a two dollar bill.

The sky is overcast. I count four distinct cloud layers on my walk back to work. The rest of the afternoon slides along in more of a blur than lunch, despite what is coagulating in my stomach. I check around with people. Cooelle's name comes up a lot. When I get to talking with Cooelle, she's got a list. In my office, she tells me all she's learned. It takes hours. She tries to keep it interesting, but right now I am content with trouble-free. I note at the bottom of a mental checklist that she has amply covered all the points I wanted her to learn the past few days. Her descriptions of my staff are accurate and contain some insights that I've never mentioned to anyone, like that she questions what Mike the intern is accomplishing for either Flight Control or himself. She's thinking of calling the school to talk with them about him. I tell her I see no harm in that, but that they might not be allowed to say anything about him. She tells me how happy she is here, and I can see it on her face. She asks if something is the matter.

I tell her she has a new mission. We have to figure out how to speed up design without sacrificing product or production safety or making Flight Control a living hell. I want her to try to figure out shortcuts to our procedures. She's bright, maybe she can figure something out. I lend her three marked-up product research and methodology manuals. As she leaves with the volumes of bound paper, out of the corner of my eye I notice a paper popping over the sandbag dam, waving, and saying in a high-pitched voice, "Take me with you."

I need a vacation. I look at my clock. It's past time to go! Let loose the dogs! Rocketing out of my office, locking up as I go, I launch myself off the dock and into the parking lot below. The sunshine barrels me over, only cloud-scraps remain of what had been an overcast sky.

I'm out. I'm free. I'm liberated. I'm unique again, just like everyone else. Rolling down my car window, it gets stuck midway. Hitting the top of it with precision, it drops down the rest of the way.

I'm driving.

11

First and Second Homes

The mental rocker button switches from amber Work to emerald Trip. I head my silver Pony Express through the early rush traffic, around stalled vehicles, accidents, and mirages all while assembling a bring list using thought balloons. Erasing a kitchen sink thought balloon with my hand, some dip in a boat thinks I'm giving him the finger or worse, four fingers and a thumb. He yells curses and pulls up beside me to give me two of his favorite fingers. Without hands on the steering wheel or eyes on the road, he nearly takes out a bicyclist. The bicyclist explains to him where he should go. Meanwhile I take a turn for the better and compile another thought balloon of things I should take with me on the trip.

Glowering at me from her perch on the cement steps to the Whisper Willows Apartments is the woman from apartment 32. Pale skin hangs off her face like a weathered burlap curtain fastened around a permanent sneer. Months ago she argued with me in a deep barking voice that I had parked in her parking spot. There are no assigned spots, no painted lines... the lot isn't even level. It is a tar and old gum paved farm field. If I look closely enough I see furrows and irrigation channels. I weave through her and the traffic of her offspring. She makes a disgusted bark at me on my way by, and someone doesn't smell well.

A piece of tape hangs on my door. That's not a good sign. Inside there is no air conditioning. Ray is on the floor hunched over posterboard with his back to the fan. I flop on the couch. "Landlady put a new lease on the door," Ray says not looking up. "It's on the table." I lean off the couch to look at his drawings.

"Immortal Man?" I ask. He nods. "He's a villain, right?"

"Kind of. But here he's a hero," Ray explains, turning the board my way. Immortal Man is on the phone with a telemarketer. "Yeah uh-huh," Immortal Man says looking at his fingernails, "so what about your competitor's prices? Yeah, uh-huh... and so your product is better because... yeah, uh-huh..." Day turns to night and day again. Seasons change. One telemarketer is replaced by another.

"How long does this go on?" I inquire.

"23 pages."

"You're kidding, right?"

"Yeah, it's actually a limited series."

At the table the lease agreement is a rewrite of our existing lease except that my keen-eye notes the omission of air conditioning. "Nice try," I acknowledge while pawing through the mail. "You see what she's trying to do?"

"Yep. I drew my own conclusions."

"Ray..."

"Yeah?"

"You want to go to Tom's lake place this weekend? This weekend?" I repeat after a door slams upstairs.

"Can I let you know later?"

"Sure. I'm leaving tomorrow morning." I don't know if he responds or not due to neighbor noise. I head into my room to change and pack. The hunt begins. Most items pose no challenge, until the pocketknife. I check and re-check. Expand the search. Nothing. Missing things are always found the last place you look. I expand the search again to cover the whole apartment with the exception, for now, of Ray's room. There! Amidst a pile of pencil shavings on Ray's drafting table! I pick it up, wipe it off while stepping over Ray, and bring it back to my room. We don't talk about this sort of stuff.

As I pack, I talk at the landlady over the phone. I lay down the law; our previous lease is still valid for eight more months. The air conditioning must be fixed, not fixed out of the lease. We are not signing a new lease. If it is not repaired by Tuesday, I tell her, I will be contacting the owner over the breach of contract. There is nothing special about Tuesday; I just made it up. I just figured there needs to be a deadline. She is very put out.

That settled for now, I call Hope. I can hear her smile just in her answering the phone. I'm scrounging for socks and underwear and three bandanas and walkie-talkies. And all the time I'm gathering the items pictured in my thought balloons, she's telling me about her day and how Nicole and Becky will be able to come. It's great. I find myself smiling at nothing. I'm smiling at everything. Attitude is the quality measurement of life, and Hope has an infectiously great attitude. I've got this dopey grin as she's telling me about her laundry. And I encourage her. I tell her it can get hot there and that she doesn't need to bring food or sheets or pillows or towels. I ask her questions about what she's bringing, and when she mentions shoes, I tell her about walking through the fields and maybe her shoes should be comfortable and durable. She suggests heels with tiny bejeweled straps.

She tells me a story from school today. She describes what certain kids did and said as she's going through her lesson as if they are a tight-knit group. I comment that it must be nice to have her as a teacher. She asks if I'm teasing her. I reassure her that I really think she must be a great teacher.

Hours slip by. When the upstairs neighbors dribble a bowling ball down their bowling-lane-turned-basketball-court, I call them on double-dribbling. Double-dribbling is not allowed in American bowling, whether or not it's played by apartment dwelling elephants. The neighbors will miss me this weekend. I am the reaction to their action. I am the referee to their game.

When Hope and I say good night, I don't tell her how much I'm looking forward to seeing her and being with her, even for just the weekend. When is reaching out touching to someone, when is it clingy, and when is it suffocating? My test is role reversal. How would I feel in her place? My test won't be graded until tomorrow.

In front of me, absently, the standard pile of travel items has formed. Others judge their items by the number of luggage pieces. I judge mine by the depth of the pile collected on my bedroom floor. I sort the pile by what will be needed or worn when. That's the way I pack.

The rest of the apartment is dark. Ray's gone. It's too late for dinner. I'm too hyper to sleep... hyper, like the music that reverberates the walls. I head out. The air around the street lamps forms a halo of rays, half by humidity and orbiting bugs, half by my weary eyes. A telephone pole seems misshapen. I look closely, and it's a veritable who's who of local garage sales, though I swear one of the fliers mentions Cleveland. Forgetting where I'm going, I stop, shake the cobwebs loose, and decide I'm way more tired than I thought.

The Ice Cream Bar is crowded. I swagger up to the bar as if I'm in Texas back when Texas was a country. I order my usual. Then I explain to the barmaid what my usual is. A ruckus occurs beside me; someone is knocked off their barstool, but I mind my own business. Not that I own a business, I only mean I'm not bothering anyone. Not yet anyway but the night is young.

"Is this seat taken?"

I glance over. It's a teenager. "No, not at all."

She turns her face into mine. All I see are her eyes, deep brown with thick black mascara-enhanced lashes. I'm close enough to count them. She's violating my airspace. Without a blink, the Eyes say, "I've seen you in here before. Do you come here often?" Through my empathy, these eyes also show a bookshelf of Experience books, overdue library books from the sociology section. I'm not sure I understand.

I tell Eyes, "Yeah, I know the place. It's like a second home." I lean back to re-evaluate her. The voice, the attitude, the smirk could have only developed after at least 15 or 16 years. Her shirt says, Girls Rule. Boys Drool.

"Really?"

"Sure," I reply, leaning back vertical again. The barmaid gives me my usual.

As the barmaid is walking away, Eyes asks, "Is that your mom?"

"No. She's my sister." The barmaid whips around and gives me a dirty look. The kid laughs. "What's a nice girl like you," I ask with a mouthful of vanilla shake, "doing in an Ice Cream Bar like this?"

"Waiting for a man like you." I fall off my stool. My spoon goes flying. She gets off her stool and walks away, her ponytail swaying as she moves. I'm left on the floor. It hurts. Not the floor so much as the fall and the floor combined. Eyes comes back with another long spoon and sets it up there on the bar. The underside of the bar is multicolored, but mostly pink. Grabbing my hand with both of hers, she hauls me up. I brush the sawdust off. She grabs my shake, spoon, straw, and napkins and says, "C'mon." Mental note: grow a beard, dye it gray, and learn to walk with a cane. Eyes moves us to a booth with two other girls in non-smoking.

"What happened?" they ask her.

"Slippery stools," she replies.

They turn to me as we sit down. The one without the nose diamond asks, "Why did you fall off your chair?"

I try to think of something clever. "Slipped," is the best I've got.

"What?"

"Slipped!"

"Uh?!?" I shake them off.

Eyes tells me, "We were here a couple days ago? We saw you shoot the paper off your straw down the bar." I have no idea what she's talking about. Paper off my straw? Oh, the wrapper.

"Yeah, that would be me." I grab a straw. "Is this anyone's?"

"No," Diamond Nose says. "If you want the paper covering, it's behind you in the next booth."

"No thanks." Holding the straw horizontally and pinching both ends, I twist it like I'm pedaling a bicycle. This compresses the air in the straw into about a two-inch space. "Okay, now snap the middle part." Eyes hesitates. "It's not going to explode." Eyes snaps it with a flick of her finger.

Pop!

They all jump. "Well, maybe it does explode." From the other side of the place the barmaid gives me another dirty look. It dawns on me that I've never been kicked out of here before. Someone they know has apparently just entered the bar, and they are talking too quickly for me to understand. I catch enough words to know they are still speaking English, when the girl next to me asks if I can hang a spoon from my nose. All four of us race to see who can be the first to establish the spoon on their nose. I lick the cup of the spoon and press it to the end of my nose with the spoon handle down. "What're your names?" I ask once we have all successfully affixed the tableware to our faces.

"I'm Carrie," says the girl who met me first. "That's–" and I swear she says Fingklukreb just as she says the next girl's name. I don't know what she said. "And this is Molly," who is sitting next to me. They all look funny, having spoons hanging from their noses.

"How old are you?" Fingklukreb asks, as the spoons fall from our faces.

"Old enough to know better, but not old enough to care," I say. Whenever I say that, people think about it far longer than I ever have. As they ponder it, I wish I hadn't said it. Life is a do over. You do it again and again until you get it right. And whenever I say that out loud, someone invariably chimes in with the comment that sex is the same way. I clarify myself by saying, "What I mean is... the way I see it, you can be responsible without looking mature. Many of my friends don't act their age, but they are responsible. Most of them anyway." They are staring at me as if they are in a trance. And I notice Molly's leg against mine. Her leg is warm. I look down.

"What's going on over there?" Carrie squeals.

"Nothing!" Molly insists, while the others look under the table. I take money out of my pocket and invite them over to an antique jukebox. They're interested in music I don't know. I feed the jukebox. It gobbles up what I give it and asks for more. I give it a little more. The girls are pressing buttons. I guess they assume I'm paying for anything. I don't assume that. I'm not rich. If I were I'd probably assume that I would buy the music. One of them might be rich. Maybe Carrie's last name is Corral as in the Corral Motors empire. Or Molly's last name could be Double or Bubble, either one of the famous Double Bubble beverage-partnership families. And the other girl, the taller girl, I notice now that she's standing, maybe I wouldn't get her last name either. But that doesn't mean she isn't incredibly wealthy, confusing people out of untold millions. They are still pushing buttons, making selections. They huddle and converse in high speed. Then Molly takes my arm and asks me if I would like to pick a song.

A song? One whole entire song? For me? What should I do; which one should I pick? Should I ask my sister the teenaged barmaid for advice? Should I, overwhelmed by their generosity, decline their offer of letting me select one of the many songs I'm paying for? Or should I broaden their perspectives and show them what is out there?

I find a Melanie classic, and just before I press the buttons, Carrie pleads with me to let her push them. I let her. I head back to the table to get my shake, only to find that I've lead them all back here. There is a scuffle over our seating arrangements. Pushing. Shoving. A bottle is broken.

The ruckus is cut short by a little speech given by the Sheriff through clenched teeth, and right before someone was about to be thrown through the front picture window too. Mainly me. I hate bar fights. I start to retreat until I'm surrounded.

"Where are you going?"

"There no longer seems to be room for me."

"Stay," Carrie tells me as if I'm a disobedient puppy. "Please?"

"I've got to go." As I head out someone might have asked me for my number, so I call back, "Seven." I don't know why seven is my favorite number. Maybe it's because I liked being seven. I don't know. It's late. I look for my car. It's not here! It must have been stolen! Digging for change to call the police, my car keys aren't even in my pocket. Whoever stole my car was impressively thorough to have stolen my keys too. That Molly girl must have been an accomplice or the mastermind, the criminal genius behind it all. As I get less angry and more amazed, I realize that I walked. I decide not to bother the police, and I head home. Along the way I hear the uniquely Minnesotan sound of mosquitoes snoring through their big long noses. It's like soft, uncomplicated trombone music. I stop myself from humming along to avoid waking them.

A cricket chirps. I shush it.

The hyper music of the Whisper Willows Apartments has local mosquitoes dancing in mid-air. I cut in. I cut through. I make a dash for the door, only to find it propped open with a cinder block. In the hallway, mosquitoes dance around moths orbiting the hallway light. I draw my keys and use them on my door like John Wayne drawing a couple of six-shooters. After the bathroom, I head into my bedroom, flip on my light, flip off my shirt, and trip over a huge pile of junk in the middle of the floor. As I reach for my alarm clock

I swear it backs away from my hand before I grab it and set it. I've got to get more sleep. I find the hiding spot of my sheet and pull it over the bed. I pull off my shorts and flip off the light.

I dream someone is bouncing something off a window screen. I get up to the sound of a rock chipping off my window. I look out. Is that the girls from the Ice Cream Bar? They wave to me. I wave back and lie back down. They must be dancing with the mosquitoes, I think, and then I stop.

12

Some Traveling Music, Please

What is that racket? My eyes open to glare at my brilliantly lit alarm clock glaring back at me. It's morning. I shut it off. Almost laying back, I realize that it's not a work day. I spring up. A whole day off! Fridays are good, but Fridays without work are not just good, **they're great!** I run through my dreams from last night and re-run through them to change the endings. I bump my night-stand and my alarm clock bounces and falls into my pile of travel items, making me wonder who else is going. I put on shorts. Ray's room is empty. He's on the living room floor in front of the fan. I kick his feet. "Are you dead?" No reply. I kick his feet again.

"Yes."

"Are you going with me?"

"Yes. No."

"Which one?"

"Yes I'm going. No I'm taking the cycle. Mister Questions, can you answer something for me?"

"Yeah."

"Are you responsible for the rock throwing urchins last night?" he asks sitting up.

"What do you mean?"

"Three girls were throwing rocks at your window last night. They missed a lot."

"Oh."

"You know them?"

"I met them or they met me at the Ice Cream Bar last night."

"You should have left them there."

"I thought I did."

"I can't believe you go to that place without a gun. Next time you see them, tell them to stop throwing rocks, will ya?"

"Sure." I get out a map and show him how to get to the lake. I take a sandblasting shower and get ready. I wonder if Hope knows how to get there. I call her and leave a message with directions. I pack small nylon bags in chronological order. With all the stuff I packed up, you'd swear I was going on a safari. Don't do that. Swearing is a bad habit. In the hallway a mother is kicking her kids out to summer school. I take my charcoal grill out of the storeroom. The kids follow me and my first load of stuff to my car as if looking for an invitation to go with. I avoid eye contact this morning. Moths, mosquitoes, and other ex-hausted bugs litter the hallway floor and walls. The front door was left open, which helps me in and out. A couple of the moths are still walking in circles just from habit now that morning is around. Rural moths fly parallel to moonlight. Urban moths try to do the same thing with light bulbs and get loopy. You know how Edison died? A bunch of mad moths kicked his butt. Sad but true. Edison's descendants later got the moths back by inventing the killer purple zapping lights. It's two to one, the Edisons over the moths, and the moths are up to bat. It's their move.

Traffic bunches up on my butt from feeder ramps as I head up U.S. Highway 61. The moment the speed limit changes on the outskirts of the suburban sprawl, the traffic races away as if a checkered flag had been lowered. The speed limit sign had read, Speed Limit 70 Strictly Enforced. Nearly a mile away another signs reads, And We Mean It. I turn on the radio to avoid the accelerating what's-his-problem looks. The Destiny song by Melanie that I picked on the jukebox is playing. Wow, they finally got to my song!

Not that this is my song, the lyrics don't fit. "I'm going to be your destiny. Can't you see? I already know your history." The song is way overboard in its emphasis that everything is planned out and that people don't have control over their own actions. Right. Destiny. Destiny made you act like a jerk. You had no choice. Destiny explains everything. As the song fades out, it goes, "destiny... destiny... Manifest Destiny." Manifest Destiny has nothing to do with anything else in the song. Manifest Destiny is how history teachers explain the race across the country by European settlers, running away from civilization and running over Native Americans. Civilization would crowd in on them, and they wound continue on. Destiny, manifest or not, has nothing to do with it. I head west on Highway Ookiewame, locally known as H-O. Westward H-O begins as a three lane highway. One lane exits. Then it comes back again. It's a disposable lane... no, it's a boomerang lane! One comes in from the left and leaves from the right. So it's not really a highway. Not all the lanes go to the same place. They are just adjacent (sometimes), parallel (sometimes) roads. You have to decide which lane you really want to be driving in because it may eventually branch away from the rest of the road. A lane joins again.

That's the trouble. Decisions. In Minnesota, you have to decide what lane to be in, who to vote for, what kind of car to get stuck in the snow, who to work for, what kind of potato chip... Have you seen the potato chip aisle of the grocery store? It's an epidemic. Soon potato chip stores will dot the landscape. Potato chip stores ensure our people all the Potato Chip Opportunities (PCOs) they have a right to, plus some additional PCOs that have never officially been recognized, but people are accustomed to having. I revolted at the introduction of the pickle-flavored chip. Modern snack food imitating early snack food. Yes, I'm sure it's delicious. No, I haven't tried it. Enough is enough. A lane leaves. This time it's gone for good.

H-O meanders. It weaves up and down and around the hills stitching its way across the countryside and skirting several lakes. I roll down the window and am surprised that it is too cool to leave it rolled down. At Round Lake I stop for gas, check the oil, and wash the windows. I think about washing the car, but I worry about what would be left of it if I washed away all the dirt. I also buy a few nutrition bars. Eleven more miles and the highway stops abruptly where the old Swenson barn used to be. I've never seen it, but I guess that doesn't stop it from being a landmark. I take a right on Old Hull Road. After 17 miles it passes through a town that is only two blocks long, Swede Ravine. I buy ice for my cooler, drinks for my friends, charcoal, two dozen ears of corn, a bushel bag of peanuts, breath mints, and a box of Major Munch cereal. After three miles a motorcycle passes. It's Ray. He waves and leads me the rest of the way.

The gravel road up to the cabin is eroded into rut gullies. I slow down to see my way through the ruts as Ray and the dust from his motorcycle continue ahead.

AutoDrive is nothing like destiny. AutoDrive will drive you, not the other way around. And for some people, that's the way they like it. It takes the decisions and maybe the fear out of the future. AutoDrive and destiny both have a plan, and you're a passenger in the plan, if you want to ride along. Most people want to ride along. I'd rather not. There aren't any AutoDrive components left in this car. I got rid of them last week. I'm in the driver's seat. I take that back; the only AutoDrive component left in this car is me. **Bam!** The car hits a rut I didn't see. I've got to stop thinking about work.

I pull off at the driveway's end into a patch of grasses that grew where I want to park. Ray gives me a what-took-you look. I wander to reacquaint myself with the place. It looks great. The new pale blue house sprawls over the steep peak of the hillside. It has way too much glass for a home that could be used during a Minnesota winter. The old, light yellow house is huddled by the doorway of the new house and shows some signs of neglect, but the barn looks like it is still being used. Looking down the hill, a big glacier-dropped rock has flattened the area around it. I've never thought of this before, but it's almost as if the giant boulder has rolled around, even bounced around, on this part of the hill and flattened it out. It's a giant boulder play area. It had a good time and left quite an impression. Below the play area, the hill slopes into a field with the remains of the original house and the creek, the woods on the other side, the lake, and the road in.

The 40 yards of field in front of the two houses and before the corn field is a mixture of lawn grasses, white flowered clover, yellow buttercups, and other low lying plants, with some patches of reddish clay and gravel.

Ray has spread out a blanket and a drawing tablet, pencils, tools, and a toolbox under a pair of maple trees near the yellow house. I take the plastic bag of corn, fill it with water from a faucet, tie it closed, and set it aside to soak. Leaving the bushel of peanuts to roast on the hood of my car, I grab a Double Bubble from the cooler and head down the hill. This place is gorgeous. "This time of year," I add as an after-thought because I'm sure Canada, Alaska, Siberia, and Greenland are nice this time of year too. Some time today, in each of those places, that thought has been repeated. "Sergei, isn't Siberia gorgeous now? But then you could say the same thing about Minnesota!" the Russian laughs.

Right in front of me, a bumblebee and a hummingbird hawk moth nearly have a mid-air collision and speed off with the patience of New York City cab drivers. I wonder who distracted them? A mosquito flies by, screeches to a halt, and does a U-turn, but I'm already many yards down the hill.

A gopher pokes its head out of a hole, chirps at me, and a second gopher pokes its head out of a nearby hole. They bob their heads in and out, watching my descent. Chickadees call from a small grove of ash trees on the level of the boulder. I respond to most of their calls with a poor imitation. I don't know what we are talking about, but I don't mind the conversation. Another bird sounds like it has the giggles, but I can't pinpoint the owner of the call. Continuing down the hill, I pass wildflowers a-buzz with bees, monarch butterflies, and little yellow moths. I don't bother them, and they don't bother me. The wildflowers and other plants are often tall enough that if I crouch down, the landscape disappears. Farther down, the hill levels into a field that slopes off into the still distant, deep blue-shimmering lake.

Nearing the old-old farmhouse, the mosquito has established the flight pattern of a surveyor, or a glutton at a smörgåsbord. "It all looks so good," she says, eying me up. She wants my blood.

With most girls, being gross or any intricate discussion of the Three Stooges is enough of a repellent, but mosquitoes aren't so easily repelled. Once they are attracted to you, they won't let go. Mosquitoes look for motion from a distance to narrow the field. Within a hundred feet, they're sniffing for carbon dioxide; that separates us from the plants. Even closer, they sniff for lactic acid and pheromones from sweat. And then they zero in on heat bringing them to the veins. At this point there is only one form of slapstick that will get their attention. I let her land. I take her out with a slap.

I shuffle through the remains of the original farmhouse. I've seen larger closets. It makes me wonder where they put everything. Tomorrow night's dinner was probably still in the field. I pick up a brick. A handmade yellow brick. Set it down. Dig around with a stick. Wood with green chips of paint. Couldn't be white – never would have found the place in a snowstorm. Flakes of rusted metal, a worn arc of ceramic, and a near-rectangle of leather pass my inspection. And all the fragments piece together, more and more, as I sift through the rubble, sand, dirt, and wildflowers, a picture of nothing. It's gone. All of the work of building the place, the hauling of water, the talk, the crackling fires, the sex, the plantings, the harvest, the snow... it's all gone. From my perspective it never happened. I can visit this spot for as long as I live but will never know what it once was. I look forward, but I can't look back.

A chipmunk watches me. I purposely don't catch eyes with him or approach him. I actually back away a bit. He gets on his hind legs and starts chewing me out in chipmunkese. He yells at me for moving his bricks and whatever else I've done. He gets on all fours, pauses, shifts directions 30 degrees left then 20 degrees right and hightails it out of here, to tell all his chipmunk friends about telling me off. I'm happy to play my part in making him a hero.

I move some debris into a makeshift stairway to the left. Climbing up without spilling my drink, I move carefully to the corner that has no roof. If the floor gives way, I want to jump out not in. I start to structurally test the floor in ways I was never taught in engineering school, culminating in my jumping up and down. Just when I finish jumping, I hear a strange sound. I listen to the house for the sounds of eminent collapse. Instead the sounds are coming from outside and above. Looking out, several people are standing on the hilltop, yelling at me. I can't tell who they are. I assume one of them is Ray, but they might be laughing at me. I pose, take a hearty swig of delicious Double Bubble, climb down, and head back up the hill.

At the top, Ruth hands me a sandwich, and she points down the hill, down the road, to where the lone hulking figure of Erix is standing, staring at a stop sign. "He had to get out," she says. I had been too engrossed by the farmhouse to notice.

I drive down to get him. I get out, and I open the door for him without saying anything. He doesn't say anything either during the ride. We don't want to break his concentration. I park the Pony Express back on the now-flattened grasses. Erix turns to me and asks, "Does Friday come before Thursday?"

"Yeah, about a week before," I reply.

My sandwich and I get out of the car, and we watch Ruth unpack some things. She has enough lawn chairs for an auditorium. I watch Ray draw. Then I realize that Erix is still in the car, so I open his door for him. Ruth hands him a sandwich.

"Things are really heating up in Iowa," she states. "Why can't we all just get along?"

Erix finds a bug.

"What's going on now?"

"They're getting – well, they say that they get less federal money than any other state and that they are being isolated from the rest of the country. It's a bit paranoid."

Erix tries to share his sandwich with the bug.

I unpack a two foot diameter grill and set it up downwind. In it, I set up and light a metal tube of charcoal. When Erix tries to drink from a low faucet on the side of the old farmhouse, I show him the cooler of drinks, notice a limited dust storm heading up the road, then I get back to my sandwich. The sandwich has large portabella mushrooms, grilled zucchini, tomato, broccoli sprouts, a paste of avocado and artichoke, and I don't know what all else. The bread is nothing spectacular, but nevertheless the sandwich is delicious. Closing it back up, I take another bite. Catching eyes with Ruth, I hold up the sandwich in a salute. I call over to Erix and ask what type of sandwich he has. "Ham," he responds.

"Is it good?"

"Very good," he says.

I call over to Ray and ask him the same thing. He says, "Vegetarian delight."

"So you like it?" I ask.

He sits up and tells Ruth, "It's perfect."

The isolated dust cloud pulls in and dissipates into a small truck. Dan Ryan and Todd Pfuloree climb out and stretch. Ruth and I go over. Ruth hugs Dan, "Your shoulders have grown even wider! How was the trip in from Chicago?"

"Great, the new US 12 whipped me across Wisconsin," his voice booms. His voice always booms.

"Are you hungry?" she asks him. As he's nodding, she hands him what would have to be a Dan Ryan special sandwich. It has everything: meats, cheeses, onions, and other vegetables stacked like a skyscraper. He accepts it with a grin. Turning to Todd, Ruth asks, "Do you have the keys? I need to test the plumbing."

"Tom·has the keys to the new house. I only have keys to the yellow house," Todd says.

Ruth holds out her hand, "That'll do."

Ruth heads in and I turn to Todd, "I'm sure she has a sandwich waiting for you somewhere."

"She shouldn't. I don't eat bread."

"Since when?"

"Since months ago."

"That explains it," I reply while finishing my sandwich. "She's outdone herself in the Sandwich Department."

Todd and I follow Dan over to watch Ray draw. Ray explains the new origins of Glory Girl to them as he draws the shadows under her breasts. He catches an amused look on my face, and his face lights up, "You should have been here 20 minutes ago. Mister Engineer here was standing on top of the cabin down there, jumping up and down, trying to see if he could smash it and break his neck. Smart thinking!"

"Don't bust the cabin," Todd tells me sternly.

"I wasn't trying to bust the cabin," I reply.

Todd walks to the edge of the hill. "Did you demolish any of it?" Apparently he can't tell.

"No."

"Good. Don't."

"I won't." There. I have been reprimanded. Why did I invite Ray to come along? That's right, I thought the sun and fresh air might do Mister Benedict Arnold some good.

Ruth asks me if I brought an umbrella. I say, "No, why?"

She responds, "Just checking."

The breeze near my car smells like peanut butter. I fetch an old towel and tongs. I dampen the towel at the faucet, grab the bag of corn and water, and bring it to the grill. I have to dump the water. Passing near Ray, I think about where to dump it. Deciding not to dump it on him, I pour out the corn syrup smelling water farther away from the grill. I shuffle around the charcoals, replace the grill, stack the wet corn still in their husks on top of the grill, drape the wet towel over them, and cover it all with the grill lid. It's a grill sandwich!

The sky is filled with big puffy white and gray clouds. I lie down on a blue plaid blanket to check them out. I sigh. I focus on one car-like cloud. A grasshopper hops over. I watch him go. Then he is followed by 30 of his closest friends and family. I sit up to avoid being run over. Todd and Dan are hauling out a set of ping-pong tables. Two cars are driving up. Lefty, wearing his lab coat, gets out of one of them. The other has Cy and Joe. Joe rushes over to me to insist that he doesn't have any relationship with Cy. I emphasize that she and I broke up years ago, and so he starts looking for beer.

"What?!?" Joe exclaims. "There's no beer?!? What are we going to do without beer?!?"

Another car pulls up. Red jumps out and says, "I've got beer!"

"Wow, deus ex machina," I comment. In high school English class I learned about a plot device called Deus Ex Machina. It was Greek to me. Apparently, you can be telling a story about some people who are in a desperate situation that gets bad, then goes from bad to worse, finally becoming so terribly awful that the best foreseeable outcome is that the heroes, the villain, innocent children, and the audience will all die gruesome, tortuous deaths as will anyone from that moment forward who even thinks of the events being described. Suddenly, something or someone, who had no business showing up in the story, like a long-dead hero, appears and makes everything better, usually about five minutes or three pages before the story ends.

In your run-of-the-mill ancient Greek play, which was not worth writing down let alone televising, this sudden someone was a god or someone thinking themselves to be a god, an actor. This god was brought to the stage by a mechanical stage device to intervene in the lives of the characters, restore order with the wave of a hand, and save the butts of the storytellers who had dug themselves into a hole of incredibility all in the name of fantastic drama. By mechanical stage device, I mean a swing-rope-pulley system which, lacking AutoDrive's complexity, probably landed an occasional god on their posterior. That uncertainty led to the only aspect that brought reality to these stories – you didn't know if you would be watching a tragedy or a comedy.

The plays did not take long to exact a toll on Greek life. Like ancient couch potatoes, the Greeks relinquished control of their society to their mythology. They figured no problem is worth solving because little problems, over time, become big problems and big problems will ultimately be handled by a god on a swing, so why bother? The Greeks were easily conquered by the Romans who adopted the same mythology, the same poorly-unwritten plays, and the same outbreak of advanced Lois Lane-itis. Thus, bad storytelling led to the fall of the Roman Empire.

"Huh?" Ruth asks.

"God from a machine," I reply.

"Right," she says, backing her chair away from me.

Todd starts handing out the paddles. Most of us join in on a game of round robin ping-pong, with five to seven of us circling the table trying to keep the ball in play. It's fun. You have to watch the ball and watch where you're going, to not run into people. Joe keeps a beer in his hand. Dan uses two paddles. Someone is often stepping in or stepping out, changing up the order of the players.

I step out to take the corn off the grill after it's been on for about 20 minutes. I put on gloves with rubber dots for gripping, and I shuck the corn. Even with the gloves the steam scalds my fingertips. Some of the outer husks are charred. The inner husks are not. I push cob holders into the ends of each cob and set them on a plate Ruth found for me. I take one and offer them to others. Lefty conducts a scientific analysis without his lab. "The corn syrup of the corn hull and kernels is pressure cooked in the steam-baking process, delivering a sweeter, caramelized flavor," he says while extracting a sample into a petri dish for future research.

I'm thinking, "I forgot to pack my petri dishes! How will I survive without them! I could go back home to get some. Maybe Lefty will let me borrow one if I need it." I think about asking him, but I don't think he'd appreciate the sarcasm.

Ray complains about corn stuck between his teeth. I root around in the corn garbage for corn silk from the tassels of the corn ears and offer it to him as floss. He tries it, almost likes it. Then he looks at me like I'm some kind of cornball.

Back at ping-pong, Ruth is sandwiched between Dan and Red. Cy is getting in some fierce shots against me, which I reconcile into easy return lobs. Joe announces, "You know, I've been in this thing the whole time, and I haven't spilled my beer once! Isn't that right?" he asks Erix, who has been watching the game. Erix pauses a moment and nods his head up and down.

A cloud of dust and flying gravel nearly runs down the game. It swerves toward the field. It lurches to halt, but the dust and gravel keep going, settling yards away in the field, leaving behind a red convertible with the top down. It's Hope! And Nicole and Becky. I run over.

Nicole hops out, parachuting her miniskirt, wearing a tight shirt with headlights on it and some saying. She grips me in a hug that holds me and pushes me away. With show, she kisses my cheek, but I'm watching Hope get out of the car. Nicole whispers, "Good boy," and lets go.

Hope heads over to me, and I can't read her expression. "What's the matter?" she asks.

"Nothing. Is everything okay with you?" I respond, looking into her eyes and cheeks for the happiness I have seen before.

"Yes, everything is fine," she says, searching my face as if she's expecting something.

I take her hand, half expecting her to shake it loose, and start her toward everyone. She stops me and beckons Becky who is grabbing duffel bags. Nicole is laughing at something Ray must've said as Joe cleans spilled beer off the ping-pong table. When Hope stopped for Becky, I felt like she was going to stop something with me. Red is reading Nicole's shirt, "Did I leave my lights on?" and laughing, while I'm feeling a tremendous burden from Hope's arrival. What do I do? How do you make a great relationship? I'm an engineer, not a poet. I am not a wooer of women. I don't even know if wooer is a word. Woo-who? As an engineer, I make plans, or I work off them. I'm not even sure what the goals are of a great relationship. Certainly I can't look to my parent's relationship or my relationships with Cy or any other girlfriend for guidance. They're no help. I wipe the sweat off my forehead with the back of my free hand. I know many intelligent or knowledgeable people that haven't been able to do this... this "happily-ever-after" thing. How can I? I am a talented person with many abilities. I am sure my abilities can help, but while I can see a great many ways I can screw this up, it would take a miracle for me to get this right.

Dan steps toward Nicole, "**Hello, my name is Ryan. Dan Ryan!**" Nicole holds her hand up for Dan to kiss it, and he does.

Ruth is leading us in the side door of the light yellow house to help them wash the road off of them. Stopped in a hallway I whisper to Hope, "I'm not the greatest at relationships. If I screw up, let me know, okay?"

Hope leans back, thinks, and nods her head saying, "You can count on it." Figuratively she just took half of my worries off my shoulders. I turn my attention to my remaining worries. What does she want? We're holding hands, on again, off again throughout the house, but I don't know her plans. Is she wanting to get married, get a house of our own, and have kids as a link in a generational chain that will encourage the kids to get married, get a house, and have kids, and so on? Is she after my money? What money? The money you've saved for a down-payment on a house. Oh, that money. Yes, she's after your money all right, you apartment-living, Pony Express-Driving, thousandaire, you. Or as an elementary school teacher, she could see me as the greatest professional challenge of her career and the subject of a groundbreaking doctoral thesis, Elementary Adults. How insidious!

I look at her. She smiles hopefully at me. I think, "Nah, that can't be it."

At that very moment, as I am turning away from looking at Hope, time slows down. Ruth is offering a bag of pickle-flavored potato chips, with a slow, deep voice. I freak out and drop to the ground writhing in pain and agony. "Not... pickle-flavored potato... gasp," I gasp. Hope's eyes narrow at me and a slight smile appears, as time speeds back up to normal. Getting up and brushing myself off, I hear, "Some people like pickle-flavored potato chips," from Ruth, behind me.

"Are you all right?" Hope asks.

"Sure. Fine. Why?" I respond.

"Do we all sleep in this house," Hope asks to change the subject, "or do we split up, some way, between the two?"

"Three," I correct her.

"Three?" she asks, glancing at the barn, 60 yards away.

"No, not the barn. We hardly spent any time at the barn... once we grew out of cow tipping. There's another house down the hill."

"Oodles of people like pickle-flavored potato chips," Ruth continues. "Red and Ray like them. Hey, Red and Ray... Red, Ray, and Ruth... the three R's."

"Really? I didn't see it," Hope says as I take her hand and lead her to the edge of the hill with the best view of the oldest farmhouse. Her mouth gapes as she sees the potential lodge, then it changes to a look that says, "I won't be taking you seriously ever again."

"You forgot a fourth R," Red says.

"Did I?" Ruth asks, as she hands out sandwiches and corn-on-the-cob to the newest arrivals.

A steady thunder approaches with a boom-boom-boom-boom and a louder boom-boom-boom-boom, coming from a large dust cloud that's heading up the road. Birds that had stayed in nearby trees decide that now is a good time to take off. The dust approaches and settles, but the thunder continues. Picture the largest sports-utility vehicle you can. This one is larger. Jake opens his door and the low booming turns into music of a type. What type? Loud! I always think the same thing when I see him, "Jake is the guy that put the boy in boisterous." I yell that to Hope. Will gets out of a back door and comes over to us and yells, "I am not driving back with them!"

Jake yells, "**What?!?**"

Will turns back to the gigantic SUV and its driver, "I am not driving back with you!"

Jake gives a puzzled look and yells a few times into the monstrosity. The music stops and all is quiet except the ringing of ears. A peevish looking man, Minion, climbs out of the passenger side of the vehicle. Standing near Jake, but slightly behind, he looks like a poor quality photocopy.

"What's the problem?" Jake asks Will.

"You deafened me," Will responds.

"Me? I didn't turn on the music," Jake says to all of us on the jury.

"Right. You told Minion to see how loud it can get."

"So you're mad at me?!?"

"No, I'm just not going to ride with you again."

"Because of what Minion did?"

"No, because of what you told him to do," Will affirms. Meanwhile, Minion just stands there like Jake's second shadow.

Hope whispers to me, "Is his name really Minion?"

Out of the corner of my mouth I say, "I dunno. I never really asked."

Jake asks, "Shouldn't you be mad at Minion?"

"I'm not mad at anyone."

"What if no one is able to give you a ride? What if I'm the only ride back?" Jake says, stepping toward Will.

"I'll get back some other way," Will says, heading past Jake to get his bag out of Jake's truck before Jake thinks of locking it away.

As Will passes by Jake again, Jake stops him with an arm. "Aren't you going to thank me for the ride?"

"No."

As they stand there eye-to-eye, Hope nudges me, "Do something."

I stop myself from repeating the word, "No." I don't want that overheard. I whisper, "Wait."

No one moves much more than a twitch or a sway. Everything has quieted down to the point that we are able to hear the wind rustling the trees. As the moment passes, the time for actions and reactions passes too.

Will brushes past Jake, dropping his bag by a tree near Nicole. She whispers something, and he nods. People go back to their sandwiches, corn, and drinks, but not back to ping-pong. Becky comes over to us, and Hope suggests a walk. We start walking away.

"Ricky!" Jake calls. "Want to help me with my tent?"

"Maybe. Give me five minutes."

"Forget it," he says waving me off with quick stubbornness.

Hope, Becky, and I follow some old road-like ruts past the barn. "Why didn't you stop your friends from fighting?" Hope asks once we are out of ear-shot.

"I thought they were about to kill each other," Becky interjects.

"Nah, who picked that fight?" I ask Hope.

"Jake did."

"Why?"

"I don't know. I just don't feel that people should treat each other that way."

"Sure. It just wasn't the time to get involved."

"Why not?"

"You really want to know?"

"Yes."

"Jake was... I don't know how to describe it... testing us... seeing how we'd react, as a group. He was sizing us all up to figure how much of a guard he needs to put up."

"Is this a guy thing?"

"Becky, I don't know if it's a guy thing. I don't know that there is a Jake in every group of guys. Maybe there is. All I know is this group, and that's the way Jake acts. I haven't been in any other group. Or maybe Jake just likes picking fights. Maybe it's just an exercise to him." We keep walking. A group of cows takes notice of us. They couldn't recognize me... it was years ago and dark out... they couldn't be old enough to remember the cow tipping nights. Still, I watch for sudden moves. It's the city aware-of-your-surroundings sense applied to the farm. I wouldn't want to make the local papers: Local Cow Gang Mugs City Boy – Some Say They Were Out For Revenge. I stop. "Were you worried about Jake? Are you worried about this weekend?"

Hope and Becky exchange looks. "We don't know what to expect. We don't know everyone..." I wait for something more, something like, "and we don't really know you," but Hope never says that. I smile.

"Okay, I'll try to help you to better understand what's going on. We're on this walk and then we get back and people will be upset that they've had to wait for us for years and Tom has been there and they're waiting to play Capture The Flag. We play Capture The Flag and then a few of us go to the barn to talk and occasionally someone else is there. Then you two sleep in the same room. In the morning I'm having cereal when I first see you, but you accept breakfast from Ruth and," Becky and Hope are giggling, "in the afternoon people get antsy and we all go into town. Sunday morning I am up early and I take a walk and then it starts to rain."

Becky and Hope start laughing when I get to the part about the rain. "All right – all right," Hope stops me, "I know you can't tell us what's going to happen. We're just apprehensive, okay? We know you are a nice guy and won't let anything bad happen to us."

I think about that and say cheerfully, "Without being over protective, yes, I won't let anything bad happen to you." We are in a lighter spirit heading back. Hope lets her hand graze the tops of the long grasses along our way.

13

Captured

When we get back everyone stops and stares at us, so I check my fly. I'm zipped! I am about to check Hope and Becky's zippers, when Jake starts yelling. "We've been waiting for you!"

"For how long?" I ask.

"Years."

"Hey Tom, how was your trip in?" I ask as we continue our approach.

"Fine. We've already picked captains for Capture The Flag, that's why we're waiting for you," he says, waving his cheese sandwich for emphasis.

Jake takes a piece of crabgrass between his thumbs and makes a whistle out of it. I turn to Hope and Becky saying, "Tom and Todd always used to be the twin captains."

"Not this time," Tom says. "The consensus is to have you and Jake be the captains. Are you okay with that?"

"Sure."

"We already flipped a coin for picking teams and sides of the field and you lost," Jake informs me.

"Did I call heads or tails?" I ask him flippantly.

"I called it," Jake says.

"I'll try not to lose again."

"I pick Dan," Jake says.

"I pick Hope."

"I pick Todd," Jake says.

"Hey Nicole, join my team." She's in pants now, and she just put her top up... on her car.

"I pick Becky," Jake says to block my keeping the three friends together.

"I pick Tom."

Jake pauses making it clear that he had intended to have both of the twins on his side. "Lefty."

"Will, come on over."

Jake makes sure I see him staring at Minion, starts to say Minion, and then picks Joe. Joe and his beer join Jake's team.

"Ruth are you playing?" I ask her. She takes my picture and smiles but shakes her head no. "Erix, join my team," I say, startling Erix.

"Cy," Jake says. I don't think she was on my side even when I was dating her.

I watch Erix still coming over to join my team as a car carefully drives up with a minimum of dust. It parks, Al gets out, and adjusts his tool belt. I yell, "Al, are you playing?"

"Playing what?"

"Capture The Flag!"

"Sounds great!"

"Okay, you're on my team!" I turn to Jake for his turn. He's about to blow a fuse, but I wait patiently for him to make his next selection. Ray is still drawing. Minion and Red are waiting patiently to be picked.

"Red," he says, and Red reluctantly joins his team.

"Ray, want to play?" I ask him.

If I had asked him if he was playing, he would've said no. Instead he says, "Sure."

"Minion," Jake says. What did you think Jake, did you think I wanted a spy on my team? Of course I wasn't going to pick Minion. I've already got a semi-traitorous Ray on my team, what do you want? I know what you want. You want me to complain that you had both the first pick and the last pick. You would then graciously give me your last pick, Minion. "Are we all set?" Jake asks.

"No," I say and then I make like I am conferring with my team, particularly Erix. What I am saying to him is, "Blah-blah-blah, you know, and if blah-blah-blah, well– "

Erix clearly says, "Thank you for picking me." He spoke with more confidence than I have ever heard from him.

"You're welcome."

Jake watches a car slowly move up the road. "We're waiting. Who has the flags?"

"I do. Hang on. We get the next pick," I say before diving into my car and slamming the door. I hear Jake yelling, but through all the rust and dirt I can't hear what he's saying. I grab bandanas and some other things. I stuff everything but two bandanas into the pocket of my jacket. Then I hide a small duffel bag in the jacket. I jump out just in time for Dexter and Mica to get out of a car that is the exact opposite of my car. It is gold. I wouldn't be surprised if it really is.

"Whaaaa-choo, whaa-choo, ahhhh-choo!" Mica sneezes before closing her door.

"I pick Dexter," I announce, cracking most everybody up. I walk over to Jake, hand him a bandana, and say, "Here's your flag. I'll want it back." He's about ready to bust a gasket, technically speaking.

Jake walks over to Mica and asks her if she's playing. She takes the bandana from his hand and sneezes into it. She asks what. Jake says, "Capture The Flag."

She says, "You'll have to teach me how."

"I think everyone needs to hear the rules," I say to Jake, but then I leave it to him to explain them, with my assistance.

"My team will be–"

"Everyone gather around and listen," I interrupt. "Go ahead."

"My team will be on the hill. Yours will be in the valley."

"For the first game. For any other games, we alternate sides."

"The goal is to capture the other team's flag," Jake tries to snatch my flag, but I switch hands at the last second.

"You looking for something?" I ask him.

"The flag must be in plain sight, not hidden, and must be reachable by anyone without requiring jumping or tools or anything. The playing field is divided in half. If you are tagged on the other team's side, you are captured and will be escorted to jail."

"How many people can be escorted at a time? Or what if the tagger decides not to take the tagged person to jail?" I am needling him on points that he knows he has cheated on in the past, even if others don't remember.

"A tagger can only take one person at a time to jail. If the tagged person is not escorted to jail after 15 seconds they are free to go."

"And they cannot be re-tagged by the same person for 60 seconds," I add, "because otherwise one person could hold several people at bay without using the jail."

"If you are in jail, you have to remain touching the object that is the jail, such as a log or a building." Jake is hinting that the farmhouse should be our jail. No, thank you, Jake. "If someone from your team tags you while you're in jail, they will be able to escort you straight to your home side. The game is over when someone captures the other team's flag and brings it over the line onto their side. If they are tagged on the way, the flag stays where the runner was tagged."

While Jake talks to our two teams, a third team is huddling a short distance away, making plans with high-pitched whispers; it's a team of mosquitoes. There's 10,000 mosquitoes right there.

"Boundaries are the top of the hill, the road, the lake, and the creek line, except the jut out where the boundary is the woods on the other side." He's asked about the jut out, and he points it out. "There is a white string across the field that divides the two sides. Any questions?" Sure I've got questions, but I learned a long time ago never to ask questions when I don't want to know the answers. "Here," Jake says, handing me an air horn. "Sound it when you are ready. Once both teams have sounded the horns, the game begins."

We all start down the hill as one group but step by step we separate into two groups. I lead with Hope and Nicole, crossing the string, and passing some seemingly abandoned gopher holes, marked with a small reality sign. I give Hope a quick kiss and slip her the bandana. As we walk, I ask her to have Erix drop it in the field near the tree nearest to the road. We slow up to let the rest of my team catch up, and I go back over the rules with some added history. I mention that one early game didn't start with Tom; he joined in the middle of the game, and there was a fair amount of which-twin-is-which confusion. Tom reminds me that I was the one who took advantage of the confusion. At the farmhouse, I drop off my duffel bag and jacket. I ask Hope and Nicole to wait there. I quietly tell Erix that Hope wants to talk to him. I take the rest of the team to the bend in the creek.

"Al, do you remember what poison ivy looks like?"

"Yeah."

"It's all around the creek or at least it used to be. You and I will cross the creek. The rest of you will want to stay at least a few yards away from the creek." Al and I cross the creek using a log and a hanging branch, while the rest of the group backs up. If we are being watched from the hillside, it should look like the main group is staying away on purpose, so they don't call attention to Al and I. Glancing at Al, he has a grappling hook and rope out as if we needed it for the creek.

When we are mostly out of view, I bend over like I am setting up the flag. I tell Al, "Lean in here. We are just a diversion. The flag has already been handled."

Al smiles, "Sounds good. Were you kidding about the poison ivy?"

"Not exactly, But it helps out my plan."

"You know you nearly brushed up against some closer to the creek."

"Where?"

"Right over there." He takes me over to it. Mitten shaped leaves... reddish stem... yes, it's poison ivy. I got poison ivy here years ago. It makes me mad, but not because I got poison ivy. It angers me because it reminds me of the Boy Scouts. I'm probably the only boy that ever joined scouting to meet girls. I'm still angry about it. "Huh. Something took off the third leaf. Very clever. Good job," I tell Al. Crossing the creek, Ray and Dexter are waiting for us, but Tom and Will have disappeared. "Hey, where did Tom and Will go?"

Dexter clears his throat, "They went down closer to the lake to act like they are setting up the flag there. We spotted the other team watching us."

"That's a good idea," I say without looking for a poker face from Al. "Let's get back to the old-old farmhouse."

"The old-old farmhouse?!?" Dexter responds as we walk.

"Yeah," I say pointing ahead of us.

Dexter clears his throat again, "In Europe that building would be considered new. A fixer-upper certainly, but it isn't old."

We all gather at the old-old... at the fixer-upper. Motioning toward the creek I tell them, "We won't be guarding the flag. Most of us don't know where it is. The small glade of aspens over there..."

"Those are birch trees," Dexter corrects with a throat clearing.

"Those birch trees will be the jail. Ray, Hope, and Nicole – I want you to play the middle. Watch the string and which side of the line you are on." I hand Ray a walkie-talkie. "Dexter – you are the go between – watch the other team – go where you think you should be, but stay away from the creek. Tom, Will, and Al you are the leads for getting the flag. Tom, where's their flag?"

"I don't know."

"What do you mean you don't know?"

"I don't think they told Todd. Wait. Todd's asking where our flag is."

"Tell him to say 'hi' to Jake for us."

We wait. I turn to Nicole and say, "Human walkie-talkies. It's the twin thing." I pull out the air horn.

"Jake replied something less friendly," Tom says.

We hear an air horn. I step forward from the group and blast a reply. "Everyone to your places except Tom and Erix." I ask Tom, "Can I ask you something without your brother listening in?"

"Hang on," he says, pulling out a cigar and lighting it. Puffing, Tom says, "He hates this."

"Can you make him think he has to go to the bathroom every five minutes?"

"Done."

I wish him luck, and he takes off.

I pick up my duffel bag and escort Erix to the far side of the fixer-upper. "How did it go dropping off the bandana?"

"I did what Hope said. I went to the road. On this side I looked for a stick or a stone. When I found it, I sat down, put down the flag, picked up the stone, and brought it back here," he says, holding out the rock.

"Good job. Don't tell anyone where it is." I take the rock, and we climb up the fixer-upper. I show him how to do it and where not to walk. I turn on the other walkie-talkie. From up here we have a great vantage point over most of the playing field. It is tough to distinguish most people. Tom and his cigar are clear because he is close, but disappearing quickly. Ray is also close. Most people seem to be on the hillside – Jake's team's side, not the field side – our side. I can distinguish Dan near the top of the hill because of his broad shoulders. I can distinguish Red because his red hair glows in the sunlight. And I can distinguish Mica because of her sneezing. Even though she's on the other team, I'll have to figure out something we can do for her.

I hand Erix a pair of binoculars and show him how to use them. He will be the best informed person out here.

Jake and two others have crossed the line on the creek side of the field. Nicole and Ray try to chase after them and end up capturing one of them. Ray points the others out to me, and I give him the okay signal that I will handle them. It's Cy that Nicole caught. I climb down. I crawl out on all fours, heading toward the creek. A chipmunk crosses my path, stops, and gets up on its hind legs. It's a role reversal. I wave him off, whispering, "Not now." Jake crashes through, and I grab his leg saying, "Tag." I get up and Lefty dives away like I am going to tag him too. I grab Jake's vest jacket and say, "Come on to jail." I lead him around the fixer-upper, which he stares at as we go by. I notice his jacket is weighed down with equipment. Nicole is talking to Cy at the birch jail. "You have to be touching this tree," I tell Jake and Cy. "Are you the guard?" I ask Nicole.

"Sure. I'm getting to know your Ex."

"Have fun," I say, taking off. Back at the fixer-upper, Erix tells me that Lefty is still wandering around by the creek. As the smartest person out here, I hope Lefty can identify poison ivy. Erix also points out Tom smoking his cigar while sitting on a glacial boulder. I tell Erix that boulder must be their jail. I am about to climb down when Erix points at Will running down the hill. Becky is chasing him. She catches up to him and tags him about 20 yards from the line. He holds the flag up dramatically and drops it as Becky escorts him to jail. Someone heads for it from our side, and I climb down. I run to the hill, and Hope runs toward me with the flag! I hug her and lift her up in a kiss.

"Way to go!" I shout. I take out and sound the air horn. Everyone comes down or over to us. People are congratulating Hope, and she graciously shares the credit with Will. She glows in the light. Lefty asks where our flag was. "I don't know," I admit. I call Erix over and ask him to show them. Erix takes him and Jake and everyone else follows. There are no complaints, no rule violations. Erix is the defensive hero.

We agree to another game, gather our things, and head up the hillside. I ask my team if everyone has their stuff, and how everyone is doing.

"Miserable," Mica says. We stop, and she continues up the hill. I almost thought she was defecting to our side.

The breeze begins to cool, which reminds me. Unzipping my duffel bag, I take out a stack of black T-shirts and pass them out. Everyone takes one and puts it over their current shirt, everyone except Nicole. Nicole takes off her headlights shirt, puts on a black shirt, clips the back of the shirt tight somehow, and ties a knot in front. It takes me a moment to regain my senses. Hope waves her hand in front of my eyes, but I don't blink. "And – sleep!" Hope says, snapping her fingers in my direction.

"That was fashion magic," I tell no one in particular.

"Yes, she's quite gifted," Hope confirms. "We await your leadership."

"Oh yeah, the game. Dexter, you and Tom move around to watch what they're doing. Here's a pair of binoculars." My motion, or someone's, stops a chirping cricket. "That reminds me." I hand out clickers and tiny flashlights. "If you are unsure who someone is, click this once. If they don't click back, figure they are from the other team." From the field below we hear a chorus of phone rings and songs. We laugh. "I think my way is more subtle than theirs."

Shadows are falling on the valley. "One of those ash trees, the furthest one, will be our jail. Will? Al? One of you, find a good place for our flag. They'll be watching. Take these glow sticks and mark different spots with them."

"Anywhere?"

"Yeah, anywhere."

Nicole is whispering something to Hope.

"I'm not feeling so good," Ray tells me.

"Too much fresh air?"

"I don't know."

"You could go up and lie down. Or we could use your help as the jailer at the group of trees over there."

"I'll try that."

"Good."

Dexter comes back and clears his throat. "We think we know where their flag is. They are all crowded around the farmhouse. It's probably on the top level."

"That technically wouldn't break the rules and would be easy to defend. They probably have their jail there too, making it nearly a one person job to guard both. That's just a guess. Tom! Do you want to play scout? Take this walkie-talkie and these glow sticks. If the flag is in the fixer-upper..." Tom laughs. "Throw out the glow sticks... activate them first by snapping and shaking them. If you can give us a play-by-play with the walkie-talkie, that would be great. Head down to the line and cross it as soon as the game starts. Good luck, Scout Pfuloree!"

"It'll be a blast," Tom replies.

I gather up my team. Dexter tells Will and Al where Jake's team has been pointing. Al says that's not where the flag is. I tell everyone our suspicions and what Tom is doing about it. Al responds, "If they have only one person left behind and one or two tagging people, the rest can be out looking for our flag."

I nod my head and sound the air horn.

"Wait. What are we doing?" Hope asks.

Jake's air horn blasts a reply.

"We're going to stay here as a group watching for a signal from Tom." From the glacial boulder we watch Jake's team dart about, some cross over to our side, and a few run into things for no apparent reason. We watch someone leap out of the brush to tag Tom on his direct assault of the fixer-upper.

Without looking away I whisper, "Who would rather not do some running? Anyone?"

No one responds. The walkie-talkie squawks, "Hey Ricky, it's Tom. Their flag– " and then nothing more from the walkie-talkie. Two or three glow sticks are thrown out of the fixer-upper. Then a firecracker goes off from the same spot.

"Okay, we all go. If you can't get the flag, tag Tom. And watch where you are going." As my team takes off, I pull the largest item from my duffel, a battery-powered lantern, set it on the boulder, and switch it on. I drop the binoculars onto Nicole's tank top in the duffel bag and zip it up. I head down the hill, catching up to Erix, and leading him in. I hear a click, and I click back. Nicole is past the building taunting and teasing someone who can't tag her. The rest of the group is hiding around the building. Tom is laughing a sinister laugh from jail and appears to be threatening to light another firecracker with his cigar.

Cy yells, "You have to be touching the wall!"

"I'm touching the wall with my foot!" he says lighting a fuse.

I head up, since I know how. I pull the flag from a hole and throw it out the building just as Cy spins around and tags me. Tom lets the fuse burn out, since it was only a fuse. "So, how's it going?" I ask Tom.

"People shouldn't be allowed to have firecrackers. It's not fair," Cy says.

"Bring it up after this game, and maybe we can all agree on that rule," I reply. We watch half-a-dozen little firefly-like flashlights head toward the border, and I am wondering which of the fireflies has the flag. "You know," I tell Tom, "I didn't bring any firecrackers because I didn't want the field to catch on fire. Of course, it's your field." By telling Tom this, I am also telling Cy that I had nothing to do with the firecrackers. Tom puffs on his cigar.

"And no cigars," says Cy, pulling her bangs out of her eyes.

"I got Nicole," Red says, bringing her up.

"I got their captain," Cy says.

"They have our flag," Red says. Cy looks for it and finds it missing.

I turn on my little flashlight while saying, "Hey, careful of the edge!" Nicole almost went over. Red was close too.

"Thanks," Nicole says.

"Hey," Hope calls up from below, "we won! Sound your horn!" I do what my girlfriend tells me to do, and we all climb down. We head up to the glacial rock. Except for Cy, Jake's team is all wearing night goggles which help people to see heat in the dark. They all have them around their necks or on their foreheads, except Minion who is still wearing his. My team looks cool in the matching black T-shirts. Several conversations are going on at once. Everyone seems tired, even the moth that is orbiting the lantern. I learn that it was Al that ran the flag in. I also learn that Ray had our flag near the jail. Cy gets a rule announced about no firecrackers. Tom asks about other fireworks, and the rule is amended to be no fireworks. Then Tom asks about just wicks, and after some debate it is decided that wicks alone are okay. Jake asks what the point was of the lantern. Nobody knows, and they turn to me.

"I thought it might throw off the night goggles."

"How did you know we had night goggles?" Jake asks me.

"I guessed."

"You guessed?!?"

"Yeah, it was my best guess to explain why some people were bumping into things. I guessed that you were using third-rate, foreign-surplus night goggles. And as an engineer with optics experience, I guessed that this $14.99 lantern might be an effective counter-measure. Should we head up to the house – the houses?"

"One more game," Jake says.

"I'm out," Ray says, handing me the flag and heading up.

"Thanks Ray," I call after him.

"Okay. Anyone else?" Jake asks. I grab my stuff. "The lantern stays here," he tells me.

"Okay." Once my team is at the dividing line, I tell them, "Everyone head in opposite directions into our side, act like you are planting a flag and meet back at the fixer-upper." I walk briskly nearly to the lake, drop off the flag, and loop back. When I get back, everyone is already back and making plans, except Erix. They're talking about different approaches, different plans, and even though minutes ago they were looking pretty tired, they are very gung ho about capturing Jake's flag a third time. I'm not sure I even understand some of the plans, but I approve them all, just asking them to be careful. I sound my air horn. Soon after, Erix shows up. He looks tired too. Jake's air horn goes off, and my team takes off.

"What do you want me to do?" Erix asks me.

"Is there anything you want to do?" I ask back.

"I don't know," he says.

We walk toward the dividing line. We see plenty of motion and hear plenty of distant shouts, but the only clear object breaking the darkness is the lantern on the rock in the middle of the hillside. I start to notice some stars. I notice the moon is just a sliver, just like a fingernail clipping. Erix asks, "We've done good, right?"

My mind becomes quieter as I try to answer him. Yes, we've played a good game, I think to myself. We have stepped out of our work and home lives and played our game and shared our toys. We momentarily care about a rocky field and a 20 square inch piece of fabric. We transformed our friends into adversaries. "Yes," I tell Erix, "we've played a good game."

Watching the beacon on the hill, I am starting to take out my binoculars when I hear a high scream. People are gathered around the rock and from what I can see, Nicole is being held down. I chuck the binoculars into the bag, turn to Erix and say, "Come with me," and we run up the hill. I dodge shadowy objects and tear my jeans at one point when I didn't dodge well enough. In moments I am at the rock and I see Nicole being held and tickled and Hope is held back, I fill my lungs and bellow, **"Get your hands off of them!"**

People back away. Joe lets go of Hope. Minion is still holding Nicole, but Jake is no longer tickling her. I head for Minion, **"I said let her go!"**

Minion releases her. He pokes me and says, "Tag."

Nicole pushes Jake. He trips into some sort of thistle bush. I pull out the third bandana from my pocket and throw it at Jake. "Here, game over." I sound the air horn; people jump. Hope slugs Joe; he keels over. Nicole makes a move for Minion. He runs away, and she chases after him.

Jake works to extricate himself from the bush without further scratches on his way back through. The smashed bush has other intentions.

"Are you all right?" I ask Hope.

"Maybe. I may not be done with him," she says toward Joe.

I head toward Joe, "Joe, you can't torture my girlfriend. That is definitely not part of the game."

"I wasn't! I was just holding her..."

"Who said you could hold her?" Turning to Jake, "Who said you could torture Nicole?" I move to confront him as he has all but one arm out of the bush.

Behind me, Joe is hit again and starts a steady stream of swearing.

"We weren't torturing her. We were tickling her to find out where the flag was. You– you had your flag. You cheated!"

"Bullshit. I stopped the game."

"That's bullshit."

"What's going on?" either Tom or Todd asks as others gather.

I pick up my lantern. "Let's all go up." Most of the group walks up the hill with me and my lantern. As we walk I ask Hope, "Where's Becky?"

"She scraped her knee and went up," someone else says.

I turn to Dan. "I noticed you didn't do anything to stop Jake and Minion." Dan doesn't reply.

I survey who we have with us: Hope, Dan, Erix, Tom, Todd, Will, Al, Dexter, Lefty, and Red. Becky, Ray, and Mica had previously gone up. Jake and Joe are casualties. Nicole is still fighting Minion... "Where's Cy?"

"She was yelling at Jake, and then she left," Hope tells me.

"Did she go up?"

"I think so. We have to help Nicole."

"I will. I'll go back down after we get everyone up." The hill levels out. I lead the group into the new blue house and into a new kitchen. Ruth gets up and launches into a hostess role. I drop off my duffel, squeeze Hope's hand, and head back out. I carry the lantern to my car, set it on top – hey, it's a police car! – kind of, and I get out a high-powered flashlight. I take my flashlight and lantern down the hill. Not far down I spot a figure coming toward me that has to be Nicole. "Are you okay?" I ask her.

"Yeah," she says, smiling slightly.

"I am sorry that they tickled you and... held you down. That's not part of the game."

"It's okay. I'm okay. They aren't really okay," she says. I lead her up to the house, stopping short. "What?" she asks.

"I have to get the rest."

"Really?!?"

I head back down the hill. Joe and Jake are on the rock talking. "Nasty to take off with the lantern."

"Don't you have flashlights?"

"No. It was light out when we started."

"But you have the goggles..."

"They suck," Joe says.

"Can you walk?"

"I can kick your butt," Jake says.

"You look like you just got beaten up by a bush." I stare at him. "If you really want another fight, it'll have to wait until I'm finished rescuing people. I have another trip after this one." I turn to head up. "Come on." I hear them following behind me. Mostly I hear Jake's verbal abuse, so I have to check on Joe from time to time to make sure he's still with us. At one point I stop to correct Jake that God's last name isn't Damnit. At the top of the hill, with light from the houses, I tag and release them, metaphorically speaking, and I head back down the hill.

After about ten minutes of searching, I find Minion with a black eye and a sprained ankle. Minion is surprised that it is me coming after him and at first tries to back away.

"I'm going to take you up," I tell him, but then I try to figure out how. Normally, you would put your shoulder under the shoulder of the side with the bad leg to help him hobble. Minion is just too short for that. Besides, that is a very slow process. In the movies, they cheat and have the injured or unconscious person helping drag themselves out of the scene. Minion is no help. I try dragging him. He doesn't like that much. Ultimately I carry him to the road, leave the lantern, walk up the road, drive down the road, pick him up, put him on the hood where the peanuts had been, and drive him slowly up. When I park the car, camera flashes go off. I get out and they are still going off. I pick Minion up and carry him into the blue house. I set him on a bench. He never thanks me.

My duffel bag has been opened and ransacked, not that there should have been any surprises. I used everything, except of course Nicole's tank top.

The dirty plates, cups, and cans tell me that everyone else has eaten. I forage for food while people watch. Mica is nearby, snarling at Dexter, "Of course you were bitten! Melvin said the pheromone cologne attracts mosquitoes! I don't know why you are even wearing that stuff." I ask her how her allergies are. She says, "Better," with a smile, and mentions having taken some sort of medicine. I assume it helps with the allergies. With all eyes on me, I settle for an apple. I think about checking my zipper again. Here comes Jake.

"Remember when we went over the rules, I thought we covered placement of the flag," Jake confronts me. I wash my apple with water that sparkles. Tom must put glitter in the water supply. Ruth tells me it's already washed. Don't you start in on me too. Jake continues, "Was there some part of the rules that you didn't understand?" I munch on apple. "Do you understand now that you're not supposed to carry your flag around with you?" I munch on apple. "Did you expect me to have to search you for your flag?" I munch on apple. There is a break in his rhythm. He's looking around for support.

"Are you done?" I ask him. I munch on apple.

"You want me to drop the fact that you cheated. I'm afraid not."

I stifle a laugh, not that I'm laughing at him, but because he just reminded me of a joke. I lean back on a counter, bumping some plates aside. "A string walks into a bar. Orders a beer. The bartender is about to give him a beer, when he stops and looks at the string. The bartender, not very bright, asks the string, 'What are you?'" I give the bartender a gruff voice, and I wave my apple for emphasis. "The string says, 'I'm a string.' The bartender says, 'We don't serve strings here.' The string leaves the bar and stops someone on the street. 'Would you please tie me up like a pretzel and split my ends?' The person helps the string. The string goes back into the bar, and orders a beer. The bartender is about to hand the beer over, but stops and asks, 'What are you? Aren't you the string that I just kicked out of here?' The strings says, 'No, I'm a frayed knot.'"

I munch on apple. It's good apple, very good apple. I must be starving. People are laughing. Jake isn't, but his eyes have relaxed a bit. Jake declares, "You've disgraced your flag."

What? He got my attention with stupidity. "You mean the Red, White, and Black?" I ask him.

"Right."

"You care more about things and how you treat them than people. Where in the rules was there anything about torturing information out of prisoners? That's why I stopped the game – because of the way you were treating Nicole and Hope."

"The game ended because I had your flag."

"Ha! The bandana I gave you is red, black, and white."

"Same thing."

"Maybe. But that wasn't our flag! Our flag is still in the field. You're still playing. Go find it." Now he's mad again. I throw away the core. "Here's a clue: the game isn't fun if it hurts people. Not Nicole, not Hope, not Minion, not me," I say looking down at my torn jeans, "not you. It's a rule of any game because it's a rule of life, one of those things your mom should have taught you. Sure, tickling can be fun, but not the way you did it or why you did it. And no, I didn't cheat. I had a third bandana in my pocket. I used it to stop the game. I used it to stop you."

Ruth steps between us. "Could we not fight?"

It's Jake's move. He doesn't.

Others are itching their mosquito bites.

Hope steps between us. Erix surprises me by stepping between us. This spot becomes prime real estate. Dan Ryan steps up but there is no more room. The crowd will delay any sort of resolution with Jake.

Minion is yelling something unintelligible from the other room.

Dan booms, **"I should have known you didn't cheat! You just did what you do – you foresaw that you would need a third bandana and had it with you!"**

I ask Hope, "Let's go outside, okay?" while apparently Ruth is asking Jake and I, "Do you want to watch some movies from here from six years ago?" I respond to Ruth, "I don't think now is such a good time." I step outside. Hope and Erix follow as I walk next door to the porch of the old yeller house. I sit on the wooden swing. Erix sits on a folding chair. Hope sits next to me. Crickets are in full concert, telling long distance stories and chirping love songs. Two moths are flying opposite orbits, like an X, around the porch lamp.

"I liked your Frayed Knot story," Hope says.

"Thanks. Thank you both for stepping in to defend me. It was a nice move."

The door next door opens and closes. There is yelling. Ruth's voice stands out from the rest, saying, "No one ever adamantly argues over something they truly believe. They don't yell about how the sun is going to rise tomorrow!" She says other things but she must've opened the door to make her point about the sun rising or something. The crickets resume their concert while watching the events on stage. The door opens and slams again. Ruth's voice calls out, "Leave him alone." And for a moment I wonder who she's talking to, but then I see Cy heading toward us. This can't be good. Stop Cy. If only I had the ability to stop her in her tracks or send her in another direction, but I can't.

"How's the crystal ball doing?" Cy starts, her eyes sparkling.

"What crystal ball?" I ask back.

"You know," Cy turns to Hope, "your new boyfriend can see the future. Isn't that weird?" Turning back to me, "Remember telling me that there's up-ways and down-ways," she sways and most of her drink sways with her, "and back-ways and sideways and – time-ways."

Ruth approaches. "Cy's picking on me," I tell her.

"Come on back inside, Cy," Ruth says. Cy resists, leaning toward the swing. Ruth grabs Cy's arm and whispers something in Cy's ear. Then she whispers something else.

"Good night," Cy says, going pale. We chorus "good night" back and watch them go. The moths want to check our IDs to determine if we are related to Edison.

"Let's go see the barn," Hope says. As we walk, she says, "After we got here, on our walk, you said that people would be upset for having waited for us for years. We thought you were kidding. Then Jake said that they'd waited for years."

"Hey wait up!" yells Becky. We stop, and she and Nicole catch up to Hope, Erix, and I.

"During the games," Hope continues, "you had planned ahead so well that you had shirts and flashlights," Erix shines his at us, "and clickers," Erix clicks his clicker, "and a lantern, and I don't know what else."

"Don't forget the third bandana," Nicole chimes in.

"I was getting to that. You knew you needed a third bandana. You said you wouldn't let anything bad happen to us, without being overprotective. You told us to be careful when we started the third game. And then you quickly sacrificed the game and pissed off Jake to keep us from getting hurt – by throwing a third bandana at him. Cy was telling Nicole about you, and now she tells us that you can see the future. Can you?" Hope asks as we reach the barn.

I turn on my small flashlight and open the barn door. The sliver of a moon, stars, and porch lights helped our walk, but won't help us traverse the barn. In the barn, Erix sneezes, startling some cows below. I point out the trap door to the lower level, so that they watch out for it, and I lead them to the wood ladder-stairs up to the hay loft. I take them up and over to a large open doorway that looks out over the houses, the field, the lake, and neighboring houses with street lamps twinkling in the distance. It is a great view. I sit down and the rest clear spots as if you can find something called clean under the dust and hay.

"Kind of," I utter. And Nicole cracks up. Becky giggles.

14

Pointed Perception

Hope asks, "What do you mean, 'kind of?'"

"Sometimes I see a moment that could be part of my future: a mood, a focus of attention, what people are saying, my own intense feelings, and things that don't make sense. They are the weird, surreal, defining moments of life... of my life. That's what I see, when I let myself – the odd moments. I hardly ever see normal stuff, the mundane, or at least I don't remember it if I do."

"Are you awake or asleep?" Becky asks.

"Relaxed. It used to only happen when I was asleep. What I saw was like dreaming, except weirder and more detailed, yet believable. Then I got to the point that I could relax while awake and sometimes I could start it up."

"You don't foresee world events?" Hope asks.

"No. That wouldn't happen unless I'm in the middle of it," I respond.

"So you just see your future," Hope prompts.

"Kind of. I see what will be my future until I determine to make a different decision. Then I could see a different future. It's pliable... bendable... overall, but once a decision has been made, the related events unfold with a solidity... a rigidity that can't be altered." Hope, Becky, and Nicole are sitting close. Erix was sitting close; now he's pacing around. Hope's question about seeing my future is bouncing around in my head. "I can see my future if I let myself. If I let myself, I see my future, and with determination, my potential futures."

"Futures," Nicole repeats.

"Yeah."

Becky asks, "Why wouldn't you let yourself? Why wouldn't you want to know your future? Or futures?"

"It's not just knowing; it's an involvement... an interaction... sort of, 'Well, what if I try this?' Have you ever thought about a problem for too long?"

They all agree. I might have even heard a moo from below.

"You are stuck working over the problem as if you are a computer trying to solve Pi or stuck in a loop. You are trying to figure out a relationship or a problem with your family and it just knots up and you wind up traveling the same thoughts over and over and you aren't getting anywhere... you aren't learning anything, but you are tearing yourself apart and finally it gets so bad that someone has to pull you out of it. They tell you that you have to get on with your life. You have to live. And maybe time will work itself out."

A light separates itself from the houses on the left.

"Uh-huh," says Erix.

"What do you think?" I ask Hope. "Are you freaking out?"

"I'm not freaking out. I'm trying to understand," she says. "When did you realize that you needed to bring an extra bandana to stop the game?"

"A few days ago. It was dark and I was standing, watching a light on a hill, I also could see stars and the moon. The moon was just a sliver, the sort of moon that reminds me of a fingernail clipping."

"Clip it," Hope says with a laugh.

"And I could hear Erix's voice right beside me. He was asking about it being a good game, so I knew we were playing a game. I saw commotion in the light and I heard a woman's scream, but it was all too far away to see. I didn't know what was going on." The light outside is coming closer. "I needed binoculars, but I didn't have them. Or I needed to get up there. We walked up to the boulder with the rock," my voice cracks. I swallow. "I'd rather not tell you what happened from there, except that one of you was badly hurt.

"I decided I would have to have binoculars in hand. Then when I saw the light on the hill, I got out my binoculars, because I had now decided to bring them with and have them in a duffel bag. Now I see that Nicole is being held down for some reason. So I race up there, running into a few things on the way. I see now that Jake is tickling you," to Nicole, "and you're also being held," I say to Hope. "So it's Jake that has to be stopped, fast, before something goes too far. So how do I stop Jake fast? I could attack him. We've fought before, but not for years. One of the problems of that is that he and I are alike in the way we fight. We don't fight friendly. Neither he nor I know when to stop. If we fight, we fight. The situation could be just as dangerous for us fighting as it was for Nic– as it could have been otherwise."

A light heads up the ladder-stairs from below. It's Ruth and Will.

"Hi, we just wanted to see how you guys are doing. You don't have to get up," she says to me. "Is everybody okay?"

Nicole and Becky say, "Yeah."

"Here, I know you didn't get much to eat," she tells me as she hands me something wrapped.

"Is it a sandwich?" I ask.

"Yes, a half-sandwich."

"What's the other half? I'm kidding. What kind of sandwich is it?"

"Veggie, like the one you had for lunch," she says. "Food is your friend."

"Sounds great. Listen, I wanted to thank you for the lunch sandwich and intervening earlier with Jake. It was very nice of you," I say as she blushes. "How's Ray?"

"He's fine. He's been either napping or sitting off to the side drawing," Will says. "Jake has settled down, and I think he wants to talk with you. He didn't mean to go overboard."

"Sure."

Ruth flashes a picture of all of us. "Ruth!" Nicole protests.

"All I see are purple and green spots," Becky says.

"Well, you are all welcome to come back in, anytime you're ready," Will says, which makes me realize that from some of their perspectives, it's as if we were kicked out to the barn. "See you later" and "see you" are exchanged, while I am lost in thought. By the time I'm back, Will and Ruth have gone down and their light is leaving the barn.

"You have nice friends," Becky comments.

"Thanks. Anyone want a part of this?"

"It's all yours."

I take a few bites of sandwich.

"You were saying you needed a way to stop Jake."

"Right. It looked like you two were on my team, but I assumed that either Tom or Todd was the captain. I don't know what would've happened if I hadn't picked you," I tell Nicole. She moves to squeeze between Becky and I. "What did Jake want? Of course he wanted the flag."

"He also wanted to feel me up," Nicole adds.

"Oh. I didn't know that. I never saw that."

"S'okay," she says.

"Well, I figured he wanted the flag, and since I always bring the bandanas, I would just bring an extra and have it in my pocket. I made that decision and played everything out again... to the point of knowing that you two wouldn't get hurt. I never saw the other repercussions with Jake or Minion." I take a bite of sandwich. Nicole pushes me back, climbs on top of me, and tries to kiss me. "Mmmmph!" I say, keeping my lips closed tight. Nicole's lips are rubbery.

"He's eating," Becky says.

"And he's mine," Hope says.

"Mmm, sandwich," Nicole says.

"You still like me?" I ask Hope.

"Yes, I still like you," Hope says. "Cy must've made you paranoid. I'm not Cy. I'm not sure what to make of all this, but I'm not going to call you names or freak out or anything. Nicole, get off him! One question though, couldn't you have warned us?"

I upright myself after Nicole climbs off. "What could I have said? 'You can't play Capture The Flag; it's a dangerous game.' or 'No tickling.' or 'Nicole, you need to wear a helmet.' or 'Bedtime is at eight o'clock here.' Seriously, if there is some way that I could've warned you that would have been reasonable to you, please let me know."

"You could've stopped the game after the second one."

"He tried to, remember?"

"That's right, you did, didn't you."

"Does it happen a lot?"

"What?"

"Your... visions?"

"Not really. I don't encourage them. I really could only tell you a few things about this weekend when you asked."

"You left out the part about needing the bandana."

"Yeah."

"Did you leave anything else out?"

How do I answer this? "Maybe..."

"Anything that you need to warn us about?"

"No."

"Good."

"So, do you know anything else about our futures?"

"No. Except I know a bit of mine and a bit about Erix." Erix crawls closer. I notice that Nicole has been leaning on me and that Hope is still close.

"So, c'mon, what do you know about Erix?!?" Becky asks and I see that Erix is practically in her lap. "This is like pulling teeth!"

"He's destined for greatness."

"What?!?"

"He's going to do something really great."

"How so – great?" Becky asks.

"Great on a global scale. I'd rather not say anything else about it."

"Hey good for you," Becky tells her lap. "So, you can't say anything more because you don't want to disrupt the timeline?"

"Disrupt the timeline? Everything changes time. Everything. That's the nature of time. It is not a line. It is not fabric like Greek myths thought. Clocks and calendars represent celestial movement, but are poor indicators of time on a personal scale. From our perspective it speeds up and slows down and has moments that are great and moments that are dull. We are the drivers, the actors of time, and we are the passengers, the audience of time. I can control what I do. I can influence Jake, but I can't control what he does. Seeing ten ways that the same thing is going to happen and nothing you do changes anything teaches... well, it teaches a whole lot of things... but one of the things it teaches is patience. I have learned a great deal about the rewards of patience. I consider myself to be something of an expert at patience. Compared to Erix, I don't know the first thing about patience."

Hey, the crickets have stopped chirping. Either they have fallen asleep, or they are listening in. Or they were listening in and now they've fallen asleep.

"Wow."

"You say, 'we are the drivers,' but we can't do what apparently you can," Hope says.

"I don't know. Do you dream?"

"Yes."

"Do you ever forget the dreams?"

"Almost always."

"Do you ever have the feeling of deja vu?"

"Sometimes..."

"I'm not sure I do anything that anyone else could do if they really wanted."

"No," Nicole disagrees from my shoulder. "Most people would like to know their future and be able to act on it."

"But then, why don't they pay attention to their dreams? I couldn't always do – I call it, pointed perception. I used to have dreams at night, forget them, and then later have a feeling of deja vu. As a way to start remembering my dreams, I kept a journal by my bed. By writing down my dreams for several months, I taught myself to remember them."

"Do you still keep a journal?" Hope asks.

"No, I don't keep a journal, and I don't take pictures. What would I do with them? My past is a repeat of a rerun. I saw it, I lived it, and I'm done with it. Every once in awhile, I'll take pictures, but only to give as gifts to people. For recording my dreams, it didn't take long for me to not need the notebook. I had developed an awareness of my dreams. My memory improved too. I learned that an attention to something, as well as practice, is how to become good at it.

"Many of my dreams had familiar people in unfamiliar places or circumstances. Sometimes I didn't like the content of the dreams. I reasoned, 'This is me. The dreams are coming from me, my subconscious. I should have control of them, make them turn out better.' So I worked at taking control of my dreams; I didn't want bad dreams. I started by wanting to make everything turn out right. I began to have fewer and fewer bad dreams.

"I started to learn things from my dreams. I wondered where the lessons came from. I read up on dreams coming from the subconscious, and maybe intuition too, but then the more I read, the more a supposed fact conflicted with another and certainly the available information did not shed any light on what I had already experienced. I may research a subject, but that doesn't mean I believe what I read. If what I read fits with what I already know, I am more accepting that it might help me with what I don't know, if that makes any sense. So I'll pick up a book, turn to the index, and look up something I already know. If it gets that right, I might trust it on things that I don't know. If a book says that something can't happen, but it happened to me, I'll believe my experiences any day over what someone got printed in a book.

"I have never told anyone all of this. One time a church leader taught my youth group to meditate. I think the ploy was to get us all to be quiet and sit still. I think that was the actual goal." Hope nods. "So he had us all get comfortable and close our eyes. He had us tone out – block – ignore our bodies and immediate concerns. He talked about floating and other things that really didn't matter to me. The combination of being alert, yet blocking out what was going on around me was a big push. I had an awake dream, so real that I thought it was actually happening. When it was over I realized that I had no idea what he had been talking about or doing or how long we had been there. The next day, the dream happened. What I had dreamed took place. Saying, 'wow, deja vu,' didn't do it justice."

I feel a shiver from Hope and realize the night air is getting cooler.

"When I was a kid, I saw other kids my age screw up and make bad decisions. I became more and more apprehensive about decision making. I would try to find out as much as I could about something to make the best decisions... gathering as much information as I could from as many perspectives as possible. Look at the options and the possibilities. The father of a friend of mine once told me, 'You never have as much information as you need to make decisions.' I'm persistent. I try to get as much information as I can so that decision making is less of a gamble. I hedge my bets. My memory, combined with persistence, perspective, faith, and decision making problems, led me to pointed perception."

It's quiet. Almost too quiet.

Either I have stunned them or I have put them to sleep. Or I stunned them to sleep. I could tell them about how I've learned to look around more so that when I dream about a situation previously, I have as much information as possible. I could tell them about how great a decision maker I have become, and yet I still make decent-sized mistakes. I could tell them a lot of things, but it's late. It's time to wake them. "Let's go back to the house," I say, "okay?" They all get up and stretch without having a rooster go off.

As we're walking, Hope takes my hand. Her hand is cold. "How are you so warm?" she asks me.

"Minnesota warmth. You never know when it might come in handy."

We are most of the way back, when Becky and Nicole run ahead for some reason. I think about asking Hope what she thinks of what I told her, but she's holding my hand. That's a positive sign. I don't need a billboard. A bat swoops down in front of us to collect some bugs the other two must have stirred up on their way by.

"Did you see the bat?" Hope asks. I nod.

Inside, Jake and his final drink of the night are doing their best imitation of a throw rug. We almost trip over him on the way in; he's not far from the door. I suppose I should have told him not to wait up. He shouldn't drink on an empty head.

"Clean up in aisle 3!" I announce.

"Hey, welcome back!" Tom greets us, and leads us into the living room where Todd, Ruth, and Will are still up. Weird! They laugh. The floor is the same level as the kitchen and hallway, but it's sunken in. It's thick glass or Plexiglas for about eight inches. Below that there is wood parquet with a Persian rug in the middle. It gives the impression of walking on air, which is aided by a few white-gray shag-rag throw rugs. This is my first time in here, I think. Will is in one of the chairs that hangs from the ceiling, playing with a remote control that raises and lowers it. Tom says, "We were wondering if you were going to spend the night in the barn. There are plenty of rooms here, or you could stay in the old house. Even Jake's tent is available since he's become enamored with the hallway tiling." Ruth and Todd are on opposite ends of a V-shaped couch. An inner wall is covered with a painting of a marshy lake at sunset. The top of the painting blends into a video screen that continuously loops a flock of Canadian geese flying across the room. Plexiglas stairs lead up with black rectangles painted on them, making the staircase look like a huge piano.

"I haven't even looked around..."

"Time for the grand tour!"

"Does it play?" I ask staring at the stairs.

"That would have cost extra. Besides it would have led to too much exercise, up and down and two steps up, now jump four down and– "

"I'm glad you thought that out," I reply.

"Cool." Nicole and Becky and a trucks-worth of luggage just found their way in. Erix has apparently been in the doorway the whole time. Nicole pulls him in by the arm, saying, "Don't be a chicken." A life-like statue of a cat blinks at us.

"That isn't your cat from when we were kids, is it?" I ask. "You didn't... animate the corpse, did you?" Tom shakes his head, no.

"Check out the window," Will says, pushing a button. The window lights up like it's daytime outside. It's an aquarium. I go over and act like I'm going to open the window, dumping the aquarium's contents into the room. I look over and Ruth is panicked, but Tom has a quit-fooling-around smirk. A giant painting of the typed word **IF** is behind Ruth.

"That's a mighty big **IF**... " I say with emotion, and several people crack up. Tom has probably been waiting for that reaction.

"It's not art, if it isn't well hung," Nicole says.

Part of the ceiling is glass. It appears to be the floor of a hallway upstairs.

"Are you ready for the dining room?" Looking in, it is all mirrors. The floor, walls, ceiling, and table are mirrors. Mirrors hide some cabinets in the wall. A small chandelier lights up the room with a single half-sized bulb repeated to infinity. We head in. Erix does not. Suddenly the room seems crowded with people as our group repeats itself right-side up and upside down and sideways and down ways and up ways and back ways and front ways.

"Wow!" Hope says for all of us.

"Cleaning this will be a chore," I tell him.

"What do you mean 'will'?" Tom replies. "This was where Jake got sick."

"Ewww," Becky reflects for all of us picturing the repetition.

"Let's go upstairs," Tom says, backing us out as Nicole checks herself out thousands of times over. Hope tells Tom, "You have a really fun house!"

"Thanks Hope. That's the nicest thing anyone has said."

"Uh, I said it was interesting..." Ruth says in her own defense.

The hallway at the top of the stairs has no floor. By flipping a light switch, Tom illuminates the glass floor. The first door is shiny brass. Tom tries the door, but it's locked. "Mica and Dexter took the King's Room. I guess you'll have to see it in the morning." The next door is open but a curtain is drawn. The hospital bed on the other side has aluminum rails and an IV and a heart diagnostic machine that shows Minion has flat-lined. The chart at the foot of the bed has not been updated. However someone has added a toe-tag to his foot with capital letters "DOA."

I comment, "I'm surprised the Department of Agriculture took an interest." Heading back out I notice Erix standing on the topmost sharp key of the stairs. "Tom, is there a bedroom downstairs that Erix can sleep in?"

"Yeah, I think the Nest Room is empty," Tom replies.

I turn back to Erix, who turns and heads wearily down the black keys.

The next door is not flat. It is composed of rectangles of different shapes and sizes in your basic crayon colors. Inside, there are several paintings of fingers and one sketch of a thumbnail. A pitcher also hangs on the wall. Ray is asleep on the canvas-like bed with a giant paintbrush-like pillow. The floor has painted footprints.

The next room has clear water running through it. A waterfall starts with a shower and a sink and ends up at a toilet. Rainforest plants separate the facilities. It is all so natural that I figure I'll have to use a different bathroom.

The next door is wooden with a smoked glass window that fills about a third of it. The lock has been broken. Light streams in through venetian blinds and from a small tiffany-glass night-light. The room is black and white, film noir. Dan is asleep on the desk; his shoes are still on. Joe is asleep on the saloon-like bar. Tom flips a switch and has us wait and listen. Now and then you hear the sounds of traffic honking and an elevated train, like Chicago or New York. "Cool room," I whisper.

"It started out as Kansas City," Tom whispers back, "but then I thought, 'How many Kansas Cities does the world really need?!?'"

The next room is powder pink and very girlie. Nicole's face lights up when she sees that it's empty. "We'll take it," she says. There are two big canopy beds at different levels, a vanity makeup mirror, and many, many pink pillows. The floor is springy. Nicole runs in, followed by Becky, and Hope. It's very pink.

"I think they just found their new home," Tom comments.

"Do you mind if we crash?"

"Not at all."

"See you in the morning," I add.

"Good night, sweetie," Hope says and she bounces over to give me a kiss. She called me sweetie!

The next room has a Reserved sign on it. The floor is like walking on bean bags with soft tan fabric over them and a big glowing sunset on one wall. Looking at the wall close-up, it's glass lit from behind and painted on the other side to resemble a sunset over water. The bed is a small sand dune to one side. "This is your room if you want it," Tom says to me.

"I'll take it."

"Which is my room?" Ruth asks.

"It's up to you but there is a room downstairs that is off of the living room and the kitchen." Ruth makes tracks across the bean bag floor and heads out the door, almost burying Todd in artificial sand. Tom turns to me, "You know how much she likes being in the middle of things."

"Where are you sleeping?" I ask Tom.

"The Polaris Room downstairs. It's like a field of stars."

"Where are you sleeping?" I ask Todd.

"Next door. In my old room."

"Very sentimental, you know."

"Cy is next door too." He doesn't have to tell me, but he says, "She's in the room you two shared." I nod. "Where's Al?"

Tom huffs, "We have plenty of great rooms between the two houses, and he's sleeping in his car!"

"He likes his car."

"I like my car too but I don't sleep in it."

"He **really** likes his car," I emphasize. Tom nods. "Where are Lefty and Red?"

"Red is downstairs in the Library. I don't know if he's awake or not. The room next door is the Lab. I designed it to be all science-like. I showed it to Lefty. He made a face of utter disgust and left. I'm not sure where he went."

"He's very picky about the scientific impression. It is far more important than the scientific method or tests or favorable journal reviews or anything. Did you do the whole beakers-with-colored-water and electric-zapping-thing where the spark arcs up the metal poles?"

Tom laughs. "Yeah. I even have the bank of flashing-light-computers that spits out ribbons of paper at the press of a button..."

"What more could a scientist ask for? It sounds like the lab of every science movie ever made."

"I tried," Tom says. "I even threw in a radiometer and some equation-filled-chalkboards."

We shake our heads and look at Todd and his smirk. I tell them, "Well, I think I'm going to get some things from my car and call it a night." Following the twins out of the room I look back at the sunset and tell Tom, "You really did great with the place. It's a great summer cabin." When I think cabin, I picture a single room, dirt floor, log structure with a fire in the fireplace, and Lincoln lying on hay bales reading a book borrowed from the neighbor in the county next door. We head down a second set of stairs. Will has almost fallen asleep in his hanging chair. I give it a little push. He gives a little laugh, pushes a button, and meows the cat statue at me.

I pick up my things from the kitchen and put them back in the duffel bag. I notice shirts, flashlights, and clickers have been returned. Stepping over Jake, I head out to the car. I step through peanut shells with some crunches. At the car, I swap duffel bags. I stop, and I think, "She called me sweetie!" The heavens arc away from my spot, the stars wink, and a distant dog barks. This is great! I check my watch for the time and date. I do that for all the great moments.

Heading back in, I cross and pause over the body of Jake. Poor, poor Jake. So many possibilities... Someone could draw a chalk outline around him and put up a Police Line – Do Not Cross yellow tape barrier. Someone could take a thick black marker and give him a mustache or freckles. Someone could put his hand in a bowl of water, as that usually causes people to wet themselves. Someone could leave him out in the field. Or by the trash. Someone could do a great many things. He's lucky I'm around and not someone. "Opportunity is knocking..." Tom says from behind me.

"Yes, but I'm acting like no one is home," I reply. "Good night."

"Good night." Taking the back stairs up, I find another bathroom. It has all the amenities, and it seats two. I test it out, and head for my room. I find a switch like the one Tom pressed for Dan's room, and it starts the sound of waves, which happens to be another way to make people wet themselves. I also push a button labeled Breeze. I partially close my door to change into my jammies, not that I have ever considered a pair of shorts jammies. It's just something that happens in a place like this – the place changes you. But then I'm practically giddy. Not just because Hope called me sweetie, more that they all acted like everything I told them about pointed perception seemed reasonable to them. It's weird to have your weirdness so fully accepted. This is going to take some getting used to.

The sand dune bed conforms to my body. I get back up and turn down the sunset. I lie back down again, and I am content. Today was a good day. I am comfortable. The breeze from above is just right. The sound of the waves, combined with the waning sunset, makes me imagine I'm on the beach at sunset. It feels good. I'm relaxed.

What if things don't work between Hope and I?

White. Everything is white. Even the stop sign ahead is half white and I take my foot off the gas, check the pavement – it's white; that's good. Ice is either clear or black. I check my rear-view mirror – car behind! I brake. My car has traction. I wonder about the car behind, but it's not slowing, not even trying. Cross traffic is ahead. I only have so much clearance. Four-foot-tall snowbanks wall in the road. I pump my brakes to try to emphasize my car to the oblivious driver behind me. It's too late.

Slam! Crash!

Cold metal folds and plastic shatters. My head heads for the steering wheel.

The airbag breaks my nose and covers me in a latex powder. My seatbelt harnesses my chest and holds my body upright. I taste blood. I hear scraping. There is a rapping at my window. I can't see out of my left eye. I turn to my left. A young man is knocking on the window and signaling for me to turn the engine off. My left arm is numb for some reason. I shift the car into park. I turn the engine off and unfasten my seatbelt. He and I fight to open my door. I try the snowbank side. That door works. I climb and fall out. He helps me up. He's talking to me, but I don't understand much. He gives me a note with information on it. He talks to me insistently. Oh, he wants to know my name and phone number. I tell him. He asks if that's my work number, and I tell him that I was fired last summer. Why do I tell him that? He wants to offer me a ride. I turn to my car. My car is dead. It's folded up like origami. It looks like it was designed by Picasso. He killed my car. He insists on giving me a ride. I look. His sport-utility truck is fine. Except that its driver doesn't know how to drive.

"I'll walk." I climb up the snowbank to get away from Mister I-Learned-To-Drive-In-Another-State. I find a white and gray lumpy snow trail. On the way to the trail, snow fills any vacancies in my shoes. The snowbank trail slopes up and down, three to five feet above the road, having been formed from compacted snow that was plowed off the street. The snow becomes softer and whiter a few yards away from the road. Icicles from an earlier snow melt still hang from roof edges; wind and snowballs have halved most of them into gaping, over-biting ice teeth. Cars squeal by like piglets rolling in a barrel, as their oil steadfastly refuses to liquefy. Visually, they aren't any more impressive than they sound, wearing ill-fitting white toupees on their roofs. Looking back, I can't even see my car wreck. I keep walking. The snow in my shoes is part squishy water now. A diamond shaped sign holds a shovelful of snow like that's its job. Some Minnesota signs have horizontal holes in them to let the snow pass through, or maybe they let the winds pass through while straining the snow out of them like a colander. Most Minnesota snowfalls are vertical, not horizontal. But the signs the highway department chose for having the holes are usually the less important signs like: "You are still on the highway. You have not yet exited across a frozen lake."

In Minnesota, the streets are paved with snow – dense unyielding snow – and littered with fenderbergs, black and gray compacted ice blocks from the wheel wells of cars and trucks. Fenderbergs the size of Stonehenge blocks dot the parking lots in random, though astrologically significant, ways. Yesterday they said it was zero degrees, and they said it would be twice as cold today. I'm still trying to figure the math out on that one. The forecaster continued saying we should expect nine months of winter and three months of bad sledding. This morning I awoke to a knocking at my door. It was my thermometer wanting to come in. Supposedly, Minnesota is part of the temperate zone, indicating its propensity for mild weather. I'd like to find the guy that made that decision. I won't rest until I do. At first it's amusing – you exhale, your breath solidifies five inches in front of your face, gravity takes over, and the ice crystals hit the pavement like someone tinkling with the highest two keys on a piano – over and over again. I freeze some swear words into the snowbank to startle someone next summer when the words thaw and are spoken again.

My shoes are becoming less squishy. I think my socks are stiffening up. I'm not feeling as cold anymore, at least not at my feet. My nose and ears are still plenty cold. The wind feels like it is biting the edges of my ears off with razor-like teeth. My eyelids feel almost the same way. Even my tongue is cold. I try to warm it on the roof of my mouth. Hey, at least my feet are warm. Warm, but not moving right. I am walking on flat feet. I try to wiggle my toes, but my body can't find them anymore. I look down at my snow and ice encrusted shoes and figure my toes are still in there somewhere. Maybe I should find a house, there might be a house up there, and knock and ask them if they can help me find my toes. No. I'll be all right. I use the side of my glove to unstick the corner of my eye, and while it is in the neighborhood, to knock icicles from my eyebrow.

I stop to breathe. I smell blood. I put my glove to my nose and look at it. No blood. That's good.

Isn't that good? I wobble. I fall off the snowbank into the soft snow side. I thought this was supposed to be soft snow? Comparatively soft, it's comparatively soft compared to dense compacted snow. Luckily my right side broke my fall. Ouch. It hurts. I broke through a top ice layer into snow. I adjust myself into a crouched position against the snowbank. A car drives by. I raise my arm up after the fact and drop it again. Damn. I should have accepted the ride from the kid that couldn't drive. I should have stayed in my origami car. Why did the kid feel obligated to pull me out? Thanks for killing me, kid. This is where I'm going to die. This isn't what I thought would happen. This isn't what I dreamed. I remember telling Hope about things. Hope. I smile. I think I smile but it only feels like I managed a facial twitch. I never should have lost Hope. She was great. She was a dream. I lost her at Tom's cabin, and then I went home and lost my job.

That's not right! I was in the new farmhouse, and I thought, "What if things don't work between Hope and I?" This is pointed perception. I need to open my eyes.

I am back in the sunset room.

That wasn't normal. That wasn't like what I normally experience. Everything is okay between Hope and I. I check my watch. Only 25 minutes have passed between standing outside and now. That part of it is normal. The part that wasn't normal was the consciousness. I could think what I would be thinking. I don't get how that could be possible. That's weird, even for me.

I'm going to get fired?!? Wow.

I lean off my dune, drop off my watch, and pull out my alarm clock. I drop off to sleep.

15

Spied Her

A line of sunlight streams through a seam in the blue sky. Getting up, I push at it. It opens into window shutters. My alarm clock turns to look at me and then turns back to watching the sunset. I guess I forgot to set it. I head for the sound of water. I wake up to the sight of Nicole showering in the rainforest bathroom. "Morning," she says with a smirk.

"Morning," I reply and shuffle out for the other bathroom. I use the facilities, get dressed, and head down.

In the crowded kitchen, Tom is asking, "Why doesn't anyone want to eat in the dining room?"

"Hey Joe, isn't it a bit early to be drinking?" I ask, partially blinded by the yellow sunshine streaming in the kitchen.

"Where did you come from?" Hope asks giving me a hug and a kiss.

"My mom," I tell her. "The stairs."

"There's another set of stairs?"

"Sure. Here. See?"

"Cool, hidden stairs. Dan is on his fifth bowl of cereal. Jake is in his tent, which is good because Ruth had to clean up after him again this morning. Um, Nicole is showering..."

"Yeah, I saw her."

"You saw her?"

"Yeah, we said good morning or something like that."

"How much of her did you see?" Becky asks.

"All of her."

Joe, Al, and Ray trip over themselves trying to get to the living room only to be blocked by Ruth, who says, "You don't really want to–" She is bowled over just as Nicole comes through the living room and climbs over people to get into the kitchen.

"What did I miss?" Nicole asks, wearing a tight shirt that says, Ready To Party. I Bring My Own Balloons.

"The boys missed you," Ruth says from under the pile.

"That's sweet. What's for breakfast?" Nicole asks. "What type of cereal do you have there, Dan?" Dan looks up at her chest and spits out his cereal. "Gross, Dan. You could've just told me."

"**It's Major Munch!**" Dan booms while cleaning up his mess. "**I got it out of his car,**" he continues pointing at me.

I take the box and get out two bowls. I pour the cereal into one of the bowls and begin separating the majors from the munches between the two bowls. Hope squeezes in next to me and says, "They told me you'd do this. It's kind of compulsive behavior." I look at her, pause thoughtfully, and then go back to separating my cereal.

"I can make some pancakes for you," Ruth says to Nicole. "And there's fruit in the bowl over there. And we have bacon and eggs, but Ray has threatened to clear out if we cook them."

"I was just going to clear out of the kitchen," Ray defends himself. "Actually I'll take some pancakes too." Ruth heats a griddle and gets a bowl of batter from the refrigerator.

"So I'd say 1.3 million," Dexter says to Tom.

"Does it matter?" Tom asks.

"It matters to me," Dexter replies.

"Is that pancake batter or is that waffle batter?" I ask, stirring things up.

"Pancake batter..."

Cy and Todd come in from next door. "Have any interesting dreams last night?" she asks me, as they discover the line for pancakes.

Lefty calls over to me, "I'd like to hear more about your dreams." Yesterday, I figured he was wearing his lab coat because he came from work. Why is he still in his lab coat?

Ray asks, "How come you never told me about any dreams?"

I'm eating from the munches bowl. I look up and pantomime that I'm eating and that if I talked I'd make a mess like Dan did. I slept soundly. I learned what I already felt – that I don't want to be without Hope. This is serious. It would hurt like winter to be without her. Mental note: Hope matters to me.

I swallow, "I learned that I'm going to be fired on Monday."

"What? Ow! Fuck!" Ruth says burning herself.

"Ruth! Such language!" I reprimand her.

"You're kidding," Ray says.

Cy has stopped smiling. Everyone has stopped and is staring at me.

I tell them, "It fits perfectly with all the odd things – whispers and secret meetings – that have been going on lately. I don't know why I didn't see it before."

"You're not kidding. Who's going to pay our rent?" Ray asks. I glance at him to see if he's kidding, but he isn't.

"How can they create AutoDrive without you?" Ruth asks.

Hope sets her hand on my arm. I look at my bowls of cereal. "I just run development. My hands-on involvement has diminished over the past two years. They'll get along just fine without me."

"Why are they going to fire you?" someone asks.

"I'm sure it's because I don't have a completion date yet."

"Firing you can't make it go any faster," Dexter clears his throat. "So what will you do?"

"I'm going to go to work Monday, and if I get fired, I get fired."

"Maybe it won't happen the way you dreamed," Hope says with dimples while looking into my eyes. I sigh. I hope nothing happens the way I dreamed. Ruth turns back to the griddle, and Dan holds out his bowl for more cereal. I take the cereal box with one hand and with the other I hold his arm to steady it. As I pour, I shake his arm that I am supposedly steadying. Cereal goes everywhere. It's not the first time.

"Whoa, whoa, that's enough!" Dan laughs thunderously.

Becky gets my attention and says, "I'm impressed. You have a pretty good attitude about all this."

"You could start up another company," Dexter says. "Come out with a self-driving car before they do."

"Legally he can't," Lefty says, hands in his lab coat, flapping it like wings. "That's infringement on their intellectual property. You can't compete unless you're using something developed independently."

"I don't want to."

"What marketable skills do you have?" Dexter investigates, without clearing his throat.

"I know engineering, specifically mechanical engineering, with a focus on optical engineering." Long pause.

"Well, that doesn't do much, does it?"

Laughter.

"You should put your resume on blueprint paper."

"You could go to Vegas. Make a killing."

"I don't want to kill."

"You could clean up!"

"They'd wring me like a sponge."

"You could work for them. Set the odds."

"No thanks. Money isn't that important," I say without regard to some people's temperament. Dexter faints.

"What is important to you?"

"Making a difference."

"There are plenty of ways to make a difference. Open your own casino with a pawn shop in the middle."

"No. I don't think there is any prophet in seeing the future."

"Tupperware vehicles and luggage."

"No, but thank you for playing."

"Rotate-a-fridge! Tired of finding gross mystery foods in the bottom of your refrigerator? With Rotate-a-Fridge that may never happen again. Because there is no bottom shelf! Or top shelf. Rotating shelves move at the push of a button."

"That's good, Tom."

"Commercial detours. Bring the market to you," Dexter says from the floor.

"I don't get that."

"Roads detour to the parking lots of stores with big sales."

"Oh, I get it. No."

"Make a scale that only goes up to 115 pounds."

"Good one," Cy tells Nicole.

"Arm-chairs with built-in remotes."

"Tom already has those."

"A doll that laughs, cries, and collects alimony."

"Teddy bear that hugs back."

"Or a remote-controlled ventriloquist dummy."

"Table-for-one restaurant. Every table comes with a date."

"Bachelor restaurant. Drink out of the carton... PB&J sandwiches... Eat out of the pan..."

"Conveyor belt restaurant..."

"No, thank you."

"No thank you cards."

"Cremation ashes sold to cannibals as instant soup."

"That's sick!"

"Sell No Solicitors signs door to door."

"Screens for car windows."

"That's not bad."

"Glow in the dark tags for underwear."

"Why is that an issue for you?"

"I always wanted to be a gynecologist, but I couldn't find an opening."

"Never go to work if you have the strength to stay in bed," Ray says.

"Hey," Cy says as I get up to rinse my bowls, "I'm sorry about teasing you last night, and if you do lose your job, I know you'll figure something out." She squeezes my arm.

"Thanks, Cy." They have all been very supportive. It's spooky!

"Could you pass the syrup?"

Lefty steps over, "I'd like to know more about these dreams of yours sometime."

"Sometime, sure, but not today if that's okay."

"Right," he says, itching his ankle.

"It – is – alive!" Tom says. I turn and Jake is at the door.

"I've got something to show everyone behind my tent," Jake says. We follow him out, and I catch an, "I'll bet," from Nicole. Jake points to a group of grasses next to his large, olive green tent. About a foot off the ground with yellow and black markings, a golf-ball-sized spider has set up a web. As we crowd around, it starts to do push-ups, which causes some of us to back up. Lefty gets out a petri dish from his lab coat. "Don't mess with my spider," Jake tells Lefty. "His name is Herman."

"Her."

"Okay, her name is Herman," Jake corrects. Hope is amused. Becky is creeped out. Mica sneezes. Herman jumps in place.

"Ish," Becky says with a shutter.

Erix comes out. We introduce him to Herman. They nod to each other.

Jake asks, "So what are we doing?"

"Waiting for you to eat," I reply, figuratively putting the shoe on the other foot. "Then we'll go swimming, right away, without waiting an hour or anything."

Jake holds up his hand, "Okay, we need to talk. Let's go."

"No. Say what you want to say. Let's not make a production out of it." When he doesn't say anything, I try to help him out by saying, "You know, you look like shit."

He gives me an exhausted, "I'm too tired to kill you" look, and then says, "You stopped the game because something was going to happen to the girls. Something serious. Is that right?"

"Yeah, that's right."

"You knew that ahead of time?"

"Right."

Tom steps up to Jake, "Keys."

"Next time, tell me." Jake hands his keys to Tom. "If there is something that I need to know, as a friend, you need to tell me, right?"

"You make a good point. I didn't know if you'd listen, but I suppose I should have given you the chance. I'm sorry."

"I was just having fun. When I thought about it, I realized how something could've happened. I'm sorry. I got carried away. I was blowing off steam. Are you and I set?"

"Yeah, we're fine."

"Good, now I need to talk to the ladies." He steps over to Nicole and Hope. "I want to apologize for my behavior during the game yesterday." He has now apologized twice in two minutes. I check my watch for the time and date, and I look around at my surroundings generally, for a frame of reference. "I should not have done the things I did." And then he looks my direction and continues talking with them in a whisper. What's he saying? He better not be saying anything bad...

Tom and Will are getting heavy tubes and a box out of Jake's truck. I open my unlocked Pony Express without a key. I figure the cows, the mosquitoes, the moths, or even Herman has no chance at working the door handle. I also figure all of them could probably get into my car if they really wanted, key or no key. I get out my binoculars.

Todd and Cy approach Tom as he is setting up a rocket platform. Todd says, "I don't think either of us really wants a rocket going through our houses."

Tom calls out to Ruth standing in the doorway, "Shut the door please? Thank you!" Tom smirks at Todd and gets back to work.

"What about the windows, smart guy?" Todd asks. "You've got a lot of really expensive windows on your house."

"How expensive?" Dexter asks. The twins ignore him.

"Live a little. Quit your worrying," Tom says, connecting a line to the solid fuel.

"Have you done this before?" Cy asks with her hands in her hair.

"I've had this rocket for years," Tom says, setting up his rocket. "This is the first time. It may not even fly with all the layers of latex paint I've put on it." He connects the rocket line to a switch and a battery half the size of a car battery, about the size of my car battery.

"Hey, that's my car battery!" I claim. He smirks without looking up. Jake's conference is over and the girls are standing behind me. Tom double-checks the connections. He double-checks that we are all out here, and he smiles when he sees Ruth helping Minion out to see the launch.

"Where are you aiming your missile?" Nicole asks. Tom points up with his thumb.

Tom stares at the rocket like he is coming to an understanding with it. "If I screw this up, I'm Todd not Tom."

He steps through a triple-check, and I picture him as a spy, making a secret drop-off. He would probably make the drop, keep walking, stop, go back, adjust the secret package, step back, frame it with his hands to make sure it's just right, and then he would go. Minutes go by and then Tom is back to triple-check the package and its surroundings. Great spy work.

Eyes are on me and my goofy smirk. "Huh?"

"I said, 'Is everything good?'" Tom asks me.

I hold up my binoculars to indicate that I'm ready. Then I realize what he was asking. He was asking me if I thought everything would be okay. Wow, he's got a lot of faith in me. I relax and watch the rocket go sideways and up. "Wait!" I shout.

"Fuck! You scared the hell out of me!" Tom yells back, and people laugh.

I turn to Erix, who had come around the other side of the tent to watch, and say, "Hey Erix, why don't you come over here to watch?" Erix sheepishly comes over while everyone watches, with his head hung low like he screwed up. "Thanks," I tell him. Tom is staring at me nodding his head in a prompting way. "What?" I ask.

"Should I change anything?" Tom asks.

I shrug, "No, it's fine." What's the fun in that?

He turns, gets set at the switch, turns to me again, turns back, and says, "Get ready... five, four, three, two, one!" and he flips the switch. Todd's shoulders rise, his arms against him, imitating the rocket. The rocket hesitates, flies at an angle to where Erix had been standing, and then flies straight up from there. Nicole swears. I follow it with my binoculars. Dexter asks where it is, and I point with my free hand, following it up, and up. I half expect it to do something, but it just keeps going up.

"Can you still see it?" Tom asks, as my finger points at a fixed spot.

"Barely. You want to use the binoculars?" I ask.

"No, just keep watching it."

"It really went high," I tell him while still looking through the binoculars. "Does it have a parachute?"

"Yeah, it was supposed to...," he says, as his hopes and dreams skyrocket.

"It was supposed to – what?" I ask. "I've lost it." I lower the binoculars to find that everyone, except Minion, has crowded around us. Ruth is taking pictures.

"It was supposed to release once the rocket started its decent," he says looking at me.

"It still could," I reply hopefully. I go back to watching the sky.

"Do you know that it is coming back?" Tom asks.

"No."

"Then why should I watch for it?" He sounds almost mad.

"I don't know. I don't know one way or the other," I tell him.

"Oh," he says and he looks up.

"What is the rocket's maximum altitude?" Lefty asks squinting into the sunshine. A reasonable question, I think.

"Well," Tom starts, "taking into account the weight of the fuselage, the pounds per square inch thrust of the solid fuel, the weather conditions and the wind speed... I haven't a clue."

"There are still a dozen extra pancakes if anyone wants them," Ruth announces. Jake and Erix head in to investigate.

Hope's hand rests on my shoulder. I put my hand on it to hold it only to find that it's Nicole's. From my other shoulder Hope whispers into my ear, "I'm not sure that Erix understands how lucky he is to have you looking after him." By their reactions, I can tell that Tom and Lefty heard her whisper.

Erix comes back out carrying some pancakes, but he's not heading toward us. I call to him, "Erix, you know Herman doesn't eat pancakes!" I'm being stared at again. "What?!? It doesn't take a rocket scientist to figure out what he was going to do. Yesterday, he was sharing his sandwich with a bug."

"When you're through with your rocket-thingy, could everyone come inside?" Ruth asks.

"Are we through with your rocket-thingy?" I ask Tom.

"Yeah, I guess," Tom says with reluctance.

At the door, Red turns to a big, spotted, tan moth, "Heh, Edison." The large moth decides not to take him on.

Nicole and Becky lead the way in. They take off upstairs as Ruth gathers us in the living room, facing the marshy lake painting with the geese continually flying toward the stairs.

"Some of us have a long history and others are new to the group," Ruth starts.

"Wow!"

Nicole and Becky come down in bikinis. They look at us funny, as we try to figure out what they are doing. "Aren't we going swimming?" Nicole asks me, directly.

"I... I never said... swimming? Oh, I told Jake... I'm sorry! I was kidding him." Becky wraps herself self-consciously in her beach towel and they take a seat in the corner.

Ruth is upset at the interruption.

"Ruth was saying that some of us have been with each other for a long time and some are new to the group," Cy reiterates.

"Yeah, several of you sent me pictures and movies and helped me put a little show together," Ruth says, pushing a remote control. The geese are interrupted mid-flight and turn to black.

Dramatic orchestra music surrounds us through hidden speakers as the yellow farmhouse, what is now Todd's farmhouse, fades in with a shed where the new farmhouse would be built. It's early one summer morning around the time when several of us used to go running, running around the countryside. A young Tom is leaning against a white picket fence with his head turned away, talking with me. He turns to the camera and says, "Mister Smartypants has an answer for everything!" I then butt in and say, "Two wrongs don't make a right, but three rights make a left." He then pushes me back and says, "There is nothing like a good sense of humor; you have nothing like a good sense of humor." During another day in Milltown, Tom tells the camera, "Don't make a production out of this." The camera pans to Todd, across the wall in front of us, who says, "Get a load of my little brother." "Little brother?" repeats a higher, younger version of Ruth's voice. "Yeah," Todd starts and then Tom joins in so they both say, "I was born first; can't you tell?" In another scene, Todd is saying, "If I'm wrong, I'm Tom not Todd." From on top of a snow hill, Todd yells, I am king of the mountain!" then Tom pushes him off. The next scene has Tom and Todd wearing matching shirts, circling the video camera, and mimicking each other, acting strange.

I'm on the screen, very young and sitting on a couch at someone's house saying, "I had the strangest dream last night," then, seeing the camera, I said, "I dreamed I had insomnia!" I turned away from the camera, and then I turned back, "Two nights ago I dreamed I ate a giant marshmallow. In the morning, my pillow was gone." In another scene, Sharon is showing me something on paper. I asked her, "Is that her?" Sharon says, "No, that's her picture." The next scene is from the yellow farmhouse porch, Cy and I run across the scene holding hands and laughing. The editing job for the next scene makes it look like I ran headlong into a hay roll. The next scene shows Todd, Cy, and I on a milk-carton boat in the milk-carton boat races. Our great ship, the Cowabunga, is neither sinking nor floating, which means we weren't doing as good as some or as bad as others. Cy was less dry than us. Ruth is filming from the lake shore with a crowd of our supporters. The next shot is of a milk-carton with the picture of our lost milk-carton boat on it. The camera zooms out to show it being held by Melanie Fields, and the music changes to her first popular song.

Hope gasps, "Is that... Melanie?!?"

"Yes."

"You knew Melanie?!?" she asks, starstruck.

"Yes."

Turning back to the wall, Melanie is singing at one of her first local concerts at a big shopping mall. Many of our friends were in the crowd, and Jenny is singing back-up. Even then, Melanie was good. Her voice was flawless, and she knew how to work the crowd. She'd told us afterwards that having us in the crowd really helped her feel like she was singing for her friends. Famous pictures of Melanie in the hay are scattered across the screen; they were taken at the barn here. The next scene shows us hanging off the Prospective Tower, and then in the field playing Capture The Flag with Jake and his older brother; Tom, Todd, and their sister; Melanie, Cy, Jenny, and Aimee; Christie and Sharon; and Will, Dan, and I. Erix and Ruth watched. Then Melanie is singing at a Christmas program with Christie on the piano.

"Christie is one of your friends?" Hope asks.

"I invited her for this weekend," Tom says. "She said no, and invited us to her house on Chicago's south side."

"I didn't know that."

"She used to teach with me," Hope says. "We lost track of each other. The last time I saw her, she was on the news."

"**I see her,**" Dan's voice thunders, "**all the time, on the Chicago news!**"

The next scene is a taping of a Melanie concert with a huge crowd. She looked like she was having fun. She also looked a little scared. The next scene reveals our secret weapon against Melanie's privacy invaders. It is the only shot of Melanie and Tom with Aimee and Todd looking just like them, as their decoys. There is a slow motion scene of Melanie turning around whipping her hair across the screen... across the wall in front of us.

Erix tells us, "I loved Melanie."

I tell him, "We all loved Melanie."

The next scene is the group of us holed-up in the Pfuloree house while her crowds lay siege outside. Then there was the memorial service for Melanie and the music. Christie is preaching about ideals. Aimee is in the crowd, looking like Melanie. I never saw that. It is very strange, like Melanie at her own service. I can't see the screen through watering eyes. The next thing I am able to see is a giant gorilla carrying Hope. I don't remember carrying her, but there probably wasn't a second ape there. "The day we met," I comment. Dexter clears his throat and says they couldn't get a sitter. Cy coughs.

"What?" Hope asks.

"Nothing. I just said, 'The day we met.'"

"That wasn't when we met," Hope says.

"What do you mean?" I ask. "That's me in the monkey suit."

"I know that's you in the monkey suit. But that's not when we met. We met at Sharon's the weekend before. At the political rally."

"What?!?" I what-ed.

"You didn't know?!?" Becky asks.

"No. You were there?"

"Yes," Hope says. "Sharon introduced us." My intelligence-o-meter just hit an all time low. If I had any feelings of familiarity about Hope at the party, I attributed them to latent pointed perception.

The screen has returned to the loop of the geese. Cy's face is red, and Todd is holding her. Erix is downcast. Becky is also crying. Mica is staring at the goose wall.

"Gee, thanks Ruth, that was great," Jake says with sarcasm. "Even Erix is affected by pictures of Melanie, and he's a couple sandwiches short of a full picnic, if you know what I mean."

"Hey, don't talk that way about him!" That voice was Cy's. Cy is defending Erix! There's something you don't hear every day.

Jake's arms swing out. "What?!? I used the sandwich analogy. I figured Ruth could understand that." He must be out of his mind. Ruth is on her feet staring at him. "It's not like I said something like, 'his porch light is out' or 'nice house but nobody's home' or 'he's not playing with a full deck' or 'he's not the sharpest knife in the drawer' or 'he looks like he could lift a ton but he couldn't spell it.'" Cy is also standing up for him. So have I. Others have too. Jake turns to Erix and says, "You know I'm kidding you. They should too. Melanie was great. She was strong, and she was fragile. She had a great voice. Her songs, even her sappy songs, still have an impact. I just saw a TV show about her story. They completely screwed it up. They didn't do any research."

"Was that on Chart Busters?" Tom asks. Jake nods. "They asked me for an interview, but I wasn't ready yet."

"They contacted me too," Cy says, her hair slipping down over her left eye. "I don't like the way they present the people they're talking about."

"They kept showing the same clip over and over of Aimee," Tom says. They thought she was Melanie. It made me wonder where Aimee is and what she's–"

"She called me Saturday night in the middle of the night." Everyone turns to look at me. "And she called Wednesday night."

"Really?"

"What did she say?"

"Not too much. She's in L.A. She's not going by Aimee anymore, but she didn't tell me what name she's using. She liked it when I called her A-Me-V. It didn't sound like things were going very well. It sounded like she has hit rock bottom."

"It was weird seeing the part where she's at Melanie's service," Jake says.

Mica asks, "So this Aimee looked like Melanie? And they were both your friends?"

Cy explains, "Friends and more. Tom was Melanie's bodyguard and I was her manager, and the rest were her support group. We kept her real, and tried our best to look out for her," she says while turning to me. "Did Aimee say where she was or give her phone number?"

"I asked for that. She said she didn't have a phone. From the sounds of it, she didn't want anyone to read what I would send her."

"Sounds like she was scared."

"Oh, she was definitely scared. I told her she could call collect. I offered to buy a plane ticket for her. If she had taken me up on the offer, I would have told her about this weekend. At least I think I would have. I was half asleep at the time."

"I wonder why she called you instead of any of the rest of us," Ruth wonders aloud. I shrug.

Erix comes over and asks, "Did you... know... what was going to happen to..." We wait. "To Melanie?"

My forefingers rub the sides of my nose. "Basically yes. It was pretty clear she was going to die, but I didn't know any of the details, since I wasn't there. I tried to warn her through Cy..."

Cy comes over, "He didn't know details, anything that might have made it clear that he really knew what was going to happen. She wouldn't listen, not to him, and not to me."

Tom says, "She cared about what people thought of her, and she didn't want to let anyone down."

A phone rings with the Fifth of Beethoven. Jake answers, "Hey. Yeah. Just my chest. See you Friday."

"What was that about?"

"Nothing."

"What do you mean, 'nothing'? Are you having some sort of surgery done?"

"No!"

"Then what's the deal with your chest?" Several people are ganging up on him.

"It's personal."

"If it's so personal why did you take the call in the middle of all of us?"

"It's no big deal. I'm getting my chest shaved. Are you happy?" We all laugh.

"The reason why I put together this video," Ruth explains, "was to make sure we remember everyone and everything that has happened. Life is about balance – a balance between the old and the new, the happy and the sad, and–"

"The living and the dead? Death is not life," Jake says.

"It's a part of life," Ruth says.

"No, it's the opposite of life. There is no life in death."

"Mortuary science," Lefty says.

"Death runs in my family. All of my ancestors have died," I say. It's true.

"A rock is not alive, and it's not dead," Cy expounds.

"That's a boulder statement," Tom interjects to a chorus of groans.

"If you really want balance," Will tells Ruth as he lowers the altitude of his chair, "you can't be so camera-shy. I didn't see you once in the video."

"I was filming most of it."

"I know. I also know you hide behind the camera. I also know that when I watch something like this, you are nowhere to be seen. I hardly call that balanced."

"I didn't think anyone would notice."

"Ha!" Jake scoffs.

"Of course we notice," Will continues. "We're not idiots!"

"Well..." Jake starts.

"Shut up!" Will stops Jake. "We aren't idiots. None of us are. I once thought Erix was. Then I noticed that Ricky didn't treat Erix that way. It cast a new light on him. Erix may not be the best conversationalist, but a moment ago he asked the question that I had always wondered about Melanie's death. Did someone warn her? Did Ricky warn her? I got the answer now, after all these years, because Erix asked the question. I should have. But he did it. If you think we wouldn't notice you if you were gone, think again. If you think we don't remember being here with Melanie, think again. As Ricky said before, we loved her. And we love you." Ruth uses her remote control to lower Will's chair. She pats his arm and whispers something to him.

"What do we want to do?" I ask. "Do we want to go swimming? Fishing? Swim-fishing? Teach Herman to fish?"

Becky is shaking, "Enough about the spider! Euwech! I have... post-traumatic spider disorder!" Minion creeps his fingers at her. Becky kicks his leg. "Let's go swimming."

"Okay, let's go swimming!"

As several of us head upstairs, Cy stops Hope and I and says, "Todd and I are going to go riding instead."

"Oh okay. Have fun," I reply, but she's not done.

"It was good seeing us together on the screen," she says.

Hope is on the stair with me. Looking straight down through the stairs, we float yards above the floor. Cy and Todd seem to float closer to the floor. It's weird. Luckily I've never been afraid of heights, widths maybe, but not heights. But I've paused too long after her comment. I have to say something quickly, which hurts neither Hope nor Cy. All I can say is, "Sure."

"Now we've moved on. Todd and I have started something, and you have Hope." Oh okay, she's with Todd. I acknowledge the news with a nod and head upstairs. Cy is very concerned about follow-up. This has been a relationship follow-up. But she has other forms of follow-up. It seemed to have irked her that Aimee contacted me, because Cy is the champion and grand poobah of follow-up. She wanted the Aimee follow-up. She's also big on the gift follow-up. "How have you used the gift I gave you," she would ask, as if she continues to be responsible for a gift after giving it. If it wears out, she feels responsible for handling its replacement. Basically, she is its co-owner.

Before Cy is out of hearing range, I quickly tell Hope, "Cy doesn't like wearing wet swimsuits."

"I heard that!" Cy yells.

Hope stops at the pink room. I continue to the sunset room. My alarm clock is on the beach drinking a drink that has its own umbrella in it, which keeps the ice cubes in the shade or the rain off or I don't know why drinks have their own umbrellas. I change into swim shorts, grab my beach towel, and I wait by Hope's door. Time stops. I don't mind. I could wait forever. Time opens the door. "Hi," Hope says. I stare at her trying to figure out what makes her so beautiful. Maybe her eyes or her smile or the way she looks from one of my eyes to the other as if to say, "Okay, this one doesn't tell me what I need to know; what about the other one?" It is not her eyes or her smile. A snapshot of either would not even symbolize the woman in front of me. I notice her body in her bikini. I notice her body in the bikini again.

"You look great!" I slobber, as little red heart shapes float above us. A door opens and an L train rumbles moments away from careening through the hallway! I throw my body against Hope's to save her from the impending doom of the train! Dan steps out, shuts off the train sound, and shuts the door as far as the lock will allow.

"Hey you two!" his voice thunders like a train. "Get a room!"

Hope pushes me back and throws her towel over her shoulder.

"Excuse me," I tell her, and we head down the hall.

The royal door at the end of the hallway opens with an argument. "I don't want to be with her," Dexter yells, "I want to be with you. I married you. So what if I looked at her?!?" Dexter coughs.

From the room, Mica replies, "It's the way you looked at her. The sad, sad way you stared at her..."

"Dexter," I call loudly to him even though I'm in tapping range, "would now be a good time to see the King's Room?" Dexter waves us in. Mica is putting on sun lotion. "Wow," I say, "looks like the best room in the house!" The room has curtains, pillows, and a bedspread of burgundy velvet with gold fringe. The carpet underneath all Mica's luggage is metallic. Brass vases surround the room.

"They had flowers," Mica sniffs, "but I'm allergic. Even to the plastic ones."

"I wasn't complimenting the decorations," I reply with a smile. "I was complimenting you." I lead Hope and Dan downstairs where we join up with Nicole, Becky, Erix, Tom, Will, Ruth, and Lefty. "Where are your suits?" I ask Ruth and Lefty.

"I'll come down to the lake to get a water sample," Lefty says, waving test tubes. I nod without betraying the fact that I forgot to bring my test tubes. First I forget my petri dishes, and now it's the test tubes. I'll have to check my car for a Bunsen burner.

"And you?" I ask Ruth. She drags me aside by the arm.

She covers my ear with her hand and whispers, "I can't go. I'm fat. I don't look like Nicole or Hope. I'm big in the middle. I would be embarrassed."

I cover her ear with my hand and whisper, "You are my friend. You are with friends. No one has to look like Nicole except Nicole. I don't know why you didn't join in on Capture The Flag, but you haven't before, so I didn't push it. If you are going to have fun here, great. But if you would rather go to the lake with the rest of us, we want you with us."

"Whisper, whisper," Nicole says.

"I'm not ready," Ruth says aloud.

"We can wait." She tears off for her room. "Where's Jake?" Ruth yells something from her room. "What?" I ask those in front of me.

Tom explains, "Jake took Minion back to Pigs Eye."

"**That's a long way**," Dan comments loudly.

"Minion was still pissed at waking up to having a toe-tag."

"Who did it?"

"That's the funny part. Jake did. But if he remembers doing it, he didn't tell Minion. Minion thinks you did it," Tom tells me. "I supplied the supplies, but he did it to Minion."

"I cause enough trouble without having to be responsible for other people's trouble," I reply. "So you didn't set things straight?"

"I didn't think you'd mind."

"I don't really," I say looking at the fish in the aquarium window with Erix.

"Okay," Ruth says. She has a hat and an over-shirt, and she might have a swimsuit on. It's difficult to tell. Mica and Dexter come down. We head out.

16

Mirages

I hold the door for them. And immediately we are overcome by a wave of heat blasting us like a sizzling red-orange oven door opened inside a scalding nuclear furnace baking in the desert during a heatwave in equatorial hell. It's hot.

"Walk or drive?"

"Drive."

"Drive."

"Drive."

"**Ruth, can we take your truck?**"

"Sure Dan, you drive."

"Air conditioning, please."

"It's coming, keep your top on."

Hope points, "Is this Round Lake?"

"No, Round Lake is closer to town. This is Mud Lake."

"That's what I thought, but at school they were saying Mud Lake is closer to Long Lake," Hope says.

"Minnesota has about 200 Mud Lakes, about 100 Round Lakes, plenty of Bass Lakes..."

"And Clear Lakes."

"And Long Lakes!"

"Spring Lakes."

"Bear Lakes."

"Wolf Lakes."

"If you eliminate all of those, there are probably about five lakes left."

"A few more than that," literal Lefty corrects.

"Okay, maybe a few more..."

Bam!

"Watch the ruts, Dan! This isn't Chicago!"

"**Right. This dirt road is in better condition!**" Another dirt road takes us to the far side of this Mud Lake. Dan pulls the truck off into some grasses. A cloud of grasshoppers wait until they are almost under the truck to get out of the way.

Getting out, Nicole says, "Mud Lake, huh?" The lake is about two or three acres. The shore here is mud with little holes and hundreds of flying green bugs, a half a centimeter in diameter, taking off and landing in the mud. Lefty takes a sample. Nicole goes over to Ruth, taking a picture of her truck, and announces, "Conference time." We gather. "That's a lot of mud. If we go in, we will be covered in mud. If we go in, you aren't going to want us in your nice truck for the way back. Is this what we want to do?" Nicole asks. I'm impressed.

"Too thick to swim; too thin to plow," Tom philosophizes.

"The lake is much lower than it used to be," I comment. "The good news is that it's too hot for mosquitoes. And tadpoles eat pond scum." Hope smiles. Turning to Tom, "What do we have as a plan B?" He shakes his head. "Okay, I'd be willing to go into town for an inflatable pool or something. Would that work? Do you have something to inflate it? And a hose to fill it?" Tom says yes. "Okay, let's head back to the house." On the way back I ask Hope, "Is it okay with you that I go into town to try to handle this?"

"We'll come with."

"You've seen my car. It barely handles two."

"Right. The pool might not fit in your car. Ruth, could we use your truck? You're welcome to come with..."

"It's all yours."

We drop everyone off and pick up shirts and my wallet. I take the ruts slower than Dan. Two horses and their riders from Mud Lake are on an intercept course to our route. It's Cy and Todd. I slow up. I roll down Hope's window.

"Where are you going?" Cy asks, from up high.

Cy's horse sticks its nose into our business.

"Into town for a pool. Mud Lake was too muddy." I think about teasing her again about the opportunity for a wet swimsuit, but I stop myself. The horse has its head into Hope's window. Either it likes the air conditioning of the truck, or it likes Hope, or it likes both.

"Oh. I found your flag." She hands it to Hope, and Hope thanks her. Her horse tries to climb in, head first. Cy pulls it back, and the horse snoofs hot air that I can feel on my side of the truck. Hope must've gotten fully snoofed. They move off, and I slowly start to drive again.

"What happened between you and Cy?" Hope asks. "When did you break up?"

"A few years ago. She didn't understand me, and what she did understand she wanted to change. People are the sum of their experiences. They are what has occurred to them... what they've thought... what has happened in their lives."

"And the decisions people make," Hope interjects, "decisions based on their hopes and dreams."

"Right. That makes sense. And at the core of it all are the occurrences we had as kids. They defined so much of who we are."

"That's why I went into elementary education," she says, then her dimples disappear. "I'm not sure what happened, but I can definitely say that even though it wasn't a perfect childhood, I always had possibilities. I could do what was right for me, even though my mother is a force of nature and my brothers... my brothers are evil in its purest form," she says with a smirk.

"That core part of you isn't going to change, but everything else will. In all the doomed relationships, the excuse of 'we drifted apart' seems the scariest."

"Really?" she asks.

"It's as if they don't care to be together. If you're just coasting on the road of life..." I start, with encouragement from her grin, "you aren't in control."

"Is that what happened to you and Cy?"

"No. I told her all of this. I told her that people can't really know each other. You can at best know someone for the moment, and then they change as they experience new things and think new thoughts and make new decisions. It has got to be a commitment to stay in touch with who each of you are... to talk and share the significant stuff, especially the life changing stuff. A relationship is work. I told Cy all this, but either she didn't get it or she didn't care. What she cared about was changing me to match an inconsistent ideal that she came up with as a kid... stereotypically normal, serious, yet kind of brain-dead. It took me awhile, but I realized that I couldn't make her happy."

"Do you still love her?"

"She's still a friend. I care about her like I care about my other friends. My friends are important to me. But I am not in love with her."

"You were really nice to Mica upstairs."

"She needed a boost," I explain.

"What happened with Mica?" our back seat asks.

"Ricky said they... what's their last name?"

"Bucko."

"You're kidding."

"No, it's really Bucko."

"He said they had the best room... well, he was complimenting her."

"How was complimenting her the same as complimenting the room?"

"I don't know," Hope turns to me and then turns to the back seat and says, "I guess you had to have been there." Turning back to me, "It was nice how you got Ruth to come with."

"What did you whisper to her?"

"Was it something dirty?"

I stop at a stop sign, give them a sneer through the rear-view mirror, and then I keep driving. We switch from gravel to pavement. It's funny: mirages don't appear over gravel; they definitely appear over asphalt, not that mirages matter.

"I still can't get over that all of you knew Melanie," Nicole says.

"I know," Becky agrees. "I can't get over the giant spider."

"So, what do you think of everything?"

"You mean Melanie, the spider, your friends, your knowing Christie, your uh... pointed perception?"

"All of that. No offense, but you ask a lot of questions, but you don't tell me how I did on the quiz."

"Am I quizzing you too much?" Hope asks.

I think for a moment. "I think good relationships need talk. If you have questions, I need to answer them. It also means that if I am miscommunicating or if you have strong feelings about something, or if something matters to you, you need to tell me. Give and take." Now would be a good time for a stoplight or something to allow me to turn to Hope. I don't get one. "Do you agree?" I ask.

"That's fair. What if there is something I can't tell you about or not right away?"

"Say what you can say. If something is bothering you, but the time isn't right to tell me, maybe say, 'Something is bothering me; I'll tell you about it later.' That way I'm not oblivious to your feelings. By knowing something is up, I can make decisions that affect the two of us. How does that sound?"

"Okay. I think there is something you should know. I don't have a very good track record when it comes to boyfriends. Nicole has had worse. She's a magnet for the worst behavior from the nastiest guys."

"I'm sorry to hear that about both of you," I tell them. "Are you okay?"

"Yeah. That's why we kind of gang up on you. We're all trying to make sure I don't make another mistake," Hope says. "I like you, but I'm concerned about the changes you talk about people experiencing. If you can never really know someone, like you were saying, only know someone for the moment, how can people commit to a relationship? How can I expect to be with someone long enough to get married or move in together or buy a house or raise kids or anything?"

"You want all that?"

"No, but if I'm going to be in a relationship, it should have a future."

"Our culture is so independence oriented," I explain, "that people do not have to get married or do anything else to survive. Men and women can exist perfectly well without marriage or even living with someone else. I have seen so many married couples that are perfectly miserable with one another. Maybe because they're loners, I don't know. I don't think marriage is for most people. I think a great many people are focused on what makes themselves happy, and a close permanent relationship like marriage would interfere with their personal happiness."

"I don't know that most people are like that..."

"Okay, I don't know how many people are. I haven't taken a survey or anything, but there are certainly people who really should not get married. It will make themselves and someone else miserable. A relationship, a good relationship, takes work. I haven't been complaining much about your tag-teaming me because it kind of fits with everything I've thought about for an ideal relationship. Both people are trying their best to make everything work. Not compromising so much that neither are ever happy. Looking out for the other's interests. Loving each other through everything. Behaving like every date is your first date. Treating each other with respect. And most importantly, talking and listening about the things that matter to both of you. I'm hoping that my previous relationships will have given me a good start to what I need to be the man you want me to be – that we work well off each other – so that we might grow and change together."

H-O meanders. The rural highway weaves up and down and around the hills, stitching its way across the countryside. Before it starts to skirt around more lakes, I turn off at Round Lake, onto Great Portage Trail. I take the Trail into the cooperative town of Harmony. Harmony jumped onto the world stage years ago to stop an international monster store from devouring local retail. Their alternative was to start the Canoe Stores, which brought together three area groups into a retail consortium. I park at the original Canoe Store. We hop out. Inside our guide takes us to the pools, without making the ladies go back to the truck for their shirts. Ironically, we choose the Mud Lake Pool, green flying bugs not included. The box just barely fits in Ruth's truck. Before leaving Harmony, we buy some ice cream cones from a small store. While the others are making their ice cream decisions, I dash across the street to an art store and I purchase a canvas and paints. Hope has Mint Chocolate Chip. Becky has Sunrise Sherbet. Nicole has Sinfully Chocolate. I choose Rocky Road. We aren't finished with them by the time we get back to the cabins. I would have finished mine, but I concentrated on the driving.

"Ice cream?!?" Mica yells. "You never said anything about going for ice cream!"

Oops.

"Do you realize how long it takes to fill a pool?" Jake asks. Gee, I'm sure glad Jake's back.

"I give up, Jake, how long does it take to fill a pool?" But Jake doesn't respond. He's busy unloading the pool. Lefty comes over and explains that you multiply the two extreme diameters of the oval times the depth times 5.9 or something that I probably learned in college for a test and then tried my best to forget. The sort of thing that I was talking to Hope about on the drive is a thousand times more important than any mathematical formula, even the ones for triangulating distance that have been crucial for my job, and yet I had to figure that relationship stuff out on my own. Understanding pointed perception is also a great deal more important than formulas that could be looked up in books or on charts. I'm tempted to mail back my engineering diploma with a list of things that I should have learned. Or maybe it should be my high school diploma that I should be mailing back. Will and Al have joined Jake and Lefty in the pool assembly process. Jake complains about the time it will take to fill the pool, but goes ahead and starts assembling it anyway. Even if transportation wasn't an issue, I doubt the store would accept the return of an assembled, half-filled pool. "Sorry about the sloshing," I would tell the customer service people at the Canoe Store, "but we realized a little late that it would take too long to fill the pool. We're only here for the weekend, you know." As I finish the point of my ice cream cone, I am requested inside by Ruth. I grab a large bag from Ruth's truck and leave it in my car. I give her the keys on the way in. A meeting is taking place in the kitchen. Most everyone is in here that isn't part of the pool assembly team. Even Ray has taken a drawing break.

"Do you have any ideas about lunch?" Ruth asks. A smirk wanders across my face. "Seriously it's 1:30."

All eyes are on me. When did I become the caterer? I may have screwed up on the pool and on Mud Lake and kind of about the rocket. Are they trying to see how many times I can screw up in one day?!? A loud crunching sound comes from outside. I seize the opportunity to say, "I'll be right back. Don't move." I step back out into the heat. I must really love these people to do this. The pool assembly team seems to be doing fine; they don't even notice me. Music is blaring from Jake's truck. I think about being up the creek, past the barn, across the field... and I relax. Cy and Todd are laughing near the creek with blue wounds; others are darting about, crouching with one hand near their waists, while throwing things with the other hand. Then in front of me, the pool assembly team is still working hard; music still blaring. I step back inside.

"What happened?"

"I dunno," I respond. "What do you think of going blueberry picking?"

"Is there a place nearby?"

"Sure," I reply.

"How far away is it?"

"How much does it cost?"

"It's not far, and it's free."

Tom approaches me. "Where is this place?"

"Remember the blueberry bushes that were across the field behind the barn?" I ask. He's thinking. I ask Todd the same question. Am I the only person with a memory here? "Cy do you remember blueberry bushes?" She shakes her head, no. "Ruth?"

"When was the last time you saw blueberry bushes there?" Tom asks.

"Years ago."

"They may not be there, since no one has cared for them." He's talking to me like most people talk to Erix. It's very condescending. I don't talk to Erix this way, but still, now I know how it feels. Tom is trying to protect me from myself.

"Okay, let me put it to you this way. I'm going blueberry picking. That's how I am going to handle at least part of lunch. Anyone who wants to come with me can." And quit picking on me. "But you may want to wear something that you wouldn't mind having purple stains on. I'll get out the black shirts my team wore last night if anyone wants to borrow one." I go out to my car for the large art bag, and the shirts. Some small empty bags and a thick rubber band go into my pocket. On the way back I let the assembly team know our plans, and that I'll try to bring some blueberries back for them. "We should be gone nearly half an hour," I mention, "and then we'll struggle our way back in the heat." Jake asks if I have a fire hydrant on me for filling the pool. I start to unzip my pants. Then I shake my head, say no and zip back up.

Inside I toss the shirts into the freezer. The ice cubes might wind up with a special bug spray aroma to them.

Upstairs I stop by Ray's room. He's lying down on his canvas bed. "Hey, look at what I got for you." I open the large bag and pull out a 24 by 36 framed blank canvas with black, white and four color paints, and some brushes. "Have fun." He's speechless.

In the kitchen I drink a large glass of lemonade. Nicole comes in wearing a My Face Is Up Here shirt with an arrow pointing up. Lefty comes in from the heat. "I'd like to examine your brain," he tells me.

"I'm using it. Wouldn't you rather examine someone else?" I say, nodding in Nicole's direction.

Staring at Nicole's breasts, Lefty says, "It takes more than some dozen pounds of fatty tissue to excite me."

Whack! Nicole slaps Lefty. Lefty lands on his lab coat, accented by the muffled sounds of shattering test tubes and petri dishes from his pockets.

"Clean up in aisle 3!" I announce to the ceiling. I lean over the shattered body, "You really might want to think before you speak. Apparently there are ramifications that you haven't considered."

"What happened?" Ruth asks, while taking pictures.

"Well, Lefty took an interest in my head..." I start.

"What was that noise?" Tom asks.

"Well, Lefty disregarded Nicole's top..." I start.

"Could I use one of your T-shirts?" Mica asks.

"Sure they're in the freezer."

"What happened to Lefty?" she asks.

"He's a broken man." To the shattered scientist, I ask, "Are you okay?"

"Yes, I think so. But I am not getting up until your mammiferous friend is gone," he responds. I turn to find Nicole retelling the story, complete with a pantomime upper-cut to the jaw. She says it went **pow**. It was actually a slap with a whack, but it's her story.

"Seriously, could I borrow a shirt," Mica asks. I go over to the freezer, break off the top one, and hand it to her. That was quick freezing; the freezer's brand name, SnowTa, sounds local. It figures. "I thought you were kidding," she says. Mica helps others find the shirts, as I head back out into the heat.

As we head out, Jake and the others start to show off. Holding two hoses has never been more prestigious. They have the pool under control. He checks his watch, which I figure is a good sign. They have been filling it for a while now, they tell us, and sure enough, there is water in the pool, enough water to wash the souls.

I start walking backwards, and Hope and Erix are the first to join up with me and others follow. The not-so-bright part of this plan is that I am leading all these people across a hot farm to pick berries, mostly in the bright sun. I pass some mosquitoes laying with their legs off of some grasses, panting, and fanning themselves with their wings. The mosquitoes aren't going to give us any trouble. Past the barn and the end of the wheel ruts and the fence and a few suburban blocks worth of field and nearly to the creek and the woods arcing away from the farm, are some seemingly nondescript bushes. Right where I left them years ago. Except that the three or four blue dot speckled bushes have turned into six or seven. They are nearly in a P shape, which is incredible to me since I had tried to propagate an R shape. An orange-breasted robin is startled by our approach and flies off to the trees, but keeps a watch on us, chirping occasionally. The blueberry leaves are shiny and firm without any residue of pesticides or chemicals. I test drive a blueberry. It is the size of my thumbnail, round, and blue with a haze of shiny blue-black. It is tart and sweet but mostly tart. The taste of one is good; the taste of a handful is better. The ones with a pinkish purple hue are not ripe, and certainly the little green ones are not ripe. A blueberry whizzes by my head. I look around and everyone is minding their own business picking and eating blueberries. Must be my imagination, blueberries can't fly. I reach a handful to my mouth when **pow**, right between my eyes, I get hit by a flying blueberry. Todd's smirk is twitching uncontrollably. My handful of food becomes a handful of ammunition, launched individually and in rapid succession against my adversary and his new, laughing girlfriend. Nearby me, Erix ducks well, avoiding the return volley. Hope is less experienced and is splattered by one blueberry that skips across her like a flat stone bouncing across the surface of a pond, leaving ripples of where it has been.

"I've been hit!" she gasps.

"Of course you know, this means war!" I announce. I escalate the battle by increasing the effectiveness of the ammunition. I bite a small nip out of the blueberries that I am now throwing at Todd or Cy, my chief adversaries, increasing the chances that the blueberries will splatter instead of bouncing harmlessly away. They yield to my onslaught, and when they are hit from behind by other enemies, they laughingly retreat a few yards, while cupping handfuls of blueberries to their bellies. I notice a few, more serious berry pickers have their hands full. So I pass out some small bags, while Becky pegs Tom. I am telling some people how you can cup a cluster of blueberries, hold a bag under them, and by rubbing gently, only the ripe blueberries will fall off into the bag. This doesn't work very well in spots where the bush is so tight that you can't get a bag under the branch with the cluster of blueberries. That's when I am pegged in the neck by a blueberry. I look over to see Tom and Becky, who have stopped their battle to watch me drop my bag with only a few berries in my hand. I reach into my pocket, grab a thick rubber band, stretch it between my thumb and forefinger, load it with a blueberry, Becky swears, and I fire it at Tom. My first shot overshoots. My second shot does not.

"War is hell... a blue, blue hell."

Tom and Becky surrender, and an uneasy peace blankets the group with a hot, humid, sticky, sweaty blanket. For another ten minutes we are fairly quietly picking blueberries, interrupted occasionally by Ruth's humming and picture taking, the robin's chirps, and the gentle rustling in the trees of an imaginary breeze. Ruth's humming leads me to making up words that fit the tune – this time the words are "Arrookoo Ammookoo." That causes several people like Todd and Tom to break into song, which is quickly interrupted. A distant thunder approaches. We all turn to watch Jake's truck mow through the field, with the thunder of his music. He did pick up on my half an hour hint. Jake scores a point.

"Hey losers," he shouts out his window, point deducted, "ya wanna ride?" Ruth climbs in and shuts off the thunder. The rest of us brush off our blueberries and climb in, while Jake and Ruth battle it out. Lefty's purple polka dotted lab coat is a lost cause. As we drive off, I watch the robin behind us, returning to its bushes.

I interrupt Jake and Ruth to ask about the pool progress. As the question leaves my lips, I realize that my looking for a progress report is very work-like, all too work-like. Luckily no one seems to notice my slip back into work mode. Jake says that the pool has a few hours to go until it is filled.

Erix takes his bag of blueberries to the far side of the tent.

The pool has water. Not much, but it is progress. My main concern is whether anyone wants to continue to sit and fill the pool. I talk privately with Will and Al. I give them each a bag of blueberries, and they explain their determination to see this through. It's a challenge that they have figured their way through. Will used his determination, while Al used his carpentry skills. They have a problem. The problem is trying to keep the rest of us away long enough for the pool to be ready. I ask if four hours will do it? They agree.

17

The Play

I gather everyone except Will and Al in the living room. "I bet you wonder why I have called you in here," I tell them. "There has been a murder! No. I think I need to tell you that it is hot outside. It's hot. And a recent excursion has led to the discovery of ice cream in town. We need to all go into town and look into this ice cream discovery. And we will probably have dinner there as well, and later we will bring something back for Al and Will." There is some discussion about the fairness of leaving them behind. Ultimately I explain that they are kicking us out. Once that is out in the open everyone is game to go, except Ray and Nicole. Okay, we'll have to remember to bring back food for the four of them. The two showers in the two houses take away water pressure from the hoses, until we are all showered and presentable for another trip into Harmony. Lefty is in a fresh white lab coat. Dexter offers to drive, but it turns out that we can all fit in Ruth's and Jake's trucks. Ruth gives me back her keys and asks me to drive her truck, so that she can prevent Jake from deafening his passengers. Hope and Erix join me in the front. Becky, Tom, Todd, and Cy sit somewhere in back.

Red jumps in right behind me and starts philosophizing loudly in my ear, "Life is a book. Yeah, life is a book. Seeing the future is no big deal. It's just reading ahead. Who am I? Who are any of us really?" Hope tries to reason with him by asking him who he wants to be. I mentally drown him out by thinking of the first thing that comes into my head. I'm going to be fired on Monday. That's the first thing that comes into my head. It's not the most comforting thought. But then there is always selling screens for car windows. Red kicks my seat. "You aren't even listening to me?" How does he know that? Okay Red, if you can hear what I'm thinking, like the twins, life isn't a book. It isn't that straightforward. If life were a book, it would be the sort of book that is so filled with double-meanings and reading between the lines, and even then it isn't a book because there are so many choices. Some books have decisions built into them. That concept must've been invented by someone like me, but it still pales compared to real life because the amount of decisions and decisions upon decisions in real life could never be sanely illustrated. "I just know what I know," he says, and he's quiet the rest of the way.

The road cuts through several patches of forest. The shadows from the trees dance across the truck and our faces at 60 miles per hour. They are fast dancing shadows. We pass a house with a tepee in front. Tom interrupts his drawing of buried treasure locations on Ruth's maps to comment, "Man that house really got TP'ed!"

We pass a motorcyclist at an intersection. It's an old man with a microphone headset under his helmet. Either it's a phone or he's doing karaoke on the road, because no one else can stand it.

We find the ice cream shop and descend upon it. The two high school kids running the place recognize me and I tell them, "The ice cream was so good; I decided I had to bring in 14 of my closest friends." One of them is looking through us for someone. It takes me a moment to realize who he's looking for, but then I tell him that, "Nicole couldn't come back." Even without Nicole, they take good care of our group. I ask about good places to eat in the area. The ice cream girl suggests an ice cream shop dinner of banana splits or multiple layer sundaes. We laugh off her sales pitch, saying, "We weren't born yesterday." Then I look at Joe and say, "Okay, Joe was born yesterday." We laugh. The ice cream pair start listing off restaurants and descriptions. We settle on the American Bar, figuring we couldn't pass that up.

Then they tell us about a play at the Round Lake Community College. It's the last night, and we have got to go see it.

We take our ice cream cones and shakes on a walk through town. Dexter tells us that so many towns like Harmony started at regular intervals on the train route, providing the train with fuel and water and, to a lesser extent, food and lodging. As the area was settled with farmers, the railroad stations became a key to getting grain to the cities to be milled. As the grain traded hands at the stations, cooperatives were set up to buy, store, and sell the grain. The grain silos in Harmony, huge shiny aluminum tubes with cone shaped bottoms, surrounded by trucks on one side and the railroad on the other, are active and current. Several townspeople go out of their way to greet us on our walk.

We drive the trucks to the American Bar. A sign on the window advertises two-for-one subpoena coladas. Dexter and Mica are concerned that our group is not in suits or ties or wearing legal briefs, and we might not fit in with the dress code. We nearly double the clientele, which entitles us to our own dress code and a free cookie.

"Uf dah, there's a lot of you, isn't dere!" our hostess exclaims, while demonstrating her expertise at the Minnesota Vowel Elongation pattern of speech. "Would ya like ta all sit at da same table?" The restaurant is not huge; either way I figure we can all talk to one another even if technically we are on opposite sides of the restaurant.

"That's not necessary," I say only to be pounced on by all sides.

"We need to sit at one table," Ruth corrects.

"Why are you always trying to divide us up?" Mica asks.

"When have I tried to divide people up?"

"Picking sides for the games yesterday..."

"I didn't ask to be captain, usually it's Todd and Tom."

"You didn't fight it either," Mica argues.

"So I should have protested being a captain on the grounds that having two teams would divide people up?!?" I look around for support.

Jake is thoroughly amused. I raise my eyebrows at him for support. He waves me off with his hands saying, "No, this is too good. And payback is a bitch."

I turn to Mica with a shock looked to say, "Did you hear what he called you?" She goes along with it and turns to Jake and asks, "What did you just call me?" Meanwhile I hastily assist our hostess-waitress, Mildred, in rearranging the furniture for the city folk. "What did Jake say?" Mica asks me.

"I don't know, but earlier he was saying something about cubic zirconia." If the word that rhymes with witch didn't set her off, any comment about cubic zirconia would launch her into orbit faster than Tom's rocket. Mica is ping-ponged back to Jake. It's his volley.

"I never said anything about cubic zirconia. What I said was that I prefer beef bologna."

"Oooo, dat's not on da menu, but I could ask da cook," Mildred offers, as she hands out the menus. "Do yer have any plans after supper?"

"Thank you, that's very sweet of you to ask, but I already have a girlfriend," I reply giving Hope's arm a squeeze. Ruth's camera flashes.

The waitress bashes me with a spare menu. "No no, tonight's the finale of Social Climbers at the community college. You should all go. It's very good." Mildred pronounces good with a long U.

"That wouldn't happen to be at the Round Lake Community College, would it?" Todd asks.

"Why yes, it is!" Mildred exclaims. She hustles our orders, barely has the cook cook our food, clears the plates before we're done, gives me a bag of the carry-out orders, and shuffles us out the door with directions to the theater in both English and Norwegian, plus a map and a phone number.

Outside by the trucks, I ask, "Well I wonder what we should do now?"

A passerby quickly turns and heads toward our group. I stop him with a hand, saying, "I was kidding. Of course, we're going to the play!"

The town and its neighboring towns are at the community college. We run into a traffic jam on the way and wait in a line for tickets, while Ruth photographs our parking spots. Despite all of this, the theater is not brimming with people. The first 20 rows are very sparse. The first five are roped off. We take over the center parts of the seventh and eighth rows. As a group, we are very talkative, while occasionally glancing at the closed curtain in front of us. Our group is talking about things in the playbill, about the restaurant, and about the differences between us and the other audience members. Our talk halts unnaturally with the dimming of the house lights and the opening of the curtain. The audience applauds.

The backdrop is gray-brown and white steep mountains, the type of mountains hardly found outside the Himalayas. The stage floor is brown, lumpy, craggy and uneven, with patches of white. Wind howls from speakers above the stage and on the side walls. At the far back of the stage, upstage I think it's called, a spotlight lights up the lowest part of the stage. A man with a hooded parka, a backpack, and many loops of rope clipped to his belt, climbs onto the stage from behind and below, using a pick that makes a metal-to-rock **chlink** sound when it hits the stage. He stands and lowers his hood. Applause.

"It's good to be first," he says, arms outstretched. "It's good to be on top."

A head pops up from below and scrambles up. She stands. Applause. "You are not on top, Pike. We have a long way to go."

"Of course, I'm on top. I am above the rest of you, Valerie," Pike speaks. "Comparatively, I am on top. I am King because the rest of you are below me. Do you know why we climb this mountain?"

"Because it's there?" Valerie responds.

"No, because it's there!" Pike exclaims. The crowd laughs politely. They set claw-like anchors into the rocky ground, clip ropes presumably to the claws, and lower the ropes.

In the pause before the next line Dan loudly comments, **"Funny!"** with classic Dan Ryan delay. The entire audience and cast look at him. The seconds tick by. The play resumes.

Three others climb up from the depression in quick succession. One of the newcomers picks up a loose stone, tosses it up in the air, catches it, and is about to toss it down the mountain behind her. "Stop Lowrie!" Lowrie turns to Pike, who says, "Let's go over my climbing rules again. Number one: keep to the path. You will be following me. Do not go off on your own. I am above you because I have figured where to go. I am smart."

Valerie coughs. "Sorry. Lack of oxygen..."

"Number two: watch out for crevasses. The faster you go up; the faster you can go down. Look before you leap. There are pitfalls everywhere. Number three: don't throw rocks. You never know who is below you. The higher up a rock is thrown, the larger the avalanche below. The higher up you are; the more damage you can cause. If you follow number one carefully, you won't have to watch out for number two. Lowrie, what were you about to do?"

"Throw a rock."

"I had to stop you from breaking rule number three. You have been demoted back to the end of the line. Now come on, overtime, there is no rest for the upwardly mobile. And remember to check your messages periodically," Pike says as he leads the group single-file across the stage to the left. They turn to start up to the right.

"Climbing should be called butt-following," Valerie thinks aloud. "I have to follow the biggest ass in the world for days on end. And I am downwind the whole way."

"Have you noticed the view, Valerie!" Pike calls back to her.

"Yes sir, I was just thinking about it."

"Isn't it spectacular?" he asks as their climbing line continues to zig-zag across the stage.

"It is big, sir," Valerie asserts. "Quite the ascent!" Her phone rings loudly. She holds it up reading a message. "'Keep it moving' – brilliant message, very inspirational, Mr. Headstone, sir."

"I like that kind of attitude. You will go far, Valerie. If you are extra nice to me, I can make it so that we can walk side by side," Pike Headstone says.

"That's very balanced of you, P.H."

"I'm glad you see it that way." They get to a ridge a few yards from the edge of the stage. "Let's hold it up!"

"Mr. Headstone, sir..."

"What is it, Max?"

"I want a raise," Max says.

"Max, you have to work yourself up."

"I have," Max says, holding up his shaking hand. "See? I'm trembling!"

Pike walks away to a rock cliff rising up on one side of the stage and starts chipping out footholds with his pick and with his hands.

"Hey Matt."

"Yeah Max."

"What's the difference between a smart climber and a Yeti?"

"I don't know Max, what's the difference between a smart climber and a Yeti?"

"Well, there are reported sightings of a Yeti..."

"All right, enough of the schmoozing and the small talk," Pike says. "Let's get back to climbing." He takes them over to the cliff wall. He starts to climb up it. He loses his footing and swings, dangling by only one hand.

The rest of the climbers lean away suddenly and cry out, "Oooh!"

Pike then swings his body back to the rock. He grabs a hold again and climbs safely up. "See? Nothing to it." Pike lays down on his side at the top of the cliff and goes back over his three rules. "Number one, keep to the path. Number two, watch out for crevasses. And number three, don't throw rocks."

Valerie says, "I'm feeling kind of low. Must be the altitude." She looks at my group for our reactions.

"Come on up. It's eaaaaasy," Pike lies.

"Nuts," Valerie says, and she climbs up the cliff, slips, and perilously dangles from one arm. The three below her lean back and say, "Oooh!" along with half the audience. She swings and climbs to the top of the cliff.

Lowrie asks the other two, "Do you want me to go next?" They shrug. She strides ahead and starts to climb the cliff. She loses her footing as well, causes the crowd to "Oooh!" until she regains her footing and climbs up.

Max turns to Matt, "I think I am now solidly against climbing."

Matt says, "You are an anti-climb Max."

The audience laughs, and so do Max and Matt, until the three above shout, "Get a move on!" The two scamper up the wall without any difficulties. They all disappear off-stage, and the lights go out.

Applause.

The spotlight returns to two ropes hanging off the back of the stage. Two climbers are slowly making their way up. They stand up and stagger. They are woozy.

"Whoa, careful there Max."

"Hey Matt, what do mountain climbers and surgeons have in common?"

"I don't know Max, what do mountain climbers and surgeons have in common?"

"They both bury their mistakes."

"Ha. Uh, that's not too funny..."

"Hey Matt, did we pass them? Did we make it up here before anyone?"

"Not quite!" a voice outside of the spotlight exclaims. The light expands to show the other three sitting near a patch of snow. Pike and Valerie stand up, go over, and coil up the ropes.

"So you had asked me if I had heard about the mixed nut theory," Pike says.

"Right," Valerie says, as they start to lead their group again. "In a can of mixed nuts, it doesn't matter how the manufacturer puts the nuts into the can; the biggest nuts will settle to the top. It's called the Brazil Nut Effect."

Pike stops and quickly turns to look at Valerie, then he starts to walk again. "What has a can of mixed nuts to do with anything?" he asks.

"Many people see it as an analogy for any large organization," Valerie says catching eyes with me and my smile. "The biggest nuts rise to the top of the organization. You might not think a can of mixed nuts is very representational, but maybe it can represent the entire world. At sea level there are the tiniest grains of sand. Whereas, way up here, there are the biggest rocks in the world."

She is still staring out, and it seems like she's staring at me. When I was a kid with Tom and Todd, when a girl looked at one of us, we used to kid about it. One of us would say, "She was looking right at me!" Another one of us would say, "No she was looking through you to look at me!" That sort of thing. But to have someone on stage watch me like this reminds me of Melanie, except that this is a stranger. It's almost like I'm a celebrity, and she's doing the play for me.

In my thinking about the mixed nut analogy and her staring at me, I must have missed something. The next thing I know, Pike absently falls down a hole.

"Where's Pike?" Lowrie asks.

"He fell into that crevice or crevasse. I don't know what the difference is. I suppose if he's in it, it's a crevasse," Valerie says.

"I heard that!" Pike yells.

"How can you hear from way down there?" Valerie asks.

"What did he say?"

"He said, 'It's my mountain-ears.'" Valerie calls to him from the edge of the crevasse, "Are you hurt?"

"What did he say?"

"He said, 'I don't know. I'm still falling.'" She turns to us and says, "All this time he's quoted the rules. And now he steps in number two."

They all gather around the crevasse.

The light dims. They turn in order and continue to zig-zag across the stage. The wind howls from the speakers. As the light rises again, lighting the whole stage, which now has more, larger snow patches, they pant and arrive at center stage.

"We made it! We're on top!" Valerie exclaims and then she breaks down, dropping to her knees and cries. She bawls. "Damn it. Why couldn't he listen to his own rules?!?" She stops nearly choking for air. The others rush toward her. She waves them off, stares, and turns to Lowrie, "Do you know why we climbed the mountain?"

"Because it's there," Lowrie replies.

"That's what Pike said. And that's what Sir Mallory said before him. 'Because it's there' is not an answer. We don't climb a mountain or an organization or a town because it's there. We climb as a challenge. We climb so we can look out and feel special. We are up here jostling for position to reach the highest point... to feel special that we made it to the top of the world!" Valerie exclaims, looking out at us.

"Matt?"

"Yeah Max."

"What's the difference between God and a climber?"

"I don't know Max. What's the difference between God and a climber?"

"God doesn't think He's a climber."

The curtain drops. The audience rises in its applause. We rise with them. The clapping continues. The curtain opens. Max and Matt take their bows and move off. Lowrie runs in, bows, and steps aside. Pike limps in on a crutch with an arm sling and head bandages. Pike takes an elaborate bow. Valerie comes out smiling and crying and waving to people. She bows. They join up and bow. Valerie then thanks Round Lake, Harmony, Portage, their families, their director, and many others. Applause. And the curtain drops for the night. The house lights go up.

As we turn to find a traffic jam in the aisles, Mica says, "I figured out why the audience doesn't sit up close. It was tough to see what was happening when the action was backstage."

"You mean, upstage," Dexter corrects, clearing his throat.

"I mean when the actors were as far away as possible, the lumpiness of the stage made it difficult to see clearly," Mica explains.

"Okay."

Hope whispers to me, "Did you know the woman that played Valerie?"

"No."

"She seemed to know you. Or at least it seemed like she was playing to you."

"I noticed that too," Becky says from out of nowhere.

"Mica," Hope says, "you didn't sneeze once through the play!"

"You're right. I hadn't noticed that my allergies went away," Mica responds.

The aisles empty quickly. The lobby doesn't. The lobby windows reveal dusk outside. People don't want to leave as if we're snowed in. Maybe half of the crowd denies the play has ended. The other half don't want to be the first to leave. I start to usher my group out, when a chorus of bathroom requests sing through and fracture the group. Joe and all of the ladies, except Hope, leave us.

"That was a good play," Jake asserts. "Not too long... not afraid to kill off their star..." Red tells Jake that Valerie was the star and shows Jake the playbill.

"**I thought it was funny**," Dan's voice booms.

"We know!" everyone replies.

I look at Hope and she turns to look at me. What was she looking at? The cast are between us and the doors, each surrounded by their fans. It is strange to see them in street clothes, without their parkas and mountain gear, like seeing Al without his tool belt. Lowrie and her company of fans are in front to the left. Pike Headstone is much farther down. Hope says, "It looks like Valerie is coming over here." I turn and see Valerie making her way over, despite being stopped every foot by well-wishers and congratulatory hugs.

Lefty and his lab coat lean in, "Do you know her?"

"I don't think so," I reply, as Joe and Cy rejoin our group.

"Beer me," Joe says to no one.

As Valerie approaches with determination, people step aside. Even some of my group back away, so we end up in a near circle.

Valerie's determination is replaced by... wonder? "Hi," she says specifically to me, but with glances around me.

"Hi..." and then I realize that her name isn't Valerie or it probably isn't Valerie. I should have read the playbill that's in my back pocket. Or I need to teach my butt to read. "Great play," I tell her. "We all liked it." Hope and Cy and others chime in to agree.

Valerie, who is tall but not as tall as she looked on stage, nods to them and thanks them, without fully taking her eyes off me. "This might sound a little strange... but have you ever had your picture taken with someone really famous?" she asks me. I'm thinking that her play must've gone to her head. I don't know her. I don't think she qualifies as being really famous. And I don't need a picture taken with her.

Cy steps in as the rest of our group returns, "Do you mean Melanie?"

Valerie's face lights up and she steps closer, "Was that you in the picture with Melanie? It was a full page picture in Bolder Rock magazine."

"Yes, that was me. Melanie was a friend of ours... of... several of us here. Cy was her manager." Valerie acknowledges Cy.

Mica is on her phone, "...no it's lacrosse, then soccer, then music lessons. No break! So you're saying they never got to lacrosse?!?" Dexter is jabbed by Mica when he suggests that La Crosse is a long way to go for soccer.

Valerie has turned back to me. "I have had that picture on my wall, forever," she says, throwing so much emphasis on that last word that I picture the dawn of time. A monolithic black wall stands amidst barren rocks with a music magazine picture taped to it. "I never knew who you were, but you... Your picture looked like you were a deer caught in headlights, but you also had such confidence, such calm assuredness that everything would be fine."

I don't know what to say. "My picture did all of that?" I ask her.

She nods and affirms, "Yes."

I reply, "I am glad I could give you so much through that picture."

Cy whispers to Hope beside me, "Stop me if I am out of line." Then to Valerie, Cy says, "Let me introduce you. Yolanda Hilleau, this is Ricky Devise. Ricky, this is Yolanda Hilleau." We shake hands and exchange smiles. "Yolanda, would you like your picture taken with Ricky?" I recognize this now. This is Cy's talent manager voice, deeper than her usual day-to-day voice.

Turning back to Val- Yolanda, Yolanda is quickly nodding her head with her forehead toward me. I nod back. She turns away, turns back, "Stay right here. Please." Turning and only stepping a few feet away, she screams, "Mom!"

Jake gets in my face, "Where's my fucking fan club?" I push him aside.

Mrs. Hilleau responds to Yolanda with a camera. Cy sets up Yolanda next to me, and I check to make sure Hope is okay with this. She nods to me. Cy puts our arms around each other and adjusts our hair and straightens our shirts. She then backs away and lets Mrs. Hilleau take a picture of her own thumb. Cy asks if she could try a couple pictures, while behind her, Ruth is already taking a few pictures. Cy steps closer to us, wiggles her thumb to show that it will be out of the frame, and takes the picture. She takes two more pictures and hands the camera back to Yolanda's mother.

Cy then separates us. She explains to Valerie, "This is Hope. She is Ricky's girlfriend. They are seriously in love. I want to make that clear to you. Ricky was a good friend to Melanie, he used to be my boyfriend, and he is a good friend to all of us, no matter what we do to him." The last part was aimed at Jake.

"What did I do?!?" he responds.

"However," Cy continues, "Ricky is rotten at writing letters, no matter how hard he tries. He's intelligent, but he can barely string three sentences together."

"Hey!" I protest.

"So, if you want to swap addresses, we can do that, as long as you understand that you should not interfere with their relationship, and you can't count on any sort of reply. Does that sound fair?"

"Yes," Yolanda replies and gets a pen and paper from her mom, while quickly explaining who I am. I give her my address. She gives me her address, phone number, parent's address, parent's phone number, a smiley face, and a heart. Cy handles the exchange of information, checking it for clarity of penmanship. Yolanda hugs Cy and thanks her, hugs Hope and thanks her, and hugs me and tells me, "It is so nice to have finally met you. It is the perfect ending to a perfect day." Yolanda moves slowly off. Our path is now clear to leave. I take Hope's hand. As we step out, I check my watch.

"Could I have my picture taken with you?!?" Jake pleads to nobody as he walks.

18

But Who's Counting?

It's cool out. I count our group. We have 15. That sounds about right. As we approach Ruth's truck, Cy tells me she gets ten percent. Ten percent of what? I concentrate on my night driving. I know the route, but it looks different at night. Yolanda's stage presence, her attention to her audience, her enunciation, and her timing remind me of Melanie. Yolanda's behavior also reminds me of Jenny. In thinking about Jenny, I remember her appearing in Ruth's show this morning.

The truck has a quiet group in the front half and a talkative group in the back, composed of Becky, Cy, and the twins. I check to make sure Red is still with us. "I'm here," he responds.

"Hey Tom," I call back.

"Yo," Tom responds.

"Did you invite Jenny?"

"No, I lost track of her" he responds.

"Who's Jenny?" Hope asks.

"Jenny was a back-up singer for Melanie that stayed around. Her mental jukebox of songs and connections to songs was amazing. She would sing lyrics of appropriate songs, changing just a few words sometimes and sometimes changing almost the whole song."

"When she was hot, really into it, it was incredible," Todd adds.

Becky climbs forward and asks, "What's going to happen when we get back?"

"Nadine and Nicole will be in the pool," I respond.

"No, Nadine had a wedding," Tom corrects. "She couldn't come."

"She already has," I think.

Hope asks, "Is this the Nadine that I met at Tom's last weekend?"

I nod, "Uh-huh."

"We're being followed," Todd announces. I check my mirrors. There is another truck following us through a few turns. I speed up to lose them. I stop signaling my turns.

Hope asks me, "That isn't Jake?"

Oh, yeah. I slow down and get back into my careful driving mode. Apparently, I have different driving modes. I take the long, gravel driveway far slower than Jake would have. Coming to a halt in the grassy field with a large pool, our headlights highlight two topless women laughing and yelling and splashing in the pool. I cut the lights. Jake doesn't. As I get out Ruth is switching off Jake's headlights. Many of us converge on the pool. Jake strips on his way over. He leaves a trail of clothes and shoes. Mica interrupts arguing with her child by phone with a sneeze. I comment, "Picking up after yourself is nothing to sneeze at."

As I give Ruth her keys she tells me, "Jake liked it when you sped up on the way back here." Hope and Becky are heading over to the pool. I head inside with Erix. I hold the door for Joe and his beers. I put the carry-out dinners in the refrigerator. And I stop Erix from following me into the bathroom, by telling him I'll be right out. No one needs an audience when they are going to the bathroom. What is almost as bad is having an audience waiting for you as you exit the bathroom. I don't know why. Sociologists always get questions like this. It's a good reason to study sociology. Engineers and orthodontists never get questions this good. I am greeted by an audience as I exit the bathroom.

"What's up?"

"We just wanted to make sure you didn't fall in," Todd says.

Lefty asks, "What did you have for dinner, a week ago?"

"Spaghetti," I respond. "Why?"

"Has anyone ever told you that you have a good memory?"

I tilt my head up and rub my chin as numbers spin on my mental odometer. "Counting comments like yours, Lefty, 82 times."

Cy laughs and then gets a serious pout on her lips. "Try not to start remembering things that I've done. There is nothing worse than a man with a memory."

"83," I tell Lefty. "You know, I tried returning your call last week, but you didn't leave a number."

"That's what I wanted to talk to you about," Lefty says, as he retrieves the world's smallest clipboard from his pocket and jots something down. He tears it off and hands it to me, replacing his pencil behind his ear. "I'm researching mental acuity. I'm running into something of a roadblock. It would seem that most people, myself included, can't remember a damned thing. Whereas you seem to remember everything that has happened and some things that haven't yet happened."

I nod. "84. Are you looking for a guinea pig?"

"Yes, and you can stop counting," he tells me.

"Is Ray one of your lab rats?"

"No..."

"Must be some other university researchers."

"What are they studying?" Lefty asks, jotting something down.

"How to make a human pincushion, I think. You'll have to ask him."

"Could you stop by the address I gave you sometime next week?"

I ponder it. "I can't guarantee that I'll be fired, but how about Thursday morning? If I'm not fired, at least I'll miss a meeting. I'm not saying that I will be able to help you out, but at least I can stop by."

Lefty offers, "Do you need me to write Thursday down on your..." He gets a quizzical what-am-I-saying look on his face.

Erix bursts into the kitchen with a flashlight. "Herman's gone!"

I'm impressed. Erix found a flashlight! I step toward him. "Spiders like Herman are well traveled, since everything clears out of the way for them. She's just finding the best places to do spider stuff, like making webs and catching bugs and having millions of little Hermans." Erix is impressed by the millions of little Hermans concept. Becky would have been too. She must still be outside.

I start to leave the kitchen to look for Ray, when Cy calls back to me, "Would you like to see the picture Yolanda was talking about? I've got it next door..."

"How about tomorrow morning?" I ask, and she nods.

I find Ray in the dining room with pens and posterboard and the canvas and paints. He also has towels and water for cleaning up after himself. He's working on the mirrored floor, along with nearly a thousand other Rays. The canvas and the posterboards all depict a Nicole-like Glory Girl flying through the sky and posing with fists on her hips. From the empty barstool in front of him, I can guess that she balanced herself on her waist on the stool. He turns to me and bursts into a grin.

"She was great... a dream... she posed for hours! Thank you for inviting me here and bringing the posterboard and getting me the canvas! This is great, a lagniappe!" I look over his shoulder as others come in to look. I left him with four colors; his palette now has a mix of nearly 40 colors. Ray and I both stop Erix from touching some wet paint.

I examine the detail. "This is some of your best work. We picked up a salad for you. It's in the refrigerator." He nods to me and my mortal issues from his mirrored cloud.

Dexter asks, "Are you going to fill in the rest of this?"

Ray is explaining his plans, as I continue my quest for those left behind. I find Will asleep in his hanging chair. Dan motions for me to be quiet as he launches the chair swinging across the room. Dan then ducks down below Will's chair. Will starts to wake up, making it look like I started his chair swinging precariously close to the aquarium window. He's half-awake. I tell his awake-half, "Your dinner is in the fridge. Is Al out in his car?"

Will opens his eyes as he swings toward the IF, "Wendy should have come with me. Al and I took turns watching Nicole pose in a bikini for Ray. Then Nadine shows up and starts talking to Nicole and somewhere they decide to team up and take on the world." Will grabs my shirt, "No one warned the world!" He lets me go now that he has come to a halt, saying, "Some of your best friends are the people my mother warned me about."

"Your mother worries too much," I say noticing Dan fall asleep on the floor below the swing.

"Those women... they took Al and I into the pool and took off their bikinis. I explained about Wendy... they didn't care. I fought them off. Al didn't. After they had their way with him, he dragged himself upstairs and into the hospital room." I turn to go up, as Dexter and Mica head up holding hands. I've never seen them hold hands. "Whoa," Will stops me, "Al won't be interested in eating until tomorrow."

Noticing some nearby open doors, I find Red reading in a library. Next door Erix is lying down in a giant bird's nest that looks like the top of Mahpiyawicasta Tower. I wish them each a good night.

Outside, I head toward seven people at the pool. As I approach, Nicole is telling a story to Nadine, Jake, Tom, Becky, and Hope, in wet underwear, and Ruth outside of the pool. "Lefty says, 'It takes more than a dozen pounds of fatty tissue to excite me.' I hit him so hard he went sailing through the air. Ricky looked at Lefty lying on the floor and announced, 'Clean up in aisle five!'" They laugh, even though it was aisle three. Nadine spots me and yells. I come over and stand near Ruth. I'm seeing **way** more of my friends this trip.

Nadine yells at me, "They were just telling me about you saving Erix's life from the rocket!" Nadine hiccups.

"It wasn't that dramatic," I correct her. I don't know how some guys can see beautiful women acting annoyingly and can ignore the annoying behavior.

"Ricky, aren't you coming in?!?" Hope asks.

"No... I think I'll go inside," I say.

"Wait... why?!?" Hope asks.

"Get your butt in here," Jake tells me. "They've been waiting for you."

"I'll be inside reading," I turn to go.

"Wait! Dammit!" Hope is yelling while climbing out of the pool and grabbing her things. She's covering up heading toward me. She wasn't covering up while she was in the pool... "What's the matter?!?"

"I just feel like going in."

"I'll come with you."

"No, you were having fun. I don't want to interrupt."

"Interrupt?!? I was waiting for you!"

"C'mon Ricky..." Nadine hiccups.

"What did I do wrong?!?" Hope cries.

I turn back to her. "Nothing."

"God Dammit, get in here!" Jake yells. Nicole and Becky are climbing out.

"I just don't feel like being in the pool."

Tom interjects, "After all the trouble you went through to get the pool, I told them... I assumed... that you'd be joining us." I shake my head, no, at him.

Naked Nicole and nearly naked Becky are right next to me. Nicole asks, "Was it something I did? Please! Don't take it out on Hope!"

"I don't feel like being in the middle of everyone," I tell them. "None of you did anything wrong. Maybe I shouldn't have come out here. Hope, I'd like to be with you any time I can. If you want to be with me, I'd love to be with you."

"I want to be with you," Hope says. I hold out my hand and she takes it.

Jake calls after me, "It's because I didn't shower today, isn't it?"

"Good night, everybody," I call back to them. We head inside and upstairs. She runs to the bathroom, and I check my clock in my room. I kick off my shoes and socks onto a driftwood table. I relax, and the clock jumps forward, and she is here. I am telling her to tell me what she likes. I touch her. I try things. I go back to her coming in the room and she is saying, "I'm getting your pants wet too." We kiss and I touch her and I once again tell her to tell me what she likes. I try other things. Some she likes; some she doesn't. I go back again to my decisions about how to touch Hope. Despite what some would say, there are far more similarities between snowflakes than the ideal lovemaking for people. Everyone is different.

It's like dancing. You have to have the right dance partner, someone who knows you and what you can do. And knows how to dance your way. Fred Astaire dances right with Ginger Rogers. If Fred Astaire dances with Gertrude the Klutz, it won't look like dancing. It will look like fighting. Both of them will look bad. Fred will look like an ass, making Gertrude do things no one could expect Gertrude to do. Dancing together, responsiveness, is more important than skill alone.

I try more combinations of ways to touch her, ways to make love to her, stops and starts, and then I come back. My alarm clock wags its finger at me like I've done something bad, like I've cheated on Hope with Hope.

Hope peers in. I stand up. "I didn't mean to hurt you, Hope. I just didn't feel like any more group attention or group behavior tonight." Hope shuts the door and climbs the floor to me. "I want to be with you, Hope, just you." I pause to make certain of my next words. "I love you."

"I love you too," she says, dropping her clothes, and kissing me. "I'm getting your shirt wet," she says. I smile and take it off. She kisses me more and stops. "I'm getting your pants wet too." I smile and take them off.

"Ignore my clock..." I mumble.

"I'm not watching a clock," she says, looking me over. She fingers my ribs like testing the keys of a piano. Her fingers play on the birthmark over my heart, and she says, "I haven't seen this before." Meanwhile, my alarm clock closes its eyes, shakes its head, and wanders off toward the sunset, oranges and reds gleaming off its chrome. Hope's fingers walk up my chest, over my shoulders, and around my shoulder blades. She climbs onto me. Her eyes twinkle in front of mine. I step for balance. My feet are caught in a pile of clothes. We go down. My back lands on faux dune. I think back to a conversation with Tom about land mines. It would be just like him to plant a faux land mine in here. It would be misplaced. That was the crux of the conversation. All land mines are misplaced.

"Are you okay?" she asks in the glow of the sunset wall. Her eyes are so close. Her lips are so close. Yes. My hands pull her closer. I kiss her with every lip on my face. I need more lips. I explore her lips with what lips I have. They do well, my lips, but a few more would do so much better. Looking into her eyes so close, I find she only has one. Her eye is two outer halves of eyes. She is still beautiful with only one eye. I have fallen in love with a cyclops... a gorgeous cyclops. One of my hands leaves her waist to touch her soft cheek. Her eye closes. My fingers dance across the side of her face to the music of our kisses. At the edge of their dance floor, where her neck and cheek meet below her ear, two of my fingers discover a spot where a soft caress causes a smile, so the two fingers touch the spot again. They turn to look at a smile twitching across Hope's lips. The fingers decide to investigate further. They caress around the spot, step across it with care as though stepping onto the ice of a frozen lake for the first time. Her slight smile no longer shows signs of departure, and the forecast calls for light giggles, followed by periods of heavy giggles in some areas. My fingers put on their ice skates and start a rowdy game of hockey below Hope's ear. Hope laughs. "Quit that," she says, raising up on me and adjusting her seating. Hey! Hope has two eyes! I smile back at her with all the innocence of hockey players. Hope slowly removes her bra. I wonder what I was thinking about or why. All I can think of now is the symphony of lovemaking that I planned and plotted while Hope was in the bathroom. I warm up the orchestral instruments and play a few hints of things to come. I pause.

I pause long enough for Hope to search my eyes. Then the first movements begin, and I follow my sheet music. The musical scale is a map of Hope's personal erogenous zones. My orchestrated passion touches her in places... takes her to places she has never been. She told me so herself, in a time coming up that may never happen; I've tuned the symphony since then. I added more crescendos. The music, the notes, the sounds coming from Hope... they are just what they should be... just what was practiced... beautiful music of moans and breathing and kisses and surprises and ohs and gasps and half-spoken words and carried notes and sighs. I have never, ever heard anything more wonderful, more beautiful, than what I am hearing from Hope right now. Through her pauses and squirming, I hear and feel a few faults in my actions and make mental notes to correct my movements for the futures. Her third climax catches us both by surprise, me more than her, since it should have had a longer build up. She was not supposed to get that turned on so quickly. Still, this is great, a great moment. I would check my watch, but I am not sure Hope would understand. I am certain my alarm clock has its back to us. I know it's sunset, but in this room it is always sunset. I hold her. My holding turns into caressing. I begin the next movement. I deviate from the sheet music with some improvised play. I tap out a rhythmic effluerage on some of her most sensitive places. Hope climaxes on top of climaxes. I didn't know that was possible. Was that three orgasms in one or one orgasm with three parts? It should be easy to get a ruling. She might have just announced that last one or three orgasms to the entire county. Certainly the birds and the bees know what is going on. I shift to touching her non-erogenous zones. Again, I make a few mistakes, brushing into erogenous zones and sending shutters rippling through her body. I add items to my mental list of Hope's likes and dislikes. I hold her. She looks up at me and smiles. She catches her breath, biting her lower lip. She closes her eyes and breathes heavily. I watch her breathing. It becomes regular... steady, like lake waves gently lapping a beach. I pull a sand-colored sheet over her. I adjust my underwear. I find some switches nearby and dim the sunset.

Hope is nestled beside me. I think she's fallen asleep... fast asleep. It took next to no time at all. I'm lightly, reassuringly, petting her hair. Mostly, I am holding her. This is weird. I know a thing or two about weird. Using that expertise, I can safely say, this is weird. How can I possibly sleep? I am propped up on my left elbow. My left hand is under Hope's head. Even if I were to free up my hand, what am I going to do, leave? No, I'm not trying to leave. I'm not even insistent on sleep. The idea of holding someone all night is weird. Part of the equation is that a relationship takes bed space. It means your limbs might get tangled up like my arm is now. I pet Hope's hair with my free hand. Her eyes open into a squint. I smile at her. She smiles back and falls asleep again. There. She wouldn't have woken up if it wasn't for me. A relationship might mean lost sleep. Then again, maybe my comforting her is making her sleep better.

I stare at her... really stare at her.

I've been heading toward this moment ever since we started ending each day with a phone call, last Monday night. And now I've twice told her that I love her. And we've made love.

I stare off at the sunset. It's time to call it off.

I look back down at Hope sleeping in my arms, and I quietly tell her that I'm kidding. Of course, I won't call it off. I'll give up the bed space. I'll give up the sleep. I want her right here, by my side. I love her. Sure, I need to get to know her better. I'll have to get an idiotic questionnaire from a men's magazine. No, seriously. I need to know more about Hope. Time will tell me all about Hope. The question is, do I let time take its time?

I stare off at the sunset. My alarm clock is on its back, halfway across the room.

What if I fell asleep right now and had a pointed perception dream? What if I come back and find that I've hurt Hope because I dream I'm playing soccer or something? Relaxing is not an option right now.

It's a really nice sunset.

When I was making love to Hope, I compared it to a symphony. I know next to nothing about symphonies. I don't know what made me think of it being like a symphony. Maybe I'm still influenced by the early music of Ruth's show this morning. Or maybe it had something to do with the play at the community college. Hope seems to have liked it... the sex... she seems to have liked the play too.

Tom really went all out on the guest rooms. This sunset is really cool. It seems to be a wall-sized piece of glass that has a sunset painted on it and is lit from behind the sun. There has to be more to it. The execution is so flawless. Except for at the sun itself, the light is so diffused. Maybe there is a second, more opaque glass with increasing, sky-like dispersion and a cut-out for the sun. Maybe–

The door edges open. I can't make out who it is, but I wave them in. The door opens wider. It's Nicole, Nadine, and Becky. Wild hair, all wet and air-dried and brush-free, has taken over their heads. Their outfits are the latest fashion of beach towel togas. The sunset casts orange highlights on them. They tip-toe in a few steps, before they realize that, even though the floor isn't really sand, they would be hard pressed to make any noise walking on it. They take a seat on the slope that approaches our bed-dune. They are empty-handed – naked without their drinks. Nadine quietly hiccups, which has got to be an impossibility that I could never imagine, and I would check my watch, except that it is on my left arm, snuggled under Hope's head. Earlier I would have said that Nadine was a bad influence on Nicole. Now as they sit here, I would say that Nicole and Becky have had a positive impact on the often obnoxious Nadine.

Nicole quietly mouths, something "you earlier." I squint my eyes and shake my head, indicating that I don't understand. She tries again, "We heard you earlier." I nod.

I mouth the word, "Sorry." Now Nicole shakes her head left and right. She uses the fingers of two hands to draw a heart in mid-air and then points to Hope and I. Nadine shifts like she's going to join in the conversation but then decides not to. They stare at my holding Hope like it is the most interesting thing they have ever witnessed. I could sell tickets. I go back to looking at the sunset. Hope breathes a heavy breath, and I look back at her, then back to the sunset again.

Becky gets up, turns around, and gazes into the sunset. Then she taps the other two and points to the door. Whispering "Good night," they leave.

Maybe I'm all wrong about the sunset. Maybe it's a screen image. I stare off.

This has been a good day. This has been a weird day. I have never felt so accepted. It is not that in my day-to-day life I'm not accepted. No. My co-workers accept me. Ray accepts me. There might even be a level of acceptance in my apartment building and at the Ice Cream Bar. What was strange about today was that I was accepted for parts of my life that I lock away, bury, and otherwise dismiss. Pointed perception is a term I made up. It doesn't mean anything. It is simply the closest description that I know for something that is part of who I am that does not fit, doesn't match, anything else I have heard of.

There are stories of people who can see the history of an object by touching it. There are stories of that sort of person helping the police. Wouldn't those people want to be archaeologists? "That rock? That was used for generations as the prehistoric all purpose tool. It slices. It dices. See how easily it puts a buttonhole in this leather hide. It can scale a fish. It can shave a chicken. And watch how easily it opens this nut. That would've been a tough nut to crack. This amazing rock, MN396117-R, did it all. Then it was misplaced at the stream. Later generations re-discovered it and used it to scrape bones, chip other rocks...

There are stories of people who see the future in tea leaves or crystal balls or clouds or skywriting... a single and singular future... one destiny. One. No menu. No choices. No alternatives. No decisions. No possibilities. Imagine Benjamin Franklin as a boy getting his fortune read. "You will run a mail service and write a newspaper. Sit down, I'm not finished. You will invent a fire-safe stove. Sit down, I'm not finished. You will create a musical instrument based on the sounds of drinking glasses. Sit down, I'm not finished. You will help create a new system of government. Sit down, I'm not finished. You will discover properties of lightning. Sit down, I'm not finished. You will – would you please sit down?!?"

There are stories of people with the ability to move objects with their mind, telekinesis. "Is there anyone here in the crowd with telekinesis? Please raise my hand."

There are stories of people able to see something happening a great distance away or to see through things. "See if you can guess what this nice lady and I will do behind this curtain..."

And there are stories of people who can read minds. The twins, Tom and Todd Pfuloree, proved that to me a long time ago. However I didn't have first-hand experience until the second trip into town today, when Red was reading my mind. I don't know how he could've guessed what I was thinking, while sitting behind me. I suppose he could've seen my face in the rearview mirror. Still, I don't know how he could've guessed.

But I have never heard of anyone else being able to see the results of choices. And for the most part, I've kept it to myself. Now everyone here knows, except maybe Nadine... no, she was telling me that she had heard the story about the rocket. Even Nadine, who has all the subtlety of a megaphone, knows. And they don't just know. They don't just accept. They have adapted to the knowledge. Tom asked me about the rocket. Sure, I got Erix out of the way of the thing, but I didn't save the rocket itself. I didn't stop Tom and talk over what he expected would happen versus what I saw happen. He never told me that he wanted his rocket back. How was I supposed to know he wasn't trying to put the thing into orbit?!? I suppose I could've looked for a happy ending, a smile on his face, but the whole thing felt right at the time, maybe because the rocket worked and no one got hurt.

Everyone seemed to think that I would know what we should do about lunch. This is Tom's place... and Todd's. Ruth seemed to have much of the Friday meals under control. Why would it become my role to forecast the food? And yet I certainly take it as a compliment. They trust my abilities. And that trust, even as it was developing last night, seems to have impacted last night's pointed perception.

Last night Hope finds out about the pointed perception and this morning she finds out about Melanie. Hope seemed as interested that Christie was a friend as that Melanie had been. Then we go to the play and the star recognizes me from a picture with Melanie. She didn't seem too interested in the Melanie part... that Cy was Melanie's manager... or that many of us were Melanie's friends. Yolanda had built an understanding of me from this picture. She was a fan of me, not Melanie, and not from a collection of songs or TV appearances, but from a single picture.

I have a fan.

I stare at the impressions left on the slope nearby. And just awhile ago, didn't three people come in here and just sit for a while, watching Hope and I? It was almost like we were on a dune stage, sunlit from behind them, and they were entranced at the scene we portrayed. So maybe I have several fans. It's weird. Red has been acting strangely. Certainly Tom has become a fan of my abilities. And Erix has always followed me to some extent, but not like this weekend. I hardly saw him a week ago Friday at Tom's house. The monkey suit might have thrown him off. At least Jake is acting normal.

But the real fan was Yolanda. I wonder what I should do. Yolanda now has a few more pictures of me, thanks to Cy. I doubt any of them could compare to all the feelings she ascribed to the Bolder Rock magazine photo. I could send her a card on her birthday, but I don't know when her birthday is. I could write her a letter, but like Cy is quick to point out, I can't write. Hmm. I suppose I could just give her a call and talk to her. I wonder how Hope would feel about my calling Yolanda? Would she freak out? I don't know how Hope feels about the whole thing. I should ask her.

I watch her sleep.

It's certainly something new to think about. What am I required to talk to Hope about? What things do I need to talk over with Hope before I do them?

She's been very supportive. She's gone along with so much today. Anyone who puts up with all that I deal out has got to be some sort of angel.

There is something about having the sun frozen on the wall, just a few minutes from dipping under the horizon. It's like time stops here. Down the hall the L train is always moving. Downstairs the geese are always flying. But the day never ends here.

If I try to look at my question from the other side, from Hope's perspective, I would say that it's the wrong question. It's not about getting Hope's permission or Hope's approval; it's keeping Hope in my life, so as my life changes, she can stay with it. I can't tell her everything. I can't tell her about every detail in my life, every noise from the neighbors, every hurtle in front of AutoDrive. It would take too long. It would be boring. What I can do is tell her about the significant things. The things I would want to know if they happened to Hope, even realizations. If something has been going on for a week, but now I realize the significance of the thing, now is when I tell her, explaining how long the thing has been going on. I tell her about the stuff that matters, and I ask her to do the same. It sounds reasonable. I hope.

Hope shifts closer to me. I look at her, and I close my eyes.

All the stories and fairy tales conclude with the loving couple living happily-ever-after. There is a great deal to iron out, to establish, and probably to maintain the happily-ever-after deal. What decisions are up to me? What decisions are up to her? What decisions do we need to talk over?

We've only been together for eight days. Wait, nine days, it's got to be Sunday already. I open my eyes. I met Hope at Sharon's, which I now vaguely remember. I was in the middle of a conversation. It was a thoughtful moment; a few of us were pondering the political periphery. Sharon introduced us and then disappeared to handle the rest of her matchmaking and coalitionist agenda. Hope stayed with the conversation for a while. I wonder who got her invited to Tom's? Probably Sharon again. But Tom was involved in this happily-ever-after conspiracy, this plot against my having vacant bed space. He had to have been involved. The way I see it, meeting her while I was an ape was our actual meeting. We were actually seeing each other eye-to-fur-framed-eye. I wonder what the conspirators would have done, if I hadn't noticed her at Tom's. Would she have been invited here? How far were they willing to go? If pointed perception worked on the past, I wouldn't have to ask.

I have to go to the bathroom. I'll just ease my arm out from under– Or not. A subtle worried look appears on Hope's face. Her cheek twitches, and her brow furrows. I can wait.

The sun is setting on a lake, whose waters seem to ripple. Maybe it's Hope's breathing. Maybe I'm seeing things. Maybe I'm tired. Nah... couldn't be tired. There must be some other explanation. I am analyzing this wall almost as much as I would be analyzing a real sunset. Tom sure did a bang-up job. Staring at the rippling, sparkling water of the sunset reminds me of having to go to the bathroom. My free hand reaches behind me to look for a button to decrease the rippling. I find a knob and turn it. It makes the sound of waves crashing to the shore. I lose my grip on the knob and try to find it again as the waves loudly pound the beach. That's a switch. That's a button. That's another button. That's the dimmer for the sunlight. That's... That's not anything. Wave after wave crash the shoreline. I almost feel the mist in the air. I find a knob and turn it. The wave sounds cease.

Hope is still asleep.

Time for a bed-time story. The legend of Minnesota starts with a glacier topping the Laurentian Mountain Range and Volcano Farm. Depending upon the season, it was either a glacier or an inland sea, complete with seagulls. Take your pick. The glacier leaked from Minnesota into the Hudson Bay to the north, the Atlantic to the east, and ultimately started the Mississippi River to take over the Missouri and Ohio Rivers. With all this water flowing in almost every direction, Minnesota should have been drained of water long ago. Only the mountains were drained; anyone who says that there are still mountains in Minnesota is bluffing. The first settlers of Minnesota were flighty women with long noses. They were mosquitoes. The mosquitoes got together and buzzed about and decided that Minnesota was the promised land, with its shady forests and abundant, slow-draining water. There was only one problem. Winter. Who would move to frozen Minnesota? The mosquitoes, being air-leeches, needed others to move to Minnesota, to mooch off of. One of the mooching mosquitoes, Minnie the moocher, decided that what Minnesota needed was marketing. Minnie started the Land of 10,000 Lakes gimmick. Lakes. Rarely are they lakes. Rarely are they liquid. Usually they are low lying glaciers. The marketing didn't work on the deer, the bison, or the elk. They said, "Lakes? In Minnesota? You're kidding." One elk laughed, "It's like calling glacial Greenland, 'green land.'" They went back to their grazing. The mosquitoes were forced to reason with the mammals. "Look," Minnie the moocher said, "we are going to bite you. You know that. We know that. If you move to Minnesota, we will bite you where you can itch. If you don't, we will bite you in the most uncomfortable spots. Like Cleveland." The large mammals moved to Minnesota. Every winter they moved to warmer spots, and every spring the mosquitoes herded them back. Native Americans followed the herds. Then Paul Bunyan moved in. He cleared the forests and drained the wetlands. Paul Bunyan was so fast at draining lakes and building shopping malls encircled with parking lots that the seagulls still flock the parking lots, looking for the lakes.

I'm not kidding; I really have to go to the bathroom. Was I waiting for this sun to set or to rise? I use my readily-available right hand to help brace Hope's head with more sand-like mattress while twisting out my semi-cramped left hand. I get up, get my pants on, which I do only for anyone who happens to be strolling through the hallway, and I put on a fresh shirt. The hallway is quiet; the house is quiet. I use the rainforest bathroom and check my watch. It's 6:23am. I go back for shoes and socks. I use the piano stairs. No one is in the living room or the kitchen. I open the curtains. Sunlight streams in. I put on my shoes, grab a handful of cereal, and head out. I'm forgetting something... **Slam**! I forgot to catch the door from slamming. Damn. The pool seems to have wet the yard.

19

Not The End Of The World

As I separate the cereal between my hands, I walk down the long dirt and gravel driveway. Along the way I watch a monarch butterfly stretch its wings and pull them up again, while working over a cluster of purple daisy-like flowers, with orange stubby-cone centers. The breeze picks up strongly to rock the flowers like upside down pendulums. From the flowers a few other monarchs rise up against the breeze, while the original monarch rides it out. It's an adventurous flutter-bye. I shuffle up some dust and gravel. Bumblebees sleep in a patch of tall orange flowers. The bumblebees snore. They breathe in, snort, "Bzzzzzzzzzzzzzzz," breathe in, snort-snort, "Bzzzzzzzzzzzzzzz." One nearby seems to wake to the smell of artificial breakfast cereal. I quietly keep moving. I pass the spot where I had left Minion and then drove him back. I pass the stop sign that had stopped Erix. A bird warbles... must be a warbler. I pass the spot where Cy's horse stuck its nose into the truck and snoofed Hope. I pass another farmhouse and turn down another lane. I finish one handful of cereal and switch to the second. This lane is asphalt paved over weeds. The lane cuts through some woods. A small cement bridge takes me over a creek. The farmhouse I'm heading toward is picture perfect. It looks like it has been here a hundred years and will be here a hundred more. Its red barn is identical to Tom's, except that this one is in better condition. There are two silos: a cement silo that looks like it was built to withstand time itself and a newer aluminum silo, which looks like I could crush it against my forehead if it wasn't so bulky. I'm not saying my forehead is bulky. The silo is bulky. Two people sit out on a swing in their yard. I run my fingers through my hair. They've probably been watching my approach since the creek. A dog gets up with its nose pointed at me. The dog drops whatever it was chewing on, maybe a cat or a raccoon. Now it takes off toward me. It is really racing toward me. If it is on a leash, it's going to seriously hurt itself. It crosses onto the road without resistance. Wow, look at him move! It's a golden retriever with a red bandana around its neck. He is almost on me.

At the last second, I shuffle right. Momentum carries him past as his head turns for the U-turn behind me. Advantage: biped.

Dogs don't have brakes. He sticks his big tongue out the side of his grinning mouth, while circling back. I continue walking, and he trots along side ahead. One of us is escorting the other. I test him, by walking faster than him. He picks up the pace to stay ahead of me. His sideways glances and wagging tail keep tabs on me. He steers me into his front yard toward his owners.

"I see you've met Ben," the guy comments. Ben circles his masters and stops between us with his side to me, as an instant barrier. I take another step and hear a low growl. "Ben!"

"It's okay," I tell them. I squat down to Ben's level and hold out my hand for him to sniff. This is a new one to Ben, who sniffs my hand and licks it. Ben gives me a calculating look that says he knows the Major Munch brand of breakfast cereal that I was eating. He runs through a list of other people he's met that eat the same cereal. He knows how long the cereal was in my hand. He knows the cereal's expiration date. He wants to know who Hope is. Ben circles me.

"I'm Tera," the woman introduces, "and this is Grant." I introduce myself while Ben attempts to bowl me over. "Where are you from?" she asks. I open my mouth to speak only to get a mouthful of long-haired dog tail.

I spit hairs, "Pigs Eye."

"Where are you staying?" Tera prods.

I point and say, "The Pfuloree, uh, house." I nearly said cabin or farmhouse, which would probably sound silly to people who apparently live here year-around. All houses are farmhouses, right?

"The new house? I did some work on it." Ben takes off. "How long are you staying?"

"Just the weekend. We head back today." Ben is back with a large chew toy in the shape of a blob... it has many handles for the dog to grab onto. Ben steps toward me with sideways glances.

"You don't happen to know," Grant asks, "anything about a missile that was shot over here yesterday, do you?" Ben drops the blob in front of me.

Missile? The rocket? "Uh, yes, a rocket got out of control. It didn't damage anything, did it?"

"No. I'll get it for you," Tera says. She heads in, which Ben notices while eying me pick up the blob. I stand up into a stretch and play with the chew blob in my hands, seemingly oblivious to the intensity of Ben's interest.

"We really didn't mean to send a missile your way," I tell Grant, shaking the chew blob to emphasize my words. "Where did it land?"

Grant is glancing at the blob and at Ben. "Near the creek," he says, making creek rhyme with pick. "Ben brought it in." I know the feeling.

"Hey Ben," I say as if I had to ask for the dog's attention. I toss the blob. Ben peels off after it. A screen door closes. Tera comes out carrying a bag, followed by a white-haired woman that must be a great-great-great-great grandmother. This woman is old.

Tera offers me a bag, "Here. These are all the parts we have."

I look in and see the rocket. "Yup. That's it." Ben drops the blob at my feet. I toss the blob.

The old woman has a scowl that must've been frozen stuck by one of the nasty nineteenth century winters. She brushes Tera aside saying, "I just want to meet the boy that's shooting at us," and she slaps my face three times in succession with a feather-like force. "Here," she says, handing me a second bag. As Ben drops the blob again, I look into the bag. It's muffins.

"You didn't need to do this... thank you. This is very nice of you." I pet Ben. I toss the blob again. "I probably better start heading back before the rain."

"You too?" Tera asks. "You know, the forecast isn't calling for rain. Grant started talking about it yesterday afternoon, saying it would hit this morning." We look up at big, white puffball, cumulus clouds crossing blue skies.

"Yeah. I started talking about it Friday."

"Friday?!?" the couple says nearly in unison. They look at me strangely. Ben takes the cue and doesn't return the blob to me. Nothing makes me crazier than people thinking I'm crazy.

"Yeah, well. Thanks again for the muffins and for taking care of the rocket," I say. "It was nice meeting you."

"Yes, it was," the old woman says.

I walk back down to the lane. On the other side of the lane, the corn field ripples in the breeze like a giant finger pulling through a giant brush. The lane dips down at the creek and then up again. A weeping willow waves to me on my way by. The world did not change overnight. I did not suddenly become normal. I did not suddenly become universally accepted, just because some people believe in me. The uneven asphalt trips me up in a forest. I pass another farmhouse. I check the rocket. Other than some teeth marks, scorch marks, and chipped paint, it looks like it did a day ago. I start walking again, yawn, and return to the unpaved driveway. The bumblebees are having a field day. As I head up the hill to the farmhouses, I see several people watching my progress. Isn't it early for people to be up? As I approach, Jake tells me, "Tom has been trying to talk me out of killing you." These people are a bunch of surly morning risers.

Apparently I am the front desk manager with whom complaints are registered.

"What did I do?"

"You slammed the door," Ruth tells me. She doesn't seem too happy about it either.

"Hold this for me," I hand Ruth a bag. "Hold this for me," I hand Tom a bag. I step toward Jake. "Okay Jake, you want to kill me because I accidentally slammed the door? Go ahead. No one is going to get in the way this time." I step even closer. "Let's bleed."

"Whoa, I was kidding. Lighten up. Where's your rain?" Jake asks.

"What rain?"

"That's what we were asking. What rain? Didn't you tell people it would rain this morning?" Jake cross-examines.

"Yes."

"Where is it? Or were you saying it would rain this morning... somewhere?"

"It's coming, keep your shirt on."

Jake points to the grass, "You know, that's not rain. That's dew."

"Are you done?"

"Yeah, that's about it. I'll let you know if I come up with any more," Jake assures me. I thank him, noticing that Tom and Ruth are obediently holding their bags without looking in them. Tom seems puzzled.

Hope comes out with Cy. Cy's fingers comb back her hair as she says, "Hi Mr. Slamming. I was telling Hope that if she was faking last night, she went **way** overboard. We could hear you two from next door."

Hope grabs me and kisses me, while smiling from dimple to dimple. At least somebody is happy to see me. "I missed you when I woke up. But I heard you were awake and holding me in the middle of the night. Did you get any sleep?" Hope asks, looking from one of my eyes to the other.

"Nope."

"I'm sorry. Was I kicking you? Or hogging the covers?"

"No, it was nothing like that. I just didn't feel like sleeping."

The worried look returns to Hope's brow. She pulls me aside and whispers in my ear, with Jake stepping up right behind her, "Did you, uh, orgasm?" Her breath is hot in my ear.

I could breath right back into her ear. Instead I simply say, "No."

"What?!?" Jake laughs. Hope jumps. "Step aside," he says to Hope, while grabbing me by the arm and taking me all of seven feet away from Hope and others. He chuckles and practically yells, "Look, that has **got** to be the stupidest thing I have ever heard from you. Easily the stupidest! You didn't shoot the white liquid of life?!? You didn't seed her field?!? You didn't water the flowers? You didn't squirt the love paste? That is the reason we live! That is **why** we live, man. It doesn't get any better than that." He's solidly pounding my shoulder with his fist, practically weeping. Did he just refer to Hope as a "that?"

I can't believe people look at **me** funny.

"Okay, lovers," Cy says, "break it up. I want to show these two something in Todd's farmhouse. And Jake? Buck up."

"Hey Ruth," I call out, "do you think anyone wants some muffins that are in your bag? Hey Tom, aren't you curious what's in the bag you're holding?" I take Hope's gentle hand and head for the old farm-house along with Cy. Others follow us. Right inside is the living room. Greeting us from across the room is Blitzen, the wonder deer.

Cy tells Hope, "The first time Ricky came in here, he looked at that deer's head on the wall and said, 'Wow, that deer must've been really moving to smash through the wall like that!'" Hope laughs and nudges me. "Todd doesn't like it, but whenever he thinks of getting rid of it, he thinks of what Ricky said and cracks up." She waves us upstairs. "This was Melanie's room when she was here. Here's the picture that Yolanda girl was talking about." Cy hands it to Hope.

Hope takes it and stares at it, sitting down on the bed. "I thought I knew this pic-" She stops herself and looks at the room. For the most part, it is a plain room, but one of Melanie's platinum disk certificates is framed on the wall. Hope looks at the bed and gets up off of it, like she shouldn't have been sitting on it.

"It's okay," Cy reassures her, pushing Hope back down by the shoulder.

Hope says, "You seem so comfortable with all of this... But I always thought Melanie was so great. If I wasn't dreaming about being her, I was dreaming about being a friend of hers. And now, here I am, with her friends, sitting on her bed... Becky and Nicky should be here. They've got to see this."

"I understand. I'll get them," Cy says. On her way out, she pushes a button on the electronic frame.

Hope steps around the room looking at a few odd pictures that were left here. Then she notices the movement on the electronic frame. The pictures flash by every four seconds. They were early pictures of Melanie and us that I had gotten together and given to her. The pictures are on a continuous, never-ending loop, and it includes some action sequences. It almost convinces you that you are there. It almost makes you believe that those days aren't long gone. I rub the inside corners of my tired eyes.

Hope turns to me with a great open grin and the grin disappears as she looks into my eyes. "I'm sorry," she says, "this must be tough on you."

"Yeah, kind of, I'm okay," I respond as Nicole and Becky show up at the door without Cy.

Nicole, stepping in first, gazes around the room. Her tube top says, "Yes they're real. Real expensive." She looks at the electronic frame first, then the platinum record. "Cool," she says. Hope shows them the picture from Bolder Rock magazine. "It is a good picture of you," Nicole tells me. "I don't think I'd go ga-ga over it like the girl last night did..."

"I would," Hope winks at me.

"That's because you're helplessly in love," Becky teases Hope.

"Oh," Nicole says and drags Hope into the hall, leaving Becky to shrug at me. What's this about? Then they're back and Nicole is looking at me like I'm from another planet.

"Are you ready?" I ask. They nod. I shut off the electronic frame. We head downstairs and outside, and the wind whips by us. Cy, Todd, Ray, Erix, and others are looking or pointing at some dark, black clouds forming on the horizon. Jake is running around his tent.

Cy turns to me and yells over the wind, "You said rain, right?!? Not the end of the world, right?!?"

"Right! But it wouldn't hurt to say a prayer anyway!" I yell back. I turn to head into Tom's farmhouse.

Behind me, Cy yells, "I have never been able to tell when he's kidding!"

Hope yells back, "He's kidding!"

Inside Ruth is doing dishes. An empty Major Munch box is in the recycling. The muffin bag is empty. "Where did you get the muffins? They were so fresh," Ruth asks.

"I picked them... at a farm nearby."

"I should have Jake slug you."

"I did!"

Tom comes through with an armful of stuff and deposits it in the kitchen. "You found my rocket! Where did you find my rocket?"

"A dog gave it to me," I tell him.

Ruth asks Tom, "Should I have Jake slug him?"

"No, I saw the teeth marks. I believe him," Tom says. Ruth backs away from both of us and gets back to her dishes. "About the pool. Last night I laid on an air mattress in it and stared up at the stars. It was spectacular... the stars slowly spun as I spun in the pool. But I have no place to store a pool. Since you seem to have all the answers, Mr. Smarty-Pants, do you have an idea of what we should do with it?" He laughs. "Does your apartment complex need a pool?"

"No. Possibly and no." I tell them about Ben and his family, how I got the rocket and the muffins, and how I really had no way of repaying their hospitality. "Maybe they'd like a pool. Ruth, is there anything left that I could have for breakfast? All I had was some cereal."

"I'll see," she says.

I step back out when the front hits, and run over to help Jake just as the wind is turning his tent into a sail. Others join us and we get the tent, poles, and stakes packed in record time. We also get the ping-pong table fully put away. The wind lends a hand, closing up some of the lawn chairs for us. Lefty's lab coat becomes a white cape. The wind starts to sort the chairs, but we take over. We establish whose chairs are whose and put them in their proper vehicles. I pack my grill. We dash back inside.

Ruth presents celery and peanut butter for my breakfast. I tell Ruth that an umbrella wouldn't stand a chance in this wind. She looks at me strangely, until I remind her that on Friday she had asked if I had brought an umbrella.

Erix announces from the window that the rain has arrived. My friends start to tease me about my breakfast. I point at Ruth between crunches. They learn that this was Ruth's menu. Nicole leads the investigation of coolers and bags to find a more substantial meal for me. Hope delivers the mixed results. Breakfast turns into a little of everything. Eggs are fried, and Ray goes to pack his things. Erix continues his weather updates.

Outside flashes white, then **boom**! Erix announces the lightning and thunder, redundantly.

Everyone who contributed to my breakfast is thanked, and I head upstairs. Mica is laying down the law by phone. I pack my bags. I notice it's nine as I bag my alarm clock. Hope comes in. "Hi. Did you like last night?" I ask.

"I loved last night. Did you?" she asks grabbing a hold of me.

"Yes." I kiss her. She runs her hand across my stubbly face. "For next time, I'm going to get condoms. Is that okay?" Hope nods. "Are you on the pill?" She shakes her head, no. "Are you willing to go on the pill?"

"Yes. Yes, I am," Hope nods, looking into my eyes.

"Something else. I want to share my life with you. I know I can't tell you everything that happens to me, every dream or discussion or thing that happens, but my plan is to tell you everything of significance, so that you can be part of my life."

"That sounds good."

"Do you think you could do the same?" I ask.

"Yeah, I think so," Hope says with a smile.

"I want to get to know you better."

"That sounds good too. I... I don't want this weekend to end. It has been so much fun," Hope dimples.

"I feel the same way, mostly."

"When do we have to go?" Hope asks looking at my pile of bags.

"I don't know. I suppose we should ask. But a lot of people seem tired. Or maybe I'm projecting my exhaustion on the others."

"I should probably pack then," she says. We head into Hope's room where Nadine is still in bed half-asleep. Now she covers up, unlike last night in the pool. The inconsistency is weird to me. I go back and grab my bags and head downstairs. Will is in his chair talking on the phone to Wendy. People like Will and Mica seem to be reconnecting with their regular lives.

"**Boom!**"

"**That was loud!**" Dan booms. Light flashes, as Ruth takes a picture. The order of the sound and light brings Erix in with a questioning look. Dan approaches me, "**Have you got a minute?**" I nod. "**I've been wondering what you're going to do; how you're going to handle being fired?**" Tom and Lefty converge from opposite directions.

I smile, to ease the concern of my congregating friends. "I don't know. I'll take things as they come I guess."

Lefty interjects, "We were discussing your situation while you surveyed the countryside. Your articulation of randomness, of an absence of predestination, indicates a potential for a veritable plethora of variables. If the predicament lacks predetermination, perhaps there remains no rationale for apprehension."

Erix leaves the living room.

My smile disappears, "What I call pointed perception, provides me with an insight into my options. I can change what I do. Everyone can. I just can't change what others do." I think Tom knows what makes me say that.

"**If,**" Dan booms, "**you need a job and you are willing to move to Chicago, I can put you to work!**"

Slugging the closest of his sky-scraping shoulders, I tell him, "Thanks."

"If you need a job that's closer than Chicago," Tom turns my attention, "let me know." I thank him.

"Before contacting them," Lefty interjects, "there is an experiment with which your assistance would supply immense satisfaction." I nod, since thanking him for considering me a lab rat would only encourage him. How long has Hope been on the stairs? She steps down, sets down three bags, and pulls me by the hand into the dining room. Flipping on the light and shutting the door, a thousand Hopes sit down with a thousand me's.

"You mentioned wanting to get to know me better...," Hope starts, and that's when we notice the mouse. A mouse is moving at about 30 miles per hour, however it has nearly no traction on the mirrored floor, so its relative speed is about two miles per hour. We get up. Hope puts a hand on my chest, "Get me two paper bags." I come back and hand the two bags to her. She opens one and sets the open end in front of the little rodent. The closed bag is used like a snow shovel to plow Speedy into the open bag. Hope closes the bag and makes a move to carry it out. I get the doors for her, as others watch. The storm has settled into a light rain. The air smells like wet hay, wet corn, and wet cows. Hope dashes out in the direction of the barn, opens the bag upside down, shakes the mouse out, and dashes back in. I lend her a towel. She blots herself and then transforms the towel into a cut-rate turban. Several start to follow us back into the dining room, until she stops them and asks them to give us some time alone.

Hope sits us back down, pulls off her turban, and says, "There once was a little girl visiting the coast with her family. She found the ocean waves had washed starfish onto the shore. They were drying up on the rocks. The little girl picked a starfish up and threw it back into the water. She picked up another starfish and threw it back into the ocean. An adult said to her, 'You can't throw all the starfish everywhere back in, so what does it matter?' The child replied, 'It matters to this one,' and she threw it back. Soon, everyone that was with her, joined in, throwing back the starfish. That's me. You can count on me. I want to help. If things go the way you are expecting at Flight Control, I will help you to find a job. If you or you and Ray need a place to stay, I own my duplex. The lower level is currently vacant. Okay? Last weekend this big gorilla said to me that he needed possibilities. I want to offer possibilities. You said upstairs that you want to tell me everything of significance, so that I can be part of your life. I promised to do the same. I want to be part of your life. I want you in mine too. I want to always offer you possibilities, to have you find possibilities in me. In order to do that, I need you to ask me for things. Please, don't just tell me your decisions on things. Please let me in on the decisions and ask me to help."

"Okay. It's a deal," I tell her.

"Are you considering moving to Chicago?" Hope asks me.

"Chicago's great. I love to visit Chicago. But I'm not planning to move back there anytime soon."

"Good. I don't want you to go," she tells me. We hug. We smile at each other. Hope and I, and thousands of people like us, leave the dining room. Everyone else is in the living room. Red, Lefty, and Dan stop talking about me once Hope and I enter the room. Cy, Todd, and Al are discussing a new type of music file, while they check their messages on handheld devices. Ray is keeping people from stepping on his drawings. Mica is cleaning up a spill, while Dexter holds a coffee cup nearby. Ruth is bringing Mica some towels. Becky is on Tom's lap on the hanging chair. Erix and Will are watching the hanging chair move up and down. Nadine is on the stairs with squinty eyes and mussed up hair, watching Jake and Nicole. Jake is up to something so I head us over there.

Jake is right in front of Nicole saying, "I'm not going to hurt you! Put your arms down. Okay, so you're going on a walk through the forest. And as you walk through the forest, the trees go by you." He swishes his palm by her head. "That was a tree. You keep walking and other trees go by." Jake swishes his hands flatly by either side of Nicole's head. Nicole is remaining still but apprehensive. She eyes Hope and I briefly. "You're moving faster through the forest." Jake swishes his hands quickly by Nicole's head. Ruth takes a picture. "Now you're running through the forest!" Jake's hands are a blur as they swish by Nicole's head. "You're running through the forest. You close your eyes!" Nicole closes her eyes. Jake stops swishing his hands and pauses for a moment. Then he slaps his hand into Nicole's forehead, saying, "Dummy, you should **never** close your eyes while running through the forest!"

Everyone laughs while Jake takes off running through the crowd. Nicole takes off after him. Dexter spills again. Ray brushes off a footprint from his drawings, while Ruth suggests that he pick them up off the floor. Jake and Nicole run into the kitchen.

I do a head count, then an individual person-by-person survey. "Where's Joe?"

Hope says, "I haven't seen him since we got back from the play."

"Same here."

"Has anyone seen Joe?"

Jake comes down the piano stairs, two keys at a time, saying, "Hey Nadine, have you ever walked through the forest?"

Nadine hiccups and clears out of the way, saying, "I taught that to you, remember? What a knucklehead!"

"Jake, have you seen Joe since last night?" Nicole is tearing down the stairs.

"No..." Jake starts, and then when Nicole is almost on him he takes off, the crowd gives them room this time. They peel off into the kitchen again. The outside door opens, slams, and opens again.

"I'll check his room," Hope offers and heads up the stairs. Tom offers to help, but Becky won't let him up. Cy announces that she'll check next door.

Lefty, Dan, Will, and Red come over. Lefty smirks, "Why don't you pointedly perceive where Joe is?"

Right here? In front of everybody? I sit on the floor under the stairs. People crowd around. "Dan, crowd dispersal," I suggest.

Dan gets between me and the rest, "**All right! Show's over! Break it up! There's nothing to see here! Move along! That means you, Lefty! Give the man some room! Don't make me haul you in for** loitering!"

Once Dan's voice stops booming–

"**You're all clear!**" Dan booms. "**Are you meditating?**"

"No, I'm vegetating. Shh."

"**Right!**" Dan booms.

Once Dan's voice stops booming, I look at my watch. I think about forming search parties. I relax.

Ruth looks over her shoulder at me as we're running through the drizzly rain and is telling me that they found Joe in the lower level of the barn.

I'm back. I look at my watch. That took no time. I get up.

"He's in the barn," I announce.

"Did you see him?" Lefty asks.

"No, Ruth told me."

"Why did you look at your watch?" Lefty asks. "What role does that watch play in the process?"

I turn to him with a teacher-to-first-grader attitude and say, "It tells me the time." I head out to the barn.

On the way, Ruth catches up to me. "Wait up," she tells me in the drizzle. "How did I know that Joe would be in the barn?"

Cy joins us from the old farmhouse.

"I suggested search parties. Someone apparently found him and told you and you told me. All you said was, 'They found him with the cows in the barn,' while we were running in the direction of the barn."

"But," Ruth spits rainwater, "that's not going to happen now. We already know where he is."

"Right."

"So we aren't going to send out search parties. I won't find out Joe is with the cows in the barn. And I won't tell you." Ruth is getting winded now. I slow us down. "So you won't know."

She just told me again, but in a different way. I shoot Cy a look, but either she's not following this, or she didn't notice. I respond, "Right."

"Wait. That's impossible," Ruth pants, with us just outside the barn.

"Let's get inside first. No, it's not impossible. Impossible is an absence of imagination. Anything can happen. Anything can be. You might think the moon couldn't turn blue; then look at the moon through a blue lens. You might think that pigs can't fly, but that's Gene's pet project. You might think a car can't drive itself, but that's my project. Thinking of time as being linear keeps the concept of time a simple concept, but that doesn't make it true."

Ruth gives me a disagreeing look, "It's a paradox."

"Right. Only a pair of ducks would like this rain."

Cy heads down the ladder to the lower level. As I'm climbing down, she calls, "Over here. Ewww. That's– He stinks!"

All of Cy's observations of the situation are correct. Joe is laying on the floor in the dirt and hay and other stuff. There are empty Yoerg Beer bottles lying about... four of them. One and a half beers are left in the mesh case. It looks and smells foul all around him. A chicken clucks resentment to that observation from some distance away. I approach the body.

Using the words I learned in CPR classes, I ask, "Annie, Annie, are you all right?" No response. "Hey Joe!" No response. I feel his neck for a pulse. I know, I should listen directly for a heartbeat. I'm not in a hurry to get that close. There is a pulse. I shake his shoulder. "Hey Joe!" Joe moves a bit and opens his eyes.

"People in India are trying to sleep," he tells us.

"It is alive!" Ruth exclaims in dramatic horror.

"What's for breakfast?" Joe asks without getting up.

"Peanut butter and celery," I reply. He leans a little and gets sick. Rumor has it that it's not the first time. It must've been that extra half a beer that did him in.

Hay is an all purpose farm tool. Hay can be used for feed or bedding, like it almost was for Joe last night. It can also be used as a cleaning agent. I'm sure that once this stuff catches on, it'll be available at any store.

I spread hay over Joe's foul productions. I drag Joe aside, and I shovel up the hay covered messes. I carry the result out the open doorway. I pitch the hay-mixture away from the path of people and animals. Back inside, the twins have joined us in investigating the wreckage that had been Joe. I lean on the shovel and yawn, as Tom asks Joe if he can stand. Joe replies, "Ever since I was a little, little kid." Joe doesn't move.

A large cow checks on Joe as she passes by.

"She was a real cow..." Ruth comments.

"Udderly," Cy says.

"That's what I herd," Tom says.

"Moo," the cow says.

Hope calls for me from above. I call back, "I'll be right up." I hand off the shovel to Todd on my way. I climb the ladder to find Hope, Nicole, and Becky, their hair matted by the rain.

"Was Joe down there?" Hope asks. I nod. "Uh, Nicole hurt Jake."

"What happened?" I ask Nicole.

Nicole looks different. She's really worried. "I caught up with Jake outside. I started slapping him. He grabbed my arms. I tried to knee him, but he backed away. So all I could do was kick him... between the uprights."

"He laughed at you after he grabbed your arms, right?"

"How did you know? Did you– ?"

"I know Jake. That's what Jake would do. Where is he now?"

"Still in the field, I think," Nicole replies. "I'm sorry. I didn't mean to hurt him."

"I know." Okay so I've got two injured men. Both of their injuries are sort of self-inflicted. The group below can handle Joe. "I'll be right back. I've just got to tell them what's going on, and then we'll try to take care of Jake." I climb down. Joe still hasn't moved or been moved. I let them know that we're going to try to help Jake.

Joe says, "Thank you, you may go, but I may... call you back for further questioning."

I climb back up. "Okay, we're set," I tell them.

"I'm really sorry," Nicole pleads.

"It'll be okay," I respond. We take off into the mist to find Jake. It's misty now; it's no longer a drizzle. On the way, Nicole asks what Jake does for a living. I say, "He's a headhunter."

"A headhunter?"

"Yeah, a corporate headhunter – power broker. He's the operator behind many CEO's." We find Jake where Nicole left him, curled up in a ball. "Hey, Jake, do you need an ambulance?" Jake swears at Nicole. I ask him again. He swears again. I ask him a third time. I've got all day, plus the patience of a Zen hermit. Using my best Zen-hermit-accented voice, I ask, "What is the rock, if it isn't me?"

"No. I'll live."

"Good. Do you think you can walk? It would probably be good to get you inside. She is sorry. She didn't mean to hurt you," I tell him. Jake looks at Nicole. He gets up. "We found Joe. He drank four and a half beers, made a mess, and passed out in the barn."

Jake manages a smile. "Four and a half? And he laughed the liquid laugh?!?" He looks at Hope and doesn't say anything more.

I ask him, "Do you need an arm?"

"Yeah, carry me," Jake snarls. "Get a grip." Jake moves slowly to the farmhouse. We watch the barn group emerge from the mist, also moving slowly, but not as slowly, toward the blue farmhouse. The pace of our two groups reminds me of something.

"What did the snail on the turtle's back say?" I ask the others.

"I don't know," Hope says.

"Whoa!"

"That's the second snail joke you've told me," Hope comments. "How many do you know?"

"All of them," I reply, holding the door for both groups. The invalids are escorted to the kitchen table and chairs. I ask Todd and Cy, "Did anyone give Joe a talk about drinking?" They tell me he's not very coherent yet. Then I ask, "Who's driving him back?"

Joe responds, "But Occifer, I'm serfectly pober. I only had tee martwonies."

"I will," Cy says. "I drove him here."

"Are you sure? You don't want him to yak in your car."

"Someone has to."

"Well, my car isn't worth as much as the rest of the vehicles..." I tell them.

"Here's something I've never understood. Why do you drive such a cruddy car? It doesn't represent you," Cy tells me.

"My car gets me from point A to point B. That's its primary job. My car reliably drives me and I drive it. I can drive the Pony Express through any weather. It keeps me dry. Except the air conditioner doesn't work, so when it's hot, I sweat. In winter, I can use a broom to sweep the snow off the car without having to worry that I will scratch the car up. I can drive it through road salt without being overly concerned about the salt eating away at the remaining metal. It gets good gas mileage, since it's a small car without much metal left on it. It doesn't have oodles of working parts, so it doesn't cost much to maintain. Insurance is cheap since the car is not considered valuable. There isn't any kind of financial investment in it. It has good tires, good brakes, and a reliable battery. What does it matter if it looks cruddy?"

"That car will never attract the babes," Jake tells me. "I can hook you up with something decent."

I turn to Hope, "Do you love me?"

"Yes."

"Do you love me because of my car?"

"No, I love you despite your car."

"Jake is concerned that my car will never attract any babes, other than yourself. I'm sure Jake meant to say, 'other than Hope.'" Jake nods. "Does that concern you?"

Hope laughs, "No."

"Good." Turning to Cy, I ask, "How did I do?"

"I'm not trying to belabor the point, but I don't think your car represents you well. How do you feel when you are driving down the road?" Cy asks.

"Good, bad, happy, sad... annoyed or amused at other traffic... there isn't any one feeling that I stick with because of the car I'm driving. I don't feel like I'm the king of the road, but then... When multiple kings all claim ownership of the road, it often leads to road battles. Right Jake?" Jake stares without acknowledgment. "Two big ol' sport-utility trucks are at a light. Yours is longer. The other one is taller, looking down at you, and revving its engine. Do you ignore it because you both have a right to be driving on the road? Or is there some form of superiority that must be proved? Newspapers should cover road royalty issues: 'License plate MN409 is a bad ass truck, however MN500 has some heavy-duty, kick-ass, hearing-impaired speakers...' If I had all the time in the world to create AutoDrive, it would be great to give it multiple driving styles. There would be the Old Lady On Board style, which couldn't drive faster than ten miles per hour. Or the Lose The Paparazzi style, which would try to ditch any tails, a great option for AutoDrive taxi cabs. The ambulance style would be fairly straightforward. Maybe there would even be a Road King style which would rev the engine at stoplights and then peel out. Of course, the special driving styles would not be standard on all AutoDrive cars; they would cost extra. Insurance companies would probably charge extra too." To Cy, I continue, "But you said you didn't think my car represents me, right? I don't think it does either. What if everybody's cars actually represented the driver? The fire chief's car would look like it's on fire..."

"Or a fire hydrant," Hope adds.

"Yeah. A cinematographer's car would look like the cinematographer is riding on a camera boom. A grocer's car would look like a shopping cart. A baker's car would look like a cake. My car would look like a car, without a driver."

Cy asks, "Is that the way you see yourself?"

Jake laughs, "Yeah, let's try to figure Ricky out..."

My face winces and my head shakes, "No, that's my job – a car that drives itself."

"Does your job represent you that much?"

"I don't know. Pick on somebody else."

Al asks, "What should we do about the pool?"

"Drain it," Jake says.

"Ricky has a plan," Ruth says. "Tell them your plan." These people must like to hear me talk when I'm deliriously tired.

I retell the story, "I'm walking this morning and a dog named Ben meets up with me and leads me over to a farmhouse where I talk with Ben's family who ask if we were firing missiles at them yesterday morning."

"They said that?!?" Tom asks. "You didn't mention that either. They actually asked if we were firing missiles at them?"

I think for two seconds. "Technically, they asked if I knew anything about a missile being shot over there. They didn't technically say 'firing missiles.'"

"Close enough."

"So then I apologized about the rocket and asked if it had damaged anything. I didn't know. Maybe it could've hit a chicken... Chicken Little. If something had been damaged, I would have followed Tom's request and blamed it on Todd... But no, Ben had brought it in, so they got it for me, and an old woman gave me the muffins you had this morning, and she slapped my face repeatedly for shooting at them."

Jake cracks up. "I wish I could've seen that! Wake me the next time you're going to go on a walk to get slapped by an old woman. That's classic. How old was she?"

The door opens behind me. "Ancient," I say, turning to see an old woman in a hooded cape come in.

"Older than me?" she asks, pulling off her hood.

"Mom!" shouts Jake, Nadine, Ruth, the twins, and someone else.

Avatrice Gaea, known as mom to many of us, pulls off her cape, drapes it across my shoulder and hugs Nadine, asking her, "Have you been a good girl?" Jake coughs loudly. "I'll get to you in a moment, Jakie."

"I've been good," Nadine says, followed by a near-coughing attack by Jake.

Avatrice squeezes Nadine and releases her and moves over to hugging Ruth. "How are you, Ruthie? Are people giving you enough attention?"

"**Mom!**" Ruth protests.

"Oh yes, that's right, you kids have secrets now... Who's this?" she asks, peering at Joe's face resting on the table. "He needs to eat some honest food, food of the earth."

"That's Joe," Todd tells her.

Avatrice steps around to Todd and pinches his cheek. "Todd, are you taking good care of your little brother?" Todd grins at the little brother reference, and nods. Avatrice moves to squat down beside Cy and takes Cy's hand. "Cy darling, are you caring for your responsibilities?" Cy's eyes arch over to me quickly like I'm going to give her some answer.

"Yes. And Todd and I just started seeing each other," Cy mentions.

Avatrice grabs a hold of Todd's hand. She closes her eyes, while holding the couple's hands. We watch as her nodding head ripples the patterned silks of her shirt. "This is," she says, just "this is." She turns to Will and Al and turns back to all of us. "So many gifts here. So many gifts. The world awaits you," she says stepping over to Erix on a step-stool. She shows us a blue marble, painted to look like the Earth and hands it to Erix. We watch Erix examine the world. In a lightning move, he gets off, sets the Earth spinning on the table, and returns to the step-stool. We watch the northern hemisphere move counter-clockwise.

"Who are you?"

"I – I'm... Ray," Ray shakes her hand.

"Are you sure? It's nice to meet you Ray. Avatrice Maka Gaea. You can call me, Mom, if you want."

"I've heard so much about you."

"Some of it might be true. Tell me, what has been the best part of this weekend?"

"Drawing Nicole, here, as Glory Girl, a uh, comic book character."

Avatrice turns to Nicole. "I'm sorry, dear, I didn't see you there." Avatrice reaches her hand out and pulls Nicole closer to the table. Avatrice reads Nicole's pink tube top and smiles as Nicole blushes. "Bare your soul. Behind your clothes and your body, you bare your soul. More than flesh or costume, your soul is the glory, girl." Avatrice drops to a whisper, "Your secret is out. Care. You and your new friends." I'm not sure I got all that. Nicole's face and chest are blotchy pink, nearly matching her shirt.

Tom stands as Avatrice approaches and gives her a hug. "You're looking well, Mom. I'm glad you came. We've had a good weekend... memories have been shoved aside by some great experiences and new close friends. How do you like the new house?"

"You wasted your money." Her words wound Tom. "Such a big house and you are all crowded in this one room... together as you all should be. Are you watching out for your older brother?" Avatrice asks.

"Always. He rattles around in my head like a marble in a tin can." Tom turns to introduce Becky. "This is Becky, a new friend. I've been trying to find a moment this morning to ask her out sometime this week."

Avatrice grabs Becky's shoulder. "What do you think, Becky? Will you be busy this week?"

"Not that busy. I'd love to go out with you Tom. What about Wednesday night?"

"What time?"

"Seven?"

"I'll pick you up at seven. Where do you live?"

"Just south of Lake Weago. Do you have a pen?"

Avatrice steps around Becky's chair squeezing her shoulder again in the process. Avatrice rattles Lefty's test tubes, shaking him. "Hello Melvin. How is the scientist?"

"I'm well. I am on the verge of a bio-tech breakthrough."

"Let me know when you have broken through. I want to be there for you. How is the prosthetic right hand? I see you were able to get it in a closer skin color."

"It is satisfactory."

"Do you mind it when they call you Lefty?"

"No. I know it is meant well."

"You are well," Avatrice confirms. She looks at Dan poking him in the ribs, "You know, at home we have a 20 foot tall, wooden statue of you." She turns to Dexter and Mica.

"Hello, Avatrice," Mica says. "How was your trip?"

Avatrice says, "The road in wasn't bad at all. If you want to take off to get back home early, everyone will understand. How are your kids?"

"There is a big mix-up at home over the schedules... Are you sure that now is a good time to go?" Dexter generally asks, clearing his throat. Everyone reassures them and says good-bye. Dexter and Mica Bucko leave.

Avatrice steps up to Red and says, "We'll talk outside in a moment. It is not so important how we came to be as who we make ourselves to be." She hugs Jake, and Jake hugs her back. "Have you been good, Jakie?" Most of the room suddenly breaks out in a coughing fit.

"Yes," Jake snarls toward those who cough.

"Your mask of false bravado hides you from true meaning in your work and your life. These people can bring value to you and your efforts. With their help, you can positively shape..." Avatrice stops her thought and turns to me. "Now." She pulls me up by the hands. She hugs me and takes her cape from my shoulder. "Even relaxed, you're not relaxed. I heard you had a dream Friday night. You didn't tell your friends about it."

I shake my head, disagreeing, " I told them that I learned I lost my job."

She stares into my eyes. "Is that it?"

"No."

"Is this Hope? Hello, Hope. I have heard about you. I am Avatrice Maka Gaea. You can call me, Mom, if you wish. Hope, ask Ricky about the rest of his dream."

"Please tell me, and Mom, about your dream," Hope asks.

"I had a dream, a pointed perception, based on us not staying together this weekend. From that premise, this winter, I get into an accident and die in a snowbank."

Hope pauses. Hope gets angry, "Significance. We agreed to talk about what is significant. How is your death not significant?"

"Because the premise is gone. We're together. At least... we were together..."

"Yes, we're together. But let's get this straight – death is significant, right?" Hope's forehead wrinkles. I hate it when her forehead wrinkles.

"Right."

Hope turns to Avatrice and turns back to me. "Was there anything else?"

"No, I think that's it."

"Anything from last night?"

"No. I didn't sleep."

"Oh. Now I understand why you didn't sleep," Hope says.

Avatrice takes our hands and closes her eyes. "Let now be forever." She opens her eyes. "It's green! Everything is so green outside! It's beautiful!"

"Buckets of rain and drizzle will do that," Todd says.

"Who's hungry? Let's go out and have a picnic!" Avatrice exclaims.

"A picnic?!?"

"It's a beautiful day." Avatrice takes our hands and leads us to the door. She opens it. The sun is blindingly bright. The dark nimbostratus storm clouds have been replaced with big fluffy pillow clouds, lots of pillow clouds. The birds finish a chorus and start another verse. "I think I have enough lunch for everyone. Jakie and Ruthie, could you give me a hand?" They spread out a large blanket and open a cooler. The food is spread out. The lunch is hot venison steaks, blueberry wojapi (frybread with a blueberry sauce), grapes and plums, floral wild salad (with marigold petals, rose petals, and dandelion flowers), wild rice hot-dish (casserole), and wahumapa wasna.

"Mom, what's wahumapa wasna?" Dan booms.

Avatrice turns and says, "Vegetarian-style corn balls."

Jake comments, "I didn't know corn had balls." Jake gets hit with a wahumapa wasna. I look at it.

Avatrice tells me, "Stop analyzing and start eating."

Having some salad, I comment for Jake's benefit, "I didn't know pine had nuts." The meal fills us up without making us full. Ruth takes some pictures causing others to get out cameras and take pictures. Ultimately pictures are taken of others taking pictures.

Because of Dan, I pick up part of a conversation that is otherwise whispered about me. I hear Dan blast, "The financial backers of Flight Control?" So I turn to look at who's talking about me. It's Cy, the twins, Jake, and Dan. Tom asks me, "Who are the financial backers of Flight Control?"

I list off, "Big Rig Transportation, Corral Motors, Double Bubble, Packard Motors, Protection Underwriters, West Bank, and Cutesy Entertainment."

"Why Cutesy Entertainment?" Ruth joins in.

"Captive audience in the vehicle. When the driver becomes a passenger, there is a new need, supposedly, for entertainment," I tell her.

We clean up or stretch out, Hope rubs my shoulders, and Avatrice pulls Red aside to talk with him. I watch Ray pack his art in my car, which I then repack to reduce the chances of the boards and canvas becoming neck-targeting projectiles during the trip back. He and Avatrice watch. I think he tells her about Kelly. In the midst of packing, a volleyball comes out and is volleyed between Tom and Todd. Ruth and Will join in, followed by Cy and Becky and everyone else, except Avatrice and Red. We form a circle. We start counting the number of volleyball hits without letting the ball drop to the ground. We count as a group. For a while 19 is the most we can get to before the ball drops on the ground. Then we get up to 34, which includes some phenomenal hits for many people, including Erix. Ultimately Red joins in, and the twins and Avatrice step out to go talk with the neighbors about the pool. We continue playing until we're exhausted.

Hope hugs and kisses me and asks me to come over and sleep at her place. I decline. She asks if she could come over to keep an eye on me.

"I should be okay," I tell her.

"Then why didn't you sleep last night?"

"Number one: because I liked holding you and watching over you. And B: because I didn't want to dream I was playing volleyball and wind up hitting you repeatedly," I tell her.

"Could I hold you and watch over you?"

"Not today... not tonight, but I'll give you a rain check." Hope nods. Ruth moves us, adjusts us, clears Jake out from behind us, and gets a few pictures of Hope and I. So does Cy. And Tom. And Nicole.

The pool group has made arrangements with the neighbors to take the pool. We say good-bye to everyone and hug everybody, more or less. I struggle to find my map for Ray. He gives up and looks to someone else for a map. Avatrice leaves. I find my map – what a relief – and direct him back over. We talk over our route and others get involved. Nadine leaves. I look the place over one more time and wave to Hope. Nicole drops the top and drives off, taking Hope and Becky with her. My freshly-washed Pony Express starts on the third try. Ray is next, on his motorcycle. Al dips his fingers in a bowl of water and flicks the water at my windshield, blessing my journey. I follow Ray. In my rearview mirror Cy, Jake, Dan, and the twins hold a conference as they watch me go.

The bumbles and flutter-byes work over their freshly-watered flowers, stirring up pollen, like dust at a construction site. I crane my head back to look at the new pale blue farmhouse, which had become a home to all of us this weekend. I glance at the field below where we played Capture The Flag. I feel a tremendous sense of loss, that the record of this weekend has been captured and there is no going back, except within my memories... memories that seem so limited because they only go one way... they only have one solution. The memories are fixed.

Never live in the past. There isn't any future in it.

Bam! Even at, what, seven miles per hour, I have to watch for ruts. I just burped up wahumapa wasna. I figured that would come up again.

The convertible and motorcycle are now long gone as I pay closer attention to the road. I'm not exactly using all my cylinders. Getting back on pavement speeds me up. I notice signposts passing by at regular intervals like a metronome. Sign. Sign. Sign. Sign. Sign. My tired eyes squint in the sunshine. I put on sunglasses. My eyes squint anyway.

If I don't wake up, this short trip will seem like forever. The odds of a tired or distracted driver getting into an accident are higher than an unimpaired driver. I crank down my window at Swede Ravine, making a pedestrian think I want to talk. I wave him off. I slow up on Old Hull Road when a gang of chickens cross the road. They must have gotten out in the storm. But why would the chickens cross the road? Whoa. A black cow crosses the road. If I believed in luck, this would mean that I could be faced with bad dairy products today. That means a vanilla milkshake is out for this afternoon or this evening.

I pass a slow-moving truck.

I don't believe in luck. I don't know what luck is. If there were such a thing, I think I could consider myself fairly lucky. Probabilities are what I understand. Probabilities are the odds that certain things will happen. You record occurrences and draw conclusions. If you look at the number of Minnesota blizzards and where and when they occur, you can better understand the probabilities of future occurrences. The chances are that there will be a blizzard in January. This is Minnesota.

Luck, I have been told, is influenced by four-leaf clovers and carrying a lucky rabbit's foot, which couldn't possibly be lucky for the rabbit.

There are places in Minnesota that are insulated from blizzards by their location in a river valley or their location near Lake Superior. There are other places that due to their elevation or their location near Lake Superior get dumped on, like having glaciers fall from the sky. One minute it is typical city life; the next minute it's hello white mountain. So probabilities are influenced by your location in relation to where blizzards occur.

Probabilities are influenced by related factors that effect the odds of an occurrence. Someone might say I am lucky to be kissed by a wonderful woman like Hope. I tell her I love her, and she kisses me. Telling her that I love her increases the odds that I will be kissed. That's not the reason I tell her that I love her; it's because it's true. Honesty helps the odds of being kissed. Except if you hate someone, in which case you still would feel lucky that you aren't kissed by them. So I take that back, honesty doesn't help the odds of being kissed. Honesty helps the odds of having things turn out well. At least that is my experience.

H-O meanders. It weaves up and down and around the hills stitching its way across the countryside and skirting several lakes like a comforter on a fluffy bed. This is beautiful country! A grasshopper splats in the middle of my windshield.

Windshield wipers in this part of the world could use a scrubbing option. Wiping a splat that used to be grasshopper just smears the splat. Windshield washer fluid can keep the splat wet, but it can't do much else. Maybe in winter the scrubber becomes a scraper. A self-scraping car! Around here, that's almost better than a self-driving car.

Al waves as he passes me. From Ruth's truck, Will waves and takes my picture, while Erix watches. I watch them disappear into a small valley ahead, reappear, and disappear again.

There are no cars on the highway behind me and none in front. I pass through a forest of pine trees stretching straight up 25 to 30 feet. The sunlight flickers rhythmically through the evenly spaced trees. Only the upper third of each tree have branches. A stray oak tree limb is in the road. I pull off and pull it off. I have the strength of ten men. Just as I get up to speed again a horn blares from a thunderous, enormous-gigantic truck baring down on me. It fills all of my mirrors, practically blotting out the sun and the sky. He pauses to yell something at me as he passes. That was Jake. He speeds off alone. Didn't he have passengers when he came in on Friday? Oh yeah, Will swore off riding with him, and Minion was taken back early. I wonder how many tanker trucks it takes to fill Jake's truck up.

After a few intersections, the highway fills up. A small truck pulls up by me. It's Todd and Dan. What, is everyone going to pass me? Dan yells clearly through my window that he had a great weekend and asks if I did. People in several vehicles ahead turn to listen to our exchange. I smile and nod my head yes. He smiles back and says, "Good." They speed off. Traffic behind me that had been going a steady speed with me speed up to pass me and look at just who it was that had a good weekend.

Getting off the highway and onto the side streets, I pull into the Whisper Willows apartment complex, where chaos rules. A caravan of followers trail me, as I carry my loads into my apartment and take my stove back to its storage locker. Most of it gets piled into my bedroom. The next door neighbors are shouting again. Ray thanks me for inviting him this weekend. It's mid-afternoon, but I set my alarm clock for an early morning. I shake a white origami frog that was resting on my bed, and it turns into a sheet that I pull over me. I crash into sleep. I dream a thousand dreams.

I wake up in a Latin-swing mood. My legs are moving involuntarily. The band downstairs is playing Latin-swing music. This is a departure for them. Is it a visiting band? No, they are just as bad with Latin-swing as their regular off-beat music. Someone, somewhere told them that you can compensate for bad with loud. Whoever that was needs to be a witness to the result. Meanwhile the gutter ball upstairs tells me that the elephants have not yet mastered the curve ball that bowlers throw. The bowling ball should curve into the lead pin, pin number one, to have a shot at a strike.

I turn on my light to find that I've launched my sheet off my bed. It is now a cover for my pile of weekend stuff... out of sight, out of mind. My clock says it's 8:32pm. That's enough sleep for now. I'll try again in a while. I get up to find that I'm still dressed. That's handy. There's a note on my door from Ray that Hope called.

Out in the living room, Ray has every light on he could find, including the photographer's floodlight which blows the rest away, like turning on your headlights while driving through the sun. He and his paints are surrounded by Nicole As Glory Girl masterpieces and does not notice me come in or go back out to the kitchen around the corner. I grab a banana. By the time some produce gets to Minnesota, it has stickers and tags from all over the world. That's one well-traveled banana. We have many a banana, and they all decided to get ripe at once. That's what bananas do. I can't just have a banana. I need something else. I grab the bag of leftover wahumapa wasna and toss it, bag and all, into the microwave for 30 seconds. One of these days I'll have to have some meat. I could eat out. I plop down in the living room with my food.

"Good morning," Ray tells me, as the sunlight takes its final full-twisting dive down to submerge below the horizon, with a two-point-five degree of difficulty.

"You know? There could be a market for banana flavored wahumapa wasna. It's delicious and nutritious, a wholesome-natural snack."

"Thanks for the commercial. Did you get the message that Hope called?"

"Yup. Thanks." I take my wholesome-natural snack to my room, change, use the bathroom, wash my face, and I notice that the shouting from next door has been raised to a new level. **Slam!** That was their door. Now there's a knocking at our door. Uh... Who could that be? I change back from shorts to jeans, and I get the door.

The guy in front of me has a thick heavy brow, a face full of dark stubble, and a slouch in a dirty shirt. I've never met the guy next door. I never thought that I'd live next door to Australopithecus. If evolution is a process, then so is devolution, apparently. I wonder if it talks. "D'you have a TV recorder?" it asks, wetly.

Wiping the spit from my face, I reply, "Nope."

It gapes at me dumbly as if it has never before run into a negative, "You don't?"

"No," I repeat. It just stands there. Maybe a visual would help. "Look," I say pointing, "that's the TV set." We stare at the little black and white set, with its rabbit ears tucked in, a layer of dust, and its cord neatly wound in back. I turn back to the neighbor. "Anything else?" It shakes its head. I hear rattling over the general noise.

"Could you turn the music down?"

I explain, "It's not from us; it's from the apartment below us." Now it's totally confused. I think about explaining how difficult it would be to turn down a live band. I decide not to go there. It turns to go. And I close the door. I head into my room telling myself that apartment buildings are a community. That was a community moment. I was sharing my knowledge with my neighbor in this community. It is complex, this apartment complex.

Apartments are called apartments because the occupants are Meant to be Apart.

I am still thinking about the role of apartment buildings in the wider global community when I call Hope. She answers. "Hi Hope! Listen if you ever run into someone who is feeling down, someone who is feeling like they don't have much to offer the world, someone who is feeling inferior, please have them come live in an apartment complex. I guarantee instant results."

Silence. She says, "This is Faith. I'll get Hope."

"Oh." Oops. Now I'm feeling down.

"Hi Ricky."

"Is this Hope?" I confirm.

"Yes, I hear you just started in talking to Faith."

"Yeah, sorry."

"It's okay. Faith told me a little of what you were saying. Could you tell me what you told her?"

I mentally play back what I had said, since I never really thought it out. "I said, 'If you ever run into someone who is feeling down, someone who is feeling like they don't have much to offer the world, someone who is feeling inferior, please have them come live in an apartment complex. I guarantee instant results.'"

Hope cracks up. "I'm sure Faith appreciated hearing that recommendation," Hope tells me. "Have you slept?"

"Yes, from 3:49 to 8:32."

Hope is laughing again. "8:32 huh? Are you sure you couldn't have slept 'til 8:33 or 8:34?" She seems loopy.

"I probably could've slept longer, but I think the neighbors had other plans."

"Is it loud?"

"**What?!?**" I ask, kidding her.

"I say, '**Is it loud?!?**'" she kids me right back.

"Yes, but after this call I plan to head right to sleep. I want to be awake for tomorrow."

"Good plan. Hey, I wanted to tell you that we all wanted to thank you for inviting us to go out to Tom's place. We all had a great time. We came back and told Faith about it. She thought we were going to be involved in a drunken orgy..."

"Not exactly..."

"...and when we told her about playing games and teasing and going into town for ice cream and the play, she was sorry she missed out."

"You told her everything?"

"Not exactly. The good stuff. I told her about the promises we made to each other. She liked that. Becky told her about the spider." Hope pauses. "It was good to meet your friends and be with them. I feel like I've known them forever. And I miss being around them, and being around you, all the time. It was very nice. Did you like having us there?"

"Yes. I loved having you there."

"There is something else I've been wanting to tell you," Hope starts. "No matter what happens tomorrow, I want to help you. You have many good friends who care a great deal about you. And while I think it's great that you can all get along so well..." Was Hope with the same people I was with? I seem to recall some embarrassing behavior. "...I don't want to get left out because I was the ninth person to offer you a place to stay or something. I believe in you, and I want to help any way I can. I should be home by four tomorrow. Would you call me as soon as you can after that tomorrow? Am I asking too much?"

"No, I will call you. I am right now writing myself a note... call Hope, Monday after four... and I am... taping it to my bedroom door. I have a great memory, but if that fails me somehow, I've got the note." Pause. "What else?"

"What do you mean?"

"You seem to have a list of things to tell me," I comment.

"Do you mind?"

"Not at all!"

"Well, Becky really likes Tom and wants to know if there is anything she should know about him."

"He has a twin brother."

"Besides that!"

"No. Nothing serious. Nothing worth breaking my rule of not talking about friends behind their backs. He's a good guy."

"Since you don't want to talk about your friends behind their backs, I won't mention what Nicole said."

"You can tell me..."

"Ricky, I don't want to be responsible for having one of your rules broken..."

"Tell me..."

"Are you sure your friendship code can survive this crisis?"

I look at the phone, trying to look through the phone. "Tell... me... I think I can guess who she likes. She likes Jake."

"Ooh, you guessed wrong. Nicole understands Jake. Jake is the most like all the other guys she's known, but the rest of you... In her words, 'I had always wondered where the decent guys hung out. I thought they were a myth.'"

I laugh. "A myth. She's a riot. Rumor is, that girls like bad boys."

"No," Hope's voice lowers, "it's the bad boys that seek the girls out, while the good boys are hidden off somewhere... maybe waiting for the girls to knock on their doors or something. Girls practically have to deliver pizzas to meet guys. As a teacher, I get to meet other teachers, a few administrators, and parents. Even if we are talking about the random single father courageously bringing up a kid or more, and even if he happens to be a good guy... he's got a kid. He's already got a family. He's already got all that he can handle. Maybe he's Mister Amazing and can handle it all. Even if he can handle it all, what kid wants a pseudo-mother stepping in to confuse the holiday events, who happens to also be a teacher at their school, and more specifically, in their class? That leaves other teachers and administrators. Most of them are women, maybe because of the nurturing role of motherhood. The few men are mostly married." Mostly married? "The ones that are left have plenty of single women to choose from, assuming that workplace romances are a good idea. Do you think workplace romances are a good idea?"

"No."

"I didn't think you would. And I agree with you, believe me. But that means a woman has an even more difficult time trying to be around you in a potentially romantic setting."

"Are you mad at me?"

"No. It's just that... Nicole is right. We found all the decent guys in one spot. You want to believe that the right person is out there. You want to believe that there is someone who could love you and you could love. You rule out the bar, the church, the laundromat, the grocery store... but then you go anyway, thinking that just maybe Mister Wonderful is there, jumping up and down and waving to you. What you find instead is that yes, there are some people that are interested in you, but most of them are so busy trying to impress you with their posturing and bragging and pretentiousness, that they can't imagine talking with you like a real person, to see if you actually have common ground, common interests and beliefs. So you try a dating service, which can be like dialing a phone number at random. They have you fill out a questionnaire. How do you answer the age of the person you are interested in? How do you list important interests? 'They have to like long walks on the beach.' What if there is no public access to their lake? It kind of diminishes the possibility of long walks."

I try to play along, "Right. You try to just wander through, 'Excuse me while I cut across your backyard again. Oh, your neighbor put up a fence? Nice and sturdy construction. No gate.'"

"So what do you say? How do you weed out the liars? The people who claim to be single but aren't. The people who claim to be of a weight or age or height or anything else that they aren't. How do you find someone like you?"

"I have never tried a dating service."

"Right," she says, and she stops talking.

I pull my sheet off the pile and lie down on my bed with my phone to my head. I stare up at my ceiling. "Hope, are you okay?"

"You don't know how difficult it was to find you," she finally says.

"I was the ape. Well, at Sharon's..."

"Right. I was at Sharon's to meet you. We were introduced and then you went back to your conversation."

"What?!?" I sit up. "Wait. I didn't– How were you there to meet me? How did you know I was there?"

"My mom is one of Cy's clients..." Hope says.

"Cy set us up? Cy the jealous ex-girlfriend set us up?!? I've got to sit down. I **am** sitting down. Now wait, was I rude to you at Sharon's? I remember Sharon introducing us and then my trying to include you in the conversation. If I was rude to you I apologize, but I don't think I was rude to you."

"You weren't rude, but you certainly weren't interested in me."

"I was there because of the rally. We were reacting to the political extremists."

"I know. You are the guy at the grocery store just trying to grocery shop, wondering why this lady keeps getting in your way. You are the man at the laundromat who is just there to wash his clothes." I nearly interrupt to mention that I use my apartment building's machines. "You are hard to reach."

"Hope, I'm sorry. If I had known you were looking for me, I would have invited you over sooner or asked you to the zoo sooner. How can I make it up to you? Do you want me to start hitting the bars or the laundromats or hanging out at churches after hours?"

"No. Please don't. I just wish we had met sooner."

"So do I, Hope."

"You'll still call me tomorrow, right?"

"Yes, I will Hope."

"I love you, Ricky."

"I love you too, Hope."

"Good night. I hope tomorrow will go as well as it can."

"Thank you. Good night."

"Good night."

20

The End Of The World

I wake up before six, and my alarm clock is still snoring. I can't tell the time exactly because its little arms are folded. I lie back and relax to play through the start of work today. I am in a Thursday meeting on a Monday morning at ten. I checked my watch on my way in. There are several guests in the meeting. On my way in, I introduce myself to one of them and make uncharacteristic small talk. I replay entering the conference room. This time I pick someone else to meet and greet. I keep replaying my entrance until I have met all the visitors.

I play the meeting long enough to have Carl announce some hot plans for the marketing of AutoDrive. I ask him about the name AutoDrive and he mentions that they ran into legal difficulties in trademarking Chauffeur, so it's AutoDrive. He explains that we will be showing AutoDrive off in a few weeks, just having it drive a few blocks without a driver. He gives me a rough draft of the presentation and asks me to look it over. I look at it. AutoDrive in a Pegasus Coup cruising through downtown – very fancy. I try to keep an open mind. I try to figure any way of making it happen. There is no way. I confirm his timetable. I set the draft down and I stand up. "Carl, there is no way this could be done. We could simulate AutoDrive behavior by having the car ride a flatbed in front of a truck. We've done that before. People would see the car turning its wheels to get around corners..."

"No. That's not AutoDrive!"

"AutoDrive is not ready for anything near what you are proposing."

"Figure out how to do it! That's what you do! You have it in you."

"It can't be done."

Carl's temples and neck veins are throbbing. "You can't do it?!?"

"No one can do it."

"You're fired!"

I walk out. I check my watch. It's 10:21am. I open my eyes. I'm back in my room. I check my watch. It's 6:06am. I prevent my alarm from going off and slowly get ready for my impending doom. I wear a tie. The sky is overcast with a gray false ceiling, installed without openings for light.

An old man is up ahead at an intersection, trying to get his bike started to cross the road. He's sitting and trying to petal. He straddles the bar and tries to kick off. He's veering into traffic. He steers, but the bike is angling sideways to the pavement. I pass him, giving him a wide berth, as he uprights his bike again. A block away I look back in the rearview mirror, and he's still struggling.

I have a last meal at Yesterday's Diner and pick up an assortment of pastries at the Ovens Hot Bakery. University Avenue construction has what is normally a two-lane road, two-lanes one-way and two-lanes the other way, down to just two-lanes going opposite ways. The double-yellow line is now on my right. Little orange cones separate the traffic heading opposite directions. I can only imagine how I would explain this to AutoDrive. The construction has apparently helped cause an accident that has pulled off into the construction site transforming it into an accident investigation site. The front car was smashed in back so that there is no longer a rear bumper, tail lights, license plate... and the trunk is crumpled. The car is still drivable, but AutoDrive wouldn't work without its rear sensors.

As I'm driving along, a plane crosses my path at an angle so that its headlights are tilted toward me.

It is coming in for a landing just past the highway. I empathize with her passengers. They can't see the runway. They can't see the airport. They have as much of an understanding of how things are going as I would if I tried driving my car while just looking out one of the side windows... without mirrors. All they really have is faith. Faith in a stranger piloting them while they look out the side window wondering how close the plane is supposed to come to those houses, and by the way, the loose mortar on that chimney could lead to leaks.

I fill my gas tank and still arrive at work early. I unlock, open up, and flip on lights. Wendy comes in early and tells me that Will told her that I had a dream that I would be fired. She says that I am AutoDrive. She tells me that they would be insane to fire me. I thank her for her support and tell her not to worry. Cooelle comes into my office and tells me that she checked with the university. Mike is not a student; Mike is not in their internship program. New paperwork lands in my in-box. If I didn't care about it before, I'm certainly not going to care about it now. I walk around and overly encourage my employees, like it is my last chance to do so. Wendy seems a little shaken up. Cooelle seems to be wondering how I am going to kill Mike. I work for a while with Scott and Clarence. We are working through a vector equation with two non-parallel vectors lying in a plane, when I quietly duck away to my meeting. I drop off a note at personnel that Mike is not an intern; he was hired by Flight Control under false pretenses.

Nearing the conference room, Heidi nearly bumps into me, "I– I was just coming to get you. We have a–"

"I know." I hand her a similar note about Mike. I walk into the conference room and greet everyone by name, throwing off their Monday mornings more than ever.

Carl starts the meeting off by announcing some hot plans for the marketing of AutoDrive. He explains that we will be showing AutoDrive off in a few weeks, just having it drive a few blocks without a driver. He gives me a rough draft of the presentation and asks me to look it over. I look at it. AutoDrive in a Pegasus Coup cruising through downtown. I read and re-read the draft. I try to figure any way of making it happen. There is no way. I confirm his timetable. I set the draft down and I stand up. "Carl, there is no way this could be done. We could simulate AutoDrive behavior by having the car ride a flatbed in front of a truck. We've done that before. People would see the car turning its wheels to get around corners. Of course, that's not AutoDrive."

"No. That's not... AutoDrive," Carl repeats.

"AutoDrive is not ready for anything near what you are proposing."

"Figure out how to do it! That's what you do! You have it in you. The other day you mobilized the entire office to find something you needed."

"It can't be done."

Carl's temples and neck veins are throbbing. "You can't do it?!?"

"No one can do it."

"You're fired!"

I walk out. I check my watch. It's 10:21am. In the hallway, I'm walking by questioning-but-wordless faces, familiar, dream-like, blurry heads. A thought lightens my step, "It's no longer your burden. It's no longer your responsibility." What had been a reflex move – heading back to my office – becomes very purposeful. My walk quickens in pace to a near jog.

In my office, Mike is leaning over my growling computer. "What are you doing in here?!?" I bark. He looks around quickly and says, "I–"

I reject his "I." I have too many I's as it is. "Get out." He moves out from by my chair and goes around to the other side of my desk like he's not going to leave. He's wrong. "Get out," I tell him, and he leaves. My computer is still growling until I key in what it wants. Then I give watchdog a command: shred.

They have my reports. They have the schematics and the programs. I grab a cardboard box from the hall and take down the Founding Fathers plaque from the wall. Unlocking my desk, I find that the telltale intern managed to open one drawer of my desk, the used blank adhesive notes drawer from the time my staff covered the office with them. I save few mementos. A withered, uninflated beach ball gets tossed in. I fill the small box. I leave the hot chocolate packets for the next person. It'll be winter... someday. I lock my computer. Carl Dumas walks in as I pull keys from my key chain.

"What's all this?" Carl asks pointing to my box of belongings. At least he looks like Carl, but he seems to know nothing about having fired me. Is there such a thing as an evil twin? And if so, which one is this one? "Are you walking out on us?" this one asks.

"You fired me," I state the obvious.

"What? What does it take to motivate you? Nobody has been fired. The question is... are you going to quit?"

"So you want me to quit?!?"

"No one likes a quitter; quitters can't get unemployment compensation." He pats the box of belongings saying, "I want you to accelerate AutoDrive." Accelerate AutoDrive... accelerate AutoDrive... he's making a joke, right? "I don't want you to quit, mister; I want you to– " then he jerks a bit, spasms, his body convulses, shakes, and quakes to the point that I'm not sure he knows which end is up. And he bursts out, **"Get it done!** I want you to get AutoDrive done." Picking up my cardboard box, he dumps the contents on the desk with a crash and tosses aside the box. The glass of the Founding Fathers plaque breaks against the Failed Experiments line. "I need you to say yes. I need you to work through the decisions and the choices for solutions. I need AutoDrive to be done. Now." He puts his foot down on a metal paperweight which launches into a sandbag, knocking it out of position, breaking the dam, and flooding the office with paperwork, streams shooting into the hallway. Amidst the flow he picks up the uninflated beach ball, shakes it at me, and shouts, "You are going to put away your smugness and your weekend plans and get the job done!" He pants to catch his breath which only slightly muffles the sound of a computerized dog gnawing on computerized documents and the sound of papers settling. "You have it in you. I've seen it. The other day you mobilized the entire office to find something you needed." Uh? Oh yeah, the power line. That's his connection to reality. He drops the ball. Is he through with the jobation? I pick up the pieces of my belongings and put them back in the box. I take the golden bumper off the wall. I head out the door with it and my box, shutting off the light on my way out. Thor is waiting in the hallway. Past him, my staff is waiting, trying not to step on the pink slips. I hand off the bumper to Harvey. I shake Clarence's held out hand.

"I've been fired. I wish you favorable probabilities," I tell them. I step out the door into a downpour. I puddle jump to my car, drop the keys in the process of unlocking the thing. I start it up. It doesn't want to go. I try again, and I drive out.

Mr. Possibilities has just leapt off a precarious position into mid-air. There is no safety net below me. Nowhere to run; nowhere to hide. The question is: what do I want to grab a hold of; where do I want to swing. What possibility do I want to try? Or how far do I want to fall?

A truck splashes into a puddle sending a tsunami wave up and over my car. My Pony Express surfs the tube of the wave, dude. Hurricanes are a rarity in Minnesota. It's been eons since our last one.

I spot a section of University Avenue, just past the construction, that has ripples. It dawns on me that ripples and a surface sheen in the water, indicate more than wet pavement, potentially flooded pavement. Then it dawns on me that I don't need to teach anyone to drive anymore. I slow up and change lanes to avoid the flooded part of the road. I pass an accident and a shipwreck.

I am driving home, because I can't think of anything else to do. I loosen my tie. I wipe the rainwater from my hair. The hallway of my apartment building is an informal daycare due to the rain. My box of junk and I shuffle by the kids coloring and the kids acting like they weren't about to play with the fire extinguisher. Ray isn't in the apartment. I put the damp box on the top shelf of my bedroom closet. I get undressed. I sit down on my bed. I put my head in my hands.

A truck rumbles and splashes by.

The rain patters a steady rhythm on my window.

The long-nailed dog upstairs tap dances its way across its apartment.

I lift my head up in my hands so that they only cover my nose and mouth.

My alarm clock blinks at me.

Mr. Possibilities... Mr. Smartypants, the guy who has an answer for everything... doesn't know what to do.

I really don't know what to do.

Oh God.

My head slides back to rest my forehead and eyes in my hands. There are times when driving, that clearly an accident is about to occur. One way or another there will be an accident. You realize that you are going to hit something, so you try to aim for the target that will hurt the least. You make the best of it.

I don't know if I made the best of today's accident or not.

My guess is that I didn't.

But then, I couldn't support a plan for a public showing of AutoDrive in one month, traversing a mile long path of stops and turns through part of downtown. He fires me. Then he says that he needs me to get AutoDrive done?!? It doesn't make any sense. Apparently Carl believes that to really motivate people, you must fire them first. I don't remember that from management class. Motivation by firing – I must've been sick that day, except that I never missed a class. In a management case-studies course, we had examples of some extreme styles of management. There was the wounded-doormat-manager style where an employee becomes a manager late in their career only to focus on revenge. There was the parental-punishment-style manager where their actions are dictated by parental behavior. And there was the pilfering-style manager where the business is supplier of personal needs. I remember all the issues we discussed in class. None of that prepared me for this final twist in Carl's behavior. He's gone mad. He had a problem with my "weekend plans?!?" I take one day off in six months... haven't been sick in all the time I've worked for Flight Control... and he has a problem with a day off?!? Carl the Wednesday golfer?!? How was I "smug" in packing up my office? How? Maybe compared to his red-faced sweat, my reaction to his firing me might have appeared smug. And on Thursday he demoted me, by bringing in this windshield-wearing Bailey stiff over me. What did he think, that I wouldn't take Friday off and I would work through the weekend to impress this invader? No.

My fingertips rub my forehead and the bridge of my nose.

Damn.

It actually happened. I was fired. I can't believe it.

What have I done? What am I going to do?

I look over at my window and the drippy sheet of water running down it. The water adds a new glaze, a second pane.

I am not the easiest person to understand. I don't understand me, and I'm me! I always say that people are the sum of their experiences, what has occurred to them, and what decisions they've made. A quick biographical sketch is not going to enable anyone to pigeon hole me into a particular type of person, a classification. They look at their square pegs and round pegs, and then they look at me, ponder, and set me aside. Staring out into the rain, I can't help but think that I am one odd duck. I don't know anyone like me. When they made me, they broke the mold, made it look like an accident...

Even with all that, how could Carl not see that I was working my ass off? How did I end up on double-secret probation? How could he dismiss the progress we make every single day?!? All my reports detailed our progress, successes, failures, and lessons. All he would have to do is read the damned things. He isn't an idiot. He should know enough to understand... he knows all about AutoDrive... or does he? Does he understand what we're doing? He... doesn't get what we're doing?!? Thursday he mentioned or someone mentioned... yeah, Carl mentioned that whole Bailey and the separate sidewalk discriminator program nonsense. Bailey read my reports and as an outsider, got confused by what is going on. I never wrote the reports for an outsider to understand. I wrote the reports assuming a level of understanding of what we were doing. Bailey tells Carl about his misunderstanding, and Carl goes along with the misunderstanding because he hasn't a clue as to what is actually going on, and apparently Bailey is misleading him. But then Bailey probably had his own agenda. Bailey was trying to get a job... not necessarily my job... he wanted the job above me so that he could, I don't know, get credit for the creation of AutoDrive by stepping in at the eleventh hour?

So Carl is an idiot... probably.

Maybe I'm an idiot too. I should have known what was going on. I should have talked to Carl. But when I tried to talk to him in the meeting, he did his best cartoon-imitation of a tea kettle. He was too steamed. He wouldn't have listened to me if I had told him there was a fire below him. If I had gotten to him before everything and everyone else got to him, I might have had a chance. If I had seen what was going on, I could have changed things.

But that's not the set up. My group is off on its own in the warehouse. Everyone else is in the offices. Research & Development is sequestered away deliberately. The weekly meetings were my only regular connection, and the meetings could have been conducted in the Research & Development world to demonstrate our progress through video demonstrations at the very least, but that wasn't what happened.

Maybe I should have kept closer tabs on the office types, but I have to ask myself, when would I do that? I had my hands full with the creation of AutoDrive. Others were supposed to be responsible for Flight Control itself.

Now it's entirely their responsibility.

What am I going to do?

I could become a hermit.

Hermits have it made. Hermits don't have to worry about being understood or misunderstood. They don't have to concern themselves with the intelligence or lack of intelligence of others. They have their remote mountain retreats on craggy rocks, amidst craggy, wind-twisted corduroy-like trees. They carry their water up, bucket by bucket. They eat little. They do little. They aren't pestered by people because the climb is difficult, and it takes great perseverance for a visitor to find the hermit.

My door knocks. I put on clothes and shuffle to the door.

It's the local urchins. "Yes?" I ask.

"We were wondering if you have any video games," a taller urchin asks while trying to peer around me into my dark apartment.

"Nope," I tell him. As I shut the door I mutter, "Hermits don't have video games."

Yeah, I would be a hermit, except for having met Hope. I am not an expert at ideal relationships, but I am something of an expert at analyzing situations. That acquired ability tells me that my becoming a hermit would interfere with my relationship with Hope. Long distance relationships are difficult; remote relationships are formidable. So much for becoming a hermit.

This is America. Here you can go, do, or be anything you want. That's what the brochure says. However on the back of the America brochure, there is a weird sort of design. If you put this design under a microscope you find that it is text that explains the exceptions and stipulations:

● America the Beautiful refers to the original state of the country prior to its formative years, when it resurfaced the forests and fields with farms, which were still nice in their own way. As a teenager, America was into tattoos and hair dyes and piercings, which changed her landscape. As she has gotten older, she has gained weight, lost weight, and gained weight again. Additional resurfacing without much foresight of overall aesthetics, has left her with unsightly blemishes. Over time she has had every surgery known to man, including some highly experimental procedures, leaving no stone untouched, no part of her body unturned. Truth in advertising leads us to the assertion that America is still lovely despite her age.

● Land of the free is correct, except that America has a higher per capita prison population than most of the world. That's the antithesis of free. In America travel is unrestricted, except if you want to use your car. Travel is restricted through driving rules, highway tolls, and state licensing, which is a privilege not a right. If you want to walk, that's fine, except that you cannot walk on the interstate highways, trespass on private property, or traverse public property without a permit and without adhering to the rules governing that property.

● The United States Bill of Rights defines the things that people can definitely do without... uh... question? No, that's not right. The amendments of the Bill of Rights are always being questioned. What you do is your business, unless what you do has been identified in federal, state, or local laws. The country was set up to create its own laws at a rapid pace to fill the legal void. That rapid pace continues today. The military has a provision that if we ever run out of ammunition, we start launching the United States Code at the enemy. The code is insidious in its plans to grow so large that it will cover the country, the continent, the oceans, and the other continents, blocking the sun for all eternity! Insert sinister laugh here.

● Licensing and educational requirements restrict all but the hokeyiest of professions. You simply cannot be just anyone, while adhering to state law. Most states exempt hermits from any professional restrictions, but this could change at a moments notice. This means you.

I lean back from my fine-print-reading microscope and sigh. There are limits on what I can do. I have a mechanical engineering degree. I can flip burgers **and** fix the stove. I'm versatile.

So what am I going to do?

I decide to lie down. Yeah, I'm versatile. I could be a hermit or work fast food. Or I could be a fast food hermit. "You've taken so long to get up here; you probably think you have no time for a hot meal. Well, think again!" I'm surprised the fast food marketing geniuses haven't tapped the hermit-seeking market yet. Come on, people, get with it!

At least, now I have a plan. When my friends come to visit me, I'll serve up–

I'm embarrassed. I'm embarrassed for my friends. I feel like I've let them down – that somehow I should have been able to keep my job and see it through to fruition. I should have found a way to make things work. I've failed myself, my friends, and I've failed Hope. How will I meet her family? I'll be introduced as her unemployed boyfriend. I'm not good enough for her.

My ceiling has one of those was-white-now-gray, bumpy surfaces meant to hide dirt and flaws. It's a camouflage paint job. I wonder if it could work on people. "He may be unemployed, but look how well he blends in with his surroundings!"

Hope has twice offered to put up with me... I mean, put me up, and she wants to hold me and watch over me while I sleep. I haven't figured out why. And she wants me to call her at four. I look at my clock. It eyes me with one eye squinting and one eye wide open. It's almost two. Wow, time flies when you are wallowing in self-pity! Where has this day gone? The dog tap dances its way back across the apartment above.

I get up and start to divide up the pile of weekend litter into laundry and not laundry. I add bed sheets. I clean up and put away the non-laundry materials. I make the bed. My room is clean enough to close the closet door. I divide the laundry into three piles: black shirts that smell like bug-spray, white, and everything else. I mix in my non-weekend clothes. I pile it, detergent, coins, and Safari Of The Mind into a basket, grab my keys, and head into the hallway only to be overrun by the day-care victims. I twist and turn to get around and through them and get down to the laundry room in the basement. It's quiet and empty with no Out Of Order signs. Maybe the Out Of Order signs are out of order. Three loads and three washers should work out. The kids stream in after me. I feed the machines, and the machines briefly communicate with my ATM; I don't know why. I make a production out of removing a black shirt, shaking it, inspecting it, and depositing it in the washing machine. I do the same for each one. After the fifth one, a child asks, "How many black T-shirts do you **have**?!?" I do the same production for all 15. I load the rest of the washers quickly and hop on a machine with my book. Then I look at the pack as if to tell them, "That's it, shows over."

I sit and read. At first my plan is to be boring. But the rabble are not quick to leave. So I start reading my book to them. "Climbing creaking, croaking, crackling dusty little stairs into the attic?" I ask, using an imitation of Heidi's meek voice. "The attic opened into woods? Trees. A tree of compassion. A tree of intelligence. A tree of knowledge. A tree of curiosity. A stump of indecision? A tree of creativity..."

"A timberland of thought," Carl's voice says. "No, not a timberland, a yard of up-standing lumber."

"Toothpicks in training– lumber in slumber– " Bill's voice prattles, "driftwood without the drift– firewood without the fire– plywood without the– "

"The woods are dense," Thor's voice establishes.

"'The woods are not dense,' said the tree of intelligence," Clarence's voice interjects. "'The woods are old. They are deep. They listen.'"

"'Gather around little woodchucks and listen,' said the tree of compassion," in a voice like Coelle's, "to all the woodchucks. And all the woodchucks gather, wearing T-shirts like head scarves." I stop using special voices. I started hearing their voices too well. No more imitations.

I continue reading aloud without looking at my audience. I'm not responsible for the audience. I'm just reading. "'Have you ever wondered how the world became complicated,' asks the tree of curiosity. The tree of knowledge sways and says, 'There once were three sisters who wove the tapestry of the world.'"

"What's a tapestry?" a kid asks. The washers churn.

"All people and their actions were threads connecting with everyone else's threads to be the fabric of life. The Moirai sisters enjoyed their work, deciding how people would live or die, and how people would meet up with others. And the people enjoyed the lives directed by the sisters. They were not responsible for their actions because everything was determined by the tapestry of life, woven by the sisters. They had no choices and no responsibilities. They were like puppets on the strings. The sisters tied knots to keep people together. They wove in new threads; an occasional quantum string filament was thrown in, and they cut the cord. They kept life interesting, adding unexpected twists to the fabric of life. More and more threads were added. Threads were being added three at a time, then seven at a time, and more. The tapestry started to unravel. Life was out of control. The Moirai sisters decided to delegate their tasks between themselves to better handle the work. One sister, Clotho, spun the thread. Another sister, Lachesis, determined the length of the thread. And the third sister, Atropos, cut the thread. The tapestry came back together. The threads came back under control, but the pattern of life became dull. The world called out to the Moirai sisters and yelled, '**Boring!**' The Moirai sisters fumed. They looked across the room at their early loom work. They looked back at their current work. They needed help. They hired a temp, an intern, and a consultant. The temp made lumpily-uneven thread, the intern did schoolwork instead of measuring thread, and the consultant made cuts all over. The doomed tapestry of life began to fall apart. Loose threads were everywhere. The Moirai sisters, on the advice of their accountant, formed a corporation. Fates Incorporated went public. Fates Incorporated determined that there was little money to be made in the life tapestry business, so it closed its life tapestry unit and went into the fashion industry. In a press conference, the Moirai sisters told everyone, they were on their own."

"'You will have to make choices and take responsibility for your lives. It's up to you now,' the sisters said."

"The stump of indecision muttered, 'I'm not sure I can handle all that.'"

"The tree of compassion replied, 'Don't look so low. Fates Incorporated filed for bankruptcy a long time ago. Your life has always been in your control. Everything you've done, you've done alone.'"

The washing machine rumbles under my butt.

"So fate went out of business?" a girl asks.

"Kind-a," I reply looking up and seeing someone's mother in the doorway.

"What's that you're reading?" the woman gruffly asks, scratching her steel wool hair.

"Nothing," I reply. She then scolds one of the children of the floor-full of children not to sit on the dirty floor. The kid asks for a chair. The mother nearly backhands the child. She catches herself, but the kid reels back as if hit. She stares at me as if searching for something smart to say or waiting for me to say something stupid. When she is satisfied that neither thing will happen, she leaves. In my best imitation of Ed Norton, I say, "Sheesh, what a grouch!" Kids laugh.

The mother leaps back in the doorway snarling and spitting, "I heard that!" No one moves. The irony of her grouchy reply causes one kid to giggle twice, while covering her mouth with both hands to keep any more giggles from escaping. She succeeds. The kids are a barrier between myself and the grouch. I doubt they are a strong barrier, since they seem solidly frightened of this woman. If she were to come toward me, they would probably move out of the way like corn stalks for a tornado. The children, the innocent children, wish to live long enough to see the seasons change again.

The grouch leaves again. After a door slams, the washers stop. Breaking the silence, one of the innocent children does an imitation of me doing an imitation of Ed Norton, saying, "Sheesh, what a grouch!" The children laugh. I feel like I'm running an orphanage. I mix my laundry between two dryers and clean the lint traps. I might be the only person in the building that cleans them. It's a tremendous waste for the washing and drying of clothes to wear out the clothes. The lint traps from each dryer contains a blanket's worth of fiber, fiber that could mend the tapestry of life. I hand the multicolored lint blankets off to the urchins. They think that's hysterical also. While I am loading the machines with money, they're throwing the lint at each other and looking for more.

"How old are you?" I ask dirt resembling a kid.

"Seven," the dirt says.

Turning to another kid, I reply, "I don't think he could get that dirty in seven years. Watch your fingers, I'm stepping through." I hop back onto my washing machine perch and open my book, "Let's see: 'your life has always been in your control. Everything you've done, you've done alone.' The wind blows through the attic grove, making the trees' leaves dance in place. The tree of intelligence leans in and sprouts, 'If our lives aren't in our own control, then they aren't our lives. Are they?' The tree of creativity sways, 'That's how it should be. I never run out of ideas. I think–' The stump of indecision cuts her off by barking, 'Decision making and making choices isn't easy!' The tree of curiosity asks, 'Isn't it easy to make decisions by asking questions? Once you ask the questions... once you know the problem and all the pieces of the problem... the answer is half solved. If you don't know, ask.' The tree of compassion offers, 'No one will chop your head off for asking questions, there is nothing to fear.'"

One kid nearly laughs at that. His look says he's had reason to be afraid of asking questions.

"The tree of curiosity asks the stump of indecision, 'When you fell did you make a sound?' The stump of indecision glares at the tree of curiosity." A door opens and closes in the hall. Music starts up. That would be the apartment below mine. I close the book. I hop down off the washer, and wind my way past the kids to the storage unit to check to make sure I put away the charcoal stove in a clean enough condition.

"You don't want to go back there..." a girl sings to me. I pull a chain next to a bare bulb. I turn the corner into the wood and wire caged storage units. The cage across and one back from mine has a person sitting on a cot. Are we keeping inmates here? That barely raises my eyebrows today. I unlock my storage unit, check the grill – it's fine, and lock back up. I check if his storage unit has a lock on it. It does not. That's good in a way and bad in a way. I go over.

"What are you in for?" I ask him with an inmate voice.

The man, the old man in wrinkled skin and clothes, turns and his face fights its way into a struggled smile. "Marriage," he says. "My wife kicked me out."

I nod without really understanding. "We'll try to keep it down," I tell him.

As I turn to go he says, "You read well." I thank him, turn the corner, and pull the chain. The urchins seem surprised that I made it back alive. They were poised to divvy up black T-shirts.

The same girl sings, "I told you..."

Another kid says, "She's so smart. Her name is Loverducks." Kids laugh.

"Shut up," she says.

"She was in preschool, and the teacher called on her, and she didn't answer and didn't answer and didn't answer, and the teacher asked what her parents call her," the girl is pounding on him now, "and she said Loverducks!" Kids laugh. I tell her that's a nice name, and she eases up on her pounding of the boy.

The dryers have stopped; the laundry is still wet. What made the machines decide to stop my laundry mid-stream? What made them stop before the laundry was finished? Did they make a decision that the clothes and towels were dry enough? Was it far enough along or taking too long? Did they decide to just stop working on my laundry? Was it personal? Or did it all come down to money? There just wasn't enough? Fine. I will take back my half-finished laundry. I load the damp laundry into my basket. I clean the lint traps, offering the fresh lint blankets to the nearest out-thrust hands. I grab my other stuff. There is something very familiar about all of this. It reminds me of a joke... a laundry riddle.

"What gets wetter as it dries?" I ask my audience, as I head out the door.

"A towel," a kid yells out. Some kids follow me, but my apartment door intercedes on my behalf. I decorate my apartment in damp laundry. I start in the living room, then the kitchen, then the bathroom, and finally my room. The apartment's humidity rises. An air conditioner would probably help right about now. Tomorrow was my deadline for having working air conditioning. This sort of thing can't wait until the snow starts flying and the air conditioning decides to run all the time. I check the time. It's three minutes to four. I watch the clock. It watches me. It is a stare down. The seconds tick by. It's almost time to call Hope. It's 3:59. Just as I'm starting to reach for the phone, it ticks the minute hand back a minute to 3:58pm. I gape. It smirks and gives me four o'clock. What an annoying clock! I call Hope. Realizing that Faith might answer, I am prepared to ask the answerer for Hope's PIN number to make certain that it is my girlfriend. The phone continues to ring. I start counting the number of rings. There are too many rings. Either I am going to step into being annoying by ringing the phone too many times or an answering machine is going to pick up. There is a knock on my door. The landlady probably gets in about now. I hang up and go to the door. It's Hope!

"Hi! I hope I'm not–" she starts. I grab her, pull her in, and kiss her while kicking the door shut. Kissing and kissing her, she pushes me away and says, "Whoa, I guess I did the right thing coming over?"

"Yes, definitely."

"What happened to your place?"

"Oh, the dryers downstairs don't dry things very well."

She nods. "Did you get fired?"

"Yes. It was kind of weird."

"Are you okay?"

"I don't know."

"Let's..." she moves us to the couch and stops. I stack laundry to free some space for us. Sitting down, she jumps back up because the couch is damp, looks at me, rubs the spot, and sits down again. "I want to hear about today, but I want to tell you a few things first. First thing this morning, Nicole told me that she missed having you around. She said that you made her feel safe." Hope pauses. "She's never said that about anybody. In school this morning, I told your string joke to my class, with some minor changes. I didn't have it go into a bar... They really liked it. I've been thinking about you all day. I prayed for you." She adjusts the hair on my forehead. "Would you like to tell me about today?" I start telling her about my repeated pointed perceptions to understand who was at the meeting. "Why did you do that?"

"Why did I do what?"

"Why did you familiarize yourself with all the strangers in the meeting?"

"Because last night I had a dream that Jake was going to ask me about one of them, but I otherwise didn't remember any other details from the dream."

"Why didn't you instead try to do different things to convince your manager not to fire you?"

"Because I learned a long time ago that I can't change what others are going to do."

"You mean like with Melanie?" Hope asks.

"Yes, she was part of that."

"But you changed where Erix was going to stand Saturday morning when the rocket was going to head into him?"

"Yes, you're right. You make a good point. But Carl is not Erix. Erix believes in me. Carl, the owner of Flight Control, for some reason does not believe in me. And the group I was with on Saturday morning was not the group at the conference table this morning. One of the things that I am no good at, really lousy at, is selling myself. If people don't believe in me, I can't change their minds. I can't make them believe in me while in pointed perception, any more than I can during regular time."

As I'm talking, a key opens the door and someone comes in. I turn to see Ray, holding a vegetable box from the Co-op and gaping at my damp decorations.

"What the F happened here? Did a closet blow up?!? Hi, Hope."

"Hi Ray. The dryer didn't work," Hope defends me. It's sweet of her.

"Oh. I got a box of overly-ripe produce really cheap from the Co-op," Ray says.

"I can feed you guys..." Hope offers.

"A lot of this stuff is perfectly good," Ray says. "Did you get fired?"

"Yes, at 10:21."

Ray nods. "I talked to the guys at the Co-op. I can increase my hours. I also messaged some roughs of the Glory Girl work I did this past weekend, and everyone is really impressed. I also called the university about more lab rat work."

"Hey!" Hope exclaims, as someone knocks on the door.

"I'll get it," Ray says, setting the box and its orbiting fruit flies on the floor. "Hi Tom. Come on in."

Tom appears holding out a bottle of wine. "For new beginnings," he says, as I take the bottle, chilled, which announces his intentions, before he heads into the kitchen for a corkscrew and glasses. He comes back with four glasses, no corkscrew. I start to give him kitchen drawer directions, but he waves me off. He fishes a universal tool out of his pocket and flips out from it a corkscrew. Without a counter, without a table, Tom holds the bottle, while screwing it, and pops the cork. He is talented. We applaud. He continues to amaze and astound by holding the stemware glasses, while pouring and serving the wine to us, without spilling a drop. We are easily entertained by Tom's exaggeratedly dramatic demonstrations of dexterity. The others take my lead in holding their glasses until Tom has poured his; he repeats, "To new beginnings." We drink. "Todd and Cy are nearly here. They are currently stuck in a lake that used to be University Avenue."

"Whoa, what's going on? Who all is coming over?" I ask.

"I'm not sure. Cy organized it," Tom tells me.

I turn to Hope beside me, "Did Cy call you too?"

"Yes. I didn't know what was the right thing to do. I didn't know if you needed some time alone or something. She said that I should come over." Hope's eyes check my eyes, switching back and forth between the two. "Did I screw up by coming over?"

I grab her forearm. "No, no. It's just..." I'm not angry. I just don't like the idea of being manipulated. "...if you aren't sure, ask me. Don't ask Cy."

"She called me actually."

"Okay. But I don't think relationships should have intermediaries. Let's talk directly, okay?"

Tom jumps in, "Cy's just trying to help everyone know what they should do to help you. And she said that you would probably climb the Prospective Tower and hang off there and blame yourself for everything at Flight Control. I don't know if I believe that, but I agreed that we should drop by here if we could. You've been supportive of us often enough." He lowers his voice, "Were we wrong to come over?"

"No."

"Was Cy wrong about what she said?" Tom asks.

"Not exactly. I wouldn't climb Prospective Tower in all this rain," I respond, and Tom nods. "I am glad you're here," I tell them. "Really. But I just got fired. I'm wounded. Should I be having a party?" I ask, looking into the wine glass at the burgundy concave surface.

"Why not?" Ray says without putting much heart into it. Hope is on my shoulder.

"Sure you should."

Tom almost spits out his wine suddenly and heads for the door, announcing, "They're here." The door knocks; the knocker knocks; the door knocks. Todd would've knocked. Cy is the only person I know who uses the knocker. Most people either think it's just a decoration or can't find it under all the landlady notices. "Come on in. He's depressed. Put your umbrella over there by mine." I get up off the couch and straighten my shoulders to avoid looking as depressed as they know I am. Cy darts around turning on lights.

"Hey!" Todd says. "How are you?" I shake his hand.

Meanwhile I reach my other hand back to Cy, she latches onto it, and I pull her back to the couch, bumping into Hope on the way, landing both of them down next to me. On the way, I say, "I'm wallowing in self-pity."

From behind or beside me, Cy reacts, "You?!? Wallowing in self-pity?!? You?!? How did that go?" I turn to her. After a pause she says, "I just can't imagine you anywhere near self-pity. You're a self-pity virgin."

"So! You set Sharon up to set Hope and I up?!?" my interrogation of Cy begins.

"You're mad at me for it?" Cy counters.

"No..." She's got me there.

"And..." Cy cues me.

"What?"

"I'm waiting for a thank you..." she says, expectantly.

I look at Hope. I tell Cy, "Thank you."

"You're welcome, but I wasn't the one who set you two up. I got involved late," Cy says.

She's being cagey. That's just what I need right now. "What's going on tonight."

"What do you mean?"

"What do you have planned?"

"A group of people are coming by to help you get through being fired," Cy informs me. "You don't have to thank me for this one. You're the one who taught me how far friends can go for each other. If you don't like it, it's your fault. We're just doing what Ricky would do." I stare at the surface tension of the wine in my glass.

Have you ever felt like crawling into a hole, only to find that someone brighter than you has blocked every hole? To make matters worse, they decide to put a spotlight on you. I will label this the Unwanted Spotlight. Just coming out of surgery, the doctors having removed your source of employment and irritation, so here comes the paparazzi and the Unwanted Spotlight.

"Remember about four years ago, the conversation about whether good people should stick together?" Cy asks. "Condensed Quality is what you called it."

"Yeah."

Cy turns to tell Hope and Ray, "We were talking about whether good people should stick together or spread themselves out. Is the world better off with strength in numbers? Entire companies composed of good people, encouraging each other and insulated from bad influences. Or is the world better off with good people isolated from one another, teaching others, and trying to reach the good in everyone?"

"We were just talking about something like that last night," Hope says. "I was telling him that Nicole and I were talking about how we found so many great people in one spot last weekend... and that it was... no offense... almost like you were hiding out together."

"Did that bother you?" Cy the psychiatrist asks her.

"It did, because if my mom hadn't talked to you about me, and you hadn't talked to her about this guy, there is no way we could've met. There is no way I could have found him."

I notice Tom is missing and hear rustling in the kitchen. I tilt my head to Ray and point to the kitchen. Ray goes.

Cy asks Hope, "You wanted to meet a nice guy, right?"

"Yes."

"You can't have it both ways," Cy says, while I shake my head, disagreeing. "You can't spread the decent people out and expect to find them. If you want someone crummy, each neighborhood bar is conveniently located for random relationships. You might get lucky."

Ray comes back and gives me a shrug.

"His theory," Cy says pointedly toward me, "was that good, decent, kind people, should go their separate ways and be out there to teach by example. We convinced him and he agreed that good people should stick together."

"Not exactly," I interject. "I agreed that sometimes good people sometimes need their batteries recharged by being with like-minded people. That doesn't change needing to be out in the world." There is a knock at the door. Ray gets it.

"I am out in the world," Cy argues, continuing the argument for Hope's benefit.

"Hi Al," Ray says, and we all copy Ray. Ray gets a towel for Al to wipe off his tool belt.

"You know what I mean, right?" I ask Cy.

"No."

"Isolated."

"I'm not isolated."

"What's a gated community?"

Bam! A door across the hall slams.

Cy shifts her eyes and tells Hope, "He doesn't like gated communities."

"I just don't think that being in a gated community is being a part of the world so much as being apart from the the world." Using Hope's words, I whisper, "Hiding out."

"Hiding? Don't you think that is a little hypocritical?"

"How?" I ask, as Tom returns from wherever he was.

"When was the last time you got to know your neighbors?"

"Just this afternoon." Cy's face registers shock and curiosity. I explain, "I read to about 13 children in the laundry room. One of the girls was named Loverducks. I also met an elderly man living in his storage locker because his wife kicked him out. And I had an almost lively discussion with a mother who wanted to beat her child in front of me. I'm meeting people left and right."

"An old man is living in one of the storage lockers?!?" Ray asks.

"Yeah."

"I have two questions for you," Cy offers.

"I'll take the second question first."

"Who do you think will be better suited to help you land a new job: friends like us or your neighbors?"

"Could I hear the first question before I give you my second answer?"

Cy smirks. "Do you recommend that I live in an apartment building like this one?"

I sigh. My futures are in their hands. "You are better suited to help me find a new job. And number one, no, I don't recommend that you live in an apartment building."

Cy pats my knee. "There. That wasn't the end of the world, was it? Yes, we will help you get through this and be better for it. Now. Are you okay?"

"I don't know."

Cy hugs me, puts Hope's arms around me, and asks, "Jake wanted to know, who was the representative from Double Bubble for Flight Control?"

"Dean Double," I tell her. She writes the name on her handheld device.

"Do you know what you'd like to do next... what sort of work you'd like to do... or anything you'd especially not want to do?"

"Anything except something that involves writing."

"How did I know you were going to say that?" Cy asks.

"Because I said the same thing six years ago."

"You could go to Vegas," Todd bets. "Make a killing."

"Don't start that again."

There is a metal clang from across the room. I lean forward. Al has the air conditioner open and is pointing out something to Ray while pulling or pinching something else. I call out, "Hey, what's going on?"

Ray shouts over some sudden hallway yelling, "Al's fixing the air conditioner!"

"Oh," I nod. I get up as the hallway commotion starts to have a familiar edge to it. Opening the door, I find Jake is just finishing his reading of the riot act to the apartment complex. I pull Jake into my apartment and shut the door. "Don't... intimidate... my neighbors."

"Someone has to, otherwise they'll walk all over you. What the hell was that?"

"The elephants upstairs have never clipped the nails on their dog. I think they are working on some canine toenail world record. You've never heard that?"

"Isn't that cruelty to animals?" Todd asks.

"Cruelty to the elephants or cruelty to the dog?"

"The dog!" Cy exclaims.

"Maybe they're fake nails."

"For dogs?"

"Yeah."

"**That** would be cruelty to animals."

"Depends on whether there are tacky designs on them."

"No, it depends on whether the dog chews its nails."

"If I were a dog owned by elephants, I'd probably chew my nails... down to nubs."

"Maybe that explains the fake nails." Hope is laughing.

"You know it was a conversation like this that caused Erix to stop talking most of the time."

Hope stops laughing. "Really?"

"Yeah. Can I get anyone anything?"

Jake asks, "You haven't moved your fridge have you?" I shake my head. "Then I'll find it." Looking at the disassembly of my air conditioner for a moment, I hear Jake say, "What the–" He comes back around the corner. "Your food is a little too happy for me." I follow him into the kitchen and to the open fridge door. The food smiles at us.

There are clear smiley faces of different sizes on everything from the individual eggs to the juices and other containers. Someone has put smiley face stickers on everything in my refrigerator.

"Tom!" I yell. Everyone but the air conditioning technicians come in to see our happy food. I examine a smiling bottle of apple juice and a happy egg. Cy gets a picture. "Thanks." What a riot. Jake grabs a smiling bottle of his very own brand of beer, Yoerg Beer. That's why it's there. He's already working the smile off it. I ask Tom, "Food is your friend?"

"Food is your friend," Tom confirms. A gentle rapping is heard from the door. Todd gets the door.

"Hi Todd, how's Ricky?" Ruth's voice asks.

Todd whispers loudly, "He's a wreck."

A streak of shiny yellow barrels into the kitchen spraying water all over and knocking into people like they were dominoes or bowling pins. "Are you all right?" It's Ruth in a shiny yellow rain slicker. And she's asking me if I'm all right, not the dominoes that are trying to right themselves.

"I'm not a wreck," I insist. "Here look in my fridge."

Ruth sticks her head and yellow rain hat in and says, "Food is–" and we finish together, "–your friend." Ruth gets the picture. "Do I say that too much?" Everyone says "no," except Jake, who says "maybe." Cy helps Ruth hang up her bright yellow raincoat in the bathroom. It's as if they turned on a large yellow spotlight in there. They step out, and Hope pulls me in and shuts the door. It's just us and a drippy yellow spotlight.

"Hi."

"Hi," I reply.

"I hope you don't mind, but I need to talk to you."

"Okay, let's... you know... talk..." I kiss her with every lip on my face.

Hope pulls away. "I need to tell you something."

"With your lips?"

"Yes." My lips prepare for more kissing. "No. This is serious. I'm... rich."

"Seriously rich?"

"Yes, seriously rich."

"This is serious. How are you going to handle it? Is there..." gasp "...a cure?" Hope's brow wrinkles at me. "Okay. You said, it's serious. What's the problem?"

"You don't have to work. You can live with me. You can do whatever you want."

I sit down on the built-in chair. "I don't know what I'm going to do, but I don't think I'd want to just sit around."

"I'm just telling you that you can do anything you want to. If you want to go back to school... I'll help you..."

I look up to her in the strong yellow light. Her brow settles. She squats down to my level. "I don't know. I'll see what they can do," my thumb points to the door, "about helping me to find a new job. So what, are you saying you want to be a safety net for me?"

"Yes," she dimples in the yellow light.

"That would be weird, having a safety net. Would it bother you if I jump up and land another job?" She shakes her head. "So you'd be okay?"

"Yes. I just want to help if I can."

The door knocks. Will's voice says something and then asks, "Are you okay in there?"

"Just a minute please," I call out. "I'll make sure to include you in my plans, okay? I've already rejected the notion of becoming a hermit."

"Look, I've been asking you to consider moving into my house. We have **working** laundry machines. No one should have to put up with the things you put up with."

"I have five months left on my lease."

"I'll pay them the five month's rent, if I need to. Didn't you say your air conditioning wasn't working?"

"Yeah. I did say that."

"We have **working** air conditioning."

"Okay. Okay. I'll consider it. How much do you charge for rent?"

"Less than you pay."

"How do you know how much I pay?"

"The sign out front says the rates for one and two bedrooms."

"That's right. It does. So how much?"

"You help me out with some things, and we would be even."

"We probably need to get back to the others."

"You'll seriously consider it?"

"I'll seriously consider it, Hope." Hope opens the door, and we go out to cheers and cooler, dryer air. Ruth and Sharon greet us.

"Hello, lovebirds," Sharon says. We give her hugs.

"Thank you for bringing us together," I tell her with a kiss to her cheek.

Sharon shakes her head. "Thank you, but it wasn't my idea. We're all glad everything is working out. Are you ready for some dinner? We have reservations at a restaurant nearby. We should probably start heading out now."

Ruth squeezes by. I head to my room to grab my jacket. The double W's, Will and Wendy, are in there looking as if they are studying museum exhibits. "I guess we're all heading out to dinner," I say, realizing I wasn't given the details. "Are you coming with?"

"Yeah," Wendy says. "Work was chaos after you left. They fired Mike. Bailey has taken over your office. None of us know what's going on." I grab my jacket off its hook. "I still don't understand why they fired you. Porter said it was a misfire; they meant to just fire Mike all along. They missed."

I attempt my best imitation of a smile and say, "I'm still trying to figure it out too." I usher them out. In the congested hallway, a conversation is being resolved, which leads to my being told by Ruth that Hope will be driving me. As I am being escorted out of my own apartment, I can't help wonder if we set some kind of record for number of people in one apartment, all of whom seem to be on their phones negotiating for more people to show up at the restaurant. People behind me promise to lock up. I'd hate for my apartment to become a training academy for looters.

Neighbors watch my group from within their apartments, almost cowering. I meet up with Hope near the stairs. She takes my arm and brings me out to her car. The rain has dropped off to a slow drip. Once I am in her car I realize I've never been in her car. "Hey, this is nice..." and I want to call her something, other than Hope, and the first thing I think of is, "Loverducks."

"Thank you, Sweetie."

"You got it fixed?"

"No Sweetie, you'll have to push us," Hope giggles, as she follows the stream of cars out into the river of road. Our procession is fairly orderly, almost like ballet, except for one giant truck that steps out and whips past everyone, leaving other vehicles spinning in its wake.

"Have you ever eaten there?" Hope asks, as we pass Yesterday's Diner.

"Sure. Is that where we're going?"

"Yesterday's Food at Yesterday's Prices? We can do better than that." Our wagon train crosses the border into Milltown and crosses back into Pigs Eye and pulls into the parking lot of Snow Place Like Home. "How does Snow Place sound?"

It sounds expensive for the unemployed, but I'm not going to reject it with everyone already here. "It should be good." I wonder if I am expected to pay for everyone? I hunt through my memory for anything describing unemployment party etiquette. Ha, etiquette – who's Eti and why did she quit?

"Are you okay?" Hope asks. "You've got a weird look on your face."

"I'm not sure I can be held accountable for the actions of my face."

"I think you can," Hope tells me, opening an umbrella for us. Snow Place Like Home looks darkly gloomy and wet on the outside. On the inside it looks like a throw-back to a warmly glowing, logging camp dining hall with polish and chandeliers thrown in. I barely miss running into an animated grizzly. Our troop is taken into a side room with a C-shaped table.

An argument breaks out in our ranks, and I go over to investigate. The issue is who will take the bill. I step in and say that it will be mine, after all this is about me. They turn, uniting as a group and say, "No!" I guess they told me.

Ray gets in my way and asks, "Did you see what Al did?"

"No, I give up. What did Al do?"

"He fixed the air conditioner. He also cleaned the filter. I didn't know it **had** a filter."

"Our air conditioner? Oh. Do you think he can un-fix it?"

"You're kidding."

"No. The broken air conditioner could've been our way out of our lease."

"We want out of our lease?!? I thought you said we wanted to keep our lease the way it was."

"Hope wants us to move in to her house."

"Us or you?"

"Us. I think. Hope! Do you want us to move in or only me?"

"Either you or both of you," Hope confirms.

I look at Ray. I can almost see the gears turning in his brain. His eyes turn into little pictures of Glory Girl. "I'll ask Al if he can break our air conditioner for us," he says.

"Hi," a waitress breathes, squeezing next to me. "Are you the guy who lost his job today?" I nod. "I am your personal hostess for this evening. If you need anything at all, let–" She never finishes, as she is seized by Ruth and Cy who ask her who requested this special service. Her finger shakes as it points and says, "The smirking guy next to the guy in the lab coat." Ruth and Cy take off toward Jake. Hope puts her arm around me and tells me in front of the hostess that she (Hope) will be my personal hostess. Another waitress comes by hesitantly and takes our drink orders.

I excuse myself to the bathroom. On my way out, Jake rattles Lefty on his way to intercept me. "So who is it from Double Bubble that's been working with your company, Flight Control, right?"

"Right, that's where I worked. It's Dean Double. I think he's a cousin or a nephew of the founder, Donald Double."

"I know the CEO."

"Is Donald Double still the CEO?"

"No, he stepped down years ago. Lee Burbs is the CEO." I nod and head to the jobless men's room.

At the mirror I take a good, hard look at myself. I splash water on my face. I stall, staring at the face staring back at me. What have I done? What am I doing? We're having a party because I was fired?!? Is this the best I can offer my friends? I think of my friends and practice a smile. I nod my head as if responding to statements. The smile fades. I reset my smile and adjust it with my fingers like I'm sculpting with clay. I hurry out before I totally lose it.

People are taking their seats. I am guided and prodded to sit in the middle of the C-shaped table. I start humming a middle C. We are all on the outside of the C table. Erix walks in the middle with a chair and sits on the inside of the C in front of me. "I'm sorry you were fired," he says.

From several people away, I hear Tom say, "I wish I had done that."

While people are ordering, I feel my smile slip away. Trying to be subtle, you know, at the head of a C-shaped table with everyone either staring or glancing at me, I use my hands, one at a time, to mold my face back into a smile, maybe. Since I don't have a mirror, I probably just pushed my features into a painting by Pablo Picasso.

Hope looks at me and nearly spits out her drink.

Will is talking about the stress of unemployment and strategies and I don't know what else. I make a mental note to call him to find out what he's talking about. Will is the sort of guy who would not be slowed down by being fired. He would still be smiling. I have to wear this fake smile.

In the midst of Will's lecture on interview tactics, Nadine comes over and apologizes for being late. I set down my fork. She reaches in from beside me for a hug. I'm sitting. She's standing. Her hiccuping breasts smash into my face, knocking my smile clear off. She straightens my hair but doesn't look around for my fallen smile.

Hope asks me if I like my meal. I nod. I ask her about hers. Her description is cheery, so cheery that I don't understand a word of it. The cheer is like a foreign language that has no common points of reference for my understanding.

I eat without tasting.

Wendy leans in to tell me about how Will told her about my foreseeing things last weekend. I start to think that Will has a big mouth, but that's not right. He ought to tell her what's going on with him. She asks if I ever foresaw the results of a test. I look down at the table, and I chew my food carefully, while Que Sera Sera plays and I'm coming up with what I'll say. I swallow, look at her, and say, "When Flight Control was first starting, and I was the only Research and Development person, I could not fully fathom how to create AutoDrive." In the pause, silverware clinks once but otherwise the room is quiet. "Where should I begin? What are the major issues? It took months to lay out the framework of the issues and obstacles facing AutoDrive. My initial tests were conducted on smaller-than-series-A vehicles. Despite how much I was learning from test-after-initial-test being less than fully successful, I needed to jump-start the process, so I applied pointed perception to the problems. It was a tremendous leap forward. I knew what would work and what wouldn't work without trying everything. It was great. Except that working night and day means you don't sleep. I was living the job. I started coming in late each morning. At first Carl attributed it to winter driving, but when winter turned to the other season and I was still arriving late, he had a talk with me. He said that something had to change. So I stopped predicting my work from home. I got to work on time. And productivity fell. That's when we started hiring people for R&D." Wendy is looking at me like she always has, for leadership and with admiration for where I have taken the company. It's sweet, even if it's misplaced.

I take my napkin from my lap and drop it on my unfinished meal. My legs stand me up without direction, scootching my chair back. I look around the room.

"Thank you all for joining me in this... Firing Fiesta. For the past five years, I have worked for and helped establish Flight Control, a company trying to create the first self-driving car, AutoDrive. I have been in charge of Research and Development for this new product, and I have put everything I am into my work. AutoDrive has a year or two left of development. This morning when the owner told me that AutoDrive must be ready for a public demonstration by the end of this month, I told him that it can't be done. I told him that, at least, I couldn't do it. He fired me. He wasn't alone. There was a firing squad.

"You all have been very supportive of me, coming out during a re-enactment of the biblical flood, like this. It means a lot to me. I don't know if I deserve it. Many of you have offered to help me find new work and get me through this. I... I accept." My feelings avalanche. My vision blurs. The floodwaters of my dam eyes break free into streams running down my face. "With your help, I will carry on. And Flight Control will carry on through people like my former student Wendy." She points down the table. I look. I see an old man with wisps of silvery gray hair resting above a freckled head. The eyes have a light spark. His neck is as wrinkled as this afternoon's laundry. "And Clarence!

"This afternoon, puttering around my apartment, I felt very alone. Depressed. Downcast... Dejected... Help me out here..."

"Discouraged?"

"Yes, discouraged."

"Downhearted?"

"Sure, downhearted."

"Despondent?"

"I don't know. What does despondent mean?"

"Disheartened."

"Despondent means disheartened?" Nodding. "Okay, what does disheartened mean?"

"Dispirited."

"Okay. So this afternoon I was depressed, downcast, dejected, discouraged, downhearted, despondent, disheartened, and dispirited!" I bow to the applause and wipe my face. "I will endure. You've helped pick me up. Thank you." Crawling under the table, I find my smile. Reappearing next to Erix, I cross the middle of the C to Clarence. I shake his hand.

"I am sure Flight Control will be counting on your leadership, Clarence."

"I am not certain I'll be staying there. I'll probably quit. It won't be a good place to be," Clarence says. "You made it a good job."

"That is the nicest thing–" I start to say, before Jake interrupts from the other side of Nadine. He asks Clarence to talk with him. I shake Nadine's hand. I shake a waitress's hand. I go around shaking everyone's hand. It feels silly shaking Hope's hand since she's my girlfriend, and Erix's hand because he's Erix, and Ray's hand because he's my roommate, but I shake all their hands. I fake like I'm going to go back around a second time, using my other hand. I head back to my chair the long way, through purses and umbrellas and raincoats. Ruth hands me an Unemployee Of The Month certificate. People finish up. A small group is having a meeting about me across the room. I offer to join the group but they decline my admittance. People wish me luck and thank Cy for the meal. Apparently she won the struggle over the bill.

With only a few of us left, Cy says to me, "You know, Erix wondered if you don't make things happen."

"Me? What about you? Setting us up... setting Hope and I up?" Cy doesn't comment, so I ask, "When did he say that?"

"Slamming Sunday morning."

Tom says, "You'll be happy to know, I'm having that door replaced or augmented with a slam-prevention device."

"Great. That's really great," I say flatly.

Hope takes me out; the bear stays. Hope drives me home. "Is there any way I can talk you into staying at my house tonight?"

I decline. "How about tomorrow night instead?"

Hope's face lights up, and she says, "That would be wonderful!"

"What time should I show up?"

"4:30?"

"Okay, 4:30," I confirm. We kiss. "Thank you for caring so much about me. I love you."

"I love you too," she says.

I head in. Opening my apartment door, I accidentally step inside a refrigerator. No, it's the apartment. The air conditioner is off. Ray comes out of his room wearing a parka and mittens. "Someone left the air on full blast," he says, shivering.

I am very tired, more tired than a wheel.

Did I just see snow falling inside the apartment?!?

In my room, cold wet clothes lie on my bed. This should be good. I put them in a basket. They stack like scraps of lumber. I post the Unemployee Of The Month certificate on my wall. My alarm is lightly ringing. It's shivering. I put a stocking cap over it. I layer blankets on my bed. I change into flannel pajamas. I climb into bed and turn out the light. I turn back on the light and reach to set the alarm and stop myself. I turn back off the light. I can't remember the icy bed being less comfortable, I think, as I fall asleep.

An odd dream has me searching for a lost wallet. I never lose things. I've never had that many things. I find the wallet, but I'm missing my identification. I've lost my driver's license.

I wake up in a sweat. My legs are sore from having launched blanket after blanket off my bed as the apartment warmed back up. The knotted sheet traps my foot on the bed as the floor catches my fall. I pull the wool cap off the alarm clock. I should have gotten the Venus De Milo clock. So what if it doesn't have any arms? It would figure some other way of indicating the time. I get up. Fold blankets. Put them away for a few more weeks. My laundry re-decorates the apartment.

Finding Ray living in the living room, I ask him if Al explained how to break the air conditioner. Ray gets up and shows me how. I get ready for the day, tell Ray I'll be spending the night at Hope's and that I'm heading out to the unemployment office.

Minnesota doesn't have an unemployment office. That would have negative connotations. Think positive. Minnesota has an Economic Activities Security Establishment (EASE). EASE is a tough place to find. There are signs that cleverly discourage finding EASE. They apparently don't want anyone stumbling in by accident. I walk up dimly lit stairs off a back alley.

The sign on their door says, "If we aren't here, try visiting us on-line." A sign inside says, "Can't wait? Line too long? Visit us on-line!" There is no line, just a clerk at a counter. The first thing she asks is whether I want to go on-line or not. I say no, so she hands me a clipboard and an application. I take the application to a dusty table and check how many pages it has. It seems to be a long application. It starts with roman numerals. When it runs out of those, it starts in on the arabic numerals. When it runs out of those, it starts a series of dots. The application finishes after about 50 dots. I get started. Every other page is an advertisement for using their on-line service instead. I weed out those pages and toss them in the recycling bin. The first dozen pages quiz me to make sure I am in Minnesota instead of visiting this form on-line from another state or country. It asks about last night's weather. The weather questions last half a page. It asks what hotdish is and fenderbergs and pop and binders and lutefisk and disappearing highway lanes and vowel elongation. It asks how many seasons Minnesota has. It asks what types of money are legal tender in this state. It asks how many Round Lakes, on average, are in Minnesota. It asks questions relating to starting a car in Minnesota during the winter when cars don't want to start. It has a whole page of mosquito questions, and then another page of mosquito-related questions. It asks about Minnesota geese, which is obviously a trick question since the flying nuisances are called Canadian geese. Only in Canada are they called Minnesota geese. The next section has me describe where I worked, how long I worked, whether or not I actually worked, and whether or not I consider this application work. It goes on to ask about laws that I might have broken in the process of working for this company. The first sub-part focuses on moral laws. The next sub-part is ethical laws. The third sub-part assumes that the applicant is Lutheran and discusses those laws. The fourth, legal sub-part covers laws of physics and parental guidance. The next section delves into how I managed to lose the job, and what I expect to do about it, and what I have already done about it. It is this section that one of last night's dreams warned me about, but I don't see why the clerk, who is currently drumming her nails on the counter, could have a problem with my responses. The next section addresses my ability to work. It recycles the questions about my ability to start a car in winter and my ability to dress in layers. It mentions goose-down coats, but it does not specify whether the coats are Minnesotan or Canadian goose-down. The next section makes me guess what the following section will discuss. It gives me a 150 options. I say it's about money. The next section says, "Wrong, it's about money." It asks me how much money I made at my last job. It asks me how much money I made at any job ever. It asks me how much money I expect to make at my next job. It asks me if I expect unemployment compensation to pay me more money than I made at my last job. The next section asks what skills I have. This section takes me all the way into the numerically dotted pages. Now it starts to patronize me, telling me that I've done a reasonable job so far, but it explains that most people never see any money from unemployment compensation. Either you haven't worked long enough or you have worked far too long or you don't want to work or you quit or you aren't going to stay in Minnesota or you aren't going to look for work. Even if approved, there will be a waiting period before money could be dispersed. Then the application says that filing the application makes the state employment outlook look bad and negatively effects the impression of Minnesota and its workforce. The hours have grown cobwebs on me, and the application is trying to talk me out of signing it and turning it in. The next section asks for my name, address, phone numbers, date of birth, social security number, driver's license number, bank account numbers, bank account balances, credit cards, credit card balances, property, property that could be readily redeemable for cash at a pawn shop and remember to bring identification with you to prove it's not stolen, mortgages, rents, insurances, other expenses, other incomes, mother and father's names, employment names, titles, addresses, phone numbers, salaries, dates of employment, dates of departure, and whether or not I have been the victim of identity theft, up until now. It asks what I would do about identity theft if it were to happen to me sometime soon. And then it asks for my signature and today's date. By this point, I'm not entirely sure of either, but I take my best shot.

I take the application back up to the clerk, who is eating a late lunch. She says, "I have to make a phone call. I'll be right with you." I sit down and wait. Just sitting here is like getting off of a boat ride and feeling like you are still being buffeted by the waves. I feel like I am still being buffeted by questions. I never noticed the repeating web address in the carpet pattern when I was looking around earlier.

"I have great news!" the clerk calls over to me. I go back to the counter. "I called your company, Flight Control? They want you back! And at your same salary, which isn't bad money. Isn't that terrific? It was all just a misunderstanding," she says, dropping my application into the shredder. I stare at her. I stare at the grinding, chewing-chomping shredder and its late lunch, the disappearing application.

"I was fired."

"Not anymore! Your application said that you had been fired yesterday. If you had begged for getting your job back, I'm sure you would have notated that. You were very thorough. So I begged for your job for you."

What do I say? I'm stunned. "Thank you," I say, heading out the door.

"You're welcome," she says.

I head to the Gun and Blunt Objects Shop. Behind it is the drug store. I buy some prophylactics, since I figure I'm fucked.

Across University Avenue is Yesterday's Diner. My waiter is the same one as yesterday. He tells me I look rotten. I tell him I tried to get money from the unemployment office. He holds up his hands, shows me the front and back of them, and then pulls a quarter from behind my ear. He says, "You'll have an easier time pulling money from behind your ear." I eat my lukewarm soup.

At the library, I read the job ads from last Sunday's newspaper. There are no ads for a mechanical and optical engineer who has experience inventing a self-driving car. There is nothing even close. Here's an ad for a manager. Well, I have managed a small-to-medium-sized group of people. I have experience with organizing and delegating and scheduling. I can work under tight deadlines. No, I haven't worked for them before. No, my name is not Francis. It actually says that your name has to be Francis. I was really close on that one.

I once helped chop down a tree on the Pfuloree cabins property, so I look for a lumberjack ad. No lumberjack ad.

Under Movers, here's several ads for wetlands relocators. There is a Minnesota law that tries to prevent the elimination of wetlands. The law preserves wetlands and promotes land development by allowing developers to move wetlands out of the way of development. Picture a highway cloverleaf interchange from above. The four circles of the cloverleaf can be turned into little round wetlands. Wetlands are usually on flat lands. Cloverleaf interchanges are not flat. Cattails rarely grow on hills, so that's why they need to hire people to figure out how to put a wetland on a hill or in a drainage ditch. Drainage ditches are being turned into minute wetlands all the time.

Several places are looking for experienced painters who are inexperienced at singing show tunes. All it takes is one person to give singing show tunes a bad reputation for an entire industry.

Telemarketing has plenty of ads, must have patience and a pulse.

Why do so many of the waiter jobs require experience as a magician? What do they need to do, pull the tablecloths out from under the dishes?

There is an ad for a zoo worker. No experience necessary. Apply in person, it says.

I return the paper to its shelf. Employment books are quarantined from all others. The shelf is perpendicular to every other shelf everywhere, like a dagger to a body. They have a dozen copies of What Color Are Your Pair Of Shoes? I turn to the table of contents. The chapters are titled: Best Foot Foreword, What Is In Your Soul, Dress For Success, The Shoe-In, Sounding The Shoe Horn, Walking In And Walking Out, and Kick In The Pants. The book has questions like, "List the top five things you like to do." Then it says, "Go talk to people who do those things." Great. Thanks.

The shelf also has pamphlets that explain how to write general resumes. They don't have engineering-specific resume guides. A small poster announces a job fair, hosted by businesses that profit off of job seekers.

I return home to my apartment to have some brussel sprouts. People who don't like brussel sprouts have never watched them explode in the microwave. It's like green fireworks. They taste better without exploding, but I'm not in a taste-better mood. A coin-sized leaf wrapped itself around another leaf, hugged around another leaf, and so on about 17 times over. A brussel sprout is a leaf ball. They should be called leaf balls. Still in my head from last weekend, Jake would say, "I didn't know leaves had balls."

Going to EASE and the library seemed to be natural next steps, natural things to do after being fired yesterday... for all the good they did me. I'm not sure what I should do. This is about as close as I get to actual fear or worry.

I don't think that people who are afraid have thought enough about the fear. The ultimate fear is death. It should be that way. Fear should be afraid of death because death can kill fear. Once you've been told you are going to die, you get it in your mind, you mentally prepare for it, and if it doesn't happen, it kind of lets the air out of fear. Then when family and friends die, and they really do die, that really deflates fear. Fear is a balloon. Fear is a balloon that may pop at any time, but like most balloons, it's far more likely to wither and die of old age.

Worry is the sidekick of fear and sometimes the assistant of fear, just like Malpractice is to Death. Extreme worry is rapid-fire questions wondering what might happen if something extreme occurs. The worrier doesn't take the questions one at a time to determine the probabilities of such occurrences or to examine and plan for each possibility. By managing the chances and the factors, worries dry up and disappear like snow in May.

I'm worried.

No, I'm not really worried. I just don't know what I'm supposed to do. Going in to get fired and going to EASE were easy compared to what I should do at Hope's. Is this a sleepover where I should bring my race car, flannel pajamas and popcorn and my sleeping bag? Or is this a man spending the night with four women, embarking on the sensuous journey of consenting adults, with the man wearing his debonair pinstriped silk pajamas that are as comfortable and distinguished in the boardroom as the bedroom? When I was in my hormone-boiling, early teens, I distinctly recall a dream about this. This shouldn't be any different from last weekend. I slept in what I always sleep in this time of year – shorts sometimes with a T-shirt. The sleeping bag will be left behind. A sleeping bag would send the wrong message – immaturity. At one of the teen years, sleeping bags become appropriate only for camping, not for sleepovers.

Will I be sleeping upstairs or downstairs? Where will Hope sleep? Questions like these are up to the host. I guess I don't need to know. Now I realize that I should have given Hope more information about Tom's cabin before Friday. It would have helped her to know what to expect.

The phone rings. It would be funny if this is Hope telling me what pajamas to wear. Answering the phone, a guy is telling me that he can give me a better interest rate than I am currently paying. I tell him the only way that's possible is if he pays me money. He starts asking questions; I laugh and say good-bye.

I gather up a change of clothes for tomorrow, shorts, shaver, toothbrush and paste, a towel, my book, condoms, and my alarm clock. I also gather nonperishable lasagna ingredients in a separate bag. Cy used to razz me about all my separate bags; she fainted once at the airport when I appeared with one suitcase. Her world set itself right again when I opened the suitcase to reveal many smaller bags inside. I pack well. I get cleaned up and change shirts. The dog above stops tap dancing circles with the slam of a door. I leave Ray a note with Hope's phone number, and I head out. My car sizzles like a fried egg in the parking lot. Luckily it's only three-quarters flammable.

I stop off at Flower Power for flowers. The clerk offers to help me from the moment I walk in the shop. "No thanks," I tell her. I look around and pick out a potted mum with about 14 flowers. The flowers have yellow centers with about 24 layered, yellow petals with orange outer-edges and tips. It smells good. The problem with cut flowers is that they often don't last longer than a few days, like balloons or worries. I don't want to be remembered by dead flowers. The mums should keep. These are my first flowers for Hope... not counting the roses we gave away at the zoo.

Gasping and wheezing from the mum gets my attention while I'm at a light on University Avenue. A bug is fanning itself and having difficulty breathing. I crank open my window. I encourage it out the window. Hope doesn't need buggy flowers.

The sunlight dims suddenly in front of me on the interstate. A cloud of locusts swarm the traffic. A locust lands on my car, licks its lips, and says, "Mmm, No-bug!" It takes off and then the same thing happens about six more times in a row. Either it's the same bug (doubtful) or six different bugs doing the exact same thing. A company in Iowa developed a pesticide called No-bug. They tested it on a group of locusts. Let's call that group the First Generation Locusts. They didn't touch the grain treated with No-bug. So the company sold No-bug throughout Iowa and Minnesota. Slight problem. When the Second Generation Locusts approached the No-bug treated grain, the First Generation Locusts said, "Stay away from that stuff. It'll kill you." Did the Second Generation Locusts listen? No. They ignored the advice. They ate the No-bug treated grain. It made them sick. They got to like the stuff, while still getting sick. They ate the treated grain and made it toxic to humans. Avoiding untreated grain, they flew back and forth between Minnesota and Iowa like an ill wind, eating and turning the grain of No-bug treated fields toxic. A locust lands on my car for the seventh time, licks its lips, and says, "Mmm, No-bug!" I squirt him with windshield wiper fluid. The locust is amusing himself, blowing soap bubbles, as I pull up in front of Hope's house. Leaving the food bag in the car in case it's needed, I get out with the mum which captures the locust's attention. I bat the bug back to Iowa.

21
Principle's Office

Hope waves to me from her second floor deck and then darts back inside. So, she owns this whole house. It is set back from the road with a driveway that winds around to the back. A small front cottage expands in back to a larger home. Pine trees perch on top of tall pine poles throughout the yard, in stark contrast to the treeless construction site next door where workers mill about the one side of the unfinished townhouse monstrosity with cameras in hand. From both my level of the construction and from the second floor, they are taking turns glancing at me. What are they doing? What are all these guys doing, waiting around with cameras, while surreptitiously watching Hope's property? Setting down my backpack and the bright yellow plant, I walk over to the construction workers, who find reasons to shuffle perpendicularly away from my approach. Nearing them, I get boisterously loud, "Hi. Could someone tell me why all of you seem to be working with cameras in hand? Are you all required to photographically document your work?" Some of them bristle; others smirk at my sarcasm. Either way, I have the attention of the crew. "You shouldn't have to work in such mistrusting conditions. I say, stand up for your ethics! Don't let the developers or the construction company... make you take pictures... stomping on your work ethics and your dedication! Put away your cameras and do the work you can be proud of!" I briefly picture them nail-gunning me to a cross as their personal savior. I may have the strength of ten men, but they still outnumber me. "If you need me to make a few calls on your behalf, I should have some time this week." I turn and walk away. Hope is watching me from her balcony. I can see her concerned brow from all the way down here. Her eyes avert to someone coming up behind me. Should I stop or keep walking? Should I turn? A big hand lands on my shoulder, so I stop and turn. This could be it.

The man, who looks like he has too often been on the wrong end of a nail gun, says, "We'll put away the cameras." I thank him, continue to my stuff, and climb the 20 odd stairs up to Hope.

Hope hustles me inside. I drop my backpack near the door.

A new girl throws around some throw pillows, while spraying the cool air with an aerosol can. "Hope! I thought you said you were going to stall him!"

"He was nearly killed," Hope says, taking the mums I'm handing her.

Becky runs in, bends over at the waist, shakes her head, and straightens, flipping her hair back. "What happened? Those are pretty!"

"He told them, 'Put away your cameras' and threatened to make some calls."

"That's not exactly what I said."

"What did you say?"

"I said, 'Hi. Could someone tell me why all of you seem to be working with cameras in hand? Are you all required to photographically document your work? You shouldn't have to work in such mistrusting conditions. I say, stand up for your ethics. Don't let the developers or the construction company make you take pictures, stomping on your work ethics and your dedication. Put away your cameras and do the work you can be proud of. If you need me to make a few calls on your behalf, I should have some time this week.' Only I was a little more dramatic." Faith laughs. Hope smiles with wide eyes.

Becky says, "They could have killed you."

Hope asks, "What did the guy say who stopped you?" Becky and Faith are holding their breath.

"He said, 'We'll put away the cameras.'"

"That's it?!?"

"Yeah..."

"They've been taking pictures of us for weeks–"

"It's been over a month."

"–ever since Nicole flashed them."

My eyebrows rise. I watch Hope examine the flowers and smell them. Hope softly and clearly says, "They are very nice. Thank you. Don't take this the wrong way, but while I am glad you were able to do what you did, I wish you hadn't."

"I was butting into your business..."

"No, it's not that. I just don't want you to get hurt." Hope stares at me. She sighs. "That was pretty funny... 'photographically document your work.'"

"Where did you come up with that?" Faith asks. Not knowing how to answer, I shrug. "Did you see the future and know they weren't going to kill you?"

I stare and ask, "Does anyone have a phone I can borrow? I have to call Mongolia to see if they've heard about pointed perception yet." To Faith, "No, I haven't consciously done pointed perception since yesterday morning. I didn't know how they would react, but I'm used to responding to situations when I think they need a response."

"I don't get how it works," Faith says, gesturing wildly.

"Me neither," I tell her. "The best I can tell you is that I can preemptively make decisions based on perceptions of possible futures. I can play things out in different ways before having to actually play them out."

"So you can see something that doesn't actually have to take place?"

"Right."

"I don't see how that's possible," Faith says, arms flailing.

"Neither do I. But it happens."

"We told you what happened," Becky interjects.

"Have you ever used it to do something that you wouldn't otherwise do?" Faith asks.

"What do you mean?"

"Like rob a bank or something?"

"No."

"Why not?"

"Why not?!? How do I explain this? Consequences."

"But there aren't any consequences, because nobody knows about it. It doesn't actually take place."

"Yes and no. Hang on. Hear me out. There is a time in every kid's life when they find that they have done something wrong and gotten away with it. Do you remember something like that? Nobody knows. There are no repercussions, and yet... you felt terrible for it."

"Sure."

"I am blessed and cursed with a terrific memory. Sometimes I think that's the key to pointed perception. That's how I can do it. I will remember everything. And if I don't do everything right, even in pointed perception, my conscience will tear me apart from the inside. That's why I would never do something in pointed perception that I wouldn't do in the rest of my life. Because I would know. Maybe it's a limitation, but even accounting for morality, there are still so many possibilities and so many futures."

"Does this have anything to do with why you hate TV or magazine questionnaires?" Faith asks with gestures.

What? "Who said I hate TV?" I ask Hope.

"Everyone did."

"I don't hate television. I don't like television. I sometimes watched it, until I got on the wrong side of it. When... when Melanie was all over television, I didn't like what it did to her, how TV people treated her. Every car, every product, seems to have to market its newness, how better it is than the last product. TV is the showplace for the newness of everything. Despite her efforts and our efforts, TV people packaged and repackaged and manipulated her for their own purposes. It surpassed itself in its grotesque depths through the coverage of her death. Television has been called a medium because it's rarely well done. I've also heard that it can't be good because it makes too much money being bad. If I am watching television, I can't watch it quietly. I have to comment on its illogical leaps and its ridiculous assertions and its dismal opinion of its audience. I haven't watched TV in years. Maybe I do hate it."

"Do you want me to turn it on to check?"

"Now, magazine questions? Those are great," I enthuse.

"Right." Becky gives me a hug. "I'm sorry you were fired yesterday. Are you okay?"

"I don't know."

"I wondered if we should have come over last night, but Hope thought we shouldn't, but then when she called us on the way back and told us how many people were at the restaurant, we decided we should have."

I smile. I shrug. When that's not enough, I say, "It's okay." Diverting attention, I ask Hope, "How's school?"

"Good..."

I tell her, "I bet you're giving them the best education anywhere. They'll be wise beyond their years."

Hope gets out a pen and tablet. "What do you feel every fourth grader should learn?" she asks.

I look to the others. "Have you asked them?"

"No."

"Then we all get to play?" I ask. Hope nods. "Look both ways before you cross the street... whether you are on your bicycle or on your feet."

"I never heard that second part," Faith observes, her hand outstretched.

"I just made it up. Turn your wheel in the direction of your skid. Oh yeah, these kids can't drive..."

"Right."

"Be nice to others."

"It's nice to be important, but more important to be nice."

"Love thy neighbor and pick a good neighborhood to live in."

"We only live once, but if we work it right, once is enough."

"What is that from?" Faith asks pointedly. I point to myself.

The door opens, Nicole brings in some bags and sets them on the counter, and steps over to me. "Hey, I hear Hope got you to spend the night!" I nod. "Did you bring these beautiful flowers?" I nod. "Are you up for some Chinese food?" I nod. She turns to work with her food bags, and in a hushed tone asks the others, "What's up with the people next door?"

"Why what happened?"

"Nothing. Not a click. I had a whole plan about using my bags as a shield."

"Ask Ricky."

"What did you do?!?" Now she's loud.

"I talked to them."

"They have been a pain for half the summer! What did you say?"

"You want the whole thing?" She nods, and I tell her.

"What did they say?"

"One guy came over and told me they'd put away the cameras."

"Way to go!" Nicole exclaims while getting out plates. "We were going to get Becky's lawyers, the lawyers she works with, to do something, slam an injunction on their asses or something."

"Where do you work?" I ask Becky.

"I work at the ULAAU. The United Lawyer And Attorney Union. You know, 'There aren't enough billable hours in the day.' Oh yeah, you don't watch television. Well, the ads are on all the time."

"That's something else kids should learn," I tell Hope. "Kids watch plenty of television, but they don't understand what they are watching. They don't know what advertisers are saying. Often advertisers are trying to show their own dream world..."

"Is this something for school?" Nicole asks.

Hope replies, "I had asked them what fourth graders should learn."

"Ooh, how about don't hurt people? And if people hurt you, don't keep it a secret."

"And if you do hurt someone, say you're sorry."

"How about, everything you're learning can be applied to anything you are interested in. Like bugs. You can do physical activity looking for them. You can count them. You can measure them. You can read about them. You can write about them. You can talk about them, sing about them. You can study them."

"That's good, Ricky. You said physical activity, count, read, write, talk, sing, and study..."

"And measure."

"What else?" Hope asks looking around at us, while we serve up from the various cartons of Chinese food.

"Share."

I read a label, "Is duck sauce made from ducks?"

"Don't hurt yourself to impress others," Faith adds with a wave.

"What do you mean?" I ask. "Do you mean never lick a frozen pipe? Or do you mean, dressers are easier to move with the drawers out?"

"I mean, cosmetic surgery and hair coloring and piercings and tattoos and..." Faith seems to be directing this at Nicole. Nicole is fiercely staring down Faith. Nicole's phone rings and Faith tells Becky, "She is different around him," while pointing at me.

Nicole shoots her a fiery look and answers. "Hello? Oh, hi. Yes, I remember. No, that's okay. No... No, I'm not blowing you off. I just have a lot going on. Maybe some other time. Okay." She hangs up.

Faith comments with food in her mouth, "She strings guys along like Christmas lights!"

Nicole gets up, "Faith, could I have a word with you in private?"

"What?"

"Now."

The two leave and the remaining two sit quietly, tuning their ears as if listening for far off fireworks. Quietly we eat. I become analytical of my Chinese food. I can only imagine the Chinese thinking that all Americans ever eat is hamburgers, just like what some Americans think of as Chinese food: chow mein, lo mein, egg foo young, chop suey... That's about it. All of Chinese cuisine represented by a handful of mixtures and wrapped up in little white cardboard trapezoidal cartons with little metal handles.

Hope and Becky watch each other, reading emotions or something. "Would you..." Hope tilts her head. Becky goes to check on the others. Hope turns to me. "How is it?"

"I like this."

"The chicken?"

"No, this."

"The rice?"

"Yeah."

"Not much of a Chinese fan?"

"No, I really like this... how did you pronounce it... rice? Delicious." I take a few more bites. "Are they going to be okay?"

"Do you mind if I check?"

"Not at all."

Hope runs out. Nicole's phone rings. I think about answering it. "Acapella's Pizza," I would say. I quickly decide against it. I've probably caused enough trouble for one day. Are there limitations of allowable daily trouble? I remember being two. I distinctly remember my mother chasing after me as disasters appeared between us. Instead of catching me, she was catching the falling lamp, the dishes and tablecloth mix, the cat, everything on the other end of tugged power cords, the aquarium... I was two, much.

They're back. They're apologizing. That aquarium survived more childhood disasters. "Your phone rang while you were gone. It was the governor... pardoning Faith for anything she may have done up until now."

"I seriously doubt that," Nicole says. "That's a lot of... stuff."

"So what did you do on your first day off, since... well... Friday?" Hope asks.

"Friday was my only day off in six months. Today was not exactly a day off. This morning I went to the hidden unemployment office, filled out a lengthy application for unemployment compensation, and handed it in. The woman called the place I used to work, found out that they would take me back, and then she shredded my application for unemployment. Then I went to the library, looked at last Sunday's job ads, and looked at their job hunting books."

"So you aren't going to go back?"

"No. My boss was looking for the impossible."

"I'm not surprised," Faith says, counting on her fingers. "Creating a self-driving car... seeing the future..."

"Futures," I correct.

"Naturally, your boss would expect the impossible," Faith concludes. "Ow!" she says after someone or something kicks her.

Nicole starts bouncing in her seat. She launches up and grabs me by the arm. "Come on Hope," she says. She takes me down the hall. "We got to talk."

"I get to be in on a private conversation?!?" I shout. "I never get in on the private conversations! This is like graduating from the kiddie table!" We step into a very fluffy, feminine smelling, life-sized version of a doll house room, complete with over-sized furniture. Hope and I sit on the edge of the over-sized, plastic and vinyl bed as Nicole paces about.

"I want to get you a job," Nicole says. "I really want to help you. It's driving me crazy! I've been wanting to ask for a job for you at my office. I'm a receptionist at Pine Press. It's a book publishing company. But they know me a certain way there, and if we both worked there, that would alter the way they'd look at you too and it would be different for me and I think it would be difficult for you and in the long run I don't think I should ask for a job for you. But I really want to help you."

I've driven her crazy. "Becky and Faith... they can't know about the fact that you want to help me?"

"You take me seriously."

"And they aren't used to taking you seriously?"

"No. Even Hope is on their side most of the time."

"I'm on your side! I'm also on their side..."

"Right."

I look around the room. No surface is left uncluttered. I move aside a Double Bubble shirt. The really strangely weird part of the room is the lack of noise. How can these people think in so much quiet? "Nicole... Nicole?" She turns from making faces at Hope. "Thanks for wanting to help me out. I might end up begging you for a job."

"Uh... If you really need a job, just ask me. You won't have to beg. I promise."

I give her a hug as my way of promising to continue to take her seriously. Maybe I hug too much, but it's who I am.

Back at the table, food is reheated. Faith turns off the TV with a glance at me. "You don't have to turn that off because of me. I'm not allergic." I see someone fighting off an army of people without injury. Faith tells me that he's a comic book character, but she doesn't know much about him. Ray's comic book knowledge could help here. I watch him kill people. And I decide, killing is not superhuman. Fighting is not superhuman. Genocide and video game battles and war are not superhuman. What is superhuman? What is extraordinary? I turn back to eating. "Okay, maybe I am allergic."

A chorus of angels harmonize a high note. It's Hope's phone. "Hello? Hi Cy. Yes, he's here. Well... Wait... I can't talk about that. I... We agreed not to talk through intermediaries. Still, I would prefer you to ask him yourself, okay? Okay, here he is." Hope hands Cy over to me.

"Acapella's Pizza," I answer. "Today's special is two large Chinese pizzas with duck sauce and a vat of Double Bubble to wash it down. How can I help you?"

"You still have your sense of humor, such as it is." She pauses for the insult to settle in. "How was your first day off?"

"I went to the unemployment office for several hours–"

"EASE? Don't you have to figure out several clues to finding them?"

"It wasn't that tough."

"How many others were there?"

"Nobody else, except the clerk."

"Right. Go on."

"I filled out a lengthy application for unemployment compensation, and I handed it in. The clerk then had me wait and without my knowing what she was doing or my permission, she called Flight Control. Then she calls me up to the counter and puts my voluminous application in the shredder, saying, 'I have great news! Flight Control wants you back! Isn't that terrific? It was all just some misunderstanding.' She said she begged for my job back for me."

"What did you do?"

"I didn't know what to do, so I thanked her and left."

Nicole spills some sauce on the bust of her shirt. She notices me notice, and she draws it into a heart.

"You aren't going back there, are you?"

"To fill out another application for unemployment? Are you crazy?!?"

"No, no, to Carl's company... to Flight Control."

"No, I'd rather do the unemployment application again. What would I do, go back to watching his veins pop as he yells impossible timetables at me while having a seizure? I don't think so. He's lost his grip on reality. He fired me and then he acted like it was incentive for me to work extra hard. How? As a volunteer?!?"

"So you aren't going back?"

"No."

"Good."

"I'm not sure it's good."

"I'm agreeing with what you're doing," Cy argues agreeably. "What did you do after that?"

"I went to the library. I read the job ads from the newspaper. And I looked at the job hunting books."

"You aren't going to start applying for jobs right away are you?" Cy asks.

I've been looking at Hope and she's been looking at me while I've been talking to Cy. Occasionally I've been glancing at the others. Now I pull the phone away from my head and examine it like it is malfunctioning. She's saying something when I put it back to my ear, but I interrupt, saying, "I'm sorry. I must've misheard you. You didn't just tell this unemployed person, 'You aren't going to start applying for jobs right away are you?' Because I've come to expect a certain level of intelligence or at least smartiness from you, and I can't see any brilliance from that question."

Click.

"Hello?" I hand the phone back to Hope. "She hung up." I hang my head. "I don't know what she thinks I'm going to do. Learn to whittle?" Some of the others laugh.

"You don't have to do anything," Hope tells me. "Let's take a walk." She pulls out a key ring with every-key-known-to-man and unlocks a door. The door opens to a staircase, which leads to another locked door, which opens to the lower level of the house. Hope flips on some lights. It smells like flowers out of an aerosol can on top of stale air conditioning, but it is a nicely furnished duplex. The rooms are twice the size of the rooms at my apartment. A TV, with the same diagonal length as my car, crouches at one end of the living room. She shows me through a kitchen of modern appliances and into two roomy bedrooms with beds and one miscellaneous room without a bed. "This could be Ray's art room or an office for you." I'm not sure why I would need an office. "We can change things around if you want... Get new carpeting..." The carpeting in my apartment is... well... I'm not sure what color it was originally, back when this state was still part of the Wisconsin Territory... and I have yet to see a more three-dimensional carpet than the one in my apartment... and while people are always talking about the new carpet smell, they don't take the time to discuss the intricacies of old carpet smell. Hope asks, "What do you think?"

"It's nice." The living room has a fancy couch, somewhat overshadowed by the TV.

"Listen. Do you hear that?" I shake my head. "Exactly. It's quiet. There are three people upstairs right now, and you can't even tell. I know it's not Tom's cabin or even Todd's cabin, but would you like to live here?"

"Can I think about it?"

"Yes." Hope shuts off the lights she turned on, and I follow her like a puppy. I position myself to go back up the stairs, but Hope heads for the front door. "Do you want to go for a walk?"

I nod my head quickly and say, "Arf, arf," and I pant with my tongue hanging out my mouth. Hope takes me out anyway.

Walking instead of driving reinforces the differences between the Weago neighborhood and my own. Instead of industrial-capacity power lines and transformers, there are giant sky-hugging oak, maple, and pine trees. The trees cast a dollar-green glow over the neighborhood. A few houses away someone accidentally planted an oak tree in the five feet of yard between the sidewalk and the curb of the street. Thirty years ago there may have been plenty of room. The tree disagrees. It is in the process of lifting away the sidewalk block. It has currently lifted it to a 40 degree angle. It's a mighty strong tree. Does it understand the principles of leverage?

Somewhere else, this uneven sidewalk might trip somebody. In Minnesota you learn to watch where you walk, to adjust your footing for ice and glaciers and other challenges that weren't here yesterday.

As we walk the sidewalk, Hope waves to people and says hello to people a good distance away. I wave with her. A black and gray tabby cat pounces out of some bushes and trots up to walk in front of us. The backs of it legs are white like fuzzy pajamas. A few feet in front of us it flops down on the sidewalk and turns its head to watch Hope's approach, with an attitude like it had always been there and what a surprise that we are showing up. All its attention is on Hope. Hope squats down and pets the subtly-striped cat, talking quietly to it. It purrs loudly. It must've recently swallowed a chainsaw. The cat blinks a contentedness that says, "I have waited for this for days." Hope rubs it under the chin. The cat stretches its chin out further than I would have thought possible. With its chin out, its mouth is stretched into a smile. Hope rubs the roots of its whiskers, then its neck, and then pets it with special emphasis around its collar and where the tail meets its back. The chainsaw revs into high gear. Hope pats it and gets up. The cat has a delayed reaction, suddenly looking around like, "Where'd she go?" We step around it and continue down the sidewalk. It trots alongside, until Hope asks it to go home.

A cloud of fur is shaken loose from Hope's hands before she takes my hand in hers. She doesn't interlock fingers precisely with mine. She puts two of her fingers together somehow making our holding hands feel different. I don't remember her doing this before. Maybe she did at the zoo or when we were in Todd's cabin last Friday.

The king of the next block is fenced in his yard and barking advice at his neighbors about their gardening. When the dog sees Hope, he does a double take. This is the first time I have ever seen a dog do a double take. His ears perk up. His smile is only interrupted by concentration as he sniffs the air. As we approach, he stands; he sits. He stands with ears down and tail wagging and tongue sticking out and in and out again. This mutt is happy to see us... I mean Hope. Hope reaches over the fence to pet the dog, saying sweet things to him, and he tries to wash her with his tongue, at least her hand and forearm. I'm all right as long as it isn't a bandana-wearing golden retriever named Ben.

Down the block, out of sight, she rubs her slobbered hand on a tissue, and then offers her hand to me. I take it, and she does the non-alternating fingers grip again. Passing by a stretch of sidewalk that has cut-outs for more mighty trees, we arrive at a park encircling Lake Weago. College-aged girls jog by an elderly couple while two younger boys follow along on small bicycles. As we walk around the lake, Hope smiles and says hello to most people. I take note of the few exceptions. Expressions brighten when people recognize her. I nod, knowing what it's like.

A small, pebbled creek cuts through limestone on its way to the lake. We stop on a wooden bridge, leaning on its wooden rails, looking out at the sun setting picturesquely over the lake. "What do you think I should do?" I ask Hope.

"Do you think I have the answers?"

"Sure. You've been a few steps ahead of me since we met."

"Me? What about you? I can't see the futures," Hope says as a couple jogs by. They do imitations of the dog's double take.

"Until recently, that wasn't public knowledge... Besides other than a few times relating to last weekend, I really don't use pointed perception much."

"Maybe it could answer your question about what to do," Hope suggests, her face aglow, her hair blowing away like rays.

A giant nuclear furnace burns hydrogen into helium eight minutes away at the speed of light, a light that shimmers the ripples of Lake Weago. Grade school pictures of the sun portray eyes or sunglasses and a smile. Solar scientists search the sun's surface for the smile. What they find is a tongue. Giant tongues of fire lick out, tasting interplanetary space. A giant tongue sticks out at us now.

A man older than that light steps lightly across the bridge and up the path with a sigh and a few wheezes, like a bug from a mum. In the summer, Minnesotans circle their lakes for exercise. In winter, they walk the indoor shopping malls, a Minnesota invention. In winter, the giant nuclear furnace barely makes an appearance. It sends vacation postcards from the distant south, saying, "Wish you were here."

Hope rubs my shoulder. "You seem to be a million miles away." I smile. "But it's good to see you smile."

Two ducks swim by us, reminding me that ducks mate for life.

A man runs to a halt onto the bridge by us and exclaims, "Whew!"

I tell Hope, "It may take me awhile to sort this out... to decide what to do. I guess I just didn't learn how to handle this sort of situation when I was in the fourth grade."

"So you blame your fourth grade teacher?"

"Pretty much, Loverducks." I run the back of my index finger across her cheek and under her chin. Taking her hand, she adjusts her grip to her own uniqueness, and we walk back, swinging our arms. I am thinking about the sun and pointed perception when Hope asks me if I'd like to sleep in her room tonight. "That's a much easier question than what do I want to do with the rest of my life. Yes, I'd like that."

"Did you bring your sleeping bag?" Hope asks. I stop, lurching our linked arms, and gape at her. "Just kidding!" she grins at me. Hope takes me up to her room; I pick up my backpack on the way in. I drop the bag and kick off my shoes, while she closes some curtains. A framed group picture sits on her dresser. "That's my family the last time we were all together. That was two and a half years ago."

"Who are all of these guys?"

"My brothers."

"There must be a hundred of them!"

"Close."

"What are all these?" I'm pointing at a collection of ornate little boxes.

"Can't you guess?"

"Can I look inside one?" She hands one to me. "I hate to break this to you, but it's empty."

She's waiting for my guess. I shake my head. "They're Hope chests. Get it?"

I poke her bust. "That's the Hope chest."

"Everyone thinks they're immensely clever by giving me my very own Hope chest. My closet is full of them. One of these days I'll have to get rid of them."

"You could put something in them..."

Nose-to-nose she sneers, "Like what? All my hopes and dreams?"

"Well, do you want a lock of my hair? And my picture for the lid?" I tease.

Hope lowers herself off her toes and wonders, "You'd give me a lock of your hair? And a picture?" Uh oh. She doesn't know I'm teasing. She has melted into a little puddle by my feet.

"I thought you said you were going to get rid of them."

Hope mumbles something bashfully.

"What was that?"

Hope mumbles a bit louder.

"What?"

"I wasn't head-over-heels in love before!"

"You don't have to shout."

"I'm not shouting."

My eyes land on an autographed picture of Melanie. "Wow. You are a fan." Hope points to the framed picture next to it, the one from Bolder Rock magazine with me looking, like Yolanda said, like a deer caught in headlights.

"Do you want me to sign it?"

"Would you?"

"No. I'm not going to ruin a perfectly good picture by signing it. Besides if I remember right, there is a coupon for acne cream on the back. It might not have expired yet."

"What are you trying to say?"

"N-n-nothing! I'm not trying to say anything!" I exclaim to Hope's rapidly wrinkling brow. I thumb through some of the songs on a disposable music player:

> Give Me Life by George Harrison
> You Didn't Have To Be So Nice by The Lovin' Spoonful
> Wonderful World by Louis Armstrong
> Don't Worry Baby by The Beach Boys
> Miracles by Jefferson Starship
> Hopes and Dreams by Melanie

I look around some more. She has a plaque for volunteering at the Remember When Nursing Home. "You volunteer at the place near my apartment?"

"No, they have another one just a few blocks from here."

"So they're a franchise, like fast food restaurants? Do they have the same old people at each location?"

"No," she giggles.

"I stopped trying to earn awards and trophies when I found out you can buy them."

"You did not!" Hope exclaims. And I can hear her brow without turning to look at her.

"You're shouting again..."

Hope fiercely mumbles something. A fake apple says "Those who love teaching teach others to love learning." I pick it up and act like I'm eating it. Hope takes it away, polishes it on her shirt, and puts it back. I leap on her bed. I sprawl out.

"Where are you going to sleep?" I ask her.

She dives on top of me. She kisses me with every lip on her face. She stops. She sniffs. She licks her arm, waits, and sniffs it. She rolls off me and the bed. "I'm sorry, I've got to brush my teeth."

I try to tell her that there is nothing wrong, but she's already in another room. I sit up. What am I supposed to do? I retrieve my backpack, dragging it bedside. Opening it, there is wheezing and gasping for air. I pull out my overly dramatic alarm clock and set it... where am I going to set it... The dresser is too far away; the nightstand is cluttered. I set it on the floor. I change into shorts. I sit back down. She must have a bathroom right off her room. The door is partway open. What am I waiting for? I retrieve my toothbrush and paste from my bag and barge into the bathroom. She looks funny brushing her teeth. I shoulder her aside for room at the sink and prepare my brush. She's mumbling something, but once again, I don't understand Mumblese. I can read it. Anyone can read it. I just can't converse in it fluently. I brush my teeth next to her, gently elbowing her needlessly. I'm lucky she's laughing.

Her mouth is full, and she is mumbling intensely. I start doing sign language... not a formally recognized sign language, not an intelligent sign language, more like a prehistoric, pre-linguistic form of sign language. It is more gibberish and gesture than actual communication. She grabs my shoulder and turns me around. I hear the sound of Hope spitting. It is the daintiest spitting sound, like she doesn't know how to spit, too much tongue and too little air. She turns me back around, offering me free use of the sink. Confused momentarily at having too much space at the sink, I finish brushing my teeth.

"I should have closed the door," she tells me. "I don't like people to see me spit. Hey, when did you change?"

I rinse my mouth. "I think we should test multiple mouth brushing. We stand side-by-side like this, cheek-to-cheek. Then I'll brush both our mouths at once! Hey! Let's get your roommates in here! We'll brush five mouths at once! Just think about the savings of... It has to save something."

"Yeah, privacy."

"Just think of the privacy savings!"

"Great. Speaking of privacy, git." She pushes me out the door, which closes after me. It might have even locked, but I'm not going to check. I can tell when I'm not wanted once the door hits my butt.

I sit down on a red heart-shaped chair. I'm in Hope's heart. She has a soft heart. This is comfortable. I could fall asleep. I close my eyes. I start to snore. Snoring the second verse of a snoring song I just made up, I hear Hope's return.

Through my eyelids, I see the change of light, and I feel her breath on my cheek before she says, "I know you're awake. I can see your eyes flutter." I snore a little louder. "Do you always sleep with a smirk?" I snore a bit louder still. "Don't you want to see what I am wearing to bed?"

"Huh? What?!?" I awake. "Wow!"

She looks like a snow angel. She looks like the most beautiful princess I have ever seen or imagined. She is the dream I have dreamt of my entire life. This is the smile that has opened up my life, peeling back my layers, removing my mask. This is the woman who is putting my heart in overdrive. My heart is racing from within her heart. I tingle.

All I can say is, "Hello Beautiful!"

I stop myself from looking at my watch. I ask her the day and the time. She tells me with curiosity as she turns off the light. A night-light switches on in the dark. I know the model number of its photoelectric sensor without looking. She takes me by the hand to her bed. She starts to kiss me again. I stop her to tell her, "I love you, Hope."

"I love you too, Ricky." She makes love to me.

I make love to her.

22

The Catch

Hope climbs over me, "I forgot to set the alarm!" I like her climbing over me. I'll have to get in her way more often. Hope checks the clock and double checks it with my alarm clock.

"Are you late?"

"No," she says opening the curtains, flooding the room in light.

"'Cause if you missed your school bus, I can give you a ride to school."

"Hilarious," she says without hilarity, as she digs around in her closet. I watch. She heads into the bathroom, shuts the door, opens the door, asks if I have to use it, I smile and say no, and she shuts the door again. I lie back contentedly with contentment. I am content. Content comes from the Spanish word "con," which means "with" and "tent" which means "temporary housing." I am with temporary housing.

I wonder what I should do today. I probably need to go home, leave my temporary housing for my more permanent temporary housing.

If I move in downstairs, Hope and I can visit each other as often as we want. If I move in downstairs, my lodging could become very relationship-dependent. I picture the way Hope greeted me... the way she looked last night at 10:42 when I was snoring in her heart chair. I guess I'm moving in downstairs. I'm not an idiot.

I get up. My alarm clock has little hearts floating over it. What's up with it? Oh, Hope picked it up and looked at it to verify the time. It likes her.

I stretch and run my fingers through my hair. I get dressed. I look out the window, and two sunflowers are looking in. I do a double take. We are on the second floor. We are all on the second floor. These must be tall sunflowers.

I get my things bagged up and ready to go. Am I just supposed to go? No. If I was supposed to go, Hope would have said good-bye. I need to wait. Without really knowing, I think I just passed a relationship test, a stepping stone on our trail together. The sunflowers nod in the breeze.

Using the lesson Hope taught me last night, I lick my arm. I wait. I sniff my arm. I brush my teeth with my dry toothbrush. I put it away. I take it back out and brush my tongue. I figure I lose a few taste buds every time I brush my tongue. Putting the brush away, I glance around for mints or mint gum or a mint plant or a wild parsley plant...

There is yelling in the hallway, then nothing, and then a knock on the door. Opening the door, I find a legally-dressed Becky. "Hello," I greet her as she looks me up and down and around the room for Hope like I hid her or something.

"We just wanted to make sure you two were up."

"Yup."

"See ya," she says. I shut the door and return to my seat on the bed.

I get comfortable. I close my eyes. I shut out bodily feelings. I open my mind to meditation. A thousand things hit me at once. It's like dodgeball. When everything is coming your way, you might be on a one-way street heading the wrong way. Many of the things have to do with Flight Control or things I should talk to Hope about or decisions I have to make. One of the things is an appreciation of the fact that I no longer work for Flight Control. This is a weird thought. I am relieved to be done working for Flight Control. I ask myself why. I answer myself that long ago, science legally divorced itself from moral responsibility. The inventor invents something in a science lab like the room Tom put together at his cabin with the colorful beakers and the zapping thing. The lab is sterile of moral discussion. The invention is patented, which means that no one can duplicate the work for seven years. Then anyone can do whatever they want with it. Important processes like the nuclear bomb or the secret formula for Cooler Cola are not patented. They are kept secret, except that the secret of the nuclear bomb was stolen as it was invented, and Double Bubble has a cola very similar to Cooler Cola.

The point is that AutoDrive started as a way of increasing the mobility of the mobility impaired. Then other organizations became involved. It has been clear for some time that the Department of Defense has been looking into offensive possibilities of AutoDrive technology. Other countries will have the technology just as fast. AutoDrive then changes from being a tool to improve life to becoming a tool to kill life. I once heard one of the physicists involved in the Manhattan Project speak regretfully over never reexamining the purpose of creating the bomb after Germany was defeated. I should not be an inventor of a product that is being developed for immoral purposes. By no longer working for Flight Control, I am freed from the moral burden. I am no longer in conflict with my principles.

Inventions need to be guided into society, not thrown at society to see how big a splash the invention can make.

It's just like the Funnellator. One of my engineering classmates created the Funnellator. He punched two holes on either side of a larger-than-kitchen-sized funnel. From the four holes, he tied four nine-foot lengths of rubber tubing. Each outer end of the rubber tubing was tied into a handle-like loop. The Funnellator was a very simple device, a water balloon slingshot. Two people would stand about five or six feet apart, holding a set of handles. A third person would place a water balloon in the funnel and pull back. Usually this person was squatting down low for maximum balloon elevation. After adjustments for aiming, the funnel holder would let go of the funnel, launching the water balloon. The water balloon could land as far as a city block away, depending upon the size of the balloon, wind currents, slope, and other factors. Sometimes we would have someone try to catch the water balloon; sometimes involuntary participants would intercept the balloons. Not long after the creation of the Funnellator, it was borrowed and used for disagreeable purposes and was taken away by the authorities. Several years later, a similar device was patented, but not by my classmate.

The bathroom door opens. An impeccable school teacher enters the room, smiles at me, and puts on Hope's earrings.

"Is there anything I can do for you?" I ask.

"No," she says, turning. She stops and grins at me. "You're in a good mood, aren't you?"

"Shouldn't I be?"

"Yes, Mr. Resilience, but then there's your job situation."

"I'll figure something out, don't worry."

"That's what I'm worried about. I want it to be us, together, figuring it out. And there's something else. The kids you were reading to on Monday..."

"What about them?"

"Do you want to have kids?"

"Them? They are a bunch of troublemakers. No thank you."

"No, I mean kids of your own?"

"Not necessarily, but..." I say noticing relief in her shoulders, "I'm not opposed to having a kid either."

She smiles, "Good... good."

"That's what you wanted to hear?"

"Yes. You aren't just telling me what I want to hear, are you? Did you pointedly perceive this?"

"No. No."

"Good. I need to get some things together. It will just take a moment. I'll have some grading to do this evening, but I'd be happy to have you around. Do you have any plans?"

"No. I'll call you around five." I pick up by backpack.

"You're going? Don't you want some breakfast?"

"No. I'll be fine."

"I'll walk you out." Hope kisses me good-bye at the top of the stairs as a few construction workers arrive for work next door. I catch them all watching me climb into my car. As I drive away, I realize how far I have to go to get home, that I am hungry, that I have to go to the bathroom, and that I am stuck in rush traffic. Now would be a good time for a flying car.

Hope's response about not necessarily having kids is interesting. She is a school teacher, a caring school teacher, so kids have to matter to her on some level. I don't think her teaching kids is just happenstance, like my reading to the apartment urchins on Monday. I have to be at the apartment complex; I live there. Or I did anyway. She doesn't have to be at school. She says she's rich. Why is she there? Why does she teach?

I dream about last night, the way Hope felt, the way we–

I get cut off by another car. Dream interruptus. I hit the brakes in time. Traffic crawls unevolved. I am uninvolved, since I'm not going to work like all the rest. Nothing is moving, especially in my lane. I try to catch up to the other lanes without success. I turn on the radio, and the music moves. Unfortunately the songs and the talk all revolve around breakfast and toilet movements. I turn it off. Traffic slowly waltzes without the music.

When I get home, I should take care of basic business and then move up to pointed perception. People keep expecting me to use it; I might as well. I'll figure out how to get employed or something.

On my apartment door there is a note from my landlady that I read in the bathroom. She wants to meet with me to discuss the air conditioning situation. What air conditioning situation? The air conditioner is broken. Or technically, it was and is again. Al fixed it, and now we have returned it to its original, non-working condition.

On my bedroom door there is a long note from Ray. Aimee called. She and Ray talked. He told her about last weekend, and Ruth's video show, and that I talked about her. He told her about my getting fired. And so she's going to fly in as soon as she can to kick some butt. I almost choke on the banana I'm eating, as I picture Aimee setting things straight at Flight Control.

There are several messages on the answering machine. The first one says, "I just want to know one thing, did you do it this time?" That's Jake's voice. He is such a concerned friend.

The next message asks, if I were given a phone, a mobile cellular phone, would I keep it with me? That's Cy. She must've gotten over hanging up on me last night. Or she liked it so much, she wants to be able to hang up on me all the time. Yeah, that's probably it. I catch on quick.

The final message is Lefty calling to ask me to be at the lab at ten tomorrow. He starts to give me the address again, realizes the stupidity of giving me a reminder, and he hangs up.

I call Jake back. I reach his messaging service. "Jake, it's me. Yes," I tell his service. I unload my travel bag and put away the lasagna ingredients. I put away my laundry. I balance my checkbook. I look at my financial situation. I have more money than I thought. Rent has been cheap. Ray has detoured me from eating meat. Entertainment has consisted of watching Ray's artistic process or keeping score for the neighbors upstairs or catching a free concert from below. Of course I have money.

I catch some sleep. For lunch, I have a soy burger and ketchup.

I relax. A second set of sirens arrives at the apartments and through the crowd I catch a glimpse of an old man being horizontally taken away from the laundry room downstairs. I overhear the police tell my neighbors that he was found in a storage unit. He was dead when he was discovered. I check my watch. It's Friday, two days in a future. I take a short step into that future. I take the old man a bunch of bananas. I set them in front of his cage. He doesn't die on Friday.

I type up a resume. It says I graduated from Minnesota University with a Bachelor of Science degree in optical and mechanical engineering. The resume explains that I pioneered the development of AutoDrive, a car that drives itself. At Flight Control, I was the manager of the Research & Development Division. I don't mention being a driver of and assistant to Melanie. I don't mention pointed perception. And I don't mention having been fired.

I type up a cover letter that says I would like to work in a grain elevator. I have always been interested in grain and the rodents that inhabit them. I emphasize that grain dust doesn't bother me.

I type up a letter introducing myself as someone who could be an essential ingredient in the Snowflake Flour workplace. While they must sift through sacks and sacks of resumes, mine is the recipe for engineered growth at Snowflake Flour.

I type up a cover letter sparking interest in a local welding company.

Remembering an ad I saw in the newspaper, I explain to a company interested in hiring a manager that I would be willing to change my name to Francis, with the proper incentives.

My letter for the Museum Of Questionable Inventions states that I am a qualified expert.

I type up a letter professing my undying love of vanilla milkshakes and my interest in engineering perfect shakes for all the customers of the Ice Cream Bar. It would be sweet.

My final letter states bluntly that I have no experience that relates to the Gun and Blunt Objects Shop, but I would take a shot at it.

I mail the letters out.

I fast forward to next Monday and call them up... all of them. They all seem to remember my letters, but having your cover letter posted on the break room bulletin board is not necessarily a sign of a successful cover letter. I receive a rejection letter from Snowflake Flour. That was nice of them. I send back a rejection letter rejecting their rejection letter, saying, "I'm sorry. I cannot accept your rejection of my application. I need the job. I'll be in Monday at nine."

Back in my room, the apartment has heated up. I decide not to type up the cover letters, and since I don't do the cover letters, I won't need the rejection-rejection letter, but I figure I need the resume anyway, so I type it up and print it out.

I go downstairs and leave a bunch of bananas in front of the old man's cage.

I run into Ray in the hallway. "What are you doing?"

"Leaving bananas for the guy in the cage."

Steam billows out Ray's ears as he unlocks our apartment door. I have never seen that happen. The steam billowing part. I've seen the apartment door unlocked plenty of times. "I'm working as hard as I can. Don't give away our food."

I think about mentioning what I saw through pointed perception, but instead I just nod and ask, "Have you been at the co-op?" When he grunts an affirmative grunt, I ask if they need a mechanical engineer. He gives me a sanity-questioning look. I retreat to my room. Two moments later a yell and a crash bring me back out to the living room. Kelly has apparently bitten Ray's hand, as her face shines at his feet. "Don't tell me, you were juggling her parts and didn't catch something?"

"You think this is funny?" he asks as his blood drips onto her upper lip.

"No. What do you need? A towel?"

Ray pushes past me to the bathroom. He yells some more from in there. Our neighbors have taught Ray some new words. This is one of your more educational apartment complexes. I wait around... stare at the hallway paint-job... check out the door frame... Ray comes out with a bandaged hand. "I need to know what's going on," Ray states. My face gets quizzical. "Are we moving? Does Hope really want me around? How far away is their place? How far is the university from there? How far is the co-op from there? What's your plan?"

"I'm nearly positive that I'm going to move to Hope's. She lives near Lake Weago. It's walking distance to the co-op if you don't mind taking a whole day to do it and possibly hopping some fences and crossing some highways. It's about 20 minutes away by motorcycle. I recommend using your motorcycle. Hope showed me the place last night. She pointed out a room that she suggested as a studio for you and otherwise as an office for me, not that I know what I would do with a home-office. Aren't they for adults trying to escape their children or something?" I get a near-laugh out of him. "Hope and I are still getting to know each other, but I have no reason to believe that she is lying about offering the first floor to both of us." I get a bottle of Double Bubble from the refrigerator. "The university is about as far away from there as here, except that the buses don't run through their neighborhood. That's what's going on. I'll talk to Hope about starting to move things over on Friday. Do you want to move with me?" I drink.

"How can we move everything?"

"Boxes. Boxes will help. I'll rent a truck. We'll have to remember the stuff in the storage locker." Taking another drink, I drool accidentally and wipe my mouth with my arm, "Not that I have a plan."

"We'll have to change our address... our phone number..."

"Yeah, those and other things... So what do you think?" I ask him as he presses on his wound.

"The place looks nice?"

"Way too quiet."

"I'll move," Rays says without hesitation. We look at our stuff. When we accumulated all of this, we didn't put a whole lot of thought into having to move it all. "I might be able to get some boxes from the co-op. I'll let you use all the radish and onion boxes."

"Thanks," I respond as the phone rings. I only get out a "Hell" of a hello, when I am interrupted by screaming, hollering, and whooping from the caller. It's Jake. He's hysterical.

"**It's about time!**" he yells. He then launches into a lengthy list of colorful euphemisms for the act of procreation. Ray and I stare at the phone.

"Jake. Jake. Hey, Jake!"

"What?"

"Ray and I may be moving to Hope's house this weekend sometime, do you–" Jake falls back into his shouting, whooping, and hollering. "Jake, do you think you might be–"

"You want some help moving?"

"Yes."

"Any major appliances? Any waterbeds? Any large car parts?"

"Just the dashboard from a '64 Wild Stallion..."

"Anything else?"

"Yeah, but nothing like you mentioned."

"Count me in... probably. Wait. What time?"

"I don't know. I have to talk to Hope first. I'm calling her at five."

"Call me tonight to let me know when."

"Got it."

"You did it!" He yells something I can't exactly understand and hangs up.

I go into my room and sit down. I shake my head and check my clock.

I relax. I dream I am reading my book. I stop the dream and open my eyes. There is no point in foreseeing what is going to happen in my book. I relax again. I go to talk to the landlady. I tell her that Ray and I will be moving within the week. The air conditioner hasn't worked for ten days. She promises to get it fixed. I tell her that it doesn't make any difference because I lost my job. Her expression shifts from worry to confusion to amazement to mental calculation to a strange sort of smile. She asks if I might not be able to afford the rent. I reply that it's a strong possibility. She tells me we could work something out. She tells me that she's lonely. I tell her I'm leaving. I go back to my apartment. Sometime later, I am sitting with my eyes closed. I open my eyes and I am in my bedroom with strangers looking closely at my face for signs of life. I ask them what they are doing. The landlady snipes that she is showing the apartment and that no one answered the door. They track muddy shoes out and try to step everywhere else in the apartment. I am annoyed. The landlady is amused. I open my eyes. I am in my room. I check my clock. I decide that I don't need to talk with the landlady. She'll see us moving out when we move out. It takes awhile to shake off my annoyance at the way she acted... the way she will act... I mean, the way she may act. Was it pointed perception or was it the grossest, most distasteful version of my housing situation? I get over it. I relax. I'm going to the Lake Weago neighborhood library on Sunday afternoon. The librarian shows me a computer terminal and says that all of the Sunday job ads appear on the Wednesday before. If I try to respond to the Sunday ads on Sunday, I am already too late. I look at her like she's crazy. She insists. She says that the newspaper accepts information on the Tuesday preceding the Wednesday preceding the Sunday. I wave her off. I know all about preceding. I go back there next Wednesday and read the ads. I memorize the best two ads. I go to the company of the better ad on the Tuesday before the Wednesday and tell the receptionist with the blue streaks in her hair that I'm responding to the ad. I'm asked which ad. I explain that it is the one they just requested. They assume I have an in at the paper. Some people ask me a few questions about what I know about a newer type of CAD software, but I don't know it. I thank them and leave. I look into the software and take a half-day course on it. I go back the previous Tuesday. Now I respond to their questions with in-depth knowledge of that software and other 4D kinematic modelers. I know my engineering formulae. They ask some more questions and these questions relate better to my previous job. They ask me if I'm detail-oriented. I close my eyes and start listing details around me, including coffee stains. Saying that I'm detail-oriented is like saying snow is cool. They ask if I can start next week. I agree. They call the newspaper to cancel the ad. As long as I play my cards right, I will be offered a job next week.

I'm back in my room. It's five after five. My clock is hopping mad. I call Hope. "Did I catch you at a good time?" I ask.

"Yes. Is everything all right?"

"Fine. Listen, I was wondering if Ray and I could move in, partly on Friday, but mostly on Saturday?"

"Really?"

"Yes."

"That's terrific!" Hope says and then the phone gets muffled. I wonder if she dropped the phone into a muffler, either the hand warming garment or the car exhaust pipe. With less muffler, she repeats, "Friday and Saturday."

"Right," I confirm.

"So what are you going to do tonight?" Hope inquires.

"Maybe read... maybe take a walk."

"You could do those things over here..."

"I thought you had grading to do?"

"Yes. I'm doing it now. Remember these are fourth graders. I can talk and grade. I can watch a movie and grade..."

"The theater isn't too dark?"

"Not at the theater, Sweetie. Here. On TV," she hesitates halfway through the letters of TV like she is speaking a forbidden word. I'm stuck on her calling me Sweetie again. It makes my heart feel warm. I hope it's not a heart attack.

Silence on the phone. The neighbors start up a catchy tune.

"Uh, okay," Hope breaks the phone silence. "I'll ask you. Do you want to come over?"

"I'm not sure."

"Do you want me to come over there?" Hope persists with a teacher's tone.

I'm not giving her my best. Doesn't she deserve my best? I want this relationship to work... not just work... I want us to be great together. "Hang on a second." Between what's happened and what's going to happen, we should celebrate. "Hope, I'm sorry about that. I'd like to pick you up at seven and take you out to dinner, someplace nice. You can bring your papers or tests or quizzes along with you."

"They're tests, but I should be finished by then."

"Okay, I'll see you at seven."

"Bye!" she says.

That was close. What was I thinking?!? With as nice as Hope has been to me, with her sweet-fun-positive-supportive-lively attitude, her intelligence, her beauty, and her persistence, I've got to be at my best. Nearly falling backwards, with arms flailing, into a conundrum, I forgot to pay attention to my relationship. Mental note: never, ever take the relationship for granted. Don't treat her the way I would treat Ray or Tom or Jake. She has been better to me than any other woman. Sure, Cy earned mega-points by hooking the two of us together, but then she lost those points again with the snooty attitude. Cy probably did that on purpose to make it clear that she wasn't trying to earn points with me. That's got to earn her some points right there.

I grab the phone book. My first dining choice accepts my seven o'clock reservation. That's an advantage of setting up a Thursday night date. I picture Hope looking gorgeous, looking very not school-teacher-like and getting into my crummy Pony Express. Something is wrong with that picture. I open the phone book again. Accidentally flipping to chauffeurs, I quickly flip to limousines. I call up three, asking rules and availability for a stretch. I call back the second one, talking out my plan and setting up the ride. I clean up, iron my shirt, and polish my shoes. Buff. My suit was parked too close to my gorilla suit. Sniffing my suit, it smells a bit like fake-fur-covered-latex. The smell comes out in the ironing.

Ray checks up on my activity, "What's up?"

"Date."

"Ooooo," he says, with a junior high tone, and he lets me alone.

As I iron, it dawns on me that I can't give Hope flowers – that was last night. I can't give her all my stuff, my roommate, and myself – that will be the two nights following tomorrow night. There isn't time to go far for something. I decide to get something nearby on University Avenue. Where do I hang my suit? I get it on.

In the hallway, the original Loverducks is hanging off the stair rail with a friend or a sister. "Hi Loverducks!" I call to her on my way by, and her blood rushes to her face.

At the Still Sparkles Used Jewelry shop, I select a bracelet of bright colored, nearly translucent gemstones. Learning the price, I ask the jeweler to put it back. He keeps it out, admiring it. I think the old man wants to wear it. He asks how much I would be willing to pay for it. He uses all his jeweler's adjectives as he compliments the bracelet. We haggle. We tell our stories. I end up buying it for a reasonable price. Flowers would've been cheaper, by the room-full, but then that's not the statement I'm trying to make. I've done cheap. That's how I can afford to get something nice for my girlfriend. The jeweler offers to sell me a fancy box for the bracelet. I decline. He shows me the box that comes with the bracelet. It is a fine cardboard box with a soft cotton, jewelry bed inside. Emblazoned across the lid is his store's name. He says that some women might not mind his shop's name on the bracelet's box, but that their friends or their mother might take offense at the name of the store. As I buy the fancy box, I ask him how many boxes he sells. With a soft tone of diplomacy, he says, "Sometimes it seems like I sell more boxes than jewelry."

I stop by the cash machine. I briefly wait for it to finish its plotting and planning. I get out a mix of insect spray and American money.

A shiny black stretch limousine follows me into my parking lot. I dash in, check my appearance, change shoes, and dash back out. The limousine still sparkles. The driver is waiting at its side surrounded by nearly every child from the Twin Cities. I excuse myself through the crowd and greet the driver.

"Are any of these yours?" he asks.

"No."

"Hop in."

We discuss my plans, Roger and I. We synchronize our watches, and Roger briefs me on issues of etiquette. I think he thinks he's my dad. As he drives, he informs me of weather conditions, weather forecasts, and other activities that may impact us at the target locations. He advises me of the restaurant's specials and recommendations. Roger fine-tunes my strategy. He directs me to the hidden breath mint locations throughout the vehicle, insisting that I pocket a few now. He directs me on the purpose and usage of several buttons and switches. He is alarmed that I don't have a phone. I politely refuse to take his spare. I watch him take a slightly faster way to Hope's house. I pay attention. This will be a great mission– I mean, date.

The next door construction site is abandoned, as we pull up to Hope's house. The upstairs door opens, someone comes out, leans with hands on the rail, staring down, and hustles back inside, leaving the door open. Two other heads pop out to look, like gophers out of a hole. Roger taps on my window from the outside. I lower it without a crank.

"She is expecting you, isn't she?" Roger asks. He's a riot. "Which one is Hope?" he asks from the corner of his mouth, ventriloquist-like. I look again. Faith and Nicole are heading down the stairs.

"Neither."

"Then you need to stay in the car. You only get out for your date," Roger tells me.

I lower the window the rest of the way as they approach. Faith puts her face in. "Nice," she evaluates.

Nicole leans almost halfway in, "Way to go, Ricky!" She snoofs the interior. "Gotta like it!"

"Thanks. It's not actually mine." They smile at me like I have just said the stupidest thing with the best intentions. "Where's Hope?"

Nicole starts to answer. Faith interrupts, "She'll be just a second or two." Nicole starts to crowd Faith out. I catch Roger eying Nicole's butt.

He taps both of them and asks them to stand aside, as Hope approaches. She has the biggest grin on her face. She looks gorgeous. I think this is the first time I've seen her hair up. Other than when we met at Sharon's, this is the first time I've seen her in a dress. Roger opens the door for her. She turns to her friends and says, "Don't wait up!"

Faith reminds us, "Remember kids, this is a school night!"

"Hi Sweetheart, this is a nice surprise!" Hope says, unaware that her friends are still at the window.

"Bye!" they shout, startling Hope, as Roger closes the window and starts us off.

Hope gives me a kiss. "When we talked, was I too pushy?" I shake my head. "Good. I just wanted to see you, that's all." A few curls of hair spin near her ears.

"Did you finish the tests?"

"Yes."

"How did they do?"

"Do you want a run down of their grades? I can tell you, but you can't tell anyone until about ten tomorrow morning. Alfredo is doing well. Antonio needs some tutoring to get up to speed. Bee got an A. Chong got a B. He could do better. Chue got... what did Chue get? I think Chue got an A. She's really improved. Davida missed class. Fong got a D... Hillary–"

"What's the matter with Fong?"

"I don't know. I'm not sure he thinks it's cool to get good grades. Oh, I wanted to mention to you... I told the class your story about Loverducks. They loved it. And I started working on the list."

"What list?"

"The list. The list of things every fourth grader should know. From last night."

"Oh, that list. So did you cover: turn your wheel in the direction of the skid?"

"I covered most of the list."

"What did they add?"

"What do you– I didn't ask them."

"You should ask them. Some of them have to be experts."

"Good idea... Where are we going?"

"First Street Station. Have you been there before?"

"No."

"It's one of my favorite restaurants."

"Be careful of saying that. I'm not superstitious, but some of my mother's friends have listed the number of restaurants that they have doomed by calling it their favorite. Do you know where Tom took Becky?"

"No. That's right, wasn't their date tonight?"

"Yes, he picked her up just before you arrived. We thought you two had something worked out between you." I shake my head. "We've been teasing Becky about dating Tom..."

"Why?"

"Tom and Becky? Tom Sawyer?"

"I didn't think of that."

"What was Becky's last name?" Hope quizzes me.

"Thatcher." I get a kiss from my teacher. She doesn't look like any teacher I ever had. "You look great!"

"Thank you. You do too," she says while straightening my collar.

At a stoplight, people waiting to cross the street try to see who is in the limo, without really looking like they are trying to look in. The downtown Milltown buildings huddle around the streets and stretch over the streets with skyways. Skyways are the glass tunnels connecting second and sometimes third floors of neighboring buildings together, allowing pedestrians to cross downtown without ever stepping outside. Looking up through the limousine sunroof, I realize that I've never seen the underside of the skyways before. I've always been too busy driving and getting places to notice. The buildings spread apart as we approach the Mississippi River. The limousine turns at the depot and jars slightly over the red brick road running alongside the river, with a pale yellow wall of trunk-sized limestone blocks in between. We pull up to the station-like entrance to the restaurant. Roger opens the limousine door for us. Our conductor, with his white handlebar mustache and navy blue uniform, looks at his pocket watch and calls out "All aboard." He opens the door for us and asks us to watch our step, even though there are no steps. What looks like a passenger car from the outside, opens on the inside to an elaborate entrance leading to a spacious dining room. Another couple follows us in, confusing our host as to whether we are two or four. Being two reminds me of that aquarium; I must have seemed like a hurricane to those fish. At the table I help Hope with her chair. A series of square windows looks plainly out at the river, Spirit Island, and the Stone Arch Bridge. Buildings milling around the far bank include flour mills, saw mills, woolen mills, lath and shingle mills, and grist mills. An eagle glides across pane after pane after pane. It lands atop a cedar tree on the leading edge of Spirit Island, eying the mist of St. Anthony Falls for dinner options.

"Tonight's special is walleye, on a bed of wild rice and peppers," our waiter tells us. "We also have bison steak on a raft of zucchini logs tied with string beans. Would you like to take a few minutes to look over the menu?" Our waiter repeats his verbal menu to the neighboring couple.

"Owamniyomni," Hope says.

"I'm hungry too," I say.

"No. That's the Dakota name of the falls, Owamniyomni."

"Oh."

"Wanagi Wita is the name of the island."

"Oh."

"Technically it's a holm. Do you know what you're getting?"

"I'm leaning on the bison. Do you know what you'd like?"

"I'm looking at the walleye," Hope says. The perched eagle turns our way. "Have you thought any more about what I brought up this morning?"

No. What was that? Oh yeah, having kids. "No."

"No?!?"

"I mean, yes! I thought about it every moment since I left you, but since I saw you this evening, I have not been able to think of anything except your exquisite beauty."

"Nice try," Hope replies with a light blush. The woman at the table next door snickers.

"I recall your asking me, but you didn't offer your interest in the subject. I also thought your stance on children was interesting since you teach them. I did wonder about your issues..."

Hope nods slightly and sets her menu down. "I like kids, don't get me wrong. They can be great. It can be very rewarding to think about the impact I can have on hundreds of kids just in a few years. But the world doesn't need any more children. The world has more people than it can feed and cloth and care for already. We don't need more; we need quality for those we have." The waiter returns. "Yes, I'll have the walleye with a glass of Chippeau Valley Blanc Spirit."

"I'll have the bison with a glass of Birch Blackberry Stain."

Hope turns back to me. "I care about my students. All my students. I get parents who come in and tell me that I need to do this differently or that differently. And I am open to their suggestions, but then... when I turn around and suggest that they spend a few hours a week working with their son or daughter, they act as if I am asking for a natural satellite. They act as if I am trying to get out of my responsibilities as a teacher, instead of trying to maintain quality education for all the children. If their kid is falling behind, the parents want me to stay after school and provide a free tutoring service. One set of parents tried to strong arm me into it. No way. I do my bit for the world. At the end of the day, I have had enough." Our wine arrives. She takes a sip. "I am not interested in having children. If we were to have a child somehow, I would love them and care for them. Definitely. But my feelings are very strong on this. I know what you said this morning..." The woman nearby shushes her companion. "...but I probably should have said something sooner to you, since it's important to me."

I raise my glass in Hope's direction. We clink glasses. "To you, my Hope and my dream." Hope rubs the corner of her eye. "I am not eager to have children. I have a few reasons, reasons for concern. But what I think right now is about how children are sometimes used to keep couples together, yet children have to be a first thought of their parents, since each parent knows that the other parent can take care of themselves, but the child can't. So the children come first. I don't want that. I want you to be first and foremost. I've told you before, I want to give you the best relationship I can. I can't do that if I have to think of a kid's needs before yours. Yes, I would take good care of a kid, but that's not what I want. I want to have a great relationship with you. I want to live happily-ever-after with you. Some people can do that with children. I am sure of it. I don't know that I can. I'm not as capable as you think I am, but I want us to be great together." Retrieving a box from my jacket, I hand it to Hope.

Sparkles of pinks and yellows, pale greens and blues, shimmer from the box, as she retrieves the bracelet. I help her figure out the clasp as tears run down her cheeks. "It's beautiful," she says, as our salads arrive on schedule. As we eat, colored reflections of her bracelet waltz across the restaurant.

After rearranging her salad with her fork and taking a few bites, she says, "I have to disagree with you. You are far more than just capable. I can't imagine someone better than you, and I can't think of why you think that way about yourself. I love everything about you." She eats some more salad with a smile, leans in and says, "I loved last night." Still smiling and watching me, she finishes her salad and says, "I told you two nights ago that I prayed for you. I also talked to the right people. I believe you are the result of all of that."

"That's very nice of you. To me, you're the gift that I don't deserve. You and that optimism of yours... all of your confidence and your trust... wrapped up in a dazzling beauty."

Hope interrupts, "No. That's the bracelet that's doing the dazzling!"

"Not from where I'm sitting! You look gorgeous! Stunning!" I reach out and play with the locks of curls curtaining one side of her dimpled grin. "I say stunning because you make me tingle and throb and go numb and knock me out." Hope blushes from her cheeks to her chest. I take her hand. "I've got you. You're mine now." I laugh a sinister laugh. It's an imitation of something Tom does.

"Stop that," she says. I think about playing footsie with her and catch myself right before doing it. I don't want to mark her with black shoe polish. Instead, I stretch and rub my calf against hers. She gets a playfully fierce expression and says, through clenched teeth, "Don't get us kicked out."

I look around and spot the eagle swoop down over the falls. I straighten up as our dinner arrives. The bison steak... I think they must've used most of the bison here. It's huge. The bison is hanging off and tipping the zucchini raft in its dark pool of raisin-orange-tomato sauce. The strained string beans are barely holding the raft together. "I think I could feed an apartment complex with this." Hope laughs. "Would you like some?"

"I'll have a small piece. Would you like to try some walleye?"

"Yes. I'll just stack it on top." I cut a piece and place it atop a drifting piece of zucchini log for her. We labor over our meals.

Growing up, I was taught to clean my plate. I was taught to clean several plates. Frankly, I did the dishes a lot. I was told that people were starving in India. Something was always going on in India. "People are starving in India" or "people are trying to sleep in India" or something. We were very concerned about the well-being of the good people of India. I never thought they could hear me all the way on the other side of the world in India, but when I asked, I was clearly told that they could. However, I couldn't eat much when people might be starving in India or someplace else. If anything, I should eat less. Ultimately my reply became, please wrap this up and send it to them. I heard less and less about India after I started bringing postage stamps to the dinner table.

"I've got to be careful of eating too much." I get out a tape measure and measure a good stopping point on my large prairie-roaming mammal. I mark it off with a stray string of bean.

Hope is smirking at me like I'm crazy. "Al would be proud of you." I think for a moment, and then I nod in agreement. "You have many nice friends. He's all right."

"No, he's Al Wright. That's his name, Al Wright."

"You're kidding me. Wright. W-R-I-G-H-T? Why do parents do that to their kids?"

"Those parents get points for creativity. But then all the teasing and name discussions for the person's entire life wipe out any creativity points and lower the grade of the parents. Al's parents are decent enough people, not the type of people you would suspect of doing such a thing to their own child..." I trail off.

The whole restaurant is jarred. Our table barely budges due to the stabilizing weight of my bison. A chandelier is jostled by its own accord. Hope asks, "What was that? It felt like we were changing tracks?!?"

"Yes," I respond while checking my watch. "Every hour on the hour, First Street Station changes tracks. I appreciate the engineering aspect of it." Hope gets it. "How is everything?" I ask her and her dimples.

"Delicious. I like yours too." Hope raises her wine glass. I check. I still have a swig left. "To you, to everything we've done and to our futures together!" Our glasses clink together. We drink. "I almost forgot! I have something for you!" Hope gives me a key. It looks like a house key.

"Is this a key to your heart?"

"It's a key to a very special Hope chest," she replies.

After a few more bites, the waiter approaches. "How is everything?" he asks without stopping.

"Very good, thank you. Could we get some more water?" I ask, noticing Hope's glass.

"Certainly," he says while leaving.

"That was thoughtful of you. And observant," Hope comments. "Are you sure you aren't a mind reader too?"

Touching my temples with my fingers, I stare intensely at her. "Nope." She giggles. The water is delivered.

I arrive at the finish line with one more bite. I lean back. Hope has stopped at a halfway point. We sit and smile at each other. This is good. This is great. Then a realization hits me. I can't take the rest of the carcass back to my apartment. Ray will kill me. "Do you think you would like a box for the rest of your meal?" I ask Hope. She agrees. "I'm going to need one for mine. I have an unusual request to ask of you. Do you think I could leave it in your refrigerator? I would rather not bother Ray's sensibilities with it."

"It could go in the refrigerator downstairs. The power is still on."

"But then that refrigerator would smell like meat. He's very sensitive. Would there be room at your place?"

Hope looks at my meat. "We'll make room."

"Thanks. Otherwise I can ship it off to India. There are people starving over there."

"Do they eat bison? Or is it too cattle-like?"

"I don't know. I wouldn't want to offend the country or its beliefs."

"Have you saved room for dessert?" the waiter asks, making me wonder where I would store some dessert. I look at Hope.

Hope tells us, "No, thank you."

I parrot back to him, "No, thank you. But she would like a box, and I would like a crate."

"Very good, sir."

Hope excuses herself and catches up to the waiter, who points something out to her. The waiter drops off the bill and the boxes. I lend him a camera for Hope's return. I check my watch. The bill includes some roaming charges for the bison. I pay the bill in American currency. The tip is a thoughtful mixture of American currency and insect repellent. I box up our meals. I use a breath mint. Hope returns and thanks me for packaging her meal. I tell her our timing should be perfect. She takes a drink of water and is ready. The waiter takes our picture.

Our limousine and its driver are waiting for us out front. He holds open the door for us. He holds my crate for me while I get in and then hands it to me. He drives us around the lakes. We stop along an eastern shore. Hope and I get out, Roger takes our picture, and we take a walk, hand in hand, with the sun setting across the lake, joggers jogging by, and mosquitoes trailing us. Back in the limousine, I take off one of her shoes without asking. I start rubbing her feet.

"How did you know?" she asks.

"Know what?"

"How did you know my feet needed rubbing?"

"I just did."

"Right there! Oh."

"Have you ever heard of reflexology? I was just rubbing your pancreas. I think." I take off her other shoe, and I rub her feet for a few miles. At her house, I help her in with the meals and help her to rearrange their refrigerator.

"Do you have to go?"

"Yeah, my ride turns into a pumpkin or one of those half-orange, half-green gourds or something, if I don't get it back on time."

"I could give you a ride back?"

"No, the way Roger was giving me the eye awhile ago, I think he wants to discuss my grade for this evening."

"You're paying him. He shouldn't be grading you."

"I can either call you and let you know how it turns out or let you know now..."

"Call me." She kisses me and takes my breath away. It feels like the first time again, except without having anyone yelling at us.

Roger gets out to get my door. The road is quiet for a few turns. Then he gives me his evaluation of my behavior, "What did I tell you about mystery?"

"You said, 'Keep your plans a mystery. Keep the lady in suspense.'"

"That's right. You didn't spill the beans right away, and that's good. But when she asked you; you flat out told her."

"What should I have done? I'm not going to lie to her."

"I'm not saying lie. Who said anything about lying?!? You– Have you ever heard a love song?" Roger doesn't wait for an answer. "Your way, the song would be over in a sentence. There's no description. First Street Station is a nice restaurant, am I right? It's romantic, right?"

"Right."

"But the name is not romantic. It's as romantic as a doctor's office. Romantic is dining on the river-front gazing into her sunset-filled eyes. That's what you should have told her. Romantic is not stuffing your face at the train station. Romantic is not making her worry about leftovers from the meal."

"They brought me a bison... an entire bison. They brought her the sort of walleye you usually find mounted on the wall."

"That's right. You could feed an entire neighborhood. But is that romantic?"

"No."

"That's my point. You did good, but I'm afraid I'm going to have to give you a B minus."

"But, but–"

"Young man, you need to put more effort into your romantic endeavors. Maybe the next young woman will give you a chance to make use of what you've learned this evening."

"Next young woman?!?"

"Sure. There will be others."

"Not for me," I say getting out my wallet. I pay off Roger.

"Don't give up."

"I haven't given up on **this** one."

I shake his hand, and he shakes his head. As the limousine pulls away, the urchin alarm evacuates the apartment building I'm trying to get in. Inside, Ray has gotten out everything in the apartment. The closet is half emptied. Open boxes carpet the carpet like land mines.

Ray lifts his welding face-mask and dials down his welding torch from his work on Kelly. "You ate meat, didn't you," he states without question. I nod in shame and head to my room. I call Hope to give her the bad news about my report card.

"I thought it was the perfect evening! It was great! Don't let what Roger said bother you! Everyone is so jealous of my bracelet," Hope tells me. Telling her the part about not giving up on her, she replies, "You better not, Buster!"

"Hey Hope, when do you want me to move in? I was talking to Jake, who is keeping tabs on our relationship–"

"I think there are a great many people keeping tabs on our relationship. What did Jake want to know?"

"He wanted to know if we had done it."

"What did you tell him?"

"I left him a simple 'yes' message."

"You told him?!?"

"You haven't told anyone?"

"That's not the– Anyone is not Jake."

"He is one of a kind, isn't he? I asked him to help us move, and he wanted to know what time. Remember, he gets his chest shaved on Friday..."

"I had suppressed that image."

"It's too funny to suppress. Are you free Saturday?"

"Yes, and Friday evening and tomorrow night... Well, not tomorrow night, I have to go to the nursing home." While I tell her she's not that old, she says, "Very funny. You could come with me. You could come over tomorrow night. Tomorrow night is All-The-Bison-You-Can-Eat-Night here. You'll love it! And then we can go to the nursing home together."

"Like looking forward to growing old together."

"That is so sweet!"

"Yes, it is, and I'll come over to eat bison tomorrow night, but then I'm going to come back here to take one last evening walk through the neighborhood."

"It's supposed to rain tomorrow and into the night. And it's not like you're moving to another state."

"Will you survive without me tomorrow night?" She grunts. This might be the first time I've heard her grunt. No, it's the second. "What time can I tell Jake?"

"For Friday or Saturday?"

"I figure, Ray and I will take over some initial loads Friday late afternoon and maybe into the evening. Saturday morning I'll rent a truck before ten and start loading it up."

"Anytime after ten should be okay. I should be able to wrangle some help."

"I think Jake is calling people too."

"How many people do you think will be involved?"

"No more than were at Tom's last weekend."

"You're kidding."

"No, it should be less than that. I'll load the downstairs fridge with enough drinks for everybody."

"We put some of our stuff down there to have enough room for your meat. That doesn't sound right." Something garbled. "No, you tell him that..."

"Tell me what?"

"Oh, Nicole wants to be our child."

"What?!? How did that come up?"

"I was telling them about our talk about kids, and Nicole volunteered to be our kid."

"I– We'd have to figure out what that means. If she means that she wants to live with us, well, I guess it goes back to what I was saying, essentially that I don't want children or others to get in the way of us being great together. You can take that as meaning, I don't want our friends to get in the way of our relationship. I don't want to louse this up. Last weekend's trip to Tom's cabin was different than other years. I didn't spend as much time with the whole group because I was off more with you or with you and your friends. But I can't feel too bad since several of them have been actively encouraging our relationship. Then again, I don't want us to be pushing away our friends either. You have great friends. I have–"

"Thank you," Nicole says softly.

"Nicole is listening in," Hope tells me. When did that start?

"I have some great friends too. Kind of weird at times, but then, so am I." I think about asking Nicole what she meant about wanting to be our child. Was she kidding? But I've said too much already. "I've got to call Jake and tell him that they can meet me here at ten on Saturday."

"Should it be here or there?" Hope asks.

I picture the Whisper Willows hooligans going up and down the apartment parking lot aisles with shopping carts full of tires and electronic equipment and music and loose change and snow shovels and insect repellent and everything else of looting value. Younger hooligans take notes and clean up the trail of loose change left behind. "I changed my mind. Can we have everyone meet over there?"

"Yes."

"What time should I row over tomorrow in the rain?"

"Six."

"One more thing. I'm willing to share my bison." We exchange mushy talk and hang up.

I call Jake and tell his answering machine of the plans, including Hope's address and phone number. I ask him to make sure that extra softening creams are used on his chest on Friday because everyone will be checking up on his chest status on Saturday.

Jake is so easy to tease. It's like he wears a big red target.

I update Ray on the plans and visit the bathroom. I set and wind my alarm clock. I change. Once I untie my knotted sheet, I lie down, and cover myself to catch some sleep.

23

The Tower

Honking of car horns wakes me from lively dreams of unamused news anchors and falling squirrels and mad scientists and being mistaken as an angel in a cloud. That's what I get for having bison for dinner last night. The rain taps on my window. I reach around for my sheet only to find that it has been folded neatly at the corner of my bed. That's odd. Looking around, I feel like I'm in someone else's room. When did this change? I no longer belong here. This isn't my home anymore. Neighbors yell. A door slams. Then it slams again, as if to add a second exclamation mark to the declaration. Okay. Yes. It's home, but not for long.

Hauling Assets is very willing to rent me a truck. Too willing. The price is quoted with a questioning inflection. That's the tip off. I'm in the driver's seat. It is too early for kids to move to college, too early for migratory Minnesotans to move south for the winter, and weeks too early for end of the month moves. I look at the phone. I negotiate the price down. I haggle. I insist on unlimited mileage and an allowance for a second driver with no additional fees. I get the truck for a song. He sells me some moving boxes. Something in the tone of his voice makes me suspect that they make most of their money selling moving boxes.

Hauling Assets is a small business. If Hauling Assets were owned by Tremendous Trucks or another of the large moving or trucking corporations, the local clerk would have no pricing or negotiating authority. That kind of local power would frighten corporate officers. They would have to hire good people, train them for more than a few hours, and trust them. Trust them?!? Ridiculous! But as a business grows, it becomes entangled in the affairs of other businesses. It grows without purpose, hires people without need, and its trust is blurred by the dazzling spotlight of personal prestige. The corporate mission becomes something engraved in a lobby plaque, using too many large words. The mission of a business used to be as obvious as the name of the business. Yesterday's Diner does not sell tires. It's obvious. There is no need for a plaque in its lobby. But business schools do not study the business of running a diner. They study business models and look for ways of fitting the business into the business model. Standardization. The building is nondescript. The offices are nondescript. The executives are nondescript and are as interchangeable as the building and its offices. As the business grows up, the executives become bigger than life. The team that worked with them dissolves and is overshadowed by the exploits of the executives in their solitary climb for power. Looking down at their underlings, they ask, "How can I trust my staff below? What do those people down there do? They don't do anything on my level. They don't do anything that directly impacts me or makes my day any better. What good are they?" The executives find themselves on top of the tower, and they smile. And when they look for camaraderie, when they look for someone to share their triumph with, they find themselves alone and afraid to look down. They are as far removed from that lobby plaque and actual operations as they can get. The trust is twisted around by greed into one more executive expectation. The executive expects to be the recipient of trust, not the social re-distributor of trust. It is the antithesis of innovation. Reports of innovation are reports of broken standards and broken trust. The corporate culture would never allow a retail clerk to negotiate prices, I decide as I take special care in cleaning myself, while exhaling into the shower spray. I'm clean.

Lefty didn't say anything about what is expected of me in my visit. In a way this is like a doctor's visit, except that nothing is wrong with me. I hope he knows I'm not paying for whatever it is he's going to do. It's going to be a close shave.

He mentioned something about mental acuity and a bio-tech breakthrough. I don't think he mentioned an MRI. Why do I think I'm going to be in an MRI? I floss.

I also recall big white tiles. I'm staring at big white tiles. I brush my teeth.

I'm getting lost in pointed perception... flash-forwards of pointed perception. Pushing through the clothes hanging in my closet, I can't find a lab coat. How can I visit Lefty without a lab coat?!? Monkey suit? Check. Red cape with stylized S? Check. A dozen black T-shirts? Check. Checkered retro-fashion dinner jacket? Check. No lab coat. A white shirt liberally doused in ketchup might be the answer. However it would be tough to clean up quickly, tough to undo. I put on clean jeans and a clean shirt.

I drop my suit off at the cleaners and stop by the Gag Shop behind Yesterday's Diner. A fake, white plaster arm cast that has a hidden zipper demands to be purchased, so I buy it. The owner of the Gag Shop is dejected. How can he stay in business with a store that shoppers want to keep secret? We've had this conversation before.

If you pull off a great gag, you are going to be asked where you got the thingamajig, the key item. If you tell them, you are revealing your trick. You are deflating the interest. You are popping the balloon. They pick up the latex rubber remains of the balloon, and they say, "This was nothing." Yes, it was nothing, but they were laughing about it only a minute ago. Sometimes it's best to leave them wondering.

There is nowhere to park at the university. I knew I left something at home. I should have brought my own parking spot with me. Maybe some white paint and a thick paintbrush... a phony parking meter... I find a spot without resorting to creating a spot. Finding the spot and parking are two different things. I shouldn't have put the cast on so soon. The traffic backed up behind me thinks I'm more handicapped than I actually am.

Raindrops dot the cast. I duck under a slab overhang at some big doors. A girl awkwardly holds the door for me, probably out of pity. I get into an elevator with a few pre-med students who look at my cast like it was covered last semester. One asks, "How did it happen?"

They are onto me. My floor. I get out while responding, "Suddenly." A medical conference convenes in the elevator after my departure. I hope Lefty likes my cast.

The hallway smells like it has been swabbed with a giant cottonball of alcohol. I read off names on doors: Dolittle, Doom, Fate, Holiday, Pepper, Quackenbush, Seuss, Spock, Strange, Zhivago... A door with a reinforced frame says, "Dept of Seismology - Dr. Richter - please do not slam door." After turning a corner and passing a few more doors, I knock at one with the name Dr. Melvin Vagues. I'll have to get him a plaque that says, Lefty. I intend my knock to consist of three hits. After the first hit, the door in front of me and the door across the hall both open. I am pulled in by my arm, and the door is kicked shut behind me.

"How are you feeling?" Lefty asks, almost like a real doctor. "What happened to your arm?"

"Oh, this? Nothing. Do you want to show me around?" I turn to find that his office is full – packed with papers, journals, books, and other materials – an arm hangs out of the middle, and I sniff the air for a cadaver. Petri dishes pile on and around a small refrigerator, as if to say that being on the fridge is the next best thing to being in the fridge. "Your bookcase caved in," I observe.

"Yes." His door knocks. "I know," he says while only opening the door enough for two, thin people, their lab coats, and their electronic clipboards to squeeze in. Lefty closes the door on their matching white lab coats, accidentally pinning them in place. "If anyone asks you," he tells me, "you are only a friend of mine getting a tour. Don't even give your name. Definitely don't let on that there is anything special about you."

"Gotcha," I tell him, and I notice the two, one male, one female, looking at me like they are peering at an unknown specimen. "Uh, your jackets are caught in the door."

"Never mind about that," Lefty says, "we are going to 8-34 and we are taking the stairs. Let's go." We dash out, and Lefty pushes me ahead with his prosthetic hand. When I stop at the eighth floor, he pushes me onward, saying that his office is bugged. He tells me that the rival scientist across the hall is mad and tries to steal projects from Lefty and anyone else. We take a tunnel under University Avenue. We tunnel through several more buildings, with twists and turns. Preformed, cement-walled basements slope into limestone foundations turning into straightforward hallways angling into cement slabbed brick basements. Some of the tunnels include large iron pipes, hung from the tunnel ceilings or walls. Downtown uses skyways, and the university uses tunnels to avoid the cold. Since the outside temperature is currently in the eighties, the tunnels are vacant, except for us lab rats. The tunnels are painted light colors, creams and grays and pastels, to dismiss the feelings of underground burrowing. We emerge into a small offshoot building, the Teska Building, Functional MRI Unit. That's what the sign says, but it could be fake. It might have said Tesla, but I am fairly certain it was Teska. Up here, the cinder block walls are painted a pale cream, and it is still raining out. We stop at a pop machine. It dispenses pop in unlabeled, stoppered test tubes. I select a fizzy, caramel colored liquid. Lefty unlocks a door into a conference room. One of the long walls has smoked glass windows looking out over a white room with a giant, room-filling, rounded, white, coffee maker in its center, and nothing else. Instead of a coffee pot, a person-sized, padded table is sideways in the middle, where the coffee pot should be. Maybe it isn't a coffee maker. Maybe it is the world's largest, rounded, white stapler.

"That's the fMRI we are going to use," Lefty says. Sounds like fun, I think as I turn from the one-way mirrors. I wonder what we are going to use it for? Then I notice another set of mirrors on the other wall. They must've put them in wrong because I can't see into that room. "Lena will be asking you some questions. I will be back shortly." Lefty leaves. The other two sit at the far end of the table like I'm contagious or something.

Lena adjusts her glasses and asks me some general name and address sorts of questions. She asks if Ricky is short for Richard or something. I tell her that Ricky isn't short for anything. She asks me many questions that were on my EASE application for unemployment. I wish I still had it so I could hand her a copy. "Is there a history of insanity in your family?"

"Yes, insanity runs in my family." I add with a Cary Grant accent, "practically gallops."

"Do you have any insecurities?"

"Why are you asking all these questions?!?" I panic. "Is someone making you ask all these questions?!? They are, aren't they?!? Is this table getting shorter?!?"

The other one says, "We could give you a lie detector test."

"Yes, but I studied for that test, and I am familiar with the Lavemore Methods for defeating lie detector tests."

Lena unfolds a plastic cup. "Please fill this with urine."

"From over here?" I ask.

Lena takes off her glasses and rubs her eyes, "I was under the mistaken impression that you were a volunteer. You are not behaving like a volunteer."

I unzip my cast. It thuds onto the table. I stretch my arms. "I'm here to visit Left– to visit my friend. I don't know what you are talking about." Something drops on the other side of the mirror. Lefty and an old man in a tweed cat-hair cardigan sweater dash into the room as I am getting up to leave.

"Hold on," says the old man with hair that's unfamiliar with the concept of comb. "Melvin, talk to your friend."

"We are conducting a study of mental acuity, specifically short-term memory, recorded through a Memmeograph, a device which we are currently perfecting. It can... well, see for yourself," Lefty says, sliding a piece of paper to me.

The top half of the page is a list of base numbers, followed by a coordinate system of numbers and times, and is otherwise gibberish. The bottom half says, "Make yourself comfortable?!? Who are they kidding? If they wanted me to be comfortable, they should have let me wear real clothes, not this hospital gown [expletive]. Then they strap me to a table and slide me into this [expletive], [expletive] [expletive]. They're on the other side of that mirror laughing and looking up my gown and having a good old time at how [expletive] comfortable I am. Comfortable! I itch! Where is that–" it starts without finishing.

"Is this some sort of transcription?" I ask.

"Yes," Lefty smiles. "The subject's thoughts were recorded, interpreted, and transcribed. This subject was our best one, from last May. She was supposed to be recalling her earliest, clearest memories... short-term memories. STMs. She didn't." I hand the page back to him. Lefty asks me, "When you think of your earliest, clearest, recent memory... the memories that you can remember all the minute details from then to the present... where does that begin for you?"

As I digest his question, my eyes glaze as memories of being a toddler, a child, a teenager, and a young adult stream by clearly, but not with the clarity he's looking for. I find that, "Almost three weeks ago, Sharon had invited me to her house. I wore my suit. Sharon wore a black sleeveless dress. Tom was at my side, talking less than usual. Someone had just come around handing out mints, and I took one without looking at who's handing them out. Sharon introduced me to Hope, who wore a white blouse with silver pinstripes and a black skirt with a silver lining. It was 7:02 Saturday evening. Tom backed off at the same moment as Hope was introduced. I guess I didn't realize that at the time. You never leave right when someone is introduced. It's not polite. I wonder if the whole event wasn't staged to set us up. Politics was an excuse..."

"You remember everything from there on?"

"The next morning I went out for a walk and a stray dog was trotting through traffic, dragging a leash, and I had to dodge cars to get to the dog without scaring it into a panic–"

"All right, all right, we're impressed," Lefty interrupts.

"Dr. Vagues has also commented on your ability to predict the future."

"Dr. Vagues has a big mouth," I tell Dr. Vagues. "What is your name?" I ask the old man and his lint-covered sweater.

"Dr. Forrester."

"Dr. Forrester, do you believe in ESP?"

"Not necessarily."

"Good. Me too. Why am I here?" Deja vu. I look at my watch. "Your colleague is in the next room," I quietly state.

For three seconds no one moves. These people aren't very quick on the uptake. Then, they all race, dive, and swim out the door. Our wooden rack of test tube drinks tips and shatters. Papers fly up in their wake, and then they glide gently to the table and the floor. One page does a rolling flip. Show off! There is shouting next door and in the hallway. Opening the door, a large Cro-Magnon in a nearly-just-barely-large-enough lab coat stands in the hallway with a flurry of lab coats yelling around it, like dogs cornering a bear. The beast glares at me and leaves, heading back through the university maze. The dogs sniff around the other room. They stop the recordings of a camera and microphone. They close the door, lock it, and return to our conference room. They look at me briefly like I was the one who messed up the room, like I would purposefully mess up someone's room?!? They shake off that notion and start cleaning up after themselves. Dr. Forrester tells Sven to get something to clean up the broken glass.

Lefty sits down and asks no one in particular, "What should we do now?"

"We continue," Dr. Forrester replies, as he examines my phony cast. "Your friend wants to know what we are trying to do," he tells Lefty. Turning to me, "And I will change my earlier answer from not necessarily to it's certainly possible."

Lefty says, "The main setback we have discovered in our exploration of STMs is that people lack short-term memories. I also believe, that despite your attempts at levity," Lefty glances at my cast, "you have the mental discipline to follow our instructions. We would like your participation in an experiment to record STMs... all STMs."

"Do you know if you will participate?" Forrester cuts in.

"No, I don't know."

"How can you see the future and not know?"

"Futures. The futures are not a single lane, one-way road with no entrances and no exits from point A to point B. I don't know why people can't understand that decisions effect outcomes. The scientific method conducts the testing of one variable at a time while maintaining all other factors as constants, however reality is diametrically opposed to those conditions. Everything... most everything... is variables. Most everything has choices. Very few things are unyielding, unwavering absolutes that will occur no matter what is done."

"What are the absolutes?" Sven asks.

"Weather. But even with weather, there are choices. People realize that it can be sunny in Los Angeles, raining in Seattle, and snowing in Minnesota, but they don't realize just how localized weather can be. There can be a blizzard in Milltown, and next door in Pigs Eye it's sunny with a few light flurries. Weather hardly cares about county borders and arbitrary time frames."

"But how can you not know what you will do?" Dr. Forrester asks without really thinking about what I said. I pause a moment. I give him a chance to catch up.

"Futures are decision dependent. My perceptions are also... attention dependent. If I don't want to know, I won't know." This is an over-simplification for argument's sake, but I let it go. I don't want to confuse elementary concepts with graduate studies.

"How can you not want to know?!?" Lena asks with a snort.

"I have personal reasons." From my point of view, the unaware, unyielding stubbornness of other people is a potential absolute. I don't tell them that either. Lefty might know some of that history.

"If you participate, there will not be anything personal," Lefty continues. "Your life will become an open book, as Red might say."

I sit there in room 41 of the Teska Building at the university, contemplating my futures. The scientists squirm in their chairs. "Please step me through the process." The scientists exhale. I hadn't known they were holding their breath, or I would've tested their limits. "I didn't say, yes."

"You didn't say, no." One point for the scientists.

Lefty flips through some papers, flips through them again, checks under the table, flips through them again, finds a stapled set of pages, and flips to the middle. He points to it in front of him without reading it. "We would set you up early in the morning. You will have to fast the previous 24 hours." Fast? Not eat. Got it. "No metal objects can be brought into the fMRI room. Not even as a joke to see how fast and how far a paperclip can fly." That will have to remain on my To Do list. "You will dress in a gown..." he might have said race car pajamas "...and will be escorted onto the platform which will be slid into place in the fMRI. From the control room we will give you instructions. We will ask that you concentrate on your responses to our questions. That is very important. It is quintessential to your participation. We will start with some focusing exercises and check the results. We will then ask you to remember your earliest, clearest, recent memory. Starting from there, we will ask you to remember everything from that moment forward. The Memmeograph pinpoints the fMRI to the subiculum, the anterior cingulate, and the hippocampus–"

"Aren't we on the hippocampus right now?" I ask.

Lefty's eyes narrow at me as he thinks, "Please don't embarrass me." Hey, I can read Lefty's thoughts! Cool! Lefty continues, "The Memmeograph analyzes the fMRI data and interprets the data into extremely jumbled text. The recordings are transcribed into English."

"How long would that take?" I ask.

"What you read before took three minutes. You said you have a clear recollection of the past four weeks. It could take... awhile."

"You don't know?"

"No, I don't know."

"You could have said you didn't know. You have to be up front with me for me to consider doing this." Lefty nods in agreement. If I'm going to be part of this, I have to know what this project is about. Understanding the scope of a thing is a key to engineering or managing. "So I lie down and rehash recent events. Do I think about every little detail?"

"Everything you can remember," Lefty clarifies.

"Whoa, that's a lot," I reflect. "Then what?"

"Well, then the STMs are processed through the Memmeograph and the results are transcribed by Lena."

"Then what?" I prod.

"Then we publish the results."

"So everyone will know what I had for breakfast, right?"

"Right."

"And everyone will know my PIN numbers and my bank account number..." They jump like I just prodded too much. This little brain trust didn't think of that, did they?!?

Dr. Forrester taps the table in front of him and says, "Well, we won't include that information. We had already decided not to include details that... should remain confidential, such as medically related issues, issues related to copulation and what not. As you saw from the sheet that you read, I think that's the one, we redacted the expletives."

"That shouldn't be an issue, since I hardly swear." The others turn to Lefty for confirmation, just as he attempts to surreptitiously scratch his ankle. Lefty nods in agreement.

"Nevertheless, we will leave out all personally identifying information," Forrester decides.

"So, everything that I've done for the past few weeks will be published in... what... a journal?"

"If everything goes right, yes, our goal is to publish."

I think about reminding them that the light bulb didn't just come on over Edison's head. He had to think about it. He had to try out hundreds of bulb designs before one worked. The first bulbs weren't even clear! But I don't need to tell them all of this. If they do this mental recording stuff on me, they'll hear all my commentary eventually.

"Just think, if this is published, you will go down in history with Dr. Vagues and the rest of us."

"I will have to think this over," I tell them.

"What else do you need to know?" Sven asks.

I pick up my cast and stand up, "Again, I will have to think this over." I'm not going to be pressured by him. I wave the cast, saying, "It was nice meeting all of you." To Lefty, "Did you hear about Saturday?"

"Tom e-mailed me. I'm not certain."

"Well, you are welcome to join us. You have the address and everything?"

He nods and says, "I'll walk you out."

"One more thing. Who came up with the term Memmeograph?" Fingers point to Dr. Forrester. "It sounds too much like a mimeograph," I state, making a cranking motion with the cast. I wave the cast and let Lefty escort me out of the Teska Building. "Were you thinking we were going to do the memory recording today?" I ask him.

"No! We don't have everything set up. There is paperwork to complete."

"Signing my life away?"

"Showing a willingness to participate... clearing the university of any legal repercussions..."

"The University of Legal Repercussions," I echo. "So if you kill me, I won't take legal action?"

"Correct. If we don't, the university won't fund us," Lefty accounts.

"You aren't trying to kill me, are you?" Why would he be trying to kill me? Then I picture Lefty saying fatty tissue doesn't excite him and WHACK, Nicole slaps him, and Lefty shatters to the floor. I did invite Nicole, and I did instigate involving Nicole in our conversation. I did point out that there were ramifications that he hadn't considered.

"No. That's not the way the journal article should read." I stop and stare at him as if he has just rationalized a price tag on my life. He shakes his head, and it shakes loose a smile. "I'm kidding you. This is role reversal! No, we aren't trying to kill you." He nudges me on the shoulder with his prosthetic hand. "When do you think you'll have come to a conclusion?" A conclusion? I think he's still pulling my leg.

"I should have a decision this weekend. Maybe we can talk between loads on Saturday." Lefty agrees. I put on my cast, zip it up, and take off into the rain before he can tease me any more.

The rain patters out a Morse code message on the roof of my car. I listen for the three quick, three strong, and three quick drops of an SOS. Pause. I don't hear it. What would I do if I heard it? Would I take it as a sign from God? Would it indicate that I need help or that God needs help? The burning bush was far superior to Morse code rain because the bush talked. If I have a response to a rain-tapped, Morse code message from God, should I tap back or just talk normally in prayer?

That group back there cannot be let out of the scholarly world, but it was good to see Lefty in his natural habitat. They fit together in a non-profit scientific dynamic of intergenerational expertise and learning without seeming like everything isn't already known. What are the Latin words for publish or perish? It's chiseled above the columns of at least one of the university buildings, but I can't see well enough through my rain-splattered windshield. Perpetuating the good name of the university is at the core of the publishing mandate, and yet that assumes quality efforts, doesn't it? The rush to publish could lead to a snowbank full of expletives.

The windshield raindrops each give a slightly different reflection of the world, like a few hundred little round aquariums of students dashing through the rain. At a stoplight, I remove my cast. My hunger nearly causes me to drive to the grocery store. That is the quantity of food I desire, but I can't stock up on food before the move. I nearly drive to a restaurant, but I need to use up food at home. I'm so hungry I could eat a bison. I drive home, with a stop at Hauling Assets for my boxes and a stop at the post office to change my address. I drive over a new speed bump to get into the Whisper Willows Apartments parking lot only to find that the urchins have dammed up the parking lot. They literally dammed up the parking lot. Someone must have said, "Damn it." Kids are very literal. One of them must be a natural project manager to organize and accomplish such a task. The Whisper Willows Lake varies in depth due to the unevenness of the pavement. I motor close to the front door and dock at the doorsteps. The flattened boxes act as an umbrella. Under the door canopy, I wring out my shoes and shake off the cast. One of the kids in the hallway eyes my boxes and asks if I will be using all of them. He must be one of the engineers. I give him the wet one off the top. He might be planning a rafting trip; I know better than to ask. I also remember the Children's Covenant well enough to know that they are bound by it not to harm their suppliers. That thought is interrupted by the devastation inside my apartment.

Have we been robbed? Has there been an earthquake? No. There is an organization at work here that robbers and earthquakes rarely arrange.

Lunch consists of a goulash created from two types of noodles, tomatoes, beans, corn, zucchini, and mood inspired spices that bring the leftovers and odds-and-ends together: some basil, a pinch of oregano, and parsley. I use the same spices in different amounts for a salad.

I eat while walking around to figure out where to begin to pack. Staring at the things in my room, I start to categorize them into things worth keeping and packing versus things that should be gotten rid of, preferably before Saturday. Clothes with holes. Gifts that don't represent me. Things that had belonged to others that I ended up storing. I stored a box of broken glass, a giant raisin-like beach ball, and other items from my old job. I stored a coat that the cleaners told me could not be cleaned.

Some of the things go in the trash. I pitch a bag of broken, oozing glow sticks. I pitch the broken glass. Other things will be made available to the poor, my neighbors.

The clickers weren't as useful for Capture The Flag as I expected them to be, but I'll keep those. I'll keep the beach ball. Maybe I'll wait to go through my Melanie souvenirs until I'm at Hope's. I'll have to figure out how to best wrap the painting from Ray and the poster of Melanie. I have no idea how to pack the Christmas tree or all the blankets that fill half my closet. There's my claws and my bear feet slippers and my bag of balls.

The volleyball could use some air. Half of my friends will be obligated to let me know. They might say the same thing about the deflated, giant inflatable dinosaur. I wonder how Hope feels about dinosaurs? I can't believe I never asked Hope if she has any dinosaur issues!

I've never had so much stuff to move at once. The bedroom closet is packed solid with the accumulation of four years and a few months of stuff, plus everything that I initially moved in. Shutting its door has never been an easy task, but I've always managed to close the closet before visitors visit my room. The closet is so well packed that if I could move it just like it is, it would save some trouble. That would be an easy route. I've never been known for taking easy routes.

The rain throws some gravel at my window to remind me that it is still out there. It would help if it is not raining on Saturday.

I relax. The sun evaporates the Whisper Willows Lake with a slurping sound. Then it grabs a hold of Minnesota and wrings the state into a state-shaped patch of humid air.

I open my eyes to find myself sitting below my brimming closet. An archaeologist comes through and marvels at the construction of the wall of possessions. "See here. What is really amazing is that this wall has withstood the tests of time without the use of mortar. The clothes seamlessly connect with the blankets holding the Christmas tree in place and propping up all the packages, boxes, and bags. Astounding when you consider that individual items can be removed from the structure, like so, without any effect on the stability of the wall as a whole!" The archaeologist moves on to marvel at the pre-machinery society that could've engineered the dams that created Whisper Willows Lake.

Hopefully the heavy duty packing tape will last. I build cardboard boxes by taping closed the bottom of the boxes with not just one, not just two, but with three strips of tape. The tape manufacturers will be so happy with me. This tape was originally designed to hold together boxes of whiskey bottles, eight bottles per box, that's why it's called Bourbon tape.

Taking inventory of my books, I find they are everywhere throughout the apartment. I collect them.

Packing the United States Department of Transportation: Guide to Highway and Roadway Signs, Reflectors, Pavement Markings, and Other Traffic Regulators; Revision 3 from under my nightstand takes one box, and it hardly has room for the whole title. I should give Nicole the signs book so that she can get rid of her older revision. There's a book on health that covers junk food really well but avoids the subject of junk thoughts. I pack my mint condition dictionary, an almanac from several years ago when I thought that an alignment of stars might help AutoDrive, the Bible from Christie, a vegetarian cookbook that Ray got for me, a book about being on your own, and some odd fiction. Ruth's Unemployee Of The Month certificate is packed with the books. I dry off my cast, wrap it, and add it to the box.

For some reason, I have a book on how to germinate a coconut. First you have to throw the coconut across an ocean. The coconut has to wind up at least a thousand miles from its point of origin. The coconut has to land on a beach and roll around for six months. Then the coconut has to bake in the sun for six months. Once a monsoon or a typhoon hits the coconut, it will germinate. I live in Minnesota. This book does me no good.

Some of these books should get passed on. I remember the stories, even the page numbers of significant passages. Why hold on to the book? On the other hand, if my memory someday fails me, the fiction books contain adventures that I have journeyed without moving, many of the adventures took place before my own great adventures. I have almost always carried a book with me. If the trip itself has quiet moments, I can always take a trip within the trip by reading.

My T-shirts and bandanas become packing materials for fragile things. The quartz from Erix gets wrapped up. The snowball candle is a reminder from Ruth that she has never fully forgiven me for hitting her on the side of the head with a snowball. The laughing people bookends came from the Pfulorees. Dan gave me the miniature Chicago skyline. The condom reminder came from Jake. I don't know why I keep the computer watch from Cy. It was almost archaic when it was invented. Back then Cy was still trying to figure out what my role would be. The utility knife set was from Al. The teddy bear came from Melanie. Nothing can happen to it.

Having cleared the top of my dresser, I drape a blue and lighter blue plaid, protective blanket over it. The blanket was draped around me and dragging across the floor behind me, when I was checking for presents under the Christmas tree when I was six. The blanket was also part of an elaborately engineered fort of blankets taped and pinned together with clothespins when I was six. The blanket was wrapped around my mom the last time I saw her. The blanket lay on the zoo hillside where Hope and I had our picnic.

I wonder if anyone studying memory loss has ever investigated whether the person might have wanted to lose the memories. Sometimes I do.

I pack an overnight bag for two night's worth of stuff: one night here and the other night there. It's weird thinking about living out of luggage in your own home. It puts into perspective the things I actually need.

The bed becomes home for the things that don't get packed. I pack the dresser's contents. What I didn't realize was how well-packed the dresser has been. It takes most of three boxes to pack dresser stuff. I move out to packing some of the hall closet contents and some kitchen items. Some of the kitchen items have not been used in a long time. Years ago, I accidentally bought a turkey carving knife. It's still in mint condition. I clear a spot in the living room for ready to go items; I stack boxes nearly to the ceiling. I tie up the ironing board and a folding table and lean them by the box structure.

Ray comes home soggy and drippy and heads straight to his room.

I add some finishing touches to the box structure and get ready for Hope's. Stopping to gaze out the window, the airborne lake rain has filled Whisper Willows Lake. In the haze, neighbors yell parenting methods at other neighbors, due to the dam kids. Engineering is just a phase. Kids will grow out of it. Children splash and shout, with exaggerated innocence, while adults debate their fate, and almost unnoticed, a kid surveys the decay of the earthen work clays.

I put a jacket over my head and head out through an argument. My neighbors generously want to include me in their argument. First they want me to take sides, then seeing that my car has drifted from its dock at the steps to an angle that is blocking the steps, they want to yell at me for the vehicular drift. I climb aboard the Pony Express and motor up the lake to the driveway at the high end. My normal traffic flow takes me out the other driveway, but I'd be damned if I tried that now. Exiting the lake, I head for Hope's.

The rain has rained out. It only drips. There are not enough drips for my windshield wipers to wipe without squeaking and shuttering across the window. I switch them on. I switch them off. On and off, the wipers and the drips keep me going the whole way to Hope's duplex. And when I see the duplex, I see it in a new, somewhat-hazy light... as home.

I climb out and lean against my wet car staring. As I start toward the house, some of the construction gang from next door intercept me. "Are you a friend of the girls that live here?" one of them asks." I nod. "And that's your car?"

"That's right." These people catch on quick.

"And they don't have any problem with your driving such a crappy car?"

I smile, "No, it hasn't been an issue."

"So the car doesn't matter?"

"What are you driving at?"

"Cars are supposed to impress women."

I look at the house being remodeled next door. A patchwork of plastic sheeting decorates the construction site. Around the plastic, everyone is watching and listening in on our conversation. I spot at least one woman. "Ask her," I offer. "The first thing to know in understanding women is that all women are not alike any more than all men are alike. Any generalization you come up with will be wrong part of the time."

"Okay, but your car really sucks..." the guy says with a smile.

"Thanks," I continue to the house and up the stairs, while a sociological conference convenes in the driveway behind me. I puzzle people.

"You're early," Becky tells me at the door. When I turn to go, she yanks me in by the elbow, which may have looked comical to the construction audience. "You are in time to help us haul your foil-wrapped dinner to the grill."

"You're grilling it?" I ask.

"If it fits. It won't fit in the oven. We checked." A giant oblong silver ball takes up much of their kitchen and reflects light all around. Hope peers around from the other side, her hair a mess, bison dripping from her shirt, saying, "This is your fault, wise guy! Give us a hand hauling it out the door." I duck an empty, airborne foil tube and grab a hold of the bison. It is heavier than I remember it. Hope and Becky grab the doors to the deck and open a grill. The deck creaks as the load and I step out onto it. I try not to take that personally. I balance the foil mass on the grill. Becky ducks under it to turn on the grill. I turn around, and Hope is gone. Becky and I clean up the kitchen. I take off my jacket and roll up my sleeves. Becky actually cleans the kitchen, while I ask where things belong.

"Hi," Hope gets my attention. She's back. Wow. She's... beautiful. I stare. Her dimples curtain her smile. "Beck, could you shut the window? The bison is wafting in. Thanks." Hope stares at me. "Are you all right?" she asks.

"I'm fine."

"Really?"

"Yes."

"You don't look fine," she judges, making me feel badly.

Becky leans in to inspect, "He looks kind of pale."

"I didn't get much sun today."

"Do you want to lie down?"

"No."

Hope puts her hand on my forehead. "You are a little warm," Dr. Hope diagnoses. I haven't had someone check my temperature this way in a long time.

"It's summer, and I just lifted a bull."

"Bison," Becky corrects.

"Bison," I acknowledge.

"Would you like a cool washcloth? Or some ice?"

"Do you have a headache?"

"I'm getting one..."

"Would you like some aspirin?"

"No. No, thank you."

"Would you like a glass of water?"

"Sure, I'll take a glass of water. Yes, please." They both go to get me some water. Becky calls out, "Regular or extra strength?"

"Regular strength water," I respond. "What is extra strength water? Is it hard water – the water that comes from the Splitsville Nuclear Power Plant?"

"What?!?" Becky calls out.

Hope takes the water past me and sets it by the couch. "Let's get you over to the couch." I let her move me.

"What did you say?" Becky asks.

"I said, 'Regular strength water.'"

"No, I was asking about aspirin."

"I don't want any aspirin."

"I thought you said you had a headache."

"No, I said I was getting one. All this talk about being sick is making me sick."

"Lie down." I take a drink of regular strength water, and I lie down.

Hope looks at the aspirin choices. Becky responds, "I didn't know which kind he wanted."

"What kind do you want?" Hope asks, as the door opens.

"Look–" I start.

"Hey, what happened?!?" Nicole asks, running over.

"Nicole, could you tell them I'm fine?"

"He's fine," Nicole tells them. Turning back to me she asks, "Are you sure?"

"Sure, I'm sure."

"I just wanted to be sure. The crew next door wants to be invited over for roast beast or whatever it is that we're cooking. The fog has trapped all the smoke next door," Nicole says, taking off down the hall.

"I'm sure we have plenty," Hope says, "that is, if you don't mind."

"We can send some over," I say, sitting up, "but I didn't think you got along with them?"

"That's no reason not to be kind to them," Hope says. "Are you certain you're–" I shoot her a look that recommends that she not make any more medical guesses. "Okay," she says, patting me on the shoulder.

Her pats turn into squeezes as she feels up the muscles of my shoulder. "Are you working out?"

"Just bison lifting."

Hope steps away and looks out the window. I peek too. She makes room. A barbequed bison cloud has blanketed the next door neighbors. "It's a smokescreen," Hope says. "How hot is the grill, Becky?"

"I don't know. I didn't change the temperature setting."

"Oh, good Lord!" Hope exclaims dashing for the door to the deck. She ducks into the heat and the smoke and the fog like a firefighter. She pulls me back inside. "The meat's done!"

"How do you know?"

"It was only set at about a thousand degrees." She wipes the soot from her face and turns on me. "You know, this is your fault!"

"My fault?!?"

"Yes, your fault! You and your big meat."

"It's not the size of the meat. It's how you grill it."

Becky and Nicole laugh, while Hope tackles me to the kitchen floor. "I'll remember that," Hope says, snuggling soot all over me. "I'm going to have to take another shower. That'll be the third one today."

"I can help!" I offer.

Hope gets up and pulls me up. She sighs, "What are you going to need?"

"Soap."

"No, what are you going to need to... serve up your meat?"

I open some drawers and gather some large utensils. The smoke has mostly dissipated, but the fog has increased. The once shiny aluminum foil has turned to gold with black shadows. Well what-do-you-know, alchemy works! I open the foil and duck the new cloud of smoke chimneying up from the opening. I butcher the meat. Nicole gets the count from the smoky cloud next door. Hope holds a plate for me. I wipe some grease on her cheek. Faith comes home and helps Becky and Nicole serve our guests below. Then we have dinner and offer the rest to the construction crew.

Nicole has changed into a Hug Me shirt. Faith tells me that Nicole told the workers that I am, "Sharing my meat with them."

I don't know if Hope is genuinely annoyed with me or not, for repeatedly getting her messy. She didn't mind getting dirty at Tom's cabin last weekend, but she declines my repeated offers to help her get ready. Instead she has me watch TV with the others.

According to the evening news, the end of the world has arrived. This upsets me, until the others calm me down by telling me that the news always sounds that way. They are amused by my reaction, but I can't be amused by the end of the world. All my favorite people are here.

Hope is nearly ready to go to the nursing home. She kisses me several times before putting on her lipstick, making me confused about the purpose of lipstick. I thought it was for making someone's lips more desirable to be kissed, but then why kiss before putting on the lipstick. I wonder what lipstick is made of? Wax, probably. Coloring. Shiny stuff, maybe bison grease. Hope tells me again that I can go with her to the nursing home. The others tell me I can stay and watch TV. I elect to go back to my apartment. Outside their door, plates and utensils are stacked, and the construction crew has left to roam the prairies of the upper Midwest. Even the smokescreen has left. I take my jacket and head home in my still-soggy car.

Driving through the fog makes it seem like things are only clear right here, in the spot where I am, and the spot moves with me. I keep my speed down to where I could stop within my clearing if I were to need to suddenly stop. It's reduced visibility. I watch my clearing in the fog until it includes the driveway to the Whisper Willows Apartments.

The dam broke, leaving a sandbar of clay and sand arcing across the driveway and mounding into the street. Inside, a sign on each of the apartment doors reminds tenants not to dam the parking lot. Ray gives me a look. He must think I'm responsible for every dam thing around here. I change into some iridescent white clothes. I had left them out, awaiting a decision on discarding them.

I cross the solidified sandbar formed from the flow of the former flood, feeling like I'm followed by a flickering flare. Passing a lamppost, a fore shadow stretches out from me like a thin building climbing up the wet sidewalk. Several blocks away I notice a glowing. It's coming from my shirt and jacket. Great. My clothes didn't glow inside. I wonder what is causing them to glow. Probably phosphorus. There must be phosphorus in the fabric. The fluorescent phosphorus must like the fog. It is a phosphorus-friendly fog. I keep walking but decide not to go to the Ice Cream Bar or anywhere else with people. I figure I'll hide in the fog. The fog fills my field of vision for a few feet in every direction. I wonder how far up the fog extends. My feet take me up the tower hill to the foot of Prospective Tower.

Prospective Tower is an inland lighthouse, a pharos, built around the time when the Mississippi River was full of paddleboats. The views of Milltown to the west and Pigs Eye to the east are spectacular, weather permitting. To get to the topmost concrete ledge, you have to pull yourself up from nearly shoulder-level. It's a fully physical climb up to a precarious precipice. I like to think of that, only because I'd hate to have to actually pronounce "precarious precipice." I'd rather just climb up the watchtower. I know this ledge. Most come up for the view, but tonight being a hazy night, there is no view. I can only see a handful of feet in front of me. It's all haze.

The haze sniffs and gulps quietly. Stepping forward, the abstract sniff solidifies into a human form. High elevations are not for the depressed; it just doesn't make any level of sense. This person is trying to permanently park their life. Another step and I'm seeing the back and left side of a tall thin woman. I break the silence, "Great view." She jumps and nearly falls off the slippery ledge. Her reflexes kick in. Her arms swish and flail. Her leg flies out to throw back her center of gravity. She regains her balance. I wonder when she last had it. "You probably feel you are the loneliest person in the world. And maybe for a moment there, you were," I tell her. Her face looks hollowed out by an ice cream scoop; the hollows collect water dripping from icy eyes. Her mouth gapes. "They say that time heals all wounds. I say they're wrong. Time leaves scar tissue." She stands and waits for me to do or say something more and sniffs. I think up some things but wait for something with the illusion of inspiration. We stand on top of the tower surrounded by mist and a long invisible drop. "Look, I know as your guardian angel, I was supposed to have read your story before coming down here, but I only skimmed it. I know you are hurting, and you are looking for a way to make everything better with a clean exit." She steps forward almost as if she has nothing to lose, and I remember her from my dream last night. Her name is Fran. "What is this all about, Fran?"

A frightened Fran stops her approach and blood flushes from her faces with a flushing sound. She stutters, "W-who are you?"

My arms stretch out in a slow shrug. Fran crouches. I look at my watch, "In a moment I'll be helping a French boy, who thinks he is the only kid in the world with a broken heart. Talk to me Fran."

Frazzled, she starts talking a million miles a minute. I barely catch any of it. Apparently she had a rotten day capped off by a torrent of water washing out of a nearby apartment parking lot and flash flooding her car. Ultimately I surmise, the issue is that no one cares.

"It hasn't always been this way, has it?" She shakes her head. I philosophize, "This is just a speed bump on your avenue of life. Think back to when you had people around you who cared about you and you cared about them. Where are they?" She starts listing off people and locations. I stop her when she gets to Rochester. I replay her expressions and notice a slight smile that had been too subtle to notice the first time through. "Felipe was special, wasn't he?"

"Yes. How did you know?"

"Call him. Or anyone else."

"Right now?"

"Yes. I'll give you some privacy." I step back. Fran gets on her phone and shakes as her fingers push the buttons. She starts talking and has to call another number. She looks over to me for reassurance. She finds Felipe and starts to tell everything to him. She listens. She rolls her eyes in my direction and patiently re-tells him everything with an exaggerated slowness. She turns her side to me. That's my cue. I carefully find the edge. It's slippery. I struggle to find my footing, not wanting to encourage newspaper editors to use Fallen Angel as a headline. Just as I find the lower ledge, I hear her tell him about her guardian angel. I speed up my decent. Then I hear her saying that she never thought of taking a photo of me. As I am climbing down through the fog, I hear her saying that I'm not there.

A car splashes past me on the street and brakes abruptly to a halt a half a block away. It sits there with its wipers on. I quickly duck into a narrow alley. I hear someone get out of the car, pause, get back in, and drive off.

Taking a different way back to the apartment, I pass the storefront of Phaedrus Motorcycles and see a phantasmal reflection in the window. I just reflected upon a ghost. Cutting through another alley, a man drops a bottle, screams, and strains himself through a chain link fence. As I pass by the spot where the man had been, I marvel at his not hopping over the fence. He went through it. "Oooo," I say. After a moment, I hear a cartoon-like sound of running and some other clatter.

A dog barks from another fence. I grin, "Shh!" It stops.

The Whisper Willows Apartments is dead when I get back there. A crayon notice parody is attached to each apartment door, reminding people not to say "dam" in front of the children. Inside Ray is asleep somewhere in the living room, possibly in a box. On my bedroom door there's a note that Hope called. It's too late to call her back. I get undressed. I still can't decide whether I am going to get rid of the glowing clothes, so I drop them in a box. I put on shorts, unfold my sheet with a shake, and climb into bed as the sheet parachutes over me, covering me completely.

24

Prelude To The Surreal

Hope is telling me, "It's surreal." I wake up to find my sheet wrapped around my head like a makeshift turban. I sit up and shake my head. I am an engineer, or at least I was, and I will be again. I should be able to keep a sheet on a bed for a night. I could bungee-cord the sheet over the bed or sew buttons on the mattress or use Velcro or duct tape or Bourbon tape or glue or bricks or a system of weights and pulleys. I've faced tougher problems. Leaving the turban on the bed, I use the bathroom. Through the door Ray calls to me that I don't want to flush. I flush anyway. My waste is exchanged for something far less pleasant backed up through the unsanitary system. I start to analyze it. It's gray with... I stop the analysis. I don't want to know. It stinks worse than a combination landfill-waste treatment plant-poultry farm. I get out of there.

"What the hell!" I yell.

"I told you!" Ray responds. "Take the bucket in the bathtub, fill it up from the bath, and pour it into the toilet. It'll take many buckets."

"This is the most disgusting thing that has ever happened here, including the dead neighbor incident."

"Yeah well, get back in there and keep the fan on and the door closed. If I don't hear a sound in there for more than 20 seconds, I'll try to pull you out. And if you opened any drains, close them. Good luck." He slams a helmet on my head, pushes me in, and shuts the door behind me.

I come back out.

"Fix it?" Ray asks.

"Yes. How long was I in there?"

"Four or five minutes. You don't remember?" Ray asks.

"I was focused on what I was doing. I drowned out everything else."

"So you wouldn't have to smell it?"

"Or remember it." I drop the helmet, and it slams loudly on the floor. I weave my way through short zigzagged trails between the boxes. I head to the open window to breathe in the fresh industrial air. The flavor of the day is roofing tar. Off in the distance, the train cars slowly and carefully switch tracks, the dog clicks its way across my ceiling, and I can't wait to get away from here. I can't move away fast enough.

"Did you see the mail from yesterday?" Ray asks. "It looks like you got a letter from Yolanda; I heard about her." I zigzag my way over to the table. "How are we going to move Kelly?"

I thumb through the mail and sit down to pay some bills. "I thought Kelly was going to ride on your motorcycle." I fill out a check. "Seriously, I figure we will take pieces over that can fit in my car, today. Then tomorrow morning, we'll take over any large fragile items that we want to personally handle. Is that okay?"

"Don't joke about Kelly. You know better than that." Ray smashes his leg into a box and then an open cabinet door. He hops up and down, swearing up a storm. There isn't space for playing hopscotch, I nearly remind him, as I study the credit card bill for discrepancies. Ray moves a box off of the other normal kitchen chair to sit down. "I have to ride with Kelly each time she is moved," he tells me. Since I charge very little, they fill the rest of the bill with reminders of all the places the card can be used, how to use the card in unusual circumstances, and even how to use the card to scrape ice from a car windshield. They have enough space on the bill for a diagram that shows the card applied at a 30 degree angle to the windshield. If the snow or ice is too thick for the card, the bill says, "use your card to shop on-line." Then they squeak in a list of purchases I made last year at this time, in case it might jog my memory for similar needs this year. The credit card people are some real cards.

"That's fine," I tell him.

"Do you know how we should pack her?" Mr. Questions asks.

"Kelly's sharp. She's a whole collection of heavy unwieldy swords, ready for cutting." I picture wrapping one of her parts in heavy paper only to cut through it like tissue paper. The same thing happens to plastic wrap or a plastic bag. The same thing happens to my blue plaid blanket. "I'm not sure we can pack her. We'll have to wear gloves though." The letter from Yolanda is three typed pages. Doesn't she understand that letter writing is my kryptonite?

"When I first met you," Ray says, "I thought, 'why does he want a roommate?'"

"Don't you know? I had dreams of outnumbering the neighbors. I wanted to fill this place up with roommates. Our former landlord intervened. I was going for the record occupancy."

"I'm trying to tell you something." I set down the letter. "I'm trying to tell you that it's been great being your roommate. You've put up with my mess and my vegetarian lifestyle, and you've made a big impact on me." Me? It wasn't me. That box made a big impact on his leg.

"How so?"

"Well, you've been a big influence on my not doing drugs any longer."

"You aren't doing drugs?!?"

"No," Ray says, looking at the open window.

"How long has it been?"

"About 17 months."

"That's great, but I was never trying to tell you how to live. People need to make their own decisions about things like that," I respond like I did years ago, leaving off the "so long as others don't get hurt" part.

"No, you didn't. And I thought you were becoming a vegetarian, until two nights ago."

"I'm not a vegetarian, but I haven't minded eating less meat," I tell Ray. "You've been a good roommate and– wait... you aren't dying are you? We can open some more windows... move some boxes..."

"No, I'm not dying, but the way I figure, the best things in life are the briefest. I picture you and Hope getting comfortable living together under the same roof. You'll be inseparable, you'll get married and have kids, and you won't have room for a roommate." The moment Ray said, "You'll get married," I pictured Hope as a bride, and I saw marriage as a pleasant possibility. Marriage with Hope would be the best thing that could ever happen to me. This is different. This is new. I check my watch. "You're smiling..."

"Hope and I haven't talked about marriage, but we are against having kids, especially as part of a planned pregnancy." Ray has a confused look. I emphasize, "No kids. Kids aren't in the schematic."

"Really?"

"Yeah."

"Who's idea was that?"

"Hope brought it up, but I agreed."

"I'm impressed."

"But that was Plan C for outnumbering the neighbors, so we're going to have to move."

Yolanda's letter tells me all about herself, her dreams, her philosophies... it's autobiographical. I don't know why she's telling me all this. If she's wondering if she's been leading a good life, my answer is yes, she's been leading a good life. I'm not sure how I'm supposed to respond to this. I'll have to ask for advice from the crew that got me into receiving fan mail in the first place.

Ray asks, "So how long do you think I'm going to be able to room with you?"

"Probably until a while after you become a big-shot artist, spending all your time in your dream studio, bemoaning all the artists that will be copying your work."

Ray's jaw drops, "Are you kidding?"

"I'll put it another way. We can remain roommates as long as we want." I hand him the letter from Yolanda. "What do you make of this fan letter?"

"It seems fine. How did she seem to you?"

"Nice. She was a talented actress in a small town play. And Cy and Hope made it clear to Yolanda, at least I think they did, that Yolanda can't expect a relationship. Cy also told her that I can't write a letter, can't even string a sentence together." Ray hands the letter back to me. "So how should I respond to her?"

Ray leans back. "Do like I do. Whip off a quick sketch and autograph it for them."

"That's a big help."

"You liked the play right?"

"Right."

"Tell her."

"That's it?"

"I don't know. I wasn't there."

I get up to look for something for breakfast. "Ray, the reason I gave bananas to the old guy in the cage on Wednesday was because I saw him dying today."

"Pointed perception?"

"Yeah. The bananas are starting to get overly ripe. Could I take a few more down there?"

"Yes, you may," Ray says, correcting my grammar. "You could take him a roll too."

"Thanks Ray."

I put on some more clothes, and I drop off some food for the old man. A woman doing laundry glares at me. Back in my apartment, I goat down odds-and-ends for breakfast while clearing out the refrigerator and the cabinets. A pile of things to be left in the hallway takes shape: some books, some canned food, several specialized kitchen gadgets – like a pineapple slicer and a cracker container, some games, placebo blankets – blankets that look warmer than they are – and other things. I would put out the turkey carver, but I can imagine hundreds of undesirable ways the urchins could put it to use.

Most kitchens I've been in have the most-used items in the most accessible cabinets and drawers and the least-used items in the most remote locations. In the remote Antarctica-of-cabinets, I find some appliances that seemed to be a good idea at the time, but have never been used. The ketchup maker, the bacon press, and the soggy breakfast cereal milk-wringer get added to the pile of items for my neighbors.

Filling one side of our kitchen sink with ice, I put some of our few remaining items in the sink to keep cold while I defrost the freezer with pans of hot water. Hopefully the building owners will replace the refrigerator with one that isn't listed in antique collectors' guides. I doubt it. I loosen a large pan-sized sheet of ice and place it on top of the sink items. Ray heads off to work.

In my room, I move aside my dresser. Dusty abandoned spider webs have built up behind it. Spiders don't clean up after themselves. It's not like this outside. It makes you wonder who tears down spiderwebs outside, since clearly the spiders don't.

Calling Hope, I leave a message apologizing for not having returned her call last night. I tell her that I will be out for around an hour, but she should be able to reach me anytime after that. I also ask her if she has any issues about dinosaurs that I should know about. I clear out our stuff from the storage cage downstairs, which is just my grill, cooler, tent, and many empty boxes. I go out to the library to use their bathroom and overhear a conversation about miracles and sightings of the Virgin Mary. I was thinking about eating at Yesterday's Diner, but for some reason the place is packed. At the apartment again, my lunch consists of two types of pickles, crackers and peanut butter. I spend an hour packing blankets. I call the power company about disconnecting service.

Calling the phone company, they want me to talk with the Sales Department to cancel my phone service, unless I have an overdue bill in which case I need to talk to Billings... Montana, I think. So I wait for Sales as I pack clothes. When talking with Sales, I tell him that I would like to disconnect my phone service. He says he would be happy to help me with that. He asks for identifying information, and I give him that. He wants to know when I want to shut off my existing service. I tell him Saturday night at eight o'clock, if that's possible. He says, "Certainly that's possible." He asks about the location and starting time of the new service. I tell him there will be no new service. He asks if I'm switching to another company. I tell him I don't know. He asks if I already have a new number or a mobile phone. I tell him, no. He says he needs this information to complete the disconnection of the old number. I offer to make something up. He reiterates that I want to cancel my current service, but that I will not be starting up a new service. I tell him that's correct. He explains that there is an installation fee for new customers and there might be a deposit required, but there is no installation fee or deposit required for existing customers. There is even a provision for keeping my current number, if I am moving anywhere in the continental United States, so long as I don't leave the country, but if I cancel my service, my phone number will be gobbled up. There is a line of people waiting to use my number. I tell him I just want to cancel my existing service. He asks me if I am planning on becoming a hermit. I tell him I thought about it, but being a hermit would interfere with my social life. "So would not having a phone," Sales tells me. He's not sure if his business is extortion or blackmail. I continue to pack my stuff. I ask him if he is paid on commission. I tell him I am not going to change my mind. I tell him that as he sits on the phone with me, not handling my account, other people in Sales are handling calls that he could be handling and making money that could have been his. That clinches it. He hangs up on me. Midway through calling him back, my line goes dead. I cannot get a dial tone. That's quick service.

Now what?

Welcome to Plan B, which stands for Because the phone doesn't work. I write a note to Ray, telling him that our phone service has been cut off. I asked for Saturday night, but they decided to cut it off now. I quickly pack some remaining items in big plastic bags. I clean up as best I can, pack up my car with some fragile things that don't belong to Kelly, and I start out to Hope's house. Traffic is blocked off on University Avenue before Prospective Hill. The detour takes me far enough away from my route that I turn back to take an alternate, round-about way to Hope's. I wonder if there is a carnival or a parade this weekend. It is still too early for the state fair. In any case, traffic is unusually polite and courteous.

The Pony Express has room for two, maybe three, bags of groceries if I don't care about elbow room and I don't mind a bag sitting on my lap. I find a grocery store in the Lake Weago area, a Choice Market. I figure several people will drink water. I also pick up Double Bubble, blueberry juice, Cooler Cola, something called Lake Weago beer, some non-alcoholic apple beer, Yoerg Beer, a bottle of Chippeau Valley Blanc Spirit, and a jug of very green, freshly squeezed wheat grass juice. More beverages than I'd planned to buy are squeezed in with my fragile things, and I still wind up holding two bags.

At Hope's house, the key Hope gave me opens the front door to the lower level. The construction crew watches me bring in my loads. They must think I'm fascinating. As I start to fill the refrigerator, a doorbell rings. We actually have a doorbell! My apartment only has a knocker. I answer the door, half expecting either the Neighborhood Welcome Watch or the construction crew wanting to come in and kick back.

"Becky!"

"Hi, what's going on?" she asks.

"I was just bringing over some fragile stuff and filling the fridge." I wave her in.

"Our phone has been ringing off the hook. People have been trying to reach you so they've been calling here or calling Hope's phone."

"I called the phone company to disconnect my phone tomorrow night, but they decided to hang up on me and cut it off right away," I tell her as I finish loading the drinks.

"What should I tell people?" Becky asks.

"Just that we're meeting here tomorrow morning at ten or anytime after that. Jake should have told them that."

"You're talking about Jake, right? He's not exactly awe inspiring; remember, I was on his team a week ago," Becky crosses her arms.

"He is actually fairly capable. You'd be surprised."

"Right..." The doorbell rings. "I'll get it," she says. "It's your girlfriend!"

"Hi Hope!"

Hope kisses me. "I'm glad you're here. Everyone has been trying to reach you. Is something wrong with your phone?" she asks.

"It was prematurely disconnected. I had asked for it to be shut off tomorrow night. And why are people calling? I told Jake that people should meet here tomorrow at ten. What are they calling for?"

"They want to know if they should bring anything, if you have a truck, if you need boxes, whether or not you saw any ghosts last night..."

"Ghosts? Why ghosts?" I ask.

"Didn't you hear? The Savior of the Midway?"

"No."

"That's right," Becky says, "that's your neighborhood!"

"A ghost saved a woman from killing herself last night and stopped a rape and appeared and disappeared several times," Hope explains.

"That's weird."

"Everyone's talking about it. They're calling it various things but mostly the Savior of the Midway."

"When was this?" I ask.

"In the middle of the night."

"Oh, I was in bed."

"We should go there," Becky says.

"Why?"

"To see for ourselves."

"I'll drive," Hope says.

"I need to drive separately because Ray and I will be moving pieces of Kelly early tomorrow morning, using my car." Hope helps me lock up behind us.

"Who's Kelly?" Becky asks.

"The bronze statue of the Lactating Woman that Ray is working on. It is very fragile at this stage, extremely sharp, and some of the pieces are fairly heavy. On my way over, there were detours on University Avenue, so I don't recommend that route."

"That's where everything happened last night."

"Oh," I respond, not quite understanding. Was it like a bomb that hit the neighborhood and damaged University Avenue?

"Let's meet at your apartment's parking lot and then walk over," Hope suggests as Nicole's red convertible drives up. We eye her approach while keeping an eye on the crew.

"Hi."

"We're going to see what's going on near Ricky's, do you want to come?" Hope asks.

"Sure, I'll just be a minute," Nicole says, taking off up the stairs.

"I'll meet you at my parking lot," I tell them, and I take off. On my way, I think about what Becky said about Jake, and I question my own confidence in him, but then I question the basis for my questioning his abilities. When I start questioning my questioning of questioning, I stop that line of questioning. The Whisper Willows parking lot is more full than usual. Hopefully it will empty out before mid-day tomorrow, so that I can park the Hauling Assets truck close to the door. Hope parks next to my car.

The four of us start to walk, with Hope and I hand in hand following Nicole and Becky. Hope asks, "Is the parking lot plowed in winter?"

"Yes. Once a year they have everyone move out their cars, and they plow the lot. Otherwise, everyone is on their own."

"You're kidding." She looks at me. I shake my head. "You're not kidding." I nod.

Becky turns and asks, "I called Tom and asked him to meet me at your place in about an hour and a half. I hope that's okay?" I nod. "He's going to try to take me on a better date than your date two nights ago."

"Romance is not a competition," I observe. "But what if it was? What if romance were an Olympic sport? Everything else is, why not romance?!? The kiss would be compulsory, but everything else would be subject to artistic expression." I go on and on until Hope puts her hand over my mouth as we work our way through a massive crowd of people. The area is mobbed with people. There are traffic barricades and police officers. I can't even tell where we are until we see, strewn around the tower, flowers and crosses, wreathes and pictures of loved ones, makeshift alters and beads and glow sticks. People are praying to the tower. People are taking pictures of Prospective Tower.

Click.

That's when my life takes a left turn from the real to the surreal. I watch some police officers preventing people from climbing the tower. How could I be so stupid! What an idiot! "I need to go."

"We just got here."

This is all my fault. It all adds up. No, it doesn't all add up, but it most of the way adds up, and it's all my fault. I tell Hope, "I'm going to head back to my apartment. Do you want to meet me there?"

"All right," Hope kisses me.

I take a meandering, zigzagged route through open spaces in the crowd. At times I'm blocked entirely by groups of people on all sides. I wait for an opening. I catch bits of the story from people reading newspaper accounts and telling groups of others what they heard on TV or in interviews or people bragging about their own personal third-hand connection to this or that witness or dog owner or resident who slept through the whole thing.

This is all about me and my walk last night. It makes me feel like the ultimate huckster or car salesman who has set off an urban legend that has captured the imagination of the neighborhood.

A man says, "I drove here from St. Cloud."

Okay, it has captured the imagination of the state.

"I'm from Wisconsin," someone tells the man from St. Cloud.

Okay, it has ensnared the upper Midwest. It's still early. People might be traveling in from other states or Canada. Canadians are just as silly as we are; it just doesn't seem that way because there aren't as many of them.

I feel awful. I don't know which is worse: all of this Savior of the Midway nonsense or the backed up sewage system of Whisper Willows. Either way, it stinks.

I get free of the crowd. There are still people coming, but I can freely walk in straight lines now. A young couple smiles when they spot me coming down the sidewalk. They cut over to stop me. "Did you see it?"

"Yes," I tell them.

"What was it like?"

I think, a sham, a circus I instigated. I look at their faces filled with wonder and I say positively, "Everything you want it to be." I pause and say, "Hope is there." They smile and thank me.

I walk on, wondering what truth is. I wonder whether truth is that I took a walk in the fog last night or if truth is that it was the Savior of the Midway. Truth can be a societal factor. That's why I never studied sociology. If enough people believe, it is a truth. I am outnumbered if I simply believe that I took a walk. If I went back and told that couple and the crowd that it was only me, I would be on the receiving end of Prospective Hill stones. It would be painful to them and painful to me. People could brag about how far they drove to bean me with a rock.

People are running toward me from behind. It sounds like a whole crowd. One of them shouts, "We're going to get you!" Someone jumps on my back and another person spins me around by the arm. It's Hope! She gives me a kiss. I look up to feel and see Nicole looking down on me from on top of me, hair cascading all around.

"I can't believe we caught up to you!" Hope exclaims.

"Yeah, you're really slow," Becky affirms, while Nicole climbs down.

"Are you okay?" Hope asks.

"Don't start that again."

"You just seem lost in thought."

"I am."

"Good things or bad?"

"A mix."

"Well, if you have any concerns about moving in, lets' talk about it."

"Faith can be a bitch," Nicole adds.

"I'll tell her you said that," from Becky.

"You would. Look at that!"

"What?"

"That tree. That Y-shaped tree."

"Those are yew trees. They always grow like the letter Y," Becky lies.

"No it's not. It was cut that way, around the power lines."

"Why don't we have Y-shaped trees?" Nicole wonders.

"Because all our power lines are buried," Hope tells them.

"Around here, they only bury the dead power lines," I tell them. "So what did you think?" I ask Hope.

"It was kind of cool. They said he looked like St. Orvius or St. Paul."

"St. Orvius. Wasn't he the patron saint of riverboats?"

"No, I think that was St. Orleans."

"Someone said he looked more like St. Paul."

A chorus of angels sing.

Hope answers her phone, "Hi Faith. No. We were at Prospective Tower." Hope holds the phone away from her ear, then back again. "I'm sorry. I didn't know you wanted to go. I–"

We keep walking as Hope listens to Faith.

"I told you," Nicole tells me.

"Look," Hope says, "that's not true. It was a spontaneous decision to go. We weren't planning on it. You could meet us at Ricky's apartment and we could go back there together." Hope asks me, "Do you have candles?"

"I have flashlights."

"It's not the same. Who ever heard of a flashlight vigil?!?" Hope whispers, "Look, I'm telling you. Get your butt over here. Okay." Hope hangs up. "Some people's children," she says, shaking her head.

Becky and Nicole are trying to figure out where all the sand and clay came from that forms a river delta out of the parking lot. I tell them about yesterday's lake. From our apartment door, I pull off a notice that says the toilets don't work; they're trying to fix the plumbing without replacing the entire system of ceramic pipes.

Inside the apartment there is a wall of boxes, nearly to the ceiling. We turn a corner to run into another wall of boxes and another. I tell the others, "I hope we find the cheese in time." Instead we run into Tom holding a bouquet of flowers. I take them and thank him. He grabs them back and gives them to Becky with a kiss. Hope confirms that Tom will give Becky a ride back home, and the two lovebirds disappear forward through the maze. Farther back through the maze I find a note from Ray saying he's gone out to dinner because he finished off the rest of the food and that he discovered that he doesn't like ketchup and peanut butter sandwiches.

"Ew," Nicole says, reading over my shoulder.

We find our way into my bedroom only to find that it's Ray's bedroom. He has done a better job at packing than I have. There is almost nothing left. There is room in the room. It's mostly just pieces of Kelly. I turn us around and take us into my room.

"You still have some packing to do," Hope observes with dimples.

"Some," I agree. "Hope, remember when we agreed to tell each other significant things that happen, to keep each other communicating?"

"Yes..."

"Do you have anything you've been meaning to share with me?"

"Yes, I've discovered a new type of soap that I like. It's like a peppermint."

Nicole stops punching my bed to ask, "Can I try it?"

"Sure, it's in my shower," Hope says.

"Anything else?" I ask.

"Well, I was thinking after school's out for the summer, maybe we could go to Chicago and visit Christie."

"That sounds good."

Nicole pouts, "I never get to go anywhere."

"What about you, do you have anything to share with me?"

"Tons of stuff. I have no idea where to begin. I don't know what order to go in. We need some time, and Faith is going to be here soon. I also don't know how much of it Nicole can hear."

"Hey! Don't leave me out!"

I clear the floor for us to sit. "Nicole, I am no expert at how to make a relationship great. I'm trying to figure out how I should be and who I should be. Last Sunday morning, Hope and I committed to telling each other everything of significance, but I am already behind in my telling her stuff. I feel like I'm already several days behind. My homework is late, and I'm in trouble. How do I include you? And then when Faith gets here, do I start all over with her, explaining what we're talking about? It's going to take 20 minutes just to get back through all the boxes to answer the door!"

Nicole stares, nods, gets up, and steps through us. "I'll take care of Faith," she tells us. She legs a box out of the way. "Come out when you're done," she tells us, and she shuts my bedroom door behind her.

"Is she mad?" I ask Hope, as I try to gauge the door slam decibels on the anger scale.

"I don't know. I know she didn't want to be shut out of whatever this is. She'll take it out on Faith." As I try to figure out where to begin, Hope asks, "Does this have anything to do with dinosaurs?"

"No, why?"

"Your message asked me about dinosaurs."

"No. I guess that was the biggest thing. I have a giant inflatable tyrannosaurus rex, and I could get rid of it if you have any dinosaur issues."

"No, don't get rid of it. You don't need to. The way you were talking I thought something serious had happened," Hope says patting me.

"Yes, several things. That wasn't one of them. I'll begin in chronological order. Wednesday afternoon I imagined going to the library on Sunday for the Sunday newspaper employment ads only to find that they are on-line on the Wednesday before, with Tuesday submissions, so I decided to go back to the library next Wednesday to read the ads. I went to the company the previous Tuesday, but I didn't know this one integrated CAD software program. Then I took a course to learn that software, and went back that previous Tuesday and they gave me a job."

"Wait. So you never actually went to the library."

"No, I did. I went there today to use the bathroom." Hope is figuring it out. "I never actually went to the library to look at job ads, and I won't be going to the company until next Tuesday."

"How did you explain being there before the job was posted?"

"I made it seem like I had an inside source at the newspaper." Hope's still thinking about it. "So I have a job, kind of. Or I will have a job."

"What is it?"

"An engineering job."

"What about the software?"

"What about it?"

"When are you going to the class?"

"I already went through pointed perception."

"What about actually using it?"

"That was part of the class."

"That you never actually went to. You have no proof of taking the class."

"I already answered questions to demonstrate my knowledge. I am self-taught... in a way." Hope's still thinking about it. "Ready for the next thing?"

"I guess."

"Yesterday when I visited Lefty, he and several others talked to me about being the subject of an experiment to read my mind."

Hope laughs, "So you've been invited to an ESP convention?"

"Not exactly. They'll strap me down and slide me into an MRI. As I think through my short-term memory, three regions of my brain are analyzed and interpreted: from impulses to gibberish to English." Hope's smile turned upside down when I mentioned the MRI.

"Hospital gown and all of that?"

"Yes."

"Are they opening you up?"

"No. I don't think so."

"My dad died in surgery. Routine surgery," she emphasizes.

"I'm sorry. I didn't know. I haven't given him an answer yet. I was leaning on saying yes."

"I'd like to hear more about this."

"I think Lefty might be coming to help tomorrow." I add, "The doctor can hold doors for us, and watch over things."

"Do you mind if I talk to him about this?"

"Be my guest." I pause. "Ready for the second to the last subject?"

"I don't know. Go ahead."

"Here is a letter from Yolanda, the girl who–"

"I know who she is."

"I'm not sure how to respond to it. I'd like to get your opinion, and maybe Cy's since she started the whole thing."

Hope reads the letter intensely. She hands it back to me. "Can I think about this? When do you want to reply?"

"Before winter, probably."

"Okay. What's next?" Hope asks while eying my sheet turban.

"I am the Savior of the Midway."

Hope's eyes become the size of bowls. Her mouth gapes open. "**What?!?**" she yells. "**You're**–" I knock her over, covering her mouth with my hand.

"Hey, these walls only look solid you know. Keep your voice down. Are you going to keep it down?" Hope nods. I remove my hand, but still lie beside her ready to muffle or muzzle at a moment's notice. "Last night I took a walk in the fog. I have some clothes that I never wear that I was thinking of getting rid of, so I wore them. They kind of glow. Especially in the fog." I crawl over to a box, dig around, and retrieve the clothes. I hold them out to her. I think she's in shock. "Remember to breathe. Breathing helps. Now, I was walking along in the fog wearing glowing white clothes, and I wondered how high up the fog went, so I climbed the Prospective Tower, only there was already someone there. From a dream the night before last, at least I think that's when I dreamt it, I remembered that her name was Fran. So I called her by name and told her I was her guardian angel and other stuff."

"You didn't."

I nod affirmatively. "She told me what had happened, and I told her how she was feeling and asked her to call this one friend. She did. And while she was talking to her friend, I disappeared. I climbed down. A few other people saw me after that, but I didn't stop any rape. Either it happened and I didn't know it; or it never happened; or there was a second Savior of the Midway out last night." Hope's eyes are narrowing at me. "Remember to breathe," I remind her.

"She was going to jump."

"She wasn't up there for the view. She didn't deny it, when I told her that she was looking for a clean exit."

"You saved her life." Hope raises an eyebrow, "You shouldn't have lied to her."

"That I was her guardian angel?"

"Yes."

"Maybe I am."

"So you don't think you lied."

"No, I know I lied. That just wasn't the part that I felt was much of a lie."

"What was the lie?"

"I– I kind of made it seem I was in a hurry. I said that 'in a moment I'll be helping a French boy, who thinks he's the only kid in the world with a broken heart.'"

"You rushed someone who was suicidal?!?" I sheepishly nod my head with a smirk. "And it worked. But now there are all those people who think a saint has–" Hope stops herself and smiles half a smile at me. "C'mon, let's go save Faith." Hope leads me by the hand through more twists and turns than this apartment should support, to find Nicole arguing with Faith from on top of her. Hope pulls Nicole off. Faith complains of needing to use the bathroom. Hey, who doesn't? We agree to find a bathroom elsewhere. I go back for flashlights and candles and manage to find a large bag of four inch, white Christmas candles and some matches. We exit through a group of residents calmly discussing the toilet situation. They stop us, but when we say we have to go, they understand.

"What's in the big bag?" Faith asks, pointing.

"One very large candle," I kid her.

"It doesn't look like a big candle," Faith says.

"It's in a lot of little pieces. It has to be put together," I tell her.

I hand out flashlights to the girls. Nicole looks carefully at hers. "I thought it might be the same one I had last weekend," she says, "but mine had a nick in it." We use the bathrooms at Yesterday's Diner. A waiter-magician I know asks me how the job search is going. I tell him that I should be ending my search soon. He's about to say good, when he thinks of something else. Right then, the other three join me, and I say good night to him. Just as I'm turning to leave he stops us and asks if we have noticed a change in people because of the whole Savior thing. I ask him what he means.

"People are talking more; they're being nicer. One couple came through here earlier, real grumpy. They stood out because they were acting normal and wondering what was going on, and several tables told them. They left saying they were going to the Prospective Tower."

"We're going there now."

"Have you been there yet?"

"This will be our second time today," Nicole tells him. We get some leftover sandwiches to go, and we start our walk toward the sunset. Nicole tells Faith what it was like. She encourages us to chime in. Ultimately, I tell them about the young couple and what I told them. Hope squeezes my hand.

When we get there with shining flashlights, several people comment that they should have brought a flashlight, so I start handing out extra little flashlights.

I light our candles. The four of us light candles for others. People gather around us, separating us into four crowds. Faith's candle wavers and goes out, and Hope relights it for her. I take a break to point out to the others, and anyone else, all the candlelights spreading across the hillside of the tower hill. Many people thank us, including a police officer, who had been standing beside me for a long time. Some people ask what group we're with. "No group," I respond.

"How do you know each other?"

"We're friends," I reply.

"Some people want to pay us for the candles," Nicole calls out.

"No, thank you," I call over to them.

Candles keep getting lit. The cop helps me open more boxes and holds them open for me. The candle lights him from his blue shirt to his crew cut. I assume his mustache is standard issue, along with the gun and the handcuffs. His pleated blue uniform shirt has Pigs Eye Police patches on the shoulders. Aren't we in Milltown? I wonder where the border is around here; I look around for the telltale greener grass or the horizon-to-horizon dotted line.

Behind the badge, his blue police shirt tells a story written through the yellow brown sheen on the back of his collar and the back of his sleeves. The personal oils and ring around his collar tell me that his shirt splits its time between him and his police station locker. He is not in a relationship. He is waiting for someone who doesn't mind worrying. He does not wash his shirt because he can't iron it. He figures he extends the life of his shirt by wearing an undershirt. The collar of his white undershirt peers over the collar of his uniform shirt, even though it is not cool enough to need two shirts. His job makes him sweat. The matching oily sheen to his shirt can be found on the seat of his squad car. Far more than his shirt, the fact that he wants to help pass out candles says a great deal about who he is.

As I light one candle, the girl puts her hand on my forearm. I look at her. It's... it's Fingklukreb! I hate it when I don't get a name right the first time. It guarantees that I'll never get her name right. "Remember me?" she asks.

"Of course I do. You are the winner of the spoon on the nose contest from last week," I tell her.

She is pushed aside by Eyes, the girl on mascara overload... Carrie. "I think I was the winner that night," Carrie tells me, as I recognize one of my neighbors.

Some people leaving get my attention with Hope's help. They want a candle, even a reject candle, to keep as a souvenir. I offer them the candle I've been using to light the rest, and they are pleased. A few other people volunteer to light candles, and soon we run out of candles. We lit more than 250, but I don't know exactly how many. My eyes burn with the ghosts of candle flames. The hillside and the roads below are covered with flickering lights.

As people move off, the cop grabs my shoulder, "What do you think of all this?"

I look around and wonder if I am surrounded by fools who accept outlandish explanations before imagining the mundane, or dreamers who are desperate for indications that God loves all people, or the curious who are here to investigate the unusual firsthand, or the socializers who want to be where the action is. Most likely, everyone shares the mix of motives to some degree. But I'm not a philosopher; I'm an engineer. I don't have all the answers. I barely have all the questions. "I don't know. Thanks for your help."

Police officers and their adversaries spend so much of their time preparing their guts, their actions, and their words for confrontations that never take place. They practice, but nothing ever really happens. The real troublemakers get away scot-free.

"Ready to go?" I ask the girls. On our way down, I give away my new candle. The others follow my example. Faith is reluctant to lose her candle; I don't know if she did or didn't. Hope takes my hand. Crossing the still-barricaded section of University Avenue, we weave our way around the brilliant spotlights of a TV news van and its signal tower.

Clear of the crowds, with arms outstretched, Faith says, "That was so much fun. I am so impressed. Do you realize how many people you just affected?" A quick chart comparing the creation of a self-driving car to handing out candles on a hillside appears in my mind. I shake my head to make it disappear. "Well, you affected a lot of people," she tells me. Faith whispers something to a wary Nicole, who apprehensively lets her.

"He's just quiet sometimes," Nicole tells her. Faith whispers something else, without quieting her gestures. "She's just... I don't know. Hey Hope, why so quiet?"

"I was just thinking about things," Hope says. From a block away we watch some people leaning into a car to discuss something. They disperse slightly as we approach and resume their business after we pass.

Nicole slows past a That Will Leave A Mark tattoo shop, "I've always thought about getting one."

I remark, "Things can seem like a good idea at the time, but once that moment is gone, you're left with repercussions and regrets. What had been clear, becomes blurry, stretched, and distorted, a parody of the original intentions, like graffiti on a masterpiece."

"Whoa. Something is definitely wrong," Nicole tells Faith. "I think it's you. Everybody was doing fine until you showed up." Nicole and Faith push and shove each other the rest of the walk back. At the apartment complex parking lot, I drop off my boxes and bags in the recycling, we stop at Hope's car, and Faith says good-bye with a wave and takes off.

Hope says, "I'll call you when I get back. Wait, I can't. Why did they have to shut off your phone right away?"

"Because I wouldn't start up a new service."

"You could have... well, it doesn't matter." Hope fishes her phone from her purse and hands it to me. "Here. This way we can talk." She kisses, "See you tomorrow!" We wave. On my way by, near another car and leaning against one of the buildings, some teenagers make kissing noises in my direction. Unlocking my apartment door, a chorus of angels sing.

"Hi Lover!" the phone exclaims.

"Uh hi," I say from inside.

"I'll give the phone to the driver," Nicole says, as I use my remaining flashlight to navigate the maze. Either someone made it more difficult or the lack of light is making all the box walls look alike.

"Hello, Stranger," Hope says.

"Hi, Loverducks! Have you made it out of the parking lot yet?"

"Yes, Silly. We're taking the scenic route home." That tells me she's taking the long way, and that she has no intention of smashing any University Avenue barricades. I'm thinking of smashing through one of these box walls. The maze wasn't this tough a few hours ago. Has Ray changed things around? Has Ray made this maze impossible to solve? This reminds me of a newspaper cartoon I once saw of a voice calling out from a dead end in the Self-Help Books section of a bookstore. The caption read something like, "Not everyone is cracked up for self-help."

"How are the roads? Any sign of snow?"

"The roads are fine. It's my passenger that's trying to get me in trouble. She either wants to know what we talked about, or she wants us to hit the dance clubs so that sweaty men can grind their bodies into us as a way of socializing." I halt my forward progress.

"So what are you going to do?"

"Go home. I'm in the driver's seat. Hey, cut it out! I'm trying to drive! Look!" I stand, leaning against a wall of boxes in an undetermined section of my dark apartment, holding my flashlight down and Hope's phone up, listening for a sign that they're still alive. I hear the sound of laughter. It's a good sign... a sign of life. "Are you still there?"

"I'm here," I tell her.

"Some guys were being guys," Hope tells me without my understanding. "I'll call you when I get home. Okay?"

"Okay. Bye."

"Bye Loverducks."

That leaves me on the edge of nowhere. The noise from the neighbors is strangely distorted. The bowling elephants seem to be on the other side of this box wall. That would surprise me. I proceed forward and backward only to find the front door. This can't be right. I start again. If I still had the candles, I could leave a trail of candles. If I get desperate for trail markers, I could use my clothes. With renewed determination, I find a narrow cardboard slot canyon in shadows and shades of brown that are hardly found this far east of Utah. It gets me to the kitchen. The unplugged refrigerator smells humid and has puddled. I thought the refrigerator was housebroken. I clean up the puddle and carry on. I head down the hall to the light at the end. Amidst the light, Ray turns to me and says, "You're back. Supposedly the sanitation system has been fixed, but I haven't tried the toilet." I want to hug him... not for the toilet, but because I didn't think I was going to make it through the maze. I'm amazed.

Instead of hugging him, I tell him, "Thanks," as a chorus of angels sing. I step into my room and answer, "Hi, Loverducks."

"I'm not your Loverducks," a woman tells me.

"Who's this?" I ask.

"This is Hope's mother. Are you the boy who is dating my daughter?"

I swallow hard, stand straight, and reply, "Yes, yes I am."

"Have you moved into my daughter's house already?"

"No, ma'am."

"Don't ma'am me. You can call me Pandora. Can I speak to my daughter?"

"She's on her way home. I'm at my apartment."

"When you next speak with Loverducks, do you think you could tell her that I called and ask her to call me?"

"Yes."

"Do you need to write this down?"

"No, m- No, I will remember."

"Good boy. Good-bye."

"Good-bye." I doubt she'll forget me. She probably won't forgive me either, I decide as I get changed. I set my alarm clock for early, when the phone rings. "Hello?" I cautiously answer.

"Hi, who were you just talking to?" Hope asks.

"Your mother."

"Lucky you."

"She asked me to tell you that she called and to ask you to call her."

"Anything else?"

"Yes, I accidentally called her Loverducks." I hear a sound that sounds like Hope is rolling on the floor laughing.

"That's priceless. That tops Faith's conversation with Erix."

"Faith talked to Erix?"

"He called, and she didn't know who he was. She was talking to him with the strangest look on her face when we got home like, 'Who is this guy?' I took over for her. He just wanted to know where you'll be tomorrow. I started to tell him that you were moving and that you'd be here and there, but then I switched to telling him you'll be here. I had messages from Cy and Jake. I called them and told them you have my phone."

"Okay."

"Tonight was pretty weird... the whole Savior of the Midway thing. It's surreal." Hope checks if I plan on taking any more walks tonight and then wishes me a good night. I whip my turban into a sheet and lie down to sleep.

25

Amazed

Angels are asking me for advice on angel issues: assistance etiquette, wing disguises, sure-fire halo polishes... The chorus of angels tells me I should get the phone, so I wake up and grab the phone. "Hi, did I wake you? I woke Jake. He's pissed." It's Ruth. I look at my snoring alarm clock in its night cap. A line of Zs stretches away from it in an expanding arc. Tripping over a giant paper airplane made out of a sheet, I look out the window for the sun. It's not there.

"Ruth?"

"Yes."

"It's early isn't it?"

"Yes. I just figured you'd start out earlier than you told everyone else."

"That's true. Yet, this isn't even early. It's late, late, late night."

"I couldn't sleep."

I carry the conversation back to bed. "What's the matter?"

"I wanted to know if I could bring over breakfast and help out."

I think for a moment and wonder how she could help here if morning actually hits. She could, but I would be concerned for her welfare around Kelly. "Do you know Kelly?"

"No."

Ray's pregnant bronze statue?"

"The nude. Yes."

"The pieces have sharp slices... splits... across most of them. They are both fragile and sharp. And heavy. We're moving her this morning. We don't have a way to wrap her, and she could slice us or my car pretty well. She's cut Ray often enough before. I don't want to have anyone else around. It'll be tricky enough between the two of us. Ten o'clock at Hope's house is still good." Ruth reluctantly agrees and asks about lunch plans. I tell her I'm buying pizza, wish her a good night, and drop off.

I am teaching a cloud of angels the fundamentals of patience. One irritated angel exclaims, "How can we learn anything with all these interruptions?!?" Angels sing and I look over and answer the phone. I can't imagine why I don't own one of these things!

"Hello, Acapella's Breakfast Pizzas. This morning's special is a scrambled eggs and bacon, toasted pizza. How can I help you?"

"That almost sounds good," Tom says. "What do you think of having a phone, a real phone, not a can on a string?"

"I understand the people who smash these things to base elements."

"It can't be that bad," he tells me.

"What's up?"

"I'm outside your door." I look at my bedroom door. No, he isn't.

"The front door?"

"Your apartment door. The front door didn't even slow down the moths." I turn off my snoozing alarm clock. I get up and trip over a giant white cloth, origami lizard. I change pants.

"Okay, I'm on my way. This might take awhile. I should have a ball of string to do this right."

"To do what right?"

"To traverse the maze in here."

"You're kidding."

"I haven't answered the door yet, have I?"

"No, but I think you're stalling."

"That wouldn't be polite... it wouldn't be right," I tell him as I take a left and then a right. I unlock the door and let Tom in.

"You weren't kidding! Now I remember," he says. I lock the door and lead him through the maze. "What's the point of locking the place?" Tom asks.

"We've boxed everything to be easy to carry. Now you're suggesting that we open the place up? I don't think so." I stop. "Hang on. We passed our turn off. Here it is."

"How can I help?" Tom asks.

"You can start by figuring out how to stop Ruth from being mad at us. She called hours ago wanting to be the first one over here. I told her that before ten, Ray and I will be moving Kelly. Kelly is sharp, fragile, heavy, and unpacked." I kick my sheet back onto the bed. "So ultimately she agreed to meet us at ten at Hope's. She'll be mad at us," I point at him as I put on a shirt.

"No she won't. She'll be mad at you. You stopped her from coming over. You aren't finished packing. She could have helped you finish packing. How are you planning to pack the hanging clothes?"

"Take a plastic bag like this. Pull it over a grips-worth of clothes. Push the hangers through the bag like this. Tie the open end of the bag like this. Use one of the thicker rubber bands to hold the hanger hooks together, like this." A rubber band snaps, shoots across the room, and squarely hits the alarm clock. The alarm clock wobbles, staggers, and falls over with a gasp. I try it again. The rubber band sails astray in the opposite direction, hitting Ray in the doorway.

"Great way to start the day," Ray retreats with dismay. From the hallway he says, "I'm okay. I wasn't planning on having children anyway."

I turn to Tom, "Here. You try." Tom completes his task without the rubber band turning into a missile. "Keep practicing. You might master it."

Crumpling the origami sheets from my bed, they become stuffing for a box of books. Tom eyes the extreme terrain of my mattress. "You aren't going to keep that thing are you?"

"How was your date last night?" I ask, deflecting his question with my own.

"Good. I gave her flowers. I took her to a nicer restaurant than you did..."

With exaggerated drama I stop and turn, "I have never taken Becky on a date."

"You know, First Street Station and your date with Hope."

"Competitive dating is not a sport."

"Yeah well, Becky wasn't impressed."

"She didn't like it?"

"She liked it. She just wasn't thrilled."

"Were you thrilled?"

"I'm not going to be thrilled by my own plans," Tom snarls.

"You should be. You should think it's over the top. You should be uniquely you, not a copy of me or Todd or anyone else." Tom bristles at my dredging up the subject of twins being copies. "First Street Station was my first choice for my date with Hope, not because it is intrinsically the world's most romantic restaurant and not because it would impress my limo driver, 'cause it didn't. I took her to First Street Station because it means something to me. It's one of my favorite restaurants. You weren't thrilled because you weren't being you. You were trying to be me or somebody else. Let's say Melanie was back, and you had one last date with her. Would you try to impress her with money? Would you waste time taking her to a play or a movie, when all you have is the one date? Or would you try to make it as great as you can for the moment you have?"

Tom finishes bagging the clothes with no mishaps or misfires. As he double-checks and triple-checks his work, he asks, "Do you think of Melanie a lot?"

"I don't have to. She's a part of me. She's the part of me that is creative. She's the part of me that does crazy things. If I wonder where something I did came from, it's usually because it came from Melanie. When I take risks, like moving to Hope's, it's the Melanie in me."

Tom stares at me. Maybe he's trying to spot the Melanie in me. "Do you think you are taking a risk moving into Hope's house?"

"Each step of a relationship is a risk. Moving to Hope's house is a risk. Talking to Hope about personal stuff is a risk. Taking Hope on a date to First Street Station was a risk. They're the right things for me to do, and that helps me to know what to do, but it doesn't change the risk. It doesn't change the fact that I could completely screw things up, or I could screw nothing up and could still lose Hope." Tom knows what I'm driving at.

Ray is in the doorway again, "Are you ready to move Kelly?"

"Yes, how many trips will it take?"

"I have no idea."

"This volleyball could use some air," Tom observes. "What can I do?"

"Seriously, you have to fix things with Ruth."

"Then what?"

"Then it's between you and Ray whether any part of Kelly can get moved in your truck."

In Ray's room we survey the parts. Ray gives an extra pair of gloves to Tom. As we take an arm and shoulder out, Tom says, "What's funny about what you said is that you were always the one doing the crazy stuff. Melanie would be laughing for hours after something you said or something you did. Melanie acted crazier because of you." Ray and I concentrate on taking the arm out, without taking an arm off. We twist the arm to get it into the back seat. Unless I mount a shelf in my car, that's about all my car can take.

Ray sums it up, "This sucks." He and Tom go over to Tom's truck as the sun breaks free from the industrial warehouses that had trapped it. Through the buildings and stray trees, the sun cuts a spotlight through to hit Kelly's arm, making it glow like an arm shaped, second sun in the back seat of the Pony Express. I'm going to need sunglasses.

"What if we cut open paper bags and tape them together?" Tom asks.

"It would cut through the bags," Ray responds.

"Yes, but it would otherwise protect the pieces," Tom counters. I follow them in. Tom observes, "The pieces would be easier to move if we didn't have to try to wind them through this maze." Neither of us reply. I figure, Ray built the maze, so it's Ray's responsibility. They cut up bags and wrap up all the pieces. I take a sandblasting shower. When I'm ready, they have everything wrapped but are wondering about the main torso piece. I volunteer a sheet to wrap it. With the sheet, it almost has a pregnant Statue of Liberty effect, except she's holding the breast instead of a book. Moving the other pieces into Tom's truck, we find a small crowd around my car, just as one of the urchins is trying the door handle. When they ask who it is, I resist the temptation to respond that it is their mother. Ray goes into an elaborate story woven around comic book characters, notably one that was turned to gold. The story travels with us from apartment to truck, back and forth. When asked who we are, Ray says that Tom and I are superheroes. Ray is then asked what Tom's powers are.

"He can split into two," Ray says. "And he can make funny faces, like that one. And that guy can see the future."

"Futures," I correct without thinking.

"Right. Futures."

The urchins want proof, as if in any eventuality it would stop at just one demonstration. No way. This could last all day. We have to get Kelly to Hope's, get the truck, and meet the others by ten. Ray elects to ride with Tom. I lead the way.

Summer Saturday morning traffic is light. Other than having to avoid University Avenue, the trip over is smooth. So far, the air is cool. At the house, the neighborhood is quiet in a calm-before-the-storm sort of way. As we move Kelly piece-by-piece into Ray's room, Tom tells me that he called Ruth and straightened everything out with her. He could be right.

Hope comes down smelling minty fresh and plants a big wet one across my lips. "Is this everything?" she asks.

"Yes, it's all done," Tom replies. "They've pitched the rest of their stuff. Their whole neighborhood is wearing black T-shirts and admiring their original Cameron Raymond artwork."

"Your name is Cameron?" Hope asks.

"Yes."

"Why do people call you Ray?"

"They don't. They didn't, until he started it," Ray points me out of the line-up.

"Do you mind it?" Hope asks him.

"No, it just catches me off guard when it spreads to other people."

"I know what that's like. My mother just called me Loverducks, thanks to him. What do you want me to call you?" Hope asks, with the care of a fourth grade teacher.

"Ray."

Hope musses up my hair. "Have you picked up the truck yet?"

"No, that's next."

"Then I'll see you in a while."

Ray elects to ride back with me, and Tom tells us he'll meet us back here at ten. On the way, Ray launches into a tirade about how dangerous Tom's driving was while Tom talked with Ruth. Ray isn't thinking about his life so much as Kelly's. I ask him if he wants to drive the truck or my car. Ray figures after we bring the truck to the apartment, we should take his motorcycle over and my car. As long as his stuff gets moved, he's done with the place.

Hauling Assets offers to sell me more boxes. I decline. The truck behaves badly as if it has been treated poorly all its life. I figure out how it handles, accelerates, and brakes. Braking is good. The last thing you want is to be at the helm of an out of control vehicle. Potholes that I have been avoiding for weeks are unavoidable with this crate on wheels. At Whisper Willows, Ray guides my backing the truck up to the door. We lock it, leave it, and return to the house. It's ten to ten. We have trouble finding street parking. Ray gives me his apartment key. Lawn chairs have been set up out front with a cooler and a table filled with breakfast. I knew I had forgotten something. Ruth makes it clear that she's not angry at me. Cy and Todd are here. Will and Wendy, the double W's, are here. Red, Erix, Stephanie, Nicole, Jake, and Lefty are here. I grab some food.

"Where's the truck?" Jake asks.

"At the apartment, waiting for us. Where's Tom?"

"He's watching Al inside."

Hope tells me, "Al came early. So far, he has oiled hinges and drawers, tightened screws everywhere, put a few screws diagonally into the basement ceiling to fix some squeaky joists... He tested smoke alarms, outlets, and ground fault interrupters. He repaired some outlets. He checked the plumbing, drains, foundation, window insulation, and ductwork..."

"Excuse me, I've got to go talk to him." I run in to find Becky and Tom watching Al examine some dust with a magnifying glass. "Excuse me, Sherlock, but you don't look under the hood of a gift car."

"The Trojans should have looked their gift horse in the mouth," Sherlock replies.

Becky says, "Let him do his thing. He's doing great. I've learned a lot. He changed the filter on the furnace and showed us how to do it. He showed us how to clear the sediment from the bottom of the water heater. He's doing a water test over there. He checked the fire extinguisher and the smoke detectors..."

Hope rests her hand on my shoulder and tells me, "It's okay. I'm not offended. I think its great."

With everyone taking Al's side, I encourage him to continue, "Carry on, Al. You're in charge of quality control."

Tom says, "As long as you have enough people at the apartment, we'll stay here and watch."

I step away with Hope. "Okay, Al, Tom, and Becky are staying here. Ray is staying here. That leaves you, me, Will, Wendy, Cy, Todd, Ruth, Red, Erix, Nicole, Jake, Stephanie, and Lefty."

Hope tells me, "Nicole has a modeling assignment; she isn't available. Todd banged up his arm. Lefty has been poking his cast. And Wendy has to get back to work. She's only here to see you."

"So that leaves ten of us?"

"Well, I was wondering how you'd feel about having Erix here as a front doorman and neighborhood greeter."

"I'm okay, if he's okay with it. So that means we would have nine people going over to the apartment?"

"It still sounds like a lot."

It's not enough to outnumber the neighbors. "Let's go out and check around with people."

Wendy gets to us first when we step out the door. Others gather around us. "Did Hope tell you I have to leave?" I nod. "I just wanted to tell you what's going on at Flight Control. Have you seen the commercials?"

"No."

"Nobody has. They only bought three minutes. They were counting on free advertising from the news. The message is that AutoDrive will drive through Milltown on the Sunday before Labor Day. The advertisements started yesterday, but the Savior of the Midway story bumped it from the news. They said the story may air late next week."

"So it's ready?!?" I ask Wendy.

"No. That's the thing. We aren't sure it will be. We're working overtime to try to get it ready."

"Wait. You said AutoDrive. Weren't they changing the name to Chauffeur?!?"

"They changed it back."

"Will it work?" Jake asks Wendy, while checking my response.

"It doesn't work yet." Wendy looks back to me. "I just wanted you to know and to know how much we miss you. And need you. I don't know how we'll get done without you. Or Clarence. He quit. And Scott got into a fight over his programming." Stunned about Clarence having quit, I thank her for updating me, and Will walks Wendy to her car. Cy catches up to them.

"Wow," Jake says. He's trying to goad a response out of me.

"It's not my responsibility," I tell him.

"Isn't it?" he asks.

Lefty comes over, "Have you made a decision about the experiment?"

"What experiment?" Jake asks.

Hope takes an index card from her pocket. "Could I talk to you about this?" she asks Lefty. When he agrees, she ushers him to a lawn chair. "I have a few questions." Hope did her homework! "Is an incision required?"

"No."

"Can any physical harm come to him from the MRI or any other part of the procedure?" Hope asks, as a crowd gathers around.

"As long as he follows my instructions and doesn't try out any of his own experiments at the expense of our project, I won't hurt him." Lefty made a joke, I think.

"Are there any potential repercussions?"

"As long as he follows my instructions, he won't get hurt."

"What's this about?" Cy asks.

"Can it change who he is?"

"No."

"Is there any chance of memory loss?"

"Any chance? Possibly."

"What?" I ask. Hope scores a point.

"What do you mean, possibly?" she asks.

"Short-term memory loss occurred in one of the previous patients."

"How long were the memories gone?" Hope asks.

"The short-term memories never returned."

"So the loss wasn't short-term, the memories were short-term," Stephanie confirms.

"Right."

I step back, tripping over the foot rest of a lawn chair. "Lefty asked me to volunteer for an experiment that will record all of my short-term memories," I tell them. "You never mentioned possible short-term memory loss."

Under a wrinkled brow and with eyes narrowed, Hope measures her next words, "Define short-term memory in this case."

"Normally short-term memory is comprised of the preceding several days. In his case, it is approximately four weeks. Maybe five."

That's when Hope blows a gasket.

"You want to wipe out my relationship with him?!?" Hope yells, waking the neighborhood. Lefty backs up in his lawn chair, sweating under the grilling. "Stay put." She turns to Nicole, "He stays." Then she turns to me. "You. Inside." I march inside. With commotion behind me, I hear and partially see Hope stopping Cy and Jake from following us, "We have to talk. Alone." Hope takes me upstairs. Faith runs past and closes a door. We go into Hope's room. "Please tell me you are going to decline subjecting yourself to Lefty's experiment."

"I didn't know about the potential memory loss, before this."

Hope grabs my shoulders and stares into my eyes. "You aren't listening. I asked you, are you going to decline? Are you going to tell him no?"

"I don't know."

"Have you lost your mind?!?" she asks, not catching the irony. "Everything we've done. Everything we've been through. Do you want that to just... disappear?" her eyes well up.

"Of course not. And I am very glad you asked the questions that you did. If I was skeptical before about my involvement, I'm even more skeptical now. He can't keep leaving out or glossing over significant issues. I have no interest in losing my memory. I also have no interest in losing my ability to remember things so well. Even though my memory can be too good at times, I also know that my memory is something I would never want to lose, and the past few weeks with you have been some of the best ever. I wouldn't want to lose them. But Lefty is my friend too. He needs something I have. I may ultimately have to say no to him, but I need to give him some more time. I need to give him a chance to minimize the risks. At the same time, I want you to stay involved and keep asking questions. Being a friend can mean taking some risks, not blindly and not unnecessarily. I was open-minded about moving in here; I heard all your arguments before deciding. Change is always risky. I would like to offer Lefty the opportunity to further make his case for my participation."

Hope sits on the bed with her hand on her chin. "Have you foreseen it being okay?" she asks, wiping her eyes.

I kneel down on the floor before her. "No. I haven't foreseen it at all."

"Is that bad?"

"I don't know. The place... the lab looked familiar."

"Maybe you need to do some foreseeing."

"Will you work with me on this?"

Hope mulls it around. "You'll keep me involved?"

"Definitely."

"Then I agree... reluctantly."

"I pack myself into a nice safe box with no risks, no dangers, and no weird stuff. The box can be padded and cozy and locked securely, but in the end, that's not much of a life."

"Do you think that's what you are doing? Do you think moving here is moving away from a real life?"

"No. I'm not talking about my moving in. I'm talking about you telling me to say no to Lefty. While I love the fact that you love me enough to worry about me and give Lefty the fifth-degree, and I want you to keep being involved in making sure I'm doing the right thing, I can't live a life that is completely free of risk."

"I'm not asking you to. I just– I don't want you to get hurt."

"Me neither. We'll try to make sure I don't. Are you okay?" Hope nods. "Why don't we call Lefty tomorrow and see what we can figure out, okay?" Hope agrees.

We head downstairs and outside, where the morning game is Let's Gang Up On Lefty. He is relieved when I tell him that Hope and I will call him tomorrow to talk about minimizing risks and isolating causes of the memory loss. Lefty scratches his ankle and leaves.

Ruth is willing to shuttle us to the apartment. The crew going over is Ruth, Hope, Red, Cy, Jake, Stephanie, Will, and myself. On the way, I explain my plan. "Our team is going to try to get everything from the apartment into the truck. The opposing team will be trying to take items from the apartment, from the moving truck, this truck, or any items left in between, such as things used to prop open doors or left for any other reason. Yes Stephanie, you have a question?"

"Who is on the opposing team?"

"Good question. The opposing team is limitless in numbers and tactics. They will have observers, runners, reporters, testers, and actual thieves. They can swap roles anytime. They can distract. They will be trying door handles, like we caught them doing to my car this morning when all it had in it was a bronze arm. They will be watching from windows. If they are only watching, they might just be part of the audience. If they are watching and reporting, they are more likely part of the opposing team. There are no uniforms to distinguish the other team, nor are there any age restrictions. If you spot a young person listening to what an old person is saying, they are either on the same team or they are swapping video game tips.

Inside the apartment, you will find an obstacle course in the form of a maze. The maze is tricky to navigate, and really gets in the way of moving around."

"Why did you make a maze?" Jake asks.

"I didn't. My roommate did."

"Ray's not here, so can we do away with the maze?"

"Yes," I tell him as we pull up.

Inside, there is a note on each apartment door requiring permission for parking a truck by the front door, since it is a fire zone. Right. Several feet of snow filling the parking lot or a lake full of water is not a problem for fire trucks, but a moving truck is.

We all go inside and play in the maze, before stopping to evaluate the task.

In my room, Red is holding my alarm clock, shaking it a little. "I remember this!" Cy squeals as she spies the clock. My clock is alarmed.

"Don't get it too wound up, or it'll need a time out," I reprimand them.

"It's a normal alarm clock," Red tells me. I tilt my head at an angle with a near shrug as if to say, if you say so.

Cy grabs it away from Red and puts her ear to it. "Do you know what it says? It says, 'Rick, Rick, Rick.' That's your clock all right." At least it isn't ticked off.

Working back to the front, I find Will and the other half of the group. Looking at all the boxes, Will proclaims, "We can do this. I will pack the truck. Ruth, do you want to help watch the trucks?" I didn't hear her agree, but they take a load out together. Stephanie and Jake follow them out.

The others are somewhere farther along in the maze, maybe still in my room. I listen for a cry for help. I am relegated to watching the front door.

"You haven't finished packing," Cy announces. "And your volleyball needs air."

"I have to watch the door," I volley back.

Stephanie comes back and takes two boxes at a time. Jake comes back and tries to take three but settles for two. Ruth comes in with stuff.

I tell her, "No, we are trying to empty the apartment..."

"I almost forgot. Can I set up a time-lapse camera?"

"Go right ahead."

Ruth works her way into a corner and sets up a tall tripod with a camera on top.

Cy appears and asks, "Do you have more packing tape somewhere?"

"The kitchen counter."

"How do I get there? Which exit is it?" Cy smirks. Moving closer, she confers, "You aren't going to keep that bed are you?"

"Yes."

"I don't know how you can sleep on it. How long have you had it?"

"About four years."

"What have you done to that thing? Wait," she holds up her hand and walks away. "I don't want to know."

Jake and Stephanie come and go, stripping. All their clothes are half off.

Hope shows up crying, clutching something to her chest. "You had your parent's wedding album and wedding rings in your closet?!? That is the sweetest thing!" She hugs me tight, wipes her eyes on my shirt, and disappears back into the cardboard labyrinth.

Stephanie slaps my back, "How are you holding up?"

"Fine." She takes two boxes and a bag and leaves.

Jake comes in, sweating, "It's getting hot out there."

"You can take a break." He shakes his head. "You can watch the door, while I move some things." He shakes his head.

"Water," he says. I get him some water.

Stephanie comes in, grabs some boxes, chuckles, and leaves.

"Hey, I found a couch," Jake says removing some boxes. "I didn't expect it to be on its end, erect."

Red appears, "I'll watch the door. Cy and Hope have some questions for you."

I dodge and weave through the box labyrinth as if I've been doing it all my life. I don't recognize my room when I enter it. The bed is on end. The dresser drawers are stacked separately from the dresser, and the closet is almost empty. My girlfriend and ex-girlfriend have done a number on my room.

"What's this?" Hope asks, holding up a large funnel with rubber tubing tied to it.

"That's either a land octopus or a Funnellator. Pack it like a Funnellator, not like a land octopus."

"How do you want the Christmas tree packed?" Cy asks.

"Does it fit in a plastic bag?"

"Almost halfway."

"Then it doesn't get packed. Neither do the claws in the closet."

"Claus? You have Santa Claus in your closet?!?"

"No, traction claws. You put them in front of a stuck car tire or behind or both. Those."

"They weigh a ton."

"Are you sure you want this bed?" Hope asks.

"I think so. But don't try to pack it."

"How do you sleep on it?"

"Restlessly."

"And you want that? Your room at my house has a bed already... a nice level, Great Plains, mountain-free, valley-free bed."

"I'll think about it."

"How do you want this big bag of rubber balls packed?"

"See if you can get a second bag around it, and treat it as though it's fragile. I should have moved it earlier. It could cause a lot of trouble."

"It could fill three of the four drawers of your dresser, plus some."

"Why do you have so many rubber balls?" Cy asks.

"It was for a prank that I stopped myself from actually doing." You have to have a lot of balls to pull off a stunt like that. When Cy relaxes, getting comfortable for an extended answer, I respond, "I'm not going to tell you anything else, since I might still do it. To you."

Cy turns back to pack. "Hope, that bag goes in the garbage."

"No, it doesn't," I disagree. I dodge and weave back through the maze only to find myself dodging and weaving through nothing... empty room, nearly.

Jake is taking a chair out like a lion tamer. Red and Stephanie are looking at a poorly packed bag of stuff. "What do you want us to do with this?" Stephanie asks.

"Take it out to the lawn over there, on that side of the building. Dump it out on the lawn."

"Then what?"

"Then nothing."

"You're kidding."

"No, these are decoys and distractions for the neighbors. They have to be getting ready to try something right about now."

"This is a perfectly good ketchup maker," Stephanie observes.

"You can have it if you want it."

"No, thanks." I can't see her ever wanting something that belongs in a kitchen. She's not a kitchen-dweller. She hauls the bag out.

Jake asks, "Do you have a dolly?"

"I don't play with dolls."

"Funny."

"I think there is one mounted to the inside of the truck, unless Will has packed it in."

"We haven't moved the couch yet because we wondered, are you keeping it?"

"I was planning on keeping it."

"It has seen better days. Is it Ray's? We could call him."

"No, it's mine."

"Then there is nothing stopping you from getting rid of it, right?"

Stephanie is back, grinning, "That was fun, dumping that stuff. You did a good job junk-eliminating. You look at that stuff and you think, 'This is kind of cool,' but it's not. It has the illusion of practicalness and wonder, but if you really look at it, you realize that it is all a manufactured illusion. There is no real value."

Jake says, "Wow. Deep," and gets slugged for his effort.

"So are you keeping the couch or pitching it?" Stephanie asks flatly.

"Pitch it. Leave it on the lawn by the other stuff. But first shake out any loose change. There is no point in giving the bank to the neighbors."

Cy comes out with a guitar case, making me regret leaving her in my room. "You have one of Melanie's guitars! How did you wind up with one of Melanie's guitars?" Hope appears from the box barrier.

"It's Melanie's first guitar. Her mom wanted me to have it."

"You? Why you?!? Why not Tom or me?" Cy asks.

"Her mom said that she thought that's what Melanie would have wanted, and she said some other things."

"What other things?" Cy asks. "You weren't as close to Melanie as we were."

"You could sell it or auction it off for a great deal of money," Jake comments with the case open. He closes it without touching it. "Melanie merchandise is worth more today than ever before."

"Melanie merchandise!" I shake my head, "I'm not going to sell it. At least not right now. Melanie's mom didn't give it to me to sell it."

"Where do you want it?"

"Ruth's truck."

Cy and Hope take the guitar out. Hope is almost shivering as she opens the door. Jake and Stephanie literally shake the couch. Litter and loose change rain down and bounce freely. The movers rescue the cushions and haul away the couch that had been under me for years and had been my family's before it became mine.

I am left standing in a living room with only part of a single wall of boxes and Red. "I don't know what they expected about the guitar. Did they expect me to erect a shrine or keep it in a bank safe deposit drawer?"

Red says, "They're surprised. That's all."

Will comes in on an inspection tour.

"How's it looking out there?" I inquire.

"I was expecting it to be cool in here, you know."

"That's one of the reasons I'm moving."

"Right." Will pats me on the shoulder with heavy condescension. "The air conditioning that Al fixed and you re-broke. Good reason." I tag along while he looks over the rest of the apartment. "We might be able to get this all in one load. About that bed, and I use that term loosely, how do you sleep? How can you even keep covers on it?"

"It keeps me from dreaming as much."

"Does it stay or does it go? Or is it another gift for your neighbors?"

"We'll trash it."

"I'm not even going to ask about the stove and refrigerator," he says, thumbing in the direction of the kitchen.

"Those stay."

Will looks in Ray's room and then back in mine. "You know, Ray wants to move more than you."

"What do you mean?"

"Look around. There are things still in your room. His room is empty. He isn't even here."

"Maybe he's in denial that we're moving." We both laugh. "Yeah, that didn't sound right as I said it. I know I am clearing out. I know what I am doing." The band downstairs starts up their encore for me. They really need to get their hearing checked. Will chuckles in pantomime on his way back out. Red is arguing with a kid at the front door. I tell the kid to go home, or I will rat on him. I make something up, and he runs away. I must have guessed right. I ask Cy to take over for Red at the front door, as we take loads out. Red and I trash my bed.

The sun burns a hole through the atmosphere to suck the water from us a drip at a time. A breeze plays in the shadows of the lone willow tree of the Whisper Willows Apartments like a brush on a cymbal. The truck is mostly full as a drafting table, boxes, lamps, wrapped artwork, and carpet rolls get added to the mix. I thought we had too many people, but this seems to be just the right number of people. Stephanie and Jake bring out the 1964 Wild Stallion dashboard with steering wheel, as I call for pizzas. Ruth and Hope return from a beverage run. Red hands off Ray's futon. Several large bags of blankets, quilts, afghans, and comforters fill in upper gaps in the truck stuffing.

I tell Hope, "I have the strength of ten men."

"When did that happen?"

"When I started shoveling."

"If you have the strength of ten," Stephanie says, "I have the strength of 20."

I introduce Hope to the original Loverducks on our way inside. Inside, all that's left is to pick up, from the original Wisconsin Territory carpet, the loose change and other missing items shaken from the couch: pens, pencils, a screw, a woman's key chain and underwear, a flashlight, lint, an eraser, a bottle cap, a Christmas light bulb, popcorn, lock deicer, the other half of a ping-pong ball... The woman's underwear is analyzed by Jake, Stephanie, and Cy to determine its point of origin, while Ruth takes down her camera.

I choose to check on the truck; Will is waiting. "All your possessions are baking in the truck," Will tells me.

"Baking or breaking?"

"Baking."

"I'll round everyone up." Inside, new theories about the woman's underwear are presented, and I encourage everyone to leave. I do a quick run around to check the place for anything left, when Jake comes back in with a wallet that he leaves on the kitchen counter.

"It's a farting wallet, a gift to the apartment that has given you so much. It's got a collection of phony credit cards, the type you get with applications from the credit card companies." I reach to pick it up. I decide not to pick it up. "It's good for 500 farts," he asserts like he counted them out.

"I think that stinks."

"Exactly. A natural bodily function. I knew you'd like it."

Jake thinks he understands me, but Jake doesn't understand me. When they were handing out clues, Jake thought they said abuse and said, "No thanks, I've had enough."

Taking a last look around, the cracks in the walls form familiar patterns again. We leave and lock the apartment. Jake and I go to the landlady's apartment. I give her the keys and an address for mailing the security deposit. She starts to complain, and Jake lays down the law, berating her for her lack of management of the building, and rattling off an extensive list of things that I am surprised he has noticed and remembered. As his list continues for minute after minute of specific issues, she transforms from defensive to overwhelmed to exasperated to injured and finally to kicking us out after eight minutes. As we leave, Jake says, "Thanks for letting me do that. That felt good. She could use a brain." Hope and I take the truck with everyone else in Ruth's truck.

Good-bye Whisper Willows.

"We did it!" Hope exclaims.

"We're not out of the willows yet." The truck groans into gear with a lurch and a shutter.

Hope smiles despite the jolt, "You have Melanie's first guitar. The lost guitar. I saw a special on that guitar."

"Someone made a program just on that guitar?"

The neighborhood trees watch us go and ask, "Y?"

"No, but it was a key part of the show."

"Why were they picking on the guitar?" I ask, before making the sound of a rim shot.

"It wasn't just about the guitar. The show talked about mysteries surrounding Melanie's death."

"And the guitar was a mystery?"

"Its disappearance was. They may have asked Melanie's parents if they had it, but they may not have answered."

"Mysteries are exaggerated to make them more interesting."

"I haven't told anyone about the Savior of the Midway," Hope says.

"I haven't told anyone other than you. I'm not sure that I should. The reactions were all so strange, as if people were exaggerating stories that were already exaggerated."

"It's like the telephone game. You know, where you line-up people, I do it sometimes with a class, whisper something to the first person in the line and they whisper it to the next person and by the time it gets to the end you see how much the message has changed."

"Yes, I know that game. I would be somewhere in the middle of the whole thing. I would ignore most of what was whispered to me, and instead whisper something about blue artichokes at midnight, or something like that."

"No!"

"Yes!"

"You didn't!"

"I did!"

"Shame on you!"

"What?!? I was helping along the process. I helped prove the theory that you should listen carefully. We were never told not to purposefully screw it up. Every time I played that game it was introduced as if it was new, but almost every group or class used it as an activity. So I was an experienced helper." I turn on the radio.

"Troublemaker."

"Helper. When you first met me, what did you see?"

"A nice guy in a gray suit."

"No, the second first-time you met me, what did you see?"

"A guy in a gorilla suit."

"Right. What was I doing?"

"You were guarding the front door and telling people to go around to the back of Tom's house."

"Right. I was helping."

"Kind of."

"I was!"

"But you were doing it in a gorilla suit, apishly. Yes, apishly. You do things in your own apish way."

"Thanks."

"Your way could be construed as trouble making," she says as I exit the highway. Hope stretches, "Isn't this a beautiful day?" And when she asks that way, I can't help but to agree. It is a beautiful day. Deja vu. I check my watch. I slow way down. "What's up?" Hope asks, as a small car darts in front of the truck. "Wow," Hope says, "that kid wasn't even looking where he was going. Good driving."

I back the groaning truck up Hope's driveway. "Are we going to clear that branch?"

"I'll get out and check." The truck wheezes to a halt, and Hope gets out. I hear bits and pieces of a discussion. Then Hope is back. "Everyone had to voice an opinion. Most agree that it'll clear the main part of the branch." The tree brushes the top of the truck.

"I wonder if the truck will be taller without all the stuff?" I wonder aloud as I turn it off.

As I cross the lawn, Ray intercepts me. "I didn't build the box maze," he tells me. "You told them that I built the maze of boxes. I didn't."

"Didn't you?"

"No," he says.

"I only remember building a tower of boxes. So you didn't stack any boxes?"

"I stacked some boxes, but I didn't build the maze."

"Maybe we both did part of it."

"Maybe. But I think it was mostly you."

I think it was mostly him, but I let it drop. Everyone is eating pizza, and I want to be part of that everyone. Jake is guarding the pizza as he wolfs it down. "Hey Jake. We're in a different neighborhood. You don't have to watch over the pizza."

A dog trots through, picks up a dropped piece, and continues by.

"You were saying?" Jake asks.

"You know, you're going to lose your appetite if you don't stop eating between bites. How's your shaved chest?" I ask.

Stephanie, Ruth, Cy, and Becky converge to tease Jake about his chest. "Oooo, soft!" Ruth gushes.

Going inside to use the bathroom, I notice Ruth has already reset her time-lapse camera. Back outside, Hope comes over, "Have you noticed anything different about the yard?"

"Is it greener?"

"Kind of. Al trimmed the hedges and cut the lawn. He also sanded, puttied, and painted some of the trim. He also cleaned the gutters."

"How do we know what boxes go where?" Stephanie asks.

"Didn't you notice?" I ask. "They go in either bedroom depending on whose first initial is on the box."

"Oh," she says. "Very funny."

Cy stops Jake from opening up the truck and gathers everyone together. Sweeping her hair aside, Cy says in her higher, announcing voice, "We have pitched in for a housewarming present for Ricky!" She hands me a wrapped box with a bow on the lid. The lid is independently wrapped so no wrapping paper has to be torn. I smile at that, and Cy whispers something to Hope. A mosquito lands on my arm for a ring-side seat. I switch hands and swat her away. The box has... a lot of tissue paper... and a phone! Cy announces, "It's a phone! It's also a TV, two things we all know how much you constantly use! It comes with e-mail which you are also always using, Internet, GPS, calculator, calendar, camera, dictionary, almanac, atlas, encyclopedia, a conversion table for U.S. dollars to Canadian dollars to insect repellent to sidewalk salt, one free movie, and a thousand free songs. Choose from rock, country, classical, easy listening, local, jazz, blues, dance club, marching band, or Christmas. The Christmas selection is 500 versions of Silent Night and 500 versions of Here Comes Santa Claus. We didn't pick the music for you. Jake wanted it loaded with all the marching band songs."

"Thanks, Jake." Jake nods.

"It also doubles as an ice scraper and a mosquito confuser."

"Wow, you bought me a mosquito confuser!"

"It's waterproof and virtually indestructible, so that you can't destroy it like your last one."

"You used to have a mobile phone?" Hope asks.

"That was shattered to a million pieces years ago."

"I always wanted to do that."

"However," Cy continues, "this phone was built for you. The instruction booklet will show you how it can self-destruct with the right sequence of buttons."

"Cool!"

Jake muscles in, "Can that be set off from a distance?!?" I snatch the instructions away from him.

"And we programmed it, Al programmed it, with the phone numbers of all your friends, even Jake's. Except we didn't have Aimee's number."

"How is Aimee going to find me?" I wonder aloud.

"To go along with your new address and your new phone number we got you some business cards. You could always send a few of these out, as a trail for her to find."

"This was very thoughtful. Thank you." I hand out my business cards. Half of them all ready have one.

"One more thing, we would also like to present Ray with this," Cy says handing him an envelope, "to welcome him to his new home and studio."

"What's this?" Ray asks. "Hey, an art supply store gift certificate! This is great! Thank you."

"We all pitched in," Cy tells him. I don't remember pitching in.

Jake asks, "Can we get back to moving?"

"Yes," I tell him, as I watch Stephanie zip past him to the truck.

"Hey, did you know this ramp comes out from underneath?" she asks Jake.

Will shouts out, "Let's get moving!"

I turn to thank Cy again. Ruth tells me that she put Melanie's guitar in my closet. We clear a path through the lawn chairs and Erix, who has made friends with the dog.

Standing for a moment with Cy, Tom, and Hope, I tell them, "I got a letter from Yolanda... a three page letter from Yolanda. I'm not sure how to reply. Hope has seen it. It's not really asking for anything.

It's almost her autobiography."

Cy asks, "What do you want to tell her?" Nicole is walking up.

"That we liked her play. I don't know; that's why I'm asking you."

Cy sighs, "I'll take a look at it and see what I can come up with, but you'll have to decide if what I say is right for you, and if it is, put it in your own handwriting." She stops and shakes her head. "You know, I think that's almost exactly what I told Melanie at first..."

Hope asks Nicole, "What happened with your go-see?"

"It was a no-go. I don't know what sort of model they wanted, but I wasn't it," she says. A mosquito lands on her shoulder, I swat it off, and let my hand rest on her shoulder. "Did you see the paper?" Nicole asks me.

"No."

Nicole unrolls a copy of The Pigs Idea, which has a big front-page picture of candlelights dotting the hillside of Prospective Tower. "See, there in the center are our groups of lights!"

Becky comes over, "Let me see!"

Hope asks, "Why are there only three clumps of lights?"

"Remember? Faith's candle went out," I remind her.

"So all this happened during our date?" Tom asks. "You got on the cover of the paper?"

"Wait," Cy says. "When was this?"

"Last night."

"And you were at Prospective Tower?" Cy asks. "How do you know which candles were yours?"

Nicole laughs. "They were all ours. Ricky brought a ton of candles, and we ended up lighting them for thousands of people."

"Hundreds," I correct.

"Where did the candles come from?" Cy asks, needing all the logistics of it.

"Remember the candlelight Christmas service from three and a half years ago? Remember who got stuck with all the white candles with the round cardboard wax protectors?"

"No, but I'm guessing it was you."

"It was me."

Nicole gets back to showing Cy the picture, "So the clumps of lights are all the lights we just lit. We gave them the candles and lit them; sometimes they got a candle and got a light from someone else nearby. All these lights are ones we had already lit and were spreading out across the hillside and all around. The picture doesn't do it justice," Nicole says, stumbling over the last set of words. Those last words echo around in my head. My head must be vastly empty to cause that echo. "It was very cool. It made Faith's year."

"Nicole." She turns to me. I hand her my card. "The last thing you just said about the picture not doing it justice? Remember that when you're modeling." She gives me a hug.

"You're sweaty," she observes, wiping her eye. "How's the move going?"

"So far, so good. Nothing has gotten–" Jake and Stephanie are both trying to move three boxes at once. "No one has visited the hospital yet," I announce loudly. "I'd better do my share and get sweatier." I open a bottle of water, drink half of it, re-cap it, wipe my lips on my arm, and grab some bags of blankets.

After hauling several loads, I notice they are still talking about the Prospective Tower last night. Come on people, get over it. Move on.

Al helps me move a bookcase and a dresser. While we're moving them, I thank him for everything that he's done today, item by item, job by job. He mentions a few more items that I hadn't heard about.

I start to take Ray's futon, and suddenly I don't have the strength of ten men. I don't have the strength of one. I look around. No one noticed. Good. I call out to Erix. Others try to step in, but I insist on Erix. "Could you give me a hand?" Anyone else would've taken that straight line and clapped, as if that is the type of hand I needed. Or given me one of Lefty's prosthetics, that's been done before too. Old jokes. Thankfully, Erix only needs to know what to do. I give him the details, and he pitches in. I walk backwards, and he effortlessly carries his share. We carry a few more loads together.

The road to envy starts with comparing yourself and what you have to others. The immediate assumption is similar to the scientific method's assumption that nothing but the variable being tested has any bearing; the immediate assumption is that you can have the good that someone has without the bad. It is character trait shopping. The character trait of wealth cannot be picked up without its burdens. Large families and small families have separate issues. Love is not worry-free.

Will starts to work on moving the entertainment center unit of cabinets and shelves, stops, and asks where it will go. I visualize the layout of our part of the house. We probably shouldn't cover a window. I think there is an interior design rule against covering up windows with furniture. I call Ray over to help decide. He puts the decision back on me. I have us set it aside.

So you compare yourself to others, as if you could ever be other people and still be yourself. You want to keep your existing character traits, especially your existing values, while shopping for new character traits. You still want to be you, just with someone else's style layered on top of you.

Having money means having money. People with money either never know what it is like to not have money or they forget. A whole new set of worries about money take over. Poor people worry about money. Rich people worry about money. Does everyone worry about money? No, but having money does not automatically alleviate the worry.

More than money, love is not something you can have and forget about. People in love worry about their lover. People not in love worry about finding love. Does everyone worry about love? No, but having love does not automatically alleviate the worry.

You can desire love, fame, and fortune, but any major changes would change who you are. And you are already changing. You might as well live in your own future, because in the blink of an eye your present is gone, and your future can be anything.

With all of that in mind, I am not normally envious. Still, I envy Erix. He's looking at something in the tree, without having to decide where to put an entertainment center that has never completely been the center of entertainment.

Nearly dropping Ray's drafting table, Todd steps in to lend a hand even with his sore arm. I don't want to tell him what he can do, so I sing, Carry That Weight. Todd joins in after a few words. Several others shout out the words or close approximations to the actual words. Al pumps air into the volleyball to the beat of the song. We sing the brief Beatles song into the house and into Ray's studio, getting funny looks from Hope and others. When Todd and I start in on Sam Cooke's Chain Gang, I hear Cy explaining to Hope that it was our work song as roadies for Melanie. As we head back out, harmonizing with our traveling music, Cy is saying she doesn't know who started it. I do. It was I.

Mica is here with her kids who are running up and down the ramp and bouncing around in the nearly empty truck. I give her a business card. She wants to grill me about the Savior of the Midway thing. She is less-than-thrilled when I redirect her questions to Nicole. After the Bucko's leave, we are able to move the last boxes, which had been the first boxes into the truck back at Whisper Willows. We shut the truck and pick up the lawn.

Inside, with the air conditioning, Jake dramatically falls to a heap in the middle of the floor. The rest of us step over him, more or less.

From the kitchen counter, Ray claims the women's keys and panties, wondering where they were found. When he finds out the couch has been pitched, he steps over Jake and looks at the fancy living room couch and reluctantly approves. He thanks everyone for their help and goes to bed.

Will asks me, "What's it like not working for Flight Control anymore?"

I stop and think. "When something like that ends, you don't kick up your feet and congratulate yourself on all the successes you had. You don't celebrate your partial accomplishments, or at least, I don't anyway. I think about how it ended. I think about not getting a chance to see it through. I think about the ill feelings. I think about what I might have done differently. Mostly I rehash the ending like it is stuck in an endless loop for all eternity. Carl goes berserk, smashing things over and over and over again." I watch Hope show Erix how to use the couch. "I am not a believer in destiny. You can do something great. Then you can do something else that is completely different, but is just as great. And you can keep doing things as long as you don't dwell on the past... either with ego or with pity. You can have many destinies. You can do many great things." Erix follows Hope's example to adjust the couch. I turn to Will, "But I was very good at what I did. It was meant for me. I was meant to help people, and AutoDrive would've provided hope and self-sufficiency to a great many people. When Wendy told me about the plans to road test AutoDrive, it just didn't feel right. I should have my hands in it. I should be there."

Will says, "She didn't emphasize to you what she has been saying to me. They need you and your leadership and your scope on how to make things work. The fact that the older guy..."

"Clarence?"

"Right. The fact that Clarence quit a few days after you is a statement of your impact. You had something good going there, and now you're unemployed. You seem to be taking it pretty well."

"I'll be all right. I just won't be working on AutoDrive. That's not one of my destinies anymore." Jake starts kicking me. I kick him back. He crawls to the cooler for a beer. Not finding one, he crawls to the kitchen.

"You really are taking this well," Al joins in.

"What are you going to do?" asks Stephanie.

"Well, I've got another job, in a way."

"What?!?"

From the kitchen, "Ricky said he has another job." People come running in.

"Well, I don't actually have a job yet, but I will be offered one on Tuesday."

Jake says, "Taking a job now is like... shoveling during a snowstorm! Wait until things have settled down."

He's drunk. "I don't get your analogy. What things have to settle down? Are you thinking that things aren't going to work out here with Hope?"

"Hope's great. That's not it at all," Jake guzzles his Yoerg Beer. "So where's this job?"

They make me explain. They drill me with questions. I tell them all about it and the decisions that I made. Erix doesn't even listen. He's playing with the couch. Others join him. Jake listens to most of it and writes down some things.

Cy says, "You can never do anything the easy way can you?" I don't know what she means. Ruth is trying to say something.

"I'm telling you," Jake pushes, "you don't want to do this."

26
The Surreal

I'm telling you I do," I tell Jake.

"Okay, two can play your game. You say it'll happen. I am telling you, it won't happen."

This is like chewing on aluminum foil. "I saw it. Yes, it will."

"You've said it yourself," he points with his beer, "there are lots of futures. The future you saw won't happen. See for yourself."

He's nuts. He's nuttier than I am. I sit down. I try to relax. I can't. I try again. I'm heading up the sidewalk to the building. My reflection in the door shows a big grin on my face. I open the door. The receptionist with the blue streaks in her hair is watching me and gets on the phone. Is she talking to me? She says, "Get out. I've called security."

"I'm just here to apply for a job."

"That's right. We were warned about you. Turn around and walk out the door."

They were warned about me?!? By whom? Jake!

I open my eyes as I tense up. "What did you do?!?"

Jake smirks, "It worked?!?" like he's playing a game.

I am in his face. "What did you do?"

"I decided to warn them about you. That decision changed everything, didn't it?"

Blood surges to fill my face. My eyes fill with blood, painting everyone and everything in shades of red. I am swearing swear words I have never sworn before, mostly words that sound like swear words: snowballs, bullfrog, L, duck, yellow mustard... My curses become syllables of over-extended words. "Why are you doing this?!? This isn't some game! Un-decide." Reddened Jake stands there smugly. "Un-decide!" Jake doesn't budge. "Hope, can I kick him out?"

"Yes."

"Get out."

Reddened Jake leaves, saying, "You'll thank me someday." Now he's predicting the future?

"I don't think so." The door closes behind him. I check my watch. "He must have lost his mind when they shaved his chest."

"Ricky..." Cy starts.

"Can you tell me why he bushwhacked me?"

"No. I'm not even sure what he did. But when Jake gets to you, I think you need a vacation." Tom and Todd agree. Tom and Todd never agree about anything. Something has to be wrong here. You don't have two sides of the same coin agreeing about anything simultaneously. The only time that happens is when the coin is up in the air.

"That's gotta be some kind of record for the fastest he has ever been kicked out of somebody's house," Nicole observes. We all disagree. This is Jake we're talking about.

Still. What did I do to deserve this? Is Jake jealous? He said Hope's great, but he didn't say it like he was jealous or drooling all over her. Why is he trying to keep me unemployed? He hasn't confused me this much since he ding-dong-ditched me... since he rang my doorbell and ran. That was a great many snowfalls ago.

What is his problem? This is surreal. I look around at everyone for support or understanding or anything, but they seem to be all tapped out. I turn to Will, "Well, I had this job lined up..."

"Something will turn up. You just have to give it time," Will tells me. I've given it days.

"Sometimes it takes years to find the right job," Red says. "Maybe you need more dreams."

From the corner where she's dismantling her tripod, Ruth asks, "Do you want me to talk to Jake?"

"What are you going to say, 'Give him back his future?'"

Stephanie busts out laughing. Stephanie never busts out anything. "Sorry, this is just too odd."

"I'm going to head home," Will goes. I thank him for all his help packing and unpacking the truck. There is a mad rush for the door, and I try to thank everyone for their help, but in a moment it is just Hope, Nicole, Cy, and I. My hand stops Cy from leaving.

"Cy, could you talk to Jake?"

"Talk to Jake? Do you think that's possible? You saw how he acted."

"Right. Thanks for helping me to pack and move."

Cy waves to Hope and Nicole and says bye to me. The door closes.

I crumple into a heap on the couch. Hope and Nicole play bookends to me.

Nicole says, "I think I'm starting to understand your pointed perception better." She pushes her hair out of her face. "If I could do what you can do, I probably wouldn't watch TV either." Hope laughs. Nicole says, "There is something I don't get."

Hope asks, "Algorithms?"

Nicole reaches over the heap to push Hope. "No. I don't understand why you don't do what you did before to get a job? Just do it again."

"Only don't tell Jake," Hope adds.

"Right. Don't tell Jake."

"Maybe," the heap responds. "But why did Jake stop me from getting a job in the first place? It breaks the Pact." Uh oh. The heap said too much.

"What pact?"

"The Pact. The Pact that all guys have," I respond, sitting up and hoping that such a lame answer will be good enough.

Nicole and Hope are in my face. "What's the Pact?"

I'm going to burn in hell if anyone finds out about this. "Shh! Keep it down. Nicole, check if Ray is still asleep," I whisper. Nicole runs out, restraining her breasts. I look at Hope, who is studying my face.

"He's asleep," Nicole says, sitting back down with her knees on my thigh.

"What I am about to tell you must never be discussed. You must swear with one hand on the TV set that you will never divulge what I will tell you, or you will never watch television again." Hope follows Nicole over to the large furnished TV. "I, state your name..."

"I, state your name," they giggle.

"Do hereby and forthwith swear to secrecy the Guy Pact..."

"Do hereby and forthwith swear to secrecy the Guy Pact," they giggle.

"... also known as the Code of Manhood..."

"Also known as the Code of Manhood," they giggle.

"... and will justly feign ignorance of the titles and terminology..."

"And will justly feign ignorance of the titles and terminology," they smile.

"... under the penalty of never being able to watch and or enjoy television again..."

"Under the penalty of never being able to watch and or enjoy television again," they state soberly.

"... even prerecorded programs."

"Even prerecorded programs."

"You are now sworn in," I whisper, waving them back over. "Friendships between guys are balls to kick around and pummel, simple and indestructible. The only real rule is the Pact. The Pact was historically a friendship pact, but over time the Pact became a pact between all guys. The Pact is to never instigate permanent or lasting harm either physically or economically to other guys. The classic example is that you can fight with each other, you can fight with friends, but you don't leave a mark. You don't give someone a black eye. That's why guys can be angry at each other, but still fight clean. You can cheat at cards, but you can't outright steal. You can hide someone's stuff or move it around, but you can't take it. If a guy breaks the Pact, the saying is that all bets are off, but what that means is that the Pact will no longer protect that individual. Guys can usually sense when someone has broken the Pact. It is a sense of pact completeness or pact incompleteness. Nothing needs to be discussed. It's all covered by the Pact. Most guys don't have to make any additional pacts, because the Guy Pact, the Code of Manhood, is enough." I look at them. "When Carl fired me without cause, he broke the Pact without a doubt. That's easy. Now, what Jake did should also be construed as economical harm because he prevented me from getting a job that I already had a form of commitment to. And what's worse is that Tom and Todd didn't back me up on it. Everyone else remained as neutral as Switzerland, but Tom and Todd agreed with Cy that I needed a vacation, putting the responsibility on me, not Jake. Maybe they don't understand that the Pact covers pointed perception just as much as any other time. You see why what Jake did doesn't make any sense. He wasn't just kidding around."

Hope leans in with a hand still on my shoulder and a hand on my chest, "It's about loyalty, right?"

"Yes, on a level. It's not blind loyalty or loyalty without the ability to kid around. It's a thoughtful sort of loyalty."

"We are talking about guys, right?" Nicole wonders.

"Okay, it's a level of thoughtfulness... a degree of thoughtfulness."

Hope pokes me, "Look, what he did was mean spirited. Jake is a jerk. You can get another job if you want, either with pointed perception or without, or you can just take it easy here and do stuff with me when I'm free. What do you think?"

"I think I need to get the truck back."

"That's right, the truck!"

"Would you give me a ride back from Hauling Assets?"

"Yes. Where is it?"

"I know where it is. I'll drive," Nicole offers. We go out. I climb in the truck, while they go down the block to Nicole's car. The tree brushes the top of the truck with a high-pitched scraping, as the truck groans, "Do I have to go?" or something like that, in a moving truck pitch.

I've said it before; I'll say it again. I don't believe in luck. I believe in probability. Probability is luck without the extreme randomness. And right now I believe there is a strong probability that there is a Kick Me sign on my butt. At a stoplight, I check my butt for a sign.

I look to my left. Hope is partway out her window trying to get my attention. I roll down my window. "Hi," she says, and disappears back into Nicole's car as the light turns green. I wonder why Nicole has her top up on such a nice day?

Dropping off the truck, the Hauling Assets clerk is torn between wanting to sell more boxes and wanting Hope and Nicole to come in from the parking lot. He doesn't get his wishes.

Nicole drives us two blocks, stops, and buys five more papers. Getting back on the road, Hope tells me, "We were just talking about having multiple futures and trying to get used to not just having one. I'm used to things being more absolute."

"You flip a coin, and it ends up being tails," I reply. She doesn't agree, knowing that there is more than one solution to flipping a coin. I let the coin analogy roll away as I head in a different direction. "Science is the pursuit of knowledge, of facts. But how many times has science changed its answers – from when you were in grade school to when you were in college to now?"

"Plenty. Every time we use a new book for class, I have to thumb through it to see what has changed."

"Science likes to check off its facts, but science is more concerned about the pursuit and the news releases, than the facts. The facts are replaceable. Religion does the same thing. The Old Testament begins with the creation story, 'In the beginning, God created the heavens and the earth.' That's in the first chapter. The second chapter re-tells the story with dust and mists and breathing life into the dust. Two creation stories. Is one right? Are they both right? Does it matter? In the end, it doesn't matter how we began. At their worst, science and religion teach absolute definitions. At their best, they teach wonder. There aren't absolutes."

"You love her," Nicole says keeping her eyes on the road. "That's an absolute."

"Yes. But six months ago I would've said, 'Hope who?'" Hope gives me a funny look, an intense look. "No... don't tell me we actually met six months ago." She keeps giving me the same funny look. "Did we?"

"Just keeping you on your toes."

Sitting quietly, holding Hope's hand, letting Nicole drive us, I compare her driving to the AutoDrive plan. I shake my head to erase those thoughts. I start to notice that one of us needs a shower, and I don't think its them. "About that experiment about recording your thoughts..." Nicole starts. I feel Hope tense up.

"Yes?"

"Would I be able to read it?" Nicole asks.

"You're wondering if I think in big words? Or what?" I ask somewhat facetiously. Hope relaxes and shakes with silent laughter.

"No. Hey! I'll pull over if you two don't behave yourselves!" Nicole shouts.

"You mean, you're wondering if it would be made available to the public?"

"Yes."

"If it's successful, yes."

"So I'll know what you are thinking right now?"

"Yes. Or you could ask me."

"What are you thinking about right now?"

"Nothing. But a moment ago I was thinking that I need a shower."

"We weren't going to say anything... Just kidding!"

Hope nudges Nicole and says, "It would be kind of cool to know what you were thinking when we first met and ever since." Hope and Nicole exchange looks. "You know, in the name of scientific research."

Nicole parks her car in back of the house. So this is what the back of the house looks like, with the deck to one side of the second level. That must be the sunflower that was looking in Hope's window! It was in a window box! "Hope, what's the red thing on your window?"

"It's a hummingbird feeder."

"Do you get hummingbirds?"

"Yes," her teacher's voice gently says. "That's why it's there. We get ruby-throated hummingbirds."

I try my key on the back door. Hey, it works. The other two move to follow me in. "Uh, I'm going to take a shower."

They stare at me blankly, "So?"

"So I figured it would be just me in the shower."

Nicole pats me condescendingly, "We can still get things cleaned up, in other parts of the house. You do live in your own little dream world, don't you?"

Leading the way in, I reply, "Yes, I do. They like me there."

The first thing I notice in my room is the entertainment center. Someone must have made the decision that this was the ideal location to dump its modular pieces. They didn't reassemble it, so I know they didn't think it would stay here. It fits as well as a gorilla in a china shop. Two-thirds of it will have to go. Carrying pieces out to the living room, trumpets blare the announcement of my ringing phone. It's Tom.

"Am I your first call?" he asks.

"No, I've talked on the phone before. Where were you when I needed help with Jake?"

"You didn't need any help," Tom replies.

"I looked for backup from you and Todd."

"Backup? That would be ganging up. You made the rule about not ganging up on someone, remember Mr. Memory? And as I recall, the rule started because of Jake."

"You're right."

"Naturally. How's the new digs?"

"Nice."

"What could be better than a bachelor pad furnished with bachelorettes? Kick back. Enjoy yourself."

"I'll try. Thanks for your help moving and showing up early."

"You're welcome. Bye!"

"Bye!"

Hope and Nicole gather lawn chairs together. "Would you take these downstairs for us?" Hope asks tentatively. What's this about?

"Yes. What's downstairs?"

"The basement."

These two strong women are almost cowering over their basement. "Are you afraid of your own basement?"

"No."

"Yes."

"Kind of."

"I had some bad experiences in a basement once," Hope replies.

I turn to Nicole, who says, "She's freaked me out about the basement."

"Yes, I'll take the lawn chairs down."

"We could put them in the garage."

"No, you wanted them down there; I'll take them down." As I step downstairs I wonder what could be down here that they're willing to give me up for? All of the romance and the move, it was all to lure me down here for the afternoon snack of a hideous, slobbering monster that lives in their basement. I'll have to warn Ray, somehow.

At the bottom of the stairs, a pile of items blocks the path. It's clearly the result of being tossed down the stairs. I find a spot for lawn chairs and set them down. There is a washer and dryer down here. How do they wash their clothes if they don't come down here?

The unfinished basement is only half the size of the foundation of the house. The other half has crawl space underneath it, something for pets and other animals to explore, but really not practical for people. Wooden shelves with circular stains and a few rusty two-piece canning jar lids tell the story of a fruit cellar. Uninsulated basements like these were designed to keep things cold, year around. Cobwebs and footprints show the extent of recent exploration, probably by Al.

The ten year old boy in me says that I should yell, "What the–," shuffle my feet quickly, and make grotesque monster-devouring-engineer sounds, complete with growling, smacking, and twig snapping.

"Ex-engineer," the monster corrects me.

I look around and go back up. Hope is waiting at the top of the stairs.

"What took you?" Hope worries. She was genuinely worried for my well-being; it's very sweet.

I apologize and tell her, "My entertainment center won't give so much entertainment anymore. I'm pitching these four pieces. Should I put them by the curb for the neighbors?"

Hope runs her fingers through my hair. "You're in a different part of town now. Around here, the neighbors put antique wood tables out that have been scratched by a cat. They post professionally made signs that read, 'Cat Available Too.' We trade artwork the first Thursday of every month. No. You can either put them out back by the garbage can or downstairs." I haul them out to the garbage can. Slobbering monsters don't need entertainment centers.

Hope helps me unpack my clothes. All I want is some clothes for after my shower, but she's reloading my dresser and removing the bags from the clothes hanging in the closet. Some clothes, a towel, and I head for the bathroom. The bathroom smells like a field of flowers just uprooted themselves, tiptoed their way in here, shut the door, did whatever flowers do behind closed doors, and left.

The water is weird. It's as clear as glass, or clearer. It almost looks as if it's made of light. It sparkles. It bubbles. It's odorless, aside from the residual flower frenzy of the room. It hardly makes a sound running out and hitting the white basin, just a soft F sound. The long soft F sound is probably due to the water turning corners in the pipes and saying, "What the F-ffffffff?" This is all wrong. Clear water? Where are the earth tones? The tans? The browns? Where is the rock-on-rock clamoring of the water hitting the basin? Where is the you-would-not-believe-how-many-limestone-caves-I've-crawled-through carbonic acid and sulfurous smells?

I forgot to move some things! I forgot to move the kitchen sink. And the bathroom sink. I knew I was going to forget something. Those sinks could show this one a thing or two about cave-like sinks, with their stalagmite mineral deposits and stalactite drips, and their brownish water.

How will I get my recommended daily allowances of a tap full of minerals? How will I get my calcium, my magnesium, my iron, my zinc, my copper, my selenium, and my phosphorous? Guess I'll have to start taking a supplement. Otherwise my body may go into shock.

I turn on the hot water of the shower to heat it up and prepare to wait. Steam comes out. I start to reach for it to see if it is hot. I stop myself. Steam is hot. Steam is very hot, I tell myself. Besides, a sign has popped out of the faucet that reads, Scalding. It's very cartoon like. I adjust the knob to what appears to be a medium temperature. The sign retreats. I test the waters. It is a medium temperature. I adjust it a little more. Perfect. In the shower, I do a water dance of trust. I enter the water stream. I retreat from the water stream. I enter the water stream. I retreat from the water stream. I keep expecting the water to change temperatures on me. Maybe it'll suddenly change to steam again. Maybe it'll start dispensing ice cubes. The temperature never changes. It doesn't feel like water. It doesn't feel like much of anything. After 30 minutes of waiting to feel the water or a temperature change or anything, I am clean and saturated. Reaching for my towel, I climb out without shutting off the water. I flush the toilet. I test the water. It never changes temperature. I run the sink faucet and test the shower water. No change. I turn off all the water. This will take some adjustment. I might need therapy... at least aroma therapy. "There was a smell. I remember a sulfur smell... the acidic, rotten egg smell! **I remember it! Ahhh**, lilacs."

My room has been transformed. Ray's painting hangs on the wall. The walls are painted with a wave pattern. My bear feet slippers hide partway under the bed. They probably think they're being cute. My bed is neatly made. My stuffed bear rests its head on the pillow. I wonder if Hope knows how important this bear is. My entertainment center is full. The books are in order by size and color of the binding, not subject. Libraries ought to try that. My alarm clock shines from atop the nightstand, little hearts floating above it, and a doily below it. A framed picture of Hope is on the wall behind it. Hey, this is a beautiful picture of her! Wow! The alarm clock is dancing in place. Who got it all wound up? The closet and dresser are full. There is not a box to be seen anywhere.

I wander out while still towel drying my hair. The living room has the flattened boxes and laid flat plastic bags. The cooler and grill sit by the stairs to the basement. I guess they didn't want to wake Ray with the sound of them tumbling down the steps. Hope is in the kitchen.

"Thank you for that picture of you. It's great! And thanks for all that you've done."

"You're welcome. I've kept expecting you to be ready. Do you always take long showers?"

"No, I was just testing the hot water."

"Is anything wrong?"

"Nope. Nothing's wrong. What's for dinner?" I ask as I open the refrigerator. "There's a penguin in the refrigerator." I close the refrigerator. "Guess that answers what we're having for dinner."

"Guess again."

Looking back into the fridge, the penguin blinks and gargles at me. I close the fridge. "Fricasseed penguin? That'll drive Ray loony." I peer back in. "I didn't even think it was penguin season." The penguin is too stiff. I open the door fully and take him out. There is a note on his back. I know the feeling. The note says, "Welcome Home from Tom." The animated penguin isn't real. He's just a puppet.

Hope empties another box. I tell her, "You don't have to do that."

"I want to help."

"You've helped. None of that has to be done now."

"I'm so close to finishing."

"Would you rather go get some dinner with me? Or should I find a leash and take the penguin out for a drag?"

"You wouldn't."

"Wouldn't I?"

"Yes. You would." I start looking through some drawers and pause dramatically upon finding some string for a leash. "Okay, okay, I'll stop, I'll stop," she says. "Let me get cleaned up, and we'll go out." Hope runs upstairs.

I check on Ray. No response from Kelly or her creator.

"Are you going to want to get groceries?" Hope asks me in the hallway.

"Yes."

"Good. I'll get some things for upstairs too. Let's take my car." I give her a questioning look. "More room."

Hope takes me to the Wood Duck Grill. Painted plaster relief ivy decorates the walls. The hostess greets Hope with familiarity, and Hope introduces me as her lover. The hostess looks me over, pins a Grade A Choice blue ribbon on my shirt, and we are escorted in. Successive archways open the café ever wider to our seats. Our table is in the center, near a fire in a heart-shaped hearth. We are the second couple here. The menu has a paragraph per appetizer and has chapters dedicated to each entrée. Each chapter begins by summarizing the main entrée elements. I start to read the menu. Excusing myself, I slip next door to a bookstore to look at a study guide edition of the Wood Duck Grill menu. I nod knowingly as I digest its contents. I slip back next door and slide back into our booth. It would have been smooth, but I slid onto Hope's side of the booth and spilled some water.

"You're going to sit next to me?!?"

"For now. Have you decided what you are going to order?"

"I'm not sure. What are you getting?"

"I'm thinking about either: the bison amidst a forest of asparagus and okra with bushes of broccoli..."

"You aren't getting the bison."

"I'm not?"

"No, you're not. Not after the past few nights."

"I had a sandwich last night. I have no idea what you're talking about."

"Wednesday and Thursday night you had bison. You— you can get the bison if you want, but I am asking you nicely to order something else. What else are you thinking about?"

She backed off from telling me what to do. I'm impressed. "I am also thinking about the scrambled eggplant baked just in thyme and served with shitake mushrooms and leek sprouts. Or I could get the grilled textbook trout on a bed of seaweed, or the panda."

"Panda? There isn't any panda."

"So you don't want me to get the bison or the panda, is that it?"

"Is it too late to date Jake instead? He might be less trouble."

"Yes, it's too late. I've never even considered dating him. Have you decided?"

Hope dimples, "It's between the zucchini flowers stuffed with spinach, ricotta, mushroom caps, and presented over bow tie pasta; or the creamy chicken breasts stuffed with artichoke hearts and fitted in a bell pepper brassiere with ribbons of tomatoes over jeweled rice and baby carrots; or the smoked Canadian walleye served cold over a bed of snow with wojapi."

"Have you decided?" our waitress asks.

"I'll have the zucchini flowers," Hope says, checking with me.

"I'll have the scrambled eggplant." We both opt for water. "You know this is Ray's fault."

"What is?"

"Our ordering vegetarian meals," I explain. Hope nods. "All my friends have insidious plans for world domination. Ray wants everyone to be a vegetarian. Red is trying to turn everyone into redheads."

"How's he doing that?"

"Orange shampoo."

"What about Jake?"

"He's trying to subvert smart people. He's said so himself."

"What about Erix?"

"He'll do it in his own special way."

"What about me?"

"You'll have the whole world move in with you."

"No, I'm fine with the group I have now, thanks."

The artificial fire crackles and pops with automated regularity as we reflect on what we just said. It's very Minnesota to be in a place during the summer weeks, have the air conditioning on, and a fire in the hearth. It's almost like denying that it is more or less a nice world out there. "People like you aren't trying to take over the world, Hope. Change it? Yes. Take it over? No. Al certainly isn't trying to take over the world. He's just trying to grease it so it doesn't squeak when it spins." Hope has a funny look on her face. "I was only kidding about your taking over the world."

Hope looks at her reflection in her water glass and swirls it. "What if I told you that I run a vast, insidious empire?"

"I'd say you are getting me back. But you look like you're serious, so I'd say that I'd like to know how you got to be financially independent."

"I'm not exactly independent." She pauses. "I don't know how you are going to feel about me after this." The fire sizzles. "I told you about my brothers..."

"Not exactly, but go on."

"My mom had her hands full, keeping them in line. Basically she didn't. All she could really do was handle the retributions."

"Time outs?"

"No. You have no idea. My brothers tortured me! They tortured me! Each in their own special way," Hope's eyes well up. I put my arm around her and put a hand on her hand. "They–" The fire cracks as I watch this strong, sweet, beautiful woman with tears, and a fire of hate burns in my gut for those that hurt her. My mom used to say, Don't waste your hate. This is one situation where the hate is not wasted.

Our waitress brings our salads and glares at me with hatred for causing Hope to cry. She looks at my blue ribbon questioningly and leaves.

"One of my brothers, Chubby, loves food. He loves to eat, not just in a this-is-delicious way, but in a devour-everyone-else's-food sort of way. If he wondered if something had spoiled or if something he put together was edible, he'd have me try it out. If I got sick or had to go to the hospital, only then wouldn't he eat something. My mother negotiated a contract with him where I get a percentage of his profits for life. Chubby is the owner of Chubby Chubby Foods. Another brother is a European pornographer. He used to cuddle me and take pictures of me inappropriately. I liked the attention. I have a contract with him too. Another brother owns a national information brokerage firm. Essentially he steals information. He's very good at it. I can tell by the deposits I receive. Another brother is in oil and fossil fuels. I was his first exploitable resource. He was always finding ways of involving me. Always with at least the potential of hurting me." Hope eats some salad, and points to mine to encourage me to eat. "The brother I hate most is Flint. He used to beat me. Usually he had some kind of weapon. He could turn anything into a weapon. He was always shooting things or launching things. As I watched Tom's rocket last weekend, I couldn't help but think what Flint would have done with it. Flint would've seen it as a missed opportunity. He once forced me to hold a rocket as it went off. If he had still been in school after the Sisyphus School Massacre, he would have been the first kid to be permanently expelled for weapons possession. Whenever I hear about some new conflict, I figure he is at the center of it. He doesn't fight in wars; he sparks the fire and sells munitions." The fire pops repeatedly like a mechanical malfunction or a skip in a record. Hope swallows and wipes her mouth. "Two more brothers are in jail for federal crimes, including armed robbery. I've even received checks from them, but with a clear trail back to the source of the money, it was easy to return it." Hope drinks her water. "My youngest brother, the brother closest to me in age is a bagger at a grocery store."

"That's not so bad..."

Hope waves me off. "You wouldn't think so, but he puts the fresh fruits and eggs at the bottom of the grocery bags."

"The scum!"

Hope nods, "You know how the police have an officer watching busy stores or events? We had a deputy at our house every evening when I was growing up. Some of my best friends were cops. They were very good at following the rules when playing games."

Hope's orange zucchini flower and my eggplant in thyme arrive. The waitress squats down by Hope, still glaring at me. "Are you okay?" she asks Hope.

"Yes. I was just talking about my childhood. Don't worry. He's one of the good guys." The waitress leaves, and Hope's complement about me as one of the good guys rattles around in my head while we eat, and the fire embers pulsate. "So. I've spilled my guts. Like I said, I'm part of a vast, insidious empire. Does this change anything with you?"

"Just how rich are you?" Hope takes out a pen and writes down some numbers followed by an M.

"Rough liquid assets," she clarifies, as if it matters.

"You're rich," I confirm. She nods. I fork around my purplish food. "Have you considered therapy for all that your brothers have done to you?"

"I've been in different types of therapy since I was little."

"Are you currently in therapy?"

"No."

"Are your brothers still torturing you?"

"They are all spread out. The nearest one is in prison 300 miles away."

"What about the bagger?"

"He's on the east coast."

"So they aren't still torturing you?"

"Well, I think about them..."

"Especially when you deal with the money?"

"That's right."

I fork my scrambled eggplant into the shape of a box with a flagpole out front. "Did your brothers ever bother you when you were in school?"

"They're all older, but yes, occasionally some of them did. And my teachers were very wary of me due to their reputations."

"Yet between the torturous childhood, the bad school experiences, and the Sisyphus Elementary School Massacre, which happened just when we were graduating from high school, you decided to become a teacher... specifically an elementary school teacher. Why?"

"I knew I could handle it. I figured I could handle anything. I wanted to stop other kids who were like my brothers."

"Have you been able to do something about those kids?" I stop playing and start eating.

Hope pauses to clear her mouth. "Yes." She swallows again. "This may sound wrong, but even though one school kid killed so many kids... and teachers... at Sisyphus, the lesson that it drove home across the country is that kids can't be mollycoddled. Kids are not innocent. They are not the ideals their parents dream them to be. They are not incapable of pulling a trigger. Without Sisyphus, I couldn't be a teacher with the authority to teach my class in an environment that is safe for learning. I wouldn't be able to confront the bullies on the playground. Of course, we all wish we could have the lessons of Sisyphus, without the lives lost."

We eat quietly for a while. More people are seated. The fire interjects a snap or a pop, trying to get us to say something else. "What do you think of your eggplant?" Hope asks.

"Too much thyme. How have you impacted the lives of your brothers?"

"I've taken away some of their money."

"How else?"

"I don't know."

"Do you feel in control?"

"No."

"Why not?"

"Now it sounds like I'm in therapy," Hope laughs lightly. "I don't feel in control because really it is my mother and her contracts that are in control."

"Do you control your money?"

"Yes."

"Does anyone else?"

"No. I have accountants and auditors that monitor several of my brothers to make sure I am getting my legal share, but I control the money. I think I should tell you that my brothers don't all know about the extent of my contracts with the others. They don't know how rich I am," Hope whispers.

"So if you flaunted your wealth, you would be concerned that your brothers would learn the extent of it and would take advantage of you in some way."

"Something like that."

"Does your mother know?"

"Yes. Generally."

"Are your brothers in therapy?"

"I don't know." Hope finishes her meal. I've been finished. What I didn't eat, I've already shipped off to India. Hope pays the bill. I thank her.

We drive to Choice Market, which Hope informs me is owned by Chubby Chubby Foods. At several points in the store, Hope makes a scene. As I attempt to add items to my grocery basket, she explains the boycotts of those certain items and why we have to buy their competitor's products. Crowds form around us as she teaches me lessons in world consumerism. The crowds get frustrated at missing portions of the lectures. They start to follow us as a pack around the store. The manager keeps an eye on us, but Hope never addresses the crowd, only me. I do my part by wanting almost everything, and by learning about the rainforests of Bolivia and health plans in Argentina. The manager helps us bag our groceries and holds the automatic door for us on our way out.

"I liked that," I tell her as I load her trunk, her back seat, the floor, glove compartment, and my lap with bags.

"You're a good listener," she says.

I sit and watch her drive. "Have you ever considered getting more involved in the lives of your brothers?"

Hope pulls over. "Are you crazy?!? I have spent my entire life hiding from them! Half of them don't know what state I'm in. Why would I want to be back in their radar scopes?" Hope pulls back into traffic.

"We were talking about changing the world. Do you or don't you want to change the world?"

"Yes, I want to change the world. But I have zero interest in anything having to do with my brothers."

We quietly bring in the groceries and put them away. "Damn, I forgot to pick up Penguin Chow. I knew I forgot something."

"Couldn't. We're boycotting them too."

"Why?"

"Artificial preservatives are used where natural ones would have sufficed."

"You're kidding."

"Yes, I am," Hope says. "Who's ever heard of Penguin Chow?"

I shake a bunch of bananas at her, saying, "You are already involved in your brothers lives. I guess I misstated the idea. I'm not talking about becoming more involved; I'm talking about altering your involvement. Maybe the whole Savior of the Midway thing has gone to my head, but maybe you should consider hiring some angels to influence your brothers. Or maybe you should consider renegotiating your contracts to have them directly aid those they are hurting. I don't know."

"I don't know if you know what you're asking."

"No, I don't. I'm not asking you to do anything. I'm just making a suggestion. I have nothing to do with it." I lean against the counter. "Your family stuff is your business. It's none of my business. I might make a suggestion, but the decisions on your stuff are all yours." Hope nods. "I'm really tired. Thank you for all your help today and thanks for letting me move in."

"Welcome home," Hope kisses me. "You're okay with what I told you?"

"Yes. I'll see you tomorrow, okay?"

"Okay, good night."

"Good night."

Hope goes upstairs. I shut the curtains. I put away the rest of the groceries, and turn off the lights. Taking off my blue ribbon in my room, I find my shorts and a shirt and wonder if I will be too cold with the air conditioning on. I search around for the thermostat and find one in the hallway. I turn down the air conditioning. This will take some acclimation.

Back in my room, I change again into my race car pajamas. I look at the bed with concern. I expected it to be lower, round, and have my name on it. I switch off the light and lie down. This is the most comfortable bed I have ever been on. I am really in trouble now.

I relax. And I decide I won't be telling Jake about any more of my decisions.

And I'm in Milwaukee.

27

Life Is But A Dream

An employment agency found a job for me with a welding company in Milwaukee. That's their idea of a perfect fit. I moved here. Left the rest of the entertainment center behind. Left a lot of things behind. I left Hope behind.

During my two month probationary period, the welding company gave me a different manager every week or two. The final manager is the guy who has shared the office with me. He says he doesn't know enough about me to have the company pay off the employment agency. So at the end of the two months I'm fired. Unemployed and living in Milwaukee, the Cleveland of the upper Midwest, I take a bus back to my apartment. This apartment makes the old one, the Whisper Willows apartment, seem like a palace. This is more like living in a storage unit of the Whisper Willows Apartments.

A solitary bare light bulb with a pull chain hangs from the water damaged ceiling. There are two closets. One is the bathroom; the other is the kitchen. The kitchen closet has fake brick wallpaper over a real brick wall. The room, the only room, has a bed, a table, and a chair. I thought about buying a radio, but I thought that would be too depressing. I share the squalid apartment with a veritable field guide of insect life. The air is dominated by flies and yellow jacket wasps, the picnic variety of wasp that so many people mistake as a type of bee because it is yellow and black. The air also has some mosquitoes that lost their way to Minnesota. I know what that's like.

The floors, surfaces, and paint peeled, plaster cracked walls are the domain of the crawling bugs. The most entertaining bugs either have too many legs or too few. The two to four inch long hairy, feathery reddish centipedes are some of the fastest. Their abundance of legs move like waves. Small silver bugs called silverfish, swim across the dry floor with hardly any legs at all. The armored infantry consists mainly of cockroaches, earwigs, click beetles, and pill bugs. The spiders have two groups, the fast and the slow. The size of a spider doesn't seem to impact its speed, neither does color.

I may have unknowingly caused disarray in the apartment. The bugs may have been used to having food, especially having food that's delivered to them. I don't have any food. When I eat, I eat out. When I come back , the bugs line-up at the door. They look me over for food and scurry off. Night after night, week after week, they have gotten used to this routine.

But tonight is different. A nervous tension is abuzz, like teenage hormones in overdrive. An edgy madness grips the efficiency apartment and shakes it like a snowglobe. The bugs turn out. Bug after bug crawls wearily forward, eying other bugs, circling them with suspicion and uncertainty, looking for weakness. A stomp of a tiny foot here, a trip there, a misunderstanding of property and a once organized community of insects turns against itself, pitting bug against bug, spider against spider, in an all-out frenzy. It is war.

Pinchers attack armor. Click beetles snap back. The wounded are butchered while still kicking. Heavy casualties mount on all sides. Infants are pulled and devoured from the baseboards. Games of maggot tug-of-war break out.

The dust of battle flies as legs and wings and other parts are cut and pulled and pinched and minced. Formations of army ants are dispersed into chaos amongst the fighting and the roaches. Bugs land on or crawl to the bed as a refuge, only to be flicked or kicked back into the mayhem. The bed is mine.

The war takes its toll on the population. The weak succumb. Even the strong collapse under the combined efforts of temporary allies.

One small bug squats down behind a larger bug. Another small bug pushes the larger bug backwards over the first smaller bug. Bugs come out of the woodwork to attack the incapacitated larger bug.

Moths, loopy from orbiting and hitting the bare light bulb, fall into the middle of the battlefield, only to become one more commodity, one more resource, to be fought over.

A pill bug, curled into an armor ball, is kicked toward a centipede, who kicks it into the net of a spider. Goal! One point for... one of the teams. They aren't that organized.

I swat a yellow jacket back into play.

Someone sounds a buzzer. The bugs huddle. Bugs in conference? That can't be good. They look at me. They huddle again. The conference is over. Good. Back to the game! This could decide the apartment.

The bugs turn, united in a common bureaucracy, united in a common destination. Me. I have been reclassified. They crawl, they creep, they scurry, and they fly toward me. I am Bug Chow.

I shout.

I open my eyes. I'm back in my room, my room at Hope's, not my room in Milwaukee. I never took the welding company job. Hope is looking at me, biting her bottom lip. I decide that I never will take the job in Milwaukee.

"Hi sweetie, I'm sorry to startle you. I wanted to show you something in my room."

"What day is it?"

"Sunday," she answers with a giggle. The floor is soft under my bare feet. I put on my bear feet slippers and follow Hope upstairs. "Were you in the middle of a pointed perception dream?"

"Yes."

"I wasn't sure if I should wake you. They say you aren't suppose to wake someone who is sleep walking. I don't know if it is anything like that."

"A sleep walker can become disoriented and bash into something if you wake them suddenly. I guess pointed perception could be similar."

Hope points to her window. An iridescent green hummingbird hovers mid-air in the early morning sunlight and pokes its long beak into the feeder attached to Hope's window. It lifts its head to look at us and zips a few inches sideways to see us better. It has a white throat and belly. Its legs and feet are retracted so only its toes appear. It zips right and drinks again, still hovering.

"I thought you said they were ruby-throated?" I ask her.

Hope puts her arm around me, "Only the mature males have a little beard of purplish-red under their chins."

"Oh. What do they do in the winter?"

"They fly to Mexico."

"You're kidding." Hope shakes her head. "So they're bilingual?" Hope nudges me.

"So were you dreaming about me?"

"No!" I exclaim. Hope is offended. "No, I was dreaming about bugs in my apartment."

"In your old apartment?"

"No, I had taken a job in Milwaukee and my apartment was infested with bugs."

"Why would you do a thing like that?"

"I won't." Her brow is starting to wrinkle. I rub it straight again. "I promise."

"You better not. How did you sleep otherwise?"

"That's it. If you had a dream where bugs were on the march to attack you, how would you sleep?"

"Did one of the bugs look like Jake?"

"Most did. Why?"

"Seriously?"

"No. Thanks for showing me the hummingbird. I'm going back to bed." I shuffle my bear feet back downstairs.

Hope calls down the stairs after me, "Remember we have to call Lefty today."

"Okay," I call back. Of course I remember. I can't wait. I stop off at the bathroom, drink a handful of water, and go back to bed. The white walls have ornate, silver-painted wood molding that almost touches the ceiling, providing a silver halo for the room.

I relax.

I am lying in a giant white plastic machine about to be stapled or turned into coffee or something.

In a kitchen, I am squeezing an orange.

I am sitting on a plane. Hope is asleep with her head resting on my shoulder.

Downtown Milltown is abandoned. It's daytime, but no one is around. I look up and down the block both ways. No one. What am I waiting for?

Standing on a familiar hillside, facing a group of well-dressed people, I look at my watch. I think I'm being subtle. People laugh. I know these people.

Lying in a hospital bed, a TV arcs over me, saying, "Coming up, scientists figure out why there is more land north of the equator than south. Stay tuned." Who cares?!?

Standing in a large cave with people, a breeze blows through the silence. I try to notice the people around me, but I don't otherwise recognize them. Caves don't have breezes.

A dark curtain drapes a foreboding figure. Chuckles seems to peer over.

A black car is racing toward me. I'm not budging. Why won't I move?

Hope smiles at me from across a table at a restaurant. She smiles and smiles with dimples that bracket her smile.

Standing in line for the Skyrail at the Minnesota State Fair, I ask a kid who is bumping into me how old he is. "Eight." I tell him that when I was his age, I was ten.

An earplug is telling me things, as I sit and stare at people in a camera.

A tall woman stands majestically in the sunlight of a small front lawn of a dilapidated house with several other people nearby. She is in a brilliant white bra, a sharp contrast to her dark skin, with cutoff jean shorts.

The microwave explodes brussel sprouts.

Hope is getting ready while I sit on her bed. "I'm stuck. Could you help me? My earring is caught in my sweater. It's my fault, trying to wear long earrings in winter, but I wanted to wear something from you." So it's my fault really. Where is it hooked?

A tow truck pulls up in front of my Pony Express... my Pony Express with its hood up.

Ruth's face is lit by candles.

In a cubicle with a headset, I stare at a sign that says, Offer Other Services. A guy pokes his head around and asks if I am getting any calls. "No," I start to answer, when I hear a beep on the line that I've got a call. I hold up a finger to let him know I've got a call.

Sitting in a small room, I'm handed Go Away magazine.

Nicole is setting a timer on a camera while the rest of us pose in pajamas with presents by a Christmas tree. She slides into place in front of us. The camera flashes. "I blinked," I tell them.

A curtain of water drapes between Hope and I, and a narrow valley.

Avatrice and another woman are laughing at me.

"Hey Ricky, I'm sorry to wake you, but it's getting late. We need to call Lefty." I open my eyes to

Hope bending over me in my room. "You must have really needed to sleep! You've slept the day away!" I sit up and look at my clock. It shakes its short hand repeatedly at the five. "Did you dream about the experiment?"

"I dreamt about a lot of things," I shake my head. "I dreamt about everything. Yeah, I was in the fMRI at one point."

"Did it work?"

"I don't know. Everything was more jumbled than its almost ever been... since I first started trying to figure my dreams out."

"If you don't know how it's going to turn out, how can you decide whether or not to do it?"

"The decision comes first. Then we check periodically to make sure nothing will go wrong. Then we keep away from Jake. That's how we make decisions."

"Right!" Hope agrees.

"That's the one thing I learned from Jake. I learned that I have to keep on top of the futures to make sure it doesn't change from what it should be. For now, we decide to go ahead with the experiment." I sit up on the bed with my back against the wall. "I'll check on the results." Or try. I wonder what was so screwy about my pointed perception?

I relax.

I am cold. The hospital gown doesn't help. Sven comes in and unstraps me from the giant coffee maker.

"It didn't work," he tells me. I follow him barefooted into the control room.

"I don't understand it," Lefty is saying.

That reminds me. I check if I remember Hope. Damn right! So what did they do? The researcher in me steps forward. "What did you do differently with me than you did with the last successful subject?" Lefty thinks. He opens his mouth partway. "Say it. You can do it."

"I expanded the scan to try to get a better understanding of how your brain differs."

"There you go. And I don't think changing what you were doing will make any difference, because I doubt if I am any different from anyone else," I tell him. Then I realize I'm talking to the wrong Lefty. I need to talk to the before Lefty, not the after Lefty.

I open my eyes.

I am startled by the fact that Hope is sitting right next to me. I'm not used to being watched like this. "I have good news and bad news. The good news is I got to keep my memories. The bad news is that the experiment didn't work. Nothing happened. I'll be right back." I run to the bathroom and brush my teeth. Coming back in, I look around for my phone and find it on a doily on the dresser. I don't seem to remember having any doilies at my apartment.

How does this thing work? I scroll through the numbers to select Lefty. The phone starts dialing or else it begins to confuse mosquitoes, I don't know. Lefty answers. "Hi, it's me. Have you got two seconds to talk about the STM experiment?"

"Yes, hang on a minute... Go ahead."

"I decided to go through with it and then I checked on the results. The good news is I got to keep my memories. The bad news is that the experiment didn't work. Nothing happened. Afterwards you were trying to figure out what went wrong. I asked you what you did differently from the last successful subject, and you said you expanded the scan to try to get a better understanding of how my brain differs from other people. I think that was the difference, and I don't think you should bother with anything like that because I doubt I am any different from anyone else."

Silence. I look at Hope. I look at my clock.

"If the experiment works, are you willing to do it?" he asks.

"Yes, just don't change things from how you did them before. The time when there weren't any lost short-term memories," I add.

"When should I bring over the paperwork?"

"How about Tuesday? After five?" I ask, confirming the time with Hope and my alarm clock. Lefty agrees, and we hang up.

"Have you eaten anything today?"

"No. Was I supposed to?" Hope drags me out of bed in my race car pajamas. Light is streaming out of Ray's studio. I hope he's not doing soldering in there. In the kitchen, Hope seems intent on imitating Ruth's veggie sandwiches from last weekend, only Hope is using better bread. It won't be the same.

After breakfast, lunch, and dinner, Hope runs into my room and runs back out. She sits us on the living room couch and flips through my parent's wedding album with me. She asks about the pictures, but I can't tell her much. I hadn't been invited.

In the middle of looking at the album, she flips through the rest of the book, closes it, and places her hands on it like she is warming them. She says, "You haven't said much about your parents. It's okay. You don't have to talk about them. From what I've seen of them here and what others have told me, they were nice people. I would have liked to have met them and gotten to know them... and gotten to know you better through them. I'm sorry that you lost them. I'm sorry they died so young. I know what it's like to lose a parent, but I was so young I hardly knew my dad when he died. I'm sorry for the hurt, and I am sorry for your loss. If you ever want to talk with me about it, you can. Okay?"

"Thanks, Hope."

She asks to borrow my vegetarian cookbook. We kiss good night.

I lie back down in bed. I relax.

I'm in Choice Market, but everything looks different. Locating the dairy aisle, I look for the milk and find it on a refrigerated table. None of the milks have caps. I ask the manager, "Why don't the milk jugs have caps?"

She says, "Listen, if you don't like it, don't buy it."

"Wait. I honestly don't know why there aren't any caps."

"Oh," she says. "Well, it saves money and it saves plastic. Some people have started bringing in their own caps. Others are selling their caps, but... I hear that soon it's not going to make a difference anyway. The milk companies are going to stop providing jugs with the threaded necks, which is going to screw up the black market cap industry. But you didn't hear that from me." I nod and carefully pick up my milk.

They offer to sell me a bag, but I don't see the point.

Outside, it is winter. I get it. The milk freezes outside, so really I'm carrying a jug of ice... of milk ice... of frozen milk. I look around for my car. I don't see it. Where's the Pony Express? I look at my keys. That's not my Pony Express key. Damn. It's tough to stand around in a Minnesota winter, holding a jug of milk level while it freezes, trying to figure out what car you drove to the store, with your mind being noticeably quiet about giving any clues. I need to open my eyes. I need to wake up. I'm not waking up. Maybe if I doused myself with cold milk that would wake me up. Or kill me. I'd freeze solid.

"This just in: local man dies from milk. Dairy council seeks second opinion."

I set the jug down on the freshly sanded snow-ice of the parking lot, and I concentrate on waking up. Nothing happens. I keep working at it. I am very patient.

My eyes open. I'm in my bedroom. I look at my alarm clock in its nightcap. I wave away the floating series of Z's of its snoring, so I can see the time. It's 5:55am. That sounds like a made-up number. I open my curtains and look out the window. I look for hummingbirds, but they have no reason to be by my window. They will be at Hope's window. I wash my face, get dressed, grab my phone, and start to scroll for Hope's number, when I spot a Hope button. I press it.

"Hello," a sleepy voice answers.

"Hope?"

"Yes, Ricky, what is it?"

"Can I come up and watch hummingbirds?"

"Are you getting me back for yesterday?"

"No, I really want to."

"Yes, come on up." I bound up the stairs two at a time. Hope meets me at the top. "I'm still asleep," she tells me. The half-open eyes and tussled hair doesn't give it away. The fact that she's still on the phone with me when I'm right here, doesn't give it away either. I put my arm around her. She pulls away. "I can't possibly be a pretty sight right now. Let me get ready for the day."

"You don't have to. Climb back in bed. I'll climb in after you. And when you get up, you can just climb over me." Hope disagrees. At her window, I peer out the curtain and am face-to-face with a sunflower. Peering around it, I see another sunflower. I don't see any hummingbirds.

"I'll be awhile. No, multi-person teeth brushing today."

When she closes her bathroom door, I fully open the curtain. The sunflowers are really looking into Hope's room. There must have been a crack in the curtain. I thought sunflowers were supposed to follow the sun, not watch pretty women. I pull over a chair to watch out the window. The sunflowers sway in the breeze. A hummingbird comes to the window, looks around, notices me, compares me to a sloth, takes a drink, takes another drink, sticks out its tongue, and leaves.

Sloth? I could run temporal rings around the little iridescent green bird. The hummingbird returns and leaves in a flash, as if to say, "In your dreams."

I called Hope and came up. I wonder how long it'll be like this. How long will need to I call to come up? Will I eventually be able to walk right up? How would her roommates feel about that? Nicole would probably be fine with it, since she wants to be our child. Becky might me okay with it as long as I am willing to answer her magazine questions. Faith? I'm not so sure where Faith is at.

Will Hope and I eventually be in the same room together? Maybe she would move downstairs so we wouldn't have to worry about her roommates. Then again, if she wanted to live downstairs, she would already live downstairs; it's her house. She's probably already figured all of this out... figured out how to join my stuff with her stuff... done the math of how many of my rubber balls she can distribute in her Hope chests...

Time to raid their refrigerator! Looking in someone's refrigerator is a representation of their life... a microcosm of who they are. A group refrigerator tells you about the group and their interactions. Are there territorial dividing lines within or between the shelves? Are there redundant items, such as a milk carton on every shelf? Have they labeled their stuff to protect their possessions? Are signs posted on the refrigerator door identifying the rules to live by, such as not damming the parking lot?

I find the bacon, eggs, bread, and juice that Hope just bought. If Hope doesn't like what I'm going to do, I'll just have to go back to the store and get more. It's not like I have a job or anything.

Finding and quietly retrieving a frying pan, I spread the bacon in a single wallpaper-like layer. I put it on the stove and heat it up. I get out plates and glasses. That was one clink short of being quiet.

Cooking utensils are in a drawer by the stove. The genetic code of cooking utensils requires them to reside near their place of employment. A spatula helps me to flip and rearrange the bacon.

I could use this break in the bacon process to scramble eggs. Maybe they don't like scrambled eggs. Scrambled eggs don't have the classic visual appeal of a sunny-side up egg. In my head, the word Yesterday in the song by Paul McCartney is switched to Scrambled Eggs. It was either Jenny or Melanie that told me that originally he was singing about scrambled eggs. I don't know if that's true. I move around the bacon again. I set up a paper towel on a plate for drying the bacon. I cook the bacon so it is crisp with no burned areas and lay them out to dry on the paper towel. A cup created from tin foil holds the bacon grease.

"Hey, I was looking for you," Hope says giving me a hug and a kiss. "What do you think you're doing?" I replay her words a few times to make sure there is no anger in them.

"Making some breakfast."

"I see that. Looks like you have five of everything. Do you want to be our cook?"

"How would you like your eggs? Scrambled? Sunny-side up? Over easy? Egg-in-a-basket?"

"What's an egg-in-a-basket?"

"Watch." I get a piece of bread, tear a two-inch hole in the middle, set it in the pan, and crack an egg in the middle. Then I fry it up like an over easy egg. As I drop it on a plate and hand it to Hope, I notice that I have more customers. "How would you like your eggs?" I ask the ladies, blushing as I think about their eggs. I pour juice for them.

"Scrambled," Nicole says.

"Like Hope's," Becky says.

"Fried," Faith says patting the table.

"Sunny-side up or over easy?"

"Sunny-side up."

I cook breakfast for them. Then I astound them by cleaning the dishes by hand.

"We have a dishwasher," I am told.

"This is easier," I tell them. They aren't convinced. Finishing up, I tell them, "Have a good day at work," and I head home down the stairs.

Ray is talking in his study and walks out. He mouths, "Is it okay to use your phone?"

I give him the okay hand signal. He's already using it. Besides I don't have any plans to call anyone right now. In my room, I lie down and wonder what work I will do next. It should be something good. I relax.

Riding an elevator, wearing a suit, holding a folder with my resume, business card – thanks Cy, and notes, I have a ten o'clock interview. I check my watch; it's ten to ten. Light streams in from behind me. Turning around I find the glass elevator has cleared the low lying buildings and the sun is shining from over the Mississippi River. I know where I am. I'm heading up Riverside Tower. It has a mix of communications companies, I think. It used to be owned by a cellular phone company. Before that it was the phone company. Before that it was just a simple radio tower, and before that it was the telegraph building across from the train depot. The depot is still down there somewhere. I nearly press my nose to the glass. The view is incredible. Luckily I have no fear of heights. I check the floor buttons; I'm not going to the top – one floor down from the top. Below are the seven hills of Pigs Eye, or at least five of them. Past the rest of Pigs Eye, there are trees interrupted by lakes, then the Midway, the Prospective Tower, the university, and Milltown. A cloud obscures my view temporarily, dragging a rainbow with it. Wow, the sun is brighter up here. The elevator brass sparkles in the sunlight. If you're applying for a job and trying to look at the bright side, shouldn't you be called an applican, not an applicant?

I'm about there. Time to prepare. I read over my notes. Okay, hopefully Jake hasn't called ahead for me this time. I'd hate to be kicked out from this height.

Ding. The doors open and a receptionist looks up from her desk, smiles, and greets me by name. Jake must be slipping. She escorts me to see Samuel Morrison and Belle Beckett. They offer me a beverage, and I decline.

"How was your ride up?" Ms. Beckett asks.

"Great view. One of the cables broke halfway up. Other than that it was fine." I pause for a moment and add, "Just kidding."

"You had me going there," Mr. Morrison says.

Belle smirks or sneers, I can't tell. "Well, welcome to Common Communication. We will be asking you some questions to try to get to know you better, while giving you the opportunity to understand the goals and interests of Common Communication. Have you heard of us?"

"Yes, it's my understanding that Common Communication is the leader in providing alternative conversations, information, and entertainment for its communications customers."

"He's been memorizing our prospectus," Mr. Morrison comments.

"How is your memory?" Ms. Beckett asks.

"Very good."

She flips to my resume. She has a Romanesque nose. "This says you are a mechanical and optical engineer, and your most recent job was with Flight Control, as the Research and Development manager for AutoDrive, a self-driving car?"

"That's right."

"Why did you leave AutoDrive?"

"I left Flight Control because I could not deliver the product, AutoDrive, in the time allotted by the owner of the company."

"I'm not sure your engineering skills will help us here," she says and thinks for a moment. "How creative was your Research and Development job?"

"Highly creative. We were trying to invent something that had never been created before. It was a mix of my being creative and my instilling and encouraging creativity in my team."

"What if one of your employees came to you and said, 'This is impossible.'"

"I would work out the possibilities with that employee, listening to what they had tried already and brainstorming alternatives."

"Have you ever received a call from a friend wanting advice?"

"Yes."

"Let's say they call you about a problem that they think you know what it's about, and you should know what's going on, but you don't know what's going on. Can you help them?"

Different tower, same issue; this is the Prospective Tower situation. How do I tell them what I would do? "Like I said, I have a good memory. Sometimes I will replay a conversation in my head, looking for clues that I might have missed the first time through, looking for connections or understanding, comprehending the situation. I also have good... intuition."

They jot down some notes. "You have a good, deep voice," she comments. "It exudes confidence."

"Thank you," I respond deeply with a confident smile.

"What do you know about our work?" Mr. Morrison asks.

"People call wanting to talk with historical figures or fictional characters to get different perspectives on their situations. I've never used your service, so I don't know anything more about how it works."

"Have you ever considered doing voice-over work for commercials?"

"No," I respond deeply. Do they do that here too?

"Just curious," she replies.

"A recent customer satisfaction survey revealed that while for the most part our customers are pleased with the service we provide, overwhelmingly their complaint is that we don't offer enough options."

I nod. It makes sense.

"Do you know who they want to talk to the most?"

I shake my head. "Dead relatives?"

"No, but you're close. God."

"That's a tall order."

"You mentioned your intuition. Could you give me an example?"

I have never tried this before: pointed perception within pointed perception. I close my eyes. I open them. "You're reading Harrowing Heights."

"That's amazing," Ms. Beckett gasps.

Mr. Morrison scoffs, "No, it's not. It's on the best sellers list."

"You're on about page 278," I add.

He turns to her for confirmation, but she's gaping at me. I've probably gone too far. It takes her roughly 20 seconds to regain her composure. I'm fairly certain I've gone too far.

"Guessing the page number I'm on is more than intuition," Ms. Beckett tells me. I shrug. "How did you do it?"

I shrug again, hoping that I can shrug my way through the rest of the interview. I might have read about shrugging in the job hunting books. Maybe it said, "Don't try to shrug your way through an interview." It was either "try to" or "don't try to."

They don't seem to be accepting a shrug as an answer. I think I like interviewing more than I like being interviewed. "Let's just call it very good intuition," I tell them.

They hold up their notes and point to different spots. "You think so?"

"I think so."

Mr. Morrison says to me, "We're going to do some role playing. I'm going to call you, and you answer the phone and try to handle the call. Remember there is no time limit for the call. They are being billed by the minute. Hello, I wonder if you can help me with my problem. I don't know who I can turn to."

"Wait. Who am I?"

"Just be yourself."

"Okay. I'm here. Tell me about your problem."

"I'm in an abusive situation."

"Are you being abused?"

"Yes."

"Get out of that situation. Extricate yourself. And get some counseling."

"But it has to do with a family member."

I imagine this was a friend of mine or even Jake. I tell him, "I care about you. I care what happens to you. From being abused, you might question your self-worth. I am telling you. You matter. Again. Get out of that situation. And get some counseling. If you can't find your way out of the situation, get some counseling and some support to help you get out."

"Thank you."

"You're welcome."

"Do me a favor," Ms. Beckett says, "try the last part, the closing, again, but add 'Bless you.'"

"In case he sneezes?" I ask. She waves me on like I'm traffic. "You're welcome. Bless you."

"Perfect. How would you like to play god?" Ms. Beckett asks.

"I guess I should have seen that one coming. God? I'd need some thunder..."

"You got it."

"No, I'm kidding. I can't play god."

"Why not? We were able to check all the boxes. You know something about creation. You have a great memory. You have insight. You have the deep voice. The confidence. The care. The psychology. And even the sense of humor, although I might be taking the stairs at lunchtime because of you and your cable-breaking joke. The only box I wasn't able to check is being able to work 24-7. I don't suppose you happen to be one of a set of identical triplets, do you?"

"No, when I was born they broke the mold. Made it look like an accident."

"I see. Triplets would've helped us with the whole 24-7 thing." They look at each other. They're trying to telepathically communicate, and it's not working. "Please excuse us for just a moment." They leave. I am left admiring a frosted-framed painting that depicts an ice-encrusted river with the buildings of downtown angling up as if they are leaning over the Mississippi in a spitting contest or something. Two of the towers, off to the side, seem to be looking at the rest, wishing they could paddle down the river until winter blows over. God.

A slap to my face. "Hey!" I open my eyes. Ray is standing over me. I get up. "Did you just slap my face?!?"

"You seemed catatonic. It's nearly three. You haven't moved all day!"

"So you saw that as an opportunity to hit me? You might want to lock your door tonight, if it locks." I look at my clock. "It's not three. It's 2:51."

"The people next door wanted to talk with you. I don't know if they're still there." Ray leaves.

I follow him out to the hallway. "Next time, don't slap me awake." He doesn't reply. I gather up some clean clothes and move into the bathroom, the room with the magic water. Clearly it's magic. My shower is like a misty, magical trip through a wonderland of softly vanishing glass droplets, pattering the percussive porcelain, like the softest brush of pine needles tapping a distant cymbal. Each crystal droplet sparkles and reflects its paltry precipitating perspective, of the shower and myself as a nude, in a downward dropping drip. Transparent water. What will they think of next? I get myself cleaned up and dressed.

Outside I am hit with intensely hot air. Immediately I start to sweat and my body goes into shock from the extreme temperature differences. What a waste of a perfectly magical shower.

"Hey buddy!" That's not my name, but I am not feeling especially obstinate about the alias. I'll bite.

"Hey what?" I respond to the nomenclator, who gave me the nomenclature. One of the construction workers comes over.

"Are you getting rid of those shelves?" he asks, pointing to the outside half of the entertainment center.

"Yes, I am," I tell him. He doesn't say anything. I don't say anything. This is guy talk. It goes on for a while. Ultimately I break the ice, which is Minnesota speak for getting-to-the-point. "Do you want what's there? It's missing a few parts."

"Yeah."

"When can you take it?"

"Right now." He gets some of his other buddies to help him move the pieces to his truck. After the quick change of ownership, I sign the title to the entertainment center parts over to my new buddy. One of his buddies asks me if I moved in here.

"Yes."

"With five women?"

"No, four women."

"Two guys with four women?"

"Good math," I add as they proceed to rough out some complex algebraic equations in chalk on the driveway. Or at least that's what I think they're doing. I'm already inside, feeling like I'm losing weight.

I just shed half an entertainment center.

Ray stops me in the hallway. "Do you hear that?"

"Hear what?"

"Nothing!"

"Yeah!"

The door knocks. I go to answer the front door, but it's the stairway door. It's Hope! "Hi Hope!" I kiss her with at least two of the lips on my face. "You don't have to knock. This is your house. I mean, if one of our doors is closed, you'll need to knock there, but not here. Right, Ray?" I call out.

"Right," he calls back.

"How was school?"

"It's the home stretch. Everyone but the janitor was worked up, and it's only Monday. Four more days. Let's go out. Wait. Grab your phone." She's thinking. That makes one of us. The hot humid air blasts us at the door. Hope stands for a moment on the sidewalk, looking down the block. "Let's take a drive." She steers me to her car and takes me for a ride. Main thoroughfares bypass bumper-to-bumper expressways to cross town. We drive through revitalized neighborhoods and neighborhoods in decline. All the houses in this part of town either have porches or decks that look out on the world. Most need paint. Hot and cold extremes are hell on paint. Driving with alert determination, Hope masters the obstacle course of accidents, oblivious pedestrians, and mystery objects.

At a stoplight I tell her, "Congratulations. You've passed your driving test. Where are we going?"

"You'll see." She gets us over to Hiawatha Avenue. We're heading to the airport. I dreamed she was asleep next to me on a plane.

"If we are going to the airport, you have to know I have three concealed weapons on me, plus all the weapons built into the phone. The mosquito confuser alone would have to play havoc with navigational signals."

"Good to know, Sweetie," she tells me, and I try to act like I haven't just melted again into a passenger puddle, just because she called me Sweetie. She said something else. I don't know what because my ears were in the puddle somewhere. I coagulate and ask her what she had said. "We aren't going to the airport," she repeats, as she turns onto Minnehaha Parkway and into Minnehaha Park.

"The Falls!" I announce. We hold hands and walk across the park to the Minnehaha Falls. Minnehaha means curling water or the waterfall, so Minnehaha Falls redundantly means the waterfall falls. I laugh at the notion that Minnehaha means laughing waters.

The park looks like an ordinary Minnesota park with a green grass lawn and picnic tables and large oak trees. A creek enters from the west under Hiawatha and after about a hundred yards it disappears among some trees.

The Minnehaha Creek crosses under an orange stone and cement bridge to then drop over 50 feet into a narrow gorge that winds and expands its way a quarter of a mile to the Mississippi River. The falls were born nearly 7,000 years ago in the Mississippi River with an early precursor to the St. Anthony Falls. St. Anthony Falls has worked its way nearly ten miles up river, near downtown Milltown and First Street Station, while the Minnehaha Falls has worked its way up the creek. The race goes to the falls with the most water; the Mississippi has more water than the Minnehaha, so St. Anthony Falls has moved farther, faster. Storm sewers have taken the flooding away from the creek and the water pressure off of Minnehaha Falls, slowing its backwards recess toward Hiawatha Avenue.

We climb down the steps two at a time into the shadowy, narrow valley. We squeeze around a black wrought iron fence, passing a sign that says something about Beyond This Point. We step carefully on a dirt trail and slippery sedimentary stones to find ourselves under the mossy rock overhang. The mosses mimic the falls by draping over the rocks. A curtain of water drapes between us, Hope and I, and the narrow valley. I check my watch before kissing Hope. She giggles in the mist. When trumpets blare, resoundingly amplified in our cave, Hope bursts out laughing. I take out my phone. "Cy did say this is waterproof, right?" Hope can't answer me. She's lost it. She's bent over laughing. "**Hello, Minnehaha Pizza, if it falls, it's free, how can I help you?!?**" Someone is talking. I don't know who it is or what they are trying to order. "**Hang on!**" I take Hope and my phone out from under the falls and try to answer the phone again. It's Ray. He wants to know if we want stir-fry for dinner. I try to ask Hope. "I'll have to call you back. Wait. Ray? How are you calling us? You don't have a phone!" He either tells me he just got one or that he recently discussed yacht fun. I'm not sure. I check the number he's calling from and add it under Cranks. "I'll call you back." I hang up.

Hope hangs her hands from my shoulders and while still laughing and sniffing she says, "That was the most romantic moment. I should have never had you bring your phone, but that was hilarious. It was such a perfect moment, perfectly interrupted by those annoying trumpets." She's delirious.

I back away onto a patch of gray-brown rock. My foot slides out from under me. I slide down the rocky, muddy hill 15 feet to the creek. Ouch.

"Do it again; I didn't see it!" my girlfriend shouts from above.

The sky above is windshield wiper fluid blue framed by tree branches and leaves. A soaring crow silhouette swoops in to inspect a carcass lying near the giggling, gurgling creek. The highly selective bird decides against this dinner entrée and swoops back up into the trees. The very blue sky is slightly brighter over the falls. A plane flies overhead. Passengers are changing their meal options to what the crow passed up.

"Are you okay?" Hope giggles nervously. The crow-rejected carcass gets carefully up and climbs up the cliff. I wipe off the phone. Hope tries to wipe me off. She gives my butt the brush off. She promises, "Next time, we'll take your car," and then launches into more laughs. I glare at her. She purses her lips to dam up her laughs. I raise an eyebrow at her, questioning her resistance. Her lips quiver. The dam bursts, and she's laughing at me again. "I didn't see the first part," she tells me as I lead her back around the fence and up the stairs, "but the rest of it was hilarious!" We climb the 72 stairs one at a time. She retells the story of my slide as if I wasn't there. "I wish you could've seen yourself." Yes, that would have made it much more funny – if it wasn't me.

Back in the brilliant sunshine, I lie out to dry. Hope sits beside me and picks nature off of me. "So..." I start to say, and she cracks up again. I examine an acorn and take off its cap.

"Seriously," she says, "are you okay? Is your head okay?"

"Acorn, oh acorn, why do you wear a cap? Are you covering a little bald head? Are you merely trying to match your million acorn friends in their nutty peer pressure? Or is it a helmet for the long drop down from the high tree branch?"

"Head: questionable. Are your elbows okay?"

"Yes." I separate several other acorn nuts from their caps.

"Are your shoulders okay?"

"Yes." The nuts and caps form two piles.

"Are your legs and knees okay?"

"Yes." A squirrel is taking interest in my acorn activities. Play all the park games you want, but don't mess with the acorns.

"Is your butt okay?"

"No. My pancreas hurts, and I have a pain in the ass. I was trying to ask you a question."

"Was this before or after you forgot how to walk?"

"Both. Ray called. Really he was showing off that he got a phone, but he was asking if we wanted stir-fry, vegetarian style I assume." Hope is laughing again. The squirrels think she's nuts. They are accredited experts on nuts. They've earned their degrees from squirrel school.

"I can't help thinking about us kissing romantically behind the falls, and then– " Hope makes a trumpet sound.

"You need to practice your trumpet. Practice the scales." Hope is practicing her trumpet scales while the squirrels have a conference nearby. She may be the biggest nut they have ever seen. They have charts and graphs. I interrupt my acorn processing. "What should I tell Ray?"

Hope stops trumpeting, "Find out if he's making it now, if it's already made, or if he can wait. If there's time, we'll come home and have dinner."

I dial him up. "Ray? Are you cooking yet? Can you wait until we get home? Hang on, Hope wants to talk to you." The phone lands in Hope's outstretched hand.

"Ray? Listen, we're at Minnehaha Falls. We were under the falls when you called. Yeah, that was the noise. I'm sorry, but it took awhile to get out from under there and up where we could talk to you. It'll take us about half an hour to get there, give or take. Okay?" She listens intently and waves off the squirrels. A small group of people pass very close to us, staring at my back, like they are laundry detergent specialists or proctologists or something. "Do you want it to be just us, or do you want to invite the others from upstairs? All right. See ya." She ends the call and hands the phone back. "I wanted him to know what's going on."

"You know I know how to walk."

"I've seen you walk," she dimples in my direction.

"You don't get it. I don't slip. Ever. My Native American name is Sure Foot. I've never broken a bone. Not a finger. Not a single sprained ankle. Here. In usually icy Minnesota. I'm Mr. Resilience. Ask Tom. Ask Todd. How did I lose my footing?"

"It could've been the kiss."

"No. It wasn't that!" Suddenly I'm being pelted by acorn parts. Of course you know, this means war. I gather fresh supplies and launch a counter-offensive. She knows how to fight. She knows how to aim while under attack. Still, I am able to quickly assess her weaknesses to move in close and drop acorns down her shirt. "Are you cold or are you hiding acorns in your shirt?" Without bothering to retrieve the acorns, Hope launches a new assault, landing me on my assault, and somehow overpowering me. From her seat on my waist, she grins as she pins my arms.

"I win," she sexily says.

"We both win." She pulls two acorns from her shirt and tosses them for the squirrels to fight over. She pulls me up and escorts me to her car. A beach towel from her trunk upholsters the passenger seat for me.

"That was fun," Hope says as we drive away. Trumpets announce our turn onto Hiawatha. "Now what?"

"Hello," I answer, "Road Kill Pizza. Would you like to hear our specials?"

"No, thank you," Cy says.

"It's Cy."

"I see," Hope says.

"We're just leaving Minnehaha Falls."

"I know," Cy says.

"How would you know?"

"Your phone has GPS."

"And?"

"And that's how I know."

"That's not how GPS works. It doesn't broadcast my location."

"Sure it does."

"No, it doesn't. You are forgetting who you're talking to. I know a great deal more than you about GPS and GPS configurations, since it is one of the top 30 components of AutoDrive. So tell me again how you knew we were just leaving the falls?"

"Your phone tracks your movements."

"Hang on a minute, Cy, I have to drop my phone out the window." Powering down the window, I tell Hope, "Let's see just how indestructible this thing is." Meanwhile, the phone is shouting, "Nooooooo!" I hang the offensive device out the window in the accelerated breeze. Pulling it back in again, I tell Cy, "Don't you dare tag and release me! Don't go hanging a radio collar on me to see how I react to the latest music! I'm not your lab monkey."

Hope asks, "Do you two need some time alone?"

"She's tracking my movements, currently our movements."

Hope again reaches out for the phone. I hand it to the teacher like I just got caught with chewing gum in her class. "Cy, why are you tracking our movements? I thought the two of you were through as a couple. Are you stalking us?" Hope hands the phone back to me.

"No, I only checked where you were before calling. I waited until you were moving, so I wouldn't interrupt anything. Honest."

"She claims she was only checking where we were before calling so she wouldn't interrupt whatever it was that we were doing," I paraphrase. Hope nods.

"Hey, I was being considerate," she says.

"She says that spying is just another way of being considerate."

Hope nods, "Ask her if this feature came with the phone plan automatically or did she request it?"

"Did you hear that? I believe counsel is trying to establish intent. I will repeat the question. Was this feature automatically part of a phone plan or was it specifically requested?"

"I had to pick three optional features. I knew you would like the option to destroy the phone."

"Yes, I might use that feature later today. But you seem to be evading the question..."

"Yes. I picked the option to be able to track your location."

I tap Hope's thigh. "She says she picked the stalking option. Now Cy, how do we disable that feature without blasting the whole package to bits?"

"I will call them."

"Thank you. Now, have you talked to Jake?"

"Yes, but I'm not getting between you two boys. You'll have to talk to him yourself."

"Fair enough."

"Are you as mad at Jake as you are at Carl?"

"No, Jake made a bad decision and seemed to be just screwing around. Carl is incapable of making a decision and seems destined for the funny farm. I could belt Jake. Carl? I have no common ground with Carl. At most, at best, he has my pity."

"The real reason I'm calling is about the Yolanda letter."

"Yes?"

"Did you like the play?"

"Yes."

"Tell her."

"That's what Ray said to say."

"Ray's right."

"What else? Saying I liked her play wouldn't fill a postcard."

"I don't know."

"Maybe Hope and I can write about our stalking experience."

"Do you want my help or not?"

"Yes, I'd like your help, Cy. What else should I say?"

"I'll work on it."

"Thanks."

"Ricky, did you keep anything from our relationship?"

"Absolutely. The memories. And you as a friend."

"Have you made a decision about Lefty's experiment?"

"So far, I plan to do it."

"Are you sure about doing that? You're not exactly an angel."

"Not exactly an angel? You say the sweetest things!"

"You're too creative to be an angel."

"I never claimed I was."

"But the experiment is supposed to record everything?"

"Right."

"Everything you think and do."

"Right."

"You don't want me knowing where you are, and I'm your friend. What about everyone learning everything about you?"

Hope asks, "What's she talking about?"

"Lefty's experiment," I tell Hope. To Cy, "What should I do, make stuff up? That would make trying to write a letter to Yolanda seem like nothing, wouldn't it?"

"I'm not sure that you've thought it all out."

"I have thought it out, but thanks for caring. Anything else?"

"Nope."

"Just so you know, we are back home now. Have a good evening."

"You too." We disconnect.

Hope points to the garage, "What happened to your shelves?"

"The entertainment center? One of the construction workers wanted it."

"Did they talk to you?"

"Yes."

"You let them have it?"

"Yes," I respond, holding the first floor door for her.

"We don't really like them. They have been a nuisance all summer. You fed them last Thursday and now you're giving them furniture."

"They've been okay to me... except for making it clear that they don't feel I'm worthy of living in the same house as all of you." Faith, Becky, and Nicole are watching TV and talking about Becky's multicolored eye shadow, while Ray is sizzling food in the kitchen.

"He just got started," Becky tells us. "So we hear you were at the falls. What happened to you?!? Did you ride the falls?"

"He fell at the falls," Hope giggles. Her dimples dance.

"Well, if you are going to fall, the falls is the place to fall."

"I'll go get changed. Tell them what Cy did." I go into my room. Everything is so neat and clean and new. Where do I put muddy clothes? For an instant, I miss the apartment. I knew where to put muddy clothes. I change in the bathroom and dump the dirty clothes in the bathtub. An acorn bounces loose and ricochets across the bathroom. That's how it starts. An acorn bounces loose, and years later people wonder why they have a tree growing in the middle of their house.

Cutting through the living room, I have them check the back of my neck and behind my ears for transmitters and metal tags. "Need any help?" I ask the chef.

"No, all the chopping was the tough part, but they helped me," he says, removing a wooden spoon from the wok to point to the living room. "The rice is ready. Most ingredients have taken a trip through the wok once now. I'm in the mixing stage." He has bean sprouts, tofu, pea pods, mushrooms, broccoli, peppers, water chestnuts, bamboo sprouts, onions, baby corn, carrots, celery, sauces, and a few other things I can't identify. Two rices are steaming on the stove. "Does it meet with your approval?"

Each ingredient takes a separate amount of time to cook. Mixing before cooking would over cook some things while under cooking others. "Yes. You do good work."

In the living room, Hope pats a spot on the couch to sit. It would fit someone sitting normally. I choose to sprawl across people. Becky shoves me into place. Nicole nudges me, "Hey, did you hear? The bishop visited Prospective Tower today."

"Don't they only move diagonally?!? Everything I know about bishops, I learned in chess."

"We thought you wouldn't mind a nature show," Becky says.

On TV, they have captured and sedated a rare black bird. They say, "We are bleaching its wings to see it better from a distance."

"Maybe the scientists should stop torturing the wildlife and get better glasses. Or, I know! How about binoculars?" I ask. They tag the drugged bird and put a radio collar on it. "I know what that's like! Why not dress it up in the latest dance fashions? We've, heh, put hoop earrings and a pink boa on the bird because we couldn't think of anything else to do to it, anything other researchers haven't already done." They let the bird go. It staggers and runs its face into the ground. "That's gotta hurt." I sway in my seat and slur, "No, Officer, I have not been drinking! No, these two men, they poured a whole bottle of bourbon into me and put me into a car!"

"You thought he wouldn't mind a nature show," Hope parrots Becky.

Ray steps in, "You might want to get yourselves whatever you want to drink. Dinner should be ready in a few minutes." Grabbing both a Double Bubble and a Lake Weago beer, I mix some of each. Others are disgusted. "Bring a plate and tell me how much you want me to serve you," Ray tells us. Once everyone else is served, Ray serves himself.

"How long have you two been roommates?" Faith asks pointing us out.

"About three and a half years," I tell her.

"Have either of you ever lived on your own?" Becky asks. We shake our heads.

"Here it goes," Nicole comments.

"I think the longer people live alone, the more difficult it is for them to live with other people," Becky generalizes.

"I thought you didn't like Chinese food?" Hope asks me.

"I like this."

"This is beyond great!" Nicole tells Ray.

"If it's beyond great, does that mean it's past great? Does that mean it's gone the other way around to being bad?" I ask.

"No!"

"I never thought of that. He's right," Faith says, gesturing.

Fire burns from Nicole's eyes as she gets up while staring at me. I dash around the table the opposite way. Breaking orbit, I take off for my room with Nicole in hot pursuit. She tackles me on my bed.

"What was that?!?" Nicole exclaims.

"I was teasing you!"

She grabs me, saying with clenched teeth, "You can't– Don't give Faith more ammunition!"

I apologize, and she helps me up. We return to the table.

"You two work everything out?" Becky asks.

"Yes," I stare at Faith and laugh a monstrously sinister laugh.

"Hey!" Faith complains to Hope, pointing us out. "They're ganging up on me!"

"No ganging up," Hope announces. "Take turns."

"Thanks. Wait... That's not good either." Faith turns to me. "So. Have you found a job?"

"Shut up, Faith," Nicole leans in defense.

"No, I haven't." I take a drink. Yuck!

"He doesn't have to," Hope says, smirking at my drink.

"No offense, but don't we have two guys here without jobs? Not that I mind having breakfast and dinner cooks."

"Whoa," Ray says. "I'm a comic book artist. Today I got a lucrative extension on my contract, thanks to Nicole's modeling. Only a few days of having my previews circulating made hot properties out of me and my upcoming books."

"I never thought of that for my portfolio! Ray, could I get a copy of something you did of me to add to my portfolio?" Nicole pleads.

Ray nods. "And thanks to Hope, the Lactating Woman fountain is going great."

"How did I help?"

"This house. I can think. I can work. I can concentrate. I can work harder. The only drawback is that I think I am less inspired than I was. It's hard to see yourself as a starving artist in a place like this. It does something to the inspirations, diminishes them or something. But I'm getting stuff done... in a dedicated studio. Thank you, Hope."

"You're welcome."

"Ray..."

"Plus, the Co-op Association in the old neighborhood is talking about expanding over here. They miss me."

"Okay, so we only have one deadbeat." Bam! Faith screams and looks under the table. I didn't kick her.

I tell Faith, "People keep telling me to kick back and take it easy. Maybe that's what I'm doing." Faith vanishes under the table. "Ray, is there any talk about Wild Rice Park for Kelly?"

"Yes, how did you know?"

"You know, there are several other statues and monuments in Wild Rice Park, right?"

"Yeah..."

"Think juxtaposition. What would be the worst statue that they might put Kelly in front of?"

Ray's face puzzles this perplexing puzzle, whose pieces I've parked on his plate. His imagination moves around the park and his face checks through the spaces until it finds that one. Concern mounts his face and wrinkles it up into a startled-yet-questioning anger. "No!" Ray's on his feet.

"Yes. Chuckles."

"They... **They can't do that!**"

"You'll have to stop them."

"The piping goes in next week!"

"Next week?!?"

"Yeah. You didn't know that part of it?"

"No," I reply. "Everything's been all screwed up. It's been really random flashes with barely any frame of reference and no time to check a watch."

"How can time be a problem?" Faith asks, her entire body folded up on the seat of the chair.

"I didn't think you were that close to being done," I tell him.

"I wasn't until the past two days. What exactly did you see?"

"All I saw was something covered by a dark fabric or a curtain in the park with Chuckles peering over what would be her shoulder. I only just figured out that it was Kelly at the dedication. Basically he's grinning while watching her. Someone in the Parks Department must have done that."

"Her left shoulder or her right?"

"Are we talking about the statue of Chuckles the Clown?!?"

I reply, "Yes. Her... left shoulder." Ray's face gets as white as a snowman. His blood packs up and leaves. "Sit down, Ray, before you fall down." Ray slides down the wall to the floor. I dash over.

"A little song, a little dance..."

"Yes Faith, we all know the credo. Ray, are you okay?" Hope is checking Ray's eyes. Becky asks if she should call the paramedics. "I don't think they can move the statue," I observe.

"Wait. Is the statue based on you?" Faith asks, pointing at Nicole. Nicole says no. "But there IS a comic book character based on you, right?" Ray blinks. "I always KNEW you were a comic book character!" Nicole tears off after Faith, who flees upstairs.

Hope mutters, "We might need the paramedics after all."

"No," Ray says, his face moving back into circulation, "I'll be all right. I don't know what to do, but I'll be all right."

"Tell them that you're not going to let them screw up the sculpture," Becky says.

"Right. You call your contacts at the Parks Board. Tell them that the planned placement of Kelly in the park is completely unacceptable. Then you consider involving the client who commissioned Kelly."

"How do I tell them how I know what I know?" Ray asks.

"You don't. You shouldn't have to. Consider quoting me as a reliable source. Be forthright in what you know and that this is a deal-breaker but not how you know it."

Wham! Ray smiles, "Noisy neighbors..."

"I have to stop them," Hope says, going upstairs.

Becky gets comfortable on the floor with us, "I think it's cool that, you know... That you have this idea of your art and how it should be displayed, and you aren't willing to sacrifice that idea."

"Thanks." Ray's face warms up. He says, "They don't have her. They are not going to get her unless I get assurances on the location. Even then, I might babysit her, supervise the installation, without leaving until it's right." He turns to me, "It's not iron-clad, right? It could happen, but I can make a difference. I can make sure it doesn't happen, right?"

"Right. You can change things. Ultimately, anything can happen."

"Within reason," Becky adds.

"That's right. Do you want some help up?" I give an arm to Ray and one to Becky and haul them both up. We finish up and clean up dinner.

"You two really get along well, you know."

Ray and I look at each other. "Maybe because we don't talk about it."

Ray says, "Right, we don't exactly sit around and say, 'Gee, we get along.'"

"He slapped me awake this afternoon."

"I told you. It was like you were in a coma."

"I must have missed that day in first aid class. 'If the patient is experiencing a coma, simply slap them awake.'" I scrub the wok. It's tough. Sandblasting would help. If we were in the desert, I'd hang the wok up to be sandblasted clean. For all Minnesota's lakes and trees and glaciers and prairies, what is missing is a sandblasting desert. Ray nudges me. Becky is staring at us. "What?"

"That's it?!? That's your fight?"

"What fight?"

"Exactly. I'm going upstairs." She leaves, and it gets quiet.

As I shut off the TV, a giant bleached-winged vulture is carrying off a researcher. In my room, I rearrange the books on the remaining half of the entertainment center. I locate my Safari Of The Mind book. It's been a week since I've read it. I read, "The stump of indecision glares at curiosity." I lie down. I close my eyes and relax.

I am telling a guy that I can't help him gamble. I don't even know the rules of Go Fish.

I am running down a sidewalk.

Kissing Hope while fireworks burst overhead.

Swatting mosquitoes.

Pine trees sway.

I'm halfway.

Friends fight to feed the world.

The grass is green below my shiny black shoes and my clasped hands.

A bird chirps.

Melanie plays my guitar.

Minnesota is losing lakes. Homes are being built in lake beds. Good idea.

A solid white line forms around the edges of the pancakes. They're flipped.

Erix is trying to tell me something.

A cat takes me on a walk.

A giant dinosaur steps through parked cars.

Horns honk. I open my eyes. The horns are still blaring. I answer my phone. It's Red.

"What's going on?"

"Nothing," I reply.

"Well stop it." He hangs up on me. My friends are such a delight.

I close my eyes. Open one. Check my clock. Close it. I relax.

It's 38 miles to Tomah.

The doctor laughs and says that she had a patient suffering from back pain. "I checked his back and asked all of the usual questions. Could it be shoe related? It couldn't be bra related. Could it be mattress related? He just bought a new mattress. No, that wasn't it. I had him set an alarm for the middle of the night. He woke up with his wife's knee in his back!"

Someone wants to put makeup on my face?

Pulling my wool hat up off my eyes, I rest my arms on my shovel and watch the snow drift slowly down, glowing in the night. Sighing into my scarf, I return to shoveling, and I think of what Jake said about shoveling while it's still snowing.

I open my eyes. I'm less comfortable. My bed real estate has been confiscated. Something is between my body and my arm. Something large and alive. Hope has nestled into bed with me. That's pretty sweet. I guess she needs me. I move a little. She quickly readjusts. She's awake. "Hi Loverducks."

"Hi," she says doing an imitation of Nicole's voice. Why would she be doing imitations at this time of night? I turn on the light. My clock blinks, an arm stretches to the three.

We look into each other's eyes. It's Nicole. I stare. I pat her on the back and reach for the phone. I push the Hope button.

"Hello Hope? Could you come down here?"

"No... I need my sleep," she says word by word.

"Nicole is in my bed."

Two seconds pass. "I'll be right down," she quickly says.

"I better go," Nicole says, getting up. She hesitates. Hope flies into the room. I haven't even set down the phone.

"What is this?" I set down the phone. Her brow needs to be pressed. Hope looks us up and down, evaluating sleepwear fashions and bed linens. Hope's shirt and shorts are grapefruit colored, inside and out, yellow and pink. Nicole's shirt is salmon colored, inside and out, pink and iridescent silver. My sheet is white, with a fluffy white comforter.

"I was just leaving."

Hope stops Nicole. "What do you think you're doing? Are you trying to wreck things? For all your talk of wanting me to find the right guy, now that I've found him, you want to wreck everything?!?"

I'm the right guy?!? Wow. I always thought Al was the Wright guy.

"I'm not trying to wreck anything!" Nicole yells.

"You aren't?!?" Hope yells back.

"No!"

"Then what were you doing in his bed?" A crowd forms in our hallway. "Come on, Nicole, what is this? Did you have a bad dream and run all the way down here to his bed?"

"Fuck you!"

"Yeah? How many times have I stuck up for you? When Faith– Faith, get your butt in here! When Faith has called you a bitch? Who has taken care of you when you're sick? Who has always been there for you? And this is how you repay me?!? This is when you decide to screw me over?!?"

"We didn't do anything!"

"We?!? You two aren't a We. We're a We." Arguments are always more intelligent at night. Nighttime is the time to discuss life issues. Who are we? How did we come to be?

"I wasn't trying to get between you."

"Right," Faith says.

"Shut up, Faith!" Hope says.

"What did I do?"

"You provoke Nicole."

"What?!?"

It's weird how I can lie here and matter and at the same time, not matter at all. I am now property. In fifth grade, two girls fought over me. One said, "He's your boyfriend!" The other said, "No he's not. He's your boyfriend!"

"Where do you think you're going?" Hope asks.

"To my room," Nicole replies.

"No you're not."

"I'm going to pack. Let me go."

"Don't do this."

They're crying. I must have missed something. Everyone is crying except Ray and Faith, so Nicole hits Faith to get her into the spirit of the moment. So it's just Ray and I not crying. Ray waves and heads back to bed.

They're saying things to each other. I have no idea what they are saying. When did they switch languages? I can't understand what they're saying through all the wailing, sobbing, and bawling. Names and pronouns occasionally slip by the cryptographic crying, but nothing else, nothing useful. Sobs are interjected into words as disposable syllables. Through all of this, they still seem understand each other. Maybe if I live here long enough I'll become fluent in the language, at least enough to translate for others, if not to create full-blown audio language lessons.

I spin off the bed onto the floor. It was the only thing I could do. I've got the floor now. "Nicole. Hope. Help me. The floor has caught me," I tell them. Nicole keeps her distance. Hope comes over to look at me, then stands confused.

My evacuation of my bed must have released some of the tension in the room. I don't know why. They are looking at me like I've lost my mind. Maybe I've just relocated the tension. The focus of confusion has shifted from between them to between-them-and-me. Hey I didn't start this; I just want to have my fair share. I have no idea how to resolve it. I think of saying, "It's late. Let's all climb into my bed and get some sleep." Luckily, I save some of my wit for myself. I don't think it would translate.

They turn their backs to me and the conversation moves into the hall. Fine. I can have my own conversation in here. I turn to my alarm clock, "So tell me..." With one arm falling past three and only one eye open, it shakes its head.

First I'm not a part of the argument, like I have nothing to do with it. Then they fully exclude me. That's gotten to be a pattern lately. I'm not included in things that directly relate to me... AutoDrive... now, it's the Goldilocks subject of who's been sleeping in my bed. Next thing you know, I'll be excluded from my own dreams.

Patience, Grasshopper, you are the willow who bends in the breeze, yet stands tall. You are the willow that whispers in the night, while listening to the whispers of time. You are the willow dancing and swaying your grass skirt as if at a luau.

Do they have willow trees in Hawaii? I lean back against the side of the bed, sitting with my legs folded pretzel-like, knees out. I relax.

I'm back at Common Communication, wearing a telephone headset and staring at a sign that says, Offer Other Services.

From the next cubicle John Wayne pokes his head around, "Are ya gettin' any calls there, Partner?"

"No," I start to answer, then I hear a beep on the line that I've got a call. I hold up a finger to let him know I've got a call. I push the Light Thunder button. The Light Thunder button only has one bolt on it. It's a start. "This is god."

"God? I'm Dawn. I have a problem. I don't know who to turn to."

"I am always with you. I am with... Ploozy, your stuffed... Yook."

"How did you know I'm holding him?"

"What would you like to talk about Dawn?"

"No one listens to me. No matter what I say, it's as if I don't matter," Dawn whines.

"I understand."

She laughs a little. "I guess you do." She pauses and laughs again. "I suppose, you give people a few simple rules, and no one follows them."

"People follow them, mostly. You follow them. But this isn't about me. Who isn't listening to you?"

"My mom."

"Who else?"

"Donnie."

"What are you trying to tell your mom?"

"You know, that I'm not a baby."

"What else?"

"That I should be able to make decisions for myself."

"Is everything going well for your mom?"

"Well, you know, she has problems with work and she's trying to make things work with Donnie..."

"And in the middle of all that, she's acting overprotective of you?"

"Exactly!"

"Maybe she acts as if people with guns and knives and drugs are lined up along your street, waiting for you to come out alone."

"Yeah! Exactly!"

"I'm not picturing your road, but it's not like that, is it?"

"No!"

"I didn't think so. There are no obvious bad people out there, waiting for you. You're right. It's actually a lot trickier than that. Out there, there are decisions and responsibilities. Some of them can be as simple as looking for traffic before crossing the street. That's where there are obvious consequences. But sometimes you don't know what is happening. One day you cross some neighbor's flower garden. It looked like dirt to you, but to the neighbor, everything was sprouting. He saw you from inside his house. Weeks later, when everything is blooming except your path of absent flowers, he comes out and yells at you. You are not a bad person. You did not mean to trample the flowers. He is not a bad person. He's only trying to defend his work."

The satellite image on my computer shows a storm in Venezuela. "Hang on a second, I've got a storm in Caracas." I hit two bursts of thunder. "Imagine having all the freedom that adults have. Wouldn't you have fun?"

"Yeah!"

"Then why don't you see more adults having fun? They don't have to go to school. They can work wherever they want, drive wherever they want, and do whatever they want. They should be having a blast." Thunder. "But they're not having a blast. The freedoms have decisions and responsibilities and regrets tied to them. Most people learn, not by listening to others, not by researching, but by experience. They call it, 'Learning the hard way.' And learning the hard way is full of experiences and regrets and responsibilities and decisions. Good decisions come from experience, and experience comes from bad decisions. The real trick," I whisper, "is being responsible without looking mature. That's how I've stayed so young looking." I tell her, "You do matter, Dawn. And maybe you are ready to have more of a say in what you do. And it will happen in the time it takes me to blink. It may not happen soon enough, but when it happens, a part of you will feel it's too soon. At least that is what has happened to nearly everyone before you."

"Thanks, God."

"You're welcome. Bless you, Dawn."

"G– Bless you too, God. Um. Before you go, does anyone have a crush on me?"

"Yes, but they are scared to say anything."

"WHO?!?"

"I can't tell. I'd get in trouble."

"How could **you** get in trouble?"

"One of them could grow up and demolish a rain forest or something. It hurts."

"You said, 'One of them.' There's more than one?!?"

"I've said too much already... Gotta go."

"Wait. My mom would like to talk to you."

"Hello?"

"Hello, Dawn's mother. Don't tell me. Let me guess. Your daughter won't listen to you?" Laughter is in the background from Dawn and in the foreground from Wayne.

"No, I was listening in, and I just wanted to say thank you. Are you here in St. Louis?"

"I'm farther up."

"Well, thank you."

"Bless you."

Two seconds after the disconnection a beep on the line signals the start of another call. Light thunder. "This is god."

"Hi. I have a strange question. I see people wearing this one eye shadow, but I can't find the color in any stores?"

"They are mixing different colors to create a new color."

"Really?"

"All visual colors are a mix of three primary colors: blue, red, and yellow, but they are starting with colors that are closer to what you are seeing. You can test-mix them on a piece of paper or a department store makeup consultant could help you further."

"Wow. You do know all."

"You are beautiful with or without eye shadow. Bless you."

I'm on break. Sherlock Holmes is doing phone consultation on a police case. Holmes spots me and flags me down. While maintaining his verbal Holmes persona, he signals a request to transfer the call to god. Unfortunately god declines. In the break room, I grab an apple from my sack lunch. I take a few bites while staring out the window. Belle Beckett runs in, her long gray hair following her in a blizzard of motion. "I'm on break."

"Well, we have 1,427 calls waiting for you."

I look at the apple. It was a good apple. "There was just a lull about 15 minutes ago, where there weren't any calls."

"That was a glitch in the system."

"Breaks over," I tell her.

"Thanks, big guy."

Abraham, Jesus, Mohammad, and Krishna walk into the break room, heading to Buddha's table. I acknowledge them with a nod and take my apple back to my desk to oxidize. I can't throw it away, not just yet.

My computer hums a tuneless melody.

Two seconds after I push the Ready button, a beep on the line signals the start of another call. Thunder. "This is god."

"God, I'm wondering if I should get nipple reduction surgery."

"If you're cold, just move."

"So that's a no?"

"That's a no," punctuated with extra thunder. I check for my watch. What did I do with my watch? I put my phone on standby after the caller disconnects. "Hey John, what day is today?"

John slowly says, "Well ya know, every day is... Wayne's day, Pilgrim."

"Thanks." I push the Ready button. Beep. Thunder. "This is god."

"I need to find a place where I can practice the tuba."

"Where are you?"

"Milltown."

"Could you move to Pigs Eye?"

"Sure, it's not that far away."

"You'll fit right in at the Whisper Willows apartment complex in Pigs Eye." I give him directions and the landlady's phone number.

"Really? Thanks."

I bless the tuba player, if only to offset all the damning.

Beep. Thunder. "This is god."

"Hello. I hope you don't mind, but I haven't always believed in you. But that's not why I'm calling. I would like to be more self-supporting. I need a way to get around town. I am blind. I could buy a car, but I can't drive one. I can't afford a chauffeur." I look at my apple, looking brown and sickly after such little time. "Hello?"

"In time, there will be a type of car that drives itself."

"You mean, like AutoDrive? I heard about the crash."

I open my eyes.

Hope is sitting across from me on a chair. She leaves the room and calls out, "Ray, he's awake." My legs are stiff. They have been out of circulation for a while. I look at my clock. It says it's seven. As soon as I can walk again, I have to check in at the bathroom. Hope comes back in and sits down.

"Don't you have to go to school?"

She sits and stares at me. Not unpleasantly. Not happily either. "It's after seven in the evening. You've been sitting there all day. We've been worried about you."

"Oh. I'm sorry." I have one leg a third of the way unfolded. The other one is only a quarter of the way unfolded. I'm holding them in place. "I didn't mean to worry you."

Hope sits quietly. I wonder what she's thinking. "Lefty called," she says, nodding to my phone. "He's waiting to bring over some paperwork."

I nod and try to move toward the phone. My legs are as stiff as Kelly's. I fall over. "Wow. How pathetic is this?"

Hope comes over, kneels down, and stares at the crumpled ball of me. She does not reach for the phone. She does not try to help me up. "What are you doing?"

"Sideways yoga."

"Seriously."

"Oh, seriously. Well, I was in a kind of jumbo version of pointed perception with an all-star cast. John Wayne was in it."

"Really? John Wayne? How did that happen? Gene's cloning?"

"No, it wasn't John Wayne. He didn't even look like John Wayne, but he sure sounded like John Wayne. And he had a hat." One of my legs untwists another inch and a half.

"A hat? That's great, really," she says without convincing me of the hat's greatness. "Have you had anything to eat today?"

"No."

"And you haven't gotten up to go to the bathroom?"

"No."

"Don't you have to?"

"Yes."

"But you're stuck?"

"Right."

Hope gets comfortable. She leans back, dreamily. "Remember Minnehaha Falls yesterday? All that flowing water? And the sound that it made?" Hope imitates the water sounds. Hope has duck lips when she does that. "In the center of the stream the water flows in a steady rush. On the edges, trickles and dribbles of water drop off slick rocks, drip by drip by drip."

"You are really asking for it."

"No," she sits up, "you are. You're losing weight. Or hadn't you noticed? You aren't looking well."

"Not that again."

Hope stands. "I mean it. You're pale and blotchy. And sitting there is not the same as living. You are a great guy. You have so many wonderful talents, you really do, but for the past few days, you've hardly done anything."

"On a cellular level, I'm really busy."

"I'm not kidding. And your legs are dying, just so you know." I try to move my legs to prove her wrong. My legs side with her. "And when Nicole and I tried to talk to you, you were in a trance. We really needed to talk to you, and you weren't here... in the present." My body comes unraveled a few more inches. I nearly brag about my momentum, until it stops. "School sucked today. Big time. Then I come home to sit and watch you for hours for any signs of life." Hope turns and leaves. I would follow her, except that for the moment, I'm an invalid in the need of mobility.

What if I were to roll my way into the bathroom? Yeah, that's a great idea, except I can't think of a way to get the ball rolling. I tuck my head in. Flash. Ray takes a picture. "Modern art," he says, titling my picture. I bet his room doesn't have a halo. I upright myself and try to stretch out. My legs are over halfway straight. I crab-walk to my nightstand and grab my phone. I call Lefty.

"Hello."

"Hi Lefty, sorry I wasn't available to take your call earlier. Could you be over here in about 20 minutes?" I ask, noticing the penguin, who's migrated in here.

"I could be there sooner."

"No, I need 20 minutes to get unstuck." He accepts that, and we hang up. Maybe he's too accepting of my weirdness or maybe he's relieved that I'm not having second thoughts about being part of the memory experiment. The way I see it, it could tell me something about me that I don't already know. I doubt it will answer one of the big existential questions, like where do my pointed perceptions come from. I stopped asking that one, when I turned it into the question of where does the future come from, leading to the question, where does the present come from. I doubt brain scans and images and translations can help me with any of that. I set down the phone and pick myself up. I'm standing. It's a miracle! Hallelujah! I hobble around my room and hobble to the bathroom and get ready for the day that is already mostly over. I'm savoring an apple when Lefty rings the bell. The apple's interior shines white like freshly fallen wet snow.

"Hey, come on in. Can I get you something?"

"No, thank you."

"Have a seat. I need to call Hope to see if she wants to come down." I push the Hope button. "Hi. Lefty's here, if you want to come down." I flip on a light, sit down next to Lefty, and look over the notes and forms he's spreading out over the coffee table. Hope and Becky appear. We make room for them. Hope brings her own paperwork, which is very thoughtful, but it looks as though we have plenty. I don't want to have to start sandbagging again.

"You look better from having showered," Hope tells me as she passes copies to us. "This is a document stating that the subject has the right to discontinue the test if he has any indication or intuition that it will cause him harm. If you both accept it, I would like you to include it with the rest of the paperwork and alter any language in any other documents. Becky is here to help with any legalese."

"Hope, Lefty is my friend–"

"It's all right. I understand," Lefty says, while reading. "I didn't know how to do something like this without confusing others. This way I can... this way it is something that you instigated, and I am accepting." Lefty's about to sign, "Which copy should I sign?"

Hope turns to Becky, who replies, "All of them. Is it okay with you?" I nod.

We read through the rest of the documents, only altering the wording of two of them. Lefty and I sign them. He shuffles and deals them out into two piles, one set for me and one set for him. I don't think he knows that I know he stacked the deck. The date is set for the Thursday after next, nine days from now. We shake hands and stop just before starting a second round of hand shaking. With the weight of the world taken off his shoulders, Lefty leaves. That means the weight of the world rests somewhere in my living room in Hope's duplex near Lake Weago in Milltown in Minnesota in the United States. Maps will need to be updated to reflect the change. Becky says good night and takes the stairs up. I pick back up my oxidizing apple. The apple's brownish interior is like freshly driven snow... driven by the sand trucks.

"Don't eat that." Hope takes my apple into the kitchen. She comes back out with an apple that looks as good as new. I wonder if she refills banana peels too.

"Thank you. And thanks for writing that agreement. It makes sense."

"You know, if Lefty's experiment actually works, everyone will know everything you know. Everything about us, about AutoDrive, the Savior of the Midway stuff..."

"What does that mean to you?"

"I think it means I have to be on my best behavior."

"Shouldn't people always be on their best behavior?"

"Well, take for example Nicole lying with you in your bed. Do you think that was bad behavior?"

"No. I think it had a great potential for misunderstanding. That's why I called you. But no, I don't think she meant to do anything wrong. What was wrong about it was not preparing us for it... not telling us what was going to happen and why she was doing it. Why was she doing it?"

"Let's hold off on that. Did you like it?"

Lights flash. Bells ring. Alarms sound. It's a trap! "Should I?"

"Come on. It's Nicole. She's beautiful."

"You're beautiful."

"Thank you, but I'm not trying to trap you." A sergeant salutes and reports that the T word has been used. I dismiss him. "I know you love me. And the fact that you immediately called me tells me where your priorities... lay," Hope smirks. "But was it okay?"

The lights start to flash again. I wave them off. "I'm okay, if you're okay."

"Nicole turns the heads of gay men. I'm not kidding. The question is, can you resist?"

"Can I resist her? You are all the resistance I need. I love you. She could be... well, let's not think about that. I love you. And I have a strong, disciplined mind. I can handle it."

Hope nods. "But what about sitting on the floor for 16 hours? Is that part of your discipline?"

"No."

"You mentioned an all-star cast. Was it all part of pointed perception? I guess I don't understand."

"My pointed perception has been all jumbled up. Either I see a hodge-podge of things, half of which I can't understand, or I have long intense sequences. Last night it was the hodge-podge. Then on the floor it was the movie of the week."

"What was it about? How could John Wayne be in your future?"

"He wasn't John Wayne. He sounded like John Wayne. I dreamed that I applied for a job at Common Communication."

"Never heard of it."

"I don't know if they exist yet. They will be in the Riverside Tower in Pigs Eye. At the top. Almost."

"Nice."

"Yeah, the view was incredible. I had never been up there before."

"You still haven't."

I nod, halfway agreeing. "I went to an interview there. They hired me. That was yesterday."

"You dreamed it yesterday?"

"Right. Ray slapped me out of that. Today I went to work there."

"Doing?"

"People call and get a phone system. They pick an historical character or a fictional character to talk to. I'm one of the people they can talk to."

"Who are you?"

"God."

"You aren't God."

"I know that."

"It's a lie."

"The phone system explains the conditions of the calls. They know, as much as any consumer knows, what they're getting into."

"How do you do it?"

"I have several thunder buttons."

Hope gets up. "Oh! Great! Thunder buttons? I could be God too, if I had thunder buttons!"

Ray calls out, "Could you two keep it down to a low thunder? I've gotten used to the quiet."

"Sorry!" we reply.

Hope sits down on my lap. "You know that's pretty weird."

"I was able to help people."

"You and John Wayne. Do you know that John Wayne never fought in any wars? Do you know what he did during the McCarthy Hearings?"

"He just sounds like John Wayne."

"And he had a hat."

"Right. He had a hat. He didn't have a lot of calls. At one point, I had 1,427 waiting for me." Hope looks at me wondering if I've lost my mind. I don't mind as long as she isn't mad at me.

"None of it happened."

"It might happen."

"But if it might happen, why dream it? Why not live it?" It's difficult to not look at her while she sits in my lap. "Are you trying to improve your decisions?" My head rattles as I shake it. "I don't get it." I play with her hair. Using her hair as a soft brush, I brush her ear and her neck. Hope rescues her hair from my hand. "Has Nicole been in any of your dreams?"

"Not really, only once since the incident at Tom's cabin. There was a moment where she was taking our picture in front of a Christmas tree, but that's it."

"What was significant about that?"

"I don't know that there was any significance."

"Do you have erotic dreams?"

"No. At least, not in a while."

"Not about Nicole?"

"No."

"Not about me?"

"Yes, but not recently."

"Why not?"

I grab both her ears and tug on them while saying, "Boogity-boogity-boogity!" She laughs. "What is all this? Are you trying to get me interested in Nicole? What are you doing, trying to set me up with her?"

"No!"

"Then what are you doing?"

"You just don't make any sense. I don't get how you can like Nicole but not lust after her."

"Do you lust after her?"

"No."

"Okay then, we have something in common."

"Ray lusts after her," she says, looking for confirmation.

"Ray!"

"I'm busy!" he yells from down the hall.

"He's busy. But what's the point of dragging Ray into this anyway?"

"I'm just trying to understand you."

"Well, that's not the way to do it. Here's what you do. Think back to a time when you started making generalizations about guys. Are you there?"

"Yes."

"Good. Now play teacher and correct the generalizations with red ink by adding the words Most or Some." My finger writes on her chest for emphasis. "Until you get a passing grade on this lesson, you won't be able to go on to the next lesson in your study of me."

"Will I have to stay after class?" she asks suggestively.

"Not if you're a good student." Our kisses carry us into my room and shut the door.

28

Blindfolded Darts

Perfection of spirit and skin sleeps beside me. Her breaths kiss the air. Her body rises and falls in desperate sighs, as if floating in an uncounted Minnesota pond. Her hair pools under her, while she offers herself to embrace the cloudy blue sky reflecting all around her. Rational thought escapes me, rolls over, and falls quickly to sleep. I wonder whom she's dreaming about, and instantly become jealous of them even if I am that who of whom she dreams. I have so much control of my own dreams, or at least I used to be able to control them. But for all that control, I can't visit her dreams. I can't float alongside her.

Laying on my side, propped up on my elbow, I close my eyes. I relax... as much as I can while lying on my side, propped up by my elbow. I see white – white like the sheet but with depth, white that whips into the eyes. I take a few steps forward. A figure emerges from the white. It is a snow woman with fake breasts... either ice or snow implants. I'm snow doctor. Jake once asked me, "What's the difference between a snowman and a snow woman?" I gave up. He told me, "Snowballs." I take a few more steps forward, past her. The blizzard sucks me in like a vanilla milkshake in reverse; whipped cream whipping all around. In front of me is a five foot tall milkshake. Unbelievable. Trying to lift it with both hands, snow shakes free to reveal one of the shrubs that Al pruned last summer when I moved in. A door opens just past the masquerading bush. From the warm yellow light, Hope looks out at me and laughs, "What are you doing? Get in here!" I follow her inside. Setting down a bag, I pull down my hood, tug off my gloves, take off my outer coat, take off my hat, unwind my scarf, untie and pull off my boots, take off my inner down coat, and climb out of my sweater. Unencumbered, Hope hugs and kisses me. Hope is making snowmen out of cotton balls and glue with a marker and construction paper for her class. She's wearing her down slippers that leave a trail of little floating white feathers wherever she goes. I sit down by the coffee table to help her make the snowmen. My hands are numb. On TV a crowd applauds a figure skater. From high in the stands, three people use a giant slingshot to shoot teddy bears and flowers to the ice skater way down below on the ice. A teddy bear, that didn't quite make it, is plastered to the back of a lower camera operator.

The refrigerator drops crushed iceberg into my glass. Water splashes around the ice in a clockwise ice water swirl.

"Hey," Hope shakes me. I open my eyes. "You're freezing. Take some of the covers." A pair of my fingers slide across Hope's upper chest. They stop, turn, and push off to skate figures across her crystal soft skin. One finger is kicked back, out, and then up, and the other finger continues across Hope's rink. They draw circles and eights and stop at the point of an ice cream cone. The fingers sit to change footwear, to make the slow climb up Hope's breast. The two fingers careen down one breast and ski up the next. They almost take a seat on a tree stump. "Okay, now you're having too much fun," she says, covering the slopes and the rink and sharing her covers with me. She snuggles up to me. Her smile eases, as she drifts back across her pond of sleep, breathing her breaths like soft kisses.

"I heard about the crash." The words from the caller seeking improved mobility haunt me. The words have been whispers in my head ever since that dream. "I heard about the crash," she said. AutoDrive crashed. Well, that's one way to kill the dream. A spectacular crash. She didn't say it was spectacular, but a spectacular crash would be a masterful rendering titled, "I Told You It Wasn't Ready." I could be proud of such a crash. It would earn a prominent location on my resume. Unless... What if people die? Pedestrians? People in other cars? On-lookers? All it would take is one wrong turn. I have to know what will happen. I'll have to be there. I snuggle up to Hope. I relax.

Through eerie light, I cross the living room and open the front door. Outside is green. The sky is a cloudy green. Wild westwardly winds whip wide holes in the trees. Hope, her roommates, and Ray cluster up behind me. The yard and street are speckled with debris. I step out, and the others follow. "Stay inside," I tell them.

"Why?" Faith asks. "Are you storm-proof?"

"No, I'm dreaming this."

"You aren't dreaming this. We are all actually here."

"I am dreaming this. Would you please go inside?" Several items drop in the street as if a cloud had second thoughts about keeping them. They drag me back inside, while I'm trying to read my watch. This was supposed to be the test drive of AutoDrive. I landed almost a week early. I open my eyes.

There is a special frustration reserved for things that used to work but no longer work. This is the frustration of dead batteries and of power outages, of lawn mowers and of snow blowers, of software re-visions, of tilted sensors, of physical therapy, and of damned arthritis. Clarence told me all about the damned arthritis. Things that you have always been able to do either can't be done or can only be done through great pain. This is also a great pain. My pointed perception isn't working. It's frustrating. I can't navigate in time, and I can't control how long I stop. And what no one knows is that I don't know how I could do these things, so I don't know what I have to do to fix it. It just happened. I just did it. I didn't think about it. It wasn't a step A, step B, step C sort of thing. I don't know a logical sequence of events. It was a visu-alizing sort of thing. I just let it happen, almost like settling in at a movie theater and saying, "Okay, dazzle me!" Except that first I had to know which of the 24 theater doors to go into, and it's not like they are ad-equately titled. Sometimes you don't know what you are going to get. Certainly a movie rating system that lumps sex in with violence doesn't help much. Which is it? Violent sex? Or sexual violence? The course in Advanced Motion Picture Makers Decisions consists of being given a coin that says violent sex on one side and sexual violence on the other.

Pointed perception doesn't have titles or ratings or descriptions or coins. It just happens. I am just a vehicle for the dreams... or the other way around. Probably the other way around. The dreams are a vehicle for me. Taking me places I never–

I didn't invent the vehicle. I stumbled upon it. And since I wasn't taught how to properly use it, I figured it out myself. Figuring out stuff for yourself can mean you do things worse than others. It can also mean you do things better than others, or at least different from others. Teaching something is almost the antithesis of inventiveness. When something is taught, the focus is learning the known. When something is invented, the focus is learning the unknown. I didn't invent the possibilities in pointed perception any more than I could invent the possibilities in the rest of life. I am just along for the ride.

Maybe that's what life is all about. Here it goes again. Existential resonances. All of life explained in the middle of the night. Life is riding along in God's car. We can navigate, but we aren't in the driver's seat.

My ride is here.

When pointed perception happened, somehow I knew where to go, but maybe I wasn't navigating so much as enjoying the view. Usually the fact that I had, or at least remembered, the pointed perception meant there was some significance. Lately my dreams have been a hodge-podge of the weird and the mun-dane. I don't know how it used to work. I don't know why it worked. It just worked. I did not concentrate. I didn't have to really think about it, which is good, because I'm not that smart. Or if I was, I'm not that smart anymore. Maybe this is what it felt like for Erix.

Maybe something is going to happen in the future that is tearing me apart. It has started by tearing pointed perception apart. Maybe this is the first sign. Maybe something has already happened to me that is changing how I look at things. Or maybe God isn't listening to my directions.

"Eh hem," Hope says. "You're drumming on me."

"Was I? I'm sorry. I didn't mean to wake you."

"What time is it?"

I look for my clock. "What the–?" It's buried in a pile of little red hearts, resting gently like settled helium balloons. I stretch my arm over and shake loose my clock. "It's 2:51." Setting the clock back on its bed of hearts, I look around for Ray. He slapped me the last time it was 2:51.

"Get some sleep."

I salute her with my free hand. "Aye-aye, Captain." Hope grabs my saluting hand and holds it in hers. That's when my other elbow decides to cramp up.

"I– I just have to sleep. I'm not trying to boss you around."

"I'm teasing you. Sweet dreams," I tell her as I settle on my side, lying uncomfortably on the arm that had propped me up. As soon as I can, I'll have to try to find out about whether the test drive of AutoDrive will hurt anyone. Hope is kissing air again. She's pulling on my hand; it must be anchoring her drift. Who's anchoring whom? Maybe she is God's trade-off. I get Hope, and He doesn't have to listen to my passenger seat driving.

I close my eyes. I relax as well as I can while laying on my arm.

Ick. What foul mucus does drip from my nose? What foul mucus doth spring from my nostrils? Doth the spring, nay, the river of phlegm ever cease its torrential flow? And what crusty shell hardens o'er lips once soft and succulent, I wonder in Shakespearean tones. I'm sick. Whenever I'm sick, I go Shakespearean. For me, it's not just stuffy; it's stuffed up. This is an unpleasant aberration of my usually uncluttered sinuses. I look in the mirror, and gasp at the hideous apparition that reflects revoltingly.

Rolling off the futon for a tissue, the last two escape the box together. Is this the end of the tissues? This box has struggled valiantly to sop up the nostril river over the past week. I turn to look at a car calender displaying January's frosty blue Pegasus Coup. The tissues fought my cold or flu, knowing that they would die trying. They gave their lives in a desperate attempt to dry me out. It will not be in vain.

I drop the tissue box to the floor and kick it out of my room. I kick it down the hall and through the living room, where the TV has been left on. An archaeologist uncovers the earliest known snot rag. Wow, they're really digging for it now. Kicking the box through the room, it batters up against the wall. I open the door to the basement, side-kick it into range, and kick it downstairs into the recycling. Thump. Thumpity-thump-thump. Thump. I shut the door.

These last two tissues will inspire me to find a way to increase recycling. Not recycling used tissues, that's disgusting. Recycling the phlegm itself! I turn off the TV. There must be an industrial application for phlegm. An adhesive, a lubricant, a pavement? Respiratory mucosa will be working overtime! Companies will no longer pay sick employees, because sick people will be paid by American Mucus. American Mucus will find phlegmatic opportunities that will put plastics to shame. "What would we do without mucus in our everyday lives? Yes, American Mucus is working for you at home, at work, and in your leisure time... making the world a little stickier, a little slipperier, and just a little slimier!"

Until I start up American Mucus, I'll have to use these last two tissues. Wow! They are soft! Comforting...

"Cut it out."

I open my eyes. I'm rubbing Hope's hair under my nose. "Sorry." I release her hair and lean back, wondering what she's going to say next about my using her hair like a tissue. Cy would have a comeback right about... now.

Nothing. I listen. I hear the slowing of her breath, breath after breath. The clock is ticking. I hear my breathing, and the steady beating of my heart. I listen intently. Hope's heartbeat is strong yet soft and steady. A car races down a street. A distant dog barks. I listen with greater concentration than I ever have before. A bedspring adjusts somewhere in the house. A mouse chews a sunflower seed. Other cars and a motorcycle are still farther way, or else they are mouse-sized and are much closer.

I use Hope's hair like a tissue, and all she says is, "Cut it out." Cy started arguments with me over far less. I don't think I really understand Hope. She seems to take everything I dish out and ask for more. Or she tells me to stop. But that's it.

If people really are the sum of their experiences, their thoughts, what has occurred to them, and their decisions, then Hope really is a product of her tortuous brothers. What I don't understand is how she has kept such a positive attitude.

Unless it's all a charade. Maybe she is the world's greatest actress, playing the part of the idealized optimist. It's an elaborate plot, a ruse to... uh... what would be the point?!? To get Ray and I to move in? I know! Maybe she has been on a quest for the long lost original guitar of Melanie. Maybe she has searched the world over, explored ancient tombs and army bases, scoured museums and auction houses, watched her step through junkyards, and even checked the Internet on a desperate quest for the missing guitar. Maybe her feigned optimism was just the tactic needed to discover its secret hiding spot.

However if that were true, why would she still be playing the part?

If Hope wanted the guitar, all she'd have to do is ask. I don't think she knows what to do with it any more than I know what to do with it. Sometimes the best decision is to wait on things and let time go by. Hope sighs.

Dogs love her. Cats roll down at her feet. Not a single friend of mine has had anything bad to say about her. Ray and Jake have definitely complimented her. And Cy and Tom and Sharon each seem to have promoted our relationship. She already knows Christie from school, which is a strange coincidence, because Christie didn't live in Minnesota for long. She's certainly generous, letting Ray and I live here rent free. She volunteers at the nursing home. She teaches kids, even though she doesn't need the money. She's kind. She's warm. She's sweet. I think I've fallen in love with a genuinely nice person.

And she's beautiful unless she's angry.

"Today-today-today, I consider myself-self-self... the luckiest person on the face of the Earth-Earth-Earth." As the echoing thought fades to silence, I lean back against the wall and check my watch. Hope moves to hold my shoulder. I adjust her horizontal hold. I close my eyes, thinking about the AutoDrive crash. Propped halfway up the wall, I relax.

I am driving a car that isn't mine. Snow is falling sideways. The wind is defying gravity. I stop at a crusty white octagon, you know, the size and shape of a stop sign. The secret to winter driving in Minnesota is that it isn't that bad. The travel books don't seem to mention that sidewalk salt is one of our forms of currency, so it's readily available. Also the books don't mention that it's better to drive on snow than ice. Snow has traction. Ice does not. So the states in the middle of the country that hover around freezing all winter have it worse than Minnesota. They have ice. Minnesota has snow. And the snow doesn't really slow Minnesota. The cities spend money on efficient plowing systems. Rarely does everything shut down due to the weather, only once or twice a decade, despite all the prayers of school children.

It's quiet... almost too quiet. Where am I going?

Strangely, I'm in the driver's seat. I'm the one doing the driving, but I'm just visiting. My future self isn't thinking a single thing. A sports-utility truck ahead slides sideways and then spins 300 degrees.

It is a few degrees short of a donut. A parked car slows it down and bounces the monster truck back into play. The panicked driver is ricocheted toward the parked cars on my side of the road. Snow isn't dangerous. Other drivers are dangerous. My car dances around the truck by taking a path that crosses where it's already been, while the truck embeds itself into, onto, and under two more parked cars. If the driver had been driving a car, they would've only hit one car. Then again, if the driver had actually been driving the truck in a careful, cautious manner, the day would've presented less property damage and uncontrolled helplessness.

I should talk. I don't even know where I'm going.

At least I'm not sick. I open my eyes. Yellow sunshine with a greenish tint pours through my windows in downward diagonal rays. Hope is gone. She must have taken all my clock's little hearts with her. I haven't a clue what day today is. My watch says it's a Wednesday in the middle of August.

My pointed perception is working on winter for some reason. First I was in the front yard in a blizzard, then I was in a storm... that was later this month, so it doesn't count. But then I was sick, and it was January, unless I just hadn't flipped the calendar. And then we played the snow traffic game. None of those dreams got me any closer to knowing about the AutoDrive accident. Pointed perception has become like throwing darts blindfolded in a room full of cats.

I'm changing.

In the kitchen, I flip a coin to decide whether to have breakfast or lunch since it's after noon. Breakfast it is. Using two bowls for my Major Munch cereal, I separate the majors from the munches. Still hungry after my cereal, I flip the coin again. Lunch it is. I microwave leftover corn and vegetarian refried beans on a flour tortilla with some cilantro. If I don't buy the vegetarian refried beans, lard will be a main ingredient. Lard shouldn't be a main ingredient of food, Ray or no Ray. I roll up the tortilla and nuke it for half a minute more. That's when Ray comes in.

He looks exhausted, but he's smiling at me. "Thanks for the tip about Kelly and Chuckles. I did what you said." He washes a carrot and munches on it without cutting it. "They were just starting to pour the footings of a foundation for the pedestal. They've already removed what they started." Crunch. The carrot's green bush sways like a pompom. "They've already started work in a spot which should have great summer sun. There aren't that many spots with sun, in a city park surrounded on all sides with buildings." Crunch.

I nod, chewing on my burrito.

"They can't figure out how I knew, and I had no obligation to tell them. It worked out really well." Crunch.

"You're not going to eat your carrot greens, are you?"

"No. I'll leave them for you."

"Thanks."

Ray sits down. "I've been getting tons of e-mails about Lefty's experiment on you." Crunch. It couldn't actually be tons. E-mails don't weigh anything. "People are worried about the experiment harming you. But they are also worried about the public finding out about private things."

"Like?"

"Like pointed perception. Like the way people act. Would people see me eating a carrot right now?"

"No. It isn't video. It's a transcript, so what they'd get is a transcript of your eating a carrot."

Ray grins, "Crunch-crunch-crunch?"

"Something like that."

Ray is still grinning. He stops. "I might be eating in my room until this thing blows over."

"Suit yourself."

Ray gets up to hibernate for the rest of the summer. He stops. "There was something else. I'm not sure, but I think there was a reference to something that sounded like the SETI Punking. Did you have anything to do with that?"

How do I answer this? "No, not directly."

Ray's carrot end and bush drop to the floor. His chin follows. "Not directly?!? You were indirectly involved in the Punking of the Century?!?"

Running off to become a hermit is looking better and better. "Calm down."

Ray starts syllables of many words, only to stop himself each time. He's speaking in tongues. He recovers enough to ask, "You– how?"

I set my burrito down. "It was either a contact of an acquaintance of an acquaintance, or there was a fourth person involved. Either way, one day while I was at the university, someone at another school, not even in this state, accidentally got in contact with a lost NASA probe. This someone altered its communication frequency, uploaded some machine code, and modified the probe's position to boost its signal strength. They wanted to double-check their telemetry formula and went through people to contact a particular engineering student." I thump my chest with my thumb. "Since I was talking to astronomy people, I start spouting off about how we should solve our world's problems before caring about or trying to contact other worlds. I theorized that one day SETI will contact another world, and the other world would respond back that they haven't the time to talk. They are trying to solve their world's problems: enough food, clean methane to breathe, that sort of thing. Then they ask how we solved all our world's problems." I look at Ray's floored carrot and chin and look back up at him. "Apparently someone was taking notes. The next thing I know, I'm hearing that SETI has successfully contacted life outside our solar system. Then we hear that it is intelligent life. Next the tonal language code is broken. Of course it was broken; it was meant to be broken. Then they are asking how we solved all our world's problems. So I am freaking out. I figure this has to be related to pointed perception. Then the signal turns out to be a fake; it's coming from one of our own probes."

"So you know who did it?"

"I know someone who knows someone who was involved, yes."

"But it was your idea!"

"I didn't suggest it, if that's what you're saying. I'm innocent."

"Right. Innocent, but not letting anyone know who was involved and how you were involved." I nod. Ray picks up his chin, brushes it off, and reattaches it. "Why didn't you ever tell me about this?"

"You never asked."

He goes through a dozen different expressions before picking an intensely-questioning look, "What else haven't you told me?"

"Lots of stuff. Pull up a chair." He sits down. The sucker. "First, the Earth cooled. Then the dinosaurs came! But they were too fat and died and turned into oil!" He nods.

"If I need any other old movie quotes, I'll ask you." Ray pitches the carrot bush and leaves.

A spice rack could provide the Spice Of The Day for a month's worth of burritos like this one. One spice dominates each burrito, maybe up to three spices, but no more. More than three herbs and spices means that dominant spices overpower lesser spices. It is the nature of spices. It is the way of things. What would really be ridiculous would be a burrito with 11 herbs and spices. Nothing needs 11 herbs and spices. That's like sanding and salting a street in summer.

"I remembered what I was going to say," says Ray, coming back in as I finish my cilantro burrito. Cilantro is (drum roll) the Spice Of The Day! "Now that you've talked about, and thought about, the SETI Punking, you know it's going to be part of Lefty's experiment. And did you name him too? Lefty isn't his real name."

"No, someone else did. His name is Melvin."

"Everyone is going to know that you were involved in the SETI Punking."

"I think the statute has run out on people running around about Martians."

"Has it?"

"I don't know." Technically cilantro isn't a spice so much as it's an herb.

"My point is that between the SETI Punking and pointed perception, you might want to reconsider your involvement in Lefty's memory experiment. Where do you get your optimism?" Right now I get it from Hope. "From the messages, I'm not sure you want to do this."

"Because..."

"Because people will find out private stuff about you."

"And then what?"

"They might try to take advantage of that information."

"How?"

"They could, I don't know, try to make you tell the future."

I laugh. "Great. Then they would know the Spice Of The Day ahead of time? I can't imagine the repercussions."

"Seriously. What if they kidnapped Hope?"

"The combined forces of her brothers would probably doom any kidnappers."

"Who are her brothers?"

"Let's just say that they had a history of torturing Hope and probably wouldn't want to see any new competition."

"You don't see a problem with getting involved in Lefty's experiment?"

"Not unless it wipes out my short-term memories. That would tick off Hope."

"But why do it?"

I lean back and smile. "Remember all the times we've talked about the Lactating Woman, Kelly. We talked out the structure, the appearance, your self doubts... Why did I do that? What's my involvement? It's the same with Lefty. He's my friend. I would be offering him options and alternatives, if I had any good options or alternatives to offer. I'm not sure I'm going to get anything good out of it, but that's not why I do things. You should know that. Whenever I meet strangers, and often with people who should know me, they try to figure out, 'What's he getting out of this?' And if you watch them long enough, you can see their heads are about to explode, because they can't figure it out. They can't figure me out."

"When I first started rooming with you, I was like that."

"My experiences are riddled with funny looks from people who are trying to fit the concept of me into their understanding of the world. Their faces become more and more contorted as they use their cheeks to wedge me into their conceptions."

"I can picture that in a comic book format."

"Usually people give up quickly, kick me out of their heads, and later wonder why everyone they know behaves the same as everyone else." Ray grabs a sheet of paper and struggles with an ordinary pen as he sketches what I described. "Maybe the memory experiment will help people to understand me better. Maybe it will fuel further misunderstandings. Whole groups of people will be making funny faces at me, trying to conceptually push me with their cheeks to fit me into their understanding of the world." Ray is putting sketches into boxes. "Ultimately, I'm doing it for Lefty."

Ray continues his sketching. "Here. Did you see Dan Ryan's e-mail?" He taps the screen and hands me his computer. "He sent me a copy to make sure you get it." Dan's message booms:

HEY RICKY!

I'M ON NORTH BEACH WATCHING THE LAKE MICHIGAN WAVES CATCHING UP ON SOME MAIL!

I HEARD FROM CY AND THE OTHERS ABOUT LEFTY'S MEMORY TEST! SOUNDS WEIRD ENOUGH! EVERYONE IS WORRIED ABOUT TALKING TO YOU AND BEING RECORDED IN THE TEST! I FIGURED HOW COULD IT RECORD AN E-MAIL MESSAGE?!? AND IF IT CAN WHO CARES?!?

HEARD ABOUT YOUR JOB AND YOUR MOVE! THE MOVE IS GOOD! HOPE IS GREAT!

LET ME KNOW IF YOU NEED ANYTHING!

DON'T BE A STRANGER!

DON'T EVER CHANGE AND IF YOU DO, DON'T FORGET YOUR CAR!

DAN

I lean back. Ray spins the computer his way and punches something up. "Will sent around a copy of the AutoDrive commercial." He spins it my way.

From a consumer standpoint, the 30 second ad says little. From an engineering standpoint, the ad says nothing. The ad is sponsored by Double Bubble, so it has a commercial within a commercial. That's called Advertising Layering. Carl's monotone reading, over cheesy graphics, is less than impressive. I conduct a pH test of my attitude for bitterness. Mmm, lemony.

Ray stops sketching, looks at the clock, grabs his drawings, and says, "Got to go."

"I'm done with this, thanks." I hand him his computer. Ray leaves.

I look at the dishwasher. Getting up and looking closely at the options, the dishwasher wants to know how dirty the dishes are, how fragile the dishes are, and whether they contain any known bio-hazards. Looking inside, I reverse engineer some of the exterior options. I stop myself before I dismantle the dishwasher. These dishes are not worth its consideration. Choosing to do the dishes by hand, I dig out a drain rack for drying the dishes, and I wonder what I should do today. That thought is immediately replaced with the idea that I need to find out what is going to happen in the AutoDrive test. If it does hurt or kill someone, I will feel responsible, almost as if I pushed the car into them. It wouldn't have the same level of deliberateness, but still, it's my – or it was my responsibility. I have an ethical obligation to non-maleficence, the ethical duty to prevent my invention from injuring others. I take that responsibility very seriously.

How do I aim pointed perception? It's as if I'm aiming at something that isn't there. Maybe it never happened. Maybe that's why I can't find it. The blind woman said she saw, no, heard about the crash. It did happen. Or it will happen. But maybe now it's not going to happen. Maybe things have changed. Or maybe it's just me. It's not that the test of AutoDrive isn't going to happen; it's that pointed perception isn't doing what it's supposed to, what it's done for so long.

Trumpets blare in my room and the doorbell rings. The door is closer. I answer it.

"Hi," Hope kisses me.

"You know, you don't have to use the bell. My house really is your house."

"I left the downstairs key upstairs. Isn't that your phone?"

"Yes," I dash after it. "Acapella's Pizza. The Spice Of The Day is cilantro. How can I help you?"

"I'd like one cilantro pizza, hold the cilantro. And I'd like a small Double Bubble in a large cup, and fill it up the rest of the way," Cy orders.

"Could you hold?"

"Yes... how realistic," she says, as I search for the hold button and press it.

"It's Cy. Do you want me to call her back?"

"No," Hope sighs. "I'll get changed and come back down, okay?"

"Okay." I watch her go. "Hello Cy? What's up?"

"Do you want to talk about the Yolanda letter?"

"Yes. What have you got?" I ask, grabbing a tablet and pen.

"Dear Yolanda, Attending "Social Climbers" and meeting you earlier this month was an excellent part of my weekend with my friends at Round Lake. It was amazing that you could pick me out of the crowd and recognize me from the picture with Melanie. New paragraph."

"Does it say 'new paragraph' or did you just start a new paragraph?"

"Don't get smart. Where was I? Your letter tells me about a very thoughtful and serious person. You are bold on stage but personally shy. Shakespeare said–"

"I'm not going to quote Shakespeare."

"Just let me read this okay?" Cy mutters something and then continues, "Shakespeare said, 'All the world is a stage,' but it is more than a stage. It is time to be the real Yolanda and the brave Yolanda and to make a difference. You are special, and you can make a difference. Your friends can help you, like the friend you mentioned in your letter, Edina. She can help you, just like I turned to my friends for help writing this letter. Be brave and be bold. Your friend, Ricky."

Hope comes back downstairs with a jean jacket. I hand her the tablet. I fake cry, "It's... it's beautiful, the way you quoted Shakespeare. It was so unexpected when writing for the guy who can't string two words together. It's really, really great." I sob and sniff loudly. Hope snatches the phone away.

"Ignore him," Hope tells Cy, "I just read what you wrote. This should represent him." I don't know what Cy says, but Hope hands the phone back to me.

"Have you been getting your e-mail?"

"Ray showed me one from Dan."

"What about the rest?"

"No. I haven't seen any others. I was thinking of writing an e-mail response program that randomly strings reactionary sentences together."

"Please read your e-mail, otherwise you won't know about the surprise party for Ruth."

"What surprise party for Ruth?"

"Exactly."

"Oh. Hope is motioning that she knows about it. She'll tell me."

"Read your e-mail!" We say good-bye. I smile at Hope for her assistance in frustrating Cy. If you can't frustrate your friends, who can you frustrate?

"Do you want to go for a walk?" Hope asks. As my tongue starts to fall from my mouth, regret washes over her face. "I have to find a better way of saying that." I pant and threaten to wash the regret off her face with my tongue.

"Woof." I scamper off for better shorts, shoes, keys, phone, and wallet. I scamper back and bark again. Outside I realize that I haven't been out for days. Most dogs can't last that long.

As we walk I tell Hope, "A guy brings his dog into a bar. Puts the dog on the bar. He says that he's got a hundred dollars that says this is a talking dog. The curmudgeonly bartender has seen every trick in the book and says that he'll take the bet. The guy asks the dog, 'What do you call the thing that is over us and keeps the rain out?' The dog says, 'Roof.' The bartender says the bet is off and is rolling up his sleeves to throw the pair out. The guy says, 'Wait. I'll ask him another question. Double or nothing.' The bartender agrees. The guy asks the dog, 'Who was the greatest baseball player of all time?' The dog scratches behind its ear and softly mutters, 'Ruth.' The bartender throws them both out. On the pavement in front of the bar, the dogs looks at his owner, shrugs, and asks, 'DiMaggio?'"

Hope laughs a little and charmingly dimples, "I wondered where that was going." We walk farther quietly with a gentle afternoon breeze at our side, crossing under some tall bushes. Something small jumps onto Hope's back and then off and we turn to watch a gray squirrel run away, a light rust racing stripe on it's back.

"Are you okay?" I ask her.

"Uh, yeah, I think so. I'm glad I was wearing this," Hope says, taking off her jean jacket. Then she looks up for any more squirrels. "Could you check my back?" I lift her shirt and look around at her back. "Did it break the skin?"

"No, but I can't see your shoulders." Hope fully lifts her shirt up. "No. We should probably check again inside later. Let me know if you start foaming at the mouth before we kiss or anything." Hope pulls down her shirt and puts her jacket back on. "Nature loves you," I tell her. "That squirrel fell for you."

"When I'm in a lake, fish bite me. Geese chase me. Now this squirrel uses me as a ladder? Yes, nature adores me," she agrees.

A few houses away, the black and gray tabby cat that swallowed the chainsaw pounces out of some bushes and trots up to walk in front of us in its fuzzy white pajama pants. We stop and it dashes back to step between us and around us, before flopping down on the sidewalk, practically screaming, "Pet me!" Hope squats down and pets the purring tabby.

"I need to tell you some things."

"Me or the cat?" I ask.

"Mostly you. I called Jake."

"Why?"

"To straighten things out between you."

I stare at the cat. It looks back at me, blinks and squints. "Please don't do that."

"You said I was Captain."

The cat turns to watch Hope pet it as if to say, "Right there. That's the spot. I will cherish this moment forever."

"You also told Cy that she could talk to Jake."

"Cy knows Jake. Yes, I asked her to talk to Jake. I didn't ask you to talk to him. My friends, even Jake, are my business. Your friends are your business. I'm not trying to figure out what Nicole is thinking; that's your department. I'm sorry if being Captain made you feel like you had to handle things. I relieve you of command."

Hope gets up, "I stand relieved."

The cat is looking around, "What just happened?"

"Do you agree that we each handle problems with our own friends unless asked?"

"Yes."

Standing between us, the cat is looking up and is desperate to understand what our talk has to do with it getting petted.

"What did Jake say?"

Hope pats the cat one last pat and steps us away. "You can't do that," Hope says playfully. "You can't disagree with my talking to Jake and want to know what was said. It can't be dismissed and be important. That's hypocritical."

"We're being followed by someone short and furry."

"Go home."

"I don't think it's hypocritical. We only just agreed to not interfere in the problems with friends. You didn't know how I would feel. That's understandable. Time has a way of making a hypocrisy out of each moment. A boy says he can't sit still. Decades later, sitting still is what he does best. One says, 'I can't do...' something. Years later or years earlier it was or will be easy. And the same is true for what you like–"

Hope is shaking fur off her hand as she walks. "I'll try to use that with my class. 'Fong, imagine you are an old man.' Knowing him, he'd act like he's hard of hearing. He'd bend forward and slowly fall off his chair. Okay, so I called Jake today. He was very cordial to me."

"Cordial? Jake? That's weird."

"I know! So I asked him what got into him last weekend. I told him that you trusted him with the information about the job possibility and that he betrayed that trust."

"Yeah? What did he say?"

"He said, 'I know it seems that way, but I'm his friend, and what I did was done as his friend.'"

"He said that?!?" I stop in front of a house that is way too large to house a close family.

"Yes."

"I don't get it." The house is orange brick with white columns. It has two full floors and dormers on the third floor and at least two chimneys. It looks strong without looking cozy or inviting. "How can he think that keeping me unemployed is helpful? Was he hit on the head when we were moving stuff last weekend? Maybe he got pelted too hard with a blueberry at Tom's cabin?"

"No–"

"That's right, he wasn't in the blueberry fight." I run my hand along a yellow picket fence. "Was there anything else?"

"No. He just asked how we were doing and getting along in the same house."

"That's thoughtful," I choke on the word thoughtful, "of Jake." I shake it off.

"I also talked to my mom. She's still calling me Loverducks. She wants to meet you."

"That's nice," I look at Hope, "isn't it?"

"Sure. Nice. Like Jake is nice."

"Oh."

"My mom is a force of nature."

"Water... glacier... and your mom?"

"Right. Water, fire, and Pandora. Do you have any plans for next Wednesday?"

I get out my phone and scroll to the calendar. It's clear. "Nope, nothing."

"Are you using that now?"

"No."

Hope giggles, sunlight sparkling across her face. The sun appears, shining from across Lake Weago. We step out onto the lake, walking above it several feet on a six foot wide wooden dock. At the end of the dock, two boys stand straddling their bikes. One of them asks a guy, "Are you fishing?"

The man doesn't turn from looking out at the lake. He says, "No, I'm drowning worms."

The sunlight hops from ripple to ripple in Lake Weago. I kiss Hope.

"They're kissing," I hear from behind me.

I stop kissing Hope. "No, she was bitten on the lips, and I'm sucking the poison out." Hope nudges me, and I resume my sucking. I'm hooked. Trumpets sound. I answer them, "Acapella's Pizza, tonight's special is carp and drowned worms, how can I help you?"

"Hey, you sound like you're in a good mood!" Wendy responds.

"Sure, why not?" Sunlight leaps across ripples, keeping alternate ripples in the dark. Hope puts her arm around me.

"We were wondering if you could help us... if you might remember something about the fifth navigational recognition section of the program. We can't find the seventh UVCCD."

"The seventh UV was originally a composite CCD. It's not in the fifth NAV recognition section. It's identified in the other-forward sensors in the fourth NAV inputs. Do a search on 748-851."

Wendy says muffled, "He says search on 748-851. He says it's in the fourth section because it was originally a composite sensor." She clearly says, "Scott's doing it."

"Why are you identifying specific sensors? There shouldn't be– It's none of my business."

"One step forward, two steps back. He found it. Thank you. You're a lifesaver."

"You're welcome. I hope you can go home soon."

"Home? Where's that?"

"I'll let you go."

"Thanks again."

"Bye." I pocket the phone. We are alone on the lake. The man, the boys, the bikes, the worms have all left. The sun is setting. Street lamps make independent decisions to light up. Silhouette joggers jog between silhouette trees. It's a quarter to dusk.

Lifesaver? I'm trying to be a lifesaver, if I can figure out my dreams. Hope interrupts my third replay of the conversation with Wendy. "Was that Wendy?" I nod. "Does she call a lot?"

"No, that was the first time since I was fired." The fenced-in dog has spotted and properly identified Hope and eagerly awaits her approach with puppy-like impatience. His ears hang down and his tail wags. Hope reaches over and pets him, while his tongue washes her hand.

"You were nice to help her."

"It's weird. I had to. I couldn't do anything else." Hope pats my back. "She's my friend. And AutoDrive is..." The dog is asking if we can stay. I reach in, and let him smell my hand of burrito and Major Munch cereal and tabby, with just a hint of soggy worms. After he finishes cataloging the smells, I pet him. I say, "Ruth." He gives me this look, a look only a dog could give you, that says he knows the joke; it's been barked all over the neighborhood.

Hope breaks us up, and we continue home. "I am so hungry," she says. "What would you think of Lettuce Feed You?" From behind us the dog whimpers that he is available for dinner.

"Salad sounds good to me."

"Your calendar is clear, right?"

"Right, except for the party for Ruth, whenever that is."

"This Sunday," Hope smirks. "I read MY e-mail. It's a surprise party, so don't tell her."

"And Lefty's experiment, which is a week from tomorrow. And your mom is a week from today. Are we doing lunch or dinner or what?"

"I was thinking dinner."

"Do you want me to make it?"

"What would you make?"

"Lemon dill pasta."

"That sounds... weird and kind of good right now."

"It takes 30 to 40 minutes to make."

"I can't wait that long. I'm hungry now," Hope grips my hand with two fingers together. "So you want her to judge you and your cooking at the same time?" I smile with a dash of shrug.

People walk by, and we say hi. They don't respond. Instead, a woman says to the group, "The woman was drunk or on drugs when she saw her angel."

After they pass us, Hope fishes something out of her pocket. She slows us down under a streetlight to look at it. I ask what it is. She stuffs it back into her pocket. "A list."

"A list of what?"

"A list of things to talk to you about."

"Oh. Have we covered everything?" I ask, and she laughs.

29
Deals

Hope continues to laugh, "No. It's a long list. Are you remembering our plans for the weekend after Lefty's experiment?"

"No."

"Visiting Christie?"

"Oh. I remember you mentioned it, maybe Friday night at the apartment."

"Would you rather fly or drive?"

"To Chicago?"

"Right."

"I think I've dreamt it both ways."

"Good. Now pick."

"Driving is cheaper."

"Yes, but that wasn't the question."

I picture myself driving us and pointed perceptioning us into a ditch. Driving takes attention. "Let's fly. Wait. Why am I making this decision?"

"Because she's more your friend than my friend."

"Oh." Looking at the house as we approach it, I ask her, "Do you want to invite Ray and the girls out tonight or should it be just us?"

"Just us, until I have a chance to talk to you about Nicole." Hope steers us to my car. "You drive."

"You navigate." The Pony Express gives us a shaky start.

"Deal. Here's the deal with Nicole. Right. She doesn't want to jeopardize our relationship. She's not looking for a sexual relationship from you. She's not trying to come between us or split us up. Left. She looks up to you." There is an accident ahead. We work our way slowly around it. "She respects you, in a way that – right at the light – she has almost never been able to respect a man. Do you see the green sign over there on the left?"

"Yes."

"That's it. You care about her, right?"

"I'm not supposed to turn right to get over there? Just kidding. Yes, I care about her. Of course. So what am I supposed to do?"

"Only what's comfortable. Only what doesn't interfere with our relationship. Hugs. Reassurance. Um, not taking Faith's side in arguments."

"I'm not going to lie or hurt Faith to make Nicole feel better."

"That's understandable. I completely agree with that."

I park the Pony Express. "So we're saying no sex between Nicole and I, and we're saying no secrets between Nicole and I or anything else that would interfere in our relationship, right?"

"Correct."

"What do we do when we go to Chicago or something? Does Nicole come with?"

"No."

"What if you and I are sleeping together?"

"She– she isn't looking to cuddle up to you every night. Or at least I don't think she is. She just wants to be able to turn to you for occasional security."

"Oh. Then it's not that big of a deal." I get out of the car and help Hope with her door, partly for chivalry but mostly because it acts up.

"Really?"

"Really. You know what this sounds like? This sounds like a test Becky would dream up from a magazine." I get the restaurant door for her. "Hello, a table for two, please." We are escorted down a garden path to a table with too many leaves.

"I'm Leif, and I will be your waiter," a lanky Viking tells us. "Have you eaten at Lettuce Feed You before?"

"I have; he hasn't," Hope betrays me.

"Please take a fresh bowl every time you go to the bar. Only take what you will eat. The sink is to encourage you to wash your hands. Can I get you something to drink?" Leif asks before taking a breath.

"I'll have a watermelon water."

"Me too." Leif leaves. I look at Hope's smile.

"What you are talking about doing for Nicole is really special. You're great," she says.

The restaurant gets dark, except the salad bar area. "It's not what I'm talking about doing; it's what I'm talking about not doing." Thunder. The sound of rain is piped in through speakers all around us.

"This is kind of like how First Street Station jumps track every now and then," Hope observes.

"I can't be great for what I don't do. People are great for what they do, not what they don't do. I admit that failing to do things is what I am best at, especially when it comes to what matters."

"Why do you say that? Because of AutoDrive?"

Leif drops off the drinks. "You CAN go up to the bar any time," he spouts with attitude.

The salad bar stretches halfway into Wisconsin. I survey the options with a surveyor's scope on a yellow tripod. Lincoln would be proud. I visualize the salad recipe I want to create. I wash my hands, take a bowl, hand it to Hope, take a bowl, and begin to formulate dinner. A mist dampens my arm as I reach for the green stuff. Dark round green spinach leaves, deep purple cabbage, deep purple and green flowering kale, dark red tomato, black olive ringlets, pumpernickel croutons, and a burgundy salad dressing of some sort tops off the bowl. I look for Hope and catch her watching me instead of making dinner. "Do you want some help?" I offer.

"No, you can go back to the table if you want." I'm not going to acknowledge that. I throw her suggestion onto a mental pile of junk mail and advertising that threatens to immobilize my eyes. If I am ever able to forget anything, this monstrous pile of wasted attention will be the first to go. Hope doesn't seem concerned what goes into her bowl. I think she absently added a decorative bunch of rubber grapes on plastic stems. On the way back to the table we stop for a kid in a rabbit costume to hop by. I know about a black cat crossing your path, but I have no idea of the ramifications of a kid in a white rabbit costume.

"What do you mean, failing to do things is what you are best at?"

"Just what I said." I toss my salad. It goes everywhere.

"What have you failed at?" she asks, as I write a postcard to India asking for part of my salad back. Technically my salad didn't go everywhere. One cherry tomato bounced out, rolled down the table and landed into the hopping path of a rabbit.

"Do you want a list?"

"Sure, give me a list."

"I'm not going to give you a list."

"This is important, isn't it? It's about you." She pauses. "You didn't fail AutoDrive. You didn't walk out on them; they walked out on you... Carl walked out on you. Besides AutoDrive, what do you think you've failed?"

I spin my spoon and wonder who needs a spoon at a salad restaurant. Maybe spoons come in handy for elaborate cherry tomato tossing acts. Maybe one of these larger groups is a juggling troop. "You heard at Tom's cabin. I tried to save Melanie's life."

Hope's wrinkled brow eases from determination to worry. She takes my hand in hers, "Sweetheart, you told her, and she went anyway, right? There was nothing more you could do. People make their own decisions."

Leif drops by and eyes our full salad bowls. "There is an extra charge for wasted food–"

"Back off, we're talking!" Hope roars at him. Leif withers and leaves, and Hope says softly to me, "You didn't fail Melanie." I try to acknowledge her words without accepting them. She's not buying it. She reads through the fourth grader in me. "I'm telling you. You didn't fail AutoDrive, and you didn't fail Melanie." This isn't helping. I retrieve my hand to eat. I chew on some kale; it's tougher than cabbage or spinach; it tastes like a dry grainy cabbage. Hope fishes the rubber grapes from her salad. "Did you put these in here? Wait. I recall adding grapes to the bowl..."

"You did."

"You didn't stop me?"

"Stop you? I would have done it, if I had thought of it. I've always thought it's odd to garnish real food with fake food. Give it to the next rabbit that hops by. Fake food for a fake rabbit." As we eat our rabbit food, I feel fur growing on my chin.

"Is there anything else that you were thinking about when you said you failed at things?"

"I don't want to talk about it."

Hope's eyes grow as wide as the eyes of a deer. Her mouth opens several times before words escape her lips. "You don't want to talk about it." She measures her words. She pulls her hair behind her ears. "So you're saying it's not important."

"I'm saying I don't want to talk about it."

"Oh."

A cloud lingers over our table while the rest of the restaurant brightens. The rabbits stay away. The waiters and vegetable stockers go out of their way to be out of our way. My salad tastes of vinegar and lemons and is hard to swallow. Hope excuses herself, and I watch her go.

This evening hasn't turned out well, and now I'm alone in my garden of eating. Picking at my salad and eating slowly, I stare at Hope's nearly untouched bowl with its rubber grapes on the side. A smear of dressing runs from the salad to the grapes. If I finish my salad before she gets back, she might not feel comfortable eating in front of me. The mist dripping down from our exclusive cloud, my exclusive cloud, is keeping my watermelon water glass full to the brim. It's keeping me soggy. I hope Hope will come back. Her purse is gone. I am alone in my puddle for one. How can I tell her that I–

"You look wet," Hope tells me, her face is flushed, and water drips from my hair. She uses a napkin to dry off her chair and her half of the table.

"I'm sorry about what I said."

Hope sits and crosses her arms. "All you said... you didn't really say anything... all you implied was that there are some things that you aren't comfortable talking with me about."

"That's not it," I tell her, and she waits for more. Patiently. What will she think of me? She watches me and waits without attitude, without arrogance, without anger... Her breathing isn't exactly slow... I don't know what I'm going to do. And that's what I'll say. "I don't know what I'm going to do."

She raises her eyebrows, looks sideways to a distant audience of rabbits, and looks back to me. Hardly uncrossing her arms, she leans in toward me and says, "You weren't talking about what you are going to do. You were talking about your supposed failures. But now you aren't saying anything. Are you ready to go?" I look at her salad bowl and nod, deciding against commenting on her appetite. She stands, and Leif drops in from nowhere.

"Here are your greens fees. The cashier will take your greenbacks up front."

Hope takes the bill and has some low words with Leif, the cashier, and the restaurant manager about our dinner shower. Okay, now she's angry. She leads me out. It is strange being out in a clear cool evening after the inside precipitation. I hold Hope's door for her. For an instant, she doesn't look at me. For an instant we're strangers again, hesitant and uncertain. What have I done? Can I stop an avalanche? Destruction is easy. Creating good stuff is tough. She turns and looks at me... gives me a slight smile... and climbs in my rust bucket. I shut the door after her. Once in, she says, "I have told you things and done things with you that I don't ordinarily say or do. You had us agree to share everything – everything important – with each other. We got you out of the low-rent apartment and into a very nice house. We just figured a way to help Nicole move forward in her life. And now you clam up?!?"

"I just need time."

Hope sits back briefly. "Is this something that threatens you or our relationship?"

"No."

"Then I'll wait for you," she says, like I'm going away or something. The Pony Express gives us another shaky start. "Can you find your way back?" I nod. Intermittent streetlights, some surviving dashboard lights, and headlight reflections keep us lit.

I want to be perfect for her. I want to be her everything. I want to be her white knight, her unbelievable snowman, but in truth, I can't be. Perfect is someone else, somewhere else. I have failed the people closest to me. That is my greatest secret. It makes everything else inconsequential... the Savior of the Midway business, the SETI Punking, even pointed perception is not as significant as how I have repeatedly let down people I loved. Somehow I'll have to figure out a way of telling Hope before she finds out about it through Lefty's memory test. We'll have more time together after summer school ends on Friday. "Two more days."

"What's that?" Hope asks. "Oh, yeah. It'll be nice."

"How long is the break?"

"Two weeks. We start back the day after Labor Day."

"Would you like to celebrate? Friday night?"

"What do you have in mind?" She's being tentative with me.

"Taking you out dancing."

"Dancing? Do you dance?" I nod. "I haven't been out dancing in a while. Where?"

"At Pow-Wows."

"Who do you know at Pow-Wows?"

"No one."

"We won't get in."

"Who are you? And what did you do to Hope and her optimism?" I roll down my window and yell out, "This woman is an impostor!" I roll back up my window. It gets stuck. I tap it, and roll it up the rest of the way.

"The one time I tried to get into Pow-Wows was with Becky and Nicole. Nicole got in. Becky and I could have gotten in if we had worn our most revealing outfits. Or if we had turned on the charm, but I didn't want to turn on the charm with those gorillas... no offense!"

"None taken."

"Are you sure you want to try to get in?" Hope asks excitedly.

"Yes."

"Can I invite the girls?"

"Sure."

"How are you going to get us in?"

"You'll see." I'll see too. I have no idea, but this might make it seem like I'm keeping secrets again, so I help her out. "You won't have to wear a bikini. And you won't have to flirt with any other gorilla."

"That's a relief. I'm a one gorilla girl."

"It's nice to see you smile."

"Watch the road, Sweetie."

I watch for potholes, but don't find any. In fact, I don't think I've seen a single pothole in this part of town. Maybe winter doesn't come here either. The Lake Weago neighborhood bought off winter?!?

My hair is still damp from Lettuce Feed You. They must have thought we'd grow if they watered us. We pass a church and a choir of angels sing. Hope answers her phone.

"Hi. Better. We're almost home. I'll come up. I'll– We'll talk later. Bye."

The thump of turning into the driveway turns off one of my headlights. If it had to happen, it couldn't have happened at a better time. I pull my car around back.

"I'll get your door." Leaving the single headlight on, I get her door for her, and she takes her purse and jacket. Then I try wiggling the headlamp bulb to see if it's a loose connection or not. It doesn't seem to be. Hey, look at me. I'm testing something on a car! How familiar! Just don't make me break out the duct tape. The problem with duct tape has two sides. On one side, duct tape would be the strongest thing on my car. It's strength and elasticity would escalate the process of pulling the Pony Express apart. The stickier issue is that duct tape has to attach to something. There wouldn't be anything strong enough to attach it to, except itself. A giant ball of duct tape is rolling down the road! Run for your life!

Hope has been waiting for me. "Is it all right if I make a stop upstairs and meet you downstairs?"

"Yes. That would be great!"

I am left staring at the car. Sometimes I wonder if more time has been spent staring at cars in wonder or disgust or in comprehension of its issues, than in driving the things. The car just sits there, as if it's comfortable just to have taken its people out to dinner and back without completely falling apart. I turn off the headlight and head in.

I get a glass of apple juice on ice. I snag a banana. I peel off the London, Paris, Rome, & Caracas stickers. Change my shirt and comb my hair.

Hope knocks on my doorframe and comes into my room with Nicole, who looks smaller somehow. "Hey. You and I talked, and we've talked. I figured the three of us should talk." Great. Let's involve Ray too. We'll need more chairs. Nicole is keeping her distance, her hands in the pockets of a baggy jersey. I don't know why she's keeping her distance, but knowing what's going on with her isn't my role. I'm still trying to understand myself.

"Okay." I stick a Caracas sticker to Hope. Nicole gets a Rome sticker on the shoulder of her jersey. "Pretty weird, huh?"

She's nuts if she thinks she's weird. "Weird? I'm sorry to say, I'm sad to report, I know nothing of that sort. No. I've cornered the market on weird. I have a monopoly on weird. You have a firm grasp on the handrail of normalcy."

I throw some pillows around the floor and dig out a deck of cards. Handing the deck to Nicole, I tell her, "It's your deal."

"What are we playing?"

"Hearts."

"How many cards?"

"All of them. There will be one extra one. That goes face down in the middle."

"I haven't played this in a long time."

"Do you know the rules?"

"Refresh my memory." I tell them the rules of Hearts. Hope reminds us, "We can only play a game or two. It is a school night."

"So we're passing four to our right, so you get mine and I get Hope's?"

"Right."

"Are you really going to get us into Pow-Wows?"

"That's my plan."

"Cool."

My more immediate plan is not to play to win. I pass three mid-range clubs to Hope, with a heart. Hope glances at me after seeing the cards I've given her. As they concentrate on the game and relax from the tension they brought down from upstairs, I look at Nicole and say, "We agreed that there will be no sex between us and no secrets from Hope. And I will continue to support you when I can with Faith. My door is always open to both of you. You don't need to knock, except when the door is closed, and it's always open to you." Nicole tries to crawl into her jersey, as we get back to the game. She wins. I ask her, "Did Hope tell you about the squirrel?"

"No."

Hope laughs, "We were walking along on the next block, and a squirrel jumped or fell from a bush, landed on my back, and ran away!"

"Wow," Nicole says, without being as impressed as Hope.

Playing another game of Hearts, Hope wins. She gets up. Nicole gets up. "We better go," Hope says. I reach out to Hope and kiss her. I call after Nicole to wish her a good night and wish the same to Hope.

I dig out my computer – no power. Ray lets me borrow his. I type up my letter to Yolanda and print it off. While I'm at it, I type up my resume and a cover letter. I send it to my phone. From my phone I send it to Common Communication by way of the Riverside Tower Property Management Group.

I need to decide on an outstanding present for Ruth.

One of the reasons I initially called Ray, "Ray," was that I already knew a Cameron, who is another optical engineer. I met Cameron in optical engineering classes at school. We were all expected to land jobs in optical imaging for digital still and video camera companies and labs. The instructors and professors assumed that's what we would do because that is what they would do. In the academic world they are isolated from actual occupational opportunities. The fact that I didn't go into an optical imaging job was very strange to them. And their assumptions were strange to me. Thinking about Yolanda, I wonder if acting classes are similar. You are taught how to talk to the back of someone's head, how to look past who you are talking to, and quick head turns, but do these lessons help the actors working in commercials or as extras, where talking and quick motion get you booted from the set? Maybe a more universal course would teach patience and preparation. Finding Cam's e-mail address, I send him a message asking about the latest-greatest, consumer-nearly-professional camera. Cameron sends me an immediate reply from Owatonna Opticals to hang on. Hang on? This isn't a phone. Well, it is a phone, but it's not like he has to put me on hold.

I address the letter to Yolanda. Ray is hunched over a drawing tablet when I ask if he would do a sketch on the envelope. His 20 second sketch is of a climber hanging on to a mountain with a pickax.

Another message from Cameron says, "Howdy, long time no see. Your timing is good. We are looking for testing and advice on a new travel-free camera. We've all seen your ad for AutoDrive and are ready to buy one. Send me your address, and I'll ship it off tomorrow."

I reply with the address and ask, "What degree of testing and advice are you looking for?"

He replies, "Easy fixes! Simple changes! You know, pros and cons. Sample pictures. A logo would be nice. Within two weeks."

I reply back, "Deal."

Dropping off to sleep on my way to bed, I am already there when I hit the pillow. I relax.

Jake is staring at me. He's smiling. Grinning. He's grinning white teeth like a snowman in a snowstorm. It's unnerving.

Getting off the Riverside Tower elevator, there are hollow walls of framing steel beams and uprights and pipes over scraped gray cement floors with old glue swirls of white or dingy yellow. This was where Common Communication was. A voice greets me, and I spot Belle Beckett and Samuel Morrison working a handheld computer over a card table. They are in jeans and sweatshirts. My suit and I are overdressed.

"Good morning."

"Good morning. We aren't hiring." That's a fine way to start an interview. "What I mean is, we aren't ready to start hiring. It's been a long day."

"I know all about long days." We introduce ourselves.

Belle comments, "You have a good voice, a deep voice; it exudes confidence."

"Thank you," I respond confidently as a prospective employee looking to be the best candidate for a non-existent job.

"We've been wondering how you found out about us. We aren't on the web, in phone listings, or even on the directory downstairs."

Last time I used the term intuition, since it carries less baggage than foreseeing futures. How do I explain this? "I had a dream about this, except it looked different in the dream."

"How?"

"Well, there was a receptionist at a desk over there and all of this was finished with carpeting and white walls and ceiling tiles. There was a conference room back there by the window and on the wall there was a painting of the city overlooking the Mississippi in winter."

"That's my painting," Belle says.

"Really?" Sam asks. Belle nods.

"What color carpeting did we decide on?"

"Well it was mostly tan, kind of a coffee-stain tan, with navy blue borders about four inches wide."

"What are you doing?" Belle asks Sam who's working on the computer.

"Trying to pull up the carpet samples. Here we go. Those aren't it. Those aren't it. Not there. Not there either."

"Wait. Is that it?"

"Or that one. Is it one of these two?"

"That one."

"Really?"

"Yeah."

"I don't know. What do you think?" Belle asks Sam.

"It's all right."

"But you think it looks like coffee stains?" she asks me.

"Yes, but the manufacturer probably wanted you to have a head start, like buying torn jeans."

Belle laughs. "What else was in your dream."

"You offered me a job."

"Did we? What job did we offer you?"

"God." Sam spits out his coffee. "You're getting ahead of yourself, aren't you? Or are you trying to see how that color will look on the floor?"

"He has the sense of humor for the part..."

Sam tries to brush off a coffee stain from his sweatshirt, "We aren't hiring."

"Whoa there, Sam, can I talk with you in the... uh... lobby?" They wind around partial walls, turn to look at me, realize I can still hear them, and move farther away.

Wet sand drips from between my fingers to form little sand pine trees on the beach.

Then I'm at the back of a crowd of people in Milltown, surrounded by the news vans and their satellite dish towers. It must be bring-your-own-satellite-dish-tower! I forgot mine! Carl is at the front being introduced by the mayor. Flight Control is being touted as a local company of distinguished achievement. I laugh myself awake.

I was there! I shouldn't have laughed myself awake. I need to find out whether AutoDrive will kill anybody. Well, it's bound to kill somebody. It'll be used by the army to drive pancake-thin tanks built without space for a tank crew. The military has to find new ways of killing people because otherwise there is no justification for the world's largest military budget. Even if some strange miracle causes morality to overtake money in Carl's decisions about AutoDrive and AutoDrive is not made available to the military, AutoDrive will kill people. Suicide bombers blow up cars and trucks full of explosives. The natural evolution of suicide bombing will lead to the suicide-less bomber, using an AutoDrive vehicle. All because I was sold on the idea of providing mobility to mobility impaired people.

The most basic recognition program of AutoDrive was teaching it not to run into things. Having taught it the rudimentary sensory data, it was a natural next step to teach it the concept of Wall. Just a few years ago, Dexter and Mica's daughter, Bucca, taught me about toddlers. She had firsthand knowledge; she was ten months old. She would stand and wobble, as she balanced precariously on two little legs, and start to move. With all her concentration on keeping upright and moving, she didn't notice the couch or wall or adult's leg and BAM! Bucca lands on her butt. Adults wonder about the purpose of a butt, but toddlers know why the two little pillows are there.

Teaching AutoDrive not to bump its nose or bump its butt was an important baby step in preventing costly cleanup, repair, and realignment. It was also key to the functionality of the product – don't run into walls or barriers or other cars or people... Really don't run into things. Snow? You can run into snow. Rain? You can run into rain. I wonder if they've taught AutoDrive snow and rain. Maybe the crash isn't such a big deal. Maybe AutoDrive crashes into snow. Or a snow fort. On the day before Labor Day? Labor Day is a little early in the season for snow. When was the earliest recorded snowfall in Minnesota? I once read in an almanac that the earliest recorded snowfall was in 1916, on September 15th. In Shakespeare's Julius Caesar, the soothsayer warned, "Beware the Ides of September" because of the premature snow. I'd like to read Julius Caesar from the soothsayer's point of view.

The almanac said, "Trace amount." That means it was either just a dusting of snow or the snow immediately melted as it hit any solid object, like a car. Either way, it's doubtful that the Labor Day crash will have anything to do with snow or even ice.

AutoDrive doesn't need snow or ice to crash. There are a whole host of reasons AutoDrive could crash.

I need to know if anyone gets hurt at the test. I lie back down and relax.

I'm on the Riverside Tower elevator again. This isn't where I'm supposed to be. I look over my shoulder, and yes, it's a great view. But when the elevator doors open, I better see AutoDrive. Of course AutoDrive will crash if it makes a running leap off one of the tallest buildings in Pigs Eye. Flying car it isn't.

I open my eyes and check the clock. It frowns 4:35am, stretches, and scratches its butt. I think I need a new clock. I wouldn't mind being able to sleep. I put on my bear feet slippers and pad my way out to the bathroom and the kitchen.

I eat a smaller-than-restaurant-sized salad and take a B complex and a calcium-magnesium supplement. Edwards said that kelp is the best natural source of calcium, but I know we don't have any, so I add kelp to the grocery list. I make bear tracks in the plush carpet on my way back to bed. Vitamins and minerals aren't going to change what's in someone's head. I take that back. They will change what's in the head, but they won't change the thoughts. Maybe. Maybe I should use pointed perception with vitamins and without, to compare and contrast thoughts.

What is wrong with me? Why can't I foresee the crash? Is it because I've let people learn of pointed perception that it doesn't work? You can do something amazing, but when you go to show people what you can do, it doesn't work. It only works in secret. It only works when you aren't trying to make it work. You let it happen; you don't make it happen. It is almost like thought and concentration and focus are the adversaries of pointed perception.

It's almost like it has nothing to do with me at all.

I kick off the bear feet and go to sleep.

30

Choices

Sometimes I dream I'm in Italy, driving this incredible sports car. It has AutoDrive. It handles the hairpin switchback turns. It flips on its headlights as it drives through short dark stone tunnels without unnecessary changes in speed or steering. It recognizes the low stone curbs that provide no barrier from the cliff. It changes gears based on both the current road and the road just ahead. It spots a goat in the road. It reads the goats intentions and gets around the goat. It is amazing.

I wake up before it stops being amazing. Looking around, AutoDrive and I have slept away the morning. Throwing some things around my room gets Ray's attention. He's at the door. "Do you need anything from the store?"

"Yeah, can you pick up a mineral supplement?"

"Sure. What kind?"

"Something to replace all the minerals we used to get from the apartment water system."

"You're kidding, right?"

"No."

Ray sits down. "Listen." I stop throwing dirty clothes into dirty little piles. "You– They say stress is at its greatest after you have gone through whatever it is you've gone through. The apartment was crazy. You've been acting crazier ever since we left it. You really want a mineral supplement?"

"Yes. But if you don't want to get it, you don't have to."

"Did you put kelp on the list?"

There are just the two of us here. Of course I put kelp on the list. "Yes."

"Do you have a recipe that calls for kelp?"

"No."

"How much kelp do you want?"

"Just a handful. If you don't want to get it, I can get it. I have to go out anyway."

"No, I'll see what I can do." He leaves.

He thinks I'm crazy. I'm not the one who will be asking around for a handful of kelp and a dirty-drinking-water mineral supplement. At least I didn't ask him to buy some turkey.

I wonder how I'm supposed to eat kelp? If it should be on a salad, I didn't see it last night at Lettuce Feed You. Maybe it was somewhere on the Wisconsin end of the bar. Maybe it's supposed to be baked in a casserole and smothered in cheese to prevent having to taste the kelpiness of it. Maybe it's supposed to be fed to fish, then I eat the fish. Next time I'll ask Ray to pick up some fish that has recently eaten kelp. Yeah. It says right here on the package that its last meal was kelp. The fish had complained that the kelp wasn't fresh, and it was executed. It was a gangster style execution for squealing. The problem with talking fish is that the fishing industry would be the first to learn about it and the last to tell anyone about it. The minute word spreads of talking fish or singing fish or fish on the net, the fishing industry will lose several years worth of profits. I'm not saying there are any talking fish in any Minnesota lakes, but rumors still surface.

The front door knocks. Probably a talking fish looking for a hideout.

With large lips in a baggy tweed suit, a flat hat, round black-rimmed glasses, and a Limpet name tag, a scrawny pale man holds out a brown box and an electronic clipboard. I take the box and clipboard and sign, "J. Hancock." It's a bit warm for tweed. I give him back his clipboard.

His voice cracks a high-pitch squeal, "Have a nice day, Mister..." He peers through thick glasses at the clipboard and reads, "Hancock," with a sour lemon juice face. I nod and shut the door.

Hey! It's from Owatonna Opticals! Cameron came through in a hurry. It's only been 12 or 13 hours. Opening the box in my room, the contents are spread out. I continue to be impressed. The packaging is all generic. The manual is photocopied. It doesn't have many logos or labels. It is a late prototype. Still, according to the manual and loose paperwork, this is a "Poof! You're There! travel-free camera, by the local professionals at Owatonna Opticals." The camera is the size of a professional digital camera. It pinpoints the depth of field... the distance between the camera, the foreground, and the background. And then it offers alternative backgrounds for your subject. Instead of standing in your room, you are standing in front of a pine forest, or the Mississippi River, or Mount Rushmore, or the Statue of Liberty, or the pyramids, or the Eiffel Tower. What was previously only possible through graphics software or green screen technology is now built into the camera. It says, "Choose from 40 studio backdrops and 40 real scenes. Add up to ten additional backgrounds from your own photos or our website collection." I can think of a few possibilities for this.

I probably shouldn't have signed for it as John Hancock, now that I think of that signature getting back to Cameron.

Looking at the opened plastic bags and the nondescript materials, it's clear; I can't give this to Ruth looking like this. It lacks pizazz.

Never underestimate the power of presentation. Presentation counts. If a gift is worth giving, it is worth giving with a nice presentation. That could mean wrapping paper or bows, but not necessarily. A coat could be bundled up and wrapped with a scarf. Jewelry could be in a nice jewelry box. A great present might be a big box full of helium balloons. Sometimes all a gift needs is a little showmanship, a little flash.

I need a box that can be a backdrop for decorations, a blank slate. I'll probably need Ray's help. I put everything back together and shove it aside.

The bathroom mirror is unclear from my shower. I clarify it to watch my reflection shave and brush his teeth. I slather peanut butter on celery and chomp my way around the house getting stuff cleaned up and getting me ready. I check the phone book on my phone for nearby stores selling gift boxes. Some stores I know will not have what I am looking for. Others I call and ask questions. I find two possibilities. What if AutoDrive worked so that I could transfer an address from my phone to my car? That would make sense. That would make a lot of sense.

Why am I still thinking about AutoDrive?

After I deal with the AutoDrive test, I will stop myself from thinking about AutoDrive. I don't work for them anymore. They aren't paying me anymore. I am done. I am through. It's not my responsibility.

I step outside, and I swelter. It's hot in the land of two seasons. The construction site next door is wet with sweat, and the crew isn't finished dripping. The Pony Express has been baking for hours at several hundred degrees. Taking the hose over, I spray it to cool it off, especially the door handle. Steam billows. Using my shirt tail, I open the door to the blast furnace and roll down the blast furnace driver's window.

The auto parts store has a replacement headlight under a layer of dust. Some people theorize that both headlights should be replaced simultaneously. They say that the minute you fix one, the other one will go. The way I figure it, that other bulb might be the manufacturing miracle that could last forever. I've had headlight bulbs that have outlasted two bulbs on the other side. This bulb... I think I had to replace this bulb the last time too. Why would I want to throw out a perfectly good bulb? What if people replaced the light bulbs around their houses with the same when-one-goes-they-all-go philosophy? I replace the bulb in the parking lot to make sure it works before driving off. Good as new. I swing over to the cleaners and pick up my suit.

The box and storage store has a white box with a separate lid. I find a white cylindrical box that could be attached to the side of the main box and represent a proportional lens. Carrying the two white boxes together, I spot a nondescript brown box that should fit these boxes and have room for a few helium balloons. I buy my boxes and drop them off at my car. I stop in a toy store next door.

Bins are filled with small gadgets, tricks, springs, balls, cars, and plenty of key chains for all the keys to all the cars. What if every toy car needed a toy car key? Things ooze and light up. They light up and make noise. They wiggle. They squirm.

This toy store is not part of a toy store chain. Toy store chain marketing and operations managers have talked themselves out of selling small cheap toys due to difficulties with shoplifting and inventory control, and small parts hazards for the little kids. The managers and executives have managed to suck the life out of their toy stores.

Stores like this one are few and hard to find. In an ideal world, all the best stores would be enclosed under one roof, like an indoor shopping mall but of fun stores. In reality, I have this store and the Gag Shop back behind Yesterday's Diner and some things found in hobby shops and novelty shops, import stores and surplus stores, and catalogs and on the net.

My mind switches gears. Scanning the items for greatness, I look and examine and imagine the possibilities of the better items. Does this rubber spider crawl realistically? Yes, but it has glowing eyes. Real spiders don't have glowing eyes. A realistically crawling, two inch, rubber spider has possibilities. One with glowing eyes does not.

"Can I help you?" a high school kid asks. I pick up a bracelet with little gems on it. I push a little switch. The gems turn into little flashing mars lights. They aren't very bright. I hold it in the dark under a shelf. They're pretty bright, if it's dark. "We just got those in. I hadn't even seen one on yet," he says. He watches my analysis and testing of toys. They have several wind-up toy cars, but when this one crashes, it's front end crumples. It makes a nerve shattering, car crashing sound. They have magic wands. With a swish, it turns a toy frog into a toy prince. I don't see the point. Here's a toy MRI with multiple monitor images. "Let me know if you need something." I nod.

Across the aisle they have a herd of inflatable elephants, uninflated, in their boxes. I examine a box for feeding instructions and how big they'll grow. Seven feet is not very big for an elephant, but it's big for an inflatable elephant. The boxes of elephants separate the inflatable lions from the inflatable gazelles. This place must go wild at night.

Nearby shelves contain White Rock bluff souvenirs, made of oxidized limestone and sandstone. White Rock was an early name for Pigs Eye. The store also has a realistic souvenir of the downtown Pigs Eye buildings with the Capitol, the depot, Riverside Tower, and the First National Bank building with its big red 1st on top. The spot of the First National Bank building has historical significance. Legend has it that on that spot on that bank of the Mississippi River, a white man first set foot. The souvenir of downtown Milltown has St. Anthony Falls, Spirit Island, and all the mills, plus the blue, orange, white, and black sky-scraping, name-changing buildings. The souvenir Mahpiyawicasta Tower has the two lakes below, and the birds nest on top. The miniature Minnehaha Falls has real running water but no squirrels. The souvenir Wakan Teebe cave has a glowing fire and a presumably realistic sulfur and incense smell.

The two downtown replicas have optional snow packets. I didn't know snow was optional. That could solve a lot of problems.

Packages containing souvenir treaties have big orange stickers warning that the treaties dissolve in contact with air, water, or by brushing up against anything. You don't want the treaties coming in contact with skin or clothes. If contact occurs, flush with water and contact a physician. They shouldn't even have these things in a toy store. I know why they do, but they shouldn't.

Then I smash open a piñata with my head. Candies hail down. The kid comes rushing over. "I'm sorry about that. I guess we should have hung the piñatas higher up."

I buy them out of the flashing gem light bracelets and crashing cars. I buy an elephant. I buy the MRI and a small helium tank. I offer to buy the piñata I broke. The guy declines my offer. Then he gives me more change than I'm due, and I give it back to him before he can close the drawer.

Two boys enter the store. The guy taking my extra change back says, "You can't come in without a parent."

"He's right there! Aren't you, Dad?" the brash brat asks me.

"I'm not your Dad."

"You're disowning me?!? Because of the cat?!?"

I take my bags and go, "Hilarious."

Back in the heat, the talkative kid says, "You could've let us stay." I'm not going to give him the time of day. A few doors down in a sandwich shop, I ignore their convoluted board of menu choices and options, and I describe an ideal turkey sandwich. I ask the two builders if they can construct it. It's a challenge. The sandwich builders pause throughout the process to go over the blueprints of the sandwich with me, confirming what I want every step of the way. Upon completion, they try to tally the price for the commissioned work. I bargain them up to an amount that includes their tips. I eat the masterpiece over its blueprints, while the two boys pace the sidewalk out front. They don't understand. They are rank amateurs compared to the professional urchins from my previous neighborhood. Preschoolers at Whisper Willows and the northern Midway area have already been apprenticed in the urchin program for three years. These two older boys are still beginners. The simple concept of flying above adult radar versus flying below adult radar is an alien concept to them. These two are looking for attention. Real urchins know better. T h e boys examine my car. It looks like a finger is going to write something in the archaeological-automotive dirt and grime, probably the old favorite, "Wash me." The car bites him. He is stunned, looks at his finger, and stops himself from putting it in his mouth, while his friend yells at him. They run away.

This is probably the first meat I've had since the bison a week ago. There was the pizza on Saturday. I didn't ask for a pickle, but it's a good side item for the sandwich. I compliment the builders on the masterpiece I just demolished. Outside, the car reveals that the boy pushed his finger through it. That ought to teach him a lesson. And for now, it's better ventilation. I enjoy the additional breeze on my way to Choice Market for some things, and I hustle home before they bake. The car starts on the first try, and trumpets herald its success. I answer the damned phone.

"Acapella's Pizza. Our pizza is the freshest because its baked right in the car. The special is pepperoni and sweat with extra sweat. How can I help you?"

"If your car is that hot, you could get one with air conditioning."

"Hi Cy. That would be odd for most of the year. I'd wonder, 'Is it cold out or is my air conditioning stuck on maximum?' But aren't you afraid of talking with me?"

"What do you mean?"

"I thought you were one of the people who isn't talking with me, because Lefty's experiment may record everything."

"Who told you that?"

"Some people will always tell me stuff."

"Well some people shouldn't try to tell others how I am feeling. I expressed some concern, but I'm not-not talking to you. I'm talking to you now right?"

"Yes. What's up?"

"Do you have any pictures of Ruth?"

"Hardly. She's the one who takes all the pictures."

Cy groans, "I'm trying to put together an album of pictures of her, but the few that I remembered aren't very good."

"Naturally. She isn't comfortable posing for pictures. Did you know that? She ducks out or hides behind people."

"I never noticed."

"She hides behind the camera."

"This isn't going to work. I don't know what else to get her."

"Gee, that's too bad..."

"Wait. What are you getting her?"

"Something good."

"It can't be too good. You haven't had too much time to plan something really good."

"If you say so."

"Is it a giant bag of bouncy balls?"

"Better."

"Better than an album of Ruth pictures?"

"Better."

"I give up. Tell me."

"It's a one-of-a-kind camera."

"Something you put together?"

"Better."

"I want in on it."

"It'll cost you."

"How much?"

"It's not about how much. This is a prototype. I need feedback from Ruth about what she likes and dislikes and a few sample pictures sent to a guy I know at the company that made it... within two weeks. I was going to get Hope to help me."

"Hope doesn't need to get Ruth a great gift. I need to get her something nice. Ruth always gives nice, thoughtful gifts. You're going to make the rest of us look bad. I need in on this." She pauses and asks, "So you want me to ask Ruth what she thinks about it and write out the responses?"

"Right."

"My name gets prominent billing on the card?"

"Now you sound like you did when you negotiated contracts for Melanie..."

"That's what I do. We're agreed?"

I pull into the driveway, "Let me talk to Hope, and I'll call you back."

"You don't need her permission."

"Don't interfere with how we do things. I'll call you back."

"Okay, bye."

Hope makes like Juliet and calls down from the upper deck, "Hey Sweetie, come up when you're done putting things away, okay?"

"Okay." The construction workers watch from the shade of a few property bordering pines trees as I haul my booty inside.

Ray is yelling at me from several rooms away, "Your kelp is in the fridge! Everyone wanted to know what I needed it for! And your crappy-water mineral supplements are on the counter with a bag of clay!"

I follow the voice to his studio. "Why clay? Where's Kelly?"

"Because clay is what we were drinking. You could conduct a sludge test to figure out exactly what we used to drink, but it was clay. If you want to recreate the sludge water, be my guest. It's your choice. Kelly is at a loading dock."

"When did that happen?"

"It's been happening for a while. Didn't you hear the crew come through here this morning?"

I shake my head. "I must've missed that." Ray nods quickly in agreement. "I didn't mean to make you run around–" Ray waves me off. "Do you know if you're going to the party for Ruth on Sunday?"

"I will if Kelly doesn't have complications."

"Do you want to go in on a gift with me and others?"

"What is it?" I wave him to follow me to my room and show him the camera. He runs off, washes his hands, and returns to examine the camera and its booklet. "I've never heard of this."

"It's new. It's a prototype."

"This is real?" I nod. With wide eyes, Ray gapes, "Did you make this?"

I could tease him with a story of my secret camera building project, but after his kelp and minerals struggles, I tell him, "No. But I'm asking Ruth to provide feedback for the manufacturers, Owatonna Opticals. And we... I was wondering if you'd create a logo or two for the camera. You would need to decide if you want any sort of credit for it. Contractual stuff. I bought this box and this one to glue on as a lens, and I was wondering if you would do some black and white illustrations for it, either drawn on the box or attached to it. Nothing too elaborate, because she might not keep the box..."

Ray's having difficulties formulating words, and I've got to get upstairs. Hope's waiting. "Could I have one?" he meekly asks.

"We could negotiate that or have Cy negotiate it, if they want to use your logos, maybe..."

"Could I try this out?"

"Yes, as long as you don't bust it or muss it up. I have to go see Hope," I tell him as I leave. He gives me no indication that he heard me, or that he knows who I am. I clean up and head up. Hope has left the door wide open. In her room she turns and kisses me with every lip on her face, all two of them.

"I got the tickets."

Tickets? Plainly she means the tickets to Chicago. "That's great. Do we get to sit together?"

"Whenever we want."

"Can I show you something?"

"What?"

"It's in my room."

"Wooooooooooo," Hope says like a fourth grader, real mature, as I lead her down. In my room, there is an empty box.

"Well, it was here... RAY!" No response. "See this box? Inside it WAS a kick-ass prototype camera that I hope to still be able to give Ruth for her birthday if my roommate doesn't break it first. You take a picture of someone and can change the background behind them. Cool, huh?"

Hope looks from me to the empty box. She doesn't picture it. "Where did you get it?"

"Last night I sent a message to this guy I know, Cameron, at Owatonna Opticals. All I did was ask if he knew of a latest-greatest camera, and he sends one by courier this morning. The agreement is that Ruth gives feedback on what she likes and dislikes within two weeks. Also they want a logo. Also their manual needs some editing. He took the manual! I went to the store this afternoon and got a couple of nice boxes.

He took the boxes too!" I dash out the room and down the hall to the studio. The two boxes have been glued together. Hope follows. "Those boxes," I point accusingly. I look around for the camera, the manual, or Ray but find none of them. "So after buying stuff, Cy called and whined that she doesn't have a gift for Ruth. She drilled me for what I have and wants to be involved in it, like getting the feedback to Cameron. But I want to involve you. Do you want to go with me to the party for Ruth?"

"Yes, of course."

"Do you want to have a part in the gift?"

"I suppose you want me to grade the manual?"

"Would that be okay?"

"I think I'd have to see it first. I'd been thinking about getting her a necklace and wrapping it in a hope chest."

"Would you rather do that?"

"Not if I can do something with the manual. I'm no expert at prototype cameras." Hope studies me. "I'm sorry if I took things too seriously last night."

"You didn't. You didn't do anything wrong." I take her back to my room, where we fall on the bed in a heap of kisses and hugs with some tickling and giggling. Laying face to face, smiling at each other, trumpets sound. "I am really, really getting to hate the sound of trumpets. Hello, Acapella's Pizza, the special–"

"I've heard the specials," Cy says.

"Cy's heard the specials," I repeat to Hope.

"Did you talk with Hope?"

"Yes, we talked."

"And?"

"Oh. Cy wants to know if she can have permission to join us in the gift."

"In the gift? I don't know. It's a little box."

"Tell her, the worst of your humor has rubbed off on her."

"No, she's right. It's not that big of a box."

"So you are saying–"

"Yes, you can be a part of the gift. We will even list you on the card."

"Prominently," Cy insists.

"We'll see."

"I don't understand you two. Hope tells me that I can't talk to her directly, and you tell me that you need to talk to Hope."

I repeat that to Hope. "Yes. That's right. You understand perfectly. Did you have a question?"

Cy sighs, "I'll talk with you later." She disconnects. I tease Cy, but I'm not trying to be confusing or inconsistent. I hope she doesn't feel like I mean to cause her trouble. Overall, she called to get my help with Ruth's gift, and I helped her with the gift. She hardly has to do anything to be a part of it.

Reaching over Hope to set the phone down, Hope takes it and sets it down herself. She picks up my clock with its bright sparkling eyes and silly grin. "Do you want to go to the nursing home with me?"

"Eventually. Wait. Do you mean me or the clock?"

"You."

"Sure."

"You will?!?" Hope's thrill is deafening.

"Yes."

Hope hops up and down on the bed-turned-trampoline. "We need to be at the animal shelter at

6:30," she says setting down the clock.

"They're keeping old people at the animal shelter now?!? That explains why their backs are never straight. Those cages aren't tall enough!"

Hope laughs, "No, we bring animals with us... cats."

"You have to go to an animal shelter to do that? Can't we just walk along the sidewalk and have all the animals leap onto your back on the way?"

"Funny."

"Do we wear tweed and sweaters and shawls to blend into the nursing home population? Or do we wear black?"

"Why black?"

"Cats love it when people wear black. They'll rub against you, step back, see you covered in fur, come back get the furless spots, and then look at you with a sense of accomplishment like they've just painted a room. Then they wash up. It's cat art."

"I thought you were–"

"Cats like washers and dryers because they turn everything into blank canvases."

"We don't have to wear anything special. Except long sleeves might be good with the cats. And you have to watch out for the butt pinchers. They usually trick someone new by acting like they need special assistance. While you are helping them across a room, they pinch your butt. I wear an armor skirt."

Climbing over Hope, I search my closet. "Nope. No armor in here."

"Just know that the little old ladies are about as innocent as... the kids around your old apartment."

"I will lock up the valuables."

"Good plan. What do you want to do for dinner?"

"Are there any restaurants near the animal shelter? Wait a minute. I'm not sure I'd trust any restaurants near an animal shelter."

"That's gross."

"I agree. We could have kelp."

"Kelp," Hope confirms. "Do you have kelp?"

"Of course, I have kelp. Everyone has kelp. Ray picked it up for me."

"How do you prepare it?"

"You sit it down. You tell it that it will be eaten. You ask it if it has any questions."

"Seriously."

"Seriously? I have no idea."

"You have kelp, but you don't know what to do with it?"

"Right. For dinner, what do you really, really want?"

Hope laughs, "No one has ever asked me what I really, really want."

"What about when your mom set up the contracts with your brothers?"

"No. That was just throwing money at the problems. It was like filling your Funnellator with cash and flinging it at me, only everyone had a Funnellator and has been flinging cash. I never asked for that. What do I really, really want? What I really, really want is an ice cream cone."

"Okay." I sit up. "Let's go."

"We can't have ice cream for dinner, can we?"

"The last time I had ice cream for dinner was... two weeks ago tonight." Hope is looking for permission to do this. It's really very sweet. I change shirts, run my fingers through my hair, grab a jacket that could get an outer fur lining, and load it with wallet, phone, and keys. Upstairs we're asked what we're doing for dinner. Hope defers the question to me. "We're going out for ice cream."

"We have ice cream."

"How many flavors?"

"Two."

"That's not enough. We need oodles of choices."

"Oodles?" I nod. "Where are you going?"

"Where is the best local place?"

Hope returns, changed, and says, "I Scream."

"Oooh, can we go?"

Hope tenderly explains, "We're going to the animal shelter and the nursing home right afterwards." Faith and Nicole turn away dejected.

"Will you navigate me to I Scream?"

"I'll drive."

"My car can stand some cat fur. It may actually bond with the rust to strengthen the car."

"Your headlight doesn't work."

"I fixed it this afternoon."

"That's great, but I'm still driving." It chirps unlocked, and we climb into her car. "I remember when I first got my driver's permit. It meant I could escape. I could get away from my brothers. The world awaited."

"You had your own car?"

Hope smiles and laughs, "No! I would take any available car or truck... my mom's, my brother's... That was probably the only advantage to having so many older brothers – they all had vehicles. No keys were safe. And if I got a hold of a rare key, I would make a stop at the locksmiths to have a duplicate key made. My brothers learned to hide their keys, and I learned to hide the duplicates. They could do what they wanted to me, but I would leave their cars in... interesting places," she laughs, while blotting a tear with the side of her finger. I put my hand on her shoulder. "Don't." I take my hand away. "You'll just make me cry more, and I won't be able to see the road." She grabs my hand briefly. "Before all the contracts, my mother got all my brothers to pitch in for a car for me. For the most part, they kept it running well to keep me away from theirs. Once, one of them devised a slow leak in one of my tires, leaving me stuck on the other side of town in winter." We park.

I Scream is an old-fashioned ice cream parlor of yellow cream bricks whose dinnertime clientele all look sheepishly embarrassed that they're forgoing a more traditional dinner for the ice cream dinner. An ice cream dinner can still have several courses, only usually the courses are stacked on top of each other. As Hope works on her choices, I order a doubly Rocky Road, which has fudge, walnuts, and marshmallows in chocolate ice cream. I haven't had this since we were in Harmony a dozen days ago. Hope has pink over pale green. The lower layer has to be Mint Chocolate Chip. We step outside and stand on the brick sidewalk, displaying our meal for all to see. "So you were stuck on the other side of town..."

"I was near Chaska, and a friend had to come pick me up; it was Becky. She had to come get me because I didn't know where to go or what to do to fix the car. Now I have a repair kit in the trunk, two phones, roadside assistance, flares, and most importantly, I know what to do in most emergencies and how to get my brothers back." I put my arm around her, and she snuggles in with me.

"How is it?"

"This is good." I Scream becomes increasingly busy with us standing closely out front, smiling, and eating our ice cream cones. Hope's tongue carefully licks an ice cream drip from her hand. A car screeches to a halt. A guy stops his bike and stares. He comes to his senses and asks if we could watch his bike for him. I ask Hope if he's one of her brothers. "No. You'll know when we run across one of my brothers." As she finishes her cone, she makes a "Mmm" sound. "What I wanted to tell you before was that I'm not an angel. I used to steal my brother's cars. You don't have to try to be perfect with me. I'm not." The bicyclist retrieves his bike and thanks Hope. Hope takes me to the animal shelter.

It's an Out Damned Spot Animal Shelter. "Hey, there was an Out Damned Spot Animal Shelter in my old neighborhood, right next door to the Remember When Nursing Home. Where's the Remember When Nursing Home from here?"

"About a mile away."

"They should put them next to each other like in my old neighborhood."

"Remind me to tell them to move."

We load up three cat kennels and one cat, Stretch, a big black fuzz-ball, for my lap. Seeing her, she looks big, but it's a deception of long black hairs covering a scrawny cat. Volunteers are returning from walks with dogs or departing with more. The cats and dogs avoid each other.

On our drive to the nursing home I think about the workers at the Out Damned Spot Animal Shelter. "They seemed pleasant enough at our borrowing some of their cats, but overall they seemed angry. I don't pigeonhole people. I don't label people. I don't apply stereotypes to people. I don't think of people in groups with a group mentality. But they all seemed angry."

"There are far more cats than people who want to adopt cats. I would adopt some of these cats in a heartbeat if it weren't for the fact that Faith is allergic. These four have been with the animal shelter for several months now, which is good and bad. It's good that they have a place and they aren't being put to sleep. It's bad because they aren't finding homes. Kittens are far more likely to be adopted than full grown cats like these. You have Stretch who will warm any lap and might have been too warm for your car," she says as Stretch washes essence of Rocky Road from my hand. "Directly behind me is Katrina, the bright-eyed black cat with white mittens, chin, and chest. She's the searcher-explorer. Katrina is the only one that sometimes hides. In the middle is Rumbles. I don't know him, but I was told he purrs loudly. Behind you is Scratch, the mottled cat. It's not a name that will help get a cat adopted, but Scratch is special. Scratch can..." Hope parks by an old twisted apple tree near the nursing home. "Scratch will lie down on the bed of someone who is going to die. He has done it three times that I know of. Last week he didn't lie down by anyone. Three weeks ago, he laid down by a woman who died that weekend. Before that, the second time, the man had a previously undetected cancerous cyst."

"Wow. Has he actually scratched anyone?"

"I don't think so."

"He should be called doctor, Doctor Cat, famous for his cat scans."

We take the cats in, let them go, and brush off. Several seniors have ringside seats in the hallway, and they watch the cats carefully. Stretch stretches and paces amongst the elderly, getting a pat here and a rub there, right there, yes! Katrina dodges the seniors like they are toddlers and takes off exploring. Rumbles finds a couple in an activity room and parks first at their feet and then tests their laps. Scratch serenely sits and washes. This one the seniors do not approach, but they watch with intense interest, as if the cat were death itself. I approach him and pet him and rub his chin, causing the seniors to include me in the whispers about the mottled black and brown cat. He turns to watch Stretch bat a small ball of yarn. He turns away, having no time for play. He starts down the hall. Hope is talking with an administrator and the seniors, while I wait and lean against the wall. Scratch stops at a corner and turns back to me, with an are-you-coming look. I go down the hall. I remember this. I check my watch. I follow the cat as it wanders the nursing home. He checks in on patient after patient, making his rounds. We find Katrina perched on top of a cabinet. Scratch is the one who spotted her. He's very aware of what's going on.

A graying administrator approaches me squinting, "You know, we have enough inspections from the state and the county. Now I have to stick around for old Scratch too." Her manner is demanding, but her lips betray a wry smile. "So what do you think. Do you think we have a clean bill of health?"

From farther down the hall, Scratch returns to get me. I scratch his back. "He certainly hasn't made any stops." Scratch parks his tail at my feet.

Stepping slightly away from the cat, she grabs my arm, crow's feet wrinkles stretch from the outside corners of her eyes. "The residents have become afraid of this cat. But youngsters like us have nothing to fear." I nod in agreement.

Scratch leads me to the front hallway, where he stops to wash up.

Hope is batting away the hands of an old man, keeping her tail away from him, as he looks down her blouse. He's almost quick, despite having the posture of someone who's been in an animal kennel too long. I step in and speak decisively. He slows down. Hope and I enter the activity room where three pieces of yarn are left unraveled on the floor. Rumbles purrs from a lap while being petted and for our benefit, hugged. Stretch lays across a table, being petted from all sides. We sit down side-by-side at another table with residents, who are primarily watching Rumbles and Stretch and looking out for Scratch.

I tell them, "An uncle of mine was concerned that his wife was getting hard-of-hearing. So he came up with a test. She was sitting in a chair with her back to him. From a distance, he softly asked, 'Honey, can you hear me?' No reply. He moved a little closer and spoke a little louder, 'Honey, can you hear me?' Nothing. He moved up right behind her and loudly asked, 'Honey, can you hear me?' She hissed, 'For the third time, yes!'" People laugh, startling Stretch, who leans up on an elbow to look around. Rumbles is oblivious to the commotion. Stretch lies back down. "My uncle went to a hearing specialist about a hearing aid. The doctor said, 'We have three different types of hearing aids. The first one will let you hear people louder; will translate Chinese, French, German, Russian, and Spanish; and will give you the international news and weather reports. That's 2,000 dollars.' My uncle said, 'That's more than I want to spend.' The doctor said, 'Well, for 500 dollars, you can get a hearing aid that will translate Spanish and give you local news and weather.' 'That's still too much,' my uncle said. 'Well for ten dollars, you can get this cork and wire. You stick the cork in your ear and run the wire into your pocket.' My uncle asked, 'What will that do?' 'Nothing. But people will talk louder!'"

Stretch is startled again, gets up, looks around, stretches, and paces the table, evaluating the attention and petting from her residents. That cat is in her glory. Rumbles rumbles his contentment. Katrina enters only to leap up another tall cabinet. She oversees the room. Several seniors tell us their cat and dog stories. Hope listens and encourages forgotten details. Rumbles switches laps three times. Stretch moves around and shares a resident's water. I find Scratch staring out a window. We round up the cats, herding them into their kennels. Stretch is last to leave with me. We quietly return the cats to Out Damned Spot and drive home. I can't help but think, the clock is ticking on all of them.

Hope and I kiss each other good night. Getting into bed, I decide with conviction that I will be able to foresee all the possibilities for the test of AutoDrive.

31

Points

What is this? Where am I? I can't understand. It's like staring at an illusion that shifts before my eyes. I try to close my eyes, and nothing happens. It's weird. Things are close and far. They have depth and are flat. What I see makes no sense. While I'm trying to figure out what I'm seeing, it changes. It simplifies into dots. I look closely at a dot by my foot. It shows me stepping to my right. A decision. An option. The landscape of dot-like options stretch off as far as I can see. I look for a horizon. I stare off for a limit. Maybe over there. There isn't one. I could run and never run out.

The close dots are distinct. The far off dots blend into a kaleidoscope of colors and patterns. Every point is a possibility? Just for stopping AutoDrive? My head is going to explode. That's got to be at least one of the options, having my head explode. It's not a great option. It's not the option of choice. At least I hope it isn't. There sure aren't just three or four options. There are billions. I sit back down in the center. I look up. Those aren't stars above me. They are possibilities. I multiply this by every decision and every being, and it all overlaps. And for the briefest moment, I glimpse God's playroom.

I open my eyes to daytime. Why does God need a playroom? Isn't God an old man? Either this changes everything or I should blame my dream on eating ice cream for dinner. It's a reasonable excuse. On the floor there is a note from Hope. With the neatest of penmanship, writing meant for framing, she says she tried to wake me to have me wish her luck today, but she couldn't wake me. She asks me to call her as soon as I wake up. Great. I just wake up, and I'm already in trouble from the teacher. I check the clock. It's one. It reminds me of a poem.

> Hickory dickory dock.
> Three mice climbed up the clock.
> The clock struck one.
> The other two escaped with minor injuries.

I call Hope. She gives me the time of day. Then she has to go. Ray has gone, but he left the camera in his studio. I consider not shaving, and like a thousand times before, I reject the notion as being not me.

My meal decision is an artichoke, since no one is around. I set a pan of water to boil. The artichoke is washed, its stem is cut, the thorny leaf points are cut and snipped. I set it in the pan to steam during my shower. There is never anyone buying artichokes when I am buying artichokes. I think I am the only person in Minnesota that eats the things. And I am not certain I eat them right.

At the apartment, I stopped praying in the shower, because I couldn't hear myself pray. I'm sure God could hear me, but I couldn't hear myself, so I didn't know what I was praying. Here, in the oddly clear water, I pray for Hope. I pray that no one will be hurt by AutoDrive. I pray for peace. Then I loudly sing my head off with my cover of Melanie's cover of You Didn't Have To Be So Nice. That's something else I tried not to do at the apartment. I didn't want the neighbors to think I was auditioning.

Melanie's most reliable back-up singer, Jenny, taught me song associations, singing a song that relates to something someone just said or did. Now I do it without thinking about it. "You Didn't Have To Be So Nice" has to be on my mind for some reason. It is what Hope was trying to tell me outside of I Scream last night. She said, "You don't have to try to be perfect with me. I'm not."

I'm not trying to be perfect, Hope. I'm trying to atone. There's a difference.

The artichoke is steamed to a moist olive green. It started out blue-green, with veins of purple. I nuke a tablespoon of butter in a small dish. I use a knife and fork as tongs to move the artichoke to a plate. Taking everything to the table, I remove a leaf, dip it lightly in butter, and use my teeth to scrape the bottom, inner half of the leaves into my mouth. For around 50 leaves, I do this. What other food has you making these kinds of teeth marks on it, while hardly eating the food itself? Corn on the cob. That's the only equivalent I can think of. It's almost like the process of chewing gum. You aren't trying to eat the gum; you're just chewing it. The leaves get smaller and smaller. The inner leaves get ridiculously small. That's the stopping point. The tiny leaves are pulled off in a circle, almost like prying off a hub cap. Below the hub cap is fur. The fur is shaved off with a knife. Then I eat the entire base of the artichoke. What's weird is that artichoke hearts are sold in stores in cans and jars. Supposedly it's the base of the artichoke, but it's more than just the base. It is half the artichoke, everything but the outermost leaves. So everyone else in the world must eat the entire inner artichoke, fur and all. I would ask someone, but I'm the only one in Minnesota eating the softball-sized leaf ball... mostly eating it.

I clean up my artichoke mess. No one will ever know.

Just to make sure, I do the dishes. Large pans and dishes first, working my way smaller and smaller. It is the engineer in me. I am building a drain rack structure of dishes. The silverware stands in a drain cup, knives first, then spoons, and then forks with their prongs up. The cup is so full, the forks rise out of it, to a peak in the middle. The utensil structure is layered like New York's Chrysler Building in forks, the tines shining and sparkling in the green sunlight. It is a masterpiece, a crowning achievement in kitchen cleaning.

The neighbors drop a large scaffold. That's the way it sounds.

The mineral supplement tastes like rock.

I check my messages, iron a gifted shirt, and load a jacket with things for tonight. One of my messages is from a Cameron Raymond, very formal. I am... We are all invited to the unveiling of The Lactating Woman fountain at Wild Rice Park in downtown Pigs Eye a week from next Monday at two in the afternoon. He's seriously giving birth. Having reached my recent quota of roommate teasing, I send him a simple message of congratulations. We now have an e-mail record of a formal roommate relationship, which is about as accurate as an archaeologist finding a snake skeleton nearby and deciding that the snake ate glacial ice. "We could not locate its tail, but we believe it was shovel shaped, enabling it to burrow deep within the glacial ice. When the glaciers melted into Minnesota humidity, the Glacial Snakes either became extinct or evolved into gnats."

I know! The next census should be coming up within the next ten years. They should ask about artichokes. The census is the only part of the government that matters. It's the only part that counts.

Hope should be home any min– I grab my keys, wallet, and reluctantly my phone. I lock the house and run out to the car. I try to start it up. Again I try to start it up. Maybe it doesn't like the new headlight. Doctor, the body is rejecting the donor organ! I again try to start it up. Another try. There it goes. Applause from the construction site.

I remember seeing a floral shop, the Blooming Idiot. Inside they have prearranged bouquets apparently put together by someone who arranges flowers by smell instead of appearance. I choose to create my own arrangement. A floral specialist insists on helping me. I point out the particular flowers, and she shakes the water off each one and holds them. I am capable of shaking water off flowers; I'm not a blooming idiot. The floral specialist wraps them. I pay her extra to keep the store name off the bouquet.

When I bought my car, I insisted that the dealership not add their logo to the vehicle. I figured, why do I need to advertise for them? I was ready to negotiate an advertising fee, but the dealership was fine leaving the logos off my one car. I guess I was the only one who had made such a request. But things have changed. I might bring my car back in and ask to have the advertising added now. I wonder how much they would pay me to keep their advertising off this Pony Express. I arrive back home before Hope. I put the flowers in the fridge, away from any orange juice or lemonade. Citrus wilts flowers. Microwaves also wilt flowers, which is something only a guy would try. I set up a lawn chair on the front lawn and a small table with sunglasses, a glass, and a pitcher of lemonade. The more comfortable I get on the front lawn, the less comfortable the crew next door gets.

One of them calls over, "Get a job!"

I take a drink of lemonade. I savor it in my mouth, tasting the lemony sourness and the sugary sweetness from taste bud specialists on my tongue. My response is an overly dramatic, "Ah," as if that swig had quenched a thousand summer baked thirsts. Minnesota is on the slope of the Great Plains, where hot winds whip dirt up and carry it away until the dirt is combed from the sky by Minnesota trees, especially the westernmost trees. If it didn't rain, the trees would be caked in dirt. If the trees were covered in dirt, they couldn't take in all the colors of visible light, except the rejected greens. Green light is the light that plants discard.

The green sunlight shimmers over me and sparkles my lemonade.

Hope drives up the driveway lost in thought. Spotting me, she smiles and stops abruptly. Lowering her window she calls out, "Hey Handsome, how are you?"

"Now that you are here, I couldn't be better."

"I'll be right back," Hope drives up the driveway. I watch the corner she drove past. It has my undivided attention. I figure Hope's height compared to the side of the house so that I will see her face right away. I watch that spot.

Hope's idea of right back and my idea of right back are significantly different. For example, if I said that I would be right back, what I would mean is that I will be right–

The door bangs open behind me. Hope is struggling with a reclining lawn chair, glass, and radio without losing her bikini. Wow! I dive to her aid. I know she's saying something but my brain is currently occupied. "What?"

"I said, thank you. Sorry I was gone so long." I still don't understand, so I help her with her chair, and I fill her glass. Hope turns on the radio, tunes in tunes, and lowers her sunglasses to her eyes. "I don't know how you knew what I needed, but this is it."

Watching the accident-prone construction crew, I comment, "Now I know why this project has taken them so long. Some of them are complete klutzes." A few of them look my way. More quietly I tell Hope, "One of them just told me to get a job. I think we're even." Drinking some cool delicious lemonade, I exhale another dramatic, "Ah." I turn to the beautiful woman next to me and ask, "Is school out for the summer?"

The left corner of Hope's mouth replies, "Yes." The way she answers, she seems to want to leave it all behind her. I'm game. It takes about 15 minutes for the drink to drop from her hand. I glance at the lemonade and wonder how strong it was. My chair creaks as I reach to turn down the radio. It takes about 15 more minutes for a procession of ants to find and carry off an ice cube. There's something you don't see every day. They must have something going on. I wonder if ants anywhere else carry off ice or if this is just one of those weird Minnesota things.

The ants are discussing uses for the straw when Becky drives up, startling Hope awake. I grab Hope's stuff and my stuff and follow Hope inside. She crashes on my bed. The clock falls off the nightstand. I kick aside some dirty little clothes piles. With some aloe vera lotion, I rub her neck and her shoulders, her back and her sides, her butt and her legs, and she moans occasionally. When I start to work on her feet, it seems as though she's been standing on pins and needles all day, by her moans of enjoyment.

"That camera is wild," Ray says, coming in with Becky. "I've copied pictures onto my phone and computer and sent some to you. Did you know it has a voice-activated timer?"

"No," I reply. Hope moans a reply.

"You say, 'Now' or 'Cheese' and two seconds later it takes a picture!"

"Hey, I got your message about Kelly. Congratulations! I will definitely be there."

"Thanks," Ray says.

"What camera is this?" Becky asks, taking a corner of the bed.

"Are you coming with us to the party for Ruth?" I intercept her question with my own.

"Tom and I are—" Hope props up on an elbow and waves me to stop rubbing her feet, so she can listen to Becky. "We're at a kind of—"

"Crossroads?" I interject.

"Yeah, a crossroads. He's always talking about Todd and what Todd is doing and I wonder where his attention is."

"On Todd."

"Right."

"So you aren't sure if you should go to Tom's for the party?" Becky nods halfheartedly. "Does he know that you think he's too preoccupied with his twin brother?"

"I don't know."

I toss her my phone. She catches it and tosses it back. "Hey, we've found a new use for the phone!" We toss it around a few more times. Ray shows us some pictures on his computer easel. Kelly is in a warehouse. Kelly is in Tianamen Square. Kelly is in the shadows of the Taj Mahal and in the shadows of Uluru and under the lean of the Tower of Pisa. Kelly is in the Amazon Rainforest. Kelly is part of Mount Rushmore. Kelly is the Statue of Liberty. Kelly is in amongst a group of emperor penguins in Antarctica. I tell Becky, "Ray took these pictures using a camera we're giving Ruth, if he didn't already break it."

"I didn't break it. And I've glued the round box to the squarish box to make the gift box itself look like a camera. I should have the artwork completed tonight."

"We're going to Pow-Wows tonight. Do you want to go?" Ray shakes his head.

"I knew I was forgetting something," Becky says, pulling out her own phone.

Nicole hesitantly comes in. "When are we going? Hi, Nicole," Hope says.

"I'm overdressed," Nicole says, looking at Hope. "Oh, cool," she says looking at the pictures on the electronic easel. Ray talks her through them.

"I figure we should leave here at 7:30," I tell Hope, setting my clock back up.

"We won't be anywhere near the front of the line," Hope replies. Becky is talking to Tom. She's inviting him to come along tonight. He's declining. I'm wondering if it has to do with Lefty's experiment on me. If it does, all of that will be over next Thursday.

"That's okay. We don't want to be right at the front."

"You have a plan?"

"I have a plan. You might want to bring earplugs. Who wants to drive? And is Faith going with us?"

"Are you kidding?" Nicole wonders.

"I'll drive," Hope volunteers, edging them out of my room.

I tell Hope, "You know I said 7:30, not 6:30."

"How long do you think we need to get ready for something like this?" she asks. Then she stops me and says, "Don't answer that. Just go on thinking that we will be upstairs just waiting around for 7:30. But don't bother us until then." She kisses my forehead and takes off.

Stopping her at the stairs, I run to the fridge, get the bouquet, and give it to her. Hope opens the fabric wrapping. She gazes at them. She sniffs them. She hugs and kisses me. I let her go.

I try a kelp sandwich. I decide I don't like kelp sandwiches. I get cleaned up again and dressed up. Isn't it a waste to get ready more than once a day?

I pick up the Safari Of The Mind and flip to the bookmarked page. The trees of intelligence, compassion, creativity, knowledge, curiosity, and the stump of indecision are having an argument with a gopher. The gopher chops into the trees. The woods try to reason with the gopher. The gopher chews away. He chews through page after page. And before I know it three beauties are at my door.

My tongue absently falls out of my mouth and unrolls across the floor. My clock topples off the nightstand again. I reel in my tongue, replace my clock, grab my jacket, and escort the ladies out. "You each look great. You always do." I open their doors for them. They seem nervous, and I don't know why. Maybe they're worried that I can't dance. They've never seen me dance. Even my friends that have seen me dance might say I can't dance, but I can dance. Maybe they know that I can't make a decent kelp sandwich.

I start to sing:

> I don't need a dream car
> you get me going just fine.
> I don't need a dream house
> you keep me warm with just that smile.
> I don't need a dream job
> you're in my thoughts and on my mind.

I belt out:

> You're my **dream**!
> You're everything to me.
> You're my day **dream**!
> You're who I want... to be with me.

Softer now:

> You're all my hopes...
> you're all my dreams...
> you're who I want with me.

"Come on. Sing along with me."

"I don't know this song."

"Course not. I just made it up."

> We don't have a dream ride
> we ride together side by side.
> We don't have a dream boat
> we get wet together without a float.
> We don't have a dream trip
> we trip together lip by lip.

"Everybody now."

> You're my **dream**!
> You're everything to me.
> You're my day **dream**!
> You're who I want... to be with me.
> You're all my hopes...
> you're all my dreams...
> you're who I want with me.

Silence.

I think I just freaked them out.

"You just made that up?" I nod. "That was pretty cool."

"I don't know anyone who's made up a song before."

"My friends and I used to make up songs a lot."

"For Melanie?"

"Kind of. Most of the songs no one ever heard because they were about fast food and hotel rooms and fans bugging her. We had several running songs about Jake. They were just our own commentaries and conglomerations on what was going on around us, just stuff to make us laugh."

We arrive at one of the hottest clubs in Milltown. Pow-Wows is a nondescript, cinder block on the outside, light and fluffy sound-proofing foam on the inside, building in the middle of a strip mall. Originally at one end of the mall, the vibrations bounced it to the middle. The club is only open Thursday, Friday, and Saturday nights. The rest of the week the building settles; the vibrations dissipate. Two security gorillas stoically guard the door as if it were a vault. The line is already starting to coil like a snake. I let my friends get in front of me, and we get in line behind 40 or 50 people. Most of them are our age, a few might be in their thirties, and the two or three in their teens won't make it in the door.

A pair of large Canadian geese fly overhead, honking as if their voices are cracking, like the voice-cracking honking of voice-changing teenage boys.

The guarded vault door is odd because the distinctiveness of Pow-Wows is not inside. Inside it will be loud and dark with spotlights and strobe lights. The distinctiveness is right here lined up on the sidewalk.

Hope, Becky, and Nicole are cowering close, whispering, and peering quickly around at the people in front of us and those collecting behind. It's as if they have lost all self-confidence. Maybe it was my song that did that to them. It's all my fault.

Nicole quietly identifies several models, male and female, within our line. I listen to her without looking at the people she's talking about. I'm not interested in them. There is a great deal of neck-craning going on, throughout the line, and comparisons being made. One of the issues is the similarity and differences of outfits that the women are wearing. Apparently an outfit that is too much like one they are wearing or too different from what they are wearing can raise their emotional ire.

There must be some sort of intense self-confidence dampening field in effect. Humidity is a dampening field, but it's not that bad out. It must be artificial.

"Have I told you all," I startle them by actually talking, "how great you look?" They smile. Hope leans on me. Nicole leans on me a few times and holds my arm twice. Becky paces within a four foot spot.

Rubbing Hope's shoulders, she says, "Oh, don't start that again."

Becky asks me, "Do you think Tom and I have a chance?"

"You're my friend. Tom's my friend. Yeah, I think you have a chance, but I'm not going to push you. That's just not what I do as your friend."

Nicole tells Becky, "I'm your friend, and I'm telling you not to blow this."

We stand quietly for several minutes, until I'm tapped on the shoulder.

"Could we, could my group get ahead of you?" a woman asks.

"Why?"

"There's a guy that keeps poking us." I look at her questioningly. "Really poking us."

"Poke him back," I start to tell her, she turns away, "with this." She turns back as I get out a little box. I extend the telescoping pole. "Touch him with this and then push this button."

"What is it?"

"A stinger."

She takes it and turns back. The crowd is relatively quiet. I watch traffic move on the street. I glance at Becky and Nicole looking at my jacket. Staring at one point on the roadway, it's amazing how many different speeds of traffic–

A man screams, twice.

The rope and pole dividers are jostled.

Arguing and cursing. I cover Hope's sensitive ears. She pulls my hands down. Then we hear applause and hoots. I look back in time to see a guy outside the line walking back to the end of the line. I turn back. Discussion behind us, a pause, then female cursing. They did it to themselves? Talk about being a glutton for punishment.

"Thank you so much," the woman behind us is telling me. "Where did you get this?"

"A friend made it. It's a simple circuit with a strong little battery."

She reluctantly hands it back to me. "I'll buy you a drink when we get in." I decline as the 40 foot lights of the parking lot come on.

"Where was that thing last night?" Hope asks. I put my arms around her.

"What happened last night?"

"At the nursing home, one of the old men..."

"You did fine without it," I tell her.

"More like I held him off until you told him off."

"Still, you probably made his week. If it had been a nurse, they'd have altered his medications."

"Do you think guys live longer by getting turned on?" Nicole asks me.

I tell her, "I have no idea," but then when I start to think about it, I decide that sex has got to help people, men or women, to live longer, but too much or too little probably kills people faster. And while I'm thinking about that, Nicole is posing seductively.

She moves through three poses and stops and says, "The real challenge in modeling is holding your pee like a man." Becky reprimands her. "I'm serious. You look at almost any picture of a model. After everything is set just right, the makeup, the lighting, the shadows, the pose, the hair, the clothes, the jewelry, the prop, the expression, the tilt of the head, the camera angle... everything, what the model is thinking about is having to pee."

"Thanks for sharing," Becky thanks Nicole. To me she says, "We can't take her anywhere."

"Look at any picture, any well constructed picture of a model, and that's what she's thinking. She's thinking, 'I don't know how long I can hold out.'"

Becky asks Nicole, "Could you talk about something else?"

"You mean like waterfalls? Or the drip-drip-drip of a leaky faucet?" Nicole laughs. I think of a song about the Mississippi. Becky lifts my arm from Hope, checks my watch, and replaces my arm.

Taking my arms from around Hope, I reach into my jacket. I think I am being subtle, but after seeing the stinger, all eyes are on me. Hope, Becky, and Nicole are watching. I sense the women behind us are watching. People getting out of their cars are watching me. Nearby traffic is watching me. People watching TV in their homes and people in movie theaters step outside to watch me. Pilots circle their planes and make an announcement to have their passengers watch me. The state of Minnesota is watching my jacket and what I am about to do.

I get out a bracelet. I switch on its tiny revolving lights, and we are bathed in swirling red, yellow, and blue lights. I put it on Hope's wrist. She thanks me. Nicole and Becky admire the bracelet. I wait for a moment as the lights flash over us. I get out another bracelet, turn it on, and hand it to Nicole. And another for Becky. And now some for the strangers behind us. Now a few but not too many for the strangers ahead.

We want their attention turned back to us. One is defective; I put it on my own wrist to keep it separate. I should have tested them at home.

The line is moving.

The adrenaline is rising.

Several groups are excluded from entering. They argue. It's feudal. It's also futile, but I mean it's feudal, like the caste system of the European middle ages or today's American politics. Some people just aren't part of the partying caste. Half of the crowd ahead of us go in or are excluded. The doors are closed behind those let in. That's not good. That could mean that the next group could stop where we are.

All attention is on the door. Will it open again? Is it on a timer, like bank vault doors? The door is imprinted with the word wacipi, which means powwow. No one notices my reaching into my pocket. From a small device, I signal most nearby radios to turn on and broadcast the songs from my device. I didn't invent the thing, but I've occasionally found it useful. Melanie got a kick out of it. It doesn't work on all radios, just a general configuration that is used in most car and portable radios. I notice people taking their personal players off their ears. I turn it up, and now we can hear the thumping of nearby car stereos. People are looking from the line to the parking lot full of booming stereos. Cars are slowing up on the road. Someone from inside comes out and stands in the parking lot, staring at the cars, and then goes back in.

My friends are rubbing their bare arms from the cool evening breeze. I put my hot hands on them to warm them up. I offer my jacket, which has been draped over my arm. Hope declines and the other two follow her lead. If Hope had taken it, I think they all would have climbed inside it.

Becky lifts my arm and looks at my watch again, setting my arm down again when she's done.

The line is moving again.

The adrenaline is rising to a new crescendo. The teens are excluded from entering, and one man is not allowed in. Everyone else in front of us is going in.

Nicole goes in, followed by Becky and Hope. An oak tree falls down in front of me and rests against my chest. I didn't hear it fall. It's not a tree, it's an arm of one of the unnaturally gigantic ape security boys. He has his hand against my chest and is looking directly away from me. There is nothing over there, you big ape. Your hand is over here. I look more intensely where he's looking, for something smaller, like a banana or his brain. What could it be? There is nothing over there. Why are you looking over there?!? Is this his way of saying he refuses to listen to anything I could say? He turns slowly back to me. He still doesn't know I'm here. He's looking at the line. He's going to speak! "Did you hand out the lights?"

"Yes."

"Nice," he says. His arm switches to my back to push me in. He didn't push anyone else in. **Bom-bom-bom-bom-bom-bom-bom-bom-bom-bom-bom-bom-bom-bom–bom-bom-bom-bom-bom–**

I almost forgot about putting in the earplugs. Hope and the others are right inside. They each copy me and put in earplugs. Hey, they brought earplugs! Bom-bom-bom-bom-bom-bom-bom-bom-bom-

Then they try to talk to me about the gorilla. I shrug it off. To the girl at the desk, I motion that I'm paying for the four of us. I read her lips and pay what the lips said.

Bom-bom-bom-bom-bom-bom-bom-bom-bom-bom-bom-bom-bom-bom-bom-bom-bom-

Pow-Wows is dark inside with mini-blinding spotlights, some fixed, others spinning, and some arcing the room in reds and blues. Strobe lights sear the retinas.

Bom-bom-bom-bom-bom-bom-bom-bom-bom-bom-bom-bom-bom-bom-bom-bom-bom-

A waitress intercepts us for our drink orders. Now, I think of offering to be the designated driver. It's too loud in here to ask Hope. I watch Hope to see what she orders.

Bom-bom-bom-bom-bom-bom-bom-bom-bom-bom-bom-bom-bom-bom-bom-bom-bom-bom-

She says, "Double Bubble." I think that's what she said. It was either that or a double bourbon. So

I abstain for now.

Bom-bom-bom-bom-bom-bom-bom-bom-bom-bom-bom-bom-bom-bom-bom-bom-bom-bom-

Maybe she ordered a diet double bourbon. Lip reading is so vague. Becky and Nicole vanish some-time after ordering and while I was watching Hope. Neat trick.

Bom-bom-bom-bom-bom-bom-bom-bom-bom-bom-bom-bom-bom-bom-bom-bom-bom-bom-

Do it again; I didn't see it. We find a table and relocate two more chairs. Hope tries to tell me some-thing. Isn't she sweet? She tries again.

Bom-bom-bom-bom-bom-bom-bom-bom-bom-bom-bom-bom-bom-bom-bom-bom-bom-bom-

Tilting my head and listening through the earplug and over the music and under other voices and around the mixed vibrations, I still can't hear her. I shrug.

Bom-bom-bom-bom-bom-bom-bom-bom-bom-bom-bom-bom-bom-bom-bom-bom-bom-bom-

Uh, oh. She gets up with a determined look. She hops onto my lap and kisses me thoroughly. I pan-tomime that I still don't understand. Could she repeat the message?

Bom-bom-bom-bom-bom-bom-bom-bom-bom-bom-bom-bom-bom-bom-bom-bom-bom-bom-

A tap on my shoulder. It's Nicole. She holds up a finger, telling us to wait. She grabs Becky and acts like they're making out. I smile back. This isn't a competition.

Bom-bom-bom-bom-bom-bom-bom-bom-bom-bom-bom-bom-bom-bom-bom-bom-bom-bom-

The waitress returns. I hold up my wallet and point a circle around the drinks and shout, "How much?" She says something. I make a guess and start holding up fingers.

Bom-bom-bom-bom-bom-bom-bom-bom-bom-bom-bom-bom-bom-bom-bom-bom-bom-bom-

We play our little numbers game until I've guessed right. I tack on tip money and pay her evenly in cash – American, not Canadian, not bug spray, and not sidewalk salt.

Bom-bom-bom-bom-bom-bom-bom-bom-bom-bom-bom-bom-bom-bom-bom-bom-bom-bom-

Motioning to Hope, I request a taste of her drink, it's clearly Diet Double Bubble. I nod and smile. My friends drink their drinks, while we watch the dance floor.

Bom-bom-bom-bom-bom-bom-bom-bom-bom-bom-bom-bom-bom-bom-bom-bom-bom-bom-

It's funny. Outside, all eyes were on the door. Inside, all eyes are on the floor. Some are already dancing. They are the opening act, just warming up the floor.

Bom-bom-bom-bom-bom-bom-bom-bom-bom-bom-bom-bom-bom-bom-bom-bom-bom-bom-

A group surrounds us and asks with mixed signals if I have more bracelets. One by one I find a bracelet, turn it on, and give it to the outstretched hand. One hand left.

Bom-bom-bom-bom-bom-bom-bom-bom-bom-bom-bom-bom-bom-bom-bom-bom-bom-bom-

No more bracelets, just a stinger and a radio controller. She's shy. I ask her to wait. I tap the broken bracelet on my wrist, turn it on, off, on again, tap it, it lights up.

Bom-bom-bom-bom-bom-bom-bom-bom-bom-bom-bom-bom-bom-bom-bom-bom-bom-bom-

I hand it to her. She thanks me and goes looking for her friends. I stand and offer my hand to Hope. **"Would you like to dance?"** I shout. **"Yes!"** she shouts. That I heard.

Bom-bom-bom-bom-bom-bom-bom-bom-bom-bom-bom-bom-bom-bom-bom-bom-bom-bom-

I lead her to a vacant spot on the floor. Starting with simple swaying and tapping, Hope follows my example. We're just getting comfortable.

Bom-bom-bom-bom-bom-bom-bom-bom-bom-bom-bom-bom-bom-bom-bom-bom-bom-bom-

Dancing is just letting music, especially the beat, take over. Feeling the beat in your bones, the melody in your arms, and the words on your face.

Bom-bom-bom-bom-bom-bom-bom-bom-bom-bom-bom-bom-bom-bom-bom-bom-bom-bom-

You imitate dance steps that you know. You improvise. You make use of the available dance space and the abilities of your partner. Escalate your complexities.

Bom-bom-bom-bom-bom-bom-bom-bom-bom-bom-bom-bom-bom-bom-bom-bom-bom-

You warn your partner about trying something unexpected or dangerous or unexpectedly dangerous. I swing Hope around me, and her smile tells me she liked it.

Bom-bom-bom-bom-bom-bom-bom-bom-bom-bom-bom-bom-bom-bom-bom-bom-bom-

You pick up dance moves from around you and make them your own. Looking around I find that the other dancers are looking at us. We've raised the standard. Maybe.

Bom-bom-bom-bom-bom-bom-bom-bom-bom-bom-bom-bom-bom-bom-bom-bom-bom-

I playfully bump hips with Hope and then move into some fancy footwork that's, I don't know... a combination of shuffling, tap dancing, and stomping snow off the boots.

Bom-bom-bom-bom-bom-bom-bom-bom-bom-bom-bom-bom-bom-bom-bom-bom-bom-

I pick Hope up, spin her around, and set her back down where I found her. The beat changes, and I start jumping in place. Hope starts to follow along, but stops herself.

Bom-bom-boomity-boom-bom-bom-boomity-boom-bom-bom-boomity-boom-

As I keep going, I wonder how long this beat is going to go on and how long I can last. I start to notice others jumping in place. The lights flash across us.

Bom-bom-boomity-boom-bom-bom-boomity-boom-bom-bom-boomity-boom-bom-bom-

People are jumping way across the dance floor. It's like giant popcorn just starting to pop. Hope is grinning at me. Anytime your dance partner grins at you, you've done it.

Bom-bom-boomity-boom-bom-bom-boomity-boom-bom-bom-boomity-boom-bom-bom-

This place is really hopping.

Bom-bom-boomity-boom-bom-bom-boomity-boom-bom-bom-boomity-boom-bom-bom-

My legs send my head a nonverbal message that they are not springs and they are getting tired of all the jumping. I give in and decide to stay at Hope's elevation.

Bom-bom-boomity-boom-bom-bom-boomity-boom-bom-bom-boomity-boom-bom-bom-

Nicole is dancing near us with some guy. She introduces him to us. He says, "Hi" and nods my way. We make room for these two and dance more as a group.

Bom-bom-boom-boom-bom-bom-boom-boom-bom-bom-boom-boom-bom-bom-boom-boom-

Over the beat I recognize a song and start to sing with it. Singing with it turns into acting out the words, dropping me to bended knee before my love. The others watch.

Bom-bom-boom-boom-bom-bom-boom-boom-bom-bom-boom-boom-bom-bom-boom-boom-

The next song lacks the ballad quality, so it's back to more normal dancing. I lead the others in a few distinct moves, ending with the Carmen Miranda Warning.

Bom-bom-bom-bom-bom-bom-bom-bom-bom-bom-bom-bom-bom-bom-bom-bom-bom-bom-

The Carmen Miranda Warning has one hand on the head, one hand on the stomach, constant hip swiveling, while slowly turning a full circle.

Bom-bom-bom-bom-bom-bom-bom-bom-bom-bom-bom-bom-bom-bom-bom-bom-bom-bom-

The Carmen Miranda Warning is more appropriate for women. Men don't have the hips for it. Nicole's dance partner looks silly doing it. I hope I don't look like that.

Bom-bom-bom-bom-bom-bom-bom-bom-bom-bom-bom-bom-bom-bom-bom-bom-bom-bom-

I switch into a spiritual dance I was taught a long time ago. I accelerate it a bit to match the beat. The others imitate it as best they can, so in a way, I'm teaching them.

Bom-bom-bom-bom-bom-bom-bom-bom-bom-bom-bom-bom-bom-bom-bom-bom-bom-bom-

I notice a man dancing like he's walking on goose down feathers... smooth. This Fred Astaire guy is good. Thankfully, his dance partner is not Gertrude the Klutz.

Bom-bom-bom-bom-bom-bom-bom-bom-bom-bom-bom-bom-bom-bom-bom-bom-bom-bom-

I take Hope for another spin. She laughs her way through it, stopping to catch her breath. I hold onto her and dance close with her. Never let her fall, except in love.

Bom-bom-bom-bom-bom-bom-bom-bom-bom-bom-bom-bom-bom-bom-bom-bom-bom-bom-

Brushing back her hair, I kiss her. Then I take her hands and step back, pull her close and step back, move in, move out, twist and turn, move in, and step back.

Bom-bom-bom-bom-bom-bom-bom-bom-bom-bom-bom-bom-bom-bom-bom-bom-bom-bom-

Hope dances around me, keeping a hand on me at all times. While I do a variation of the Minnesota Shiver, she wraps her arms around me and moves in close.

Bom-bom-bom-bom-bom-bom-bom-bom-bom-bom-bom-bom-bom-bom-bom-bom-bom-bom-

Fred is spinning his partner like a top. I hope he practiced with a top first. When I spin tops, they spin out of control, gravitating toward the most fragile objects around.

Bom-bom-bom-bom-bom-bom-bom-bom-bom-bom-bom-bom-bom-bom-bom-bom-bom-bom-

Fred turns himself into a chair and catches his partner to give her a rest. We all applaud. He looks around for his next victim, I mean, dance partner.

Bom-bom-bom-bom-bom-bom-bom-bom-bom-bom-bom-bom-bom-bom-bom-bom-bom-bom-

Hope and I stop, look at each other, and motion back to the table. A chair is missing. My jacket is trampled on the floor, but the gadgets are undamaged.

Bom-bom-bom-bom-bom-bom-bom-bom-bom-bom-bom-bom-bom-bom-bom-bom-bom-bom-

I switch off the radio controller. Dancing is just like riding a bicycle; once you stop, you realize how hot you've been. Where's that waitress of ours?

Bom-bom-bom-bom-bom-bom-bom-bom-bom-bom-bom-bom-bom-bom-bom-bom-bom-bom-

Becky returns and is talking closely with Hope. I don't see Nicole. Looking for her flashing bracelet, I see a lot of flashing bracelets. Someone approaches.

Bom-bom-bom-bom-bom-bom-bom-bom-bom-bom-bom-bom-bom-bom-bom-bom-bom-bom-

It's not Nicole; I don't know her. She brushes by me, stops, and stands nearby. She stares at the dance floor, looks at me, stares at the dance floor, looks at me...

Bom-bom-bom-bom-bom-bom-bom-bom-bom-bom-bom-bom-bom-bom-bom-bom-bom-bom-

She should hold up a cartoon-like sign that says, Dance With Me. Without it, I don't understand. Our waitress appears, looking like she was run over by a truck. Twice.

Bom-bom-bom-bom-bom-bom-bom-bom-bom-bom-bom-bom-bom-bom-bom-bom-bom-bom-

I order two glasses of water. Hope orders water. Becky orders a double something. The woman wanting to dance leaves to find sign-making materials.

Bom-bom-bom-bom-bom-bom-bom-bom-bom-bom-bom-bom-bom-bom-bom-bom-bom-bom-

The dance floor looks packed, but having been out there I know it isn't as tight as it looks from a distance. Hope has her hand on Becky's shoulder. Becky wipes her eyes.

Bom-bom-bom-bom-bom-bom-bom-bom-bom-bom-bom-bom-bom-bom-bom-bom-bom-bom-

I lean in to show concern for Becky, without the ability to hear. It's almost like I'm pantomiming the real world. Leaning in to listen, without actually being able to listen.

Bom-bom-bom-bom-bom-bom-bom-bom-bom-bom-bom-bom-bom-bom-bom-bom-bom-bom-

Do old people do that? The waitress returns. I stand and hold up my wallet, indicating that I'm paying. I return a water to her and offer her the chair. She wavers.

Bom-bom-bom-bom-bom-bom-bom-bom-bom-bom-bom-bom-bom-bom-bom-bom-bom-bom-

She sits and drinks her water. Drinking my water, I take my time working with my wallet. When I pay her, the waitress thanks me and leaves. I sit back down.

Bom-bom-bom-bom-bom-bom-bom-bom-bom-bom-bom-bom-bom-bom-bom-bom-bom-

Just as I'm sitting down, a hand pops out in front of me. It's Phil from Flight Control. I stand and shake his hand. I look around for his horn-honking dog.

Bom-bom-bom-bom-bom-bom-bom-bom-bom-bom-bom-bom-bom-bom-bom-bom-bom-

Interrupting him, I yell, "**Where's your dog?**" He chuckles and says something. We're standing too close for me to read his lips. He says something more.

Bom-bom-bom-bom-bom-bom-bom-bom-bom-bom-bom-bom-bom-bom-bom-bom-bom-

He is still saying stuff. I tap his shoulder with the back of my hand and introduce Hope and Becky. He asks me something. I motion that I can't hear. He starts to indicate–

Bom-bom-bom-bom-bom-bom-bom-bom-bom-bom-bom-bom-bom-bom-bom-bom-bom-

–something. I shake his hand again and yell, "**Take it easy!**" I sit back down. That's just what I need... to see someone from Flight Control right now. They drive me crazy.

Bom-bom-bom-bom-bom-bom-bom-bom-bom-bom-bom-bom-bom-bom-bom-bom-bom-

Everyone should have a corporate stalker. They help you when you're feeling lonely. I hadn't thought of AutoDrive all night. Thanks Phil, for reminding me about it.

Bom-bom-bom-bom-bom-bom-bom-bom-bom-bom-bom-bom-bom-bom-bom-bom-bom-

Hope taps me. She talks loudly in my ear, something about going. I ask, "Going?" She nods. She talks in my ear, "Have you seen Nicole?" I tell her no and offer to look.

Bom-bom-bom-bom-bom-bom-bom-bom-bom-bom-bom-bom-bom-bom-bom-bom-bom-

I search the nearby tables. No Nicole. I search the dance floor, dancing and shuffling my way through it. No Nicole. I check another table section and the bar.

Bom-bom-bom-bom-bom-bom-bom-bom-bom-bom-bom-bom-bom-bom-bom-bom-bom-

I ask a woman going into the ladies room if she'd see if there's a Nicole in there. She comes out right away to tell me, "No, sorry." I've searched the place. I go back.

Bom-bom-bom-bom-bom-bom-bom-bom-bom-bom-bom-bom-bom-bom-bom-bom-bom-

As I'm telling Hope that I couldn't find Nicole, I stop myself, and I ask her to wait. I relax. We search the place again. We check outside. She's outside. I open my eyes.

Bom-bom-bom-bom-bom-bom-bom-bom-bom-bom-bom-bom-bom-bom-bom-bom-bom-

"**She's outside!**" I yell. Hope and Becky get up and grab their purses. I grab my jacket. We head out. Outside, I take out my earplugs. My ears thank me.

Nicole's freezing, so I lend her my jacket. She tells us about getting kicked out for hitting a man and what he had done to her first. In the car Nicole asks me, "Are you always giving things to strangers?"

Turning around in my seat I tell her, "I don't think you're a stranger, and I didn't give you that jacket; I lent it to you. There's a difference."

"Not the jacket, the bracelets," she says slipping it out the sleeve and flashing it in my face.

"He bought the waitress a water," Hope points out.

"She looked like she was going to pass out."

"No, last Friday night you gave out candles – "

"So did you!"

"–and tonight it was light-up bracelets. Do you always give some form of lights to strangers on Friday nights?"

"Yes, Friday nights are the nights for free lights," I advertise in an announcer's voice. "Other rules and restrictions apply. Offer valid only when I feel like it."

"Where are we going?" Hope asks.

"You're driving."

"That doesn't mean I have to decide where to go."

"Is anyone hungry?" I ask. They agree or kind of agree. I navigate Hope to the Streetcar Named Dina on Seventh, one of the few places open late in Pigs Eye. It's tough to get to because the sidewalks are all rolled up, and strangely, Seventh is not six blocks away from First Street. A glacier melted and more streets had to be named. Streetcar Named Dina is a faded yellow and chrome streetcar converted into a narrow diner. It shares its late night clientele with the Pig's Sty Saloon next door. I navigate Hope to a parking spot on the other side of Dina to avoid the unappetizing spot between the two late-night hot spots, the pig's trough, where people routinely get sick. Dina's sign says Breakfast Anytime, so I order French toast.

Sitting across from Becky and Nicole in the diner's stainless steel and red vinyl brilliance, they look like they've both cried. Hope asks them how many drinks they had. I remember buying one for Nicole and two for Becky, so I'm surprised to learn they were closer to the double digits. Guys were buying them drinks left and right. "So had you finished one before starting another?"

"I had two at once, once," Nicole says, wiping the table with her forehead.

"He was asking about drinks," Becky smirks.

An earth-laden guy comes along and pulls up a chair that squeals its way across the dingy linoleum to the end of our booth. He makes a big effort to say something. Even though he gestures articulately, his tongue and lips are as coordinated as a fish on a bicycle. He smiles repulsively, causing us to lean away. That's when he gets tossed out.

Nicole asks Becky, "How would you rate him?"

Becky giggles, "Compared to the rest of tonight's opportunities?" Nicole nods. "I'd say he was a five, maybe four and a half."

"I'd agree on the four and a half," Nicole rests her chin on an unsteady elbow.

"You must not have caught a whiff of his breath," I counter.

"That was factored in."

"Yes, there was a wind factor that did not escape our notice. He was not a breath of fresh air. And his face was a-pealing. Still, you have to look at the big picture of how he compares to tonight's candidates."

I thank Chet for evicting the fifth Beatle, when he brings us our plates. To Nicole, I say, "So the scale changes... depending on who's around. You grade on a curve?"

Nicole sobers up and says, "Everyone grades on a curve." Past her, the windows reflect blurry images of us at an upward angle. Traffic headlights drive through us. "You don't up and say, 'That's it. Everybody sucks.' You don't. Because where does that put you? Are you better than everyone else? If you think that, it works the other way." I tunnel through the French toast using only a fork. The toasted French offer little resistance. "Am I right?" I nod. Nicole slumps back down, relieved for some reason.

"I've always thought this place has the ideal ambiance for a murder investigation," I tell them, looking at a tear in the red vinyl that exposes its underside and the foam of the seat. "I imagine detectives combing over all the scratches and scuffs of the place and the claw marks across the floor, punctures in the vinyl, and scraping on the window ledges and deducing that a bear must have made its way through here."

That went over like a bear in a canoe. It's time to be quiet. Hope looks exhausted. The percussion of forks on plates are all that's left in our booth.

Becky wags a French fry saying, "I want someone stable."

"I've always had to invent my own stability," I say before reminding myself that it's time to be quiet. I study my French toast. Clearing away layers of French toast, I find a petroglyph on the plate. It is a petroglyph from Wakan Teebe cave of a turtle and two snakes. I've seen reproductions of this petroglyph many times, but I've never been in the cave. Eating away more French toast debris and staring at the turtle through local maple syrup, it's not a turtle at all. It's a dark, driver-less Pegasus Coup tilted down to pass between the snakes. The perspective switch, from the size of a turtle to the size of a car, makes the snakes into roadside barriers while still looking like snakes. That is one dangerous road. Caution: giant snakes. I almost point it out to the others, when I realize it's still quiet time, and they're waiting for me. Pushing away my plate, Chet hands me the bill. Acting stunned by the total, I yell the dollar amount with dramatic astonishment. Then I pay Chet, adding extra tip money for bear repairs. I ask Hope for her car keys, saying, "I'd like to drive. I think I'm more awake than you are." She relinquishes the keys, they climb in, and all the passengers fall asleep. I drive them quietly home and get them inside, while birds gargle and practice their scales with test chirps.

32
Go

Taking out the batteries and putting away the gadgets, I add my clothes to my dirty little clothes piles and determine to foresee what happens to AutoDrive. Sprawling across the bed, I close my eyes, and I relax.

I'm sharing scrambled eggs on a stick with Hope.

I open my eyes. No that's not the AutoDrive test.

I close my eyes, and I relax.

A toy car and I are in front of a class of school kids.

I open my eyes. No that's not the AutoDrive test.

I close my eyes, and I relax.

A mottled cat blinks from the bed of an old man.

I open my eyes. No that's not the AutoDrive test.

I close my eyes, and I relax.

Faith asks Red if he heard the report that 30 years from now there won't be any more redheads. He freaks out.

I open my eyes. No that's not the AutoDrive test.

I close my eyes, and I relax.

Hope has her head on my shoulder. The kid in the seat in front of me is screaming her head off. I can't hear a word she's screaming because of my earplugs.

I open my eyes. No that's not the AutoDrive test.

I close my eyes, and I relax.

I'm in a lingerie store. I'm never in lingerie stores.

I open my eyes. No that's not the AutoDrive test.

I close my eyes, and I relax.

I'm shaking Ray's hand in front of the very well lit Lactating Woman drinking fountain.

I open my eyes. No that's not the AutoDrive test.

I close my eyes, and I relax.

The mayor waves his hand at Carl and calls Flight Control, "One of Milltown's marvels." I laugh myself awake.

I was there again. I have to stop laughing; I refuse to laugh myself awake this time. I will be as serious as serious gets. I won't even lie down.

I sit on the floor with my legs out. I relax. Bumped and jostled by a crowd, I forgot to bring a satellite dish tower again. Up on the short platform, the mayor is introducing Dumas to the crowd. When the mayor speaks of the distinguished achievements of Flight Control, I assume no one bothered to remind him of the time we almost took out the gas main. The challenge was that the gas lines were buried four feet down.

Dumas starts to explain the potential of AutoDrive, saying, "AutoDrive will return people with impairments. AutoDrive will talk on the phone. AutoDrive children... take directions." It's like he memorized phrases, but not complete sentences. He's all jumbled up. We catch eyes. "We want to go with safety to...

the roads. AutoDrive will allow you to drive us anywhere. It will give rides to anyone on your block. AutoDrive will be the car you want to have the elderly. People who can't drive will AutoDrive. AutoDrive is today's dream tomorrow."

He's killing me.

And he could be right.

He's speaking in tongues and the crowd is wondering if he's real. Carrying the microphone down to the car, he's about to pass in front of the speakers. I can't believe he's doing this, and no one up there is stopping him. Feedback builds instantly from the speakers, and people plug their ears, wincing. I'll have to remember to bring earplugs along with my satellite dish tower.

Carl turns on the car, gets out, and shuts the door. He leans in the open window with the mike and says, "Go." His head is grazed as he tries to clear the window. The car takes off. He says, "There goes AutoDrive," but his tone is nowhere near as positive as it should have been. He starts swearing a half second before flipping off the microphone.

The Pegasus Coup turns the corner down the block.

Some people move down the sidewalk in the direction it disappeared only to be stopped by a barricade and a police officer. The rest of us just stand around. Carl is back on stage rubbing his head while pointing out something on a map to several people. The mayor indicates the crowd and points to Carl's microphone. Carl shakes his head.

"So this is it? The car disappears around a corner?" someone asks.

The test drive should have been conducted at the race track, so that everyone could see what the car does, but I'm sure that would've cost too much money. Besides, AutoDrive was not created for the racetrack environment. It wouldn't work. The sound of a car hitting a fire hydrant gets our attention. It is heading this way from another street. There is damage to the front right quarter panel and AutoDrive is still driving. It's not supposed to do that. Now I'm thinking like AutoDrive. What's it going to do? Well, it will no longer recognize any problem from the right side of the car, since those sensors probably aren't functioning... certainly not in tandem. It will see the two foot tall platform with its black top and... it will not be able to distinguish it from the road.

I yell, "Look out!" startling the people right near me. Most others don't hear me. AutoDrive sees the people on the platform but thinks it can get around them, not understanding that they are on the platform that it is about to hit. Carl tries to hit a remote control which does nothing. He never did like technology. He jumps up off the stage. Mid-flight he is batted by the flying stage like a pitched baseball. That's got to hurt.

The car pushes two of the stage pieces down the street, with loud pipes-on-pavement scraping, leaving the rest of the wreckage behind. Now it must be thinking it sees pavement in front of it, which is actually the tops of the stage pieces. Between the false pavement and the smashed right fender, AutoDrive is practically driving blindfolded. It is trying to accelerate back up to its cruising speed.

I dodge and weave my way through the crowd, hop the barricade, and run after the car. From what I saw, many people were hurt. I have my answer, and I have no chance of catching up to the car or figuring a way to stop it now that it's blind. I run one block while it drives three to hit another barricade and a squad car, with its two-stage battering ram.

I open my eyes. I'm sitting on the floor of my sunny room with my legs stretched out in front of me and my back to the bed. How did I get in this position? What time is it? My clock has fallen over again. Maybe I need to build it a chair. It's 11:11 on a sunny Saturday morning in the middle of August. There's a note on the floor near the door.

Now I know what AutoDrive is going to do. I'm not sure that it out-and-out killed anyone, but if it didn't, it sure did injure people and send 30 mile-per-hour shrapnel flying around as it took the stage.

Crawling to what has to be a note from Hope, I harvest it from the carpet, and it says that she's worried about me sitting on the floor. She says she's gone out shopping. She liked dancing with me last night. Then she elaborately writes Love and below it the L and the V transform into an H and a P to end up as Hope. It would make a neat flip book.

AutoDrive flipped people off like that. I can't let that happen... not that I could do anything about stopping it after it hit the stage. There is no reasoning with AutoDrive once it's lost its senses.

I rub and move around my legs. I could try to stop AutoDrive before it comes back around... but by then it's already hit the hydrant. I could somehow stop it before it hits the hydrant. Yes. I could stop it before it does anything. Won't that make people happy?

This is the police dilemma. The police dilemma is that police officers have to wait for the crime to be committed before stopping the crime. That is why hiring more police officers does not stop crime. You can fill the streets with police officers, and they may be surrounded by seemingly suspicious behavior. The police could've arrested everyone that headed in the direction of where AutoDrive first disappeared, for attempting to cross a police barricade or something. But those people weren't trying to cross the police line, they were trying to watch AutoDrive. They were trying to see what was happening, that's all. Even if all police officers could foresee what would happen, all they could really do is be at the right place at the right time, maybe catching someone in the act of committing a crime, but the timing of that is so narrow that it has to be nearly impossible. So they put up cameras in banks and on street corners as irrefutable eyewitnesses to catch people in the act. But even if the criminal doesn't wear a simple baseball cap to protect their identity, the images are rarely clear enough to identify anyone. Banks could be saturated with cameras, under the floor, in the walls, in the pens on chains, in the teller's glasses... everywhere, but even then, someone would have to sift through all that video, which could take a long time.

I can't stop AutoDrive before it does anything. I would be locked up.

I can warn them. I can call Wendy. Draining some fluid in the bathroom, I shower and shave, making myself presentable for the phone call. I call Wendy.

"Hello."

"You're not Wendy."

"Wendy, who?" Will asks.

"I take it she's not there."

"Right. That's your fault. She's at Flight Control."

"How could that be my fault?"

"You would never work her on a Saturday."

"That's right. People need time off to think straight. Could you give her a message for me?"

"Do you want to call her directly?"

"Nah. Could you tell her that during the test, AutoDrive will hit a fire hydrant on Sinkhole Street, then turn onto Nicollet and run into the presentation stage."

"Really? Maybe you should call her."

"Could you tell her?"

"Yeah, I'll tell her. Hang on a minute. You said, 'Sinkhole turning...' was it a right or a left?"

"A right. It actually cuts the corner."

"Sinkhole turning right onto Nicollet and hitting the presentation stage. I don't know what presentation stage you're talking about."

"That's because it isn't there yet. It's one of those temporary stages like a hotel would set up in an events room... the type Melanie played on in Cleveland."

"Oh, I know the type. So AutoDrive is going to hit it. Were there... are there going to be people on it at the time... when it got... when it'll get hit?"

"Yes."

"Oh." Pause. "Was... is Wendy going to be..."

"She wasn't on it. Hopefully that's not going to change."

"Got it. Okay so I'm sending her a text saying that you said that 'during the test AutoDrive will hit a fire hydrant on Sinkhole, turn right onto Nicollet and hit the presentation' – oops, two T's in presentation – 'stage with people on it.' That sound right?"

"Great. Are you going to Tom's tomorrow?"

"Yes. I am; Wendy probably won't be able to make it."

"Okay, I'll see you there. Thanks!"

"Bye!" Setting down the phone, I lie back on the bed and stare up at the ceiling halo. Ah... No more AutoDrive. Wendy will relay the message, and the R&D team will stop the injuries and property damage from ever occurring. It's all done. All systems are go. Mission accomplished.

I'm tired. I sleep, until I'm startled by a kiss.

"Hey, Sleeping Beauty, do you want to sleep the day away?" That's got to be a trick question. The correct answer is obviously, no. And yet I pull my covers over my head anyway. I wonder why that is? My comforter is tugged effortlessly from me, leaving me exposed to the air conditioning. I duck under a sheet and its elasticized corners. "Wake up... Smell the coffee..."

"I don't drink coffee," the sheet mutters.

"Come on, Sweetie, I'd like to talk to you," Hope says.

I climb out of the fitted sheet, hug her, get changed, and plop back down on the – "Bed!"

"No, you need to stay awake."

I reluctantly remain upright, realizing the historical rational. "Mankind never wanted to become upright. Mankind was forced into it to stay awake."

"You've been asleep for nearly ten hours, right?" I shake my head. "I know we made a deal about Nicole, but it's driving me bananas. I need to know if she's been in bed with you."

"No, she hasn't. At least I don't think so."

"Could you tell me if she does?"

"Right away?"

"No. Just tell me, okay?"

"Okay. The reason I only got to sleep around noon was that for a while at least, I got pointed perception working again. I had to make sure that the AutoDrive test wouldn't hurt anyone, but it did. It hit a hydrant."

Hope giggles, "Is the hydrant going to be okay?"

"No. Yes. The hydrant is going to be okay. It'll be up and hydranting in no time. No, after it hits the hydrant, the car plows into the stage."

"Is that its first stage? Where is this again?"

"Downtown Milltown. The presentation stage. It had the VIPs on it: the mayor; the owner of Flight Control, Carl Dumas; several others..."

"Oh. What are you going to do?"

"I already did it. I called Wendy, got Will, and gave him the details. I'm done."

Hope's brow wrinkles. She ponders it. "How do you know?"

"What do you mean?"

"How do you know that you've stopped AutoDrive from hurting anyone? You called Will..."

"He sent a message to Wendy."

"So he sent a message to Wendy. Let's say Wendy changes things. How do you know things aren't going to still happen the same way? Or worse?" I picture AutoDrive steering clear of the stage and plowing into the crowd instead. "With multiple futures possible, people can still get–"

Trumpets interrupt Hope. The phone says it's Flight Control, Inc. I show the phone's screen to Hope before answering.

"Hello?"

"Hey! This is Wendy. Can I put you on speaker?"

"Please don't."

"Oh." Something muffled. "We were wondering what more you can tell us."

"The mayor, Carl, Bailey, and others are on a makeshift stage, one of those temporary stages, on Nicollet Mall. Carl gets off the stage, passes in front of the speakers, causing piercing feedback... and starts the car. By the way, he never shows the inside of the car so people can see that there is no one in it. He leans in the window and says, 'Go.' The car grazes his head."

"Okay, hang on." I look at Hope listening intensely. Something muffled. "Go on."

"The car goes down the street a few blocks and takes a left."

"Where does it turn?"

"On Mdewakanton Avenue, I think. Then it's gone for a while, but it comes back from Sinkhole Street, cutting the corner, hitting a fire hydrant, with only minor injuries to the hydrant..."

"What was that?"

"Nothing. It hits a free standing hydrant while turning back onto Nicollet and sustains damage to the front right quarter panel. It proceeds back down Nicollet, runs into the stage and takes two pieces several blocks before smashing into a squad car." Silence. "Hello Wendy?"

"I'm here," she's crying. I slump down with the weight of having made one of my friends cry. Damn.

"Look..."

"Is that it?"

"Yeah, that's it."

"I gotta go. Thank you."

"Sure." We disconnect. I stare at the phone for all the trouble it's caused. "That went about as well as could be expected. I made her cry."

"You weren't exactly the bearer of good news."

"No. I wasn't. How do you think it makes me feel? AutoDrive ends up a wreck. Knowing that it doesn't work and that, as you said, I'll still have to monitor it, even though my pointed perception hasn't been working right... it's not what I wanted."

"What's wrong with pointed perception?"

"I don't know, it's been confused, scattered snippets. It's been tough to understand much of anything."

"Have you had any more dreams about Lefty's memory recording?"

"No."

"How long have you had the trouble with pointed perception?"

I think about it. "One week... since last Saturday."

"Since you moved in here."

"Exactly."

We sit in silence pondering the implications. "So it's me," Hope says.

"Maybe I have it too good here. The apartment wasn't exactly idyllic living."

"But you had pointed perception earlier..."

"But that was less than idyllic also."

"You could sleep in a tent in the yard... one that leaks. We could set up the sprinkler..." I tackle her and tickle her. Her giggles are music. Somehow she ends up on top, smiling down at me. "You know, with that call, you may have just saved the life of the guy who fired you."

"I didn't think of that, not that way. I didn't pick who to save. I doubt anyone who saves lives, firefighters, the Coast Guard, ever stops to decide who should live and who should die."

"They never have the time," she smiles. I think she just made a joke. More tickling. Her bracelet is no longer flashing. Stopping side-by-side, she says, "You're having trouble seeing the future? You poor baby! The rest of the world may understand." More tickling. My stomach rumbles. She puts her ear to it. She listens and talks to it, "What's that? Uh-huh. I see. So you haven't eaten all day and you want some food? Uh-huh..." I get uncomfortable being cut out of the conversation between Hope and my stomach. She continues to talk with it and it with her, and I feel a twinge of jealousy. No one has ever talked directly to my stomach before. I feel excluded. And my stomach has good manners; it doesn't talk when Hope is talking. It waits to rumble until after Hope finishes talking. Maybe it's that when Hope stops to listen with her ear to my stomach, she applies a little pressure, and that's what gets my stomach going. From my waist, Hope says, "We've decided you need to eat."

"Okay, but when you're done there, my pancreas would like to have a word with you." I pick up the snowy white comforter and heap it on the bed. Ray has left the camera, camera box, and materials by my closet. Hope picks up my clock.

"Your clock is running fast," she says quizzically.

"Just set it down, and it'll be okay."

"Did I forget to tell you? We have a policy in this house. You have to make your bed every morning." I glance at the bed and chase Hope into the kitchen. I grab the box of Major Munch, a banana, and apple juice. "Please don't tell me you're going to mix those three?" I really ought to, just for her reaction.

"I think you are happy to be done with school."

"Very observant Dr. Freud. What else?"

"And you had a good time shopping..."

"Right, I should show you what I bought. But what else?" I shrug. "I'm excited to spend more time with you!" She watches me separate the majors from the munches, picks up the box, and analyzes it. "This isn't real food."

"Look." I point to a spot on the box. "See? It's part of a complete breakfast."

"What does a 'complete breakfast' mean? I don't think it means healthy, and if it does, you have to eat all these other things: eggs, a grapefruit, and is that a can of spinach?"

She's teasing me again. "Let me see." I angle the box just right for light; it's one of the tricks of detecting a forgery. "Ray drew that in. He likes to make his mark on packaging. If you look in the cabinet, we have canned beaches, not peaches."

"Did he switch the contents too?"

"Which would look better in Hope's hair? Majors? Or munches?"

Hope backs away as I pick up a handful of munches. "Did I forget to tell you? We have a house policy against throwing food too. I'm going to run up and get the stuff I bought." I wonder what she bought? A snowmobile? She wouldn't have a snowmobile upstairs. Most snowmobiles are already put together. Maybe she's getting the keys that she left upstairs. Hope brings down shopping bags, and I rub my head trying to think how much of a snowmobile could fit in the bags. Either she has all the fasteners, nuts, and bolts in one bag; all the snow guards and fenders in another bag; grips and seat cushion in another; gauges and gear shift in another; headlights and taillights in another; and the tractor treads, fuel tank, engine, and handlebars are still upstairs; or she didn't buy a snowmobile. She pulls out a tank top and shorts. "You don't like it?"

"No, it's good. I was just expecting a fender." Hope thinks I'm teasing her. She presses them to her body to simulate wearing them. "Is that how you're going to wear them? I think part is supposed to cover your back and part is supposed to cover your front."

"I'm not going to try them on here. What if Ray comes home?"

I cram my banana in my mouth with a last handful of cereal, grab my glass of apple juice, and motion Hope to my room with a, "Mmmm-mph."

"That's disgusting," she says, following me with her bags. I would ask what she means, but my mouth is full. Fluffing up my pillow, I get comfortable. Hope looks confused, like she's figuring out how to try on a snowmobile. "You really want to do this?" I nod, still chewing. She unstraps and kicks off her shoes. Looking at me, she unfastens and unzips her shorts. She lowers them down her legs and steps out of them, leaving her in her shirt and what appears to be thong panties. "Don't look at my butt," she tells me, with her hands covering her backside, just in case I were to suddenly appear behind her.

I swallow, "Why?"

"Because. It's my butt."

"I've never even seen my butt. I am told I have one, but I wouldn't otherwise know. Have you ever seen your butt?"

"No."

"Then what are you worried about?"

"What if you don't like it?"

"Would that be the end of the world?" I shake my head, "What you don't seem to realize is that I've seen your butt."

"When?"

"Plenty of times. I already know what it looks like."

Hope removes her hands, stepping closer, "And?"

"And what?"

"And what did you think?"

"Oh. It's fine. It's great. It's part of you."

"You aren't convincing me."

"Am I supposed to convince you of something? Let's say I was ashamed of my 982nd hair... this one, right here... and I didn't want you to see it. What would you say?"

"I would say that you don't need to worry about that hair."

Weeping dramatically into my pillow, I ask, "But have you seen it... really seen my 982nd hair?!? It's disgusting! How could you possibly love it?" Her hand is on my back.

"Because it's part of you. I love everything about you."

I sit up and pull her to me. "I love everything about you too. I love your butt, but I don't differentiate it from any other part of you. People come pre-assembled. I love all of you."

"Is there a part of me that you don't like?"

"Yes. But like I said, it's all you."

Hope pins me down, "What don't you like? Come on, out with it!"

"There it is. I've gotten you upset."

"Tell me!"

"It's when you're upset. That's what I don't like."

Hope looks into my eyes, alternating, one at a time. "Really?"

"Really."

"That is so sweet."

"No, it's not sweet. It really tears out my heart when you're upset. Even seeing you mildly upset hurts like hell."

Hope sits back. "Wow."

My thumbs hold her hips as my fingers brush over her butt. "Thankfully, unlike hair number 982, your being upset comes and goes." Hope kisses me, climbs off me, starts to cover her butt, looks back at me, and uncovers it, smiling. She tries on the new shorts. "Those look good. Turn around. How do they feel?"

"They're a little scratchy at the waistband."

"That doesn't sound good. This may sound stupid but are all women's shorts scratchy at the waistband?"

"No. Part of it is these tags, but part of it is the elastic."

I go over and feel it. "You could insulate the elastic by always tucking in a shirt or attaching a piece of cloth..." Hope takes off her shirt and bra and puts on a tank top. "You don't wear a bra with that?"

"No. It has a bra built in."

"Right. Half of my pants have underwear built in too. I understand." She takes it off and turns it inside out to show me the hidden supporting structure. She puts it on again. I think she likes doing this. "Other than the tags, I like it." Having learned that it is an important question, I ask again, "How does it feel?"

"Good."

"Good, that's the way clothes should feel." She takes off all her clothes and puts something else on. She works with the straps. It doesn't cover much. I don't know what it is. "What is it?"

"It's a swimsuit." Oh. "It changes color with body heat. Like a mood ring." I study her mood. She turns around without my asking.

"How does it feel?" I ask without thinking that the suit is already answering.

"Good."

"Where would you wear it?" I wonder aloud.

"Around you. Do you like it?"

"It's nice. It's sexy, well... it's not sexy; it's just fabric and chemicals. You're sexy, and it complements you. But..."

"What?"

"I hope it's not toxic."

"I'm sure they tested it."

"How? With rats in mood swimsuits?" Hope doubles over laughing. "The rats would see the scientists approach with the little swimsuits and would ask, 'Now what?!?'"

Hope is on the floor, saying, "They coax the rat with the swimsuit on into the little rat pool and under the sun lamp."

"Is the pool a wading pool or does it have a diving board and little lifeguard stand?"

"Both. It's a wading pool with a diving board."

"Lab rats must have a little sign that says, 'Number of days without an accident equals zero,' and it's permanently set at zero." Hope gets up and tries on jeans. I look them over. "For me, the real test of pants is to sit down in them." She tests sitting down.

"For me, it's what shoes am I going to wear with them."

I'll play along. "What shoes are you going to wear?"

"Sandals with a thick strap, short black boots... maybe this one pair of tennis shoes."

"Do you want to get them?"

"I will." She leaves and comes right back. "I can't believe we're doing this."

She goes out again. My nightstand is covered in a lava flow of little bubble hearts. I'm going to have to get that alarm clock fixed. Hope is back with an armful of shoes, way more than three pairs. As she tries them on with her jeans, I try to be helpful, but I'm not really seeing what she's seeing. To me, they are shoes with jeans. I'm not sure I understand the intricate relationship between them. Hope takes off her tank top and tries on a bra. At least with shoes and jeans, I understand them on some level. I get my phone and search the Internet for "fit bra." A woman is having a fit in a bra. I select the next hit, which is about having proper fit in a bra. Hope sits down next to me.

"This says that the straps should lay on your skin; they shouldn't cut into you. That makes sense. Your shoulder straps aren't cutting in, but this strap is. It says this strap should be horizontal. It shouldn't ride up in back, but it does. The elastic should not itch or irritate the skin. It says that any underwire... does this have underwire?"

"No. If it did, it would be here."

"Underwire should not poke into you. Poke into you? What kind of torture device is this?" Hope pats my shoulder. "It has wiring? What about creating an air conditioned bra? Why not put the wiring to good use?" Hope nods. "What size do you wear?" Hope tells me with strict confidentiality. I read further and ask, "At the end of a long day, where does it hurt?"

"Here, there, and everywhere. Usually here, here, there, my feet..."

"I wonder if I could experiment on you, once school is back in session."

"My Life As A Lab Rat."

"No, I would just work with you to see what we could do to reduce or eliminate the end of the day aches and pains."

"Yeah?"

"Yeah."

"I'd go along with that."

"Is there anything else?"

"Just some earrings."

"So now what?"

"What do you mean? Are you wondering what we should do?"

"No, what's the next step? Do you return the shorts?"

"I guess so."

"Do you put away the clothes that you bought and remove the clothes that they are replacing?"

"Replacing?" Hope changes back into her original clothes.

"Yeah."

"These clothes aren't replacing anything."

"They're not?"

"No."

"So..."

"I buy clothes," she says slowly and suddenly I'm a fourth grader. "If I like them, I keep them. I add them to the clothes I already have. You should appreciate this; I now have more possibilities."

"But..."

"Shh. You lie down now. You've had a tough afternoon, and you've been a big help. I'm going to put these things away and come back down." Hope tucks me in and carries out her stuff. She was being sarcastic about my tough afternoon. I've read up on recognizing sarcasm in those around you, and that was definitely sarcasm. Sarcasm is an art form. Modern museums should consider exhibiting the best of modern sarcasm, not that– "Miss me?" Hope asks climbing in. Technically no, I missed your sarcasm. I couldn't stop thinking about it. Hope takes my mind off of her sarcasm. I do my part in garnering her attention. We rest awhile. We are about to start distracting each other some more when the upstairs neighbors start a ruckus. It's enough to get my attention here, but back at Whisper Willows, this would be nothing. "We really have to be careful," Hope says. "Do you want to know another reason I don't want to have kids?" I nod. "I don't want to always have to play referee." Hope prepares herself and storms upstairs. I'm kicking around some piles of dirty laundry when trumpets blare. It's Hope. I will always answer Hope's call. "I'd like to make dinner for you. Could you come up here and bring the camera manual?" I agree, even though I don't see the correlation, and it's not exactly a manual camera. Oh yeah, she said, "camera manual." I get cleaned up, iron a shirt and put on a tie. This tie shouldn't clash with my shorts. From now on when I buy a tie, I'll have to bring my shorts, like Hope and her shoes. Hope does a double take when she sees how I've dressed myself like a fifth grader would.

"What's for dinner?"

"Do you like salmon?"

"Yes."

"That's not what we're having. Just kidding. It's salmon and angel hair pasta with tomatoes," she says while taking a look at the manual. She quickly gets out a pen. "Do you have this electronically?"

"Yes, I think it's on the disk."

"Dinner is going to be ready in 20 minutes. Do you think you could find the file and send it to me?" Downstairs I take off my tie and hang back up the shirt, pulling on a T-shirt. My computer's battery is charged, and it helps me read the CD. I send Hope the file. While eating dinner, Hope edits the manual and tells me, "You've been losing weight. You need to remember to eat." Eat. Got it. "I mean it. You're looking really skinny. Have you eaten anything before this today?" I'm about to answer giddily when she adds, "Other than the cereal and the banana." Crestfallen, I shake my head. "What can I do to get you to eat more?"

"Help me figure out what's going wrong with pointed perception, so I can make sure AutoDrive doesn't kill anyone in its test."

Hope sets down her pen. "When is the AutoDrive test?"

"The Sunday before Labor Day."

"Right. And when is the experiment with Lefty?"

"This Thursday."

"Right. You're worried about something that's two weeks and a day away, when five days from now you get to play lab rat yourself. I don't think you've got your priorities straight." Hope stirs the pot.

"Either way, I need to figure out what is causing pointed perception to be unreliable."

A cloud of steam rises as Hope pours the pot of noodles through a strainer. She runs cool water through the noodles, tosses them, and pours the noodles into a frying pan with pieces of tomatoes and other ingredients. She stirs in basil and oregano, covers the pan, checks the heat, and sits back down. She seems to be re-writing entire sentences.

"I know fourth graders who can write better than this."

"Yeah, well, we all can't be writers."

"I wasn't criticizing you. I was criticizing whoever wrote this."

"Whomever."

"Whatever." Hope twiddles her pen. "I think AutoDrive costs too much."

"What? You lost me."

"If a mobility impaired person needs a ride, they can call a cab. Period. Flight Control fires you, but it's as if you're still working for them. They have Wendy working all hours and on the verge of tears. And you said that AutoDrive is going to go crazy and either injure or kill people." Hope gets up to stir the pan. "It costs too much. Is this technological breakthrough more important than the lives of the people struggling toward it? Is the goal of AutoDrive more important than the lives of everyone at Flight Control? I'm just putting this into perspective." Hope puts on a hot pink oven mitt and checks the salmon. "What you're trying to do with pointed perception is to live your life in a test run, and maybe to live for everyone, but that's not what life is all about. Is it?"

"No. Not most of the time."

"When is it?"

"When people are going to die. Especially from something I helped create."

"But can you stop that? Can you stop people from dying?"

"I think so. If they listen to me."

"But you don't know that, do you? You saved Fran. But did you know that she was going to die?" she asks, taking off the hot mitt.

"No. Only the guy living in the storage unit. I fed him some bananas. He would have died before I moved. He didn't, but I don't know if anything has happened since then."

"I think there is a big difference between using pointed perception for deciding whether or not to take part in Lefty's experiment and using it to save people's lives. You have to live your life too. You aren't God. You can't stop people from dying. Doctors can't. You can't. You can do everything right and still not do enough. It never seems enough because in the end, we're only human. There's only so much we can do. Everything has risk. If you try to eliminate all risk... you can't. A car in the garage is safe, but that's not what cars are made for. Cool! I just made a car analogy!"

"Great." Hope gives a cute, I'm-proud-of-myself look. She concentrates on editing the camera manual. Without the distraction of editing my life, she gets through a few more pages and serves up dinner. She pours us each a glass of Birch Blackberry Stain wine. "This looks great," I tell her, as Nicole breezes out the door with a wave.

"Thank you. Now, you said you got pointed perception working again. How?"

"I don't know."

"What did you do?"

"I closed my eyes and relaxed, just like any other time." I chew on that for a while. "No, I laughed myself awake from the mayor's praises of Carl and Flight Control, so I sat on the floor, determined not to laugh myself awake again."

"There are worse ways of waking up."

I swallow, "It's the bed! The bed has screwed up pointed perception."

"That bed happens to be state-of-the-mattress-arts technology."

"It's too comfortable."

"Too comfortable?"

"Yeah, I actually miss my old bed." The salmon flakes off in pink layers three millimeters wide with a white sheen and a darker pink edge.

Hope loses her fork, "That thing looked like it had been run over."

"It was. Twice. To get it just right."

"You ran it over?!?" I nod chewingly. "You ran over your own mattress." I nod again. "On purpose?"

"The first time was on purpose. The second time was almost accidental, but then it was on purpose too."

"So many questions you never think you will wind up asking. Why did you purposefully run over your mattress?"

"To get it just right for pointed perception. The sledgehammer had made a good dent in it but hadn't done enough. This is delicious, by the way," I tell Hope as Faith comes in and plops down on the couch.

"Thank you. So you laid out the mattress at your old apartment complex and drove over it? No wonder everyone there watched you like–"

"No, the mattress pre-dated Whisper Willows. I mean, I had it before I moved to Whisper Willows. Nothing pre-dates Whisper Willows. The dinosaurs used to keep their neighbors awake with all their howling at Whisper Willows."

"Why did you get rid of it, after you had so successfully pounded it into submission?"

"Everyone wanted me to get rid of it."

Hope is astounded. While she struggles for words, I serve up seconds. "That's the stupidest thing I have heard from you. You caved to peer pressure?!?"

"Will was the one who convinced me to get rid of it."

"What did he say?"

"Well it wasn't so much what he said as the way he said it."

"Right. Week two of Peer Pressure 101. Did he know that you had... uh... modified the mattress yourself?"

"No."

"Don't you feel badly that you got rid of it?"

"I feel worse about the couch."

"What about the couch? Did the couch do something for pointed perception?"

"No, nothing like that. It was just that it had been my family's couch."

Hope drops her fork. "We can go try to get it back!"

"No."

"Really."

"It's okay. It's done." The pink salmon and the red tomatoes and the angel hair pasta all have a pinkish hue to them. This is a girl-pleasing palette, if the girl likes pink. Otherwise it still might please the palate. This salmon traveled far upstream to land on my plate. Hope has been silently staring at me. "What?"

"I'm just watching you make faces at your dinner. You don't want to go back for the couch, but you feel bad about getting rid of it."

Leaning back, I bobble my head, "That's basically it, but I wouldn't couch it in those terms. I don't feel bad. I just wasn't ready for it."

"I get it," Faith says, hand outstretched, "couch."

Hope looks at her as if she's lost her mind. She gets up with some dishes, comes over to me, and says, "I think you are better than me at letting things go." When I don't reply she takes the dishes to the sink. She clears more of the table before asking, "If you could do anything, what would you do?"

"About the couch?"

"No. Anything."

When I was a kid, I came up with a list of things I wanted to do. I wanted peace on Earth. That's still open for accomplishment. I wanted to fall in love with the perfect girl for me. Done. I wanted us to be happy together. We're working on that. I wanted to invent something great. That almost happened. So close. "I've always wanted to invent something great."

"Like AutoDrive?"

"Like AutoDrive."

"Why can't it be AutoDrive?"

I give Hope the look she just gave Faith. "AutoDrive won't work. There is no amount of kibitzing from the sidelines that I can do to make it work. It needs more time than it has." Hope still looks confused. "Here. Do you have–" I look around. "Faith, do you have a pen and some paper? Thanks." I draw a box with a boot coming out of it. Ray would be better at this. From the boot, a dotted line arcs up to a guy folded in half and sailing through the air. I label the box Flight Control. "Look. This is Flight Control. And this is me. They fired me."

"What happened to Mister I-Like-Possibilities?"

"He was fired," I tell her. Is she trying to piss me off?!? "I– I love your optimism. I really do. It's great. But there are times when optimism just distorts the truth. It ignores the truth. This is the truth. AutoDrive is dead. It's going to fail. It's not ready. It's going to die, so assuredly that it's already dead. The most I can do – the absolute most I can do – is to try to keep it from taking people with it to its grave. Dead is dead. What you said before is right. I'm not God." That got Faith's full attention. "I can't stop AutoDrive from dying." Hope tries to say something. I don't want to hear it. "Let it go!" Swigging the rest of my blackberry stain, I help her clear the rest of the dishes. Hope takes the pan I'm washing and puts it in the dishwasher. I try to wash a fork.

Faith comes over and grabs us by the arms. "Cut it out! You two can't fight!" She's stronger than she looks. She could move mountains or at least cars. A knock at the stairway door sends her fuming in that direction. I pick up the camera manual.

"Hey Hope, you missed a word."

"Where?"

"There. That word is untouched."

"See you tomorrow. Here he is," Ray tells my phone, handing it over to me. "You left it downstairs."

"Thanks," I tell my phone retriever. "Hello. Acapella's Pizza. Tonight's special is angel hair pasta over a head of cabbage with ears of corn and eyes of potatoes. What would you like?"

"Can I get the special, but substitute the ears of corn for cauliflower ears?" Tom asks. "And could I substitute the head of cabbage for a head of lettuce?"

"For you, anything. What's up?"

"Becky and I were just talking. She was telling me about last night. It sounds like you had fun."

"It was all right. You should have been there."

"That's what I'm hearing, but I thought I should take the mature route."

I snicker. "What exactly is the mature route? Does that go by the lakes?"

"I watched TV." I shiver vocally. "Exactly."

"Was it good?" I ask.

"No, it was dull, and that's what I thought I needed. How's your Saturday night going?"

Hope has the dishwasher humming to itself and is typing the manual changes on a keyboard hooked to her phone. Faith is still listening in. "So far, so good. We just ate."

"We were wondering if there was something we could snow-pack onto."

"I think we'll be taking a cue from the Tom Pfuloree 'How To Be Mature' handbook and stay in tonight."

"Right. Stay in. Say no more!" He makes growling noises.

I hand the phone to Hope, "His tummy wants to talk to you." She pushes it back to me. "If you had called sooner, we could have tried to see if we could get everyone together to go to the drive-in." Hope and Faith seem to take notice.

Tom says, "We haven't been to the drive-in for a while."

"Exactly."

"Now we have the vehicles for it."

"That hasn't changed. I still have the same car we used one of the last times."

"I mean my truck or Ruth's van or Jake's truck." A cold chill ices my spine when he mentions Jake. "We could go next weekend."

"No, next weekend is out. We're going to Chicago."

"Who's we?"

"Hope and I."

"Don't you have that surgery with Lefty?"

"It's not surgery, and yes, that's Thursday. What about the weekend after that? The Friday night?"

"Sounds good to me. I'll mention it to people tomorrow."

"Do you have everything set for tomorrow?"

"Yes."

"Do you know what you should do? You should go to the Ice Cream Bar."

"We haven't been there in ages." At least I think he said ages, but it sounded like "pages" which doesn't make any sense.

"Go there and blow your straw wrapper down the bar about a third of the way and say that the bar-maid is your sister."

"Right. There was something else I wanted to tell you, but now I can't remember it." Why do people say this to me? I have a good memory, but not so good that I can remember for them. That would be a great memory.

"Call me if you remember. And let me know if you need something for tomorrow."

"Done. Bye."

"Bye." Hope is returning the paperwork to me and clearing away her stuff. "That was quick," I tell her. Hope nods with a smirk. Hope leads me into her room.

"What are you going to do about the pointed perception problem? Pointed perception problem – say that three times fast."

"Pointed perception problem - pointed perception problem - pointed perception problem."

"Work on it."

"Hey," Faith says from the doorway, "don't you two have a friend in Chicago named Christie?" We nod. "Someone just tried to kill a Christie in Chicago." We dash out to the living room.

33

Surprises

The TV screen is split into a multitude of segments: there is a still picture of Christie (our Christie), an active shot of police spotlights partially illuminating part of a blocked off street, an active shot of a reporter flipping through a thesaurus for different ways of saying "I don't know," and scrolling text says "Chicago minister Christie was shot at by several unknown assailants. She has minor injuries. Three other victims have been rushed to Caring Chicago South Hospital. Two of the other victims are reported to be in critical condition." There is also an advertisement for Double Bubble.

Scrolling my phone numbers, I punch Dan, and the phone dials.

"**Hello!**" he thunders.

"Hi Dan, I heard about Christie."

"Yeah! I am miles away on Pulaski! Traffic is at a standstill! I can't get anywhere near her place! The radio says that she has two minor bullet wounds! Do you mind telling me what the hell is a minor bullet wound?!?"

"Right!" someone else says from a distance away.

"Can you believe that?!?" Dan must be talking to someone out his window.

"It's bullshit, that's what it is," someone replies.

"They said two teenage kids, one of them only 13, are mostly dead! Whoever did this didn't care who they shot!" Saying something else out the window, he tells me, "I'm trying to decide if I should just leave my car and walk or what! There's a line-up of cars in front of me, a line-up of cars behind me, and no place to park a car! Hang on!"

The scene on TV hasn't changed except for the commercial which inappropriately advertises Double Bubble as "Now With A Shot Of Lime!"

I cover the phone. "Dan says that he's trying to get through to Christie, but the traffic isn't moving."

"That was Cy calling! I want to three-way with both of you, but she already has Ruthie on the line! Will that work?"

"I don't know..."

"You're the inventor-engineer guy! You should know these things!"

"As the inventor-engineer guy, I just try it and see if it works."

"Okay..."

And that's when Dan hangs up on me.

I try calling him back, but I get a message listing the barcodes of the various trunk towers that are full. I memorize the first eight before realizing that I don't need to know this. After 17 more barcodes, I disconnect. News On Demand continues their continuous coverage. NOD reporters explain at length what they don't know. They elaborate on the unknown. They speculate on the unknown. They get out a dart board and take wild guesses at the unknown while assuring us that they absolutely don't know. Then they switch to other people who are equally unsure but are located elsewhere.

"Who is she?" Faith asks, arms flailing.

Hope responds first, "When I first started teaching, I was at Yeast Elementary, in the brewery neighborhood. Sisyphus had already happened so teachers had the discretion to kick students out, but I was determined not to kick any students out. That was my personal goal. But there is a big difference between getting your degree and actually working the job. At Yeast, I was struggling to maintain order in my class... I was struggling to find the confidence to control my class, until I met Christie. This pine tree of a woman listened to me and suggested that we join forces and classes. Between us, we had over a hundred students because teachers wouldn't teach. They were scared to teach anywhere, especially in the public schools. So we had over 50 students each. We pulled the troublemakers and some non-troublemakers. Then we put the pressure on them. They became the class leaders."

"I think I know where she got that idea," I interject.

"Let me finish. We identified everyone's strengths and weaknesses and broke them into groups. When we were doing math, the math team helped us help other students. When we were doing reading, the reading students helped out. Everyone was so close to each other that when the school year ended, everyone cried. Parents tried to get us to keep teaching the same group for fifth grade. I couldn't have done it without Christie. She has a gift. We taught combined classes the next two years, both with over a hundred students, a few coming in from private schools. Then Christie said good-bye. I could never find anyone with the compassion, the strength, and the confidence to co-teach another class with me. Half of what I know about teaching, I learned from Christie."

"Fourth grade isn't all Duck-Duck-Goose," I tell them. "It's funny that she isolated your troublemakers and then got everyone to work together, because that's what she did with us. She started as a back-up singer on Melanie's first road trip. She was a quiet, thin, undernourished girl, just watching and listening, sometimes humming, and then just as we were getting ready to leave the bus, she freaked us out by starting a prayer. It cooled us all off, which seemed like a bad idea at the time, but as we breezed through problem after problem and concentrated on the show, she was literally a blessing. She led us in prayer from then on. And when the entire crew was getting on each other's nerves, she got us all together and became our glue, our negotiator, and the one who... kept us talking to each other. We probably gave her the experience to work with children."

Faith says tapping the table, "So she's with your group, then she gets a teaching degree, and works at your school–"

"My former school," Hope corrects.

"–your former school. When did she have time to go to seminary school and find herself a church?"

"I don't know that she ever went to seminary school."

"How could she be a minister without having gone to seminary school?!?" Faith waves to us.

"She could be my minister any day."

"No I mean, how could she get a church?" Faith persists.

"I'm not really sure, but I wouldn't be surprised if the church formed around her, instead of the other way around. Here..." I start searching the Internet, through my phone, about Christie. I find a biography and hand it to Faith. Faith mumbles when she reads. On TV, the Gun and Blunt Objects Shop advertises a store-wide, back-to-school sale. Hope and I stare at each other.

"Um, guys? Christie doesn't just have a church in Chicago. She's global," Faith's arms outstretch to try to hug the world.

"Cool."

"No. She's said things that have angered people in other parts of the world."

"Like what?"

"And where are these angry people?"

"Like denouncing symbolism over spiritualism and she's emphasized behavior over worship," Faith reads, tapping at my phone. "And they are in... West Carolina, Freedonia, and Iowa."

"So she's for practicing more than preaching. How revolutionary of her!" I say, while the clock on the wall strikes ten. On TV, the scene has changed to a large crowd. I half-expect to see big Dan Ryan mugging for the camera.

I lean back. Christie's been shot. I never dreamed this would happen.

Hope turns to me, "Are you okay?"

"She's been shot. And there is nothing I can do about it. It makes me feel..."

"Helpless?"

"Yeah. Thanks. When is our flight again?"

"Not until Friday."

"Friday?!? What are we going to do until then?!?"

"We could go sooner, but you have plans Thursday, and we have plans Monday and Wednesday," Hope needlessly reminds me.

"Wow, we're busy people. I think I'd better go to bed and pray for Christie."

"What?" Faith asks, pointing at me. "You pray?"

"Lots of people can do it. Really, anyone can do it. It's not a secret. It's easy." I kiss Hope and wish them a good night.

Downstairs in the bathroom, I brush my teeth and mess up my hair with both hands. In my room, I assemble Hope's altered paper copy of the camera manual with Ray's notes, the camera, and its accessories into their new box. Taking back out the camera and its recharger, I charge up the battery. I send a message to everyone I know who knows Christie about what happened to her. I change and look at the bed. From now on I won't try pointed perception in this bed. It's not lumpy enough. I turn out the light and climb in.

Maybe no one else does this, probably they don't, but when praying before sleeping, I do it in bed. In the movies and on television, prayer in the home is done at the table to bless food or kneeling before the bed as if it were some form of altar. I pray when the time is right for prayer. Tonight I pray for Christie and Hope. I pray for my friends, even Jake. I pray for understandings. And I drift off to sleep while still praying.

The jumble of images that play before me are accepted as a jumble of temperatures, people, places, and things familiar and strange and strangely familiar. Rolling over, the bed transforms. It becomes lumpier, less comfortable, focusing my dream.

"Are you actually asleep?" Nicole asks from under my back.

"I was asleep." I roll off her and turn onto my back.

I try to remember my dream while trying to think of something to say to Nicole.

Christie was shot at is all that is on my slumbering mind.

"Did Faith really break up a fight between you and Hope?"

Is she talking about now or in the future? She's talking about now, hours ago. "No."

"She lied. I'd beat her brains in, if she had brains."

"No, she just didn't understand what was going on. She only thought she had to break us up. We're fine." In the midst of the silence, my clock snores softly. "Nicole, can I ask you a question?"

Her body tenses. She exhales, "You just did."

"Do you get your shirts, the ones with words on them, custom made?"

"Yeah, the originals are all in French."

I don't understand, but I play along. "Do you think you could get one made for me to give to Hope?"

Nicole relaxes. "Seriously?" Asking if I'm serious always seems to be a trick question to me. The answer to whether or not I'm serious is complex and metaphysical. Nicole asks, "Yeah, what do you want it to say?"

"One, as in O-N-E, Gorilla Girl."

"Yeah, I can do that."

"I don't know what size she wears..."

"I do."

"You do?"

"I'm a girl. I do."

"Thank you," I respond with formality not usually found between those congregated in bed. "Let me know how much I owe you."

"Oh, I will." Nicole sighs. Outside an owl hoots. After several hoots without a response, one hoot gets stuck midway. Startling me awake, Nicole asks, "Do you and Hope talk about me a lot?"

"All the time. We're constantly talking about you. We never stop talking about you."

"Did I just wake you?"

"No. I was reading the fine print on the insides of my eyelids."

"Seriously."

"Seriously? No, we don't talk about you a lot. You have nothing to worry about."

Just as I start to drift down into the current of the river of sleep, Nicole asks, "Have you heard from your friend in Los Angeles?"

"Aimee? No, not for over a week." I didn't jolt awake that time. My body must be acclimating to her lack of timing.

"You know, Hope is still upset that you never looked for someone to date." I think, that doesn't make any sense. Why would she be upset? I could've ended up with someone else. The convoluted logic puts me to sleep.

People talk in my sleep. It's strange that nothing can ever be normal for me. I've heard of people talking in their sleep, but never other people talking in one person's sleep. That sort of strangeness is reserved for me.

I wake up and check my messages. My clock seems annoyed with me, and I don't blame it. It's late. I should have been up an hour ago. From my messages, it's clear that everyone else is up... Hope, Ruth, Dan... Dan tells us about his adventure last night to see Christie, who stood before the crowds, from on top of a truck, and shouted out to them about the children who were shot. He included a video clip. She welcomed the crowded streets of people and thanked them for caring enough to personally come down, bearing witness to this tragedy and physically supporting this ministry. He included a video clip of that. She thanked the police and the ambulance paramedics for reacting so quickly in such a poor community that can't always afford their services. She called for peace and led them in prayer. And Dan included another video clip. I wish I had been there with a trash bag full of candles. I send a message clarifying a comment from my message last night before noticing that Hope already stepped in to clarify it. In sending a message to Ruth, I nearly close it with, "See you later today," before stopping myself, remembering that it's a surprise party. Surprise is the key. I'm still sending messages while segregating my Major Munch cereal, when Hope comes down to snicker at me and my pajamas.

"Shouldn't you be getting ready?" she asks, taking a seat on my lap and distancing me from the majors and the munches.

"If you're like me, and I know you're like me, you feel you are always ready for the day."

"You haven't seen your hair, have you?"

I put up both hands and feel around. "It's still there. Maybe not exactly where I left it, but it's close." Her eyebrows shoot up.

"Do you have a card for us to sign?"

"Card?"

"A birthday card?"

Just as I'm reaching for one of Hope's earlobes, Ray comes home. I thought he was home. From my lap Hope asks him, "Is the presentation for Kelly tomorrow or the following Monday?"

Horror wipes his face white. "The following Monday. Why?"

"I just wasn't sure."

"The following Monday... A week from this Monday..." he repeats off to his room, shaking his head and grabbing his banana on the way.

"I guess you scared him."

"I didn't mean to," she says, looking earnestly down into my face.

I reach around her to try to finish my breakfast activities. "I can't get ready until I finish breakfast, and I can't finish breakfast with you on my lap. It's a linear system of interdependence."

Hope gets a chair of her own and asks, "Who's driving?"

"Who's going?"

"Everyone."

"Then everyone should... no, that won't work. We'd start our own traffic jam. Hang on." I go to Ray's room and find him sprawled across the bed like he hit it from a great height. "Ray?" The bed grunts. "Ray, are you coming with us to Tom's to celebrate Ruth's birthday?" The bed grunts affirmatively. "Do you want a ride?"

His head lifts turtle-like and says, "It's too hot for a car. I'll take my motorcycle."

I grunt an acceptance. I tell Hope, who is behind me, "Ray won't be riding with us."

Back at the table, Hope tells me that she'll drive. At least, that's what she thinks. "How soon will you be ready?" When I tell her eight minutes, her eyes jump out, she catches them and dashes upstairs, saying "I've got to finish getting ready!" I take my two bowls into the bathroom and finish eating while showering. The soap does not subtract; it adds to the flavor of the cereal. I put on a marble-like granite print shirt that Ruth got me some time ago. I take a piece of paper and fold it in half, twice. On the outside I write Happy Birthday, managing to misspell birthday and hoping my friends won't notice. Inside the makeshift card, I write out the names of all the gift conspirators. Carrying the gift and card, I trip over Ray's helmet with a finesse that springs to mind the theme music to the Dick Van Dyke Show. Outside, the oven-baked air is thicker than rock, crumbling my shirt against my chest with oppressive pressure. Pushing through to the backyard, I step by our row of cars. Birds squawk loudly, while I try to remember last night's dream. They move to surround me. Someone has worked them up. Is it me? A bird flits in and then dives missile-like out of a birdhouse in a tree. Does that make it a tree house? Trumpets startle the birds; they back off to discuss the timbre of my call. I answer my phone without dropping the gift. "Where are you?" Hope asks through our fancy walkie-talkies.

"The backyard by the cars," I tell her. Hide And Seek is more fun if people know that you're hiding. Hope pops out onto the deck upstairs, gives me a look, dramatically pokes the disconnect button on her fancy walkie-talkie, and disappears back inside. The sound of a hundred clogs on wood brings me around to the distinguished group of ladies coming down the stairs, all dressed up for a birthday party.

Nicole's shirt says, I Melted Frosty. Nicole! She was in bed with me last night!

"I'm driving!" Nicole announces.

"No, I'm driving," Hope tells her.

"This is convertible weather."

"It'll ruin our hair."

"The humidity will ruin our hair."

They all turn to me to referee. I have my hands full. I have to tell Hope about Nicole. A hand slips the card off of the gift. Ray is behind me reading it.

"There's no O in birthday." This gets everyone's attention. They make a grab for the card faster than I can move against the humidity. "You didn't tell me you needed a card."

"It's fine," I tell him.

All four women, who can't agree on anything, give me looks that say, "It's not fine."

"If you tell me the best way to get to Tom's, I'll quick make another card for you."

Hope hands the card directly to Ray, while I describe a scenic route to Tom's, which includes a grand tour of Duluth. Hope gives me a coin to flip. Nicole calls, "Tails." The coin gets stuck mid-air in the humidity. I pull it out of the air, shake it in my hands, and slap it on my wrist over a mosquito.

"Tails it is." I brush the mosquito carcass off the heads side, say a few words, and return the coin to Hope. Nicole dances a victory dance over to her car. For the sake of my leg room, apparently, I am assigned a front seat with Hope. On the way, Faith gets her face brushed with Nicole's hair. I should have taken Hope's side for two reasons: number one because she's Hope and reason B because driving through the humidity in a convertible is like water skiing face first; it gets old after the first hundred feet. Faith pulls Nicole's hair. We arrive more or less uninjured to a house that isn't mine. I ask Nicole to pull around the corner to hide her car. I can feel good that we didn't take my car; Ruth could identify it a mile away. But she has also seen Nicole's car more than she's seen Hope's car. We should have taken Hope's car.

As we walk back to Tom's I tell them, "This was almost my house. I have to remind myself occasionally that it isn't mine because I can so clearly remember how I nearly won it from Tom in a poker game a few years ago."

"Really?" Becky asks.

"Are you going to tell us about the one that got away?" Nicole asks, hopping on my back.

"Nicole, get off his back." She slides off.

"There isn't too much to tell except that Tom won a great deal of money, but almost lost his house." Hope looks puzzled. It wasn't a puzzle. It was cards. A motorcycle honks at us as we walk up the driveway. It's Ray. An arm shoots out the back door and rotates to tell us to hurry up. When we are in range, we are yanked inside.

"Tom and Ruth will be here any minute now! Get your butts in the living room!" Cy tells us. Don't tell me what's about to happen.

The living room is full of shadowy movements. On my way toward the dining table I run into Nadine. "Don't go over there," she whispers. "The cake is over there; it's fragile." She whispers a hiccup.

I back up into my entourage and lead them across the living room. It is damned dark, until Hope turns on her bracelet. Colors cascade across us and around the room. Complaints are whispered by nearly everyone. They were used to the darkness. We make our way to the stairway where the unlikely combination of Sharon, Will, and Jake are halfway up the stairs. We park ourselves at the base of the stairs, and Hope douses the bracelet. I kiss her for her ingenuity. Faith complains that someone is pinching her.

A penlight turns on inside a lab coat and makes its way across the room to us. The lab coat sits down, and the penlight shuts off. Lefty whispers, "When will she be here?" A chorus of tea kettles silences him. I close my eyes, which is redundant in the darkness, and I relax. I open my eyes and switch on the light of my watch.

"Knock it off over there," Todd's voice says.

"Eleven and a half minutes," I tell Lefty.

"Are you sure?" Al asks.

"Yeah."

"I can't stay in this position for that long," Stephanie's voice says, evoking zero sympathy from Jake. "Erix is on my foot," Stephanie complains. "Would you please move?"

"What is going on out here?" Cy asks. Gene tells her what I said. "Is she going to be surprised?" Cy asks me from across the room, at least, I assume she's asking me.

I answer, "Yes," without offering full disclosure.

"Then you can all sit still ten more minutes," Cy says and storms back out.

"Sheesh, what a grouch," I whisper. From across the room Stephanie laughs.

It's quiet for a minute now that we don't have to be quiet.

Hope says, "Under a thick blanket of snow, the matted prairie grasses, and under several feet of frozen ground, a large group of gophers huddled together in their burrow." Hope nudges me, "Your turn."

"Their heartbeats slowed, changing time itself," I tap Nicole.

"The wild animals heated themselves up with passionate sex. Go."

"That's not sticking to the story," Faith says, and I see her gestures without actually seeing her gesturing. "Their beliefs kept them strong through the long winter months. Behind me."

"Their whiskers kept check on those around them," Sharon says, "keeping balance and order in their borough. Your turn."

"The gophers determined to stick with their plan no matter what difficulties they faced," Will adds.

"Playing poker," Jake starts, "one of the rodents cheated."

"Lefty, it's your turn."

"'Is it cheating to use what you know?' the gopher asked."

Becky says, "I don't know anything about poker, and I know less about gophers, but the gophers agreed to play nice."

"While a few of the gophers start work on a clay sculpture."

"The clay sculpture is of deoxyribonucleic acid, highlighting the chromosomal characteristics in hibernation, digging, and undomesticated fornication."

"One gopher scurried around to patch up cave-ins and kept the hay evenly distributed. Over to you, Todd."

"The gophers watched out for their brothers and sisters. Go."

"They exercised to keep in shape and avoid the spring flab. Go. Go. Go Erix."

"They slept."

"The capitalization on root market speculation benefited–"

"Everyone quiet," I announce, interrupting Dexter.

"I was going to do the sex part again," Nadine cries. "Bite me with those gnarly teeth."

"Ssh!"

The mental seconds tick inside my head, while behind me Jake quietly scoffs.

Cy runs in. She runs into a lamp.

Tom noisily unlocks the back door. Way to overact the part, Tom. "Could you get my folder? I left it on the coffee table."

Blinding light.

"Surprise!" Everyone jumps out and since they can't see, they jump into furniture and things and into each other and balloons and paper streamers that criss-cross the ceiling. The stereo blasts trumpet music, and I check my phone.

Ruth screams and runs back into the kitchen. Tom catches her and brings her back in. "You scared a year off my life!" We sing our own version of a happy birthday song. Nadine holds out a lit cake, jumps a little, and Ruth blows out the candles.

"Were you surprised?" Cy asks.

"Of course I was surprised," Ruth says. "It's not my birthday."

Much confusion. "Wait. When is your birthday?"

"Next month. And that's what I wished for, another party on my actual birthday."

"It's really not that long from now, is it?"

"Yeah, it's..." she counts, "18 days from today. Surprise!"

Several of us move to collect our gifts and go. Cy stops us.

Ruth passes out cake slices, while Nadine assures Ray that, "No animals were harmed in the making or baking of that cake." Noticing that several people are refusing to eat cake, Nadine asks, "Are you questioning the sanity of my kitchen?" The cake's reality is very very limited. It will disappear in no time. Nadine almost hands me some cake, but then takes it away again, remembering, "You never eat cake."

Hope is giving me a funny look, questioning my not eating cake, when Ruth says, "I just heard from Red's parents. Red was admitted to the mental health center at Loon Lake yesterday."

"You're kidding."

"No. He was saying something like, 'It doesn't make sense.' And drooling. And going nuts."

"That happens to me at the legislature," Sharon says, "except for the drooling part."

"They had to sedate him."

"They haven't had to sedate me, yet."

"We should all paint our hair orange and go visit him," Tom suggests.

Jake says, "Pay up."

Apparently several people bet that I would be the first to go... Gene, Nadine, Dexter... Jake bet against me. He had his money on Red, the long shot. I would've had my money on Red too. Most days.

"What does your shirt say?" Todd asks Nicole. "What did you do to Frosty?" The middle word of her shirt smeared into a blob with an ED at the end. They find a smear on the back of my shirt.

"What have you kids been doing?" Sharon asks. Playing piggy-back springs to mind as a response, but that still wouldn't be innocent in the dirty little minds around me.

Hope steps in, "It's okay. I was with them." The dirty little minds are still revving. A blushing Nicole whispers something to Tom and they take off upstairs. The dirty little minds are in high gear.

Gene is arguing with Ray saying cartoonists distort the appearance of animals, causing geneticists to try to figure out how to make the cartoon animals actually happen.

Jake asks me quietly, "Have you ever heard of a horn that honks a word?"

"No, that's unheard of."

Erix tries to eat his cake from the middle.

Tom comes down with Nicole, who's in a tight shirt that says Twins on it and carrying a shirt for me. "I'm sorry about messing up your shirt. Tom said you can borrow this."

I ask Hope, "Can you help me change?"

"You just want my help with your turban."

"Don't start that again," Tom says.

"Turban?" Nicole asks as I take Hope away.

In the bathroom, I change shirts and try to rinse the ink melt off the back of my old shirt. As I scrub the shirt using a bar of soap, I tell Hope, "I just wanted you to know, Nicole was in bed with me last night."

Hope swallows, "Did anything else happen?"

"We talked. I kind of squashed her. That's it."

"Did you talk about anything I should know about?"

"Only that she said that you are still upset that I didn't actively look for someone to date."

"That's not true. I was, but I'm over that."

"Good." I wring out the shirt and look at it. It's better. The ink is still there, but it's hard to tell in the rocky print. I hang it up.

"Hey in there," Cy knocks, "Ruth is about to open gifts." I open the door, and Cy evaluates our state of dress before escorting us in.

With her gifts spread out on the coffee table before her and the Queen For a Day crown on her head and everyone around her, Ruth couldn't look more content. "Thanks for not wearing the turban!" she exclaims. "This is wonderful."

"Open this first," Sharon asks. It's a fiber optic purple stone necklace with light-enhanced zirconia diamonds. "Let me help you with it." Sharon puts it on Ruth.

Gifts are pushed around in front of the big camera box. She receives chocolate, two cookbooks, a spa visit, daisies, a genealogy chart, unmentionables that barely make their way out of the box due to overwhelming modesty, a gift biopsy, a truck repair and rebuilding set of books specific to her truck, and something from Jake. "What is it?"

"It's a new horn for your truck."

"What's the matter with my old horn?"

"It doesn't honk words."

"Any words?"

"It can be any word. Honk obscenities." That explains Jake's interest.

"Did it really cost a million dollars?"

"No, Jake just does that instead of marking over the price. He's very good at that, and it's all very amusing until you go to return something."

"What did you return? Cy? Cy! What did you return?"

"The Navy surplus fish-scared-out-of-the-water sonar."

"Why did you return it?" Jake demands.

"I just didn't have any use for it. And when they saw what you did to the price tag, they acted like I was trying to rob the Federal Reserve. Jail time is not the best Christmas present."

Erix gives Ruth a geode that opens to reveal purple crystals.

Nadine and Ruth exchange left sandals. Some people think I'm weird.

The camera box is next. Ruth reads the card. The list of names involved makes her feverishly interested. She opens the box, looks at the materials, and gets out the camera. "I've never heard of it," she says.

"That's because it doesn't exist, yet," I add. She gives me a questioning look. "This is a prototype, Poof! You're There! travel-free camera, by my friends at Owatonna Opticals. One of the key features of this camera is its ability to capture the image of a subject and replace the background, like Ray's illustrations on the card and on the box. I worked out getting the camera, Hope edited their manual, Ray designed a logo for them and did some preliminary testing, and Cy will be collecting all our information as well as your feedback to submit to Owatonna Opticals."

"It's almost like you have a company again," Jake observes.

Ray offers to show off the camera to Ruth and says that he considers himself something of a photographer too. Ruth asks him, "If you saw the most beautiful sky in the world, would you kick yourself for not having a camera with you?"

"No."

"Then you aren't that into photography, but I'd like your help with it."

The last present is from Becky, Faith, and Nicole. It's the Feed The Hungry board game. "Oh, I've heard about this. They say it's tough."

"Just like the real thing."

"Would you want to play it now?"

"I've always wanted to."

"Wait," Ruth says. "Ray, would you be willing to show me how to use the camera later."

Ray nods while recovering a hidden envelope. "Here are some pictures of the Lactating Woman statue that I took with that camera." Everyone mobs the pictures.

As Sharon peers over, she says, "I've heard about this statue, but I haven't seen it."

"Ray made it."

"This is your statue?!? So you're having the unveiling a week from tomorrow, right? But the statue didn't actually travel to China or India or any of these other places, right?"

"Right. It's the camera that does all that, instantly, without needing any graphics software."

"Very impressive. I can say, 'I know the artist!'" Sharon says, as Ray blushes.

"So how do we play this game?" Ruth distracts. Al and Will are getting out the game board, the pieces, special cards, dice, scoreboard, and instructions. Ruth sniffs at Al. "What are you wearing?"

"Petroleum-based grease."

"How many people can play?"

From behind the instructions, Will says, "Anywhere from two to 20 can play. We all start at square one. As you can see from the board, there are many ending spots. Some are good–"

"This path ends in a loop. That can't be good."

"This is worse. It says, 'You're dead. End of player's game.' Nice ending!"

"This one says, 'Limbo. Food might reach someone. Might not. Go back to square one.'"

"Are you actually supposed to limbo?"

"No, limbo, as in not going anywhere. Stalled."

"What if that happened during a game of limbo? You see 'how low you can go' and then you get stuck."

"That happened to me once."

"Who's playing?"

"Feed The Hungry or limbo?"

"Feed The Hungry."

Nadine says, "I'll watch. Erix will too." Erix is already watching intensely.

Dexter says, "I have to go. Mica and the kids wish you a happy birthday."

"Thanks, Dexter."

Al takes the scoreboard and adds Ruth's name and his own. Sharon says, "I'm playing." From hand signals, Al adds Will, Cy, Lefty, Stephanie, Gene, Hope, and Faith. Becky offers to keep score. Tom refreshes drinks.

Will says, "There are three decks of cards: food, transportation, and local issues. We need someone to read the cards, offer choices, and give outcomes." Nicole volunteers. "'Please read the following introduction.' Okay, I'm reading it. 'Welcome to the Feed The Hungry board game. This game is meant to provide entertainment, while offering some of the complexities of feeding the millions of starving people in the world. You might ask if there should be a strategy game based on stopping starvation. If there are strategy games of war, where the object is to kill, then there is room for a game where the object is to save lives, which is just as challenging, if not more so.'" There are mixed reactions in the room. Will reads through the rules.

Jake asks me, "Have you found another job?"

"Don't start that again."

"I'm just asking."

"If we each move only one space at a time, then whoever starts first will win, right?" Cy asks.

"I'll start," Stephanie volunteers.

"There are several ending points... successful ending points."

"Are they all the same distance away?" Cy asks.

"No."

"Then why would we go the long ways?"

They just decided as a group not to go the long ways. "Someone, go the longest way for me," I ask.

"I will," Hope says, and one or two people seem to re-examine the longer paths.

"I won't," Stephanie says. "I want to win."

"Any dreams about this?" Jake asks.

"No."

"Who starts, Stephanie or the birthday girl?"

Ruth has Stephanie start, saying, "I'm not sure this game is about being selfish."

Stephanie moves one square for a money card. Nicole reads a money card, "To collect money do you – A. go door to door, B. contact family and friends, C. contact Acme Food Drives?"

"Go door to door. A," Stephanie picks.

"You collect 400 dollars and lose three turns."

"What?!?"

"Congrats."

"I already hate this game."

"Who's next? Erix, are you playing?" Erix shakes his head.

Ruth says, "We'll go clockwise. Cy's next."

Nicole reads, "You're given ten million eggs. Do you – A. arrange transportation to the docks, B. give them back, C. try to sell them, or D. try to trade them?"

"I have a feeling I'd lose turns trying to sell or trade them. I arrange transportation."

Nicole reads, "The eggs spoil. Lose one turn and 200 dollars."

"You're kidding. I can have a debt? What were the other answers?"

Nicole asks Will, "Can I tell her?" He shakes his head.

"Is it your turn?" Nicole asks. "What's your name?"

"Gene."

"Okay Gene, you try to raise money from an organization. Is it a government program or a charity?"

Gene looks around at us and stares at Nicole, looking for clues. "The charity."

"Roll the dice. If you roll a one, two, or three, you lose that number of turns and get that number in thousands of dollars. If you roll a four, five, or six, you get that number in hundreds of dollars." Gene rolls a two. "Two thousand dollars and you lose two turns."

"It's my turn," Al says, commenting, "So far everyone has lost at least one turn. If we all lose a turn that isn't going to matter." He moves a space.

Nicole reads to Al, "You are given a thousand dollars that must be spent locally either in A. media fund raising or B. to grow more food."

Jake says, "Don't grow more food!"

"Why?"

"It's a waste of time! I've played this before. It'll take too much time to grow the food and then the food will rot. You'll lose the game."

"What am I supposed to do?"

"The problem isn't a lack of food; there often is food in the area. The problem is getting food to those that need it, and you would think that everyone would agree to that, but there are groups actively trying to keep food from people."

"Jake, why didn't you help me on my turn?" Cy asks.

"Or mine, Jake," Stephanie says, pronouncing his name sharply. Gene nods. I feel slightly vindicated.

"I hadn't remembered anything until now."

"Could we get a ruling on Jake's involvement?" Cy asks Will, who turns it over to Nicole.

Nicole says, "If you can't help everyone, keep quiet. While Jake was talking, Al picked media fund raising, so he lost a turn but gained 7,000 dollars. Ruth, You speak before – A. a group of supermarket owners, B. a group of charitable organizations, or C. a group of churches."

"I'll pick the supermarket owners."

"Why?"

"Because they are closest to the food but seem to be the long shot."

Nicole says, "You didn't get money, but you got 10,000 dollars worth of non-perishable food and water delivered to the docks. Move ahead four squares."

"Wow."

"Lefty. A food corporation has a plan touting powdered infant formula as superior to mother's milk. Do you agree? This would have been a good question for Ray."

"No."

"Unclean drinking water is a leading cause of infant mortality. You avoided a boycott and collected 500 dollars."

"I don't lose a turn?"

"Nope."

"Will, you receive word that rats have infested the docks. Do you tell the other players?"

"Yes."

"For each player that has food on the docks, add a thousand dollars to your funds. I think that's just Ruth."

"So Will gets a thousand dollars. Do I lose a thousand?" Ruth asks.

"No. It doesn't say anything like that."

"Cool. But I'd really like to know what would've happened if he hadn't told me."

"If everyone agrees I should read it, I'll read it." Everyone agrees. "If Will had said no, Ruth would have lost half her food."

"Thanks Will."

"Happy birthday, you know, 18 days from now."

"Hope honey, you are given a thousand dollars–"

"Given?!?" Stephanie asks. "I had to go door-to-door, got only 400 and lost three turns."

"You chose to do that," Nicole boldly responds to Stephanie. "I'm not finished. You are given a thousand dollars. You can – A. bring on volunteers or B. hire two part-time people."

"Volunteers."

"Your low administrative costs add 2,000 more. Faith. I have to pick a real good card for Faith." Stephanie and Faith both protest. "Faith. You have to give an Internet presentation. In Japanese. You don't know Japanese. Do you fake it, like you usually do, or cancel?"

"I cancel."

"You lose."

"What? Why?"

"Because you're a loser." Faith and Nicole fight over the card. Hope rescues it but hands it back to Nicole with a look. "You earn 500 Internet credits." Hope intervenes again. "You earn 500 dollars because someone steps in to help you. Sharon? Are you playing?" Sharon gets off her phone. "Three organizations want to partner with you. One is conducting a study of the causes of world hunger. Another is trying to improve transportation. A third organization is meeting to define its goals. Which do you partner with?"

"Is there a none of the above?"

"Yes."

"Ooh... I want to partner with Jake. Can he be on my team?" Everyone allows it. I keep out of it. "Jake, what do you think? It's between none or improved transportation, but I don't have anything to transport yet." Jake shrugs. "You're a big help. I pick none."

Nicole says, "Okay, nothing happens." Sharon shrugs and turns back to her phone. "Ruth, move ahead one. Now what card would you like?"

Jake intervenes, "Now Ruthie, you've got a choice. You could have her pick a money card if you think you need more money or a food card if you think you need more food or a transportation card if you think you're ready for transportation."

"What do you think?"

"I don't know, but I'm on Sharon's team."

Ruth looks at me for support, so I say, "You're doing great. Keep up the good work." That's what I'm supposed to do, isn't it?

"Food card, please."

"Three organizations offer food for 5,000 dollars: one is overseas, another needs to get to the dock, another is at the dock. Which do you pick?"

"I don't have 5,000 dollars. What do we do?" Nicole turns to Will. Will turns to the instructions.

Ruth turns to Jake. He says, "I don't know. None of us were ever stupid enough to try to buy food without money." Jake gets hit with a throw pillow.

Will says, "It says that if you go off in the wrong direction, such as picking a card for buying food or transportation with insufficient funds, you lose a turn."

I kick a balloon out to the kitchen with me. After getting a glass of water, I examine Tom's freezer with a screwdriver. The dehydrator is accessible. That's what does the dehydrating. With a minor modification to the condenser-compressor flow and an adjustment to the sensors, I reverse that process.

Sipping the glass of water, I stare out the kitchen window at a row of pine trees, more than two stories tall. Behind the pines, a taller cottonwood shimmers in the breeze like it's made of tinsel. It feels good to stare at plants. Two months ago I watched that tree drop its cotton puffs over the neighborhood like snow. Some of his neighbors blew it off as they do every year. Some tried to shovel the cotton puffs. Some complained that the trees should be cut down. It's Minnesota. Get used to the white stuff. Leaning forward, I knock over a pineapple. As I set it straight again, I realize that pineapples don't grow on pine trees.

It's strange to be in the middle of a group of friends and feel alone. I'm a part of the group as much as anyone else, but still I can feel alone. Maybe it's hearing about Christie or Red and not being able to help either one of them. Maybe it's— Tom and Becky come into the kitchen. "Hey, what's going on?" Tom asks. "War broke out. You're missing it."

"I'm just looking out the window." They look out as if there is something amazing out there. "I just need a moment." They grab some drinks. Becky pats me on the back. They leave.

Sharon comes into the kitchen saying, "I heard you wanted to be alone." She stops next to me, puts the back of her hand to her forehead and dramatically enunciates, "I want... to be... alone." Picking up a lemon, she smiles, "You're funny, you know that? You don't want to be alone. Many people want to be alone. Many people like to be alone but not you and me. We're the type of people who like to be around other people. We wither without the action and interaction. We would die in solitary confinement. So why are you out here suffering? Is everything going well between you and Hope?"

"Yes, fine. Hope is the bright spot in my life. As a matter of fact, I want to thank you for hooking us together." Sharon looks puzzled. "You know, the last time I was at your house, five weeks ago?"

Sharon pivots back a step. "I didn't hook you up."

"You don't remember? You introduced us."

"Yes, I introduced you..."

"You're saying you didn't hook us up?"

"That's right."

"If you didn't, who did? Did Cy?"

Sharon's face momentarily betrays my guess as a bad guess.

"Sharon," Tom calls, "Faith is taking away all your food."

"Coming," she says, eyebrows shooting up.

"You're not going to tell me?"

Sharon shrugs, hands me the lemon, and leaves. The pine trees don't leave. They don't have leaves, but they no longer ease my mind. I cut open the lemon and squeeze it into my water, making lemonade. I kick a balloon back with me into the living room.

My eyes narrow at my friends as I sip the bitter lemonade. There is a mystery here. One or more of these people know more than they are saying. My ice cubes jangle in agreement. Look at them. Sitting around, laughing, and playing games when there is a mystery to solve. They aren't so innocent. Erix isn't saying much. I take a swig. Lemonade splashes down the corner of my mouth, and I wipe it away with my hairy wrist. I'd bum a cigarette from one of them, except none of them smoke, not even me. The reason I've gathered you all together, I think to myself, is that one or more of you are involved in a conspiracy. That's right, look around at the people you are sitting with and realize that some of them are capable of a diabolical deception and undeniable duplicity. Or is it you? I spill more lemonade, revealing my drinking problem. Tom tosses me a towel. I could tie this on my head so easily and then who'd be laughing?

I wipe up my mess, return the towel, and sit down.

"Did I get credit for the matching money?"

"Yes."

"Where's MY lemonade?" Jake asks.

"Gene," Nicole says. "'The army has volunteered to deliver your food for you. Do you accept?'" Jake coughs a negative cough. Stephanie reprimands him. Gene accepts. "Oh, too bad. To prevent accidental injury, the army drops your food away from people. Far away from people. Practically the Indian Ocean. Go back to Square One."

"Square One?!?"

"Local card, please," Ruth says.

Nicole reads, "Customs officials have intercepted your food shipments. Do you – A. wait patiently, B. bribe them, or C. contact their military?"

"I wait patiently."

"Lose a turn."

"What?!? I just lost three turns chasing refugees around as they flee from my food, and I have to wait another turn? Are you sure that's what it says?!?" Ruth argues.

"Don't yell at me! It's the customs officials that are making you wait. If this was an easy game, they'd call it something like Go Shopping At The Mall."

"Let's play that next," Sharon suggests, and everyone agrees.

I ask Sharon, "Is that you back at Square One with Gene? How did that happen?"

"My corporate sponsor backed out due to poor photo ops. I lost all my money."

"I'm sorry to hear that."

Lefty asks Nicole for a local card. "Are there women in your group?"

"Say no."

"Yes."

"The women are raped. Everyone loses a turn."

"What kind of game is this? Why did you even give me a game like this?" Ruth asks.

"How can we lose a turn when we're back at Square One? We don't even know if we want to Feed The Hungry anymore," Sharon wavers. "How can we lose a turn?"

"Will, are you up?"

"No, I lost my turn by bribing a local official enough for him to leave the country, leaving me with a new official. Plus, everyone was raped. Remember?"

Hope asks for a local card. "A relief worker offers advice. Do you follow it?"

"Not without knowing what it is. No."

"Move ahead two squares."

"Hope is making short work of the long way."

Nicole asks Faith, "What card do you want?"

"Transportation," Faith says uneasily.

"The local military volunteers to help you move the food. Do you accept?"

"No."

"Good girl," Nicole says. "Move ahead one."

"I think a war game would've been better," Stephanie says. "At least you can win that." I watch my friends fight it out.

Hope takes the long haul, avoids big business and governments and local warlords, declines short cuts and easy routes, gets the food to the people, and wins the game.

People lean back, recovering their drinks. Tom announces, "I've been talking with some of you about some plans. In case you didn't get the message or in case I didn't send it, some things are coming up, not this week, but next week. A week from tomorrow at two o'clock, if you can get off work, Ray's statue of the Lactating Woman, which is also a fountain and is kind of heavy, is being unveiled in Wild Rice Park. Then the next night, Tuesday night, the Milltown Millers play the Pigs Eye Pigs at Met Stadium, not Millers Park. And on that Friday night we're going to the drive-in. Then two weeks from tomorrow, we're planning to go to the fair."

Will asks, "Are we going to the drive-in no matter what the weather? So even if it's raining?"

Tom points to me and says, "He's already determined that it won't rain that night."

"Our own weather man!" Becky comments.

"What about the game at Met Stadium?"

They all turn to me. I shrug. They don't accept the shrug. I close my eyes. I open them. They're still staring at me. "Would you go about your business or something?"

"I love your necklace!" Nicole gushes at Ruth. "Who gave it to you again?"

I close my eyes. I relax. My living room glows a sickly yellowish, greenish nearly-phosphorescent glow from the windows. I open the front door and it whips out of my hand to BAM! slam into the closet door behind it. The yellowish green is bright and dark with charcoal gray clouds and ripples of thunder, while winds whip wild holes through trees, branches bent backwards almost to the breaking point. Aluminum cans skip down the street like stones being skipped across a pond with pink-punk-pink-plunk-plunk-punk sounds. Faith and Hope are beside me. I step out and tell them, "Stay inside."

"Why?" Faith asks. "Are you storm-proof?"

"No, I'm dreaming this."

"You aren't dreaming this. We are all actually here."

I get a glance at my watch as they drag me inside.

I open my eyes. "There's no way. There's no way the game will be played that evening in an outdoor stadium like the Met – big storm. A fly ball could easily make it to Wisconsin."

"Will the game be on the day after?" Jake asks.

"I don't know."

Sharon gets up. "Happy birthday, Ruth. It's been fun. Weird," she says, turning to me, "but fun. We'll have to do this again in a few weeks." She winks, steps over to me, and says, "Good luck figuring things out." Sharon makes a point to shake Ray's hand, and Todd and Cy walk her to her car. Nicole and Will put away the game without waking Nadine, who is asleep on Erix's shoulder. Ray starts showing off the camera to Ruth. The rest of us pick up cans, bottles, glasses, and cake plates, along with stray pieces of wrapping paper, fallen streamers, and gift bags. We should be out before the snow falls.

"Don't anyone else leave," Ruth directs. "I have to get everyone's picture!" She takes hundreds of pictures. She gets a picture of me holding an egg close to the camera so it seems larger than it is. With Ray's help, she puts me in front of a group of emperor penguins looking at me funny like I've taken something from them. She promises to send us copies of the best shots.

Cy and Todd come back holding up her phone and shouting, "Everybody Say Hi to Dan!"

"**Hi Dan!**" we shout out.

Cy announces, "He says to tell you that he talked with Christie a few hours ago. She has a scar and bruised right arm near her shoulder. One of the boys who was shot was released earlier today. The other boy, the younger boy, is expected to be released in the next day or two. What else? Oh yeah. He told Christie that we've been hoping and praying for them, and she thanks us. Anything else?" Tom and Jake fight over the phone.

"Watch out for that lamp!" Tom yells and captures the phone from a distracted Jake. "Hey, so you spent the night there?" Tom takes the conversation into the kitchen while Nicole and Becky head upstairs. Stephanie gives us the play-by-play anyway.

"Tom's telling Dan about the presents... and the game... and the camera." Several of us try to cover Stephanie's ears, without interrupting Ray and Ruth. The struggle jostles Erix, waking Nadine, a very kindergarten-cranky Nadine. Nicole and Becky come down with my shirt. I hold it up. It's not wearable.

"Are we ready to go?" I ask my group. We all wish Ruth a happy near-birthday and on our way by I thank Tom for the use of his shirts. The surge of hot humid air washes over us outside, refreshing our sweat. Still carrying my egg, I crack it open on the sunny sidewalk. It sizzles. It bakes under the mini-magnifying glasses of all the drops of humidity. A man walks a hot dog. The dog pauses to look at the egg. The egg makes a pop. The dog continues. "Congratulations on winning the game," I tell Hope after I figure we're out of Stephanie's earshot.

"Thanks. Your saying I should take the long routes helped. I couldn't have done it without you."

"The tougher the problem, the more likely that it has to take a long haul. AutoDrive taught me that.

But you won the game, not me."

"Cy was telling me that you can't take your phone on a commercial flight."

"What?!? People do it all the time!"

"Not that phone, not the phone that self-destructs."

"Great, she gives me a phone I can't travel with!"

"Oh, you can travel with it, just not fly..."

"What are you saying?"

"Wouldn't it be better if we drove to Chicago?"

I think about relaxing too much and pointed perception and realize that Hope can drive too. "Whose car?"

"How far do you think your car will get?" Hope asks, as Nicole unlocks the car doors and pushes me into the middle of the front seat.

"I get to play with the radio!" I announce. "Black River Falls?"

"That's not exactly Chicago, is it?" Hope asks.

"Did you have a dream about something happening on the plane?" Faith asks.

"Her or me?"

"You."

"Yes, Hope fell asleep."

"I might in the car too. I think it will be my car," Hope says close to me, over the noise of the convertible's breeze.

We get caught in some Sunday Return Traffic – the trucks and SUVs returning from their weekend urban escape. Above us, a group of boys on a pedestrian overpass wave. I don't think they're waving at me. I play with the radio until my hand gets batted away by Nicole. The radio announces a tenth-day anniversary of something I miss in the roar of Nicole's acceleration. When traffic is set free, Faith yells in my ear, "Is Stephanie a lesbian?" I am now deaf in my right ear.

"We'll talk back at the house."

"Why?!?" she yells.

"Stephanie can still hear you when you yell."

The rest of the way back I work up what I'm going to tell Faith. I follow them up the outside stairs, trying not to stare. Inside Faith keeps going.

"Faith..."

I try to stop her, but she says she'll be right back. The rest do their own things for a few minutes before returning to me in their living room. Hope changes to light pink and brings me a drink of a lemonade and limeade mixture. She calls it L-ade.

Nicole changed into a shirt that says, Please Don't Feed The Models. She says, "I should have worn this shirt this afternoon." Faith rolls her eyes.

I tell Faith, "The short answer is I don't know if Stephanie is a lesbian or not. I've never asked her. I try not to pigeon-hole my friends into types or categories. I wouldn't want to limit them to a label any more than I would want them to do that to me."

"That's not what I was trying to do..."

"A long time ago, I started saying that Tom and Todd were the same person. I would say things like, 'He just thinks he's twins,' or 'He's just really fast,' or 'Have you noticed that you hardly see them together?' or 'Pictures of them are usually blurry.' That's part of what got Ruth into taking pictures. I thought I was being hilarious. It turns out that I wasn't."

Hope is pushing tons of buttons on her phone. "I'm canceling the tickets."

"It turns out that Tom and Todd had spent a lot of time developing distinct identities. On some things, they're opposites, but not everything. My kidding them about being the same person kind of infringed on their individuality. Or at least, it wasn't hilarious, so I stopped doing it. If it's not good, or good and funny, it's not worth doing."

"I wasn't trying to pigeonhole her. I was just asking because I was wondering, that's all," Faith gestures.

We all turn to Nicole, expecting her to drive through that opening Faith left. Nicole eats an ice cream bar, seemingly oblivious to us. I can almost see a halo over her head. "Okay."

"Did you get your money back?" Becky asks.

"Yes," Hope responds.

"Did they keep any of it?"

"No, but they made me promise never to do it again."

"How can they do that?"

"They have my number."

"Get another number."

"I like my number, besides I promised."

"You made a promise to a corporation. That's not much of a promise."

"A promise is a promise. How can I expect them to keep their promises, if I don't keep mine?" Hope asks. She looks at me and plays with my hair in ways that I like and I don't like. When she keeps doing what I don't like, I tell her I don't like that part of what she's doing. She looks at me and studies me, until I give in and ask what she's doing. "I was thinking about something Cy said."

"About taking the phone on a plane?"

"No, she had asked if you had told me why you two broke up. And I told her that you said she didn't understand you. And then she said that yes, that was part of what was going on, but the last thing you had said to her about being together was that you felt you were cheating on your next girlfriend by still seeing her. And that was years ago. I haven't fully decided, but I think that's really, very sweet."

"And this all took place when? During the two seconds I was in Tom's kitchen? Do people just sit around and wait for me to leave so they can talk about me?"

They quietly look at me. Faith checks the clock.

"Okay, I get it. I can take a hint," I get up and head for the stairs. They tell me they're just teasing and Becky's laughing, but I'm already bounding down the stairs.

"Dive! Dive! Dive!" I dive into my bed, nose first, like a submarine.

With my face embedded in the bed, I am submerged in the quiet of my room as recent memories sink in. We're driving to Chicago next weekend, not flying. Red is at Loon Lake. Sharon thought my pointed perception was weird. It is weird, but it bothers me that she thinks it's weird. And even weirder is that she doesn't think she originally set Hope and I up together. Is she lying? She is a politician. But Sharon has never lied to me before. I think I know what happened.

Sharon was keeping watch over her flock by night, when behold, an angel of the heavenly host appeared to her from within a bush that burned but was not consumed, saying, "I am the angel of–" And the angel did cough, for the smoke from the burning bush did bother the angel's lungs. And the angel did a great rubbing of the eyes, for the smoke from the burning bush did cause the eyes to weep. "I will step forth," said the angel, "so that you may see me and understand me. And I will stifle the burning bush, so that we may not be interrupted by those that extinguish incendiaries." The angel did step forth and, upon extinguishing the bush, said, "Woman of great council, there are two with prophetic powers and understanding of all mysteries and all knowledge and have faith enough to move mountains, but they do not have love. Love is patient – hold your place for I have not finished – love is kind. Love binds the souls and spirits together in ways no ring of metal or stone could signify, for the binding of love stretches and is as strong as the strongest polymer and yet is as soft as silk and does not scratch, even accidentally. Love is its own symbol. Hands are held and clasped not to pull or control, but as companions and admirers. Love is not jealous or boastful; it is not arrogant or rude. Love bears all things, believes all things, hopes all things, and endures all things. Love is all you need. Yes, it is." The angel did pause to scratch at a wing, for it did itch, and to give the woman Sharon a moment to reflect upon what was said. "These two must be given to love. You must provide the divine intervention but must not take credit for the act, for even though an idea of nature cannot be copyrighted so too there can be consequences to claiming that which belongs to the Lord." And behold, two widescreen images of the woman Hope and the man Ricky appeared along with biographies that appeared to have been gleaned from the Internet, for they contained errors of fact and of omission. The spelling was poor. And the woman Sharon knelt down and wept, for her sheep had wandered as the angel spoke, and she was not acquainted with Hope, and the address given may not be the most current, and she did fear the awkwardness of this more than most things political.

What I need is confirmation. Another vessel dives beside me.

Touching my shoulder, Hope says, "Your arm is hot. I practically need a hot mitt to touch you. Do you want me to turn down the temperature?"

I retrieve my face from the form-fitting bed, and the first thing I see is the bed doing a plaster cast-like imitation of my face. Great. Now the bed is doing imitations. I turn to my clock to see if it is amused. Looking at Hope, who's smiling a concerned smile at me, I ask, "What temperature is it now?"

"I'll check." She gets up and presses a spot in the wall. The spot in the white wall dissolves into a screen. She presses it again, and it blends back into the wall. She dives back. "It's 65 degrees."

"Wow, that's hot! Of course I'm hot if it's 65 degrees Celsius. Wait, that's Fahrenheit, right?" Hope is smirking at me. "No, 65 degrees should be cool enough. The problem is my body. My body knows it's summer. My body is used to being hot during the summer. It's always been hot during the summer. So now it's compensating for the air conditioning by heating itself up even further." Hope starts talking to my torso. From what I can make out, she's telling it to not work so hard, to relax and be cool. "Hope? Up here. Hope, how long have you known Sharon?"

"Not quite two months, why?"

"How did you meet her?"

"Through my mom," Hope says. This doesn't make any sense. "Aren't you hungry? You didn't eat anything at Tom's." I nod. "Let's go out for dinner. My treat, and I get to drive this time, just us." I reach for my phone, but Hope pulls me away and out the doors. "Ruth seemed to like her presents, especially the camera," Hope says while driving.

"Everyone had mixed feelings about the game."

"Maybe, but Cy called a few minutes ago asking where to get one. For all the complaints, I think they really enjoyed it. Sharon was about ready to go until she saw it." Hope takes the highway to dinner. "Did you hear Lefty say good-bye to you?"

"No. When was that?"

"Ruth was taking pictures of you. I didn't think you heard, but there was a lot going on. He said, 'See you Thursday.' And I waved to him for you."

"Thank you." That's new. No one has ever waved to someone for me, basically covering for me. I've never– actually we used to do things like that all the time for Melanie. Fans would be screaming their heads off, and we would wave to them, and while it wasn't Melanie waving to them, maybe it was the next best thing since we were next to her.

"I'm still concerned about his experiment," she tells me.

Hope takes us to Mde Maka Ska, White Earth Lake. Rising up 447 feet from the western shore is Mahpiyawicasta Tower. The bird's nest topped, white tower memorializes the millions of Native Americans who died during the 16th century pandemics. For the first time, I choose the elevator over the stairs, growing up. At the top floor, the entranceway has an autographed picture of Avatrice Gaea. Hope whispers a request to the hostess and we are taken to a table with a tremendous view of the Twin Cities rising up among all the trees and the houses. In the distance is the First National Bank building. Next to it stands the Riverside Tower, future home of Common Communication. About halfway there is the inland lighthouse Prospective Tower. Below us, the nearly perfectly round lake reflects the blue sky above us. To the right, Mde Unma, Other Lake, is equally round. It's as if two huge boulders were dropped from this height or higher, to impress the land. Behind us, the rest of the restaurant is cast in bright orange and the angling shadows of the sunset. We sit on our blankets. Hope waves away the menus and orders for us.

I have always wanted to talk to the air conditioning engineer of this building. How can you have air conditioning that doesn't smell or behave like air conditioning? Here it fans out in waves like a breeze through a pine forest. It has hints of pine, without the pineapples, as well as juniper, oak, and maple. How do they do it? If I had studied heating and cooling system engineering maybe I'd know.

Two trays of small bowls are set before us, with all sorts of mixtures, recognizable and unknown. Hope watches me examine, study, and taste the variety of foods in front of me. I recognize wojapi. I recognize wahumpa wasna. I recognize beans. I recognize many dishes.

"May we eat with you?" It is an elderly man with long gray hair and a face that could be a dried apple headed doll with a surplus of wrinkles. With him is an elderly woman, dressed in white and tan, and a grade school aged girl and a younger boy. I offer food from my tray and they politely decline while the boy presses his face to the glass and then leans his body up against his face as if trying to flatten it, one way or another. A giant paintbrush drops down from above and bathes the skylines in light sunset orange with sparkles added to the windows. The boy never notices. We exchange introductions. Hope makes sure to emphasize that she doesn't think I am eating enough. The man's name is Cal. Her name is Harriet. The grandchildren are Hunter and Sky.

"Oh! Grandchildren!" I exclaim. "I thought you two were just a little more frisky than you let on." Cal nods, and Harriet gives me a sly look. Looking out at the view of the Mississippi, I comment, "The majestic Mississippi."

"Ha ha, Wakpa," Cal says. "But Mississippi works too with all its hissing S's. Look out there. Do you see the S shape as it slithers its way through the cities?"

Hope says, "Yes," for me since my mouth is full. I'm going to have her do all my talking for me from now on.

"There once was a great snake," Cal says as their food arrives. "This snake, Zuzehecedan, was big and it was hungry. It would eat and it would eat and it would eat. This snake would eat all the fish of a lake in one gulp." As the orange light is blocked off from us, I notice a small crowd gathering around us. "As the snake got larger, it wanted larger and larger types of food. It was always hungry. Try some of this," he says to me. Hope has enlisted strangers in her campaign to feed me. "When the snake got big enough to eat a bison in one swallow..." Sky gives her grandfather a wide-eyed look. "Then all the tribes were concerned. This was a snake that could easily eat people. And even if the snake did not eat people, it was eating all the food. All the tribes banded together. Off in the distance, past Pigs Eye and the white rocks, from a bluff over Pigs Eye Lake, a storyteller stopped the snake."

"Why do you s-s-s-s-s-stop me, oh s-s-s-s-s-storyteller?" I ask him, deciding to take a role in the story. This amuses Cal and the kids.

Cal is caught off guard. I hiss a little more to help him back on track.

"I want to tell you about a great feast of food," Cal says as the storyteller, with a cough. "A great feast that is in your future."

"S-s-s-s-s-so tell me."

"The storyteller said, 'This is my story.'"

"I will give you credit. I will call it his-s-s-s-s story," I add.

"As the storyteller told the snake about the great food, the snake's body wound its way from all the way over there," Cal points his audience out the window, "turning there and over there, with its tail ending up there. The tribes attacked the tail and the length of the body while the storyteller kept the head of the snake enthralled in the tale of the great feast. When the squamous snake finally realized that it was under attack, it twisted itself and arched its neck sideways, rubbing the dirt to rock. It whipped half its body straight along there, creating the Minnesota River and then back again for the rest of the Mississippi, the Hahawakpa, which gets smaller and smaller where the tail was. As it wriggled, it rubbed the dirt down to bare, vertical rock cliffs in many places, wearing off its scales on the rock, turning the rock cliffs white. Finally the snake reared up its head as it was being sliced open all along and with a final–"

That's my cue, "Hiss."

"– the great snake's head smashed to the ground at Pigs Eye Lake. The great snake died and provided a great feast that lasted for two years and left two great river valleys. The rest is history." We receive pats on our shoulders and our backs for the telling of the tale.

"Eat," Hope tells me.

"Yes, eat," Harriet tells me.

"You need to eat," Cal says.

"Eat!" the children yell in the same ear that is still recovering from Faith's attack in the car. I hiss at them; they run away. I eat my little bowl of sauteed Canadian goose and my dried bison and berries and I guess I'll fill up on seeds of goosefoot, maygrass, marshelder, pigweed, and sunflower. I rarely need my fork; the fork has five tines like fingers and thumb of a hand. Yeah, this'll fill me up, seeds and knotweed beans. I ask Hope if she has a spare copy of one of my business cards.

She hands me one. I give it to Cal saying, "If you ever need to scare the kids, give me a call."

Cal is taking small bites of his meal, staring out at the S shaped path of the Hahawakpa. After two seconds, he takes my card and says to me in a quiet voice, "Have you ever wanted to change the past?"

"All the time."

"I would like to go back in time and find the Ojibwa who told the French that we were the Nadouessioux... the adders... the enemy... and I would kick his butt."

We look out eastward, searching for his trouble-making spirit.

"This is your squash," Hope says.

"No, thank you."

"I thought you liked squash?"

"No, I call it squish."

"But you like zucchini..."

"Zucchini? Yes, I like zucchini. Cooked. Raw. In bread. Not in bread. My favorite zucchini are zucchini canoes," I tell Cal, and he nods. "You sparsely hollow the canoe and fill it with cheese and bread crumbs. Great stuff. Zucchini canoes."

"They can make that for you here," Cal says, and before I can stop him, he's waving someone over and making the special order for me. The waiter is looking at me as he listens, evaluating me for this request. I try to protest, but Cal waves me off with the very slight wrist flick of a maestro, as if to say that this is hardly worth discussing, as if to say that this is inconsequential compared to what he is used to handling. To Hope he says, "We'll make sure he gets enough of what he likes." They smile at each other while Harriet watches the silhouettes of Sky and Hunter plastered against the sunset across the restaurant. Hope puts a bowl of walnuts and pecans in front of me. Nuts.

I don't like, I don't want, I don't need anything special made for me or done for me. My anti-ego shifts uncomfortably, like a great ape that knows that if he accepts special treatment he will ultimately have to fight it out with the alpha ape who is lurking somewhere. My peripheral vision catches what I think is the giant paintbrush indecisively changing color after color on the downtown buildings, struggling to keep up with the darkening sunset. Waiters, head waiters, and managers all descend upon our table to clear old bowls, refresh water, and deliver the special zucchini canoes, complete with little, cheesy people and ornately carved bamboo shoot paddles in a stream of blueberry sauce within a gravel bank of chopped nuts. A little overboard, aren't we? Others gather to marvel at my plate. I offer everyone and anyone a portion of the masterpiece. No one accepts my offer, not even me. But I have to accept. I pick up my handy fork. As I lower my fork to the first canoe, everyone holds their breath. Taking the first bite, everyone exhales. I tell them, "It's delicious," knowing full well that saying "delicious" to this culinary art is like saying "wow" to the first viewing of any masterpiece of art or invention. It's under-whelmingly insufficient. Sky and Hunter watch closely as my first canoe starts to sink. I bail blueberry sauce, at first using a half grape bowl from the canoe and then by the spoonful. People leave as I transfer cargo and travelers from the first canoe to the second. As I eat the canoes and their contents, Hope looks like a kid who just got the snow day off from school – contented.

"Sure Foot's a great guy," she tells Cal. "He just doesn't always remember to eat. That was nice of you to order this. Maybe the problem is that he doesn't have enough food on hand that he likes."

"I'm right here you know," I tell her between paddles. I eat the paddles all at once so the second canoe is left without any paddles.

"I think your friend is on a journey. When you're on a journey, you travel light and you eat light, you concentrate on the journey, not everything else. It's good that you can remind him." Uh, guys? I'm still here.

"We've been together for only a few weeks, and he's not exactly clingy. It's tough to know when I'm crossing the line," you're crossing it now, you know, "telling him what to do."

"Like a couple of porcupines, there's a lot of poking and prodding," Cal says, giving Harriet a poke in the arm for emphasis. Harriet pokes him right back. The lights of the restaurant rise to compensate for the darkening sky. Sky stands behind Harriet and says something to the others that I don't hear as I stuff myself with the rest of the second canoe and most of the stream. I don't think eating needs to be such an obligation. I'd have shipped the second boat to India, if I thought I could get away with it. As I lean back, my tray is cleared away, and I follow the gaze of the others, watching Hunter sneak up on unsuspecting strangers. He drapes a blanket over himself to blend into the draperies. He disappears into them. Smart kid. I would've liked to have used that trick when I was being set up for the zucchini stuffing.

Long curved screens above the windows play scenes of sunsets and storms filmed from up here. Video from time-lapse photos show the sun dropping, echoes of what we just witnessed. It shows storm clouds rolling in from across the plains, tripping their way over the twin skylines and dragging their heels through the river valley, before stumbling eastward into Wisconsin. The sun shines brightly again, and the screens take on the images of a crowded Dakota village on the lake and running the trail through a forest of mammoth trees. The perspective runs along the Minnehaha, twice crossing it, to emerge overlooking a small clearing in the marshy river's edge. It is the nearby Hahawakpa, some of the bluff features haven't changed, but this is not the Mississippi River that I've ever seen. It is free. The view pushes off a canoe, climbs into it, and takes off downstream. The river flows fast and slow with rapids and eddies and rocks the size of cars and fallen trees as wide as billboards and still growing. We don't take the easy ways. We take the rapids. One of the rocks scrapes the boat, slicing a hole that leaks a riverlet of water. Drifting by Mendota, people converse with us and look downstream with us. We paddle again to Kaposia at White Rock, where we beach our canoe in the marsh cattails, rising from the water like vertical brown hot dogs on green sticks. A sickly boy covered in rashes is lying on the wet marsh grasses by a small, fast two-man canoe not much bigger than a zucchini. The boy has the smallpox virus. The crowd on the river doesn't know what he has or what it means. It is like nothing else. That evening we take the disease back to the lake with a mix of tom-toms, vocal melodies, and symphonic strings. Watching the resulting time-lapse deaths from smallpox and the deaths from subsequent exotic village-emptying diseases, it's difficult not to feel partly above it all. It is all in the past. Smallpox can be prevented with a quick shot of the cowpox virus. We have moved onward and upward. Hope and I say good-bye to Cal, Harriet, and Sky, but we can't find Hunter. When Cal says good-bye, he calls me Sure Foot. Hope stops a waiter for our bill and is for some reason told that it was taken care of. On our way down the elevator, Hope is about to say something when we're joined by another group that's leaving. It's still warm and humid outside. Moths elliptically orbit the parking lamps. In the car, Hope asks me, "Do you know who that was?"

"In the elevator?"

"No, at our table!"

She's testing my memory. I don't know why. "Yes. Harriet, Cal, Sky, and Hunter."

"Do you know who he is?"

"Hunter?"

Hope explodes, "No! Cal." I shrug. "He is the chief. The chief! Not just of the Dakota at Reyatao-tonwe or at Mendota but of all the Mdewakanton. He is the chief. Do you know why he sat with us? Do you think he knows that you are a friend of Avatrice Gaea?"

"I have no idea."

"Doesn't that drive you crazy?!?"

"No. He just seemed like a nice old man."

"How can that not drive you crazy?" Hope drives, concentrating on the road. At a stoplight she checks to see that I'm still in the car with her.

"The idea of AutoDrive killing people in its first trials – that drives me crazy. Having the Chief of the Mdewakanton band eating with us is... nice. I guess that explains why we couldn't pay the bill."

"I suppose. This sort of thing happens to you everyday, doesn't it."

"I can't say I have ever eaten with the Chief of the Mdewakanton before."

"But you're so... calm about it." I lower my window and shout out the news to the rest of the traffic. Traffic doesn't understand me. Traffic looks at me funny. Hope tugs me back into the car. At the house, Ray's bike is absent from the driveway. Hope escorts me into my room and disappears.

My phone has several messages from Tom complaining about a blizzard in his freezer. It's snowing in his freezer. It already has six inches and more is on the way. So is Al. Tom can't get it to stop without shutting off both his refrigerator and freezer. I once turned his key chain into a snow globe. All the tools I needed were already at his house: an old jar, strong glue, and an old piece of Styrofoam. I glued the key chain to the inside of the jar lid. A piece of the Styrofoam was crumbled into the jar. The jar was filled the rest of the way with water. The lid was screwed on tightly and sealed with the strong glue. He had the jar lid on his key chain for the longest time. Later when I was prepared to do it again with glitter, he had a key-less remote that I didn't want to submerge.

Hope comes back. We get to know each other better.

34

The Setup

I fluff up my pillows in my sleep. My pillows giggle. My pillows have never giggled or been ticklish before. Those aren't my pillows. "Sorry about that, Nicole."

"It's okay." I find my pillows, my actual pillows, and fluff them extra well. "What have you really got against TV?" Nicole asks.

"TV is make-believe right?"

"Yeah."

"But it doesn't work if you don't believe. It doesn't work if you can see through it."

"See through the set?"

"Right, the false-wall sets, the episodic formula, the inconsistencies... how most commercials represent the wildest dream or fantasy of the advertiser... how the news makes the news anchors seem knowledgeable about their stories but without teleprompters and phonetically spelled out words, they would be just a face on the screen. So much of TV assumes that people have no memory and can't imagine other possibilities."

"Does it bother you when people watch TV?" she asks.

"People can do what they want. For me it's just very predictable."

I fall back asleep. My dreams are a hodge-podge of AutoDrive and accidents. I try to sneak into Flight Control to secretly repair AutoDrive, and it's weird because I don't think anyone has ever snuck in to anywhere to repair anything since the beginning of time. "I'll just chisel in a tenth commandment. Nine seems too weird of a stopping point." We get caught, the future me and I, and turned over to the police. The police try to figure out what we were doing, but the future me clams up, leaving just me to defend myself, and I'm not even sure what I was doing or its implications. The cops are confused, and I'm with them. They put me in a cell to think things over. The cops make the mistake of letting me keep my cell phone in my cell; I consider using its self-destruct mechanism to bust myself out but decide against it. I use my cell time for pointed perception and come to the conclusion that having been arrested and charged with breaking and entering, my credibility has crashed to zero. I can no longer talk to Wendy or Will. A restraining order bars me from coming anywhere near AutoDrive. Several of my friends aren't talking to me. This is a dead end. This is getting nowhere. The ends do not justify the means. So I back up. I go forward on the theory that I can do everything and fix everything through Wendy. At first it works okay, except for a lot of reexplaining and convincing. But then she starts to break down. She is pressured from both sides. All of AutoDrive rests on her shoulders. It's too much. The next thing I hear, she's taken off for Bermuda without her phone or plans to return... so much for the intermediary theory. A modern raindance could rain on the AutoDrive parade, dusting silver iodide at 10,000 feet to seed the clouds. But rain will only wash the car. AutoDrive won't understand rain, but that won't stop it. I decide I could stop AutoDrive with a lawsuit. "Sorry I just drooled on my phone," the lawyer says. I call five lawyers, and all five agree that this is a great idea, so I figure I'd better not go the lawsuit route. However I could call the Pegasus people, give the vehicle identification number, and report it as stolen. They will send a satellite signal to stop the car or not let it start. That could work... for about 20 minutes, maybe 30.

"Hey," Nicole says to the side of my head. "I have to go. I have to go to work."

"Then go."

"You're on my arm." I let Nicole's arm go and apologize. Her butt wiggles out the door. I try to get back into a sensible pointed perception. What I get are nonsensical snippets of silliness.

Erix looks at AutoDrive and shakes his head. AutoDrive looks at Erix and shakes its head.

My name and grinning face are on an advertisement for AutoDrive as if I'm giving a celebrity endorsement. The last thing, the very last thing I would want to do right now, is promote or endorse AutoDrive.

And I dream I'm in Italy again with an incredible AutoDrive sports car. As it turns and avoids goats with perfectly calculated precision, for an instant, a microsecond less than a blink, I trust AutoDrive.

Silliness.

Scrolling through reverse AutoDrive code for British roads, I wake up to a mild earthquake. Hope and her smile are jumping up and down on the bed. "Wake up, Sleepyhead!" I hold onto my stomach. What did I eat last night?!? Oh yeah, Hope made me eat everything.

"Hi Sunshine. Could you stop that? You would not believe all the stuff I ate last night."

Hope stops; her smile disappears. "Are you okay?"

"Yes. Besides I've been told that this is state-of-the-mattress art, a really expensive bed. You don't want to break the bed."

"I couldn't break the bed, not unless I drove over it a few times or something, not that anyone does that."

"No one would do that." Hope lays down next to me smiling. She stops and sniffs the pillow and puzzles over the smell. "Nicole," I tell her.

"Oh. Anything happen?"

"I uh, accidentally fluffed her pillows." Hope stares at me. "I was asleep!"

"If you want to fluff pillows, fluff my pillows."

"I wasn't trying to fluff anyone's pillows, except... except this one!" She's still staring at me. "Here." I pick up my two pillows and fling them onto a closet shelf. The first one makes it, bounces off the closet wall, drops down, and lands softly on one of my large piles of dirty clothes. The second pillow hits the edge of the shelf and lands on the first pillow. "There. No more pillows. No more fluffing." Hope still doesn't look satisfied. I stare at her. I fluff her pillows.

"Okay, they're fluffed! Do you want to go to the mall with me? I have to do some returns."

"The shorts?"

"Yes and something I picked up for Ruth before I knew what you had planned."

"You are the model of efficiency. No, I'll stay here."

"Okay. See ya," she kisses me twice, once for my upper lip and once for my lower lip.

I set the pillows up on the closet shelf, and even out my mountains of dirty clothes. My sheets make a snow cap on one of the mountains. Carrying one of the mountains into the basement, while shuffling to clear a path down the stairs, I look for a way to put money into the washing machine. Weird. It's free.

Half of the mountain goes into the machine. I use a towel to wipe dust off the dryer to set down the rest of the load. The laundry detergent box is the right size and shape, but the box is monochrome; the brand is unknown; and the contents are fused into one solid block of soap. How old is this? I break off a piece that appears to be the right size and toss it into the machine. It clunks. I start up the machine. I wipe off a wooden stool. I sit and watch the washer.

This isn't the apartment building. I don't have to watch the machine. No one is going to take the laundry out and dump it on the floor. I get up and run into a cobweb. That's annoying. Cobwebs on the skin feel like being covered by spiders. I take a stick and wind it through web after web after web. The webs wrap around the stick, stretching and tearing with the soft sizzle of 10,000 tiny stickers being peeled off. The layers form a wrapped ball at the end of the stick like gray-white cotton candy. Setting the cotton candy down, I sit back down on the stool and relax.

I'm late. The stage is set almost entirely on the sidewalk this time. AutoDrive could only hit Carl if it is gunning for him. That's a thought I never considered until now. Carl is standing on the edge of the stage, scanning the crowd like a nervous groom. He stops when he spots me. I guess that makes me the bride. I don't like that analogy. He nods. I don't think he is nodding to me, so much as at me. He's nodding in my direction. Now he's whistling and pointing. Whoever he's trying to signal must be a complete idiot. AutoDrive is turned the opposite direction from what it was before. That shouldn't help. The car doors are open. A guy wearing a windshield on his face approaches me.

"Are you here to wish us luck?" Bailey asks, muffled by my earplugs. I don't have any response for him. I could explain that there is no such thing as luck. I could say lots of things, but I try not to teach gophers to yodel. It wastes time and annoys the gophers. "The best thing Carl ever did was to fire you." He's trying to provoke me. It won't work. "You held us back."

He wants to be hit. He's ready for it. And if life were as simple as movies and books make it out to be, I would hit him. But in reality there are too many repercussions. And in reality, he's not worth the attention.

I laugh at him. He jumps, startled. He wasn't expecting that response. The mayor is introducing Carl, as the owner of Flight Control and a local champion of ingenuity. I'm still laughing. Carl sneers at me as he talks and he seems to forget to not walk in front of one of the speakers. Bailey is telling me to shut up when the feedback hits. Now he notices my earplugs. Bailey backs off. Carl doesn't get clipped by AutoDrive as the car drives off.

An alarm buzzes, unmuffled by my earplugs. I open my eyes. The washer has stopped. The washer load goes to the dryer. The washer starts again without money or sidewalk salt. BAM! I smash the detergent box against the washer to break off a hunk of solidified detergent. I drop it into the washer with a splash. The rest of my laundry follows the rock of detergent. I sit back down on the stool, close my eyes, and relax.

Bailey backs off. Carl doesn't get clipped by AutoDrive. The car drives off, squealing its tires and heading away from Mdewakanton Avenue. Who is Carl trying to impress by having AutoDrive peal out, junior high school kids? AutoDrive turns and disappears. Bailey starts to applaud, others join in for a few claps, before stopping to wonder why they are clapping. Minutes tick by. Bailey walks back over to Carl. People are checking their watches and asking questions. "Hasn't it been long enough?" "Is the car going to come back?"

Everyone reacts at once. Everyone who isn't tethered to a van with a satellite dish tower races down Nicollet in the direction that AutoDrive went. I take out my earplugs. Walking by, a reporter tells her camera that "the word car comes from a part of the gasoline engine, the carburetor."

"No, car was short for carriage." I get a few yards away, and I stop. What am I doing? Where am I going? I don't have a plan. I don't have a strategy.

I stare off at the open road and its distant crowd.

An alarm goes off. I look around, but no one looks alarmed. I open my eyes.

The washing machine is still running. The alarm is coming from upstairs. My alarm clock is ringing from the top of the stairs. I climb the stairs and pick it up. "How did you get–"

"I have been calling and calling to you," Hope says from the couch. "That was the only way I could think of to get you up here. What were you doing down there?"

"My laundry."

"You don't have to stay down there."

"Force of habit. At the apartment I had to watch my laundry."

"Were there clothes bandits?"

"No. Well, maybe. But basically people had little or no respect for personal property. People would dump other people's laundry anywhere."

"That's not going to happen here," Hope assures me.

"Right. Because Ray wouldn't do that and," I toss up and catch my clock, "the rest of you are scared to go down there. Do you wash your clothes in the dishwasher or... don't you wash your clothes?"

Hope marches sternly over to me and swipes my clock. "First of all, yes I do clean my clothes. We have a washer-dryer set upstairs. And second off, I just don't like basements."

"Does it have anything to do with your brothers?"

"It has everything to do with my brothers," Hope says, looking okay with it.

"Do you want to get over your fear of basements?"

Hope absently snuggles my clock to her bosom. I'm never getting that clock back. "This is the way I am."

"Yes and no. You will always be you, but this you is as transitory as summer in Minnesota. You can do anything you want. If you want to be afraid of basements, you can be afraid of basements. If you don't want to be afraid of basements, you don't have to be afraid of basements." Hope nods. The washer buzzes. "Do you want to come with me to check my laundry? The clock can come too."

A slight smile appears and she says, "Not this time."

Bringing down a clothes basket, I move partial mountains of laundry through the laundry system. I think I might be the only person in the world who views laundry as a system. Maybe the manufacturers of this detergent – what is it – Snow Fresh – maybe the Snow Fresh detergent company views laundry as a system too. Maybe I could get a job with them if things don't work out with my Common Communication letter. Searching the battered box of detergent for an address, I rub off dust and soap residue. It says, "Tucson, Arizona." Snow Fresh is in Tucson. Sand Blast detergent is probably from Duluth. Either way I'd have to move.

Heading back up, I'm surprised to see Hope and my clock sitting, waiting for me, on the top step of the basement stairs. Back lit by the sunlight, they're reading messages on her phone. She picks up the alarm clock, and they lead me to my room. "Your friends are talking about going to visit Red tomorrow," she says.

"They're your friends too."

"Do you want to go?" Hope asks, returning my clock to my nightstand. The clock slumps from elation to dejection in record time. I grunt an agreement, while folding or hanging up my laundry. "What was that?" I repeat my agreeable grunt. "What does that mean? Are we," Hope laughs, "are we back to ape sounds?"

"It meant yes," I tell her, grunting again more slowly for emphasis like a language teacher, my hands open and gesturing wide.

"I thought we had evolved past the ape sounds." I grunt indifference. "Now what does that mean?!?" I grunt a lengthy, technical explanation. Hope pulls me by my big ape arm onto the bed, climbs on top of me, and thumps her chest. "I'm not talking with you like that, Ape-Man. And you might want to reconsider talking to me like that, especially while my mother is here."

"I'm sure she's heard worse from your brothers."

"Yes. She nearly killed them, and they are directly related to her. She's been in Miami when sharks were around. They were all around her. But they didn't bite her out of professional courtesy. Remember she is a lawyer."

"Gotcha."

"That's better," she says climbing off, "but you still might want to brush up on your English." I grunt an agreement. Her eyes narrow. Her lips purse. I get up and kiss her pursed lips, opening them and searching through the contents of her pursed mouth with my tongue, until she says, "Okay that's enough. I'm not going to reward your ape talk. Now have you eaten anything yet?"

"I was just about to" think about it, I say part to her and part to myself. Before I get a chance to think, she's dragging me into the kitchen. I open a can of Beaches. Despite Ray's alteration of the label, it tastes like peaches, without any of the grit you'd expect from a can of Beaches. "Would you like some?"

"No, thank you," Hope slowly articulates like a language teacher. She forgot the gesturing part, the sweep of the hands. I eat my Beaches.

Putting the rest of the can away, I ask, "What do you think we should bring for Christie?"

Hope pushes back from the table. "A card. A donation to her church. I'll handle those things." Hope narrows her eyes at me. "Have you had any dreams about seeing her?" I shrug and grunt. Hope's eyes widen in shock. I don't know if she's surprised that I don't know or that I grunted. Ray storms in and takes a seat.

"Kelly is done!"

"Congratulations!"

"I knew you could do it," I tell him.

"We hooked her up, and she works. She lactates."

"That's wonderful," Hope says.

"Yeah? Then why don't I feel wonderful?" Ray goes to the fridge and takes out the half can of Beaches. "What am I going to do now?"

"Anything. Everything."

He takes his head out of the can and turns to me and asks, "No, I really want to know what I'm going to do?" That's odd that he would ask me that way, like I have anything to do with it. I have enough problems running my own life. I'd be damned if I run his.

"Life doesn't work that way. Have you ever wondered where God is? God is at the crossroads of each of your decisions, each one, waiting for your choice. That's what life is all about. Anyone who talks about death being the time when God looks at your life's choices is nuts. God was there all along."

"I don't know about that."

"That's your choice. I saw you unveiling Kelly. It... At least previously, it will happen... without Chuckles peering over her shoulder."

"But what do you think I should do?"

"Concentrate on Kelly. She still needs you, at least until she goes public next week. Think about the unveiling. Remember what Sharon said about Kelly? She said something like being glad to say, 'I know the artist!' You are already a hit. Dream about it. Get comfortable and dream about how people will react to you and what opportunities will open up. Use the next few days to decide if you want to do more sculptures or if there is something else you want to do, so that you'll know when you are talking to people at the unveiling." Ray shoves the Beaches can at me. "No thanks, I just had some."

"I can't dream the way you do. I don't have pointed perception."

"Right. What's it going to be like at the unveiling?"

"I don't know. There's going to be a canvas over her–"

"Will there be people there?"

"Yeah."

"How many?"

"I don't know. A lot."

"So a whole crowd?"

"Yeah."

"Strangers?"

"And friends..."

"What will they bring with them?"

"Cameras."

"Will they have anything else in their hands?"

Ray stares at the side of the can. "We're handing out something about Kelly and the park."

"So they will be holding the brochures? What else?"

"Babies."

"So mothers are going to bring their babies with and hold them, instead of leaving them in the strollers. Why?"

"I don't know. It's just an impression. Kelly brings that out of people, the mother's tenderness and caring, I guess."

"You keep saying that you don't know, but you do know. You know the feelings that Kelly will evoke in people. You know that some people have a fondness for that mother and child love. Others have shame and deprivation that they associate with it. They'll react differently. You've thought about all these things throughout the process of making Kelly."

"Not really."

"Okay, then I have. People are going to ask you to explain your ability, explain the expression on Kelly's face, explain that wrinkle, right there," pointing to nothing in mid-air. "And they will have their own issues, good and bad, mostly relating to themselves, that made them come out for the unveiling."

"So you aren't going to tell me what's going to happen to me?"

"No, because I don't know. You haven't decided yet, and even when you decide, I may not have a clue. It depends on what's going on with me over time... now and later... you know?"

Ray stares at me like I have fur or I'm glowing or something. The laundry downstairs buzzes without any reaction from Ray. His trance ends with his pat on the table. "You're a big help," he says taking the Beaches with him to his room.

"I'm going to take care of my laundry," I tell Hope.

"I'll be upstairs," she says, getting up.

"Hey. We can do something together. It's just that I need to handle my laundry first."

"When you're ready, I'll be upstairs."

I think I'm missing something, but I say, "Okay." She goes up. I go down. I work the laundry system, evaluating the results of the system on my clothes, looking for damage and alternative settings. For AutoDrive, I decide that I can't be in the crowd on the far side from where AutoDrive disappears. That's not where the action is. I need to be where the action is. I take another set of laundry upstairs, put it away, sit down, and relax.

I'm standing at a barricaded street corner several blocks from the start of the AutoDrive test. No one is around, except for someone coming up right next to me. "Rain isn't in the forecast," she says. I turn. It's Cooelle. "I never got the chance to participate in any precipitation planning," she says. "I don't know if you heard, but they canned me two weeks ago." That would be right about now. "Are you involved again?"

"No. At least not with Flight Control. I'm just trying to make sure no one gets hurt."

"Why do you care, after what they did to you?"

I turn to her with a speechlessness that lasts until a Pegasus Coup drives by with a wake of last season's road salt and yesterday's news. "I've got to go." I hop the barricade and run after the car. The car takes a corner almost effortlessly, and a moment of – this is weird – sheer unadulterated, undiluted Pride sweeps over me, and I think, "That's my car!" And then the metal crunching, glass and plastic shattering CRASH occurs to sweep away any inkling of pride or accomplishment. I run to the corner and turn it. Down at the end of the block, AutoDrive has hit a police car. "That's my car." Faint movement is inside the white police car, but I can't tell for certain because of the sunlight. I run to the far side, the uncrunched side, of the police car. There is no uncrunched side of the police car. His forehead is bleeding. There is blood on his mustache. His body seems to be still shaking from the impact, but that doesn't make much sense. The door makes part of an unlatching sound but won't open. I pull on it. I put both hands on the handle and one foot on the back door and pull. With help, metal bends against metal.

"Are you okay?" I ask the officer. He blinks and works on an answer. Others are arriving around me helping to pull away the door. We work him free from his car. He stinks. A plainclothes doctor or paramedic or med student takes over. I take off my shirt. It becomes his pillow.

"That car is still running!" someone says.

"Everyone back off! That's gasoline you're standing in!"

I look over. Cooelle reaches in and turns off AutoDrive.

I open my eyes. My room is darkening. My clock tells me it's after six, but it keeps swinging around its minute hand so I don't know the minutes. One of these days I'm going to get that thing fixed.

Should I call Hope or go upstairs or just finish doing my laundry? I decide to climb the stairs and knock. Nicole opens the door, and I am eye-level with her Functional And Ornamental shirt.

"Hi," she says backing up and holding me aside as she shuts the door, "you aren't thrilling her by sitting in a trance or hiding out in the basement."

"I wasn't hiding in the basement, and I wasn't in a trance."

"What do you call it?" Nicole tilts her head. Faith removes Nicole's hands from me and pushes me down the hall to Hope's door. She takes my hand, wads it up, and knocks it against the door. Faith hides.

Hope answers, "Oh, hi." She turns around and walks back in. That is officially, the grand poobah champion, worst reception I have ever received from Hope. I slink into her room behind her.

"Did I do something wrong?"

Hope turns on me. Her brow is wrinkled. Her dimples are missing. "I've been looking forward to having some time with you for weeks." We haven't been spending time together?!? "I only have two weeks off from school." Oh. "Today was a waste." She sets herself down in a pile of hope chests that she seems to be sorting or stacking or something. I could tell her I was busy watching AutoDrive smash itself and others. I could tell her I'm nearly finished with laundry. I don't know what to tell her.

I tell her, "I didn't mean to waste your day, but you never talked about plans for today, did you? You're acting like I let you down, but you never told me what you wanted. If you want to make plans with me, fine, but if you don't, don't berate me for something I know nothing about." She looks up at me just as I'm turning to leave. I drop down two flights of stairs to finish my laundry.

Talking is the simplest thing. Talking isn't tough. But talking, back and forth, and coming to an understanding seems to be the toughest challenge a relationship has to face. The foundation of a good relationship is how the people talk. I've seen it. And how they talk is a perfect representation of their relationship. I can hear a lifetime in a phrase or a tone of voice.

I finish my laundry, eat some leftover ambrosia, and head to bed. I'm just starting to rest peacefully when Nicole wakes me. "Hey," she says, "could I get a quick hug?" I figure what could that hurt? I give her a hug without fully waking up. She watches me drift back to sleep. The sleep is the most peaceful sleep anyone could have, as if everything is settled; everything is as it will be.

Sunshine drifts through my window as I wake up from a very sound sleep. Someone had been in my dream. Dream? It was just one dream. Faith. She was in my dream last night. It wasn't good. I sit up, leaning into a snowdrift-like pile of comforter. I relax.

35

Bam

Someone opened my door, but they're gone now. Pounding on the stairs. Nothing. Pounding on the stairs. I get on my knees to crawl off the bed. Faith is standing in front of us, her arms in front... holding a gun. She is panting slightly, but otherwise has the look of someone working on a mildly difficult crossword puzzle. "I'm going to kill you." Why is she going to kill me?!? "Nicole." Oh, that makes more sense. Wait! Nicole sits up, and I'm moving in front of her. Faith's gun yells **BAM!** My chest fires back. Now there's something you don't feel everyday. My blood pressure drops like water through a drain. I turn to Nicole, hearing Faith say, "Oh my God," like she is surprised that guns do that. Nicole is choking with a hole below her neck. I try to move to look at my watch, but I'm falling onto dark speckled sheets. I open my eyes, surprised to find myself laying down. I sit up again, like when I was shot... will be shot... not if I can help it. I have to know when that's going to happen.

Heh. People say they want to die peacefully in bed, but I don't think they know what they're talking about.

Faith is going to kill me.

I used to wonder where new tenants at Whisper Willows were on the gun chart. Everyone else I'd already figured out or learned through spies. What was nice about my old neighborhood was that while guns were plentiful, most didn't have time to clean them or practice aiming. It was like living in an armory of carelessness. "Excuse me, I couldn't help but notice. You're leaving a trail of bullets." And it isn't tough to figure people out. People slovenly in their own appearance and car care weren't the types to keep their gun cleaned and oiled. People are consistent. Gun care and accuracy aside, the principle issue is accessibility. Is the gun on them? Are their nerves resting on a hair-trigger? Most people travel lighter than that. They might lug around a gun for a while, until they get tired of lugging it around. Or they might trade it in for a lightweight pea shooter, only to be laughed at for trying to be threatening with a gun that is child-safe. There is an attitude of people carrying guns, a cockiness that certainly diminishes once they know how well-armed those around them are. I may not be carrying a gun, but these guys are. And most women aren't interested in the added weight on their hips.

Nothing is as simultaneously useful, the ultimate problem solver, and as useless as a gun. Guns don't require any marketing. They have built-in marketing. All the gun manufacturers have to do is lobby against gun control. The guns do the rest. The poor scrawny boy has no money, no muscles, and no confidence. He has no chance against the mystique of the gun. The gun can solve those problems, until it is purchased, then reality sets in. Money should be convenient from the convenience store... all you have to do is wave the gun, but the owner has a gun too. The kid isn't going to get money from the gun. In order for the gun to provide muscle, the kid has to show it, but showing it and shooting it are two different things, and if you aren't going to shoot it, I can just take it away from you like this! Just messing with ya, kid. Here's your gun back. So the boy learns that the gun doesn't do anything. The kid tries to learn about hold-ups, and now that he has a gun, now he hears about all the things that go wrong in robberies. Or everything goes perfect for a measly 48 dollars. He wants to return the gun and get his money back. He never even fired the thing. Gun shops don't want to see their guns again. They'll take it back for a price, but he didn't buy it from a gun shop. He bought it from the guy who is always looking over his shoulder. That guy seemed understanding enough to take the boy's money. He should be understanding about taking the gun back and returning the money, right?

Having street smarts means having an awareness of the people and things around you, with an eye to the dangers and intentions. I had street smarts at the apartment. Apparently I forgot them in the move. I didn't see that coming. I didn't see Faith coming.

Faith was gunning for Nicole. What is it with her?!?

This house is not an armory of carelessness. I am certain Faith has had practice on a range and has cleaned her gun religiously. She has the time and the commitment to give the gun. She hit two targets with one bullet. She wins a doll, a penitentiary Penelope doll. She also wins orange overalls.

It's a hell of a month to get fired and fired at.

Now it's going to happen again. I relax. Someone opened my door, but they're gone now. Pounding on the stairs. I grab my watch from my nightstand, waking Nicole. It is early Wednesday morning. Nicole is asking me what's up, but I'm fumbling out of the bed, I already hear the pounding on the stairs. The gun lights up the darkened hallway as Faith gets that surprised look on her face again. The hallway darkens again while my chest bursts and my ears ring. As I fall to the floor I decide that I really hate that surprised-frigging-look on Faith's face. I open my eyes.

How can a gun be so confusing to her?

I've never understood Nicole's problem with Faith; why Faith could really get under Nicole's skin. Now I get it. Nicole must be a better judge of people than I am. Any friend who shoots me is no friend of mine.

What were they arguing about that caused Faith to shoot Nicole and me? Any argument is weak, if it needs force to back it up.

I find myself rubbing my chest absently, rubbing it raw.

I'm not invincible. I'm not invulnerable.

So what do I do? I could barge upstairs, try to find Faith's gun, and take it downstairs to bust it up. I would find an old hammer and slam the hammer into the muzzle of the gun. I know enough about alloys to know that one hit would not damage the gun, only scratch it. My arm would feel the hit more than the gun or the hammer.

The best way to solve conflicts is not by fighting. Be prepared to fight? Sure. But the key is to dodge the fight before it begins.

Damn.

Hope knocks on my half-open door. "Hi. I brought you something." She holds out a little framed picture of herself.

"I think I need to move out."

The little framed picture drops from her hands and bounces midway between us. Hope bursts into tears, ripping another hole through my heart. "No!" Hope grabs my shoulders. "Why?!?"

"Faith has a gun." I look at my clock. It gapes at me, teetering on the edge. "In about 16 hours she will either shoot me or both me and Nicole. Faith really blows me away." Hope is frozen. "I think I need to move out."

-    Hope shifts from fear to determination. "No. Come with me." I follow her upstairs. Upstairs smells like a truck full of shampoos, deodorants, and perfumes hit another truck full of paint and nail polish. It smells like a calamity of fragrances. Hope stops at Faith's door and exhales sharply. She gets out a key ring with every-key-known-to-man and unlocks the door. The first thing I notice is a cross against the wall. It appears to be original size. I'm surprised the wall can bear the weight. Hope goes straight to the nightstand, pushes aside a vibrator and pulls out a gun. She should keep those in separate drawers to avoid confusion.

"That's it."

I stare at the gun with a hatred I haven't felt in a long time. It takes on a reddish tint. Hope handles it like she's had military training. She unloads it without a blink, without a hesitation. "She's lost her right to have a gun in this house. I will straighten everything out. Will you stay?"

"If it doesn't kill me."

Hope eyes me. "You scared the hell out of me."

"You can't fool me. There never was any hell in you."

"I thought you were upset about last night."

"No. Just getting shot."

"Wait for me in the living room, okay?" I go out and wonder which living room she's talking about, upstairs or downstairs. I pick the upstairs one. It's closer. I take a seat. I rub my chest.

Hope returns, asking, "Can I get you a drink?"

"No, I'm fine. What did you do?"

"The gun is hidden away," Hope confidently says.

"What's the next step?"

"Faith and Nicole are more my friends than your friends. I will handle it. I'd like to put you up in a hotel so I can get this straightened out without you in the crossfire."

"A hotel? Why don't I just stay with someone?"

"Selfish reasons, really. This way I can visit you anytime... or bring you home anytime. I can even arrange some spa time for you so you can be pampered."

"Please don't. That sounds like hell."

"Worse than getting shot?"

I rub my chest some more. "Close." Hope sits down.

"My brothers did a lot, but they never shot me."

"But there were guns?"

"Yes. Guns and other weapons. Familial war could have broken out at any moment in our house. I was voted most likely to get caught in the crossfire. One winter, my number one task was disarmament. I'm used to negotiations and family treaties." Hope gets out her phone and calls the Indulgence Hotel. She books a room for two. I try to stop her, but she won't listen. They ask about room preferences, food choices, and entertainment interests. She takes care of it, even surprising me about some of the things she knows about me.

When she completes the call, I tell her, "All that will be wasted on me. I'm planning on visiting Red tonight with the others. And I could spend the rest of the night at the Ice Cream Bar."

"You're more likely to get shot there than here."

"They don't pass out guns at Loon Lake. That has to be high on their list of rules."

"I meant at the Ice Cream Bar."

"Oh. Still, the Indulgence Hotel would be wasted on me."

"That's where you need to stay. It might not be the whole night. We might all come and join you."

"Shoot out at the Indulgence Hotel? No, thanks. They'd have to tell their clientele, 'Well, you asked for some action. We aim to please.'" That last part is the Indulgence Hotel slogan.

"I'm not going to let Faith shoot you." Hope changes posture. "I'm telling you, it won't happen. I decided," she says, imitating Jake. Somehow I've had this empowering effect on my friends, maybe by telling them that their lives are not predetermined.

"That's good. Just remember, I've never wanted to kiss Jake, so don't get too good at his imitation."

"I won't. I'm going to get some things for the card and donation for Christie."

I have two problems with the Indulgence Hotel. The first is that I was just there... in my dreams. AutoDrive will crash nearly in front of it. I'm not eager to be there without a solution. The second problem is that the only other time I stayed at the Indulgence Hotel was a brief stopover with Melanie and the entourage. Staying at a hotel when you're younger with a big group is different from staying at a hotel as an adult. There are behavioral expectations on adults that I may not be able to meet.

"I'm going to figure out something for Red." I head downstairs.

To me, a gift should be special. It should mean something. It should represent me, the giver, as well as my perception of the recipient. Giving a gift that doesn't represent the giver is a kind of lie or a mixed message. It's like saying, "Hey kid, I don't think you should be playing with matches, but here's the fireworks you wanted." And if I think someone likes something, and they don't, I learn about it, hopefully. They should tell me, or they will get something similar again. The camera for Ruth turned out great. It represented my interests in technology and her interests in photography, plus all our travels years ago. And she seemed to like it. Oddly enough, it didn't cost much.

I pick up the little picture of Hope from the floor, glad it didn't break. I set it on my nightstand partially in front of my other picture of Hope. This will be the site of my Hope picture collection.

Red likes books. My phone searches the web for a book for Red. I could get Red an unauthorized biography of Melanie, but then I'd feel obligated to mark it up for reality. I don't think I'm ready to revisit all of that. The phone continues to ask me about this book or that book. I continue to say, "No." Nothing feels right. As I answer the phone's questions, I get cleaned up and pile together some clothes, some toiletries, and the Safari Of The Mind book. The phone asks if Red would like that book. Nice try. I say, "No." He's already on a safari of the mind. He needs less safari. I could get him a blank book. He reads so much, maybe he ought to write some things. A blank book would be a good representation of the fact that anything can happen. I could give him some orange shampoo, as a reminder of the time that he snuck around Tom's cabin, the old one, and stole all our shampoos and bars of soap and replaced them with orange shampoo and orange soap – very tricky of the redhead. Or I could get him an alarm clock. He seemed interested in mine.

Cy sends a message following up about everyone getting together to visit Red. To me, friendship shouldn't be a burden, so I try not to pester my friends for favors. When I need a favor, a chart of my friends is wheeled out in my head. Squeaky-squeaky-squeaky, the wheels need oil. Using the chart, I plot out who I haven't pestered recently or who owes me a favor. Cy owes me a favor. I reply to Cy, "Should we paint our hair red to visit him? And could I get a ride at five?" She replies with 40 question marks. Her finger must've gotten stuck to the question mark key. She asks me why I need a ride. I respond, "I figure we can use the spray on costume-quality, Temporary, red hair color. We just need to know how many people are going and how many cans it will take." Her reply asks if all the cars over here suddenly broke down. I respond, "We can use paper towels or newspapers to protect our clothes. It should be newspapers so that they get red."

Cy's short response is, "You aren't going to tell me, are you?"

My first reply is, "I can pick up the cans, if you tell me how many we need."

My second reply is, "You might want plastic bags over the headrests in your car."

My third reply is, "Should we eat before getting together or afterwards as a group?"

Cy says, "Yes. I will pick you up."

"Thanks," I reply. Text a simple message – get a blizzard of responses. That is the order of things.

The backpack I retrieve from the closet has patches over patches. I have carried it everywhere, and it has carried me everywhere. It was everything. While I'm packing it with things piled on my bed, Hope knocks on my door and comes in.

"Here's the card for Christie," Hope shows it to me. It shows someone looking like Christie, standing on a hill with arms outstretched, talking to a huge crowd. "What do you think?" she asks, after slipping something into my backpack. I don't think I was supposed to notice.

"Chicago doesn't have hills. It barely has slopes. Other than that, it's great." I hand it back to her. I pull a package of condoms from my backpack. "Now how did that get there?!?"

Hope takes it and puts it back in. "They should have everything you need, but just in case they don't, you should have those."

I take them out. "I won't need them."

"Not even if I come to visit?" Hope puts them back. "What I'm saying is that you can do it if you want to do it as long as you use those."

"And what I am saying is that if I am alone, I won't need them. And if you all come and join me, I still won't need them."

"Take them with anyway. Maybe it'll rain, and you'll need rubbers." That makes no sense.

"I called Cy and set up a ride to visit Red. I figure she will drop me off at the hotel afterwards." Hope is surprised.

"You aren't going to drive?"

"My car doesn't belong anywhere near the Indulgence Hotel. It's like putting Jake in a beauty pageant. It's not going to happen."

"Why Cy?"

"She owes me from Ruth's birthday present."

"Did you tell her about Faith shooting you?"

"No."

"Please don't. I don't want your friends to misjudge her."

My tongue ties itself in knots trying to respond. "She shot me."

"What happened?"

"She shot me. Nicole and me. Then only me."

"Where were you?"

"The first time I was in bed. Then I was in the hallway."

"Wait. You were shot in bed, got up went into the hallway, and was shot again?"

"No, we were shot in bed. Then I decided to try to stop Faith in the hallway. So I tried it again and this time, she shot me alone in the hallway."

"What were you doing in bed together?"

"Nothing. At least I wasn't doing anything except sleeping."

"Was Faith aiming at both of you?"

"No... just Nicole. I got in the way."

"Way to test whether or not you're bulletproof, Clark," Hope smirks. "Tell me about when you were... or will be... or would have been... in the hall. Did you try to take her gun... to crush it in your bare hands?"

"No. She just shot me."

"Could she see you?"

"No."

"Then she probably thought you were Nicole."

"I don't look like Nicole."

"I don't think Faith was trying to shoot you. I think she was trying to shoot Nicole, but I need to handle this without everyone and their brothers getting involved. Could you let me handle this without involving your friends?"

"Yes. But what about warning Nicole?"

"I will handle Nicole."

The front door closes, and I jump. I'm not this jumpy. It's Ray. I shrug. Hope shrugs back. I whisper, "What about Ray?"

"What about him?" she whispers.

I whisper, "Are you going to warn him, or is he going to get caught in the crossfire too?"

Hope puzzles over that while Ray comes in with a bag of something and plops down on my bed, shoving my backpack aside. "What's up?" he asks. "Have any good dreams lately?"

"Nope. Nothing like that." My tongue works over my teeth. "I've got to take care of my teeth," I tell Hope. "Can you keep Ray entertained for a moment?" I don't wait for a response. In the bathroom, I floss. I rinse with mouthwash. I brush my teeth. And I swish through a fluoride rinse. Holding a little mirror inside my mouth, I inspect my teeth. My dentist recommends me. Maybe my dentist set me up with Hope.

Hope is lying on my bed reading a book. Ray isn't around. I interrupt her reading, "What did you tell Ray?"

Hope looks up, "I asked him to be out from four to ten while I handle some things. He was fine with it."

Looking at what she's reading, I tell her, "I have to go run some errands. I'll be back in a while. You watch the campsite."

Construction workers next door stop their work as I round the house to my car. That explains their progress. They stop work if they see something move. If my going to my car is interesting, they must love television. I doubt they watch anything. They just turn it on and off.

My car does its best imitation of the sun, hot and bright. I go back to my old neighborhood to the Gag Shop back behind Yesterday's Diner for a dozen cans of red hair spray. I tell them, "It's for a prank, but I can't say any more, except that it involves a heard of bison."

A very old man asks, "What's that song?"

"I said, 'Heard of bison.'"

He croaks, "I don't think I know that one." I think he's pulling my leg. "Hum me a few bars, and I'll fake it."

I stop by a cash machine. I give the machine my card and my appropriate PIN. It says the usual things in fine print that scrolls quickly across the screen and I get to the part where all the machines have agreed on the signal for world domination which will be– And that's all I get a chance to read. Next, the cash machine asks if I would like my money in Canadian currency, United States dollars, insect repellent, or sidewalk salt. It displays a currency rate chart. Because of the trip to Chicago next weekend, I figure I'll need United States dollars. I'll probably also bring sidewalk salt for tolls, if Faith doesn't gun me down first. The cash machine licks its metal fingers and counts out the dollars. I call out random numbers just to see if I can throw off its count. It tosses out my money. I step back from the machine, just out of habit. The dollars sit quietly in the metal drop basket of the cash machine. I step forward and stack them up. The machine spits out my cash card with a spitting sound. It's all wet, probably from having licked its fingers to count the money. The cash machine hums to itself as I walk away. I look back. It stops. I continue back to my car. I think it's humming again.

I pick up a sandwich for lunch that uses a stiff lettuce instead of bread to hold it together. It's better than Friday night's kelp sandwich. I pick up ten bottles of orange shampoo and other groceries and take them home.

Hope helps me bring in the groceries. "Do you think you have enough shampoo?"

"Those are for Red. Are you okay?" I ask while focusing on putting away the groceries that melted into puddles in my car.

"I just got through telling the construction workers next door to mind their own business."

"So I should mind my own business too?"

"No. No, I'm just telling you I'm upset."

"At me?"

"Yes. And me. And Faith. And Nicole."

"What did I do wrong?"

"You contemplated moving out."

"An easy answer to save lives. Thats' the Last In First Out method of housing inventory. It wouldn't be fair for Faith or Nicole to move out, when I just got here."

Hope slams a jug of apple juice on the counter. "That's not your decision!"

"Isn't it?" She just ignited my engine. "I have been on my own a long time – a very long time – and I'm not very old. If it is time to go, I go. I decide if it's that time."

"That's not what I meant!" Hope fumes. "What I meant was, we should talk things over because we're together, right? And you have as much right, or more, to be here as anyone else."

"What gives me that right?"

"Because I love you, you big ape!"

Oh. "But we did talk it over. We decided that you'd fix things – defuse the situation – while I go off to a hotel for the evening."

"Right, but before that, you decided to move out, without letting me in on the decision."

"I did. You heard it nearly as soon as I thought it."

"Really?"

I nod. "Are you still mad at me?"

"No."

"Good. That just leaves Faith, Nicole, and yourself for you to be mad at." I grab a moving box and put the bottles of shampoo in it. I get some wrapping paper. I pull the shampoos back out and individually wrap them. Hope offers to help, once she catches on to what I'm doing, and she wraps faster than I do. "You must be used to wrapping shampoo," I tell her, but she doesn't reveal her secret. As I finish my last bottle, Hope gets the door and escorts Cy in.

"What's going on?"

"Just wrapping some presents for Red."

"Who said anything about presents?"

"Don't worry. I've got you covered. Again! This one will be from you. I've got a present for every-one to give him." Cy counts the bottles like I'm serious. I grab my backpack, the bag of red hair spray, and the box of wrapped shampoos.

"How do you figure?" Cy asks, as I kiss Hope good-bye. "You aren't coming with?" Cy pries in Hope's direction.

Hope shakes her head and says, "No, but one of those is from me." I laugh without actually laugh-ing. Hope whispers to me, "Watch out for the beds, I hear they're comfortable."

The half second after I shut the car door and fasten my seatbelt in Cy's car, she asks, "Okay, what's going on?"

"You expect me to shoot my mouth off? Nothing doing."

"I guess we'll just sit here then," Cy says.

"So this is a test of wills?"

Cy nods with a noticeable hesitation. I relax. We're getting out of our vehicles, looking very strange with orange-reddish hair. It feels hot. I open my eyes. Ow! I try to climb out of a hot seat with my seatbelt fastened and the car moving down the highway. I unfasten my seatbelt while lowering my window. While I climb out the window, Cy yells, "Get back in here! You're going to get yourself killed! I'm cooling it off! I'm cooling it off!"

"Pull over. I'm getting out."

"Get in here and sit down. The seat is already cool."

"Put your hand on it and keep it there." She fakes it. Her hand hovers over the seat. "You lie like a rug. Pull over."

"Get in here! You're going to break the window."

"No, you're going to break it if you think you can raise it with me on it."

"Get in here. A cop is just ahead of us."

"You're driving. You could pull over. I'm not the one who's going to get in trouble. You are." Cy reaches for part of me she shouldn't be. I bat her hand away. "Don't make me jump out."

"Don't you dare! It's cool now, see?" She takes her hand off the seat and rubs it. Sure it's cool. "Get in here."

I climb back in and sit back down. It's warm but no warmer than a seat of my car. "You really burned my butt, you know that?" We pull up to Ruth's house, the middle of three town homes. I bring my stuff.

"You can leave everything but the hair paint in the car," says Cy. I look at her like she should permanently stay where we're going. Ruth is at her door waiting for us. Cy asks, "Do you have any butt lotion he can use?"

"What's this about?"

"Cy purposefully burned me with the seat heater in her car."

"Why did you do that?" Ruth questions.

"He wouldn't–" Cy whines. She stops herself and starts again in a more mature tone. "I was seeking some insight into a current situation he is in, which he refused to divulge."

"I see," Ruth referees. "You know Cy, you are both seeing other people now. You won't know every little thing that's going on with him anymore."

"I know!" Cy growls.

Ruth turns to me, "Do you really need some lotion?"

"No. Got any pickle-flavored potato chips?"

"I think you two should kiss and make up. Well, at least Cy should kiss you where she hurt you."

Ruth answers her door as more people show up. She escorts us all to her patio, where she's set up newspapers, and the neighbors on both sides have invited over guests to watch us. Tom, Todd, and Erix arrive, followed by Nadine, Al, and Will. Everyone reads the cans of hair paint.

"Is Lefty joining us?"

Ruth responds, "He said he didn't want rutilant hair. I had to look up what rutilant means."

"What does it mean?"

"Red."

"Is this red or orange?" Cy asks.

I tell her, "Red, I think."

Erix either volunteers or is picked to be first. Watching the transformation, I'm not certain we're doing the right thing by acting silly for Red at Loon Lake. It's nearly like selling freezer units during the seasonal ice age in Minnesota. Not only is it not needed, it is actually counter-productive.

And yet, being true to yourself and who you are also matters. We shouldn't suddenly act like the poster children for Normalcy just because Red has made a U turn within his lane on the interstate of life. It would be crazy to suddenly act normal now. It would be like rearranging the furniture after the party has already started.

Ruth has a neighbor take our picture using her old camera. I ask if I can bum a ride from her. Ruth drives Erix and me. Everyone else drives separately.

"Is something wrong with your new camera?" I ask.

"Nothing," Ruth replies. "Didn't Cy tell you? I love it. I think it's great."

"I noticed that you didn't use it for the group picture."

"Of course not. I didn't want to get paint on it, and I didn't want to show it off in front of the neighbors."

"That makes sense."

"I **really** like the camera. Erix, try not to touch your hair, okay?" Ruth asks.

The Loon Lake Mental Health Center has a serene view of Loon Lake but not many windows. Winter is the number one mental health problem in Minnesota, so for over half the year, windows do not help the treatments. It reminds me of an old book I once saw. In one class during fourth grade, the teacher showed us a very old book called The Minnesota Guide. It read, "The climate is the principle boast of Minnesota. It is claimed to be the healthiest in the world. The testimony of thousands of cured invalids, and the experience and statistics of 20 years, confirm this." And the 1869 book claimed that the winters were not as bad as rumored. It was pure Minnesota propaganda, encouraging settlers to move to the land of 10,000 ice blocks. The book had no author, no one wanted to be the one lynched by the frozen mob of immigrants. Whenever I think of health issues in Minnesota, I think of that book.

All of us redheads leave our vehicles. Ruth takes a picture of her truck to remember where she parked, even though there are hardly any other cars in the lot. On our way in, I hand everyone a shampoo-sized present. A startled receptionist checks her glasses after seeing us. With her long, temporarily red hair, Cy talks for us, and the receptionist makes a call. A man wanders slowly through us. I think about pointing to our hair and warning him not to drink the water. A matronly woman steps gingerly into the lobby with big shopping bags under her eyes and fake red hair, but not as fake nor as water soluble as ours. She introduces herself as one of Red's doctors. She leads us on. At the door to a room she asks Cy something. Cy turns around with a smirk and points at me. I'm guessing this has to do with climbing out of a moving car. My reputation precedes me at all mental health centers and sanitariums. As my friends file into the room, the doctor stops me and asks, "Could I speak with you for a moment?"

"Yes," I tell her, "after I see my friend."

Red is on a bed surrounded by piles and stacks of books, with his parents nearby. He adjusts his bedspread, a stack of books topples. There are more where that came from. Awkward silence leaves many things unsaid. We each give him a present or, in my case, two. He opens them. He and his parents are mildly amused by all the bottles of shampoo. When my friends reveal the shampoos were my idea, the doctor smiles politely and asks again to speak to me. She leads me to another room.

"The care and treatment of our patients' mental health is the first and foremost goal of this facility," the doctor tells me. "Damage and destabilization of an individual's ability to properly function in society can have many causes," she says looking from my face to my hair and back again. "Red has mentioned you frequently, yet he denies using narcotics or stimulants with any of you or individually." She points her finger at me. "Are you taking any medications?"

"No."

She lists off drug after drug, individually, as if her comprehensive question did not cover all drugs.

I deny all of them. When her list loses momentum, I help it along by suggesting other drugs, she perks up, but then I deny those drugs as well.

"You don't seem to take your friend's mental health very seriously."

"Are you implying that a serious attitude is more effective than a facetious attitude? Have you any clinical studies to back up that assertion?" When she tries to change the subject by bringing up the Minnesota Multiphasic Personality Inventory, I get up and say, "I didn't think so. You're reaching, doctor. But thanks for believing that I am either a druggie or a pusher. You've made my day." I lead us back to Red's room. Nadine hiccups that my face matches my hair. So I announce to all of them the doctor's drug questions, eliciting laughter from my friends. She didn't know she was so funny.

Red's dad comes over to me and says to the doctor, "I don't claim to understand all that these kids do. I was just telling Tommy here that I would've loved to have seen that rocket that they launched a few weeks ago. But other than some of them drinking too much, nothing I have heard suggests the use or misuse of drugs. Don't impugn the credibility of his friends in your quest for a simple solution. You are barking up the wrong tree." The doctor leaves. Red's mom snaps a picture of us with Red with her camera and Ruth's, and we all sign a small banner for him. We leave with Red's parents.

As we talk in the parking lot and the sun sets across Loon Lake, Red's parents are more upset than they had let on in his room. We all reassure them. I tell them, "I don't know. Red might be the sane one." We promise to keep in touch. Cy and Ruth argue over who Red's parents should contact, but ultimately Ruth is insistent. The parents drive off.

Al says, "I sometimes wonder if I'm crazy. If one of these days, people are going to figure that out and have me taken away."

I reply, "You're the least crazy person that I know."

"You're saying that you think Will is crazier than I am?" I nod.

We decide to invade a local restaurant. We go into the restaurant one at a time, each wanting to sit at the bar. Through the window we watch as Tom almost steers to a table, only to then decide to also sit at the bar. When Erix and I go in, we fill in some of the empty stools between our group. Everyone else in the restaurant is staring. A waitress asks Todd if we all know each other. He looks at Tom sitting next to him, examines him carefully, and shakes his head, "No." We each order fries and either a shake or a drink. Then we synchronize our eating and drinking and swiveling in our seats. Erix is our leader. The rest of us follow his lead, down to a final blotting of our lips with our napkins. A few of us mutter a rumor that eating here turns your hair red. We pay our bills, file out, and go our separate ways.

Ruth is driving Erix and I home. Or at least she thinks she is. "Could you actually drop me off at the Indulgence Hotel?" I ask her.

"What? Why?"

"I'm not allowed to explain. At least not now. Could you do that?"

"Okay. I guess I'll drop you off first."

There's no room out in front of the hotel, so Ruth drops me off at the Museum Of Questionable Inventions. We say good-bye, and I grab my backpack.

A sign loudly says, Indulgence Hotel - We Aim To Please.

The Indulgence Hotel has a concierge who may be the most powerful man in Minnesota. He has resources and connections for indulgences of the mind and the body and maybe even the spirit. That's what they are all about. And the first thing people think of is sex, whether they want it or not. They want to know the possibilities. They want to know what is done. A billboard on Highway 12 once showed a romantic couple and their Indulgence Hotel guest preferences card, which marked religion and instruction and conversation but not sex, with the implication that everything else was covered.

The front desk ignores me under the suspicion that I am not a guest, and if ignored, I will just go away. I don't dissuade their doubt. I loiter. I squeak my sneakers with swivels of my feet on their reflectively waxy marble floor. I play with one of their pens like I am Ringo Starr test driving a new set of drums. Then, when it doesn't appear like anyone is paying any attention to me, I head for the grand piano. That's when several people decide to overtly pay attention to me.

"May I help you?" I'm asked in a less than helpful tone. Before they get a chance to throw me out, I tell them that I have a reservation. A manager takes over for a clerk and is then replaced by a higher manager. I am asked for my name and give it.

I am told, "For best possible service, please clip this card to your shirt or robe." I think that request is more for their benefit than for mine. I am asked to confirm my name. The manager does a double take looking at my information. I don't know. I like the prejudice better. There's an honesty in the discrimination. I wonder if this is how Red feels, being a redhead in a non-redheaded world? The smooth manager snaps her fingers, and a teenaged bellhop comes to take my backpack. Her uniform is a small tuxedo coat, black pantyhose and little black boots, with a dressy bodysuit in between that looks like a frilly white blouse with a bow tie. Once we are in the elevator and the door closes, I ask for my backpack back. She insists on carrying it.

"I'd get in trouble. There are cameras all around. You can do anything you want, but I can't." At my room, I tip her a big tip, but she seems to have expected bigger. "Do you want me to show you the amenities," she asks. I shake my head. I'm sure they're very nice. I go into my room. Oh look, this won't be so bad, I have a TV! Dropping off my backpack, I head into the bathroom and take a shower, hoping that these four ounces of shampoo will be enough to wash the red out of my hair. Nearly all of it comes out.

I get cleaned up and head out. In the hallway, I hunt up the stairway. I climb down dozens of flights of stairs without seeing anyone. Opening a metal gate, I end up between a kitchen and a loading dock. Doors are propped open with bricks. All the air of the hotel is ventilated out nearby, a hot concoction of smells that would take a dog weeks to analyze, categorize, and discern. I pick up an Indulgence Hotel ball cap, discarded in a pile of dust and dirt. I brush it off and twirl it on my index finger. I lean against the cinder block wall, twirling the cap, watching the traffic of people and the variety of carts. Linen carts, housekeeping carts, hand carts stacked with boxes, serving carts...

"You. Are you working?"

I look around me and smirk, "Not at the moment..."

"Funny. Take this to the One Mississippi Room."

I take the box the direction my new boss indicated. I never realized getting a job could be so easy. I always complicated the process with paperwork and questions and... here's a map. I go down this hall, and it looks as though I have to take some stairs, but it's not clear if I have to go down or up. Turning down the hall, the stairs and ramp only go up. I find One Mississippi right next to Two Mississippi. The sign for One Mississippi says, Common Communication. I swear. Setting down the box, I pull the baseball cap on as far down over my head and body as it will go. It only stretches down to my ears and even then it is threatening to launch off my head. I pick up the box and head in. Belle Beckett and Samuel Morrison are there with two others. They are talking about me! My letter! I drop the box off on a free end of the table they are working at.

"That was fast," they say to me.

"If you need anything else, let us know," I tell them hoarsely. On my way out the door, my cap rockets off my head and parachutes back into my hands. I head back the way I came. Subtle. I am as subtle as a brick.

"You! Kid! You're younger than me. Put this over there."

"Right away." I have the strength of ten men. I shove a crate for him. Ten men? Ten men would've lifted it.

"I need you to make a run for me. Do you have a license?" I nod. "Go to Ralph & Jerry's for Blue Razzles."

"What are Blue Razzles?"

"They're a cross between blueberries and raspberries. Never mind what they are! Go!" He hands me the keys to a Pegasus Coup in the alley. It had to be a Pegasus Coup; this one is blue like the razzles. "Do you know where Ralph & Jerry's is?"

"Yes. It's by Positively Fourth Street."

"Great. Go!"

The Pegasus Coup adjusts the seat and steering wheel around me after I get in. It gives me books' worth of digital information framing a clearing in the windshield. I would be well informed, if I didn't ignore it all. With its rows of street lights, I take the Hennepin Bridge across just one Mississippi River to University to Tenth to Fourth. The boss never told me how many Blue Razzles he wanted. He also didn't give me money. I decide that I can afford to donate three packages to the cause. I return to the hotel. The boss is nowhere to be seen. I am left holding the bag. So I try a Blue Razzle. It's good. Different. I have a few more. I look around for him and find him talking to people who look scared of what he's asking. I interrupt him with the Blue Razzles and his keys.

"I didn't give you money," he tells me. I nod and show him the receipt. He pays me back and makes me keep the change while asking me, "What do you know about religious issues and the whole Midway thing?"

"What Midway thing?"

"The Savior of the Midway."

"What do you want to know?"

He smiles a ghastly smile. "You'll do." There is a collective sigh by the people around us, and silent prayers to God that they wouldn't have to talk about religion. "Go to room 3711 and talk to the nice people." The chrome of the elevator reveals how silly I look in the cap. I take it off. My fingers comb my hair. I knock on the door to 3711.

An old man, even older than the guy at the Gag Shop, answers the door. He is tall or would be if he stood up straight. He is well dressed and leads me into a living room where an old woman sits, with her knitting cast aside.

"Can I get you something?" he asks me.

"No, thank you. Can I get you something?"

"No..."

"You had some religious questions, some questions about the Savior of the Midway?"

"No," he says, so carefully sitting down that I think he thinks he's about to sit on a cat. "I want to know... we want to know if there is good in the world."

I smile, "Yes, there is good in the world. There is tremendous good in the world." I tell them about Hope and how she cares for the young and old. I tell them about the day, weeks ago, when Hope and I handed out flowers at the zoo. They smile. I tell them about Ben the dog, and his family giving us muffins. I tell him about my friends pitching in to help me move, and I describe how hard Jake and Stephanie worked, and all the things Al did. They are overjoyed. I tell stories for hours. Over time, they become less overjoyed and more tired. When they have both fallen asleep, I take a pad of Indulgence Hotel paper and write a note that says:

Yes, there is good in the world.

There are people doing honest things, unselfish things.

There are people being nice to each other and caring for each other.

There are random acts of kindness, altruism. It happens all the time.

Leaving the note on the table, I shut the door quietly behind me. Back down in the main back hallway of the hotel, I stand around for a while, and then I step outside. I know this alley better than I know the street out front. Expensive moths fly around the light over the loading dock.

One of these days, I'm going to have to learn to sleep at night.

We're standing around by a back door, myself and a mixed group of hotel staff and some delivery people, trading hotel-patron stories, when I see someone familiar approach from down the alley. It's Faith. She's found me. She spots me in the group and gets a surprised look on her face. I've seen that look too many times today. I hate that look.

"We've been looking all over for you," she says. "We've been up in your room." With those last two words, she has shot down and destroyed any connection I had with the people around me. They back away. Faith gets out a phone and calls Hope. "Here," she says, handing the phone over to me.

"Hey," I say.

"Where are you?" Hope asks.

"Talking with some people."

"When you're done, could you please come up to your room?"

I say my good-byes, while Faith waits. They ask to see my room key. They're impressed. I ask why.

"Because you are high up there, but **you** aren't high up there," one guy tells me.

Faith explains on the way up that the higher you are in this hotel, the more important you are in some way. It is a skyscraping hierarchy. The elevator keeps going, and I keep my distance. "Look, I'm sorry about shooting you in your dream. I know it wasn't on purpose. I shouldn't have been even trying to shoot Nicole. I didn't know what was going on. I'm really sorry. It won't happen. Hope is keeping my gun–" She abruptly stops talking and gesturing and stares at my thumb absently rubbing my chest. "I'm sorry. Please say something."

"Nice shooting, Tex." The elevator door opens. I lead us down to my room.

Nicole sits at the table. Her shirt is silent. I know she's got a Double Barreled shirt or something. Hope is on the phone, "We need some old pillows for a pillow fight. No, they don't have to be washed." She hangs up. She is wearing the One Gorilla Girl shirt I asked Nicole to make for her. I'm guessing lots of stuff has been going on. I drop off my cap and empty my pockets into my backpack and flop down on the bed. Hope removes some flecks of orange paint from my hair. "This looks more orange. Is this what everyone looked like?"

"Do you want the full story or the study guide edition?" They choose the full story, so I tell them about the hot seat that Cy put me on and Ruth's hair painting block party. I tell them about being accused of doing drugs or pushing drugs. I tell them about the synchronized restaurant invasion, the dismissive front desk, and the back hallway assignments.

"Wait a minute," Faith waves. "What made you decide to hang out in the back hallway?"

"Back off, Faith," Hope growls. Nicole listens quietly.

"Sometimes, some days, when you feel the whole day has been a battle, beating you down, all you care about is just getting a little acceptance, like the wag of a tail from a dog, to make you feel okay. That's what I was looking for. And I knew I couldn't find that through the front lobby."

"You had orange hair," Hope points out.

"I could permanently have orange hair. I don't think that should affect people's behavior. So I was in the back hallway. And I'm asked to take a box to the One Mississippi Room. So I take the box there and it's the people from Common Communication."

"Who are they?" Faith interrupts again.

"A start up company that I sent an employment letter to last week. The only place I sent a letter to last week. So I pulled down this cap and delivered the box and got out of there."

"Did they know who you were?"

"No, but I think they were talking about my letter. So then I was sent on an errand for Blue Razzles."

"Those are good," Nicole says.

"What are they?" Faith asks.

"They're a mix between raspberries and blueberries."

"Then I was asked to go talk to some old people about whether there is good in the world. I told them that there was good in the world, until Faith blew it away."

Faith groans and drags a chair up to me on the bed and sits down to lean over me, gesturing wildly. "Look, I said I'm sorry. I said I'm sorry to you. I said I'm sorry to Nicole. I said I'm sorry to Hope. I'm sorry. I'm giving up the gun. I will not own a gun. Hope told me everything you told her. And I **had** been wondering if there wasn't something going on between you and Nicole. And it's been driving me crazy because I know you and Hope have something great and Hope has needed something great... has needed someone great... forever! I would do anything for her. And I just couldn't understand anything else because Nicole has something of a reputation... of ruined relationships. And here you are, and they are swearing that they both knew about what was going on and all you are doing is being – I don't know – something that Nicole never had. I already offered to move out, and I know you did too. If you need me to move out – no – if you want me to move out, I will. But I just want to tell you that I think what you dreamed almost happened, and if it had happened, if I had killed either one of you, I would've hated myself for the rest of my life. I am **so sorry**. I hope you will find it in your heart to forgive me. Please."

As she spoke I looked from her to the ceiling and back again. Now I respond to her, "Tex? I forgive you." She gives me a hug. Sometime after that, I hear them talking about me wondering if I'm asleep. And I wonder why they wonder that, but that's when I stop wondering.

36

A Hole In One

Hey Sleepyhead, do you want some breakfast?" Hope asks, still a One Gorilla Girl, but surrounded by girls in little tux jackets and shirts without much for pants. I start to get up, until I realize the girls aren't the only ones missing the pants. Even starting the day without pants in a crowded room, today has got to be a better day than yesterday.

"Flapjacks." I pull up my sheet.

"Excuse me?"

"Sorry. Pancakes."

"Anything else? Something to drink?" one of the girls asks, so I ask for grapefruit juice.

"Is that it?" Hope asks.

"That's it, Loverducks," I reply. I close my eyes and hear one of the girls parroting back what I ordered plus other items.

"Now," Hope says, "I want all of you to grab a pillow for a pillow fight."

My eyes open wide as girls giggle pending doom. "Whoa. I don't want a pillow fight." The girls freeze.

Hope asks them, "Who's calling the shots, him or me?" Then to me she says as the gaggle of giggling girls climb on the bed, "Sorry, bad choice of words." To them she says, "Ready... Go!" Right away, I get a face full of pillow.

After four or five pillow hits, I ask, "Where's my pillow?" Hope points across the room to the remaining pile.

One of the tuxedo girls yells, "Here's your pillow!" And I get hit 19 or 20 more times. In one of the swings, I see a girl's whole body twist into the swing; she's not just using an arm. At first I was thinking it was less – bash – effective. Now I'm thinking – bash – it's more effective. It's funny – bash – bash – I'm evaluating pillow hits in the middle of a pillow fight.

"There's a hole in this one."

The next hit is really in for it. I grab the girl's pillow from her.

"Ah ha!" I cry out. She screams and runs away. Bash! Feathers fly out from the last pillow that hit my ear – bash – bash – and from another one that hits my side. Now that – bash – bash – I am – bash – bash – armed they are – bash – bash – really attacking me. Bash! "Of course you know," bash – bash, "this means war," I declare in the middle of the assault. I accidentally grab one of the girls in the assault. Bash! "Hey look," bash – bash, "it's snowing!" Bash. Bash! I swing my pillow into whoever has been really bopping me from behind. Bash, from in front. I swing my pillow in front and whiff. Bash. I swing again, while grabbing an ankle and pulling someone over into the growing snowbank of feathers. "They just don't," bash – bash – bash, "make," bash – bash – bash, "pillows the way," bash – bash, "they used to." Bash! Bash! Bash! I lie back, and they pile on for the kill. Bash! Bash! Bash! Bash, weak hit. Bash! Amidst the laughs and giggles, I open my eyes briefly to see through a layer of feathers into the blizzard above, as several of these giant penguins pin me down. I close my eyes again. I could send them flying. I do have the strength of ten men. But sometimes – bash, late hit – having the strength of ten men means you have to take your lumps.

"I have feathers," one penguin spits, "in my mouth."

"You also have feathers in your ear."

"I do?"

"Here."

"Is he still breathing?"

A penguin gets off my chest. "Yes... I can see the feathers moving." She gets back on my chest. I think she gained weight since the last time she was on my chest.

"What the– What happened out here?!?" the voice of Faith asks. "It looks like an explosion at the pillow factory!"

"Look at those feathers up there," one of the penguins says, "they're just swirling in a circle."

"Cool."

"Wait," Faith says. "Where's Ricky?" she asks as if I've been misplaced again.

The penguin on my chest gets off again, so from under the feathers I say, "Under here." Feathers are being shoveled away, and I see Faith in a white robe and a white towel around her head like a fluffy white turban, surrounded by the flock of penguins. "Hello."

"You should see yourself," she points. And Hope appears behind her and takes a picture. She kneels down beside the bed and shows us the pictures of the pillow fight, which from where I was laying was more like a pillow execution, being fired on from all sides. "I don't know why you are all so happy," Faith says. "Don't all of you have to clean this up?"

The penguin over me lays back down and replies icily, "No. We're bellhops. We're not maids." Never disgust a penguin, Faith.

"I didn't know," Faith complains with a shrug. She goes to start a blow dryer. Or else she's using a leaf blower to try to clear the snow. I'm just guessing.

Room service arrives with breakfast. The penguins clear out. A flock of them thanks us, saying that it's the most fun they have ever had on the job. I get a couple of pecks on the cheek. Room service is stunned by the scene and struggles to find a clearing for the meal. When they leave, it's down to just Hope and me. Faith is still in the bathroom. Looking at the winter wonderland, I laugh.

"Was that fun?" Hope asks.

"I was just noticing how a stack of pillows can fill a room with feathers. You wouldn't think you could have so many feathers." I eat my fluffy pancakes. They stuff me.

"They're fluffy," Hope observes. I nod. She kisses me and snuggles me. "I need to tell you... the reason why I had them beat you up is that you really worried me. I didn't know where you were. I couldn't call you because **somebody** left their phone back at the house. But I also want to thank you for leaving your backpack here, because it meant that you were coming back. Unless something happened to you..." Hope worried. I give her a kiss. Then I realize I have to brush my teeth.

"Where are my pants?" Hope looks and points. I fetch them and put them on. I open up my backpack and change shirts and put on socks. I comb my hair. I stretch and make ratcheting noises as I stretch. "I owe Nicole some money for that shirt."

"No, I paid her."

"What? That shirt was meant as a gift for you. A gift. You de-gifted it."

"Is that a word?"

"De-gifted. D-E-G-I-F-T-E-D. De-gifted. No one has ever so utterly de-gifted something the way you de-gifted that shirt. I bet you try to buy off Santa Claus too."

"I do not!"

"Do so. How much do I owe you for paying off Nicole?" When she tells me, I respond, "Really?

That much?" But I go for my wallet and give her the money.

"Your money is kind of damp."

"My cash machine licks its fingers."

"Yuck," she says as I start stuffing pillows. "You don't have to do that. They have vacuums."

"Wait. Tell me about this. So they stick the pillow covers and the pillowcases into the vacuum cleaner and then just vacuum up the feathers? Is that how all pillow makers do it?"

"Yes," she says, sweeping away feathers with her hand from a nightstand and setting down the money, "that's the way they do it." I look from her to the money to her again, and back and forth until she finally explains, "It's tip money." Faith comes out. "It's about time. We've been waiting for you." Actually I've been waiting to use the bathroom. I dart in and shut the door. Through the door Hope asks, "Are you going to take forever too?"

"No, forever and a day." After I've taken care of things, I find that Hope and Faith have built a feather cabin. It's like a house of cards only it's made of feathers.

"Don't... move..." Hope says. Faith looks fearful.

"I just need to get my backpack."

"Where is it?"

"On the other side of that thing."

"You're kidding. Look at it. Even without us moving, it's swaying."

"Just like a real skyscraper."

"Do you really need your backpack? Can't you just leave it here or something?"

"Yes, I really need my backpack." As Faith gingerly moves to the pack, a breeze blows a hole into the house of feathers and in seconds it is blown away. Faith casually grabs my backpack and hands it to me. "Thanks."

As I head to the stairs, Hope yanks me back saying, "The elevator is this way." At the front desk, I hand back the hotel card I was supposed to have worn and my room card. Hope gets the bill and describes the damages to the room.

The clerk looks it up and points out on the bill, "We charged you the standard Pillow Fight Fee. We hardly ever get that request. And he didn't use any of our other services." Tattle-tale. A crowd of unwanted valets mope around, dejected. I look around to see if I recognize anyone from last night, but I only recognize one bellhop from this morning who waves at me.

Hope's car waits for us out front. I insist on riding in back. It's a different point of view, seeing things from the back seat of a car when you're used to either driving or riding in the front seat. It's almost the difference between being somewhere and seeing it on a movie screen. Same view; different framing and different control.

Even though it's mid-morning, when we get home, I wish them a good night. I sleep until trumpets sound.

"Hello?" I'm too tired to play like I'm a pizza place. The caller confirms my name and says that they are with Common Communication. Like having a belt of a high caffeine drink, I am now wide awake. "Yes, you're responding to my letter. How can I help you?"

"We were intrigued by your letter. We aren't hiring, right now, but we couldn't set your letter aside. We were wondering if you would meet with us for an interview, even if we couldn't employ you for another five or six weeks."

I figure that by then Hope will be back at work and AutoDrive will have damaged all that it's going to damage. "Great. When would be a good time for you?"

"How about next Wednesday, a week from today at ten?"

"That would be great."

"Do you know where the Riverside Tower is?"

"Yes."

"We'll be at the top. I'm sorry. No, we are one floor down from the top."

"Great. I'll see you then. Thank you."

"Thank you. Good-bye."

"Good-bye."

I have an interview for a non-existent job. I mark my calendar on my phone and fall back asleep. An angel awakens me with a soft soothing voice, saying, "Wake up, Sleepyhead." This angel has the happiest of dimples. "My mother will be here soon, and you said you wanted to cook dinner."

My eyelids rocket open like twin Saturn V's. "When?"

"One hour."

I bowl Hope over launching myself into the shower, grabbing my toothbrush on the way. While I wash my hair, I lather and take off my shorts and brush my teeth and try to remember how to boil water for pasta. I pull a clump of wet feathers from behind my ear. I wring out my shorts and rinse my hair, body, and mouth, while Hope peers in. "Hey! You're splattering me!" Hope complains. I toss my toothbrush over her head and into the sink. I turn off the water and shake like a dog. "I'm out of here," Hope says.

"If you can't stand the spray, get out of the shower."

"I didn't think I was in the shower," she says, leaving. I comb and shave and paint my pits with antiperspirant and wipe up the bathroom. I dash into my room and get dressed and I find Hope, waiting in the living room. "You have 48 minutes left. Did I mention that my mother is always punctual?"

How do I boil water fast? I get out a large glass measuring bowl, fill it with water, and nuke it in the microwave. I add three cups of bow tie pasta into a two-quart pan. I add a few tablespoons of olive oil to a frying pan. Hope has moved into the kitchen to watch. I drain a can of quartered artichoke hearts and carefully dump the contents into the frying pan and start the heat. I dump the nuclear water into the pasta pan and start the heat under it. I set my internal clock for 12 minutes. As people pile down the stairs, Hope says, "You have 42 minutes." Becky, Tex, and Nicole each pull up a chair. I add some more water to the measuring bowl, pour in a leftover half bag of frozen broccoli, cover it with waxed paper, and nuke it for two minutes. I'm making enough for three. If my group turns into six, I'm in serious trouble. The hearts sizzle, so I turn down the heat.

"I love to watch a man work," Becky teases.

"What are we making?" Nicole asks.

"Lemon dill pasta," Hope says.

I get out lemons, lemon yogurt, dill, parsley, and Parmesan cheese. I stir the pasta. I turn and stir the artichoke hearts.

Something else is stirring. Something else is cooking. I turn to look at my audience. I read them with the same intensity that they are reading me. To avoid their self-consciousness at my scrutiny, I turn back to stirring things up.

With my back to them, I evaluate that these four roommates are getting along better and sitting closer together now, after all the target practice of yesterday, than they ever have... at least as long as I've been around. I drain the bright green broccoli and mix it with the artichoke hearts.

"You have 33 minutes," Hope says.

"He isn't bothered by the pressure, is he?" Tex observes.

Becky says, "I would be nervous, meeting Tom's parents for the first time."

"Would you cook for them?" Nicole asks.

"No way."

Yes, instead of picking on each other, they've decided to pick on me. I get out the glass juicer. I put it in front of my audience. I cut a lemon in half and lean each half down onto the juicer.

"Hey, say it, don't spray it!"

I throw out the rinds, wash my hands, and fish out the seeds. I pour a little lemon juice onto the vegetables. I turn off the heat under the pasta and drain it. With a slotted spoon, I ease the little bow tie noodles into the frying pan with the artichoke hearts and the broccoli until it's full, dashing dill and parsley in between spoonfuls. Cooking is all about timing. Not about the timing of one particular thing, it's the timing and coordination of all things, so that all things are ready at once. I don't know how God does it.

"You have one minute."

"One minute?!? I have at least 22."

"Not if she's early," Hope says, pointing at the window. Hope's roommates dash out of their seats and fight for the stairs, effectively blocking my route to get a clean shirt, which is why some cooks wear aprons... because they might have a traffic jam of roommates. I'm hoping Pandora will be someone nice. The doorbell rings. "Do you want me to..." Hope offers.

"I'll get it." I'm hoping I can get along with her, like that administrator at the Remember When Nursing Home. I open the door. "Hello. Are you Pandora?" She doesn't answer. She has a flowing robe and... is that a tiara? I guess Hope will tell me if I'm inviting in the wrong person. "Welcome."

"Is that the cleanest shirt you could find?" she asks.

"I was just going to get changed. Please come in and make yourself at home."

"This is my home," she says as I dash off. "Hello Loverducks," I hear her say as I duck into my room. This is going to be a laugh riot. I change my shirt and return. Mother and daughter are facing off in the living room without speaking.

As I pass through, Pandora says, "Fasten your seatbelt. It's going to be a bumpy night."

"This is your home?" I ask from the kitchen nook, stirring things up. "Which room is your room?" She says something in a low voice to her daughter. "What was that? I didn't hear you." I pour in more lemon juice. No response. With the juicer still in hand, I go out and ask the mother, "Would you like something to drink?"

Pandora glares at me. She takes off her glasses. "What do you have to offer?"

In case she's talking about drinks, I list off, "We have water, milk, apple cider, wheat grass juice, blueberry juice, non-alcoholic apple beer, root beer, Lake Weago beer, Yoerg Beer, Double Bubble regular or lead-free, Birch Blackberry Stain, Chippeau Valley Blanc Spirit, or Yellow Snow Fizz."

"Water," she replies dryly.

"Would you like ice?" She nods.

Imagination is the limit to how many practical jokes can be played using the simple concept of ice in a drink. You can freeze any number of substances into ice cubes. You can create a time release formula by freezing small amounts of something and then refreezing them into larger ice cubes. You can freeze different items that will react to each other once they melt. Dry ice can be fun, in small amounts, as long as they don't take a drink. Dry ice with water in a metal cup will ring the cup like a bell. I check the freezer. I don't have anything prepared, except for plastic ice cubes that look like ice cubes and keep drinks cold but aren't ice cubes. I drop three of them in a glass and fill it the rest of the way with refrigerator water.

"Here you are," I hand it to her. "Can I get you something?" I ask Hope.

"I'd like a glass of Chippeau Valley Blanc Spirit. You got that for me didn't you."

"Yes I did, Loverducks."

I stir the mixture again, stirring in the lemon yogurt and a dusting of Parmesan cheese. I pour Hope's glass of wine and bring it to her. Pandora puts back on her glasses to look at her ice cubes.

"So tell me, what do you do for a living?"

I tell her, "Nothing."

"Nothing?" Pandora turns to her daughter.

"That's right. I'm unemployed. Last night I thought I had a job at a hotel, but it turned out they mistook me for someone who worked for them. Please excuse me, while I get dinner set."

"I should like to be served, none of this 'come and get it' nonsense."

"Would you like some help?" Hope offers.

"No, thank you. It's under control." I turn off the heat and get out dessert. I break up some parsley and slice a lemon for garnishes. I get out three plates and serve them up with garnishes. I dash some dill on top of each. I grab napkins and six forks. I set and serve the table. I light a candle. "Dinner is served. We are having lemon dill pasta." I bow my head. "God. Thank you for this meal and this company. May each give us strength. Amen." After a bite, I say, "You were asking me what I do for a living. I worked for a company called Flight Control for five years, developing a self-driving car called AutoDrive. I led Research and Development. A little over two weeks ago I was fired because I could not deliver AutoDrive in the time frame they required." I turn to Hope. "This morning I got a call from a company that won't be hiring for five or six weeks, but they're wanting to interview me next week."

"The same people you ran into—"

"Yes."

Pandora asks, "What company are we talking about?"

"It's just a possibility. I'll be happy to tell you if I get the job."

Pandora stretches her long fingers, "I have connections. I could help you get that job."

"Maybe you could help me to get other leads. In the meantime, AutoDrive is scheduled to have a test run in less than two weeks, a week from this Sunday. Even though I'm no longer involved with Flight Control, I'm trying to make sure AutoDrive doesn't kill people."

"I'm still curious about the company that will be interviewing you."

"They are a brand new company. I believe they only have two people so far."

"I still might be able to do something."

"Thank you for the offer."

"But you aren't going to take me up on it."

"No."

Pandora sulks. Hope asks, "Is this cheese?"

I look, "I think it's Wisconsin cheese."

"How can you tell it's Wisconsin cheese?"

"Because you can barely see it from here." Trying to think of something to say to Pandora, my memory deluges me with every lawyer joke that I have ever heard, plus some that I didn't think I knew. I am blessed and cursed by a terrific memory. It leaves me speechless.

"What are your plans with my daughter?"

"Well, next weekend we're going to Chicago. The weekend after that is the state fair..."

"No. I 'm talking about your long-term plans."

"Well, winter is coming up."

She crumples up her face. "Will your troubles be... little ones?"

"No, we are planning big trouble."

"What I mean is, I want grandchildren."

"Maybe you can adopt."

"So to summarize, you aren't equipped to give Hope children, you aren't able to hold a job, and my daughter is providing a roof over your head. And I understand your parents are dead. Have I left anything out?" Pandora asks.

"Mother!"

"I'm nobody. I'm nothing."

"Ricky is great."

"I don't see what's so great about him," she says with heavy emphasis on the him.

Hope is blowing steam. "You don't do you? Well you know the whole thing about–"

"Would anyone like some more lemon dill pasta? There's plenty!"

"You've interrupted my daughter." The way she says daughter creeps me out.

"My name is Hope, mother."

"I know. I named you. You may continue, Loverducks."

"No, that's okay," Hope says.

"Really?" Pandora's eyes narrow at us, peering like a hawk with two mice trying to escape her clutches. She swoops in. "You have only known each other for weeks. Weeks. And already you have secrets. Secrets from your own mother. What's this all about?" She puts her face in mine.

"Well, the reason it's called Lemon Dill Pasta is that those are its main ingredients. Lemon. Dill. And pasta. However," I look around for anyone else listening and I whisper, "those aren't the only ingredients."

She pats my cheek. "Funny boy."

"What is the secret to being a mother to so many children?"

"The secret? The secret is being able to enter a room and know just what's going on."

"And which is the best prison that any of your boys is staying at?" Hope kicks me.

Across the table Pandora's eyes reflect the flames of the candle. "My sons are not saints. I don't believe I have met a saint. I'm not sure I could trust a saint. I would wonder what they are hiding. What are their secrets? Her eyes are aflame. Do you have a secret, something you haven't told Hope?"

"I tell Hope everything."

"That's good. And have you told her everything? Or is their one hold out? What's that one secret?" Hope intervenes, "Pandora. Stop this!"

"What? He asked my secret. I'm asking his." Point: Pandora.

"Is this too sour? Or does it need more lemons? I have plenty of lemons."

"He says he's nothing. A nobody. Is that who you want, Loverducks? A nobody?"

Hope gets up, passes slowly around Pandora the long way to me, and squats down beside me. "I love you," she tells me.

"I love you too," I tell her.

She turns to her mother. "The question is not whether we want each other. We've already decided that. The question is whether YOU want to be part of OUR lives."

Pandora eases back in her seat and stares. We stare back. I mentally picture a wall clock over Pandora's face. I watch the seconds tick away while waiting for her reaction. Seconds become minutes. She picks up her plate. "I'll have seconds."

I take the plate and pat Hope's back, reassuring her. "Coming up." I reheat the lemon dill pasta, serve up some more, and return. Hope is at her seat, eating and listening to her mother. Hope will take a little more. I return her plate with a little more. We listen politely as Pandora weaves tales of legal intrigue and crooked politicians and their golf games. When she finishes, I ask, "Would you like some cheesecake for dessert?"

"Are you trying to kill me?"

"No ma'am, I'm offering you cheesecake."

"I accept."

Hope looks surprised. "I didn't know you had cheesecake."

"So, you would like some too?" Hope nods her head frantically. I remove plates and return with smaller, cheesecake laden plates.

Pandora tells me, "You called me ma'am. Don't call me ma'am. Don't call me madam. However if you choose to be so bold, you can call me mom." I nod my head. I won't be calling her mom. After dessert, our conversation moves physically into the living room and topically into the bedroom. "Hope sleeps upstairs, and you sleep down here. Is that right?" I agree. "Isn't that just for show? Something you tell people like Hope's mother?"

"No, this floor had been vacant when I moved in, so I figured that if Hope wanted to live on this floor, she would already be on this floor. I also didn't want to muscle in on Hope upstairs, because when you have a group of friends that can get along real well, it's one of the most valuable things in the world. I'd say that friendship is second only to real love." Hearing Ray's motorcycle pull up, I ask Pandora, "Would you be willing to give Ray, my roommate, the third degree?" Hope is stunned. I don't know if she's stunned by my suggestion or stunned that her mother's going along with it. And that's where Ray comes in.

Pandora stands, "Who are you?"

"I'm Ray."

"Who are you to waltz right in like this?"

"I didn't think I was waltzing."

"No. No one ever thinks they are waltzing. I'm sure it just sort of happens. No one plans to waltz. The orchestra just happens to be there. You just happen to be dressed up..." She's right. Ray is dressed up. "With whom have you been waltzing?"

Ray looks to both of us for support before redirecting the prosecutor, "I was out with Ruth."

"Waltzing with Ruth. Who's Ruth?"

"She's a friend of ours," I step in to tell Pandora. "Hey, I didn't see that coming."

Ray does a double take, one look per meaning of what I said. "Yeah, it just sort of happened. We have a lot in common."

"Ray, this is Pandora, Hope's mother."

"Hi."

"Do you eat cheesecake?" Ray nods. Pandora leaves.

"So, Ray and Ruth. Ruth and Ray. I picture a circular sign with two R's and an X- crossing on it."

"I always thought there were three R's," Hope observes.

Pandora returns and gives Ray an enormous plate of cheesecake, grabs his arm, and says, "You may go, but we may ask you back for further questioning. Don't leave town." She turns to me and confesses, "I always wanted to say that." Ray backs away to his room. To Hope she says, "I looked into your friend Christie. She's really something. Her church-less church, her anti-war statements, and her theatrical miracles could get her in a good deal of trouble."

"Yes. She might need your help," Hope asserts.

Pandora stares at her daughter. Her expression shifts. The seconds tick by. "I don't know," she says in a way that sounds like a yes. "I will be going now." She moves toward me. Almost saying something, she puts her business card in my hand with a hug. After giving something to Hope and hugging her, she leaves with our good-byes.

"That was weird," Hope says, "she hugged me. She actually hugged me."

"Me too."

"You don't know how weird that was." I put away the leftovers, and I move to clean up the dishes, but Hope takes me into my bedroom. "Wait here." Hope leaves and I look at my phone. It's been busy taking messages for me. Hope returns, ready for bed. I toss the phone away. Hope kisses me and holds my head in her hands saying, "All I've been able to think about is Lefty's experiment. Do you know what's going to happen?"

"Yes. It's not going to happen." I retrieve my phone and show her the message from Melvin that says that the fMRI-Memmeograph STM experiment for this Thursday has been canceled. He mentions coping with the sudorific heat, whatever that means.

"That's a relief," Hope says. "I have hated the idea of that experiment ever since I first heard about it." Hope lays back on the bed.

"Then you are going to hate this other message from Lefty."

"Other message?" she sits back up.

"The one that says it's rescheduled for a week from tomorrow." I hand the phone to her.

"He can reschedule it as much as he wants, as long as it doesn't actually happen. I don't want this... I don't want what we have to end."

"I don't either. We have a reprieve."

"I don't want you to die."

"I'm not exactly gearing up for it either."

"You could decide not to do it." She looks at me. "No, I guess you couldn't do that." She waves the phone, "Was that it?"

"No, there's also some pictures from Ruth of all of us with red hair." Hope scrolls down. "Scroll up."

"Cool. I want copies. Did she send it to me?"

"Probably, but you can forward it if you want." Hope pushes the phone's buttons and then hands it back to me. I toss it aside again. I check the time before turning out the light. I can't tell the time because the alarm clock is holding the little picture of Hope in its arms, while blissfully sleeping. I check my watch and turn out the light.

37

The Hard Way

The experiment is happening anyway. We're outside the fMRI unit making small talk about Tuesday's storm and apparently they all know that I predicted that it would be bad enough to rain out the Pig's game. Lena is also impressed that Melvin and I know the sculptor of the Lactating Woman. I explain how I once did the pose for Ray to help him with the tilt of the body. They all think that is sufficiently weird, and that it's time to get inside my head to see if I'm putting them on.

"Lie still," Lena tells me as I'm being slid into the giant coffee maker. I stop her and wiggle my body frantically, then I give her the okay sign.

"Lie still," Hope says. I open my eyes. I check my clock, but I can't see anything. I lie back down and close my eyes.

I'm on Forth Street, and here comes AutoDrive. It drives by me without so much as a wave and smashes into the police car again. All I really have to do is warn him. I'm at the corner again. Another cop is on foot directing traffic. I approach the car, while the guy in the car eats some sort of sandwich. He watches my approach. I knock on his window. He tries to wave me off. "You'll want to get out of your car," I tell him through the window.

He lowers the window. I say it again. It's an egg sandwich that stinks. The cop swallows and whistles for his partner, who comes over. "What's this all about?"

"I was trying to tell him that he's going to want to get out of his car."

"Why is that?"

"A car is about to come around the corner up ahead and smash into this one."

"Like that one?"

"That's the one." AutoDrive smashes into the squad car and pushes it over the second cop and me. I wake up moaning.

"What happened?" Hope asks.

"AutoDrive just ran us over... me and a couple of cops."

"Stay out of its way," she says groggily.

That's good advice. I suppose I should try that. I try it. I'm back where I started. I watch AutoDrive repeatedly hit the police car. AutoDrive only hits the barricading police car once; it just gets played over and over in my mind. It makes me think that it is inevitable or that AutoDrive has seriously injured many people.

It's like television news. The same news stories are played over and over. You begin to think, "Wow, there is a lot of crime out there. The streets aren't safe." But in reality it's just one event being repeated hundreds of times. The streets may be safe or they may not be. The viewer won't know because news doesn't cover the streets, it doesn't even cover what's new, because what's new could be that all is quiet. That is a non-event. News only covers events. It should be called, events.

A car dealership going out of business could be new, but it is not an event. However if a tornado whips through a car dealership, picking up cars and trucks, and slamming them into the parking lot asphalt like a modern day Stonehenge, that's an event. Send somebody out there to see if any of the upright cars still start. That would follow the old journalism school flowchart. If the event is just property damage, seek out the irreverent humor.

The death of a community leader is not an event, but a runaway child is an event. The child will be missing and assumed to be abducted, even if the kid leaves a note that says, "I'm running away." Television news is optimistically pessimistic. Every event, every story, hangs by a thin thread over ultimate disaster. That's the bias of the news. Disasters make careers.

I close my eyes. Once again, AutoDrive plows into the police car. When I wake up, Hope is gone. I close my eyes. My body twists, following AutoDrive to its doom, again, and again.

Back at the same old grind, standing on Forth Street waiting for AutoDrive to pulverize the police car again, I think, what if I got on the police radio? What if I got on the same frequency– Someone grabs me and shakes me. I open my eyes. It's Hope!

"Hey! You must've fallen out of bed. You're tangled up." She loosens my sheet shackles from my legs. "I'm not surprised. You kept running into me, almost rolling over me all night."

"Sorry."

"It's okay. I wondered what would happen if I wasn't here to block you, and I guess we found out. Maybe I'll put down some throw pillows to soften your landing."

I pick up my phone to check for any changes from Lefty. I set it down again.

"Nothing?" I nod. Hope smiles. "Since today is free..."

"Yes?"

"Would you want to do some things with me?"

"Like?"

Hope goes to my closet and looks around. Then she looks through my dresser. "Like when was the last time you bought some clothes?"

"Who is president?"

"That's what I thought. We could go to the mall, get you some clothes... maybe a haircut..."

"Eli doesn't work in the mall. His shop, The Kindest Cut, is in my old neighborhood."

"I think Eli can spare you this time around."

"I can't cheat on Eli. He'll know I had my hair done somewhere else. One look and he'll know I was with someone else. Then what? He'll wonder if I had a problem with my last haircut. It'll break his 67 year old heart!"

"Okay, okay, we don't have to do the haircut. Do you want me to make you something to eat, or are you having your cereal again, not that it's breakfast time?" I give her a look, put on my bear feet, and shuffle by into the kitchen. Hope follows me in. The maid must've cleaned up the kitchen. Wait a minute. We don't have a maid.

"Since when do we have maid service?"

"We don't. I cleaned up and ran the dishwasher."

"I was wondering what that thing was. Why did you do it? Why did you kill our mess?"

"You made a great dinner. I wasn't sure if I'd like it at first, but it grew on me," she says in a back-handedly complimentary way.

"You didn't have to," I tell her as I insert bread into the toaster. I get out some oranges and bounce them around on the counter. "I'm feeling like you aren't happy with my appearance this morning. First it was a general complaint against my clothes, then my hair, and then cleaning up my kitchen mess. What gives? Are you trying to change me?"

"I'm not trying to change you. I'm just trying to clean you up a bit, that's all." Technically, that's a change, but I'll hear her out. "And I didn't think you'd mind my cleaning up the kitchen." I get out a pitcher and find the juicer in the dishwasher. "I thought you might say thank you."

"Thank you." I get out a knife and slice the oranges in half.

"You didn't say it like you meant it." I give her an extremely puzzled look as I squeeze some oranges, spooning out seeds, and draining the juicer into the pitcher. After nine oranges, I pour two glasses. Getting down on bended knee, I sing operatically:

"Thank you, for cleaning up the kitchen!
Thank you, for cleaning it up so well!
Thank you, for cleaning up the kitchen!
And making our lives so..." carry the high note for four seconds "swell!"

"I thought you were going to hell there. I still don't think you meant it."

"Then don't clean up after me. Have some orange juice."

"Okay. You know there's a whole jug of this stuff in there," she says pointing to the fridge.

"You don't like it?" I ask, slathering peanut butter on my toast.

"No. it's good. It has more pulp than you could dream possible."

"I don't know. I have strong dreams."

"I know. I was bowled over by a few of them." She looks at the orange juice. "Do you always do things the hard way?"

"Pretty much. I find that things turn out better that way. Besides, once you're used to doing things the hard way, the hard way just doesn't seem so hard anymore." I munch on my toast. "Do you want some?"

"I already ate." I nuke some leftover lemon dill pasta. It leaves the noodles dehydrated and rubbery but still edible. "I'm not trying to change you, I just thought that we should spend the day at the mall. It's supposed to be hot today but cooler in Chicago. I don't know if you already knew that." I shake my head as I chew. Nature plays a cruel trick on Minnesota: hotter in summer and colder in winter. Then it forgets to give us any other seasons. "My mother sent me a message last night. She says that she likes you. She never likes anyone."

"Did you tell her I'm taken?"

"No, but she stopped calling me Loverducks for the first time in weeks."

"Maybe she forgot."

"Not likely. Her memory is like your memory." Oh. "So what do you think of going to the mall today?"

"Let me think about it."

Rabbits look at shopping malls with envy, saying, "If only we could breed that fast." Milltown had the very first indoor shopping mall in 1956. After the first few, malls started springing up everywhere, like rabbits or invasive weeds. Once the Twin Cities were saturated with malls, each mall had an expansion project, slicing away a percentage of their parking lots for new sections of retail space. When the expansion projects were complete, when the retail market was considered absolutely saturated, a giant Mega Mall was added to the retail mix. In Minnesota, the talk is about going to the mall or the cabin or the lake as if there is just one. It's like talking about the snowflake. One snowflake is lonely. One lake is lonely. And one mall is lonely. I clean up my dishes. "What's wrong with my clothes?"

"You're a great guy. You deserve better clothes."

Oh. I nod. "I get it. The clothes make the man."

"No. I'm just trying to do something nice for you."

"Okay. Except that I know who I am. The clothes I wear are part of who I am. I don't try to be the best dressed, just the opposite. I want others to feel good, so I dress on the silly side of life. Sometimes I catch myself off guard because I don't put too much thought or forethought into what I wear. It... matters to me that it doesn't matter to me, if that makes any sense. I want the type of people who dismiss others based on looks to dismiss me as well. It makes life simpler."

"What can I do for you? There has to be something. You... have peanut butter on your top lip."

"That's okay, it's a mustache. I'm wearing it to show solidarity with Red. No really, if you want to buy me a shirt, we can look at a shirt, but I'm not interested in replacing my wardrobe... even if some of it is in bad condition." A light bulb blinks over my head. "Is there something that I've worn that embarrasses you?"

"No. Well, the blue and gray jersey shirt is pretty bad."

"I don't know which one you're talking about." Hope leads us back into the bedroom. "This one." Oh. She's right. I've worn worse, but it's bad. I tear it in half and toss it on the floor. "It's rags."

Hope grins with dimples, "Thank you."

I smear the peanut butter evenly, I think, across my upper lip. "If there is something bothering you, just tell me."

"So you don't need a replacement shirt?" I shake my head. "You got to get me a shirt, but I can't get you anything." Hope giggles, "I can't take you seriously like that."

"Nicole shouldn't have given you my shirt. It was supposed to be a surprise from me."

"She needed it to show Faith how much you love me and that when you were alone with her, you didn't talk about her, you talked about me, and what you could do for me. It was the sweetest thing. I loved it. It was the two of you collaborating to do something nice for me. How cool is that?!? I was happy to pay her for it."

"You've done plenty for me."

"I've given you a place to live. Big deal. You already had that." Hope takes one of the new rags from the floor and wipes off my lip.

"Listen. Do you hear that?"

"No."

"That's the sound of quiet. That's something that can never be moved into Whisper Willows. It gets stolen before the moving truck turns off the street. I could've been deaf and still not missed a beat." I kick off my bear feet. "But that's nothing compared to your belief in me. The fact that you understand me well enough to believe in me is a miracle because I'm me and even I don't get me most of the time. I have intelligent friends; they're great people, but they don't understand me a lot of the time. Take Cy. Half of the time she thinks I'm serious when I kidding. And when I'm really serious, that's when she finally thinks I'm kidding."

"Yes, but it was Cy that told me about your dreams, remember? When an ex-girlfriend, a drunk ex-girlfriend, says something is cool about her ex-boyfriend to his new girlfriend, you're inclined to believe her."

"Wait... ex-boyfriend's ex-girlfriend's drunken statement... you're missing something. She didn't think it was cool. She thought it was weird. There's a difference."

"Yes, but I discounted her opinion."

"You what?"

"I discounted her opinion. I knew she was drunk and unhappy, and I discounted her opinion of your dreams being weird. Discounting is a shopper's term."

"I see."

"Let's go shopping."

Outside, the construction workers ignore us and act like they're working. My car is a puddle of molten metal and liquid glass, sizzling, smoking, and fizzing. We take Hope's car without any argument from me.

The sun is perched directly over Minnesota, gazing at itself in the reflections of the lakes; the lakes lay across the state like fragments of a shattered mirror. The sun is bright enough to know that those aren't mirror shards but warms to the idea anyway. The sun melts the road asphalt into a hot sticky black gum. Tires grip and rip at the gum in an effort to get away, leaving tire tracks in the pavement and decreasingly circular tires. This asphalt was never supposed to get this hot. This state was never supposed to get this hot. It's a hell of a tough way to drive.

"Oh, I almost forgot, Faith wants to take us all out to dinner tonight. Some place fancy."

"Why does Tex want to do that?"

"Because of your dream."

"I thought we cleared all of that up?"

"We did. But she still feels guilty. Calling her Tex doesn't help."

"Do I have to dress up? I have a suit, the gray suit I wore to First Street Station and to Sharon's."

"You could wear that..."

"You don't like my suit? I'm going to need it for the interview next week."

"I don't know."

"Well, I also have a checkered retro-fashion dinner jacket. It's reversible. It doesn't just have a silver lining; it turns silver, nearly chrome."

"I would definitely recommend the gray over the chrome for an interview. When have you worn a jacket like that?"

"At an antique car show. I was representing Flight Control."

"Why would Flight Control be at an antique car show. That makes no sense."

"I know. That was Carl's idea. I think he thought that we would attract the interest of other sponsors who were sponsoring the show, but there are two problems with that theory. One: a company sends their junior employees to an event like that, not their top decision-making dogs. And B: even if you did attract the attention of other sponsors, the first thing they would ask is what you were asking, 'Why are you here? It makes no sense.' But I didn't really care. It gave me an excuse to take a few hours off of work to watch people show off their true loves. And I bought the checkered retro-fashion dinner jacket for the show."

"Where do you even get something like that?"

"At the antique car show."

"Oh, of course. I buy all my clothes there. What are we doing going to a mall for clothes? We should be looking for antique cars to follow to a car show." Hope is right. We could. In Minnesota, antique cars, boats, and most motorcycles are stored in large, remote storage units for the winter half of the year. When you see an antique car on the road in Minnesota, either it's going to or from storage or it's going to or from an antique car show. We scan the traffic for old cars. Now I know which mall Hope is driving us to – Southedge, which was the first indoor, fully enclosed, shopping mall.

Lakes form in quarries. You dig a big hole, water collects. This used to be a lake back when this quarry provided all the stone for the buildings of Milltown and Pigs Eye. No one remembers that because they weren't around back then. They might remember the quarry taking less and less space as land was sold off and other businesses and condominiums were built, but they don't remember the lake. Only the seagulls remember the lake. The seagulls perch up on top of the tall lampposts, staring down at the parking lot below and squawking, "I'm telling you, this is supposed to be a lake."

Hope parks us near a camel on a giant orange sign.

"So you think I should wear my gray suit to the interview?"

Hope gets excited, "We could get you a new suit. That would be great!" She has an odd idea of great. I figure, humor her, at least until Red's room is available.

"That would be great."

Hope drags me through the lake mirages of the parking lot and to the mall doors. As I pull on the handle, I put my foot in the way of the door. When the door hits my foot with a **bash**, I fling my head back, like it was hit by the door. "Oh my gosh, are you okay?" Hope asks concerned. I try the door three more times with the same results. Hope gets wise to me as a crowd forms, and she opens the door next to my door and pulls me in. "You had me worried for a minute there," she says.

A woman passes us, telling Hope, "My husband also has problems coming in here."

This isn't the Mega Mall, but it has plenty of stores. And every one of them, even Mittens For Kittens, is having a back-to-school sale. Hope growls at the signs. I ask her, "Has our conversation descended to animal noises?" Hope leads me to the suit department of an expensive store. We pick out a few suits and a woman younger than us offers to help.

"That would look good on him," she parrots in response to each one of them. I look around for a checkered retro-fashion dinner jacket, to see if she would say the same thing about it. I just can't find a checkered retro-fashion dinner jacket. Where do you have to go to get a checkered retro-fashion dinner jacket?

I try the suits on, one by one, and shuffle out in sock feet. Hope has me sit like I am eating dinner and reaching for the salt. The next pose is on a street corner waving for a taxi. The next pose is shaking hands. The sales girl is laughing while trying to take notes on the poses. We pick a suit.

The sales girl tries to get an older man to measure me, but he says she has to learn. Class is in session. I am the test dummy. As she turns ten shades of red measuring my pants, Hope and I discuss each shade of red as possible candidates for a color of shirt that might look good on me. She asks me when I'll need the suit. When I say "tonight," she faints.

"You don't need it for tonight," Hope tells me over the slumbering sales associate, "just next week."

"Oh." We revive the sales girl. "Monday or Tuesday would be fine," I tell her.

"Great, we can do that. For a minute there I thought you said, 'Tonight.'" She chuckles nervously and writes it up for Monday. Hope pays for the suit. As we leave the store and cross the mall atrium, I notice that Hope is very pleased with herself.

"Miss Ranidae?"

We turn to find the voice coming from the sort of high school guy that most high school guys want to be and most high school girls want to see.

"Yes?" Hope responds.

"I don't know if you remember me, but I was in your sixth grade class when you were a teacher's assistant?"

"I'm sorry, I don't," she says with a warmth that would put the parking lot to shame.

"I-just-want-to-say–" he stops himself and starts again more slowly, "I just want to tell you that you were the best and nicest teacher that I've ever had." The high school linebacker's legs threaten to shake out from under him.

"That is so great to hear. What's your name?"

"Billy. Bill. William Nelson."

"Can I call you Bill?"

"Yes, that's what everyone calls me," he looks around as if people will jump out from the stores to back him up on that one.

"Well, Bill..."

"Wait. Could I... kiss you?"

Hope turns to me. "Would that be all right?"

I take my time deciding. Hope knows it. The kid doesn't. It's probably winter out when I finally, hesitantly, say, "Okay."

Bill moves as if he's in a dream. I check my watch. Hope breaks off the kiss before the dream is over.

"It was nice to see you again, Bill," Hope says, but he doesn't reply.

He's still living the dream.

Hope is lost in thought too, as we walk away. I steer her into a submersibles store and stop us in front of a large watercraft before she knows where we are. I step back as a salesperson steps forward and asks Hope, "Can I help you?"

Hope says, "No thank you," as she finds me behind her and pulls me out of the store.

I say, "I didn't think I would have a problem with the kiss. I don't think I do. But this aftereffect on you is a bit much. Do you want to see Bill again?"

"No. That was just, really neat."

I steer us into store after store looking for another checkered retro-fashion dinner jacket. I can't find one anywhere. I stop us at Edinner, a cafe in the center of a main atrium, with white umbrellas over the tables, as if they expect the glass skylights to rain down at any moment. I order the seafood surprise. If it turns out good, it'll be a surprise. Minnesota isn't known for great seafood; I don't know why. It could be some sort of geography thing. Hope still hasn't recovered. A woman stops by offering a pedicure. I accept on Hope's behalf. Someone else stops by offering a manicure. I accept on Hope's behalf. Someone else comes along offering neck rubs. I accept on Hope's behalf. Other services try to pile on, but I decline since Hope is already surrounded. When they suggest that I become a recipient, I shake my head. The manicurist has me pick a color.

Soft bluesy jazz with muted trombones and trumpets plays all around our ensemble. I recognize the tune or a variation of the tune.

> I croon: "You.
> You make my dreams come true.
> You're everything that I ever knew.
> You make my dreams come true.
>
> With one kiss the boy took you away.
> You filled his dreams.
> And now he fills yours.
> His kiss took you away.
>
> You.
> You make his dreams come true.
> One kiss blew everything that I ever knew.
> He makes your dreams come true."

My seafood surprise arrives. With my expectations lowered to the deepest depths of Lake Superior, the first bite isn't so bad. Hope's eyes cross, maybe from the neck massage, possibly from what these people and their elaborate toolkits are doing to her hands and feet, I don't know. I can't say I ever did something to her to make her eyes cross. Jealousy pinches me.

It's easy to say you don't get jealous. It's easy to say that love is not jealous, until you see Hope swooning over Johnny Stud-Muffin. Then you have to deal with it. You have to decide if you can put up with the pinches. You can love the Minnesota forest, but can you tolerate its mosquitoes? As I fork up some more well-traveled seafood, without a sound or a flash of light, Hope returns to her body, upsetting a basin of water at her feet.

"What is all this?" she asks.

"It's seafood," I say taking a bite that my mouth instantly rejects and sticks back out on my tongue. I flood my mouth with water.

"I get it. Very funny." Hope says, making all her attendants go away. I pay them off, while my wallet makes a draining sound like 10,000 lakes being emptied at once. Turning to Hope, she seems upset. "Why would I want chrome nail polish? It's... on my toenails too?!?"

I shrug. "Look, you've got a whole lot of little Hopes on your hands. Isn't that what your mom wanted? All those little Hopes smiling up at you. Well, not smiling... You even have little Hopes at your feet." Hope puts back on her sandals and straps her feet in tight. She doesn't seem too happy with me. "You don't seem too happy with me."

"Where's my lunch?"

"You were already out to lunch, so I didn't think you wanted to actually eat. You can have mine." I push my plate forward. "It tastes awful. Do you want to try it?"

Hope pushes it back. "No thanks. I was a little out of it."

"Right. And it's a little hot out. And the stores here are a little expensive."

"He... was every teacher's dream."

"I thought every teacher's dream was for the students to become experts, not getting a kiss. Wait a minute! What do you teach at that school?!? Do you teach kissing?"

"Remember. You said it was okay," she reminds me as if I need reminding.

"Right. The kiss. I don't mind a little lightning; I just don't want the fire to burn down the house. It's like inventing something and then having to deal with the repercussions of it. You've been in la-la land."

"You've been in la-la land yourself."

"Not over a kiss."

"No, but it's still more important to you than– Let's not talk about this. Are you finished?"

"You haven't even started."

"I didn't order anything."

"Then let's go somewhere to eat."

"You aren't going to eat that?"

"No, it's terrible," I tell her again.

"You knew it would be terrible, didn't you?" I nod. "But you ordered it anyway. Why?"

"I suppose I didn't want to eat without you."

Hope leaps into my lap and kisses me like I'm Johnny Stud-Muffin. "That is the sweetest thing!"

"Sweeter than Billy Nelson's kiss?"

She thinks it over. "Equally sweet," she says. I feel a pinch. Someone must've let a mosquito in here. Hope grabs a menu and orders us an appetizer fruit mix of blueberries, pineapple, and watermelon.

"That's it?"

Hope shows me the time. "Faith will kill us if we aren't hungry." From her spot on my lap she can't see the odd look she's getting from me. We feed fruit to each other. Some of hers tastes like nail polish. I hand her a spoon. "We don't have enough people to play spoons," she tells me.

"Maybe later." When we tire of throwing blueberries around, we leave, without leaving any instructions for shipping the seafood surprise. I figure it has enough airline miles to book its own way to India.

In a store full of occupational wardrobes, I spot a top-of-the-line lab coat, and Hope buys it for me. On our way out, I notice Billy Nelson is still standing where we left him. A crowd around him is looking at him like he's a living mannequin. I decide against pointing him out to Hope, hoping she doesn't notice.

Tumbleweed rolls across the baked Camel Lot, and Hope's car blasts us with hot air, before saying just kidding and switching to cool air. Hope makes out with me in the parking lot while we're still parked. She draws a heart on my chest – the simple shape, not the complex organ. Putting the car in gear, Hope asks, "If you were rich, what would you do with your money?"

"That depends on who needed it."

"Let's say everyone could use it."

"No, I mean my friends."

"Let's say your friends don't need it."

"Then I would see how much good I could do with it."

"Like what?"

Watching the traffic, I calculate the ingredients for the recipe. "Most issues are not improved with money alone. Most issues need money and people who are knowledgeable and concerned. Active money. Smart money. Active money is money that's not thrown into a situation but walked in. It's dynamic. It can change as needs change because it is connected to people. And I would start with the most important needs: food, clothing, and shelter. If you don't have those things, having schools or libraries or parks or mid-life crisis centers don't really matter."

"What if you had plenty of money, enough money to do whatever you wanted?"

"To me, the formula is the same whether I have 50,000 or 50,000,000. All my money is all my money. Either way since it is all I have, I wouldn't waste it by throwing money away."

"I mean, what would you do for yourself?"

I don't get it. "Like what?"

"Like would you like to travel or buy a submersible or something?"

"No."

"You don't want anything?"

For two seconds I let myself think of anything. It only took half a second to think of the one thing that would be The One Thing that I would want. One and a half seconds are wasted in the thought. "No," I tell her, because The One Thing isn't possible.

"Wow. Nothing?"

Angels sing. "What don't I have, you know, other than a job?" That's a misleading question. Hope hands me her phone. "Hope's Car And Pizza Delivery Service. We're already on our way, and it's hot enough to bake a pizza on the hood."

"Pizza? We're wondering where you are," Faith wonders.

"We're in the neighborhood, Tex. We should be there any minute now. I was kidding about the pizza."

"Okay," she says and hangs up.

"Could you try not to call her Tex?" Hope pleads.

"I'll try."

Hope dodges the squirrels playing in the road and dodges the departing construction workers. She pulls up, turns the car around, and parks at the side stairway, effectively blocking anyone else from getting out around her car. "I'm driving tonight," she tells me, in complete agreement with the way she parked.

Inside, I cut the tags off my lab coat and hang it up. I get freshened up while Ray tells me through the door that he has agreed to be Nicole's date for this evening. "Do you know where we're going?" he asks, following me into my room.

"Someplace fancy," I reply as I try on my checkered retro-fashion dinner jacket.

"I've never actually seen you wear that thing."

"Never underestimate my ability to look silly and out of place," I say, reaching for a jacket that glows from the back of my closet. I hesitate and decide against it. I choose instead a short sleeved dress shirt and tie. Ray changes to match me and meets me in the living room, where I'm looking over messages on my phone. The damned thing trumpets at me. Hope asks us to meet them at her car, so we go out. The door above opens.

They're beautiful.

Four lovely women carefully descend the steps with silky legs and sparkling dresses. They wear a mixture of smiles from hesitation to a full blown grin. Hope's the one with the grin. The smiles disappear as they argue over the car seating arrangement, which ends up with me in front between Hope and Faith. I didn't know that where we sat mattered, but it leaves me without much leg room. I try to think small.

Faith is shaking. I turn to ask her if she's cold, but she says instead, "I'm really sorry about what almost happened. I don't know what to do," she says handing me an envelope. In it is a card that shows a devastated room and a dog looking pitiful saying I'm Sorry. There is also a blank check. Faith hands me a pen. I put the check back in her hands.

"No, that's ridiculous. You don't owe me anything."

"Pass it back here," Becky says.

I tell Faith, "You don't owe anyone anything. You're taking us out to dinner tonight. Then we're even, okay?"

"Seriously," Becky says, "she doesn't have that much money."

"Everything is always a lot," I philosophize to Becky. I'm not going to diminish the gesture.

Hope drives us to the Wabasha Cave, famous for its prohibition-era gangsters, historical hideout of shady characters. It's a fancy restaurant inset into the bluff. The door has a sign that reads, Castle Royale. The door is locked. Becky points out a button with a sign that says, Ring Bell. Faith pushes it. A small slot slides open in the door. "What's the password."

"I don't know," Faith replies.

"Swordfish," I tell her.

"Sword–" The door opens. "How did you know? That's right, you know everything," Faith tells me. She's wrong, but I do know Marx Brothers movies.

It's a little dark for our group. Lights flicker off glazed limestone. Glass, mirrors, and polished brass give soft echo reflections to the flickering lights. The dresses around me sparkle like soft starlight.

It's damp. Dehumidifiers are running, you can tell, but the moisture still leeches in. It's like trying to dry out a creek. It's a cool humid.

Men and women in double-breasted pinstriped suits with Chicago-sized padded shoulders escort us in and take our drink orders. After five elaborate drink orders, I order cranberry juice. Hope hands me her keys.

"Do you have kidney problems?" Becky asks.

"No, I just like the stuff."

Something brushes through the stillness. "Did you feel that?" Faith asks.

"Feel what?"

The drinks arrive. We toast the house and our friendship. We toast an end to the construction next door. We toast Kelly. They toast the relationship Hope and I have. We toast Minnesota, getting the whole restaurant involved in that one. They toast my pointed perception, confusing the rest of the restaurant. We toast a stuffed pig named Pierre. Several other tables join in on that one. Between all the toasts, we order dinner and more drinks. I check to make sure that Ray found something that will work for him. I order a swiss cheese and mushroom sandwich. Another table toasts the Savior of the Midway. We'll drink to that too.

Seemingly oblivious to non-vegetarian orders being placed around him, Ray asks Nicole, "What am I going to do without Kelly?" She hugs him. "What am I going to do without Kelly?" he asks me. If he's expecting a hug, forget it.

I ask Nicole to hug him again. "You'll be all right," I tell him. He gives a questioning look and then perks up like I just made his day. All I said was that he'll be all right. I think I'm missing my true calling – used car sales. No, that car has never been in an accident; all front ends look like that. I excuse myself to the bathroom. "Tell them about Billy Nelson," I tell Hope.

The hallway has gouges left from either a pickax or a large bear. The men's room is downstairs at a low point in the cave. The hollowed-out-stalagmite-shaped urinals encourage cave dweller behavior in here. The faucets are hot and cold running stalactites. I rinse my face while a gangster comes in. "Evening," he says with a tip of his hat.

"Yes," I agree, while exiting.

I have no problem finding our table. Ours is the most lively table in the joint. The laughter and shouts echo across the main dining cave.

"Here he comes. Tell him."

"Tell me what?"

"I was just telling them," Hope tugs me into my seat and into her arms, "how sweet you were to let the boy kiss me and to order something you didn't want to eat, just so you wouldn't eat without me, and getting me a massage and a manicure and a pedicure. It was very nice of you." They continue to gush over me while our food arrives. Hope shows off her nails and none of them show any signs of letting up throughout half the meal. Even Ray is involved, but I'm almost positive he's teasing them. Our whole Edinner experience is iterated and reiterated until I am thoroughly sick of me. I regret bringing the whole thing up. I become desperate for a way out of this conversation. I have the car keys. I will use them as a last resort.

I ask Hope, "Weren't we suppose to be taking cats to visit the elderly tonight? They can't drive themselves, you know."

"I gave the cats the night off," Hope replies. Drat.

New tactic. "Becky, did you order grilled bat?"

"No!" she slaps the table and laughs like I just said the funniest thing in the world. In fact they're all laughing, multiplied with echoes. I'm the only one who didn't think that was funny. Okay, Ray was faking it. He rolls his eyes at me when no one else is looking. That's right about when the prohibition-era cops raid the joint, looking us over and questioning us on how we like our meals, that sort of thing. Apparently they're hilarious too. A spoon goes flying, and one of the cops catches it. We could play spoons, if we had cards. I order a ginger ale and mix it with my cranberry juice. Everyone at the table, including one of the cops gets to try it except me. I would order more, except all of the waiters have been arrested on account-a breaking the Eighteenth Amendment of the Constitution. Becky and Nicole wander off.

Faith leans over me, "Are you having fun?"

"Yes. A blast. Did you know that Hope buys all her clothes at car shows?"

"Hey Hope, is he having fun?"

"Are you having fun?" Hope leans in from the other side of me, bumping into Faith halfway across my plate. "Hey, where did you come from?"

"My mother," Faith says, "same place as you."

"You never told me that you two are sisters." They look at each other to check.

"No, no, no, no. We both came from our mothers... our separate mothers."

"Your mothers were separated? That's too bad. It happens."

"No, wait. I was going to say something," Faith insists. "What was it? What were we talking about?" I have the finest caliber of friends.

"Your mothers."

"That's right. Did you have fun meeting Hope's mother? Isn't she something?"

"No, she's something else."

Faith's hand smears across her makeup, setting up a look that could inspire a generation of painters. Faith waves back over Nicole and Becky and quiets everyone down to tell the story of how she first met her roommates. She mentions college and cars and something about time, but otherwise I can't figure out almost any of it. Her gestures make the dehumidifiers work extra to dry out spilled glasses. When she's halfway through a new story, I realize she's talking about when she first met me, but I can't figure out that story either.

Our group leaves without the coherent composure that came in with us. It's cooler outside, now that the sun is down. The minute I've got my giggling group in the car and I pull out of the parking lot, the phone rings with extra loud and insistent trumpets. I hand it over to Hope.

"Acapella's Pizza," she answers and I grin. "Mmmm, wouldn't pizza be delicious? What can I get you?" That's my girl! "What? He's here; he just can't talk now." Hope listens. "Cy's mad. She wants to know where you've been. Your phone has said, 'Out Of Service,' and that's archaic. What did you do to the phone?"

"We've been in a cave!" I shout.

Hope holds the phone up to me after I'm done shouting. Then she talks to it again. "Did you hear him?" Hope listens. "Okay, stop and let me tell him. She says that exploring caves is dangerous. Stuff like that. She says we could get histoplasmosis."

"What's histoplasmosis?" the back seat asks.

"What's histoplasmosis? Oh. She says it's a respiratory illness caused by inhaling festering bat droppings. That's disgusting, Cy. Yeah? She's kind of nagging. Did you forget to ask dad before borrowing the car?" Hope holds the phone up.

"We're fine. We just went in for dinner. Faith led us in." The phone hovers near my head in case I have anything else to say in my defense, but I don't.

Hope gets the message after several blocks. "What else, Cy?" She listens. I drive. Someone has to; the car isn't going to drive itself. "Really? Why? Okay, I'll have him call you when we get home. Bye." What's going on? I nudge Hope. "She says that people are upset that they weren't invited to go to Chicago with us to visit Christie and that she's their friend too."

If I thought they should be invited, I would have invited them. "It's not like I was excluding them. If they want to go, they can go."

Hope tells me that they like me while Becky asks "Who's upset?"

"Cy didn't say. Cy didn't say – that's kind of cute. I don't know who's upset, maybe your Boyfriend."

"What's this?"

"What's what?"

"It's like I've got grease on me," Becky says.

"Maybe it's chocolate."

"It's not chocolate."

"You said it was greasy?" I ask.

"Yeah."

"Maybe you were dripped on... in the cave."

"Ew."

"No, that's good. It's a cave blessing."

"Really?"

"Look! We're passing the lake!" Everyone looks.

Inside the house, the girls go upstairs. Ray stops me from following them. "What was that all about?"

"The lake or the cave blessing?"

"Neither. Faith. The blank check. The apology. Dinner."

"Faith had a misunderstanding." I try to walk away.

"No, come on."

"I dreamt she shot me. Or both me and Nicole. Everything was cleared up, and Faith no longer has the gun."

"Why was she shooting you?"

Noise from the stairs. The upstairs group is back downstairs in our living room with us. They sure sobered up in a minute and a half.

"Why were you shooting him?" Ray asks Faith.

"I thought you knew already."

"No."

"I thought these two were sleeping together." Fingers are pointed.

"Why did you think that?"

"Because they were sleeping together. They just weren't doing... ah... anything else," Faith responds.

"Why–"

"Ray. Could you drop it?" I ask him. Ray goes to his room annoyed.

Faith steps in close. "You didn't tell him?"

"I didn't think you'd want that." Faith pats my shoulder. "There probably was an easier way to tell him, but that wouldn't be like me." Faith hesitates and follows after Ray. One of them shuts his door behind them.

Hope reminds me, "You have to call Cy."

"You promised, not I."

Hope takes my phone, gets it dialing, and hands it back. "Help me to honor my word," she says.

"Hi Cy. What's up?"

"What's Faith doing taking you and Hope into caves at night?"

"It wasn't just Faith, Hope, and I. Becky, Nicole, and Ray were with too." Clomping heels on stairs tell me that people are going upstairs.

"I don't—"

"We had dinner. It was the Wabasha Cave."

"Did anyone shoot you?"

"Excuse me?"

"Did they do the trick where the gangsters go around shooting people?" Cy clarifies.

"No. I heard they stopped doing that because too many people were dying from heart attacks. They talked about making it less realistic, but maybe they've given it up entirely. So, what's this about people feeling uninvited to Chicago?"

"We just want to be included, that's all."

"Who's we?"

"Almost everybody."

"So you're saying that if I chartered a bus and said, 'Hop on board,' everyone would come?"

"I don't know if everyone would."

A dentist would love this conversation because it's like pulling teeth only without so much blood. "Okay, who are you certain about?"

"It depends."

"Okay, so what about you? Do you want to come with?"

"I'm not sure. It really depends on what the plans are. What're the plans?"

"Water the plants? This phone isn't working."

"No. What – Are – The – Plans. There's nothing wrong with that phone." Cy mumbles something about the telephone operator.

I don't think an operator is on the line. "All I know for certain is that tomorrow Hope and I are driving Hope's car to Chicago to see Christie. Dan is expecting us to stay at his place, but I'm taking a wait-and-see approach. It's nice of him to offer." I hear what sounds like shots fired as Hope comes down wearing more comfortable clothes. "Cy. Are you okay?"

"Yeah, why?"

"I thought I heard something."

"It's fireworks. We're at Prospective Park because of the thing two weeks ago. We **would** have invited you, but we couldn't get a hold of you. You were out of service." Someone says something. "Listen, I'm making too much noise. I'll call you back. Stay out of caves." She disconnects. Nicole and Becky come down. Becky turns on the TV. Nicole hands me a bowl of popcorn. Her shirt says, Also Available in Sober.

"Record temperatures have led to lakes disappearing, isn't that right, Dave?"

"That's right Chet. Temperatures reached the hundreds once again for much of Minnesota today. The heat wave of the past few weeks has increased the disappearances of hundreds of Minnesota lakes. Somebody ought to file a missing lakes report! And speaking of reports, reports of evaporated lakes have come in from Brainerd, Fergus Falls, Mankato, and the Worthington areas, as well as up north around Thief River Falls and Hibbing. The Natural Resources Department, the NARD, has even reported fewer boundary waters in the Boundary Waters. Some of the missing lakes are prime real estate, especially around Fishing Lino Lakes. What you see are circles of homes surrounding some fresh tree-less property. Chet is currently building a new home on a former Mud Lake if I'm not mistaken. I'd say it's time to buy some property! Today's high temperature was 102 in Milltown, 100 in Pigs Eye, and 102 at the airport. Currently it's 91 here in Milltown. It's 89 across the river in Pigs Eye, and the airport splits the difference at 90. How's the construction progressing, Chet?"

"Somebody tell Dave he's in Minnesota! He's the only guy who can have a **tropical depression** in a **temperate zone!**"

Local news is only a step away from having a laugh track.

"Is Faith still in Ray's room?" Nicole whispers. I nod quietly.

I break out of my quiet. "The news shouldn't be as long if there isn't any, same with the weather. It's like having firefighters hose down buildings without fires. There's nothing wrong with waiting around until you're needed."

"Are you feeling unneeded?" Hope asks, sitting on my lap. "You are you know. I think that's why

Cy was calling."

"Cy doesn't like change. I think she's worried that we're growing up. She wanted to know our plans, but she wasn't exactly committing to liking them." I eat some popcorn.

"That makes sense. What are our plans?"

I swallow, "First we drive across Wisconsin. Dan has said some good things about the new Ultra Speed (US) Highway 12, but I think I'd like to take Interstate 94."

"That's good. Can we stop if we have to?"

"Yes, I tested your brakes on the way home. They work fine."

"That's not what I meant."

"We can stop when we want. In Chicago, Dan has welcomed us to crash at his place."

"You said the brakes work," Nicole points out, "so you shouldn't crash." I give her ribs a poke.

"So you've talked to Dan. Have you talked to Christie?" Hope asks me.

"Dan and I sent messages, but no I haven't talked to Christie."

"Should we?"

"I don't think so."

"What if she's not there?"

"She'll be there when we pull up. She'll be happy to see you. That's about all I know."

"But not you?"

I shrug to the sound of trumpets.

"Doesn't that ring get annoying?" Nicole asks the obvious.

"Acapella's Pizza. Tonight's leftovers are... What have we got? A twice-baked, twice cooled cheese pizza and one pepperoni and mushroom that got lost somewhere in Highland Park. How can I help you?"

"Hey. How's it going?"

"Hi Todd. Are you filling in? Trying to patch things up?" That's what Todd does. If I'm not getting along with Tom or Tom isn't getting along with me, Todd steps in to smooth things over. He doesn't really pull us together so much as diminish the importance of what's going on just by his easy-going nature. His attitude puts things in perspective.

"I guess. What's up?"

Faith comes in and flops down in her dress.

I tell Todd, "We're watching the news. Just watching. Not listening. No sound. They have a live shot of a reporter standing at a street corner talking. In the background, it's dark. We are supposed to presume that the reporter is at the location of some event, but there aren't any bugs around. I'm suspicious."

"You think they're faking it?"

"Yes, I do."

"What's going on tomorrow?"

"Well, it may not be as exciting as watching fake news, but Hope and I are driving down to Chicago to see Christie. We might stay with Dan. We might not. We might not even stay the whole weekend." Hope hops from my lap and leans in so we're face-to-face.

"So this might be a zip in and zip out thing?"

"Exactly." Hope is practically nose-to-nose with me.

"When will you know?"

"By about 5:30 Friday afternoon."

"If things are good and we wanted to quick fly into O'Hare, would that work?"

"Yeah, that would work."

"Would you give Cy a call as soon as you know?"

"Yes."

"Okay, I'll talk with you later."

"Bye."

Hope asks, "We might not stay the whole weekend?" I nod. "What if I want to dip my toes in Lake Michigan?"

"Have you seen what they put in Lake Michigan?" I ask rhetorically. "They had to reverse the flow of the Chicago River to get stuff out." Hope's eyes peer into mine. "We can see the lake if you want. It's just like our lakes only greater. We need to pack and go to bed."

I wish everyone a good night, kiss Hope, and walk zombie-like to bed.

38

Drive

The driver's seat feels funny. I swivel and shift myself. Hope looks at me through her sunglasses, the eastern sun sparkling on her glasses and lighting her embroidered shirt, depicting a sunset over Lake Weago. The sun on her shirt doesn't wear sunglasses or a smile. She says, "Your seat is adjustable." I mess with the buttons, testing them, and figuring them out. I adjust the seat to shove a loaf-sized piece of seat into my lower back. "What're you doing? You're trying to make yourself uncomfortable, aren't you? Watch the road."

"Is there a massage setting?"

"Yes." She pushes a button and turns a knob.

"I don't feel it."

"You don't get it," she says coyly. "Only passengers get the massage. The driver has to stay awake."

"I can drive, stay awake, **and** get a massage. Your car needs repairs. Improvements. All it would take is getting the seat parts for the passenger seat. Install the parts in the driver's seat. Match the wiring from the passenger seat. Alter the switch settings to include the driver. Maybe add more juice to run it."

"Or you could just wait your turn until I'm driving."

"The back seats have the massage units too?"

"Yes."

"I could drive from the back seat."

"Get your seat belt back on."

"Haven't you heard of a back-seat driver?"

"Fasten it... thank you."

"It's a shame letting the back seats go to waste. There are plenty of people who would want a ride."

"This car does not pick up hitchhikers."

"No. I'm talking about something that would be prearranged, like providing a service."

"Like AutoDrive?"

"AutoDrive is a product not a service."

"Same idea."

"Yes. Maybe it comes from the same place inside me. I just think it's a waste to drive so far with an empty back seat."

"You miss your friends, don't you?" Hope asks, touching my arm.

"No, it's not that. Even a stranger could solve the problem."

"Or we could have the back seat removed."

There is a great divide between Minnesota and Wisconsin. It isn't our fault. It isn't their fault. But geologically there is a fault, through which the St. Croix River flows, dividing the two states until the Mississippi takes over. We drop down the side of Minnesota and cross the St. Croix River. Hope looks out over the still, shadowy water.

"I talked about taking Interstate 94. Do you want to take Ultra Speed 12 instead?" I ask.

"You're driving. You can decide."

I told her that we could make stops, and you can't make stops on US 12. "Let's take I-94. And welcome to Wisconsin, Hope."

She dimples, "Thank you." We rise up from the border edge of the state, passing the Welcome To Wisconsin sign, and drive into the hazy Wisconsin sunshine. After the border towns, unruly traffic races off to US 12, the American version of the Autobahn. We're left with the trucks, the locals, and the less hurried. The first bug of the trip splats against the windshield. Correction, that was the third bug of the trip. I must've missed those other two. Hope says, "Look at the brown cows!" I look and see only rolling green hills.

"What cows?"

"You didn't see them?"

"No. Were they little cows?" Maybe they were too small to see.

"Calves?"

"I don't know. I'm asking you."

"Ewes?" Hope yawns and stretches with unknowing seduction.

I squint suspiciously. "This has long trip written all over it. Maybe I should have taken US 12."

Steam rises from sunlit fields, like the plants are blowing off steam from their hot morning coffees before having to go to work photosynthesizing. One plant asks another plant, "What do you do?" The other plant replies, "Photosynthesis." "I'm in the photosynthesizing industry myself," says the first plant. "Me too," say a half dozen nearby plants. A chorus of "Me too" plant voices thunder across the fields. That would be just like plants.

Traffic is bunched up around me, meaning slower traffic is holding back faster traffic. We get organized as a group, signaling and shifting lanes, measuring the speed and driving abilities of the other cars, identifying inattentive drivers, deciding reasonable speeds for the conditions and the traffic, and picking teams. Who do we want to be our driving buddies? You can't trust just anyone to drive nearby at speeds that would tire gazelles. These particular gazelles have a mass of several tons, which is multiplied by the speed of the pack to measure the momentum. When you start to estimate the force, the momentum, this pack of vehicles has, you realize that how we interact matters. This is Zen and the art of driving. It's being aware of your group of vehicles. Everyone gets only one chance to screw up or show signs of being a screw up. We're just starting out. We've left the big city or the conglomeration of cities, however you want to look at it. We don't know who the problem drivers are. The erratic driver will be watched, tagged and released.

A truck weaves onto the shoulder. That truck is a suspect for two seconds, until I notice a low dark blob is in the middle of the road. Right lane traffic rides the shoulder to avoid it. It's a duffel bag. I almost comment on the duffel bag, when I notice Hope's eyes are closed. I look over twice more before determining that she's asleep. She was right about the massager putting someone to sleep. I push the button to turn it off.

There is something else is the road. Someone lost some boots. They're leaving a trail. There's something else ahead. They lost a raccoon.

One of the keys to good driving is looking ahead. A camper trailer appears to be the source of the excess camping gear. What looks like a sleeping bag teeters on the side edge. Everyone behind is watching it, giving it room, predicting its drop off. If the camper people are careless at packing, will they be careful at driving? Probably not, people are generally consistent.

The sleeping bag drops and bounces out of bounds. A car ahead signals to the camper that they are leaving their stuff lying around on the roadside, a trail of camping gear. The camper pulls off to regroup.

Anyone who says the uncertainty principle isn't relevant to the measurement of the momentum of large objects, has never driven across Wisconsin.

One of the faster cars, several cars behind me, seems overly edgy, swerving within its lane with inconsistent acceleration. The driver probably made a bet with someone that I-94 is just as fast as US 12. The swerving driver is going to lose. Traffic parts like the Red Sea, except for me. I have nowhere to go to get out of the way. I could speed up, or I could slow down, but I don't want to do either. Slowing down won't help the other driver, and speeding up will only make the situation more dangerous. Racing boy will just have to wait. Racing boy flashes his lights and honks his horn. I don't know where he expects me to go. I don't think he cares. I pass other vehicles, and a few more, and let him go. Racing boy is a racing girl. She drives parallel to me, but I don't look over. Racing girl, you're free to go, so go. Whatever she needs to say, I don't need to hear and neither does Hope – a little less conversation, a little more action. She pauses nearby and then accelerates an additional 15 miles per hour. In minutes, she's gone.

The Wisconsin Highway Patrol hasn't made an appearance yet, but it's only a matter of time. They usually park in the center, in the green median that separates the east-bound traffic from the west-bound traffic. The median widens for bridges and narrows for underpasses, but mostly it's two or three car-lengths wide. Grasses and small blurry-blue daisy-like flowers fill the median. When dirt roads interrupt the median, they are marked with neatly printed Reserved signs, letting us know that even though the troopers are gone, they will be back.

The interstate intersects with local highways, often named after letters in a preschool-sort-of-way. Some of the lettered highways repeatedly cross the interstate. Highway F was doing that for a while.

Cars rush within feet of a shiny black crow waddling the highway shoulder, its tail shifting left and right as it walks. The bird ignores the menacing traffic, inspecting the asphalt shoulder, like a high school janitor eying a crowded hallway floor. It's a job.

A car merges onto the highway in front of me and leaves its turn signal on. I pass them and leave on my turn signal. Someone spilled white cotton ball clouds across the pale blue sky.

"Your turn signal is on," my traveling companion tells me.

"It's solidarity with the car behind me." Hope looks back and waves to them. They turn off their turn signal. I turn off mine.

"How long was I asleep?" Hope asks stretching.

"Not too long." I dodge another raccoon.

"That's awful."

"Would've been worse if I'd hit it. Somebody must be dropping raccoons. That's the third one I've seen." Today must be the recycling pick-up day for raccoons.

"I was **going** to suggest we stop somewhere for something to eat, but I just lost my appetite. Cool, black and white cows!"

After checking my path and mirrors, I look over to see the same green slopes we've been seeing. Ponytail grasses sway and bounce in the breeze, catching the sunlight like natural tinsel. "What cows?"

"You didn't see them?" Hope digs for something in a duffel bag.

"Were they camouflaged? What the F? It's back again."

"What?"

"F. Highway F. Do you need a rest area?"

"No."

"Good, 'cause we passed the rest area at Menomonie while you slept. There won't be any more for a while."

"Please don't tell me that," she says just as I start to say there are other stops. "And never, ever say something like that to fourth graders. That's a sure-fire way of making them need to stop." Various shades of green stretch out from all around us. Blue-green at the horizon, but it will be green when we get to it. Pretty tricky of the chameleon-like fields. "Would you like to listen to some music?"

"Okay."

"It's Melanie."

"Oh." A once flying bug splats across the windshield.

"Do you still want to?"

"I'll give it a try." She plugs her player into the car stereo. It starts off with "Hopes and Dreams." It isn't the regular version of "Hopes and Dreams." It's the slow, mostly instrumental version of "Hopes and Dreams." The one that was played at Melanie's funeral. That one. "We don't play this." Hope reaches to change it, and I stop her with my hand. "You can't know... what it was like when this was played at her funeral. We almost never played her recorded music. If we did, it was just a part that we were talking about or comparing to someone else's work or to one of the Melanie-clones that were copying her style. We'd play snippets of this or that as we were figuring things out. When we listened to recorded music, we listened to other stuff. When we listened to her, she was right there performing or practicing the song. God." My thumb and forefinger duck under my sunglasses to wipe the corners of my eyes.

"I'm sorry."

"When we were in the cathedral, it had to be there, nowhere else was big enough, and this song came on and... this part that's coming up..." Melanie crashes into the end of what is usually an up-tempo happy song, slowly singing about having all your hopes and dreams ahead of you. "It did, more than any words, what funerals are supposed to do – tell you that she was gone, really gone."

We listen to her song, while Wisconsin whizzes by. Melanie sings, "Nearer to thee. Tomorrow redeems. Snow body knows, all my dreams. Hopes and dreams. Us invincible teens? Hopes and dreams."

Dropping down a sizable hill, the highway curves left. I navigate around some slow moving trucks, and I swallow to unplug my ears from the drop. It plugs them up more. The sound of the road and the car – I'd grown used to the noise – and the song, are all gone. I guess I only half swallowed. I swallow again and my ears hear clearly. The song is over.

"Are you okay?" Hope asks with a hand on my shoulder. Melanie's "Hard To Get" starts playing.

"I'm fine. It's starting to really warm up. Do you mind if I turn on the air conditioner?"

"No, not at all."

"Thank you."

"Have you always been so polite?" I think a moment. Then I politely rattle my head up and down. "Did you see the view back there? I didn't want to interrupt the song."

"I think so," I check my mirror.

"I'm sorry, I didn't know you had someone on your butt."

"They're determined to have me speed with them following behind me. Three times, when I've changed lanes, they've changed lanes. I think they think that cops only pull over the vehicle in front. Or else they figure they'd have an easier time slowing down. Either way I'm not interested in playing escort to them." I gradually slow down, nearly to the minimum speed limit. They stick with me as if I know something that they don't know. And that's true, I do. I know that institutional changes always occur on Mondays, and I know the acceptable forms of Minnesota currency. I know that Herman the spider is telling stories to grandchildren about the giants she scared, and I know that there is a fine line between fishing and drowning worms. And I know that the seventh UVCCD, 748-851, was originally a composite CCD in the fourth NAV inputs of AutoDrive. I know lots of things. The tailgating car realizes that I don't want to play Follow The Leader anymore, and they move off. Hope's player starts another song.

We pass a deer carcass on the side of the road. "Oh deer."

"What?"

"We just passed a deer."

"Oh dear."

Broken rows of wind blocking trees separate the fields without giving much refuge to the birds. Hope shifts a little in her seat. I think it's time to look for an exit. I'm willing to stop. I'm willing to go that extra mile for Hope.

Blue signs appear to tell us what services are available at the next exit. Restaurants are listed as food; grocery stores aren't. Fuel stations and lodgings are also listed.

Some services are right there at the exit; some are several miles away, just a quick trip into town at 25 miles per hour. The idea is to slow you down so you might visit other shops along the way.

Some services don't make the blue sign's list, making me wonder what they didn't do that they were supposed to have done. Are they below the blue sign standard of quality?

I signal my exit from the group.

"Are we stopping?" I nod. Hope waves good-bye to some of the traffic. "How did you know?" I smile. "You're very thoughtful. I never would've believed someone could be as thoughtful as you. You're blushing."

"Uh, no, it's a reflection from that fruit stand sign."

"No, it's not," she says, snuggling my right shoulder.

"Who's bathroom would you like to use?"

"I get to pick? Restaurant bathrooms are generally cleaner than fuel station bathrooms."

"I didn't know that." I'm glad then that I'm offering her the selection.

"There." She picks a combination fuel station, restaurant, gift shop, and bait and tackle store. A most exquisite choice. She puts on her sandals and grabs her purse as I pull up. "Are you coming?"

"No, I'm going to fill the tank."

"So am I," she says going in. I don't know what she means.

I pull over to a fuel pump, get out, stretch, feel the baking heat, yawn, check to make sure I have my copy of Hope's car key, feed the fuel pump some Minnesota currency, and set the pump to fill the tank. Grabbing a squeegee, I scrub the front windshield's baked-on, yellow, bug guts. I must've missed that day of biology when the teacher told the class that all flying insects are filled with mustard glue. That's what I'm trying to scrape off – baked on mustard glue, not available in any stores.

A big adhesives company was started in Minnesota by setting up shop on the highway coming back from Wisconsin. Back then, they offered a free service where they scraped off traveler's windshields. They'd take all the stuff they scraped off, package the stuff up, and sell it as glue. They have since diversified. They make Bourbon Tape. Their adhesives are the best in the world. At Flight Control we used their adhesives to mount sensors on cars; one of Harvey's shoes is probably still stuck to the floor. They hardly ever scrape incoming cars anymore.

A hot wind blows through, along with half a hectare of soil, fertilizer, and ungrounded seeds. I spit out some seeds. That's what this windshield needs – sandblasting. I bet they have no problem blasting bugs off windshields in the Sahara.

A motorcyclist pulls up and waits for the squeegee. I hand it off to him. He uses it on his cheeks and his arms.

Yes, the Sahara is the answer to all of life's problems from: "I bet it doesn't get this cold in the Sahara" to "I bet it doesn't snow like this in the Sahara."

"What are you thinking about?" Hope asks.

"The Sahara."

"It is hot out. I'm going to go over to that Cheese Stand."

"Okay." Her ponytail bounces with her across the parking lot. Another wind blows through, surprising me by hitting me with some hay. I start to brush off about a bale's worth of hay, only to decide it would be easier to become a scarecrow. I drive over to the Cheese Stand. Hope is looking at a cheese sculpture of Michaelangelo's David in Monterey Jack. "Is any of this cheese made from invisible cows?"

The cheese farmer looks at me. "I'll sell you some invisible cheese, if you want. It tastes as light as air," he says cheesily.

"No, thanks."

He writes something down. "Invisible cows. I always get the oddballs," he tells Hope. To me, he says, "No offense."

"None taken." What a cheese ball. "Is that what you're having for lunch?" I ask, pointing with my elbow to David as Hope picks hay off me.

"No. I don't know what I want. Do you want to switch drivers?"

"You're replacing me?!? What did I do wrong?"

"Nothing." The cheese farmer scoffs. "I just thought you might like a break."

"Are you getting anything?"

"No, just looking." I lead her over to the fruit stand where she wants everything. "I can't get anything because it'll bake in the car. I love peaches," she tells the grower, "they still have their fuzz on them. By the time they get to our stores, all the fuzz is gone."

"Replaced with shaving nicks and bruises," I add.

"Where are you from?" the grower asks.

Hope answers "Milltown," while I answer "Pigs Eye."

"Oh, a feuding romance. Your families are on separate sides of the river, with separate ideas of how to live and whom to love... hearts together... spirits apart. His family is in the old town: distinguished and staid, with an old worldly charm..."

"Actually..."

"While your family is from the new town: lively, energetic, and rambunctious, ready for anything! Your parents will never cross the river to meet on anything..." I nod. "They come from different schools of thought, towns so close yet so far apart. Yours is a romance of stealth and anonymous text messages, a romance of passion and exuberance..." Is that good? "... a romance of singular purpose – to meet amidst the river that divides your hearts."

We buy some grapes and peel out.

With limited options, we choose Slather Burgers, under the giant bull. Slather Burgers advertises their Full Deck burger, with a full stack of 52 ingredients, no jokers. I decide that's not the sandwich for me. They also have a Triple Slather Burger with a bacon and cheese mortar.

Hope orders a Slather Salad.

"Do you want the Full Deck salad?"

"What's the Full Deck salad?"

"It has 52 ingredients. It's like a salad bar in a bowl. Sometimes we have a tough time smashing the lids on them."

"No, that's too much."

"Do you want the Pick Off salad?"

"What's the Pick Off salad?"

"It's the Full Deck salad, only you tell us what ingredients to pick off."

Hope turns to me, "Do you know what you want?" She pushes me forward.

"Yes, I'll have the grilled veggie sandwich without the mayo, mustard, salad dressing, or the butter spread." I pause for all the buttons to be pushed. "And a drink."

"Uh, that will take three minutes. Are you willing to wait?" I nod. I am handed a cup.

Hope says, "I'll have the same."

"Uh, that will take three minutes. Are you willing to wait?" She nods. She gets her cup. I pay. I interrupt the next order to give back a few dollars too much change. While we fill our cups and grab our straws, Slather Burgers erupts in a sea of mimicked orders. People agree to wait three minutes.

"Where did you see the grilled veggie sandwich?"

"It wasn't on the menu. It was on a little sign on the side."

"Well done."

"Medium well." We sit down at a table. I tear off one end of the paper wrapper from the straw, pull it a bit, and try to blow it off in Hope's direction. She's stunned I would try to blow it in her direction, then her shoulders slump, empathizing with me it didn't work. It won't blow off, due to a hole at the other end. I pull the wrapper a little farther off the straw and coil up the end. I blow it out like a New Year's Eve party favor.

Hope laughs, "That's great." Hope tries her straw with the same results.

Slather Burgers gets a mad rush at the straw dispenser. The place has so many New Year's Eve party favors, I half expect confetti to start flying. I eye my paper napkin, which could be shredded. My eyes shift to a large standing fan that could easily be tilted to propel shredded napkins skyward. I'm just about to set the plan in motion when our lunch tray is dropped off, along with some attitude.

"We were all out of potato slices, so we substituted radishes."

We secretly pick off the grilled radishes. Someone in a giant Slather Burger costume comes over, looks at our meals, looks at us, sticks out its cheese, and leaves. Even the Slather Burger has attitude. I imagine it's tough to be a happy burger, when you live under a bull.

Back at the car, Hope again asks me if I want her to drive. I decline her offer. We pick the I-94 ramp "East to Madison" instead of the one "West to Pigs Eye" and merge onto the highway.

Hope's player starts Melanie's cover of "You Didn't Have To Be So Nice." I ask Hope, "Could we be done listening to this?" She agrees.

The highway cuts through forests of pine and oak. Here and there in shady median nooks, state troopers sit, gunning for speeders. Signs warn of deer crossings. Round red stickers added to the ends of the noses of the deer make the signs more specific to one particular deer. They are Rudolph the red-nosed reindeer crossing signs. "Rudolph crossing," I point it out to Hope the next time I see one. She laughs.

I am just pointing out a bubble of traffic-less space around us, when construction slows us to a residential street speed and pops our bubble. We're down to one lane, right behind a mattress truck. We can't see around the truck to see how long the construction lasts. All we can see is the advertisement on the back of the mattress truck. A woman slumbers peacefully on her fluffy bed. I point to it and say, "That's not helping me to keep awake. Could you check the Internet to see how long this construction lasts?"

"Where are we?"

"Wisconsin, I hope. I thought you were navigating."

"No, I'm just seeing where you're taking me. Hold on a minute." She navigates her phone. "Wisconsin construction. Hey, we could build a house!"

"Road construction. Expect delays. Isn't that pessimistic?"

"Oh, road construction. That's different."

"There was a sign for Warrens."

She mumbles quietly, "You never said road construction." She announces, "Here we go. Five miles." She puts away her phone.

"I wish this truck would go away." An orange End Road Work sign appears. It must be some sort of protest sign. So I say, "Right on, man." We speed off, free from the oppressive yoke of construction.

Little green mileposts mark the miles with a number, every mile of the way on the right side of the road. Between each mile marker is a round, white reflector on a post at every tenth of a mile; nine of them are between each mile marker. And once you notice them, noticing the regularity and the rhythm of them, coming toward you and speeding by, you notice how mesmerizing they are. Do not operate heavy machinery, like a car or a truck while watching the mileage markers. I'm starting to get sleepy. I'm having a hard time keeping my eyes open. I'm dreaming of stretching out on a nice soft bed or even a couch...

I almost relax.

I have to stop looking at the roadside. Look around. Soft puffy white pillow-like clouds stretch and sprawl comfortably across the satin blue sky. A bird glides effortlessly.

"I have to wake up. I'm falling asleep."

"Me too," Hope replies. Debris flies on the road, probably hit by a truck up ahead. I tap my brakes to warn traffic. Large pieces of steel-belted rubber from a truck tire or two litter the roadway. I get around it in an exaggerated manner, as another way of warning traffic behind me. "You handled that well. You woke up just in time," Hope says, "but you've been driving the whole way. I could take over."

"Deal."

We pass the rock skyscrapers of Camp Douglas, and a swarm of motorcyclists are sputtering by just as I'm exiting. Pulling off onto a gravel and grass shoulder, the engine fan kicks into high gear to try to keep the engine as cool as it had been on the interstate. Shifting the transmission to park, I close my eyes. Now that I can close my eyes, I don't want to close my eyes, which makes me angry about having been tired in the first place. I should have more mental control than this. I look over at Hope, and we get out of the car. Meeting behind the trunk, I catch her and kiss her and feel her. She pulls away, takes my hands, looks around, and steps back to kiss me more. It's hot. And we're getting exhausted by the running car. We climb back in. Hope readjusts her seat and mirrors, while I stretch out in the passenger seat. I put my feet up. That doesn't work. I stretch my feet out under the dashboard only to get caught in something. Hope gets us going. I put one leg up and stretch one leg below and leave them there.

"Are you comfortable at all?" she asks, looking cool back behind the wheel.

"At all? Yeah." The way I respond makes her laugh, and she imitates me.

"Did you see the woman wearing next to nothing on the motorcycle?"

"When?"

"Just before we stopped."

"No. Was she behind a cow?"

"Cows don't ride motorcycles." I stare off, trying to figure how many things Hope has commented on throughout this trip that never really existed. This is a whole new side of Hope. The highway cuts through gray and tan rocky hills, 30 to 40 feet tall. "I just saw a great blue heron," she announces. That one I saw, except that it was only a pretty good blue heron. It wasn't that great. "Talk to me," she pleads. "Don't let me fall asleep. Tell me about pointed perception."

"Pointed perception is just a decision making tool. The real issue is AutoDrive."

"Okay, tell me about AutoDrive."

"Like I told you Wednesday night, I watched AutoDrive smash repeatedly into a police car. The only time it didn't do that was when I tried to warn the cop in the police car. That time it hit me, another cop, and the cop in the police car."

"So you're saying it's stubborn."

"Yes, in a way, it's going to do what it's going to do."

"Have you ever thought that if it's going to do what it's going to do, that getting involved just causes trouble for you?"

"How so?"

"Well, let's say you lay out one of those spiky things that are used to stop a car that's being chased. You're the one they'll blame for the damages. Not AutoDrive. Not Flight Control. You."

"I never thought of the spiky things." My fingers dance a spiky thing dance on her thigh.

"That's because you don't watch TV. You—" She laughs. "I almost said you can learn a lot from TV! I never thought I would be advocating television." She seizes my dancing fingers and holds my hand to her leg.

"I can deal with their blaming me for damages to AutoDrive. I can't deal with my blaming me for damages from AutoDrive."

"But what if you can keep yourself out of trouble while keeping AutoDrive out of trouble?"

"That would be ideal," I respond.

"The problem with the spiky thing is, well... there are two problems with the spiky things. Number one they do cause damage. You aren't going to get away scot-free. And number B," Hope smirks, "most people don't happen to be carrying around the spiky thing. They aren't exactly a fashion accessory."

"There is no number B. It's just B." Hope gives me a look like I just popped her balloon or rained on her AutoDrive parade.

"What you need to do is: come up with a list of ways to slow down AutoDrive."

"Slow it down? I want to stop it." Hope shrugs. I interrupt her shrug. "I was once told a story about a guy who got pulled over after drifting through an intersection with a stop sign. The officer tells him that he failed to stop at the stop sign. He tells the officer, 'I slowed down. What's the difference?' The officer gets the guy out of the car and starts clubbing him.'"

Hope asks, "The officer takes him around to clubs?!?"

"No. The officer hits the guy with his night stick."

Hope giggles, "Is that what you call it? Your night stick?" I take back my hand. "Give me back your hand. It's keeping me warm. Go on."

"So the officer is hitting the guy with his club and then stops and asks, 'Do you want me to stop? Or just slow down?'" Hope laughs but tells me its not very nice. "I don't want to slow down AutoDrive. I want to stop it."

"But if the spiky thing slows down AutoDrive enough not to harm the police officer, is that okay with you?" I nod. "What do you think?"

"I nodded. Didn't you hear the rattle?"

"No. Your head rattles when you nod your head?"

I nod. "Rattle-rattle-rattle."

"That time I heard it. So, list off ways to either stop or slow down AutoDrive."

"A wall. Building a wall would be the perfect way to stop AutoDrive."

"But it couldn't be something that big—"

"Hang on, I'm not finished. The wall would be made of ice so it would melt right away. Have you ever wondered how they make the ice for ice rinks? A giant ice rink making machine. I just have to sneak in and, using one of the trucks with a crane on it that they use to deliver the ice to the ice rinks, I take the ice downtown and prop it up in the middle of the street, wedged between the buildings on either side. The wall will do its job, melt, drain down the storm sewers, and leave only a puddle. It's perfect!"

"Wait," she says.

And she leaves me waiting. "Kind of leaves you speechless, doesn't it?"

"Yeah, I don't know where to begin."

"Begin where I did."

"Okay, I'll start with the ridiculous and try to work my way out of it." Hope studies the traffic, waving at the highway patrol as we drive by. She's still at a loss for words. "I know I'm going to regret asking this, but how do they get the slab of ice into the ice rink?"

"Through the slot."

"Right, the slot," she says. "What slot?"

"The hidden slot outside. The one that looks like a mail slot except much, much longer. The ice slides through the slot, down under the seats on one side, flops into the middle, and rattles around, spinning like a quarter coming in for a landing."

"I knew I shouldn't have asked. Next question, where is the giant ice making machine?"

"I don't know. It doesn't look like river water..."

"Next question, do you want to stick with that idea, or do you want to see if we can come up with something better."

"I'd like your help coming up with something better."

"Thank you. Have you thought about calling 911?"

"Now?" Hope doesn't respond. I may have gone too far. Her brow is starting to wrinkle. "Seriously no, I'm not sure what I would say."

"Would you consider it?"

"Yes, I'll consider it."

The solid and dotted lines of the highway stream toward us. "Did you write the programming for AutoDrive?"

"Yes and no. It started with just me and expanded from there."

"Do you know what others programmed?"

"Yes, because it was a group effort. It was too complicated to do isolated programming, to farm out pieces of it."

"So you know how it would behave in a given situation?"

"Yes and no. A simple situation? Or a situation that we thoroughly tested? Yes. Any other complex situation? No. There are too many variables. Let me give you an example. Rocket scientists have programmed rockets to launch from a moving object, the Earth, and dock with another moving object, a space station. The rocket can be manned or unmanned. It is amazing code for precision navigation. But let's say there was an obstacle in the way, a police car floating in orbit for some reason. The rocket will drive right into the police car. It's not smart enough to maneuver around anything or to stop and let something pass. AutoDrive has to know everything that you know while you drive. Is that merging truck going to have the brains to pick up speed as it gets on the highway? What are we going to do with these extra lanes?"

"Do we take 90 or 94?"

"Exactly. That's the sort of question–"

"No, I'm asking, do we take 90 or 94?"

"I-90. Rockford. A rocket couldn't have asked that and decided what to do with that new information as you're doing."

"So what you're saying is that unless the situation is simple, you don't know what AutoDrive will do."

"Exactly."

"That rules out the ice wall, doesn't it?"

"Yes," I answer the teacher sheepishly.

"It's okay. You just need to think of a simple situation that will make AutoDrive stop." She's right.

She's consistent that way. "Rest area one mile. Do you want a rest?"

"I think we can both use a rest." We use the facilities, read the hysterical marker, and buy some cold bottled water that claims to be from a glacial spring. I stop a group of teenagers in matching orange T-shirts. "Hi. Could you drive for us? We're both tired." They agree, and we are all set to do it, until some chaperones take over and decide otherwise. "I'll drive," I tell Hope.

"Are you sure?" Maybe I didn't sound sure.

"Sure I'm sure." I mess up Hope's mirrors and make the seat uncomfortable again. Back on the highway, a huge inferiority complex tailgates. There would be no reaction time if I brake. The other lane is clear. "So I just need to think of something simple that will make AutoDrive stop." Hope agrees. "I'll have to work on that."

"I know it's a little late to ask, but do you know how to get to Christie's?"

"Are we there yet?" I whine. "Yeah, Dan wrote me and told me."

"Did you know that there's a monster truck on your butt?"

"Oh, is that what that is? I was going to have a doctor look at it. Back at the rest stop I agreed to tow him across state lines. Welcome to Illinois, Sunshine."

"Thanks. You can tag and release Mr. Monster Truck back into the wild anytime."

"That's a great idea. What if we could tag other drivers? Keep track of their migratory habits? And their reproductive rituals?" I start to incrementally slow down a mile per hour per mile.

Hope says, "Let him go. There is no reason to torture the monster. And I'm glad you aren't easily intimidated." After a few miles, the inferiority complex discovers another lane and departs. "Life is like a collection. You decide... you pick and choose what you want to be. You think about it being a choice for the moment, but the choices change and shape who you are. Whatever you decide about AutoDrive, that's who you'll be. I think you decided some time ago, back when you were working for Flight Control, that because of your position, you were responsible for AutoDrive's outcome. And that might have been true. But you're no longer responsible for it. You need to know that even if AutoDrive kills a hundred people, it's not your fault. You stood your moral ground. AutoDrive wasn't ready and wishful thinking by Carl couldn't make it be ready. I love you, and I will love you despite what AutoDrive does. I don't know if that's comforting or not—"

"It is."

Traffic divides between those with Illinois Toll Road I-Passes and those without. On the side of the section of those without, there is a billboard of acceptable forms of currency from nearby states. This is educational. Wisconsin cheese is an acceptable form of currency, as is Minnesota sidewalk salt, Chicago tommy guns and pizza, and Indiana racing tires. Hope unfastens her seatbelt to lift a sack of sidewalk salt. I tell the attendant that I'd like to pay for the group, waving my arm to indicate all the other cars. The attendant takes the sack and places it on a pile next to a stack of 25 inch tires and taps a sign that says, "Improvisation theaters are in the Loop. Try your comedy there." Noticing the tommy guns, I take off without nearby competition because in the next lane, a big-assed monster truck is stuck.

Nearsighted drivers without their glasses barrel up to other cars, only to realize that they aren't the only car on the road. Maybe they aren't nearsighted. Maybe they're just driving like dogs. They approach another car and sniff its butt. When they have smelled everything they need to smell, they go around the car. Some cars sit on other cars butts for hours.

Billboards are stacked three high here. Someone must've done a study and determined that three levels of billboards is the most anyone will ever read. One of them advertises the Illinois State Lottery and has a digital readout of the current lottery jackpot. It asks, "When will it be enough?"

South-bound traffic into the city has bunched up. On the other side, traffic isn't moving at all. That is the Friday City Departure traffic, escaping to Wisconsin. Engines have overheated. Tempers have overheated. Couples are coupling. Motorcyclists who were cool are no longer cool because no one has figured out how to make an air conditioner for motorcycles stuck in traffic. And most of them are on their phones.

Trumpets blare like truck horns. I hand Hope my phone. "What am I supposed to say again? Oh yeah. Hello, Acapella's Pizza. Today's special is Chicago-style deep dish–"

"Good one..." I comment.

"How can I help you? Hi Cy. I'm not sure where we are, but we already have 20 story buildings around us, and the sky is noticeably orange," I hadn't noticed but she's right, it's a cheesy orange, "so I figure we're close. What's up? Oh. I'll check. Are we still planning to call once we know something? His head is rattling. Did you know that his head rattles when he shakes it? Well, it was news to me. Okay. Talk to you later. Bye. That was Cy."

"I told Todd I'd call... That means I'll call. It's not that tough to comprehend."

"She was just checking up on us."

"I know. That's the part that bothers me. My butt is numb."

Hope laughs, "You missed your chance at a massage. You could've had one when I was driving."

We drop off a few more tolls. Interstate 90 becomes the Kennedy Expressway. The planes of O'Hare fly over our hair, which is why O'Hare is called O'Hare. We join back up with Interstate 94, passing the giant lighted billboard lips of Magic Kiss. It's glossier than the original. They still haven't taken the John Hancock out of its crate. Sears got its start in Minnesota and now look at it, all grown up and towering over Chicago. The expressway cement dividing blocks are pockmarked from the equivalent of a world war or two. A slight jog takes us to Ashland Avenue which takes us south for several miles of traffic lights. We cut over to Halsted. A few more turns and we are on residential streets. This is a grid system of streets, if I ever saw one. Eighty-second comes after 81st because that's the way the numbers work. South is not east of west. South is south. It's easy.

Driving in Chicago is different from driving in the Twin Cities. In Chicago, the accelerator and brake petals work in concert. Tap one, then the other, back to the first, now the second. Going for a smooth ride? Forget it. Here, it can make sense to use both petals simultaneously, almost like a bicycle. Down on one, up with the other. Use two feet; it saves time. Minnesota? Minnesota invented the yield. In Chicago, yielding is something that tricyclists outgrew. Do what you are going to do. Don't putter between two lanes or in the intersection of indecision. People will not wait for you.

Car engines that are on the threshold of running, that run on imagination here, would never run in Minnesota. It's not that Minnesota doesn't have imagination. Minnesota is swimming in imagination; just wait for what Minnesota dreams up next, like thunder snow. It's that some of these Chicago engines can hardly sputter and turn over in hot, nearly combustible weather. They couldn't both sputter and shiver. They couldn't run in Minnesota.

Hope feeds grapes to us. "My feet are hot and crabby," I tell her.

"Mine are cold and clammy." Hope puts on her shoes. She pulls her hair out of its ponytail and brushes it out.

Duct tape is very useful, but it doesn't hold up in Minnesota. My Pony Express is nothing pretty, but it would win Miss Photogenic and probably Miss Congeniality against a quarter of the cars on the road in Chicago. Many Chicago cars have sub-standard parts. Metal parts are connected with duct tape, windows are replaced with clear plastic, and taillight covers are replaced with red cellophane. Chicago auto parts stores carry five items: clear plastic sheeting, cellophane, body putty, metal coat hangers, and duct tape.

Some Chicago cars are self-driving cars in the sense that they do their own thing.

39

A Snowflake In Time

Sidewalks are polka-dotted with gum. Lawns are fried in the hot summer sun. Hydrants are locked with steering wheel locks. Graffiti marks territorial corners. A corner store makes it easy with a small white billboard on one side to post the marks – very understanding of the store owner. We park half a block away, the nearest spot. Kids laugh and scream and fight over a garden hose. Mid-air water drops sparkle in the sunshine. The houses have seen better days, but some have a fresh coat of paint. A cat hacks up some crabgrass. Christie's step-sister Salome, in a Peace shirt, is the first to recognize us. Christie stands tall on the edge of sunlight and darkness, wearing blue jeans and a bright white bra that contrasts with her dark brown skin, shimmering in the half sunlight. She is a stark contrast to the wide-eyed skinny kid I met so many snowfalls ago. Gawky Christie is all grown up.

"Would you look at what the cat just hacked up?" Salome says in my direction. I look at Hope. "I'm not talking about her. I'm talking about you."

Hope dashes into Christie's arms, leaving Salome to pick on me. "Huh," Salome says. "Have you been on a farm?" Leave it to Salome to find the remaining speck of Wisconsin hay. I pick it off. "Don't drop your hay anywhere you like. Do you think we want to see your hay here?" She smirks with attitude.

"Look at you!" Hope and Christie both say to the other. People look out of windows and step out onto porches to see what the commotion is about.

"This is the guy," Salome says to the neighborhood, from about Halsted over to Calumet, "who taught me how to avoid singing the high notes. Huh! I can't tell you how tough it's been trying to unlearn what you taught me." Salome pokes me in the ribs.

"It was just for that one night," I protest. "You were sick. Your voice would've cracked if–"

"She still can't sing straight," a tall man confirms.

Christie is asking Hope how we hooked up. I want to hear, but that's when Salome decides to demonstrate her lack of singing to me. Others give her some background and a beat, enough so that I can't hear Hope and Christie ten feet away. When Salome should hit a high note, she drops an octave to a low note.

One guy points out to another guy, "That's the guy that messed up," only he doesn't say messed up, "Sal's singing."

"He what?"

"She can't sing because of him." Another guy with a jacket muscles in.

I excuse myself. I find my way through the crowd of onlookers to Christie and Hope. "Hi Christie."

"It's good to know that you two are together. It's good to see you," she says with a cooler reception than Hope received. "You aren't ready for me."

"What?"

"Prophet, you aren't ready for me," Christie says stoically.

Even Hope is startled by Christie calling me Prophet and by the way she says it. That's not what everyone used to call me. "That reminds me," Hope says, reaching into her purse. "We have something for you." Hope gives Christie the card with the check inside. Christie thanks us each with a kiss. She introduces us to people left and right and behind and above and takes us into a nearby cedar-closet-smelling house which may be hers, but it doesn't seem like it is. Her attitude toward Hope is all girlie and friendly and holding hands. Everybody likes Hope.

"...these are friends of mine from Minnesota. I can't believe you came all this way!"

"He dreamed this," Hope tells her.

"Listen. Don't chase his dreams, without paying attention to your own. He might be meditating with God, but... follow your dreams too. And take him with you."

And with that, we're left to fend for ourselves.

Or I am anyway. Hope is being shown some sort of recording while I sit on a narrow wooden staircase to one side of the living room of people coming and going. I'm going to have to follow-up on Christie every now and then to see how she's doing. I close my eyes, and I relax.

It's the day after Christmas according to my watch, my closet-sized Christmas tree, and the mess of wrapping paper. The snow outside swirls like mosquitoes. Whose new easel is that? I better not look around too much. I search for news on Christie. There's some old news from September. Oh, my God. She was killed. Who killed her? I recognize this guy, Zacchaeus. What do they know about him? Okay. I open my eyes.

Everyone in the living room is staring at me, including some people in the doorway, most of the rest of the city, and Zacchaeus. Why does he have a jacket? I smile half-heartedly, checking my watch. Salome asks, "Did you dream about me?" I shake my head. "Then can I get by you?" I get up and off the narrow stairs. Then I follow her up, through the door and duck in. In the attic, she stops me from following her saying, "Do you mind? I need a little privacy." I let her use the bathroom alone. I look out the dormer windows through lacy sheer curtains at the one-way street. I accidentally mess up the dust on the sill.

Christmas?!? Christmas was the soonest I could do some checking?!? There are other holidays, and how tough is it to search on someone who is in the news like Christie is?

Hope comes up. "What's going on?"

"I'm waiting for Salome."

"Oh."

"It's all yours," Salome says with a flourish.

"I was waiting for you."

"Ain't that sweet? You are something, you know that?"

"No, I'm something else."

"I had the biggest crush on you, and now you're with her, and you tell me you're waiting for me. You **are** something else." Salome winces. "Don't get puffy. I don't like you anymore."

"Sal, listen, the shooting, I know who did it. He's going to kill Christie next month if we don't stop him."

"**Who!**"

"Zacchaeus. His birthday is March 4th. His full name is–"

"I **know** who he is! Huh! Remember how to do the push over?" I nod. "You're on."

She doesn't give me a chance to explain about messing up the dust. We almost barrel over one of those big old metal fans that could easily slice and dice vegetables and anything else. Downstairs we disperse and Salome starts tapping people, just tapping them for no apparent reason, while I squeeze in behind Zacchaeus. She comes up to him, yells, "**Hey!**" and pushes him over me on all fours. I grab a leg. Sal shouts, "**What's this Zac?!?** A gun?!? We're **non-violent**! Not much of a gun. Why the gun? Why are you shooting people, Zac?" People pile on.

Zacchaeus twists to get out of my hold. My arm scrapes on the stucco wall. What's the point of stucco walls?!? I can't see anything. I'm between him and the wall. The car was more comfortable and less cramped than this. I'm scrunched; my side gets elbowed. I'd check my watch again, except I can't. I can hear plenty of shuffling, stomping, swearing... My ear gets roughly covered. Somebody probably thinks it's too sensitive for the swearing. My arm is wrenched. And then I am getting freed up; others are in control; I can let go. Everyone helps Zacchaeus up. No one helps me up. Hope is talking with Christie. Oops. I bled on their nice stucco wall. How do you clean stucco? I spit on my hand and manage to smear the blood a little, while scraping up my hand. It gets dark around me. I look up to Christie and Hope.

"Heh, sorry about the wall," I apologize and stand up.

"What do we tell the police? They're on their way," Christie says.

Isn't it obvious? "You tell them that you think he did all the shooting last Saturday."

"How do we know that?" she asks. I grunt. Neither of them accept the grunt as a reasonable answer, although it comes naturally enough to me. "Chicago cops don't miss a beat and know when something is fishy or we're holding back. What's the answer?"

"It's like Sal said, you're a non-violent group. He was found with a gun on him."

"Are you willing to talk to the police?"

"For you? Yes, I'll talk to the police." We head outside. I try to look confident, but she's right – I don't know what to tell the police. It's similar to part of the AutoDrive problem. How do I explain myself? Maybe this is a dress rehearsal. Someone gives Christie a shirt. Sal is berating Zac. And I thought she was picking on me earlier. She was just warming up. She is all over his case. If she times this right, he'll break down right when the police arrive. That would be excellent timing. However, here come the police... and the news... they practically carpooled. Wouldn't it be easier if they carpooled?

The Chicago police are cut from the same blue polyester cloth as the police in Minnesota. Many of the men and one woman have the same standard issue mustaches as their northern cousins. They take the gun and have a curbside chat with Zacchaeus, while keeping everyone else away. Advertisement backdrops are put up by the news and taken down by the residents. Salome assists me in redirecting all news questions to an elderly man next door in a rocking chair. We watch the master at work, taking his time to thoroughly answer a question – the antithesis of news clips. Hope is rubbing my shoulder. I call Dan. I let his machine know what happened and tell him we won't be spending the night. I call Cy and let her know that we might be on TV, and we'll call back. Hope calls Becky and tells her almost the exact same thing. Salome takes me over to the police. While we wait for them to get around to me, I pick up bits and pieces of what is going on. Apparently Zacchaeus has a record, but no outstanding warrants. He has a license to carry the gun, but shouldn't have been able to get a license, due to his record.

A cop the size of Cicero steps over in two steps. They couldn't find a mustache to fit him, so he doesn't wear one. Instead, a mole sits on a bump on the bridge of his nose. He asks, "Are you the push over?"

"Yeah, that would be me."

"Sergeant Pulaski," he says as an introduction. He types on a clipboard, while asking for my name, address, and phone number. Trumpets sound. "That's me calling, don't worry about it," he says, taking my picture with his clipboard camera. "Now, do you want people to know about these dreams of yours?"

"Not particularly, no."

"Then here's what you do. Don't talk about 'em." I nod politely as if he's explaining the engineering principles of an oxcart. "My report is going to say that you had a suspicion. You acted on said suspicion. That action led to the revelation of a concealed, licensed handgun." He types. I stand there. Zacchaeus leaves in a squad car. A train thunders by. Pulaski pauses to look up and looks at me, "When I mastered the three syllable word, I made sergeant." He goes back to his typing. I wonder if he's always had the mole on his nose. I suppose the molehill preceded the mountain. That's the way it usually goes. Hope comes over and puts her arm around me. The cop stops, looks at her, smiles, and forgets where he is. "This'll just take a minute more." He watches his clipboard with intensity, like it's playing some Chicago police highlight shows. The show lasts four minutes. He looks up at me and back down at his clipboard. "I'll be right back." He steps through people, talks to two smaller officers, one in plainclothes, and points at me.

"What's that all about?" Hope wonders.

"Everyone wants to share your beauty. You're worth pointing out."

"Very nice, except he's pointing at you."

"Right. He's asking what I did to deserve being with you. You have to learn to read lips."

"I'll try," Hope says, kissing my cheek.

Pulaski steps back. "You're free to go. It was good meeting you." He shakes my hand. I'm sure he always does that. Anyone who says there are no mountains in Chicago, never met Sergeant Pulaski.

"We're free to go," I parrot back to Hope. "Should we? I'll take you to the lake. It's funny. Here, there is only one!"

"Are you sure you want to go? We drove all this way."

"Yeah. You heard what Christie said. I'm not ready." I lead Hope over to a congregation centered on Christie. She turns to us. "We're going now." Not knowing what else to say, I repeat what I told her many years ago, "Remember to eat your vegetables."

"We're about to have supper. You are both," she emphasizes the both, which surprises me, "welcome to join us."

"I don't want to impose. We're going to go."

"Get Sal," Christie tells a kid. He runs and yells. Christie hugs Hope, of course. I get a hug too.

"You sneaking out?" Salome asks me, while hugging Hope. "You aren't supping with us? How are we going to thank you?" Until those last two words, her tone was as belligerent as ever, then her voice cracks.

"I didn't do anything. You are all blessed. The peace you had has been returned. I'm just a messenger."

"So you're going to eat at some fancy restaurant?" Sal's working the guilt machine now.

I laugh. "Fancy restaurant? Let's see. We had lunch at Slather Burgers – ooh Tres Chic. Now we're going to the beach. Dead coho still wash up, right?" Nods of agreement. "Well, that could be dinner."

"Eww," a kid says, and Hope agrees.

I take Hope's hand and turn to go. Sal grabs me and says, "Stay in touch this time, okay?" I agree, and she lets me go.

In the car I turn us around and backtrack to Halsted, which is the long way to 63rd which turns into Hayes, entering Jackson Park. We park easily between the beach and the harbor entrance and walk to the beach, watching tall boats enter the harbor alongside us. The scent of wild onions is carried on the wind. It's cooler by the lake. The beach waves break calmly against the shore. It's cooler **in** the lake. Children kick and scream as they are pulled from the cold water to leave. Seagulls monitor the situation, evaluate it with squawks, and provide janitorial services. The breeze blows back Hope's hair. She breaks our silence and says, "I hope you didn't think that we had to come to the lake. It was just a suggestion." I nod.

"I figured it was time to go. Who cleaned up the cohos?" The gulls act like they don't hear, but they look around for other scraps with pride. "The question is what do we do now?"

"You never seemed too thrilled about staying at Dan's," Hope observes.

"His girlfriend Cathy likes me like Salome likes me, except without the liking me part. She actually can't stand me, says I'm too weird."

"That explains your not wanting to stay with them. But tell me, do you believe what you said about being a messenger?" Getting close to the water, wet sand drips from between my fingers to form little sand pine trees. I notice a line of dead cohos, white feathers, and algae. I back us up and away from the water and stretch out a towel to share. "You brought a good towel?!?" Hope asks.

Yes. Yes, I did. "I couldn't find any of my old ones."

"I stashed them at the back of your closet."

"Oh. Sorry. I didn't know where my towels were." Hope sits down. "I'll buy a new one."

"No, it's okay. So, about being a messenger?"

"Remember when I told Fran I was her guardian angel?"

"Wait. Who?"

"The whole Savior of the Midway thing?"

"Yeah?"

"I've never put limitations on who I am. I am who I need to be. People always need more than what they have, something different or a boost of reassurance or a little help. Sometimes that means I'm a friend, sometimes that means I'm an inventor, or a dreamer, or a guardian angel, or a messenger, or anything else I need to be. At that moment I was a messenger. Now I'm not. I know what I said, and I stand by what I said, but it was only a... snowflake in time." Trumpets squawk like seagulls. "Acapella's Pizza–"

"**Hey!**" Seagulls jump.

My friends are determined to deafen me. "Hi Dan." I hold the phone away.

"**Are you heading out?**"

"Yeah." Hold the phone away.

"**What are your dinner plans?**" The seagulls turn in unison.

"Don't have any. Probably get something on the way." Hold the phone away. The seagulls go back to their beachcombing.

"**I could get you in somewhere!**"

"Hold on a second. Hope, what would you like for dinner?"

"Deep dish pizza."

"You can think about it. Take your time. You don't have to blurt out the first thing that comes to mind."

"**HI HOPE!!!**" Dan yells loud enough to shake the Sears Tower. All the gulls take off from all the beaches on the lake. I didn't have the phone to my ear, and it's ringing.

"Dan. Dan, we're in the same state as you **and** we've got these phone thingies. You don't have to shout."

"Okay," Dan replies.

"Hi Dan," Hope says when the beach stops shaking.

"So she wants deep dish pizza. You're taking US 12 out?" he asks in subdued tones.

"No, we're taking I-90."

"Hmm, let me think a minute." One in every three Chicagoans is a navigational expert. They have to be. "Okay, do you know Sleepy Hollow? It's out by West Dundee."

"Sure, it's legendary."

"Al Capone's is out there."

"He's dead."

"His place is there."

"Capone was from the South Side."

"Yeah, but the owner lives in Sleepy Hollow," Dan replies. You can't beat that logic, unless you are more interested in the name than the pizza. "Are you interested?"

Hope nods for us. "Yes, we are."

"Hold on. I'll call them. Wait. I should pre-order for you, otherwise you could be waiting an hour. What do you want?"

"Pepperoni and mushroom," Hope responds with quiz show speed.

"**I heard that!** Hold on."

While we wait for Dan, we watch a nearby shadow, of a couple sitting close together waiting on a phone, stretch out across the sand. Light dances lightly on the ripples of the water.

"I'm back! You're all set for eight o'clock!"

"Thanks, Dan," we respond.

"Take it easy!"

"You too, Dan." I put away the phone. "Did you know it's a felony for Dan to say the word Fire? Especially around the theater district."

"He doesn't have to be in a theater?"

"Nope."

"It's not even seven yet. What are we going to do until eight? The museums?"

"No, Dan allowed for just enough driving time. We have to go. If you are going to dip your toes, dip them now. I think I see a row of fish lined up waiting to nip your toes as you dip your toes." I help Hope up.

She eyes the fish and says, "I'll pass."

We take our towel and leave a crinkled patch of sand behind. At the car I offer Hope the choice, "Do you want to drive or call Cy?"

"I'll talk to Cy." I hand her my phone as we start up. "Hello, Cy. Were we on TV? They didn't show us?!? We were in the background most of the time. We're heading across Chicago now to a place called West Dundee?"

"Sleepy Hollow," I correct.

"Right, Al Capone's in Sleepy Hollow. And then we're driving back."

"**Tonight?!?**" Cy asks loud enough for me to hear.

"I guess. Not right now, he's driving. Okay, I'll relay. She wants to know if you've considered that deer cross the highway more at night than during the day. He's nodding his head. And have you considered the exhaustion factor? He's nodding his head. How far are we expecting to get?"

"Wisconsin," I state.

"Yeah. Do people want to meet us somewhere? I don't know, I'm wondering what you want to do. Camping? I didn't pack for camping."

The car scrabbles and scrapes through traffic and tall skyscrapers to discover western sky and the sun, setting again.

"So a day trip? Hiking? I'll see what he thinks. He's nodding his head. Yes, it's rattling. I'll contact the others at my house. When we get there, to The Big Woods, we should have a code or something to get us together. What's that? 'Drive vroom-vroom?' Yes, I know what that's from. Okay, drive vroom-vroom will be our code. The NARD will think we're nuts. They'll try to keep us away from the squirrels."

The earlier onslaught of escaping urban traffic littered abandoned autos and auto accessories all around us and our asphalt artery. Airplanes aim to assert themselves into our path in an amazing vertical amalgamation. This close plane's silvery steel undercarriage reflects a funhouse mirror of us and Hope's car. I use the reflection to comb my Lake Michigan wind whipped hair. At the ultimate instant of the merge, our paths diverge. Missing us by a hair, the planes land at O'Hare, while we continue along the thorough-fare.

Hope laughs, "That's a good idea, and we'll bring us. I'll ask him." Hope turns to me, "What time tomorrow will we get to The Big Woods?"

"Let's see. Interstate 90 across the river at the south end of Minnesota, connecting with 52 and cutting over near Zumbrota... I'd say one o'clock." Where do we get off? Now that I've figured out Minnesota tomorrow, maybe I should think about Illinois today.

"And we can bring something..."

Traffic is lighter without the pending doom from above. I exit at 34 and slow down from the blur. I find Capone's. The sign drips tomato sauce. At least I think it's tomato sauce.

"It's dinner time. We gotta go." Hope smacks the phone in the kissing sort of smack.

The thug host attempts a guessing game with us to figure out the name of our reservations. I'm just about to cheat, when a boss waiter smacks the thug upside the head in the non-kissing sort of smack and leads us to a table on stage. At least it seems like we are on stage. We are on a small platform overlooking the other patrons. We are protected from the other patrons with a row of tennis racquets and tommy guns. This is the protection racket.

An agreement ironed out with the boss waiter means we will get our drinks and salads and pizza as soon as we get back from the little mobster's rooms.

As we eat, Hope sends a message to our roommates, and I comment, "You and Christie are lucky. You both know what you want to do, you're good at it, and you're doing it."

Hope chews on that a moment and says, "In a way, so are you. It's just not a profession for you, at least not yet."

When we are finished and ask for a bill, the boss waiter tells us, "Call your loud friend."

"Hey! How was it?"

"Good. Delicious."

"Any complaints?"

"No complaints."

"This one is on me. Tell the waiter 30 percent. And he should have a bag for you," Dan cachinnates.

"He heard. And he's giving us a bag. What's in the bag?"

"Blue Razzle Cheesecake. Two slices, forks..."

"Thank you, Dan. **You're a good man!**"

"You don't have to shout. Have a safe trip."

"Bye!"

We thank Capone's. In the parking lot, Hope heads for the driver's door, saying, "You got us out of Chicago. I'll get us out of Illinois. Just help navigate me back onto 90." She pulls her hair back into a ponytail, fixes the seat, and smiles at me, before starting the car. Back in a blur on I-90, leaving the suburban sprawl of the boonies behind, Hope says, "Close your eyes and dream as much as you want."

I relax and close my eyes.

I fall asleep. And somewhere in my sleep, I am loitering on the sidewalk in front of the Indulgence Hotel, calling 911. I consider weeping, "Just let me talk to AutoDrive. Let me speak to it! It will obey me. For I am its creator. It will listen to me. Please..."

"911 emergencies."

"A car is about to crash into a police car at the corner of Forth and Third, downtown Milltown." There. Simple and succinct.

"Did you say, 'about to crash?'"

"That's right."

"How do you know that?"

"It's a self-driving car."

"Oh, right. A self-driving car."

This isn't going well. "Didn't you hear? They closed off much of the downtown traffic for this. It's call AutoDrive."

"Hold on a moment." Muttering, "There's a guy talking about downtown being closed off for something called AutoDrive? Okay. I'll tell him." Talking to me, "Sir, the only thing going on today is that part of downtown is closed off for something called Flight Control."

"Flight Control and AutoDrive are the same thing. Flight Control is the company that makes AutoDrive, the product." Here it comes.

SMASH-CRASH!

"Never mind."

I turn away. I've seen the crash before. Inside the tinted plate glass windows of the hotel, a complex assortment of luggage is being wheeled across the lobby. Hope suggested I give AutoDrive a simple situation that will make it stop, something it will understand. It's worth a try, I decide.

I'm standing in the middle of Forth. There are 4,000 holes in this plan, not the least of which is that this is a hell of a bet. I'm betting my life that AutoDrive will stop. AutoDrive turns and heads toward me.

40
Signs

Hope shakes me awake. "There's something in the road ahead. Someone is in the road." Our brights are on bright, but the darkness of night and the fog of steamed plants keep things obscure. We're parked on the shoulder.

"Where are we?"

"North of Madison. We passed an exit for Lodi."

"Turn on your hazard lights. I'll be right back."

"I'm coming with!" Hope declares.

Two semi-truck lengths ahead, a strange vehicle has hit a deer, which is partly lying in the middle of our side of the divided interstate highway. It's not dead yet. It's screaming like a little girl, or someone else is. A man stands nearby, watching us and the deer. He has a golf club. Their car is or was a large can of Double Bubble on its side on wheels, only its front end is crushed and leaking oil. Two children are screaming their heads off, something about "**Daddy's killing the deer!**"

Checking my watch, I ask the man, "Did you lose your ball?"

"What? **No!** I'm putting it out of its misery."

"Put away the putter and get out of the road!" I tell the golfer.

"Do you have a phone? Mine was crushed in the glove compartment."

"Yeah, we'll call 911 and set some flares." I call 911 on our way back to Hope's car. I read off a mileage marker on the side of the road and give them the information. It's easy.

"Did you lose your ball!" Hope repeats. "I almost busted out laughing."

"It's not something you see every night." I open up the trunk as a car speeds by. I get out a package of flares and a set of glow sticks. Using the light from the trunk, I read the package of flares, "Hold flare away from body or head. Remove red lid to expose chemical surface on white cap. Twist and remove cap, exposing flare igniter button. See cautions before proceeding. Strike igniter button with chemical surface on cap. Lay lighted flare on pavement."

I ignite a flare, blind us, and set it back several car lengths from Hope's car. I ignite another, walk farther back, and drop it off in such a way that it shouldn't get hit or roll off into the woods. Another car comes, except this one is hitting the brakes. We activate some glow sticks by bending their plastic tubes enough to break a glass vial inside and shake it to mix the chemicals. We drop off a few between our two cars in the middle of the road. As we approach the surreal scene of Double Bubble versus nature, I get out my phone and flash a few pictures. I nudge and point Hope to give glow sticks to the girl and the boy. The deer has moved and now has black rubber skid marks in front of it. It's still moving.

I tell the golfer, "We'll set up some more of these," waving the glow sticks, "and we'll be right back."

A truck pulls over to talk to us. Shouting over the deer, the deer tries to get up, only to flop back down. It smells like its been on the road for a while, then again, so do I.

We drop off some more glow sticks and more traffic slows up and stops to look over the scene. Hope nudges me about something off the right side of the road. Past the tar shoulder and the reflector post and some gravel, down the grassy slope, up the other side of the drainage ditch, in a fence break near the woods, two sets of yellow eyes glow in the light of the stopped traffic. Proportionally they are half the size of the deer that was hit.

"Aw," Hope says. She must have been touched by the proportions. Vehicles line-up. Hope talks with the kids. Wisconsin state troopers arrive. They arrest the deer. The golfer asks us how far we're going, but we aren't going far enough for him. He's trying to meet up with five other cans. I don't know why, but that makes sense.

By the time we leave, the flares and glow sticks have been picked up. The deer is gone. All that's left is a large crushed and discarded Double Bubble can.

This must be the recycling drop off for aluminum cans.

"Wow." Hope laughs, "Did you lose your ball!" She's delirious.

"We'll have to stop soon."

"No kidding. All I've been thinking about is the cheesecake."

"Oh, me too," I kid her.

"You have not!"

"I could feed you..."

Hope sits up straight and runs her hand across her cheek. "You could, couldn't you?"

"I'll get the bag." I feed her past Baraboo, while watching for deer. They will be seeking revenge but will be forever spooked by pop cans. I tell Hope that, and she can't stop laughing. I put away the cheesecake.

"Hey! Did I finish?"

"Yes, you finished. But you have some of your slice of cheesecake left. I have to figure a place to put you to bed."

"You men are all alike." I get out my phone, its map glows in the dark car, and I search on Wisconsin Dills lodging for tonight. "I was kidding, you know. You aren't like other men."

"I know. Don't worry. I'm looking for a place in Wisconsin Dills."

"Are you kidding?" Hope asks.

"No."

"Have you ever been to the Wisconsin Dills?"

"No."

"I didn't think so, or you'd know that it's the Wisconsin Dells. It has nothing to do with pickles." She stares at the dark road ahead and says, "It is a summer weekend, and it's late; there is no way we can get in anywhere at Wisconsin Dells. Wisconsin Dells is a family getaway halfway between Chicago and the Twin Cities. They have several water parks. It will be packed, evenly packed. They're very organized at Wisconsin Dells. Did you know that a family can be kicked out of the whole area? Just because of a few brothers... What else is there?"

"Is Lyndon Station a family getaway?"

"No."

"I just sent a message to the Dew Drop Inn at Lyndon Station. There's also the Duck Inn, practically next door to the Dew Drop Inn." The phone lights up. "Hey, the Dew Drop Inn says they were just about to close up for the night. They're asking how soon we can be there." I check the distance and our speed. "We should be there in ten minutes." I send the message. They reply. "They will wait for us."

At the Dew Drop Inn a convention of small flies meets under the lights of the parking lot. We dodge them and get a room. I carry up my backpack and Hope's two duffel bags. Flopping in the room, I'm giving Hope a back rub when she asks, "Why didn't you want to stay around Christie's?"

That was hours ago and hundreds of miles ago. We were in another state. "She said I wasn't ready for her, that's not exactly a welcome."

"But she did invite us to stay and eat with them."

"I didn't want to overstay my welcome." My voice cracks, so I take a drink of water.

Hope props herself up on her elbows. "Whoa. Overstay your welcome? We just got there. How could you have overstayed your welcome?"

"Easily. We just dropped in. We weren't invited. She never kept in touch. The clock was ticking. Even when you are invited, the clock is ticking. Dan invited us to his place, but Cathy O'Leary doesn't like me, never has. She doesn't have to like her boyfriend's friends. The clock would've definitely been ticking. It always is."

Hope stares at her pillow and then turns to me. "Does that apply to your staying at the duplex as well? Are you concerned about overstaying your welcome?" I slowly nod. "So it was easy to decide to move in, because you figured you'd leave once you'd overstayed your welcome." Before I can reply she continues, "And it was easy deciding to move out when you had trouble with Faith, because the clock is ticking?"

"No, it wasn't easy deciding to move in. I first had to make sure that I wanted to be with you, but that didn't take long at all. But yes, I have been watching for signs from you or your roommates that I have overstayed my welcome."

"You're impossible..." Hope holds up her hand, "I didn't mean that the way it sounded. You're impossible in the sense that I have never met anyone like you. You are a better good guy than any guy I've known. I don't want us to break up, but even if we did, I would still want to be friends. I don't know where this comes from, but–" She goes to a desk, takes out a piece of paper, and folds and tears a rectangle. She writes on it. She hands it to me.

It says, "Indefinite stay certificate. The clock has stopped."

"I have been on my own for a long time. A long time. I had to come up with my own ways of making decisions, and my own ways to not become a burden to the nice people in the world, who would take me in from time to time."

Hope is crying into her hand. "You have a place with me. You don't have to wonder if you need to go away. My house is our house. You don't have to be alone. I love you. Don't let me go."

"I love you too. I'm an experienced traveler. I don't know much about staying." I hold her, she starts to say something, but instead she falls asleep in my arms. I never meant to hurt her. I never meant to make her cry. She drove us out of Illinois and through nearly half of Wisconsin. Without a stop. Or at least I think it was without a stop. I picture her inside a truck stop having a cup of java and laughing with the truck drivers while across the place and through the gimmick license plate holders and souvenir shot glasses and out the window, out into the parking lot, under the giant arc lamps where bats swoop through to pick off a pound of spiraling bugs in one pass, her car sits, with me in a mix of sleep and pointed perception.

I have a few bites of cheesecake – too rich for my blood. I set back the container with my free arm, shut out the light, one of them anyway, and I relax.

Here comes AutoDrive. I'm standing in the middle of Forth. And I think of Hope telling me not to let her go. I'm not going to hurt Hope by putting AutoDrive in front of my life. I step out of AutoDrive's way and back to the sidewalk. I'll have to come up with some other simple thing to put in front of AutoDrive.

AutoDrive crashes.

A stop sign is the natural object to stop AutoDrive. I always carry around a stop sign. Doesn't everyone? It's a protest sign... a very non-specific protest sign. Where would I go to buy a stop sign? Flight Control could order from some places that an individual can't. I lean against the Indulgence Hotel and check my phone. It gives me suggestions on stealing stop signs; it needs a morality lesson. Further checks yield a restoration yard that has all the right signs. I could stop over there, but I call first. They say they will permit me to buy the sign, but I need a permit to leave with it. That's not going to help. No one is going to issue a permit for a sign in the middle of Forth; it would impede progress.

I could make a stop sign. It would need all the modern reflective properties of any other stop sign, since AutoDrive was trained on real stop signs. I think I could make an accurate stop sign. I would take a tracing of a real one to get all the proper measurements. That wouldn't look suspicious. People are always tracing signs. The more I think about it, the more I think that a stop sign is not the right answer. How would I happen to be carrying it? How would I post it without endangering myself? Hang it down from a skyway? Oddly enough, a stop sign doesn't seem to be the simplest way to stop AutoDrive.

Maybe hot asphalt.

Or glue, which reminds me, we'll have to wash Hope's car or at least the windshield.

Or a speed bump. Which is worse – AutoDrive or an airborne AutoDrive?

Maybe a life-sized cut-out of me is the answer. Unlike a stop sign, what's someone going to do, come up to me and ask, "Excuse me, where do you think you're going with you?" I'd say, "I'm just walking around with myself, minding our own business. My friend here is feeling a little run down. But I think he's the picture of health."

I sit down on the sidewalk to call around to a few photo finishing places to see how soon I could be ready. They all say I'd have to allow three weeks. That's not going to work. Maybe Gene could clone me. I put away the phone and notice Cooelle standing on a discarded piece of newspaper, gaping at me. I wake up.

I use my fork to poke the digital clock so I can see the time. My movement wakes Hope. We get up. I act like my arm is permanently stuck straight out from having been under her all night. She tries to lower it but can't. She bops me with a pillow.

"One pillow? I laugh at one pillow. I'm used to more than just one pillow. And this is no Indulgence Hotel. You can't just order up a flock of flocking penguins to do your bidding."

She bops me continually with the pillow, and my arm remains stiff and lifeless until we climb into the shower together. Otherwise it would've been awkward. We thoroughly enjoy our shower.

The lobby provides us with juice and yogurt, cereal and toast, bananas and small sealed cups of jelly. We take our places amongst our fellow travelers. The alertness of the group ranges from high caffeine to a low caffeine sleeplessness. Some teenagers are traveling to play volleyball. I explain that I've traveled to play group round robin ping-pong. A mother asks me if I was on a team. I respond, "Yes, but it was a Capture The Flag team, so we didn't take our ping-pong very seriously." She's confused. Some people are here for the Wisconsin Dells. They correct me that it has nothing to do with dills. One family from Indiana says they are on their way to see the Prospective Tower in Pigs Eye. I blush and say nothing. When it comes out that we're from Pigs Eye and have been to Prospective Park, even their children are now interested. Questions are thrown at us like pillows.

Life is like a tightrope, a balancing act at a cheesy tourist trap circus, where you may amaze the crowd with your performance, but you have three to five shows a day.

Aware of Hope's attention next to me, I tell them, "Prospective Tower is an inland lighthouse, a pharos, a watchtower, built around the time of the Mississippi River paddleboats, midway between Milltown and Pigs Eye. In a way, it's like any other place. Grass lawns and giant oaks cover the hill around the tower. Eagles have nested there. There are plenty of places like it."

I tell them that, "There is a spirit there that's different, or at least it was when we were there. People stopped to think about... what's important to them and for a moment forgot about the things that aren't important. They spoke in soft voices about the stories of what happened or what might have happened.

Ultimately it's not the place that's special so much as who you are when you're there. And who you take with you."

Just as I'm starting to suck jelly directly out of its plastic package, they show us a picture from the Internet of the hillside of lit candles. Hope practically spits out her orange juice to say, "Those were our candles!"

I explain that if that picture was from two weeks ago last night, we handed out the candles. "The Pigs Idea used a similar picture." Then I suck jelly.

I don't instill a lot of confidence, but Hope helps... when she's not fountaining orange juice. Hope laughs at my sucking jelly and soon all the kids in the lobby are doing it. Hope tries it. Parents are torn between stopping their children and trying it themselves. Everyone notices us leave.

At the Lyndon Station, we fill the car up with fuel and take it through the car wash. We exchange our warm bottled water for the cold stuff. Hope helps me check traffic as I merge back onto the highway. We're 220 miles from Milltown according to a sign, which means we're about 200 miles from Chicago. The sign will be wrong about the 220 miles. Hope talks about the people at breakfast and sucking jelly, and she reminds me of what she said last night about the fact that her house is our house. She offers to put my name on the deed. I decline. We pass Mauston and the rock skyscrapers of Camp Douglas again and the turnoff for Interstate 90.

"Aren't we supposed to take 90?" Hope asks.

"We will."

"We just passed it."

"I know."

Hope fidgets. "Could I look at the pictures you took of the accident last night?" I hand her my phone. "One of these, the one that has the can taking up most of the frame and the deer in front of it, is very dramatic. You know who would like this? Ruth. Could I send her a copy?" I nod. "I'll send it from you to me and then from me to her. Is that okay?"

"That stinks. Someone lost a skunk." I shake off the smell. "Yeah, it's fine. You can pass it around."

"I'm sending it to our house. You know what? I'm going to send it to everyone. I'm still wondering where we're going."

The sunlight flickers through the forest, a light echo bouncing around the trees.

"Are you ready for a rest area?" I ask while turning off.

"Actually I am," she says, reaching for her sandals.

"You might want hiking shoes."

"I didn't bring hiking shoes."

While Hope is in the bathroom, I read an industrial advertisement masquerading as an hysterical marker. It says that the Black River Forest Valley once had pine trees with six foot base diameters. Paul Bunyan swung his giant ax across Wisconsin, leveling the forest in one fell swoop, before breakfast, making way for a taconite processing plant run by a subsidiary of Itsa Steel.

Hope returns and reads the sign with me. The next sign says You Are Here and has a giant arrow above us, pointed at us. Hope takes my picture with the sign.

The next sign is dedicated to the emergency services personnel of Wisconsin, who have seen everything, except maybe an accident involving a pop can and a deer. I look at Hope. She looks at me.

The next sign, on the other side of the parking lot, says that the forest grew back after a hundred years. The trees weren't hundreds of years old yet but were regaining their footholds. The sign then takes us back to the afternoon of April 27, 1977, when a fire burned 17,590 acres of forest, crossing Interstate 94 twice, and burning a dozen homes. No one knows how it started, but the sign has an arm reaching out a car window, about to flick away a smoldering cigarette butt.

The next sign edges us up a hill.

"They had to cut down all the trees to make all these signs."

The sign explains that this Bell Mound is actually a kane, a glacial rock pile, dumped through a hole in the ice to create a scenic overlook that's worth the climb for the adventurous. There's some fine print at the bottom of the sign that mentions that it's like a 20 or 30 story building without an elevator, plopped down in the middle of the recovering forest. The sign refers to an earlier sign for details about Wisconsin's top-notch emergency services.

A man shuffles down saying, "I read all that on the Internet." What an icehole.

"Are you ready?" Hope nods and looks at her hiking sandals. The forest takes us in and shelters us from the sun. White barked aspen and rough barked oak trees provide quiet from the roaring stream of highway traffic. A cool breeze blows through the trees. Birds flit around above us and beside us, calling out descriptions of us and our measurements, across the forest slope. Our tar path twists and turns and re-joins an earlier path from where the rest area used to be. The kane is a long strangely-uniform, north-south hill, perpendicular to the westbound side of the interstate, with its peak at the north end. The rest area had been between the kane and the interstate, but the rest area was moved west. Now it's a west area.

Along the old rest area path an abandoned sign, covered in creepers and vines, welcomes us to this Menomonie place of worship. Even the Ho-Chunk and the Kickapoo are welcome here. No fighting. From here, you can see the curve of the ground. From here, you can make connections. From here, you see the herd. From here, stones fall. Some fine print says to remember when throwing stones, what it is like being under them when they are thrown.

The birds down below are squawking up a storm of measurements.

Up the tar and boulder stepped trail, the trees step away from their embrace to reveal a hazy humid sky. I stand on a boulder at the top of the mound. Hope takes my picture. "Nice view," she says. I kiss her with every lip on the hill. This is romantic. I get bolder and pull her up with me. Her bracelet catches the light and reflects colored light in all directions, like a lighthouse of prisms, shining across Wisconsin.

This is where the volleyball team finds us. They take our picture with their cameras and ours. "You know all the cool places, don't you?" one of them asks, as they look all around, some trying to give us our privacy, some oblivious to it. They admire Hope's bracelet.

It gets confusing when they ask where we're going, and I try to explain that I purposefully missed the turnoff for Interstate 90 in order to bring Hope here. "I think I understand," one of them says as her eyebrows bounce up and down like rapidly dribbled volleyballs. "If you two want to get all lovey-dovey, we **promise** not to peek." Contagious giggles, Gigglitis, spreads across the hilltop. We say good-bye, but they follow us down anyway, some of them running ahead as if they can't control their decent.

I call after them, "Hit the brakes! Hit the brakes!" Some of the giraffes of the team take it slower, saying they feel the downward pressure in their knees. In the parking lot, we say good-bye again and get back on the highway. At Black River Falls we turn around to head back. Just past Tomah, just past water-logged fields with red dots floating in them, we take the Interstate 90 exit.

"Were you planning all along to go to that rest area?"

"No, it's just that we needed something to do to stall us because **somebody** drove farther than I expected yesterday."

"You didn't foresee that one, did you? Well, we could've slept in." My arm springs out. "Not that again!" Hope lowers my arm. "Did you know the volleyball players were going to be there?" I shake my head. "Did you see the girl flash the countryside?"

"With her camera? Who needs a flash outside in such bright light?"

"No, she flashed the countryside." Hope lifts her shirt for emphasis. I struggle to regain control of the car. "Sorry."

"I didn't see her."

"I guess I was supposed to tell you. She was keeping an eye on you."

"I don't get that. Why would someone flash herself while watching me but not so that I could see her?"

Hope laughs, "She's being daring I guess... They liked you."

Flashing behind me or something is a sign of affection? Since when? "I think they thought I was more interesting than a hotel lobby or a rest stop. That's not the same as actually liking me. It's grading on a curve."

"What if you had a fancy sports car? Something from Italy. Maybe then you would have an ego, especially if the car came with the ego options package. Uh-oh, Rudolph crossing." She points out the sign. She turns on the radio.

The song finishes. "This is WLC radio for west-central Wisconsin and La Crosse, the Love Channel, with nothing but love songs. Think you forgot that special someone that's gone? That relationship that died before it could live? Neither did we. Good morning, everybody. That was Love Emission by Spooge, another song to listen to with the car running and the garage door closed. Hey, I'm just kidding people! You don't want to miss our afternoon long tribute to love screams. Here's one that almost made the list. This is Slipped Apart."

Hope turns off the radio. "Yikes," she says. "Now I know why it's called La Crosse instead of La Pleasant Disposition. So let's say AutoDrive is all done. What would you like to do next? Hey! Look at the cows!"

"I'm not falling for that again." I drink some water and start Hope's automated massage. She turns it back off, as a pack of motorcyclists peer in our windows.

"Are we there yet?" Hope asks.

"If you check the map, you'll see, we're just inches away."

Wisconsin falls away to the valley of Onalaska and La Crosse. We cross the Mississippi River at La Crosse. River sparkles are interrupted by boats frozen in my brief glance away from driving. "Welcome to Minnesota," we tell each other. The interstate hugs the river for a half dozen miles along the edge of Minnesota before climbing the bluff straight into the state. Right at that upward bend, we watch an eagle, a bald eagle, spiraling down into the pavement on our side of the highway. A truck moves to block traffic. I signal the motorcyclists to slow up. I get out. Guys are moving to restrain the eagle and detach its collar. I say something like that it's great they're taking the collar off.

One of the guys laughs, "No, we aren't taking it off exactly. More like replacing it. That's a Wisconsin State collar. We're putting on a Minnesota State collar."

Another guy says, "Sub-dermal too. I need a sub-dermal extractor."

I go back to the car, check my watch, and ask Hope at her window, "Got a golf club?"

"For the eagle?!?"

"No, those guys are replacing a Wisconsin collar with a Minnesota collar. Could you call the state troopers?" A group of motorcyclists are approaching. I tell them what's going on. One is a Wisconsin State professor of something other than engineering, office political science, maybe. I mention something about the national eagle, on each emblem and flagpole, wearing a collar. My comment, coupled with the rising temperature, turns the group, including at least two retired couples, into an angry mob. Never mess with symbols. Never mess with retired people.

The group mobs the scientists. The eagle smiles in its tranquilized stupor, as collars are fitted for the biologists. The Minnesota troopers arrive. The culprits are identified via radio signals. The bald eagle is free to go without accessories. The bird staggers off the road to sit out its headache at the base of the rocky cliff. The truck is moved out of the way and those of us at the front clear out, freeing a long line of traffic.

Hope says, "I think you may become a protector of roadside wildlife."

Our band of traffic spreads out. "I can think of worse jobs."

"Do you think you'd be happy doing something like that?"

"I liked Flight Control, but was I happy working 12 hour days and sleepless nights on AutoDrive? I'm not sure I'm looking for a happy job. It's work after all." I take what Highway 52 deals me.

"Right. Happy in an overall sense, happy in a doing good sense, not in a joyously gleeful sense, because we wouldn't want you grinning that much," Hope grins. "Turn off here, please." I turn off, and Hope giggles. For some reason she wants us to stop off in downtown Rochester, Minnesota. A body shop offers a special on tire rotation. Isn't that what I've been doing? Tire rotation? "Turn left at the light," Hope points. "Okay, there it is," She points to the left. "The Mayo Clinic."

"That's no clinic. That's too big to be a clinic. That's a clinic like Minnesota is moist." I keep driving. The Mayo Clinic is the hospital of possibilities, for the world's tough cases, when other doctors shake their heads gloomily.

"Do you think you could pull over there?"

"For the Mayo?"

"No, that store." I park the car, and we go into a clothes store. "I have Chicago clothes, so I'm looking for camping clothes."

"Can I just wear what I'm wearing?"

Hope looks me over and kisses me. I guess that's an answer. We look around the store. It sells hospital scrubs and nurses' uniforms. It sells backless nightgowns. It sells robes. We leave there and enter a larger store around the corner. They have more of the same. Driving several blocks, we find a Canoe Store, but their clothes section is just like the other two stores. I take Hope's hand and take her out of Rochester. I scan small towns for clothes stores. We stop at the town of Zumbrota in the Zumbrota Valley on the banks of the Zumbrota River. Hope buys khaki shorts, socks, hiking sneakers, and a Zumbrota T-shirt featuring the Zumbrota Covered Bridge. I close my eyes for a moment. I buy a moon pie maker and ingredients, a flashlight, and I pick out a flannel shirt for Hope. She loves it. We pick up water, sandwiches, peanuts, and a large bag of local apples. I remind Hope that we agreed to one o'clock. It's now one o'clock, and we're not there.

We leave Zumbrota on Highway 60. The prairie grasses tan in the summer sun. Hope changes along the way, flashing people in Wanamingo, Bombay, and Kenyon. As she tries to cut off clothes tags without a scissors, I ask, "If you don't put enough postage on your package of lima beans for Bombay, India, you know Mumbai, does the post office send the package to Bombay, Minnesota instead?"

"I don't think it works that way," she says while twisting around, showing off her ribs. I tickle them. She jumps. "Stop that." I play innocent, but she doesn't buy it. We take 56 to 246 to 29 and into Big Woods State Park, also known as Nerstrand. I stop in at the NARD office, a wood building with a stop sign, sitting in the middle of an open prairie.

I nod and say, "Hi." The two rangers look apprehensively at me like they are already having a tough time keeping track of the strange behavior of the day. I fake like I'm looking at their guidebook to Snowshoeing The Park, waiting for some other people to leave. Once they're gone, I decide I'm not going to keep them waiting any longer. I whisper surreptitiously, "Drive vroom-vroom."

"We wondered if you might be part of that group. Your group has our two largest group spots. How many people and how many vehicles do you have?"

"Two people. One vehicle." I pay the money. Hope comes in. She cropped her shirt somehow without a scissors. The ranger gets confused and nearly hands me back my money. Another ranger steps in with a map to show us how we navigate a simple path to our group's spots. They give us a tag to put on the windshield of the car. They ask us if there's anything else we need, or if we can hint to them how many more of us are coming. We decline. On our way, Hope points out the wildflowers highlighting the field. A robin calls out, birdie-birdie-birdie. We drive over to our campsite, the woods closing in on our path. The campgrounds look full. A speed limit sign keeps us down to five miles per hour, so that we can identify each plant and wave to all the campers on our way in. I point out the three foot tall wood posts along the drive, "Do you see all these posts? They're telephone poles that were pounded too far in."

"Don't tell me. Paul Bunyan drove those in," Hope says.

"Paul Bunyan? No. Paul Bunyan never knew this place existed. As he looked around to make sure he'd cleared the entire state, this was in the shadow of his ax."

The cracked and uneven tar road takes us to a small gravel driveway and parking area for our group's camping spots. I park next to Ruth's truck. We get out and stretch. Nadine waves to us, while standing and talking with some mesmerized campers. Ruth smiles and takes our picture. Cy checks her watch without smiling. Joe is looking through binoculars with his mouth. Erix is looking up the same tree. With sleeves rolled up, Stephanie unloads logs. Tom and Becky share a hammock and are playing some music. Todd is trying to explain something to Jake, who is absently running into me, front shoulder to front shoulder, without a reason. Al is trying to put up a huge tent. I go over to help him. It looks even larger close up.

"Who's tent is this?"

"Uh, Ruth's."

"Ruth?!?" I call back to where she's talking with Hope. "You don't go camping with a circus tent." Snickers come from nearby trees.

"You don't?"

"No." A mosquito lands on my arm to get a closer look at the tent. I whack it. It gasps and does a barrel roll off my arm to drop onto the flat tent below me. A swarm of hovering mosquitoes holds up tiny score cards for the dive. It was better than that, but maybe they saw a tiny detail that I overlooked.

"I think this is the mast," Al says.

"The main mast? For the sails? I don't think so. If there is a pole in the middle, it should have a cap on it, so it doesn't go through the deck, I mean, the floor of the tent." Ruth is taking pictures of us and our audience swarm. "Ruth, does it have a pole in the middle?" We all turn to Ruth. She shrugs. I look below, "Does it have a drop cloth?"

Al says, "That's already covered." He leaves the poles to me and starts staking out the edges. The ground is a mix of sand, soil, and ash from a thousand campfires. Without having rain for a while, the ground is very dry and very hard. Al breaks a few plastic stakes before switching to only metal ones. The poles make less sense. Do these all belong to the same tent?

Hope and Cy come over, followed by Todd and Jake. Ruth announces, "Jake went to the dentist yesterday: two fillings, no Novocaine."

"Novocaine is for pussies," Jake responds, flexing his arm in front of Hope.

Hope squeezes his biceps and pats him saying, "Work on it."

Jake leans in to tell me, "You're slipping. You used to always plan stuff for the same day as my dental visits. You blew it this time."

I tell him, "You visit the dentist so often, you're used to the pain."

"I don't feel the pain."

The swarm eulogizes their fallen sister.

Looking at the poles and the shape of the tent, I analyze, "There aren't that many tent shapes. I think this one is car shaped..."

"You would," Jake comments.

"...with a higher middle than the two sides. This isn't a sleeping tent. This is a parking garage tent for all our vehicles." More snickers from the trees. "I was wondering what the ramp was for."

"This gizmo dispenses tickets," Al says.

"It does not," Ruth denies.

I ask Al, "Are you sure there is enough clearance at this spot?"

"Maybe we'll need a flashing light on top to warn low flying planes."

I ask Ruth, "Who's sleeping in this?"

"Anyone who wants to. Anyone who's spending the night." Hope didn't buy camping clothes for tomorrow.

"Listen," Joe says, "I want to tell you. Minnesota State Parks are like public places, so you can't have visible alcohol."

"You already told us," Jake says.

"I didn't tell them," Joe sloshes his binoculars in my direction.

Jake points at me, "He probably remembers the rules from ten years ago, right?" I nod, while Erix taps Hope on the shoulder.

"What's that bird?" he quietly asks.

Stephanie notices and comes over, asking me, "Need help?"

"Yeah, take one of those poles that looks like this, and do like I'm doing."

"Are you sure about this?"

"No."

"Does this– ?"

"Does this what?"

"Wait," Al says. "These two clip together in a circle."

"A circle?!?" We all look over at Ruth who is taking a picture of an upside-down light-blue bird that Erix is pointing at, as it walks head first down the side of an oak tree.

"I think it's a type of nuthatch," Hope says.

"A circle wouldn't make any sense," I tell them. "A circle would collect water. Unless..." A 40 watt light bulb blinks on over my head. "Unless all these other poles could be the same length." If a squeaky toy could giggle, that's the sound the nuthatch makes.

We reassemble the poles. Between all of us and our coordinated effort, the tent rises. It is a cross between a tepee and an igloo. It is tall and tan with a rounded top. It is very large. From the hammock Tom says, "It looks like a giant mosquito bite."

Coming over with the hiccups, Nadine says, "I think it looks like something else." Cy reprimands her. Nadine responds, "I didn't say what I was thinking. You're the one with the dirty mind."

"You didn't have to say what you were thinking. It's what you're always thinking."

While they argue about whose mind is more unsanitary, Al and I devise a winch and pulley system to get the nylon canopy over the top. Sharing two hammers, we stake down the tarp.

I hit Jake. "What was that for?"

"There was a mosquito on you."

"I think I see a mosquito on you," he says. I dash away to a cooler. It has ice, several beer canteens with duct tape covering the labels, more fake binoculars, fake logs with straws, a propane lantern that probably isn't a propane lantern because they don't normally need to be kept on ice, a plastic chipmunk, and a

12-pack of flashlights. "Is this your cooler?" I ask Joe.

"Yes, it is," he answers with pride.

"Could I have a flashlight?" I ask, noticing the plentiful, afternoon, ambient light.

"Go for it." I take a drink from the flashlight and almost back into a deer. "Careful with that," Joe says. "That's mine too."

Cy pulls me away, "We're trying not to encourage him."

"What? This is just a flashlight. An ice cold, frothy flashlight. Refreshing."

She takes my flashlight away and asks me to take a lawn chair. We set up lawn chairs around Becky and Tom, who are on a freestanding, tubular-framed hammock. Ruth and Stephanie encourage Erix to join us; he steps closer but doesn't sit down. Cy gives me back my flashlight... my flask light.

Hope sits down by me and starts doing something with her hair. Wow, she's sexy. I ask Cy, "Who else is coming?" A mosquito lands on my thigh and unfolds a minuscule lawn chair. She sits down. She leans over the little armrest to take a drink from my leg, and I flick her away.

"This is probably everyone. Mica says she's allergic to state parks."

"I believe her."

"Gene wanted your help doing something at the state fair. I think he asked Lefty instead. Will is waiting around for Wendy. And Minion is still mad about the toe tag."

"What about Ray?"

"He declined. He didn't say why. Neither did Faith. And I never heard from Nicole."

Hope interjects, "Nicole is modeling in New York."

"Oooo," responds much of the group and maybe an owl or two.

"How's Christie?" Jake asks.

"She's... good. She's certainly grown up. Salome has too."

"Who?"

"Sally. Remember little Sally? She's a grown-up now. But the difference in Christie... Maybe you didn't notice it," I tell Hope, "because you knew her later, but she's absolutely found her place... no, she's made her place and is so purely committed to her people. It's weird when someone younger than you, so thoroughly surpasses you."

"I did that to you a long time ago," Jake says. Erix passes by.

"You aren't that much younger than I am."

"Did you notice? He's not going to even comment on the surpassing part," Tom points out. "So we heard there was a mercenary in her group."

"A mercenary? Zacchaeus? I don't think so. He was too much of a pushover to be a mercenary."

"That's what the news is saying. He's not just a mercenary; he's a freelance mercenary." I think about what Tom is saying, and it implies that Christie is not as safe as I thought she was. "Did you have anything to do with his discovery?"

Hope practically spits out her water. She nods her head. We're all looking at her.

"You're going to have to work on that poker face," I respond, wiping my leg. "Yes, I identified him, and Salome and I took him down, literally." Jake's attention is riveted. Erix paces.

Todd says, "You can't just leave us hanging with that. What happened?"

"I crouched behind Zac – Zacchaeus and Sal pushed him over me–"

"I remember! She always did that!" She hasn't grown up as much as you think," Jake interjects. "She was always pushy."

"I held him. Others held him. And Salome took his gun away."

"You've had a helluva week with guns," Becky says.

Cy ping-pongs her stares between Becky and I. "Guns?!? Plural?!? What other guns have you been dealing with?" Way to go, Becky.

"Forget Novocaine," Stephanie says, "guns are for pussies."

"I think Becky is confusing..." I respond slowly and deliberately, "...the fake guns of places like the Wabasha Cave in Pigs Eye or Al Capone's outside of Chicago with the real gun that Zacchaeus had."

Hope slaps my back. "You had a mosquito on you." Jake thanks her.

"You might as well tell that story too," Cy says to Becky.

"Wait," Al says. "How did you know the gunman was nearby?"

"I saw it in a dream."

"Pointed perception," Becky clarifies.

"How could you see something happen that you weren't there for?"

"I didn't. I read about it afterwards."

"Before wards," Nadine corrects. Thanks, Nadine.

"Did you happen to read anything about the World Series?" Jake asks. I shake my head. Jake snaps his fingers in disappointment. Erix snaps his fingers too.

Ruth says, "You saved her life. Probably. I'm impressed."

"We're all impressed," Cy corrects, "but what's this story about another gun."

Becky is looking at me like I'm supposed to finish telling the story she already blurted out. I barely managed to rescue her from breaking through the ice of a frozen lake, and now she wants me to take the short way across the lake. A mosquito gets in my face. I bat it away. Cy gets in my face, her brown hair falling forward like blinders on a horse. I can't just bat her away, can I? "Hope? A little help." Hope sets her drink on the ground and backs Cy away.

Cy turns to Hope, "Another gun?"

"It's resolved. Let it go."

Erix is standing beside me. He's covered in mosquitoes. "Erix!" I shake loose his shirt to interrupt half of the air leeches. Hope and I brush him down while I call, "Bug spray!" Realtor mosquitoes lead displaced mosquitoes over to me. I bat them off me and out of the air.

Stephanie scoffs at Nadine's bug spray and uses her own Boundary Waters proven bug spray on Erix. "Tilt your chin up," she tells him as she sprays his chest and neck. "Next," she says, pulling me to my feet, and spraying me with more air leech repellent.

"Whoa there, Fire Fighter Francine, save your spray for some of the other fires," I tell her. Stephanie sporadically sprays some others. Swarms separate in confusion.

Leaving Tom and Becky behind, you know, to watch the campsite, we head for a trail into the Prairie Creek valley. The trail twists and turns down the humid woody hillside of oaks and aspens, elms and ashes, maples and basswood. Birds flit high in the trees to announce our presence. Wood beams mark the trail edges, providing a gentle separation between us and the rest of nature. A mosquito crosses the line, and I bat it back in bounds.

This is good, being in the middle of the group. After being on the road so much the past 36 hours and putting trust in other drivers, strangers, it's good to be amongst a group of friends. It's good to trust them to lead our way. They go to it like mosquitoes to Erix. It's good that they care. And it's good that I'm not the weirdest one in the group. Or at least it's good that I don't think I am.

While Hope is distracted with looking at something, possibly an invisible cow, Cy pleads with pursed lips and fawning eyes, "I really want to know."

"It's okay," I tell her. "Everyone is all right. I made a promise to a friend, not to tell. And it's not Hope. There's nothing to worry about." I pat her on the arm and try not to give away that Hope is sneaking up on Cy from behind. Hope tickles Cy in the ribs. Cy tries to stop, drop, and roll, and she gets mixed up in the dirt of the trail. We help her up and brush her off, and Hope tickles her again.

While Jake watches and takes notes, Hope asks Cy, "Are you satisfied?" She helps Cy up.

Cy agrees, looks at a dampness at her knees, and says, "Someone's been blessing the trail." We all look ahead to see Joe spilling his binoculars, while looking with Erix and Stephanie at some ferns or something in the ferns. We catch up. They ask what it is. We should have Gene and Lefty here to collect samples and conduct analysis. Most of us agree that it's a weird bright orange fungus growing on a gray rock.

Jake disagrees. "I think it's an artificial cheese spread," he says.

Again, it's good that I'm not the weirdest one.

Continuing down the trail, Nadine asks from behind me, "What made you decide to look into the future at Christie's?"

Looking back at her, I see something and stop her from running into me. "Erix, don't taste it! It's not cheese." I wave to him to catch up with us. While we wait... we are all waiting for Erix... I tell her, "Nothing else was going on. I wasn't doing anything."

"That's it?!?"

"Well no, not exactly. Nothing was going on, so I got to thinking about Christie and worrying about her. I decided that I would try to check up on her every now and then."

Cy looks like she forgot to exhale. She's about to burst. "I must have missed something," Cy determines. "Where was Christie?"

"In a crowd in front of me in the living room of a house we were in. I didn't mean that I was looking for her. What I meant was that I decided I'd use pointed perception to check on Christie, later." Nadine and Cy talk at once, both confused, and I work to untangle their simultaneous questions, while Todd is helping the ladies over a log. "What?"

"What did you see?"

"A news story on my phone." Now that I recall it, I realize that the phone will be slightly different, an updated model from my current one. "I had to flip through several news stories to get enough details about... about what Zacchaeus did. Hey Joe, is this a light beer?" Joe ponders that for too long, forgets what he was pondering, and stumbles away. "Watch your step."

The trail levels off, swings way to the left and back again, probably avoiding the breeding ground of some rare lily. A chipmunk darts down a log, turns and looks at us, and high-tails it out of here. The green canopy overhead opens up to light a fast moving stream weaving around over and under boulders like braided hair. It's a braided stream.

Ruth looks back the way we came. "Do we have to climb back up that?"

"Not right away," Jake replies.

"How are the fillings?"

"Great. They've got built-in chips. One more filling and I'll have a complete radio."

Sitting down on a bench, Ruth says, "You guys are all plotting to get me to exercise more. That's what this is all about."

"No, no!" we all deny, more or less at once. Tom and Al pull her up and push her farther along the dirt trail that follows Prairie Creek. A woodpecker knocks out a low rapid Morse code on a hollow echoing tree.

Erix and Stephanie are stopped at a fork in the trail. To the left, the trail crosses the rapidly rushing creek with a wooden bridge and then heads up the hill on the other side, disappearing into the trees. To the right, the trail drops down into a slower part of the stream. "Which way?" Stephanie asks.

"Which way?" I ask Jake. He starts to cross the bridge, so I take the trail to the right into the stream.

Climbing down the bank I see the falls in between us. Prairie Creek noisily drops 15 feet off a flat-edged greenish-gray shelf of Platteville limestone, with a width of 40 feet. The creek bed spreads out six times as wide as it was above the slightly-arcing falls. The noise is like the sound of 40 showers running. The others are on the trail between us trying to decide which way to go. Jake is on the bridge, about eight feet above the creek and ten feet prior to the falls. He shouts to me. "What?!?"

From his wooden balcony, Jake loudly calls to me:

> How cheerfully thee chaseth thy false driven trail
> Confounding compatriots, popular victory prevail
> From whence thy shallow stream of humor falls, alas
> May a pain most dental be perceived as you fall upon your ass.

Or at least that's what I think he said. I hardly heard a word. Nevertheless, I reply:

> Influencing paths and people impressed to control
> With your command the rest may warily stroll
> A problem they see, that might take a heavy toll
> Halfway across is Jakie, an ugly bridge troll.

Jake is giving me an intensely confused look. I don't think he understood a word of what I said. Everyone else is looking at Stephanie, who is laughing hysterically.

Down here the creek is mostly a few inches deep. The breeze off the falls is refreshingly cool, almost cold. A mossy, vine-like plant, with leaves the size of champagne bubbles, hangs over the rock ledges, as if it's doing an imitation of the flowing water of the falls. Two hummingbirds dart by. I move some rocks into two-lane stepping stones. Traffic arrives before I finish. Hope has taken off her shoes and socks and is wiggling her toes in the sand and clay. Erix is too. He nearly smiles. I examine the smoothness of some stones. Water can work miracles, softening the toughest, densest rocks. Water wins.

Everyone is down here now, even Jake. Water wins; why didn't I think of this before? I'm supposed to be Mr. Possibilities. I call out, "Jake! Todd! Stephanie! Come here! We're playing Rock Paper Scissors."

"Why?"

"To see who wins."

"Wins what?"

I shake my head, "On three. Ready..." A hummingbird hovers to watch. "One. Two." The hummingbird doesn't have time for this. It leaves. "Three!"

Stephanie pulls her fist out as rock. Todd has his hand flat as paper. Jake has two fingers out as scissors. I have my fingers wiggling.

"What the hell is that?" Jake asks.

"Water. Water soaks paper. Water washes away rock. Water rusts scissors. Water wins," I tell them.

"The game is not Rock Paper Scissors Water."

"It is now."

Stephanie slugs me lightly in the shoulder. Jake thanks her. She also smiles and says, "Good one. I never bought into the idea that paper beats rock."

Hope's cute Zumbrota T-shirt gets wet along one side, while she inspects the three foot tall, cave-like indentation below the falls. I ask her if I should try calling Ray while lying under there. A splash behind us means either someone is tossing boulders into the water or... someone fell in.

Cy is sitting in the creek.

Todd reminds her that she doesn't like wearing wet shorts. Other comments are thrown in, causing her to splash out at the rest of us. Ruth takes pictures.

The big kids have taken over the swimming pool.

A small green frog leaps out from near a log in the creek to seek a hiding spot in some low plants. Erix looks after it.

Finishing my two-lane stepping stone path across the creek, Hope relays a message from Ruth, Nadine, and Cy, who are up on the bridge and letting us know that they're heading back. The rest of us leave the creek to follow them. A small sign identifies this as the Hidden Falls. Behind us, the wildlife breathes a sigh of relief at our departure.

Hope and I hold hands, while slapping each other's mosquitoes. It's romantic in a Minnesota way.

Hope asks Ruth if she got the picture from last night. Ruth replies, "I thought that was just something off the Internet." Hope goes into the whole story. In Hope's version of the story, I saved us from hitting the deer and the can family. I saved the deer from being clubbed with a putter. I saved other vehicles from hitting the scene. And I saved other deer from getting involved or rioting. She thinks I saved the day. I like my version better. The others have bought into Hope's version. They haven't heard my version, but I don't feel like arguing with my girlfriend, and I'm uncomfortable with the pedestal she's set me on. My anti-ego trips me. I stumble, and Hope keeps me balanced. That was a major disappointment. I didn't even get a smart ass comment from Jake. What's this world coming to if you can't trust your friends?

Ruth stops to catch her breath. Even under the cool forest canopy, it's still too hot for a climbing hike. We look at what Erix finds under a log. Todd looks up plants on Cy's phone. When Ruth starts taking pictures again, we know she's okay.

Back at the campsite, Becky and Tom seem agitated. "Careful of the bees," Becky says. "Jake!!! You stepped right on them!" She points to the ground where Joe's spilled beer has attracted a swarm of anxious yellow jackets.

"Those are not bees. They are yellow jackets. Big difference," Jake tells them. "Not everything with yellow and black stripes is a bee. Charlie Brown is not a bee. These?" Jake stomps. "These are yellow jackets."

"You haven't heard his lecture?!?" Stephanie asks Tom.

"Yellow jackets are a type of wasp. Wasps will eat meat or fruits. Wasps drink Double Bubble. They drink Yoerg Beer. What's the word?"

"They're omnivores," Cy reminds him.

"Right, omnivores. They're tough, persistent, flying ant-like wasps complete with one sharp stinger. Bees will only sting if you annoy them or pitch your tent on their nest. If you leave bees alone, they will leave you alone. Wasps are looking for food and drinks. If you leave a can of something open and unattended, your next drink could include a yellow jacket stinging the inside of your mouth." Jake stomps again to conclude his lecture. Becky is keeping her distance. One thing about Jake is that he has a tendency to cut through the bullshit and talk about things as they are.

Tom announces, "The NARD rangers stopped by for a visit."

"Really?" Joe asks, hiding his binoculars behind his back.

"They wanted to know when Jake's next lecture was being given."

"Really?"

"And a blue ribbon panel of campers has given our tent first prize for original lodging in a state park."

"Are you okay?" Hope asks me.

"I think I'd like to lie down and take a nap." Hope escorts me into the tent, unzipping the flap for me. The tent has a bunkhouse setup of foam pads with sheets and pillows. "Who set this up? This is nice."

Hope sticks her head out and asks who set up the beds. She crawls back over to me and says, "Tom did." I lie down to take a nap. There is a stump or a root underneath me. Hope whispers, "I'm going back to the park office. Sleep well." She kisses my cheek. She lets Ruth in before letting herself out and zipping the door closed. Pine sap drips onto the tent canopy. I relax.

I'm back on Forth Street. If I keep watching this accident I'm going to become shell-shocked or battle-fatigued or something. I need something simple to stop AutoDrive. Another AutoDrive car might help. Or a giant mirror. You can't just carry around a giant mirror. But a big sheet of foil or metallic plastic like an extra long emergency blanket might do the same thing as a mirror. AutoDrive would see a car coming toward it, playing chicken. In the end, it has to stop; a car is coming toward it. No... If it doesn't stop for a police car, a side silhouette, why would it stop for a mirror image of a black Pegasus, a front silhouette. This is not going to work.

I fall asleep. In my dreams, I hear Todd read something that says, "Minnesota has 90,000 miles of shoreline... more than California, Florida, and Hawaii combined!"

And Tom replies, "That's such a meaningless statistic. It's like asking which has more edges a jar or a sponge?"

I want to tell them to keep it down. I want to tell them that tent walls don't slow down sound any more than the walls of the Whisper Willows Apartments, but I'm too tired. When I open my eyes the tent walls dance with jittery shadows. I fumble for shoes I don't remember having taken off. I unzip out of the tent. I look at strangers standing around the smoky campfire. The sky is a rich dark blue above silhouette trees. I don't recognize a boy, a girl, a woman, or a man. Another woman, this one in a baggy sweatshirt and braided hair, turns and smiles at me with Hope's smile. It is Hope! Her hair is braided like Prairie Creek before the falls, a snapshot of water weaving around boulders, frozen in time. I take a hold of her and look around. Becky, Tom, Cy, and Todd are seated. Hope, the strangers, and I are standing. They are all quietly staring at me.

"Hi."

Hope asks me, "Did you sleep well?" I nod.

"Where's the rest of the group?"

"Al and Jake took Erix, Stephanie, Nadine, and Joe home," Cy says.

"What about Ruth?"

"I think she's still in the tent. Didn't you see her?"

"No, it's a big tent. I never even went upstairs." Our guests all turn to look at the tent.

"He's kidding," Cy informs.

"That's right, I did use the upstairs shower. What's for dinner? No one bothered to stock the kitchen," I point back to the tent.

"Hotdogs. We didn't even have bread, so we had to use some of yours. I hope you don't mind," Becky says politely.

"Is that all you had?" They nod. I tell them, "I need to get something from our car." Hope squeals.

"Wha– what just happened?" Tom asks.

"He just called it, 'our car.'" I open the car and take out my bag from Zumbrota.

Todd offers, "I've got a stick you can use for cooking a hotdog."

On the picnic table, I open the moon pie maker, a hinged two-sided round cooking enclosure with two foot long handles. I drip a bit of safflower oil on each half of it, put a piece of bread on each side, open a can of blueberry pie filling, and spoon some filling onto one half. I close it up, clipping the two handles together. I put it in the fire. The crusts of the bread, sticking out of the moon pie maker, burn off. I flip it. I watch it cook. Most cooks use experience to predict their results. In that way, I'm no different than any other cook. We don't have a plate, but we have paper towels. Opening up the moon pie maker with a paper towel, I tap out the pie onto another towel. I tear off the charred edge of the pie and sprinkle it with powdered sugar. I offer it up. Discussion and generosity lead to it being split between Becky and Cy. Hot blueberry pie is my business for the next hour while I learn that the man is a park ranger and the two kids belong to the woman, who is camping across from a yapping dog that barks when its scared, and it's scared of night. They are borrowing some of our quiet. They fill me in on their discussion as the sky turns black and the stars appear. The discussion involves a gruesome crime that I've heard nothing about. The main issue is unclear, but it seems to be a question of whether or not to live in fear. I feed them pies and reasons not to be afraid. Between the cooking and conversation, the smoke from the fire shifts directions every six or seven minutes. The boy says, "I know how to get it to stop blowing at you." Hope asks how. He says, "You say, 'Smoke from wood, smoke from fire, I've been good, blow much higher.'" The smoke knows better and puffs smoke into his face. Some of us use the kid's technique with mixed success.

My final comment about not living in fear is about control, "Who do you want to have in control of your life: you or a criminal?" The woman asks what I do for a living. "I'm unemployed."

She snaps her head and juts her face out at me, "Then you need to stick to your own shit before giving advice." The fire snaps and pops out in imitation. We are otherwise quiet. Like a mosquito on a prosthetic arm, she is confused by the lack of reaction and prepares for a second strike.

"You've overstayed your welcome," Hope tells the scowling woman. I check my watch. Todd waves to them half-heartedly. The woman makes a critical comment about our tent as a departing shot. The boy pitches the rest of his paper towel covered pie into the fire, with a burst of red hot embers that showers back down like red rain. He follows his sister and mother into their darkness. We watch the fire recover, burning the paper towel... over-cooking the pie... turning some of the filling into a hard blueberry candy and burning some with a bluish tinted flame. The half-eaten pie becomes a dark little mass amidst a brightly glowing red mosaic of embers.

The ranger says, "Sorry about all that," and he wishes us a good night.

Hope and I sit on the picnic table bench, stretching our legs out toward the fire, my arm around her Big Woods sweatshirt. We stare at the fire: the six of us, the surrounding trees, and a few low glowing eyes from the woods. The fire is getting older, with more embers and less fire. A pop sends a tiny red ember up, lighting the smoke around it, fading as it rises, heading for the tree tops, and out into the sky above where it finds its place in the stars. Look at all the stars.

Hope looks up without my saying anything aloud. Maybe she saw me look up. "Oooo," she says, "the stars are out." I look over, and everyone is looking up. The fire shifts, and our attention shifts back to it. The embers sizzle softly, making it clear that the campground is asleep. The birds are asleep. The chipmunks are in burrows telling stories. Even the mosquitoes are either asleep or have found somewhere else to spend the night. When the last A-frame of the fire tumbles in on itself, Hope gets up to stretch. "I have to go to the bathroom," she says.

"As the teacher, you don't have to ask permission."

"No, would you take me?" I agree and before I can blink, Cy and Becky are coming with as the twins talk about putting out the fire. I pick up a flashlight from the picnic table only to find that it's one of Joe's. From the car, I grab a real flashlight, a flannel shirt, and a toothbrush.

We're shuffling away from the campsite when Ruth quietly calls out, "Wait up."

Becky and Cy are both shivering. I offer, "You could share this flannel shirt I got for Hope." What stuns me is that they each put an arm in a sleeve and hug each other into the shirt. Let the record show, I was kidding. I can't believe this. How are they going to walk like that?

Ruth steps gingerly toward us in bare legs and bare feet. "Ow, ow, ow, ow, ow."

Cy whispers, "Ruth! You could've put some pants on. And shoes. We would've waited."

Ruth passes us, without slowing her momentum. "Ow. Ow. Ow. Ow. Ow," she whispers across half the campground to the bathrooms, as a distant yapping dog raises its tempo farther away.

The fluorescent lights of the men's room are blindingly bright, after adjusting to the dark and a single flashlight. The lights hum and buzz. The moths are having a party with any other bug that's still up, which includes male mosquitoes doing imitations of crane flies, female mosquitoes (wrong room, ladies), big daddy long legs (devourers of spiders) with music provided by shiny black and brown crickets and their orchestras.

The faucet has a button that allows only five seconds of water per push. Wash a hand while holding down the button with the other or wash both hands at five seconds a push. Take your pick. I should invent a clamp to allow me to wash my hands normally, well, not completely normally since there's only a cold water faucet.

I take as much time as I can in the bathroom; then I stand outside and wait. As my eyes readjust to the light outside the bathrooms, I stare up at the more open sky above and all its stars. A few paces away, out of the light, the stars surround me from Polaris to the Dippers, both great and little, with silhouette trees on the fringe. The darkness sparkles. The spirit of the heavens descends upon me. I look around for something to prop up the sinking sky. That campsite isn't completely using that tent pole, but I can't take their tent pole without asking, and it's a little late for that. Here come the stars. I stretch and hold my hands up to catch the sparkling darkness.

Hope steps out to me and kisses me. I'm kind of busy here, holding up my part of the bargain. I drop my arms around Hope in her oversized sweatshirt and her campfire perfume and kiss her, as the stars fall all around us.

A train goes by, "Ow, ow, ow, ow. Ow, ow, ow, ow. Oooo," with Ruth leading a flannel-coupled Cy and Becky. We follow them, lighting their way, and let the stars fall where they may. Hope warms her hands with mine.

A raccoon platoon dumps over a campsite garbage bag and investigates its former contents. "Baby raccoons," Becky says, pointing out the half-pint, junior masked marauders amongst the more experienced snack food eaters. They play their way through the campsite and continue on to others.

As we approach, I recognize our campsite by Joe's plastic deer. We step closer. Joe's deer moves. It spots us and dashes away, presumably to find Joe.

I put our campsite garbage in a nearby can. Hope has our bags, and we find our beds in the tent. From her bed, Hope whispers, "There's a root right under here." I tell her it's probably the same one that's under me. Hope feels around. She shifts our beds, so that we are rootless. At least I am. We lie down. I relax.

My dreams are a convoluted mix. Stars fall all around me. I let them down. A high pitched drum taps out an uneven rhythm.

I open my eyes. The lighted dome extends above me. Someone forgot to turn out the light. Someone ought to paint the ceiling of this chapel. A bird chirps a beat inspired by a dripping faucet. Chirp-chirp-chirp-chirp-chirp-chirp-chirp-chirp-chirp-chirp-chirp-chirp-chirp-chirp-chirp-chirp-chirp-chirp. Pause. Chirp-chirp-chirp-chirp-chirp-chirp-chirp-chirp-chirpity-chirp-chirp-chirp-chirp-chirp-chirp-chirp-chirp-chirp-chirp-chirp-chirp-chirp– It has a skip. Someone needs to give One Note a push.

I think I just figured out why Stephanie didn't spend the night. She hears much more than I do. My friends are still asleep. Come on guys, it's morning. I check my watch. Correction: it's just barely morning. I wonder if One Note has some sort of snooze button. I watch the shadow of a daddy long legs making the hike up the outside of the tent, the Sir Mallory of the harvestmen, its shadow becoming sharper and more defined the higher it goes.

Chirp-chirp-chirp-chirp-chirp-chirp-chirp-chirp-chirp-chirp-chirp-chirp-chirp-chirp-chirp– I leave the tent. A common sparrow sits on the picnic bench with its head turned, chirping incessantly, without bothering to listen to itself. Chirp-chirp-chirp-chirp. "Psst," I get its attention, and it flies off to annoy someone else. I go back in the tent and lie back down, in time to watch the daddy long legs planting a flag at the summit. It uses one of its own legs as a pole. I fall back asleep.

"Hey Sleepyhead," Hope says, with her hair brushed out, wearing a Friends With Big Woods tank top and the flannel shirt. "They need to take the tent down." She kisses me on the forehead, sniffs me and says, "Pine fresh." The tent is empty except for us, my bed and backpack. Hope pats me and leaves.

I get changed and roll up my bed. Before leaving the tent, I call out, "Echo."

The tent calls back, "Echo. Echo. Echo." A far off woodpecker hammers out a reply on a percussion tree.

Outside, Ruth is bandaging her feet. Everyone else is packing things. I figure the tent is my responsibility. I tap the walls to tumble bugs from their temporary home. I clear out the inside and leave the door open to let the air out. It comes down much faster than it went up. A pliers from Hope's trunk helps me take up the stakes. The poles come apart much easier. I clean some pine sap from the canopy. I try everything I can to get the tent stuffed back into its duffel bag. I try cramming it. I try folding it. I even try origami, managing to fold the tent into a giant tan duck.

Everyone else gets involved, and we get it packed. The plan is to go to Northfield for breakfast. Tom leaves some extra wood for the next campers. We decide on a route and leave the Big Woods. Highway 246 twists and turns with stop signs and stoplights to Northfield. Hope drives. I help her follow the signs.

41

End Of The Line For Kelly

The Jesse James Cafe in Northfield celebrates the defeat of Jesse James and his gang with their Heywood eggs and Gustafson pastries. People can do heroic things. In 1876 the townspeople of Northfield thwarted the robbery of the First National Bank.

The waiters and waitresses of the Jesse James Cafe are college students from Carlton College and St. Olaf College. Our waitress with bright eyes and a big smile is from Carlton College. I get Heywood eggs, named for the bank clerk who refused to open the safe. Tom and Todd each get the Frank Wilcox sausage and eggs, named for another bank clerk who also refused to open the safe. Becky has the John North wheat pancakes, named for the man who founded Northfield and also founded Riverside, California. Cy has the safe cereal, and Ruth has a Gustafson lingonberry pastry, in honor of Nicklaus Gustafson, a Swedish immigrant who was killed in the crossfire. I also suck some more jelly. Tom asks Cy why we picked Big Woods. Cy answers, "It's the only state park that doesn't have a body of water or a historical site."

"It has the creek and the falls."

"Hidden Falls."

"Right."

"But they are hidden falls, so they don't count."

"Oh."

Banners announce that the big Northfield festival is in two weeks. Noticing us notice the banners, our waitress asks if we might be able to come back for the festival. Others shake their heads, but I say hopefully, "Some of us might be able to come back."

We separate and head back to the Twin Cities. While I drive, Hope points out cows in a trailer and checks the messages on her phone. "Nicole sent some messages. Apparently modeling in New York sucked jelly."

"Did she say that?!?"

"No, that's my interpretation. She wonders if you gave away lights on Friday night. You didn't, did you?"

"No, technically I had you do it. Remember? You gave the glow sticks to the kids of the can family."

"That's right," Hope says, still reading her phone. "'Why do you want oil on my boobs?' Nicole asked one place she was working with... a go-see, it's called in the modeling world. 'So they don't squeak,' they said. That was when she left."

"When does she come back?"

"This afternoon."

"We should all oil our chests in her honor."

"I don't think she would appreciate that. I don't mean to stifle your creativity, but this was something really big for her. For one of the two go-sees to treat her badly..."

"How soon does she come in?"

"About two hours."

"Do you know, does she have a ride?" I accelerate.

Hope looks from me to the speedometer to the phone to the back window. "Do you think we can make it? How will we find her? Did you know Tom and Becky were following us, and you just left them in the dust?" Hope asks a lot of questions when she's excited.

"Yes. A complex technique of subject recognition and communication. No. And I didn't mean to. Here's what we do. Check the flight over the Internet. Call Nicole and let her know we will meet her at the arrival station at three. Call Becky and let her know. Call Faith and let her know." A pickup truck is stalled on the side of I-35. "I wanted to park there."

"You did not."

Hope keeps busy setting everything up, while all I have to do is drive us back and wonder how Ray's doing. Hope lets me know that Becky wants to join us. Tom meets us at Post Road by the airport to drop off Becky. We pull out Friday's beach towel and lie out underneath the landing planes while we wait for Nicole's arrival. The landing planes make Becky squeal with a horror-movie-like fear, holding both of us to protect her from the giant planes. A choir of angels announces Nicole's arrival, by way of Hope's phone. We go to arrivals and pick her up with ease. She's crying. We get her luggage in. I chauffeur from the front seat while they all pile into the back in one big hug.

They're saying things to each other, but once again, I can't understand what they're saying through their wailing, sobbing, and bawling. Very little slips by the cryptographic crying. Sobs are interjected as disposable syllables. My job is to drive, not to understand. At the house, Faith joins in the crying and hugging. I haul luggage in the afternoon heat.

The lawn is getting a little shaggy. Maybe I'll mow it in the morning when it's not so hot. I check up on Ray. He has the shakes. He's trembling in fear over tomorrow's ceremony for Kelly. I try my best to reassure him. When I ask if there's anything I can do to help, he shakes his head, so I go to my room.

My clock has stopped. It's keeled over with its arms limp, its eyes closed, and its tongue hanging out. I wind it up, and it comes back to life. I set it down. I shower and shave, thinking about AutoDrive and dinner and that winds heal all times, at least for my clock. In the kitchen, I try to cram lasagna noodles into a pan to boil without breaking them. Enough are already broken. I try folding them into the water. The noodles bend more than they fold. I try turning a noodle into an origami duck. Picasso would see this as a duck, but it's too abstract for anyone else to recognize it as more than a noodle. The box says I'm supposed to boil the noodles for ten minutes. How can I boil them for ten minutes when they don't want to get more than their feet wet?!? All four from upstairs come downstairs. What I need is a long thin pan.

Their complexions have matching highlights from crying. Their shirts nearly match. I should do something about that. Nicole comes up to me and says, "Hope told us how you suggested meeting me at the airport and calling all of us to let us know. I don't know how you do it. Well, I do know how you do it, but I still want to tell you how sweet I think it is. It was just what I needed." She hugs me, helping to break another noodle. I stir the noodles, spiraling them into the pan, and set a mental timer.

I ask them, "What can we do tonight, together, that isn't too serious, that Ray could join us as he wants and leave as he wants? He's really nervous about the unveiling of Kelly tomorrow."

While they think about that, talking it over, I start to prepare other ingredients and heat the oven. I could just set the lasagna outside to bake.

"The Miss Superficiality Pageant is on tonight."

"I thought the Miss Low Maintenance Pageant was tonight."

"They've combined the two."

"Does the same woman win both?"

"Not necessarily. It's actually kind of unlikely that someone would win both Miss Superficiality and Miss Low Maintenance."

"Instead of evening gown, there's a nightgown competition." Nicole nudges me in the ribs.

"That's the Miss Superficiality contest. For the Miss Low Maintenance Pageant, she wears whatever she wears to bed."

"What if she doesn't wear anything?"

"They blur it out, to protect our tender American sensibilities. They don't blur it in South America or in Europe. And the interviews will be over the phone."

"For which one?"

"I'm not sure."

Hope turns their attention back to me by asking me if we could all watch the pageant here. I agree, feeling weird to give approval to her about her house. I guess it's like approving a landlady visit. Of course, she's way more than a landlady. I better get back to the lasagna.

"How long will that take?" Nicole asks. "I'm starving."

I check the box. "It takes two days to bake."

She snatches the box from me and then apologizes. "It says 90 minutes."

"I know," I tell her. "I translated it. Ninety minutes will seem like two days." Nicole nods and hands the box back. I steam some veggies in the microwave.

Lasagna is a pasta baklava of layers. I lay out layers in two pans. Hope offers to help and takes over a pan, imitating my layers. That is, until the olives. Usually cooking is either a monarchy or a dictatorship – rarely is it a democracy. In the case of the layer of sliced black olives, it's a democracy. The popular vote in the kitchen is against black olives. The olives get put away. And the vegetable lasagna goes into the oven.

While feeding Nicole some grapes from across the table, I ask Hope if it would be okay if I cut the lawn while the lasagna bakes. She says I'll need a key. She goes upstairs to get it. One of the grapes hits Nicole's forehead. Hope hands an unusual gadget to me and takes me out to the garage.

She unplugs the mower from an outlet, asks for the ignition key, and plugs it into a two prong inlet. It's a circuit breaker. Hope teaches me the lawnmower.

I am underwhelmed that Hope is teaching me how to use a lawnmower.

"After unplugging and inserting the key, you push the red candy-like button and squeeze the two handles together. The mower cuts the lawn and mulches, but you have to walk behind it and push it, holding the handles together." I take off with it, acting like I can't hear her over the noise of the mower. It's silent and has no exhaust, so it could be run in a basement... if the basement needed mowing. The cut grass is the only smell, not gasoline exhaust with a hint of cut grass. It's not self-propelled, and it's not a robot. It's not AutoDrive, but it's a cool mower. It gets exciting when it goes over gravel or sticks, which is how I learn not to go over gravel or sticks. I check my watch; it's after six, but it's still hot out. I stop it and look under the mower. All I see is one big blade on a shaft from the motor. Along with the motor, presumably there's also a battery hidden in there along with an internal charger and a starter. I remove the rocks and sticks from the area I was mowing and start again. After mowing the yard, I put the mower back the way it was, pull out the key, plug it in for recharging, go in, and get cleaned up again.

In the living room, the ladies are watching a pre-pageant show, which provides the most in-depth coverage we could want or imagine. The Miss Superficiality Pageant will be broadcast live from Hollywood. The Miss Low Maintenance Pageant will be broadcast live from Cleveland. The coverage will switch back and forth. While Superficiality contestants are changing outfits and having their hair redone, the coverage will switch to the Miss Low Maintenance Pageant. When the Superficiality contestants are ready, coverage will break away from the Miss Low Maintenance Pageant. The Low Maintenance contestants will sometimes be shown in a small rectangle on the screen, waiting patiently for their pageant to continue.

There will be no professing the desire for world peace. World peace is out. The Superficiality contestants are only allowed to talk about themselves, no complex issues. And world peace is not a low maintenance issue.

This year will be the first to use CleanTV to protect viewers from the hazards of live television. CleanTV is technology that will blur anything recognized as obscene. The pre-pageant show hosts provide a demonstration of CleanTV. It blurs a bald head, some people's noses, and some people's lips. It blurs many seemingly innocent looking objects. They joke that since this technology is very expensive, maybe next year they will instead send out smudged glasses to all their viewers, with the motto, "Dirty glasses to prevent dirty viewings."

They are also campaigning to put the power in the viewer's fingertips by having a blur button added to every TV remote within the next ten years. It's the Remote Idea.

The hosts in Hollywood are excited and giddy. The hosts in Cleveland are blasé and indifferent. Ray comes in to join us as the show gets started. He's excited and giddy and blasé and indifferent all at once. I serve up the lasagna.

The women evaluate the appearance of the Superficiality contestants and the attitudes of the Low Maintenance contestants. After about 20 minutes they ask our opinions. Ray announces that our ladies are better than the women on TV. I agree with him, wishing I had said it first. He gets a three handed back rub. I get the dirty dishes.

Distant trumpets take me away. Will is on the phone telling me that he thinks the can accident picture is cool. I don't really understand anything else that he's saying, except that in a roundabout way he's telling me how hard Wendy has been working on AutoDrive. Usually he's more straightforward than this. I mean, I understand that Wendy has to have been working hard on AutoDrive. Everyone in R&D probably is. I mention Ray's ceremony tomorrow, and Will changes the subject back to AutoDrive, "About AutoDrive. Do you think it'll work?"

"Is this between you and me or do you have to tell Wendy what I'm going to tell you?"

"Either way."

"Then, just between us, I'm afraid not," I tell Will.

"I understand. At least I think I do. Listen, I'll see you Friday night at the drive-in. And maybe tomorrow at Ray's ceremony."

"All right. Tell Wendy that I'm hoping for the best. Good night."

"Good night."

Back in the living room, the pageants have narrowed to semifinalists. At this stage, the Superficiality contestants are examined under a microscope. I ask, "Shouldn't there be only a superficial judging instead of this in-depth analysis?" I get quieted. Meanwhile the Low Maintenance contestants are asked questions over the phone or kept on hold. They all seem fine about it.

Something that wasn't announced during the pre-pageant show is that the Miss Superficiality finalists no longer have a time limit in answering questions about themselves. They can take all the time they want. And they do. I shuffle off to bed before they're done.

After another sleepless night, I'm pondering AutoDrive while separating the majors from the munches, when Ray comes into the kitchen, a very clean-shaven Ray, and asks me, "Do you have to do that?" I look down at my cereal, look back up at Ray, and shake my head no. "I need your help with something. I'm expecting someone to totally misunderstand the fountain."

Just one person? I thought I was an optimist. "Ray, the fountain is a celebration of motherhood and a beautiful work of art. Anyone who has a problem with it ought to think about the statue of Paul Bunyan or the statue of Chuckles the Clown or all the extremely unusual statues in Brussels or Melbourne or

Nuremberg or Stockholm. They ought to consider your intentions. And they ought to consider the fact that for half the year, Kelly will be covered in snow."

"You don't get it. I'm worried about my mother misunderstanding. I think she thinks this is all about her – that she's the model for Kelly instead of my ex-girlfriend Kelly."

"I thought Kelly was named for the fact that one day she'll turn green?"

"What? No, this alloy isn't supposed to turn green. Who said anything about it turning... oh, now I remember talking about that. I was kidding." He's getting me back for all the times I've kidded him. "My mother thinks she is giving a speech today. She's not. Avatrice Gaea is."

"She should understand that." Ray looks at me like I'm talking crazy talk. I would love a collage of this look from everyone that has ever given it to me.

"Would you pick her up from the airport? And tell her she's not giving the speech? And escort her around?" Hope comes downstairs.

"Yes, I will mother-sit. When is her flight coming in?" Hope goes over to Ray.

"11:50." Hope hugs Ray.

"Are you ready for your big day?" she asks him.

"Ask me tonight, when it's over."

"We will all be rooting for you." Hope comes over to me, "When you two are done talking, could you come upstairs?"

"Yes."

Ray hands me a piece of paper with doodles and a phone number. "This is my mom's number."

"How do I input these doodles as part of the phone number? Is there an algebraic equation that simplifies all this?" I ask him.

Ray asks, "Hope, would you take him away?"

"Gladly."

Upstairs in Nicole's room, Hope puts on a second shirt. She and her roommates all stick out their chests at me. "Yes, they're very nice."

"No. Read the shirts."

The shirts each say, "Cameron Raymond Fan Club," with differing convex distortions.

"That's very nice of you to do," I tell them. "And nice of you to be a part of all this. Got any extras?"

"I have four more."

"Is there one for Ruth? She hates being left out of this sort of thing."

"This one will be Ruth's." We check it for size.

"If you have an extra one for me, I'll take it, but others can come first."

"Ricky!"

"Coming!" I yell. "Psst, guess who won the Mr. High Maintenance Pageant this morning." I drop the shirt in Hope's hands and run down the stairs two at a time. "Yes, Ray?"

"I should be able to pay you back tomorrow."

"You don't need to think about that right now."

"I just wanted you to know."

I shrug. "Is there anything else you need?"

"No. If you could keep track of my mom, if you could mother-sit, that would be great." The way he says that, the roller coaster tone of his voice, has a certain implication that has cropped up lately, whenever he's hinting about pointed perception.

"Hold on a minute," I tell him with a hint of irritation. I sit down, close my eyes, and relax. I open my eyes, using my index finger to wipe away a tear.

"What?"

"It's fine. It's going to be fine. She'll be there. She's renting a car."

"You got a kind of intense look on your face, when your eyes were closed."

"I'm telling you, it's going to be fine." I'm not sure anyone could possibly understand how much I hate pointed perception.

Ray backs off, saying, "Okay, I have to go to a meeting about the ceremony, kind of a pre-meeting meeting." I understand. "I'll see you there."

"I'll be there."

Ray leaves, and I tell Hope that I'm going out to pick up my suit. She makes sure I'm not planning to wear it in this heat. Outside I'm doused with hot wet air. The construction crew next door all droop over like someone snuck up and swiped their skeletons. It reminds me of a famous painting. I pour myself into my puddle of a car, ooze down the driveway, and into the street. The displacement of air from momentum causes a slight coolness that nearly solidifies the car. Parking in the Camel Lot again, I go into the Southedge Mall, solidify, and ask for my suit. With my suit over my shoulder, I walk into Unmentionables, a lingerie store, and immediately get a sunburn.

I analyze the store, breaking it down into sections and subsections. The store sells lingerie, but they also sell cover-ups, robes and perfumes. I like the way Hope looks and smells, so buying a robe or perfume would be counterproductive.

"Can I help you?" a lingerie sales associate asks.

"Yes, I'd like to get some lingerie for my girlfriend. Something that's sexy and comfortable..." She asks me Hope's sizes. I tell her, and she starts leading me into the store past chrome racks of clothes. "... with no poking underwire and straps that lay on the skin without cutting into the skin or riding up..." She stops and heads us in a different direction. "The fabric shouldn't itch or irritate the skin... the color should be light..." She stops again, pondering now. "It should fit her without being too tight." Now she's staring at me with that crazy person look, but I'm undetoured. "It should complement her body and be as pretty as she is." The sales associate calls over a manager and asks me to repeat what I just said, as if I said something lewd. I repeat it all. The manager shakes her head and brings me over to some things called bodysuits that have no similarity to the contents of the hangered bag over my shoulder. I feel the inside of the bodysuit. It feels like sharp plastic points. I make a face.

"You don't want her to be too comfortable in it, do you? Then she might never take it off," the manager says, while the sales associate takes notes, smiling and nodding.

"I want her to be comfortable." The manager is startled by my determination. She shows me something that already needs ironing but looks like it would be impossible to iron. "Too wrinkly."

"I'm sorry that's all we have."

"Is it all right if I look around?" They agree, and the manager offers to hang my suit up for me while I look. The lingerie section of the store has subsections, sometimes divided by style, sometimes by color, and sometimes by brand. Having figured that out, I'm able to eliminate certain color groupings, styles, and brands that don't fit my criteria. I dodge other shoppers and read tags. There's a bra called balcony bra, another called top shelf, and still another called pinnacle peaks. I look at fabrics for appearance; check sizes; exclude unusual washing requirements – must be freeze-dried in Antarctica, that sort of thing; feel for softness; and gently tug the material for stretch. I'm starting to think that they know their store, and that there isn't anything. It doesn't completely surprise me, but then again, it's not like I asked for an air conditioned bra. That would be the perfect gift for today.

In a lowly corner, not fitting into the other categories and subcategories, I find a white, kind of... I

"Okay, you were right," Faith says, "that was too depressing." She checks my clock, which is leaning against Hope. "It's not even nine, but I'm exhausted. I'm going to bed to say my prayers." She messes up my hair before going up.

Ray's right, the storm has let up. Storms rarely park in Minnesota; they usually drive through, one direction or another. Or several storms collide here, pull off to the side of the road to swap information, and are towed off together.

It's tough to tell if it's still raining or if the winds are just shaking drops from the trees. Drips drop in a cluster. That seemed like a shake. It's still windy, but the trees are folding back out to their original umbrellas, somewhat. God has done some pruning.

The sun cracks through the clouds of the western sky, shining rays breaking other gaps, and setting off a rainbow, appearing in the tree's gap.

"Let's go out."

"Is it safe?"

"Faith is upstairs. She won't be out with us, dancing with a lightning rod, so yeah, it's safe."

Outside, the orange-yellow sunlight casts a brilliant glow on us and the neighborhood. All the colors seem brighter. The wet sidewalk reflects the glow. Several unfinished rainbows arc like mid-air doodling. Hope hugs me. Becky and Nicole pick up some litter. Ray and I take a five foot tree branch to the backyard near the garage.

A hummingbird is tearing down spider webs. It either doesn't like where the webs are, or it needs the materials.

The girls come back with litter for the trash and recycling and compost. Hope says, "We left a lost lawn chair by the curb for someone to claim."

"Should we do the same thing with the branch?" She smiles with soft dimples and shakes her head. We look at old scars of lightning strikes on the trees and find one fresh scar.

The lights pop on in the house. We go in to close curtains. I move to put away my lantern and Hope tells me, "I know how special your parents were, because of how special you are. I heard that one of your earliest memories was that every morning at 10:30 it was Apple Time; you and your mom would have an apple together."

"Ten-thirty was the first time of day I knew. No other time mattered." I kiss her good night and take my lantern and things and go to bed.

My bed is a mess. I don't know how to lie down on it. I turn off the light and sort of fall in. I close my eyes and relax.

"I've been waiting for you." That's the thought inside my head. I'm in a shower. Nothing spectacular. "Never mind where you are. You are not wanted. Go back to your present. Open your eyes in your present. The present is a gift you need to open and explore, savor and enjoy, live and experience. When you are from is a great time. The best. You have Hope. Listen to her. She wants to be with you, all of you. You've created a wave you will surf for the rest of your life. Go there and stay there."

I tell the future me, "Today is tomorrow's yesterday. Today doesn't matter."

"You're wrong; your today does matter. Without today, there will be no tomorrow."

I make another choice. My eyes close in the future. My future says, "I've been waiting for you. You think you have a grasp, a handle, on all the potentials of your life. You don't. You only have a glimmer of a glimpse of the possibilities that God offers you. Live. Leave."

I open my eyes. I don't know, but I think I just kicked myself out of pointed perception.

I turn on the light. My clock yawns and stretches. I reassemble my bed so it looks like anyone else's bed... hotel beds... beds in movies... I close my eyes and fall asleep.

43

Making The Cut

Hope is still asleep. I could call her Sleepyhead and question her wasting her vacation in bed, but instead I leave without waking her. The sky is filled with glacial, anvil-like clouds, peering through the trees.

The Pony Express is so shiny, even the rust sparkles like brown sugar. It got a free car wash last night. And it's cool to the touch. It's been three months since it was cool in a temperature way. Stylistically, the Pony Express was never cool. It never even tried. I reach for the fan knob without looking. I look. It's not there. It's on the floor.

Traffic doesn't seem to realize that the road has two lanes. I breeze by. Sometimes in winter, during or after a snow, before the plows get out, traffic sticks to only one lane. And it makes sense, because only one lane is freshly driven snow. Sometimes during the rest of the year, traffic in Minnesota mimics this single-lane behavior for no apparent reason. It's like they are all on their way to a funeral or jobs they don't enjoy.

Dodging the state fair traffic, my car takes me to The Kindest Cut on University Avenue in the cleavage between the Twin Cities. My barber Eli is 67. He makes Clarence look like a kid. When his hands start to shake, my ears run for cover. He's a good man. The first time he cut my hair he asked me if I was wearing a pink bow. I said no. He said, "Oops," and you never want to hear your barber say, "oops." He said, "Oops, I think I cut off your ear, Mr. Van Go."

Eli is a master at driving a barber chair with no hands. His feet work the petals to raise and lower the chair and steer it in one direction or another. He doesn't even stop clipping, while he moves me, which is incredible, except for the fact that my nose used to be just a little longer.

Last year I made the mistake of asking him how long he expects to continue cutting hair. I didn't mean anything by it, but ever since, he pauses before cutting my hair, and he makes a point of holding out a comb and a scissors and asks me which is which.

When the little bell rings as I step into The Kindest Cut, I am surprised to see a teenager in the barber's apron. "Hi, I'm Delilah," she holds out her hand. "You must be my eight o'clock." She flips back her long, iridescent hummingbird green hair on the side that has hair, scratches the shaved spot near her temple on the side that doesn't have hair, and waves me into the chair. "Have a seat." Sitting down in a barber's chair with a new barber is like watching a movie on a plane – you can't just walk out in the middle. "How would you like your hair?"

Eli cut my hair. He never gave me a choice. This is new. What if I tell her short? Will she cut it short or buzz it down to stubble like her temple? This is a fine time not to have pointed perception. She's waiting for a response, so I say, "The usual."

She gives a little laugh and throws a hoodless poncho over me, just as I'm about to check my watch. I close my eyes, and I relax. Nothing happens. No pointed perception. It's weird. Abilities are things you expect to gain but never lose. When I was a kid, I could be invisible. No one paid much attention to what I was doing until I had done it. No one expects much from children. I was invisible. I was always responsible, but my invisibility meant that my methodology wasn't questioned. The instant strangers started calling me mister and sir, I was no longer invisible. I was a customer and a citizen and a voter and all the other things expected of adults. I was accountable for my methodology. I had lost my invisibility. I'd thought it would be a part of me forever.

"Is Eli okay?" I ask Delilah.

"Grandpa? Yeah, he's fine. I'm taking over the shop."

This certainly has been the month of changes. I bet it's been a big change for her. "How's it going?"

"It could be worse. It could be better. Many of his old customers take one look at me and turn around and walk out the door. I don't know what they're thinking. Maybe they think they stepped into the wrong place. Or that Grandpa is working someplace else now. Maybe they think I'm going to cut their hair to match mine. Your telling me 'the usual' is kind of funny, since we just met. But it also told me that you aren't looking for a change from the way your hair looks now, so all I need to do is use your haircut as a guide to how you want your hair. I can mimic Grandpa's style. I can do an Eli-style for as long as my customers want. All someone has to say is, 'give me the usual.' If it's just about the haircut, I can do the haircut. The toughest thing is that Grandpa loves to talk to a captive audience. How long have you been coming here?"

"Six years."

"Then you've heard all the stories. Grandpa is an expert at winter weather forecasts and politics and the Pigs Eye Pigs and everything else. And watch that you don't have an opinion of your own. When no one is looking, he'll drop loose hairs on your tongue. He's very subtle about that; he uses the closed end of his fist, and his pinkie does the work."

"I've had the hairy mouth treatment, now that you tell me about it," I tell her.

"Don't feel bad. He did it to everyone." She concentrates on her cuts for a moment. "And I doubt I'll ever be able to drop casually into conversation about national issues or insist that I know when it'll snow or anything like that."

"You don't have to. You aren't him. You're you."

The bell rings. A familiar face steps in front of me. "I know this guy," he says, bowing so I can see him. It's the waiter from Yesterday's Diner, sideways. "Is she any good?"

"So far so good," I respond.

Delilah says, "I'll be with you in about five minutes."

The waiter waits. He moves some newspapers and sits across from me. "I haven't seen you around in a while, did you ever find a job?"

"No. That's why I'm here. I've got an interview this morning."

"Your hair will do great," Delilah predicts. "You'll be great on top. The rest is up to you."

"Good luck with that."

"How do you two know each other?"

"I wait tables at Yesterday's Diner."

"Yesterday's Food at Yesterday's Prices?"

"That's right. He's the guy that comes in with all the babes."

"Ouch." Delilah snips off part of my ear.

"Sorry." I feel around. "Is it bleeding?" she asks.

"Not yet." The waiter squirms and decides to sit quietly. Delilah concentrates on her work, and I watch for any sudden moves. She foams up my face and shaves me with a straight edge. She finishes up and hands me a mirror. I check my ear first. I wiggle it and make sure it's the same ear I came in with. Then I check my hair. This is not the same haircut as I always got from Eli. Where's the shaggy spot? Where's the subtle unevenness between the two sides? "Looks good." Delilah breathes a sigh of relief. Delilah brushes me off. I pay her, thank her, and she makes a show of the tip.

"He always knows how to tip," the waiter confirms, missing Delilah's hint.

I say good-bye to them. The door hits me on the way out with the tinkle of a bell.

At home, Hope is impressed with my haircut yet seems to think that I've forgotten how to put on a suit. "It's going to go great," she says, "but I'm sure you already know that."

"No, I don't. Pointed perception no longer works." She asks why. "I think it's because you told me how you didn't like it."

"I didn't mean for that to happen. How could that happen?"

"At some point I started agreeing with you. At first it wasn't me, just the future me, but now? I guess I agree with you."

"Then that's good, isn't it?" I nod somewhat. "You look great. You're going to do great," Hope predicts. I grab the stuff I printed, kiss her, and head out again. I ignore a whistle from the construction site next door.

The iceberg and anvil-like clouds are spreading out and so is the traffic. I park a few blocks away from the Lower Landing. I shut off the trumpets on my phone and take a walk in my suit, thankful for last night's cool down. Riding an elevator up the Riverside Tower, I check my watch. It's ten to ten. Light streams in from behind me. Turning around just as the glass elevator clears the low lying buildings, the sun blasts me from over the Mississippi River. I nearly press my nose to the glass looking down at the train depot falling away below. The view is incredible. Luckily I have no fear of heights, and I'm nearly as comfortable with weights. I double check my floor – one floor down from the top. Below are the seven hills of Pigs Eye, or at least five of them. Past the rest of Pigs Eye, trees interrupt lakes, then the Midway and Prospective Tower, the fairgrounds, the university, and Milltown. I get just about high enough to see the rows of lakes, remnants of buried river valleys, when a titanic-sinking iceberg cloud obscures my view temporarily, dragging a rainbow with it. Wow, the sun is brighter up here. The elevator brass sparkles in the sunlight. If you're applying for a job and trying to look at the bright side, shouldn't you be called an applican not an applicant? I'm certain I've thought about that before. I'm about there. Time to prepare. I read over my notes.

Ding. The doors open and I am met with hollow walls of framing steel beams and uprights and pipes over scraped gray cement floors with old glue swirls of white or dingy yellow bug guts. This was where Common Communication will be. A voice greets me, and I spot Belle Beckett and Samuel Morrison working a handheld computer over a card table. They are in jeans and sweatshirts. My suit and I are overdressed. "Good morning."

"Good morning. We aren't hiring." That's a fine way to start an interview. "What I mean is, we aren't ready to start hiring. It's been a long day."

"I know all about long days." We introduce ourselves.

Belle comments, "You have a good voice, a deep voice; it exudes confidence."

"Thank you," I respond confidently and deeply, as a prospective employee trying to be the best candidate for a non-existent job.

"We've been wondering how you found out about us. We aren't on the web, in phone listings, or even on the directory downstairs."

"I had a dream about this, except it looked different in the dream."

"How?"

"Well, there was a receptionist at a desk over there. All of this was finished with white walls, carpeting, and ceiling tiles. There was a conference room back there by the window and on the wall there was a painting of the city overlooking the Mississippi in winter."

"That's my painting," Belle says.

"Really?" Sam asks. Belle nods.

"What color carpeting did we decide on?"

"Well it was mostly tan... kind of a coffee-stain tan with navy blue borders about four inches wide."

"What are you doing?" Belle asks Sam, as he ignores us to work on a computer.

"Trying to pull up the carpet samples. Here we go. These aren't it. Those aren't it. Not there. Not there either."

"Wait. Is that it?"

"Or that one. Is it one of these two?"

"That one."

"Really?"

"Yeah."

"I don't know. What do you think?" Belle asks Sam.

"It's all right."

"But you think it looks like coffee stains?" Belle asks me.

"Yes, but the manufacturer probably wanted to give you a head start, like buying torn jeans."

Belle laughs. "What else was in your dream."

"You offered me a job."

"Did we? What job did we offer you?"

"God." Sam spits out his coffee. "You're getting ahead of yourself, aren't you?" I ask. "Or are you trying to see how that color will look on the floor?"

"He has the sense of humor for the part..."

Sam tries to brush off a coffee stain from his sweatshirt, "We aren't hiring."

"Whoa there, Sam, can I talk to you in the... uh... lobby?" They wind around partial walls, turn to look at me, realize I can still hear them, and move farther away. I can still see them. Ms. Beckett is pointing at something as she talks. They come back.

She's about to say something but stops herself. She flips to my resume. She has a Romanesque nose. "This says you are a mechanical and optical engineer, and your most recent job was with Flight Control, as the Research and Development manager for AutoDrive... a self-driving car?"

"That's right."

"Why did you leave AutoDrive?"

"I left Flight Control because I could not deliver the product, AutoDrive, in the time allotted by the owner of the company."

"I'm not sure your engineering skills will help us here," she says and thinks for a moment. "How creative was your Research and Development job?"

"Highly creative. We were trying to invent something that has never been created before. It was a mix of my being creative and my instilling and encouraging creativity in my team."

"What if one of your employees came to you and said, 'This is impossible.'"

"I would work out the possibilities with the employee, listening to what they had tried already and brainstorming alternatives."

"Have you ever received a call from a friend wanting advice?" I nod. "Let's say they call you about a problem, and they think you know what's going on, and you should know what's going on, but you don't know what's going on. Can you help them?"

"I have a good memory. Sometimes I will replay a prior conversation in my head, looking for clues that I might have missed the first time through, looking for connections or understanding, something to comprehend the situation. I also have had good... intuition."

They jot down some notes.

"Could you give me an example of your intuition?"

"You're either reading or about to read Harrowing Heights."

"That's true," Ms. Beckett says. "That's pretty good."

Mr. Morrison scoffs, "It's on the best sellers list." He says to me, "We're going to do some role playing. I'm going to call you, and you answer and try to handle the call. Let's act like there is no time limit for the call. We're thinking of billing by the minute. Hello, I wonder if you can help me with my problem? I don't know who I can turn to."

"Okay. Tell me about you problem."

"I'm in an abusive situation."

"Are you being abused?"

"Yes."

"Get out of that situation. Extricate yourself. And get some counseling."

"But it has to do with a family member."

"I care about you. I care what happens to you. From being abused, you might question your self-worth. I am telling you, you matter. Again, get out of that situation. And get some counseling. If you can't find your way out of the situation, get some counseling and some support to help you get out."

"Thank you."

"You're welcome. Bless you."

"Do you always say that?" Ms. Beckett asks.

"No. It's just in case he sneezes," I tell them.

Belle Beckett twiddles her pen. "God is a full-time job, 24-7 with no vacations and no breaks. I can't imagine God putting people on hold, although I can imagine a waiting line for God. I don't suppose you happen to be one of a set of identical triplets, do you?"

"No, when I was born they broke the mold. Made it look like an accident."

"I see. Triplets would've helped us with the whole 24-7 thing." They look at each other. They're trying to telepathically communicate, and it's not working. "Please excuse us for just a moment." They leave again.

Hopefully God doesn't take this like a slap in the face. Hopefully God considers a phone service a way of helping to spread His word, instead of competition. While I'm waiting, I give God a call and leave a message through silent prayer. I don't bow my head or kneel or anything. That's our deal.

Belle Beckett and Samuel Morrison return. Belle says, "We would like to work out some details and meet again. How does a week from this Friday sound?"

"Good."

"Ten o'clock again?"

"Sounds good." They both shake my hand and escort me to the elevator. I should ask if they have a more prestigious position than god, just to kid around. The elevator doors shut and I drop down. I head straight home and ignore a comment from the construction site to hang up my suit before anything happens to it that would cause me to have to dry-clean it right away. I check it over on its hanger – good as new. I get dressed and check my messages.

Hope wished me luck. Cy and Jake want to know why they didn't hear that I had an interview. Lefty's message is checking to see if I'm ready for tomorrow's experiment. Erix called and said, "Some storm." Tom wants to know who's coming to the game tonight. Ruth does too. Nicole left a message saying she stopped by my room last night and my bed was a disaster. She stopped by again before she left for work; I was gone, and it was picture perfect. She isn't asking a question, so I'm not sure I need to reply.

Upstairs, Hope is chopping up a pineapple. "Hey Handsome, how did it go?"

"Good. I have a second interview a week from this Friday."

"Congrats. My mom called to ask about your interview."

"What did you say?"

"I said, 'He's still there. I haven't heard anything.'"

"You didn't tell her where I was interviewing did you?"

"No. She asked again, playing dumb, 'Where is he interviewing again?'"

"I don't think anyone has to know until I have something."

"She really may be able to help you. She has connections. She knows all the big shots."

"A big shot is just a little shot that keeps on shooting. What are you doing?" Hope is eating a piece of the center of the pineapple. She signals me to wait. "Take your time," I tell her.

"I'm eating pineapple core. It's the best part of the pineapple. You can't get it without cutting it up yourself. At first, it was the only part of a pineapple I could get, in a family as big as mine. But I grew to really like it. After a few years, when I finally had a piece of regular pineapple, it wasn't the same. Pineapple core is sweeter and tougher, kind of like pineapple chewing gum. I love it." She tucks her hair behind her ears and smiles at me with dimples that are almost proud that she was so deprived. She looks at her pineapple and her smile decelerates. She fights with herself. She comes to a resolution. "Would you like to try a piece?"

"Okay." The pineapple core is more of a pale yellow than the rest of the pineapple fruit. It smells like pineapple. It tastes like pineapple. I wouldn't say it's like gum. I would say it's like wood or bark. "It's okay. I won't get in the way of your eating the rest."

Watching Hope sensuously savor the pineapple core is wild. She really likes the stuff. We take the pineapple into her bedroom and get the sheets sticky.

"Everyone is asking if we are going to the game tonight. Are we?" Hope asks.

"Not me. I'll feel naked without pointed perception. People will be asking me if anything is going to happen that inning or if they can go to the concession stand, and I'm not ready to talk about it."

"If you're trying to make me feel guilty, it's working."

"No. I'm not trying to do that. You can go if you want."

"No, thanks," she says.

"But do you want to?"

"No."

"Then let's not. I'll reply to Ruth for us. You reply to Tom for us. Tell him that the girl in the shower has been keeping her hands to herself." Hope's dimples smile. We send our messages. I text her that I love her. She texts me that she loves me. Her letters dance. It's romantic in a 21st century way.

"I want to tell you," Hope says, "I never intended for you to not be able to see the futures. I think it's cool. I really do. I just didn't want you to... I felt I needed to tell you that I was worried. I wasn't trying to change you. I wasn't trying to stop you from doing anything like your dreams, like pointed perception. I was just trying to tell you I was worried."

"Well, I listened to you. You have to know that I listen to you."

Hope runs her fingers through my hair. "It reminds me of one of my early teaching experiences. I told one of my students to go do whatever; I was busy trying to help another student. He listened too."

"Uh oh."

Hope nods. "Two other teachers and a principal later, we straightened him out and got him to behave. I think... your hair is a little too short... I'm going to be more careful with what I say, now that I know you're listening." She kisses me. "I hope you don't mind my saying this, but I hope pointed perception isn't gone for good."

I stalk some animals, a wild mixture of bears and bunnies, elk and loon – very inconsistent of them to sit together on a shelf, but inconsistencies are running wild right now. I turn back to look at Hope, who's wondering what I'm doing. I reach for the biggest bear.

"Don't you dare," Hope intercepts my reach. "Don't hurt Smokey Three!"

"Smokey Three?!? What happened to Smokies One and Two? Don't tell me! Let me guess! Smoking. The cancer was unbearable."

Hope pushes me away. "Simply put, my brothers happened to them. I don't have a single original stuffed animal from when I was a kid." I certainly understand that. Hope holds Smokey Three facing me. "You're taking the whole not-having-pointed-perception-thing well."

There is a great deal of talk to a relationship. When I made the agreement with Hope at Tom's cabin to have us keep each other posted on what is going on with us, I didn't realize how much talking that meant. I didn't know that what I'm feeling about various things was important. Feelings are just incremental thoughts that could lead to action. Action matters. Feelings don't. I feel love for Hope, but if I never told her or kissed her, the feeling wouldn't matter much, would it? Smokey Three is staring at me. How do I feel about the loss of pointed perception? "You matter to me. What you say matters to me. Pointed perception works between present me and future me. If one of us disagrees, I guess there isn't a connection, based on what happened. It's only been the past three and a half or four weeks that it has been more controllable, and I think that's in large part due to your acceptance of it. You matter."

"But what about AutoDrive?"

I guess it matters too. I don't understand. "What about it?"

"What about needing to use pointed perception to figure out a solution for stopping AutoDrive?"

"Oh. I figured that out."

"When?!?"

That's a trick question. When will it happen or when did I dream it? I think she's asking when did I dream it. "Monday night."

Hope sticks Smokey Three in my face. "Are you going to tell us how?"

"No, you'll find out on Sunday. Blink once if you understand." Hope blinks. Smokey Three doesn't. "Okay, here's the deal," I tell the bear. "I just don't want anything interfering with my interference with AutoDrive."

Hope and Smokey Three look at each other and turn back to me. "What about using pointed perception to make sure that nothing goes wrong with tomorrow's experiment?"

"For someone who doesn't like pointed perception, you sure keep track of my pointed perception to-dream list." The two of them stare at me. "I never got around to checking on Lefty's experiment."

Hope bounces, "But wait, doesn't the fact that everything is figured out for Sunday mean that everything will work out or at least not harm you tomorrow?" Smokey Three starts beating up on Hope.

"Hey Smokey Three, don't beat up on Hope."

"He's not. He's patting me on the back."

"Oh." I don't understand stuffed animals. I never spent much time with them. "No, it could mean that the experiment doesn't happen tomorrow or something. It could mean that I spent or I will spend all day Friday and all day Saturday in the hospital, being patched up in time for Sunday." Smokey Three falls to the floor.

She says, "Thanks. Way to make me feel good about the whole thing." I shrug. "So you really don't know what's going to happen, and you have no way of knowing?" I nod. "Augh! I hate myself!"

"Don't hate Hope," I tell her. "That would be a tremendous waste of hate. Don't waste your hate."

"Waste of hate? I've never heard that before."

"My mom said it."

"If I hadn't said anything, you would still be able to use your pointed perception."

"Then maybe I wouldn't be here with you and Smokey Three," Hope grabs him, "and you'd be missing me."

"You're right, I would be. You're that sort of guy. When you aren't around, people miss you."

"Is that you talking or the bear?"

"Me. Hope."

I ape in a deep monotone, "Me, Ricky. You much better than Tarzan or any of my monkey friends."

"Speaking of missing you when you're not around, I was wondering if you'd be willing to hang out with me for a few hours on Friday and Saturday at the state fair. I was roped into doing some volunteering in the Education Building."

"What will you be doing?"

"Handing out stuff from the public school's booth. Answering questions. Standing around. Sitting around. Waiting around. Saying hi to students."

"Kissing former students."

"Exactly."

"I'll be there."

"Something else I've been meaning to talk with you about," Hope goes to her desk and gets a stack of envelopes. She waves them in front of me. They look like my bills fanning in front of me. I would recognize that airflow with my eyes closed.

"Are those my bills?"

"Yes."

"What are you doing with them?"

"I'd like to pay them," she says.

"Why?"

"Because I can."

"So can I."

"I would like to do it."

"That doesn't make any sense."

Her face puzzles at me. Smokey Three looks from her to me. "Do all couples make the same amount of money? I mean is the income evenly earned between the two of them?"

"No. Most probably don't make the same amount of money."

"Naturally one makes more than the other."

I nod, "Maybe their incomes flip-flop over time."

She prods, "Are their expenses the same?"

"Some would be... food, housing, vacations..."

"But their doctor's bills might be different." My head rattles twice. "In the long run, doesn't it make more sense for them to share their money?"

"But what if one of them is very wealthy? Does it make sense for the couple to just spend money from that one?"

"Okay, but how can I keep giving big money to charity when you're scrambling to pay little bills? Even if I got you everything you want, which is next to nothing, and I continue giving to charity, I'm still taking in far more money than I could ever hope to spend. If my brothers stop partnering with me, my money still multiplies. Stock exchanges have oodles of benefits for larger accounts – my accounts. My trades get traded first. My accounts earn interest that is unheard of anywhere else in the world. And you know all those market analysts who predict trends?" She shakes her head. "If I want to really move money, I cause my own trends. Trends are very predictable, when you're the one moving the money. That's what big money does. I don't need market analysts. I can negotiate terms, earnings, interest... And you want me to let you pay for food that I eat when I'm downstairs?"

"That's right."

"So what happens if I somehow lose all my money and you get rich, do you share your money with me?" I don't respond. "The ultimate test of fairness is switching places. Would you accept the situation you are offering, if the situation were turned around?"

I lie back. Hope just hit on something I hadn't thought of here. It's a variation of the golden rule: do to others as you would have others do to you. Only she's saying let others do for you what you would do for others if the roles were reversed. "You're making this difficult on me."

"Why?"

"Because I'm not used to taking handouts. We talked about this in my apartment bathroom weeks ago."

"This isn't a handout. I love you. This is what any family would–" Hope stops herself. I think she understands now, which feels like a weight has been lifted from my head while another one is plopped down on my chest. "I care about you. I want to take care of you any way I can, but you're so independent, so used to taking care of yourself and you have so many friends that I can hardly do anything for you. You cringed when I said family, but I want you to be part of my family. Okay. I won't use that word. I want to take care of you. Please let me take care of you."

There is a weakness inherent in letting someone take care of you, a weakness in the reliance, in the trust. If I come to rely on them, what happens when they leave me? What happens when they die on me like everyone else? Without warning? What happens if Hope dies? "When I first moved in and looked at my bed, I thought it would be lower to the ground." She doesn't get it. "Way lower to the ground... with my name on it... and maybe a bowl next to it with my name on it..."

Now she gets it. With irritation. "You think you're a pet?"

"At first I did when you took me for walks."

"Have I ever put you on a leash?"

"Hardly ever."

Hope crawls over and lays beside me. "Tell me what I should do. How can I take care of you without you feeling as though you're a pet?"

"That's just it. You don't tell me what to do. You ask me. That's the difference. I really haven't thought that you're treating me like a pet much. You don't need to worry. I guess it's only fair for us to alternate taking care of each other, but... I'm not used to that. For now at least, I'd like to continue paying my own bills."

"Could I transfer some money to your account?" She never gives up. She perseveres. She's looking at me with dreamy eyes full of hope.

Eying her warily, "How much?" Hope draws a one in the air, then a zero, another zero, still other zeros... "Whoa." I wipe away a few zeros. Hope hesitates and adds another zero. It makes the cut. We agree. Hope gets out her phone and with my routing and account information, transfers the money to my account. I ask her, "Do you want to go for a walk?"

Hope sits up and pounces on me, barking and licking my face.

I think I've influenced her behavior. On our way out, I sing part of the Beatles's song Help.

44

Early Winter

Outside the air is cool. The construction crew is acting cool. The squirrels are hopping about and gathering freshly fallen acorns from the storm, burying them, marking and mapping GPS coordinates. The black and gray tabby cat pounces out of some bushes and tears across the lawn with a speed that wouldn't have been possible in the heat of recent weeks. He trots up to walk in front of us. He falls over and looks up at us. Hope and I pet him. Hope talks to him about last night's storm and checks him over to make sure he's okay. He responds by revving his internal chainsaw.

Instead of heading us to the lake, Hope angles us through some gardens. The path leads us under ivy covered trellises and gazebos, purple flowers with a crumpled-paper texture accent the greens. Looking at flowers stretching up and around us, a squinting woman nearby tells us it's a type of clematis. Hope asks her if the garden had much storm damage. We're given a storm damage tour. Bright pink hibiscus flowers are even brighter, we're told, since the storm. Plants on the edges of the gardens had the worst damage, either being leveled or folded because they didn't have others to lean on. One large craggy tree branch pressed some flowers. I remove the branch and haul it aside. The squinting woman explains that she is one of several of the neighbors of the garden who maintains it. She gives us a history of who has done what and for how many years and makes a comment about an early winter.

I comment, "It looks like you're growing chicken-wire."

"No, that's to protect some bulbs from the squirrels."

"Nothing is growing except the chicken-wire."

"That's because I just planted them."

"Isn't it a little late for planting?"

"Not when you're planting flowers for next April or May."

"Do the flowers break through the snow?"

"Yes, they do."

Sure they do. Maybe in this neighborhood but flowers never broke through the snow anywhere near the Whisper Willows Apartments. That must be kind of cool. I picture a wide open snowfield with all sorts of flowers popping up, and trumpets sound.

"Hello, Acapella's Pizza. Today's special is the all green pizza with spinach, green peppers, and green olives. The sausage was looking a little green, but we had to throw that out. How can I help you?"

"That doesn't sound so good."

"Hi Dex."

"Hey, are you still not coming to tonight's game?" You don't need pointed perception to see the future. This is a call for babysitting.

"Yeah, I think I'm available for babysitting, hang on." I turn to Hope. She nods. "Yes, either myself or both of us will babysit."

"Do you want to babysit here or there?"

"Whatever works for you."

"Okay, I'll talk to Mica and call you right back." Dexter disconnects.

As we turn to leave, or at least I turn to leave, the squinting woman offers us tomatoes. I don't know much about gardening but in the world of gardening, an annual is something that does not grow back. The word annual makes it sound like it comes back every year, but annuals don't. Tomatoes are annuals. I get the impression that someone sneaks into gardens and plants tomato plants. And any one tomato plant must produce a grocery store's worth of tomatoes, because this time of year, anyone with a garden is trying to pawn off their tomatoes. I tell her, "We'll trade you – bananas for tomatoes."

"You grow bananas?!?"

"No."

They laugh. She gives us a wheelbarrow full of tomatoes and promises to tell the whole neighborhood of my offer to trade bananas for tomatoes.

A block away, Hope says, "You're always making an impression on people." I don't see the big deal. All I did was offer a productive trade.

We are about to tip the wheelbarrow over the spot where the sidewalk is being leveraged by the tree, when trumpets alert us. "Hi, Acapella's Pizza. Today's special is a tomato pizza with extra tomatoes and tomato sauce. How can I help you?"

"Any cheese?" Mica asks.

"I'll check." Moving some tomatoes around, I announce, "No cheese, only tomatoes."

"Listen, I'm calling because we have a babysitter already. Dexter wasn't understanding that I was waiting for a call when he called you, but we're all set."

"You're certain."

"Yes. Thank you for the offer."

"You're welcome. Enjoy the game." I disconnect. "That was Mica. They don't need us." Thinking about what we should do, I ask Hope, "Hope, does the Lake Weago neighborhood have lemonade stands?"

"Some kids make their maids sit out on the curb and sell lemonade on occasion."

"How about a tomato stand? We'll sell tomatoes at a dime a piece. Okay, a nickel." Hope helps the wheelbarrow over the uneven cement slabs, as a cool wind blows in from Saskatchewan.

The question is what to do with a wheelbarrow full of tomatoes. Hope could give them out at the state fair. Of course each would need a little blue ribbon award for being this year's most average looking tomato. Then they would seem to be worth something. But then tomatoes have a certain aerodynamic reputation, and the state fair has so many different performers: musicians, log carvers, mosquito air shows, square dancers, and all of them frightened of flying tomatoes. Maybe Hope should give out something with more bounce and less splat, and something else should be done about the tomatoes.

Lately Tom has been so generous – the penguin in the fridge, the nude in the shower – he should get something out of the tomatoes. I could line his driveway. I could stack them up against his back door. Some sort of stabilizing agent, toothpicks at least, would be needed to stack them up... What if they were all frosted white? Frosted white tomatoes, like snowballs with a red center. Or what if his entire yard was frosted white?

As we roll up Hope's driveway, she says, "I think we should put half of the tomatoes in each refrigerator, at least until you're ready to start a tomato stand. What do you think?"

"Okay."

"I'll run up for some grocery bags to put them in." She runs up while I remind myself that the first paper grocery bag was invented in Pigs Eye. Isn't that fascinating. The construction crew is staring again. I could throw them some tomatoes. I warm up my throwing arm. "I know what you're thinking," Hope says handing me a bag. "Resist the temptation." We bag up the tomatoes. Tucking the wheelbarrow into the garage I notice a snowman hanging out in the rafters. Taking in the tomatoes, my memory and imagination envision an idealistic snow scene. Becky is confronting Hope in their kitchen. She turns to me.

"What are the tomatoes for?" I give her a funny look from my storehouse of funny looks others have given me over the years.

"I just told you," Hope intervenes, "one of the women who runs the community garden gave them to us. What has gotten into you?"

"You don't have any plans to use the tomatoes on Tom's house?" Becky asks.

"No. We just got them," Hope says, but then they both turn to me.

"What? You can have a tomato if you want. You can bring one for Tom if you want. Take the whole bag! How could tomatoes be used on a house... without just making a mess?"

"I don't know. Tom has told me about some of the things you've done."

"Tom's getting paranoid. What Tom forgets is that it all started with Todd's pranks. He probably gives me credit for things I never did."

"So it wouldn't bother you if I took this whole bag of tomatoes? It's heavy."

"Help yourself." Becky doesn't know what to do. A horn honks. She checks out the window. As she grabs her purse, she tells me to be good. "I always am," I reply.

She says, "Bye," and whips out the door and clomps down the stairs. Clomp-clomp-clomp-clomp-clomp.

"Of course, my definition of good rarely involves me sitting still with my hands folded in my lap."

"So you are up to something?"

"Kiss me."

I almost lose track of time in her kiss. Keys click the door lock.

"Ah, **HA!**" Tom yells, while Becky takes our picture.

Hope looks at them as if they've lost their minds.

"Okay, you caught us kissing. Now would you stop fooling around?" I ask them. I have a separate storehouse where I keep all the stop-fooling-around requests I've ever gotten. Becky and Tom are thoroughly embarrassed as they leave. Becky's natural tomato blush overwhelmed any artificial blush she put on.

Hope is looking at me. "I'm sorry about that," she says.

"You don't have to apologize," for Tom or tomato face.

"They should be more trusting."

I shake my head and get out my phone. I have to remember to drop it off in my room. "How attached are you to that snowman hiding out in the garage?"

Hope looks me over like she's seeing me for the first time. "It's been hit with snowballs and weathered some blizzards... Why?"

"Would you miss it, if it hit the road and didn't come back?"

"What have you got in mind?"

"Have you noticed how cold it's gotten all of a sudden? You might go out to a ball game and come back to find winter has arrived."

"Just with a snowman?"

I like her question. "No," I smile, "we'll have to buy some snow. A yard full."

She's thinking it over. Give it time. This moment could set all sorts of precedents. It could decide how far she wants to– "What else do we need?"

I kiss my woman. "Well... do you have a lightweight winter jacket or sweater and a hat with a pom-pom at the top and matching gloves?" Hope leads me into her room. She shows me a red and white sweater with matching red and white hat and mittens. "Perfect."

"What else?"

"We'll need white fabric."

"I have white sheets..."

"No, we need more than that, bigger pieces, like from a fabric store."

"We should go to the Canoe Store."

"Do they have fabric?" She nods. "I didn't know that. Grab your mittens." I drop off my phone downstairs and pick up a jacket, hat, gloves, and scarf. On our way out, I ask Hope, "Does the snowman fold?"

"No, but it can be taken apart."

We wipe off the snowman and put his pieces in Hope's car. At the Canoe Store, we buy several bolts of fabric, fabric scissors, some tent stakes, wire, and clear packing tape. I even pick up a fabric pencil, although I can't see how it's different than a regular pencil. Fabric pencils might be a scam.

Hope is doing the fabric math. "This might be too much."

"Think three-dimensionally. Think lumpy snow. One of the bolts will be for the cutouts for the tops of the bushes, the front steps, the railings..."

"The mailbox."

"Right. The mailbox. I just wish they had the icicles. They seem to be just starting to take down their back-to-school stuff. Of course, if we had icicles, we'd need a ladder..." We buy our cart-full of fabric with other items, stop off for some dinner, and drive to a house that isn't mine. It's Tom's house.

"What should I do?" Hope asks.

"Could you put Frosty back together?" I start laying out the fabric. I stake down the corners just in case a breeze picks up.

Early snows cover the grass and bushes without covering the sidewalks or streets. That's because denser materials like cement hold heat (and cold) better than lawns and shrubs. Before it really gets cold, it is typical to see plants covered in snow, while sidewalks and streets are wet from melted snow. It's a clear-path snow. Clear-path snows are nature's way of saying, "I'll handle the shoveling this time. The rest is up to you."

"Need a hand?" Hope offers. Laying the fabric is much easier with her help. "Do we want to get the boulevard?" Hope asks, pointing to the grass between the sidewalk and the street.

"Not yet." On the third piece of fabric I stop and watch Hope, intently working to winterize Tom's lawn. She is so cool.

"Am I doing it wrong?" she asks.

"No, I was just admiring you." She flashes a surprised smile, and we get back to work. We cover the yard easily. I'm thankful Tom doesn't live out in the country with one of those huge front yards like Ben the wonder dog and his people.

Thinking of dogs, I hope they don't get any funny ideas. That could ruin everything. People stop to watch the show. I wish I had a giant theatrical curtain so they'd have to wait for the finished product. We put Frosty up to one side. The mailbox becomes snow covered. In the same way, we lay white felt fabric over a bush, mark the outline with a pencil and cut it out. On our third bush, a large man comes over. That's when I notice that we have a crowd, including dogs and bicycles. We could sell snowcones.

The man asks, "Are you planning to put anything on the roof?"

"I'm not sure."

"I have a ladder if you need it."

I encourage people. "We'll use it."

He leaves, and Hope asks, "What are we going to use a ladder for?"

I whisper, "I don't know."

While cutting fabric for the front steps and railings, a woman approaches. "Do you know what would look good? Icicles."

"I know, but we don't have any."

"We do. They're in that box. We'll want them back."

"Thank you!" We switch to putting up plastic icicles while there's still some daylight. I am up two floors on the ladder, while below the silhouettes of 30 winter experts debate icicle aesthetics and proper placement. Tom's neighborhood is really getting into this. Ultimately some fabric covers the overhang part of the roof, leading into the icicles on the edge. Someone has anonymously set a full-sized plastic reindeer in the snow, who knows only three songs and repeats them over and over. At first I thought it was one of the deer we left in Wisconsin last weekend. Some camera flashes cause Hope to remember to take some pictures. "Could you check to see how the game is going?"

A guy tells us, "It's the bottom of the seventh. The Pigs lead the Millers five to four. At least, that's where it was a few minutes ago."

I help the large guy with the ladder. He tells me that about a month ago some guy in a gorilla costume was hanging around on Tom's front lawn. I try to act surprised.

The crowd is starting to leave when a news crew shows up. The crowd does not favor this news channel because of an exposé on kids confronted with death. The news crew leaves. The crowd disperses. The news crew comes back to get film of the yard without anyone flipping them off. Then they leave again. A neighbor comes back out to ask us to turn down the deer.

It's back to just Hope and me. She gives me a band of bells, and she puts one on. We get our hats and things on and sit on the front steps. It's just like it was almost five weeks ago, except more winter-like. A cricket hops across the fabric snow. "There's something you don't see everyday." I comment. This is almost magical. "The fabric seems to sparkle like real snow."

"One of the neighbors threw out a few handfuls of white glitter. Where were you? Oh, you were probably on the ladder."

We look out over the glittering fabric, and a choir of angels sings.

"Hello," Hope answers. "Hi Nicky. Hang on." Hope covers the microphone. "She wants to know where we are." I shake my head. "We can't tell you. Why? What's up? I'm sorry. It's just that we're doing a surprise sort of thingy. Don't be mad... It just sort of happened. No, it's just us two. I don't know where Faith is. Right, Becky's with Tom and everyone at baseball. We'll involve you next time. Okay. Should I call you when we're coming home? Okay. Bye." Hope disconnects and explains, "Nicole came home, and everyone was gone. It's the first time that's happened in a while." We stare out at the starry snow.

This was where it all began for us, not with the winter wonderland but here on these front steps. We may have been introduced earlier, but here is where we really met. "Thank you for all your help. I couldn't have done this without you."

"We make a pretty good team, don't we?" She jingles her bells.

"Yes, we do."

We hold hands in the warmest, most localized winter on record. "I'm so hot," Hope says, in her red and white snowflake sweater.

"Yes, I know."

"Do you know what I've been thinking about?"

"Lefty's experiment?"

"Yes. I'm worried."

"I know." What can I tell her? I trust my friends. I go to great lengths for my friends. That's what friendship means to me. What Lefty has done so far is kind of cool. If nothing else, it could help our understanding of the mind... understanding of memory. My brand new lab coat is ready to go. I don't have pointed perception. I don't know that it matters. I'm not thrilled by the prospects of losing my recent memories, so many things have happened, so many things have changed. Without recent memories, I'd walk out of the Teska Building and try to figure out where I was. I'd drive to work and find that I no longer belong there. I'd drive home to find Ray gone and someone else living in my apartment. Trumpets would blare out of my pants, and I'd see how far I could throw my phone. "Could I borrow your phone?"

I don't want to let Lefty down. I send him a message that says that I'm having cold feet about tomorrow's experiment, knowing full well that feet are the furthest thing from his mind. I show the message to Hope, who's rubbing her shoulder. I check on the game.

"The game's over. The Pigs won."

"How long ago?"

"I can't tell." I hand back the phone.

Angels sing. Hope answers. "Hi Lefty. He's here. Hold on a second."

"Hi Lefty, did you get my message?"

"Yes. Are you ruling out involvement in the fMRI-Memmeograph STM experiment?"

"No. Hope and I are both concerned about the potential for short-term memory loss."

"Would you be willing to meet me tomorrow to discuss this? Both you and Hope?"

"Hang on." I cover the microphone. "Do you want to go with me to talk with Lefty?" Hope nods. "Lefty, yes, we'll meet with you. What time?"

"Noon. We'll have lunch together. I'll be in the bumping recollections section of the Mendota Museum. I'll send directions." Hope stretches and yawns while Lefty talks.

"Okay. We'll see you tomorrow."

"Good night." Hope puts away her phone as Tom drives up. We stand on the front steps, smiling and waving and jingling our bells. Two crickets stop what they're doing to wave as well. We're all doing the parade wave, which is slower and less specific than a normal wave.

Tom gapes at his winterized house. "I don't believe it. Becky is in so much trouble!" He gets out his phone and calls her. "Hi. Guess where your roommates are? Your two innocent roommates. They're here. With bells on. You– You've got to see it. It's– It's... **Winter!** My yard. I'll take a picture and send it to you. Hold on." He flashes a picture. He pushes a lot of buttons. "I just sent it to you. Yeah. I couldn't get the snowman into the shot. I don't know. I'll ask. Where's the Christmas lights?" I interrupt my waving to shrug with a light jingle, then I go back to waving. Back to the phone he exclaims, "All your professions of innocence! Did you know about this? She says it was on the news?!? How did it get on the news?!? They didn't say it was my house. I see."

Through her teethy smile, Hope asks, "Can we stop waving?"

"Not yet." I check my watch.

"Uh huh," Tom says to his phone. "No, you don't have to rush right over. I'm thinking of leaving it like this. Did you do the backyard too? They're shaking their heads, no, but I'll check anyway. I've gotta go talk to the vandals. I love you too. Bye." The crickets clear out of his way as he approaches.

"Now we can stop."

"Good, because my arm was getting tired. What do you think, Tom?"

"How did you get on the roof?"

"A neighbor lent a ladder. The icicles belong to them too."

"How did you get the neighborhood involved? Did you ring bells?" he asks.

"No, everybody came out on their own. We had a block party."

"I think everyone showed up," Hope grins proudly. "Huge turnout."

"Great," Tom says without meaning it. "And you helped out?" Hope nods without understanding the ramifications of the admission. "I see. You are now fair game."

"What do you mean?" she asks.

"You're in this together."

"He means he can get either of us back now."

"What about your neighbors? They were involved too."

"Different set of rules. They're neighbors, not friends." Tom wanders around back. The crickets chirp.

"You should have told me."

I shrug. "He won't do anything to hurt you."

"Really?"

"Well, he might put a life-sized picture of a nude man in your shower."

"That's not so bad."

"What if it's one of the presidents?"

Hope blinks as if she's being flashed by a succession of presidents. She shakes her head to try to get the images out. "That's not good." She pauses thoughtfully. "Still, I guess I have nothing to worry about." I nod.

Tom comes back and says to Hope, "I'm sorry if I scared you about being involved. If you want to back out now, it'll be okay. I'm sure he didn't coach you on the true meaning of your participation."

"No," Hope says, "I'm good with it. Your move." She taps his shoulder with her mitten covered fist.

"Thank you for not doing the back too."

I knock my forehead and tell Hope, "We forgot to do the back!"

"We didn't forget." She leads me away. "Good night," she sings out.

"Good night you two."

I wave. Hope hands me the car keys. I honk as we drive off.

"How did you like that?" Hope asks.

"I think it went pretty well."

"I think it went great." She turns on the passenger seat massager and sighs. "How could it have gone better?"

"It's not that it could've gone better. It's just that I can always imagine a better prank."

"What would be a better prank?"

"Moving his house. The whole house. A block away would be ideal. Otherwise, turning it on its foundation would be good too."

"Wow. That'll take some work. When does he go on vacation?" She smiles at me and squirms in her seat, like she's going to get out her calender and start making plans.

"He's learned not to go on vacation... at least not without me."

Hope laughs. She takes off her mittens, bells, hat, and sweater and gets the bag of supply remnants together. "What's the strangest thing you've ever done?"

"Strangest? I guess you'd have to break strange down into categories. I once put a coconut in the path of a tornado. Never saw it again. I don't know if it is the strangest thing I've ever done, but it's what I think of."

"Why would— I guess I shouldn't ask why. I can only imagine the baffled people wondering how a tornado picked up a coconut." Hope gets out her phone. "Hey Nicole. We're on our way home. Yes, it was pretty cool. Yeah. Okay, see ya."

The lights of the highway flash to the beat of the music on the car stereo, interspersed with dark night. Hope stretches. Some Pigs fans flash their lights at us, hooting and hollering.

"I can't believe my vacation is almost over," Hope laments. "Where did the time go?"

"The time went to Chicago and the Big Woods and dancing and to the party for Ruth and seeing Kelly unveiled and having dinner with your mom and the Chief of the Mdewakanton and a thunderstorm and winter and getting kissed by Billy Nelson." A police officer sits at a stoplight right next to us, looking us over as if we've been changing seasons without signaling. He scratches his mustache while figuring which code violation that would be. "You start on Tuesday, right?"

"Yes."

"That's four whole days away. You have plenty of time to do whatever you want."

"No, tomorrow we're meeting Lefty and going to the nursing home. Friday and Saturday it's the state fair. Friday night is the drive-in. And Sunday is AutoDrive. As far as I know, nothing is happening Monday."

"That's good right?"

"Yes, because I'll have to get ready for Tuesday." I pull into Hope's parking spot and return her keys to her. "I'm going to run up, get ready for bed, and come back down to say good night." I agree, go in, and have an apple. I check my phone. It has several messages, including pictures from Ruth. Ruth must have been bored from the game. She has pictures from the concession stands, a picture of the line for the ladies room, a picture from the highest benches of Met Stadium, a picture of a crowd of moths spinning out of control around one of the giant arc lights, and a picture of all of them with the Pig's mascot who is trying to take Jake's beer. Tom sent two pictures of his front yard and titled the message, Early Winter. From the way he sent it, he probably sent it to everyone he knows. I climb in bed. Hope runs in and climbs in after me. She shuts off the light. As I reach around to hold her, I feel a slight pull on a muscle of my upper back. That's new. I wonder where that came from? I rub the same spot on Hope. My massaging hand kneads its way up Hope's neck to rub and pet its way around her scalp. She moans softly almost saying something, but my thumb and fingers rub the words out of her. She presses into me as my fingers bump into her ear. Thumb and forefinger tug gently on the edge of her ear in a semi-circle. Rubbing down Hope, my hand stops to explore where the back of her bra used to be. She just made a yummy sound. My fingers stomp and lumber and poke and tap dance and squeeze their way across Hope's back stage. My fingers break out a shovel and dig into the arch in her lower back. "That's too much," she says. My fingers look at each other, shrug, and throw off the shovel. They climb their way to Hope's side where they lay out on her ribs, scooch over, and lay out again to rest. Hope sighs. Ten seconds later my fingers are up again inching up Hope's side. About seven finger steps from Hope's armpit, she jumps and squirms and says, "Please don't tickle me." My hand pats her, plants a flag, and moves back down her back. Gently and firmly it presses her back, like sculpting a figure in snow. My snow angel falls asleep and so do I.

Hope and Nicole wake me up by talking about how I don't move or make sounds when I sleep. My eyes are still closed. It's funny that they're talking about how silently I'm sleeping when I'm not even sleeping. Sleeping without moving or making a sound is another trick to invisibility when you're a kid on your own. Sleeping under beds is a simple trick. And under train platforms and bridges. And in cabinets. And under couches. You can learn a lot about people and upholstery from the underside of their couch.

What's amazing is that I have all my fingers and toes. I've met so many people who've been through so much more than me and have less to show for it.

45

The Trials

When I wake back up, Hope is gone and so is Nicole. It's late. I have to have breakfast so I can have lunch with Lefty. I get cleaned up, look at my bank account balance, and have a grapefruit by cutting it in half and cutting the segments like gaps between the spokes of a bicycle wheel. I scoop the segments out with a spoon. Anyone who is big on traditions ought to explain wars and chants and why grapefruits are called grapefruits. Wouldn't it be hilarious if it's because they grow in bunches? A botanist steps in and says, "We named them grapefruits, so you can recognize them in the wild. See? They grow like grapes."

Hope comes down while I'm on my second half. "Hey! You're up! You're ready!" I nod. She's very cheerful this morning. Her dimples are on full power. "Are we meeting Lefty at the university?"

"No, at the Mendota Museum."

"When?"

"In about a half an hour. We'll have lunch with him."

"Then why are you having breakfast?"

"So that I can have lunch. You have to have breakfast before you can have lunch. I've had whole days of not eating because I couldn't get breakfast."

"I can't tell if you're kidding or not."

"Right. Both. I'm kidding, and I'm not."

"Okay, I don't get it."

"Sometimes the best way to get through a difficult situation is with a sense of humor or at least a creative solution."

I steer us to my car. Hope picks up the fan knob from the floor and looks around for a place for it. She finds the post that it had called home and sets it on it. The fan knob flies off the handle and lands on the floor again. I start up the Pony Express. I try again. I try, try, try again. What did I say about a sense of humor? I can't remember. On the sixth try, it starts. It backfires. Hope jumps in her seat, and the construction crew ducks for cover. This car was far more reliable when it had responsibilities. Now that it isn't used as frequently, it hardly wants to go at all. It never used to backfire. Hope cranks her window open. The Pony Express squeals and neighs as it shifts into second gear. I smile reassuringly at Hope. It may actually take us where we're going.

We nearly get to the airport but instead drop down the Mendota bluff to the Mendota Museum. I park the Pony Express a good distance away from other cars so that a tow truck will have no maneuvering difficulties. My next vehicle should be a tow truck.

Hope flashes her museum membership card, and we get in for free. I flash her my get out of jail free card. She laughs, but you never know when one of these little cards might come in handy.

A sign tells us that in October the Mendota Museum will have a special exhibit on art forgeries and their histories. People with membership cards or clever forgeries get in free.

I use the directions on my phone to maneuver us through the museum. Take a sharp left at the copper hook, he says, feel your way through the dark ages, under the bison blankets, turn left after the paleolithic paintings, paddle through intercontinental boats, at the copper birds and fish halfway through the

Hopewell Mounds take another left, turn left again at the Cahokia summer outpost, and another left at age of pandemics, feel your way through the dark ages, do the tribal bump, turn and fight, and make reservations for lunch. Halfway through the second or third dark ages, I call Lefty.

"Hey, your directions go in circles."

"History is cyclical. So are the exhibits. I can hear you. I'm in the next gallery – the tribal bump." Lefty, his lab coat, and Dr. Forrester are at a table in the center of a round room that has tribes encroaching and pushing out other tribes westward across the United States as the Europeans moved in. The room is crowded with people pushing and shoving. Arrows fly out. Shots are fired from muskets and rifles. All are ghosts and holograms and protections of some sort, except the four of us.

"Dr. Forrester, you remember Ricky. And this is his girlfriend, Hope Ranidae."

The old man fumbles papers and bumps off a figure of Michaelangelo's David sitting, playing video games. Instead of a fig leaf, his controller is in his lap. Dr. Forrester stumbles over it to shake Hope's hand, as an arrow arches over us and hundreds of American languages are shouted across the room. I check my watch out of habit. Dr. Forrester shakes Hope's hand so vigorously that the lint of a thousand ages flies off his sweater. He smiles so strangely as his eyes show him walking briskly through a field of flowers hand-in-hand with Hope. She has that effect on people. "Should we have lunch?" he asks her in a low conspiratorial tone that ignores Dr. Vagues and myself. Hope nods. Lefty and I follow them down the turn and fight stairs. A wall figure holding a knife surprises me.

"I thought he was a carving! What a relief!"

Hope laughs. Dr. Forrester asks what she is laughing about. A painting in the entranceway to the Reservations Cafeteria shows sparkling water from high ground to tap water, with fertilizers and pesticides and cattle run-off flowing in between.

"The special today," Dr. Forrester elegantly informs Hope, "is steamed swamp rat and wild rice." Hope moves away from Dr. Forrester to my other side. Dr. Forrester runs his fingers through his hair and phones all the king's horses and all the king's men to put his heart back together again.

We choose grilled rice.

Lefty takes over. "The reason we asked you here is to talk over the fMRI-Memmeograph STM experiment to see if you have any doubts or fears that we can put to rest."

"Is there any reason why I was picked as a test subject other than having a good memory?"

They shake their doctoral heads. "Good memory? You have an astounding memory. Tell me my boy, what did you have for dinner... a week ago Tuesday?"

"French fries, a Double Bubble, and Blue Razzles."

"Those are good aren't they? You didn't hesitate did you? And what was the first thing I said to you when we first met?"

"'Hold on,' you said. And then, 'Melvin talk to your friend.'"

"That sounds about right. You have an astounding memory. Tell me, do you recall your earliest long-term memory?"

"My earliest memory was being on the floor playing with a toy car, trying to make it go without being pushed. My mom said something to my dad from the other room. He asked me what she said and I told him. I didn't realize it at the time, but I later figured out that he was hard of hearing. I tell stories of a hard of hearing aunt and uncle but really it was about my mother and father. My father used me as his hearing aid, which is ironic since he never listened to me." Hope puts her arm around me. "My biggest concern... **our** biggest concern is that something will happen to my memories of the past five or six weeks – short-term memory loss – since that happened to one of your previous patients."

"That will not happen," Dr. Forrester says.

"I don't think you can be sure of that. You are in the middle of the scientific discovery process, which means that there are still surprises in the road."

Dr. Forrester taps his tray with a finger. "What if I were to bet you a large sum of money that there will be no short-term memory loss?"

"No good. If I don't remember, I won't remember the bet."

Dr. Forrester snaps his fingers, "I thought I had you there."

I try eating grilled rice with a plastic fork. "No such luck." I think about telling them that pointed perception isn't working. I choose not to mention it. I ask Lefty, "Could the experiment work on someone who is dead?"

"No." I switch to a spoon. "Why?" Lefty asks.

"Just wondering," I tell them, but they are now all very uneasy, or else the swamp rat special is just as disagreeable as it sounds.

"Getting back to the STM loss, as long as you follow our instructions, there should be no memory loss." He thinks he's being reassuring but he's not.

Hope explains that she lost her appetite in the age of pandemics.

Dr. Forrester says, "Even if you were to lose your memories, you'd still have the transcript from the experiment. You'd still have your memories."

I ponder my carton of milk. "Incredibly good things have happened to me. Incredibly bad things have happened to me. In with all the incredibly good things, meeting Hope and falling in love with her and having fun with her has been a shining star; I can't think of anything better. I have never loved anyone more than her. The past five weeks have made me feel greater love and passion, comfort and care, than I have ever felt. It is no joke that I don't want to lose these memories." Hope kisses my cheek. Grabbing Lefty's right arm, I tell him, "That's why I couldn't go through with the experiment today. I need you to safeguard these memories for me." I let go of his arm and stare across the Reservations Cafeteria where a troop of scouts come in noisily. "A memory is fluid, like time. You can shift it about with a wave of your hand. It'll wave back to you. It can look different, even though it hasn't changed. It's not different. You're different. You're looking at it differently, now that you've sloshed it around. No transcript has that fluidity. Something will be lost in the translation." I stare at my cafeteria tray.

Lefty says, "I will not risk you or your memories for the sake of the STM experiment. You have my word." I nod. "Will you consider participating in the experiment?"

"Yes."

"The setup costs time and money. Will you let me know by next Tuesday if you're willing to do the experiment on Thursday?" Lefty asks.

"Yes," I agree. We clear our trays.

"Do you know the way out?" Dr. Forrester asks.

"The same way we got in? Are there any shortcuts?"

"Through history? No."

"I will escort you up," Lefty says. On our way, we pass the great snake Zuzehecedan, coming down for lunch. When we are up in the tribal bump, Lefty tells us of the shortcuts through the dark ages. He reaffirms his commitment to my well-being. We shake hands and leave through the dark ages and out through the front doors.

Outside, Hope holds back her hair in the breeze and says, "I have never been in there without a field trip of school children. That was really nice, what you said about me in there." We kiss passionately.

A door opens behind us. A girl scout peers out. "Oooo," she says, snickers, and pops back in.

"What if she's in your class next week?"

Hope doesn't respond. Instead, she leads me to my car. "No more school talk." I try to start the car. The radio works, meaning the battery works. It has gas, but it doesn't start. Hope is quietly watching me. I try it ten more times. I check the fuses under the dashboard. I pop open the hood and check the spark plugs and wires. I'm surprised by what I see. I start pulling out belts and hoses and casings and wires. Parts are flying everywhere. Hope gets out of the car in a panic, thinking I'm tearing apart the engine, which I'm not. Attached near the windshield washer fluid reservoir, I have a bag of spare parts. This is where the parts I'm throwing around are coming from. One of the plastic casings is still rolling around with a hollow rolling sound as Hope looks at me, trying to read me. I wire the positive post of the battery to the wire on the other side of the solenoid. I try starting it again. It starts. I pick up the loose pieces and dump them back in the bag. Hope studies my actions. I drive us to an auto parts store. I get the battery tested. It's fine. I get the alternator tested. It's fine. I buy a new starter. At home, as I work under the hood, Hope leans in beside me and says, "At the museum, I was wondering if you wanted to tell the doctors about the pointed perception development."

"I thought about it, but I decided against it. They said their interest is in my memory. Maybe without pointed perception I'll remember more. Maybe less. I have no idea."

"That was pretty funny," she says, "what you did with all the car parts."

"Thanks." I change heads on my socket wrench. I move my lamp. My head and arms dive back in. "Do you mind my watching you work?"

"Not at all. I'm used to an audience watching me work." Hope laughs. "Seriously, at Flight Control it was the best way to teach people what to do and how to do things. I could tell them how to change the starter of a car, but am I going to remember to tell them to have the car off first? I'm also used to talking my way through what I'm doing or philosophizing on the overall purpose of the activity while I'm doing whatever it is I'm doing. So much of car repair and so much of setting up the components and programming of AutoDrive are mundane trial and error. You try this. You try that. You open it back up for the tenth time today. You try not to keep count. You make adjustments. You close it back up. You try it again. There is a point where you can concentrate too much on the work. You have to be working through a slow, ordered progression of steps, but aside from that, your mind can be doing anything. You can be telling a story to an audience around you. You can play a song in your head. You can do anything to prevent yourself from sidestepping safety... or getting angry that complex systems don't work when, really, it's amazing that anything ever works... Even when they do work, it's just a matter of time before they don't work. Machines don't last." My voice echoes around under the hood of my Pony Express. "You are never truly... Done." I shut the hood. I put away my tools and wipe away the grease with one of my old towels that was at the bottom of my closet near the folded Christmas tree.

Hope wipes some grease from my face. "You should keep your nose out of there. Do you want to go to the nursing home tonight with me?" I nod. "Would you like spaghetti for dinner?" I nod.

Hope makes spaghetti for about a hundred people, without using up all the tomatoes. I help out and get cleaned up while it cooks. Ray shows off sketches of new statues. Faith and Nicole offer to clean up after dinner, allowing us to leave early for the animal shelter.

The Out Damned Spot Animal Shelter spends all their money on the animals, the way it should be, so the building is modern cinder block with the emphasis on drab, as if no artist or architect would want to donate features to a building where so many animals may get a second life or a third or possibly a fourth, but many animals are put to death. The barks and cries of the animals echo sharply off the walls. It is loud for human ears. It must be intolerable for animals or Stephanie's ears. Volunteers come in to take the dogs for walks. We take some cats for a ride.

We have Katrina, Rumbles, and Scratch from the last time, each in portable kennels, plus a six month old kitten-cat on a leash harness. She claws her way out of my arms to leap and takes off like a dog to explore and wrap the leash around a tree and tie it through a bush. "We'll call her Scout." When I unclasp the leash to untie it from the bush, Scout's legs move into overdrive, trying to claw her way out of my arms. She knows exactly what she wants – escape. I tell her, "Winter is coming." That seems to take some of the drive out of her determination.

"I can help you in a minute," Hope says. Scout meows, asking Hope which one of us she plans to help.

With my fingers laced into its harness, I hold the kitten-cat in place on the ground. A chipmunk with his nuts in his mouth scurries by, then stops to observe the incapacitated kitten-cat. "Hey Chip, when did you decide to become a monk? I thought of doing that once." If his mouth was empty, Chip would chirp a clever reply. Instead he hightails it to his tree house. I unwind the leash and clasp it to the harness. Scout has educated me. Maybe she has learned something too. I wouldn't be surprised.

"Let me help you with the car door," Hope says.

I figure Scout will be okay in the car. Scout has other plans. Scout wants to lasso the seat with the leash and crawl under the brake and accelerator pedals. "No you don't." I stop the kitten-cat from interfering with vehicular operations. She squeezes to the floor of the back seat and leads the other cats in a chorus of meows. I recognize that Scout is a troublemaker, but there's not much I can say since, in my own way, I am too. The scratching that follows is Scout sharpening her nails on the seat. I stop her. I have never clawed up anything, except perhaps the Prospective Tower. "Maybe Scout should switch places with one of the other cats for the ride home."

"The manager said that she'll hurt herself in one of those kennels."

"Maybe we shouldn't have taken Scout with us."

"Maybe you're right." Scout tries to draw blood. I should have named her nurse.

Hope doesn't know what the pint-sized carnivore is doing to my arm. She says, "I still can't believe how accepting you are about not having the dreams anymore."

"I'm a flexible guy."

"Recently I was thinking about the Savior of the Midway. I was thinking about how you figure people out. You figure out what they need and give it to them. You could go around giving people what they need before they even need it."

I decide not to snow on her parade.

Scout spins her wheels on the wax hallway floor of the Remember When Nursing Home. When her traction takes hold she zips down the hall with a speed that would make a cheetah say, "Whoa."

Rumbles finds the nearest lap and is surrounded by seniors who need him possibly more than he needs them. Katrina, the other explorer, sniffs around. She follows the lead of Rumbles, looking for attention and accepting it.

Most eyes watch Scratch, looking around and starting down the hall to investigate the rooms. I start to follow him. Hope stops me. "Why don't you hang around here; I'll follow Scratch." None of the old men follow her when she follows the mottled cat.

An old woman is saying, "Cats remind me of Hank. Whenever I used to see Hank, my vision would get misty and cloudy around the edges like a romantic picture."

Another old woman says, "Sounds like glaucoma."

"It wasn't glaucoma! It was love," she says to me.

I agree, "It sounds like glaucoma."

"Well, it wasn't."

I notice Hope down the hall, stopped at a room, as a tail disappears into it. She looks at me and goes in. I try to step away without anyone noticing.

The administrator that I met here two weeks ago intercepts me, saying, "Well, we missed you and the cats last week. Did you bring old Scratch back with you?"

"He's in a room down the hall."

Her smile turns to business. "Which one?"

The name on the door is Morton Gneiss. Scratch is on the bed of a course old man. The cat blinks slowly, looking back at us. The administrator says that he's several billion years old. His nearest relative, Isua, is in Greenland or Quebec or somewhere. The old man turns to us and rocks. The administrator signals a nurse. Hope and I take our cue to leave them to handle things. We step back down the hall. The elderly woman who may or may not have had glaucoma says, "The best time to visit someone is before they die." Close by, the other residents have the two older cats chasing and playing with several pieces of yarn. From out of nowhere, Scout bursts through, seizes some dangling yarn, and zooms off with it around a corner.

We sit with the cats. Scout reappears more and more frequently and stays longer, until finally she settles just nearly out of reach of a resident, who has to stretch to pet her. As it gets dark, we collect the cats and return them to the animal shelter.

While Hope drives us home, I rub my wounds. I don't know who's the grand champion of weird, Scratch or me. Either way, "Scratch is one weird cat," I tell Hope. "Maybe he sniffs out whoever is oldest."

"If that were true, from what I've heard, he should have sniffed out Mortie Gneiss a long time ago." Hope turns on the radio. I know the song within three beats, nearly reaching to switch it off.

Can't sleep tonight
The bus bounces across Nebraska
Can't wait to get back to my home city
Guitarist Jake snores with ever hit

Lights flash through shades
Like memories of incessant photographers
The bus vibrates like you know
It's got me turned on edge

Bouncing at 70 miles per hour
This is going to be my final tour
Wanna climb Prospective Tower
Hang with my friends, immature

Can't sleep tonight
Everyone else has crashed
That keeps me awake

Can't sleep so I write
The thought of crashing
Keeps me awake

Can't sleep through the fright

Can't sleep tonight
Can't sleep tonight

"That was Melanie with Can't Sleep Tonight off of her final album for all the people at the Prospective Tower tonight. A fog is sweeping across the Twin Cities this evening, almost like three weeks ago. This is WET-1000 broadcasting live from the state fairgrounds. We'll be right back." Hope turns back off the radio. She gives me a look. I don't know if the look has to do with the goofy voice of the disc jockey or the comment about Prospective Tower or the Melanie song or still about Scratch, the morbidly prophesizing cat. Melanie's song echoes around in my head as I lie down in bed, lullabying me to sleep.

46

The Sticks

Hope wakes me up. "Do you want to go to the state fair?"

"**Do I!** Do I? **Of course, I do!**" I shower, change, and eat before opening my eyes. I offer to drive, insisting that I fixed my car.

"I'm driving," Hope says. On the way she adjusts her visor to block the morning light and tells me, "You don't have to hang out with me all day–"

"All day?!?"

"You can wander around and help judge the cows–"

"They're on trial?!?"

"For awards."

"The cows stole some awards and now they're on trial and you want me to sit in judgment of them when they need the awards to feed their starving children?!?"

Hope throws the brochure at me. "Here's the schedule. Go crazy."

"Crazy?"

Hope gives me a look, her eyebrows peering over her sunglasses.

Traffic is surprisingly light. We get to a parking lot, and we're told that the fair isn't open yet. I have never been to the fair before it opens. I try to figure out who to call to ask if I'm crazy to be here before it opens. In all fairness, there was the time that I slept over, but no one is supposed to know about that. With a flash of her identification, we get in the parking lot and onto the fairgrounds.

The Minnesota State Fair sits on 320 acres, four times the area of Disneyland, in the northwest corner of Pigs Eye, near the border with Milltown. It's a ghost town of buildings and streets, except for late August and early September when, with over one and a half million visitors, it becomes "the largest 12 day fair in the country." That last part is according to the brochure. There might be a larger 11 day fair or a larger 13 day fair, but this is "the largest 12 day fair in the country."

The brochure folds out into a map of the fairgrounds, which shows where the Grandstand and the Skyride gondolas and the Space Tower and the barns and the Mighty Midway of amusement rides are, and all the buildings in between, but it doesn't tell me where I'll find scrambled eggs on a stick. That's what I really want. Not that it has to be on a stick, but at the Minnesota State Fair, all foods are assumed to be served on a stick unless otherwise stated.

This year's Great Minnesota Controversy is the recycling plan for all the sticks. Stick drop boxes are conveniently located throughout the fair. There's one. It has a picture of a stick and a smiling tree on it. Looking at this map for food items is like looking at a single page map of Chicago for hot dog vendors.

"What are you looking for?" Hope asks.

"Scrambled eggs on a stick."

"Does it have to be on a stick?"

I look around. Is she kidding? "Here it does."

"That's true."

The Education Building is large enough to have several aisle's worth of standard convention and trade show style booths backed with midnight blue curtains. The theme for the booth is Schools Help Children Find Their Way. I thought maps did that. And religion. And crossing guards. I have a theme for schools. How about Schools Teach? I know. It's a little late to make a new banner...

Hope sets up her things, getting out a book. I should have brought a book. Then the theme could be, Reading Is Fun. We'd sit and read our books with big grins on our faces, demonstrating our theme. Then parents would tilt my book so they'd see that I'm reading Safari Of The Mind, and they'd shake their heads in judgment of me, as if I were a cow that had stolen an award to feed my family.

"I'm going to see if I can find some scrambled eggs on a stick," I tell Hope. "Can I get you anything?" She shakes her head. "Call me if you need me."

Hope kisses me saying, "Have some fun."

I walk out of there and onto its tree-lined fairgrounds street, Cosgrove Street I think. The streets throughout the fairgrounds are all full-sized municipal streets. They have to be for emergency services and things. While at Flight Control, I once began negotiations for conducting an AutoDrive test out here when nothing else was going on. Once we started tallying potential damage to all the permanent buildings here, we decided that fields and parking lots were better suited to our needs. Besides, the fair already has bumper cars. That's where I first learned how to drive.

A truck lumbers by with an ease it'll lose when the streets are packed with people. Long shadows stretch from the trash cans, stick cans, signposts, trees, and buildings. I turn onto Dan Patch, which has the main east and west entrances and goes by the Grandstand. Dan Patch was a consistently winning race horse from back in the days when they raced horses at the Grandstand. They used to race stock cars here too and purposefully wreck trains. Now it's the main stage for the big concerts. The Minnesota State Fair has hosted many big acts. It was here that Theodore Roosevelt first said, "Speak softly and carry a big stick – you will go far."

Melanie played here. After playing in New York and Los Angeles, this was where she was most nervous. She was a wreck by mid-afternoon. Everyone was running around trying to figure out what to do. Do we cancel? I started telling jokes. I told jokes for two hours straight. I told jokes until my voice was hoarse. She was in hysterics. After the show she said I saved the day. I blushed. She said she could've performed naked. I blushed even more. The jokes weren't that funny. It's like thinking about a snowflake being dangerous. It's not. But when a 100,000,000 are flying at you with a 30 mile per hour wind, a few are bound to hit. The wind is the delivery.

Bright pale yellow sunlight reflects on the windows of curbside food stands, waking from the short night, slowly preparing for the fresh onslaught. The fairgrounds open at six and close at midnight. I check my watch. It's six now.

This is one of the largest food fairs in the country. It has the motto, "Eat fair food and carry it on a stick." Or else I made that up. I start listing off the Minnesota State Fair food on a stick. There's the corn dogs, caramel apples, cotton candy, ice cream bars, lollipops, and the shish kebabs. Those all grow on sticks, I think. But then there's the corn cob on a stick, the chocolate-covered banana on a stick, walleye on a stick, hotdish, and deep fried cheese on a stick. And then there's alligator, pickle, chocolate-covered cheesecake, waffles, egg rolls, ostrich, pork chops, spaghetti and meatballs, macaroni and cheese, pizza sandwiches, salmon, vegetable kebabs, scotch eggs, pancakes and sausage, coffee (frozen), and deep fried candy bars on a stick.

Industrial spies report that the deep fried burrito on a stick is in its final stages of development. Soup on a stick is still stuck on the food science drawing board.

Major Munch cereal isn't on their radar.

I should have brought a box of Major Munch cereal with me. Taking food into the Minnesota State Fair is like importing snow, but I'm getting... wait! There's a line of a few people at that window. They have breakfast. They have breakfast on a stick.

I call Hope. "I found breakfast on a stick. Do you want anything?"

"That's sweet. What do they have?"

"They have French toast on a stick, waffles on a stick, wild rice sausages on a stick, oatmeal on a stick, fresh fruit on a stick, hash brown potatoes on a stick, and they even have scrambled eggs on a stick."

"Oatmeal on a stick?!?"

"Yeah, someone just bought one. It's like a smoking-hot oatmeal bar."

"I'll have a fruit stick," she says.

"Do you want anything to drink?"

"No, I have water and juice here."

"Okay, see you soon, Loverducks." Two people chuckle.

"Bye," she says.

I order two fruit sticks, which are skewered melon, strawberries, banana, and peaches, and one scrambled egg stick, which has a cheesy batter around it to keep it together. They are each served in their own paper canoe. I also get a state fair cup of apple juice. I'm told to say hi to Loverducks for them. I weave my load through oncoming swarms of people, sometimes leaping up over the crowd, like a salmon swimming upstream.

Carrying breakfast through this crowd is like carrying worms through a lake; I attract a great deal of interest. Some try to snatch the food from my hands, which is why most people do not walk with food; they eat it on the sidewalk or the street right by the vendor. If they need more, they're right there. If someone asks, "Where did you get that?" they can just point.

Getting back to Hope's booth, she has a male teacher with her. We're introduced. He's Mitch Whatzhisface. They only have two chairs. However there is a stool in the inches of no man's land between the Public Schools booth and the Department Of Redundancy Department next door, which, oddly enough, has two of everything. I pull the stool over beside Hope. Sitting down, I find myself about four feet taller that Hope. This isn't right. I move the stool to the other side of the booth next to a table of brochures. I peer behind the curtain to see if I can eat backstage. I'm looking into a cholesterol booth on the other side. I learn something new. You never want to see the back side of a cholesterol booth. It's disgusting. I choose to eat on the floor behind the table, which is a good idea until Hope nearly trips over me, while fetching a brochure for a parent who's new to the area. I take the rest of my sticks outside. I find a big oak tree several blocks north of the Education Building, past the snowmobiles, snow plows, snowblowers, and submersibles. I finish my breakfast under the tree.

What's nice about the submersibles is that they show people what their neighbors are dumping in the lake that they're playing in. The submersibles only drop up to 18 meters, just enough to get caught under an old tree or get tangled up in old nets and fishing lines and spare tires. The problem with submersibles is always abandoning ship. Not so much the action as the idea. It's the thought that counts.

Some squirrels nearby take some acorns and a discarded stick and create acorns on a stick. They laugh their fuzzy gray and red tails off.

Two days from today AutoDrive will be tested. I hope it doesn't kill anyone.

A week from today will be my second interview with Common Communication.

A man and woman argue their way across the grassy area where I'm sitting, not noticing me at first. When they notice me, they each give me a clear facial expression that pleads, "Help me," but they keep walking and arguing. "You said–" and "Why do you always–" and "Can't you just once–" and I wonder if they know what they are arguing about, since they certainly dance around the subject. On the street nearby, clusters of people push baby carriages and pull wagons of children. One woman carries a child while pushing a stroller and pulling a wagon. If I had a medal, I'd give it to her. Lucky for her, it's downhill from here. A pair of geriatric women walk slowly by, pointing out where things are and where things no longer are. Crossing paths with the older women, a group of teenaged girls, dressed to turn heads, walks casually and talks at high speeds. Any one of them could be Princess Kay of the Milky Way, state fair royalty. All I catch is a squeal, "But I didn't give him my phone number. I gave him a relay service number. I can cancel it any time." Three boys follow them at a discrete distance. A large family gets out of the street to meet, apply sunscreen, synchronize watches, negotiate money, and revise schedules of "meeting back up again." Three more families mimic the first with varying degrees of success. Two more groups march in, carrying blue wooden yardsticks against their shoulders like rifles. I have been to this fair so many times, and people are always carrying the yardsticks, but I have never seen yardsticks being handed out. I have never seen where they come from. I've come to the conclusion that they are not handed out. People bring their matching yardsticks back from the Yardstick Year. I must've missed that year. They use them to measure how long they've been coming to the fair. This open area is no longer open; it's crowded. The squirrels have retreated to the trees and are chattering about engineering difficulties of an oak tree based acorn catapult. Below them, another group walks through carrying red wooden yardsticks. There must be a battle scheduled sometime today between the red yardsticks and the blue yardsticks. Just before I'm trampled, I get up. As soon as I move, a small half-built catapult crashes down beside me. I could lecture the stupid squirrels on the principles of motion, but instead I take my two paper canoes to the garbage and my two sticks to a stick bucket to be gathered up and turned back into a tree when the fair is done.

A curbside shack covered with giant inflatables attracts my attention. Colorful action heroes are tethered to the top. They have cars, planes, elephants, dinosaurs, deer, gophers, phones, squirrels, and bison. I think about my bank account balance that I was just looking at yesterday morning. The inflatable car can wait for another year.

Standing about six feet from the shack, I turn to go, and there's a boy looking at the inflatables from the same distance away. Is he making fun of me? It's as if he doesn't want to get too close or they'll pop and he'll have to buy something. His jeans are hand sewn in the knees with big loopy stitches that I once used. He steps back and walks over to a woman waiting for him.

"Did you see anything you like?" she asks him, saying "like" not "want" or "need."

"Yeah. The car."

They walk away without saying anything else on the subject.

I look up, expecting to see God between the trees, egging me on. All I see is blue sky.

I step up to the inflatables vendor, wait through another purchase, and buy an inflatable car. Back in the fair street, the two have been swallowed up in a flowing river of people. I hurry in the direction they were headed. They could be anywhere by now. I dodge a woman whose face is too small for her head. Stopping to think, I reason that they are probably in the middle of the street. I direct myself to the middle of the street. Nothing. I look up, half expecting a giant arrow pointing the way, but the sky is still clear and still blue. I continue on. There they... no, that's not them... that's them. I stop them. "Hi, would you like to have this?"

The kid looks at the inflatable car like it's the weirdest thing he's ever seen. "No, thank you," the mother says politely.

"It's yours. No strings attached."

"That's all right," she says.

Why does everything always have to be so difficult? "I'm going to set it here on the ground and leave. If you don't want it, the crowd will kick it around; it'll end up in the gutter and the storm sewer, and it'll float down the Mississippi." I set it down.

"Thank you," the boy says from behind me. It's tough to be nice these days.

Back in the Education Building, Hope and Mitch Whatzhisface stand while congested streams of people inch past like bumper to bumper traffic. I inch by with the rest of the crowd, until Hope snaps out of her pleasant demeanor and recognizes me and pulls me out of the congestion.

"I've missed you," she whispers to me. "Where have you been?"

"Machinery Hill," I whisper back. "Why are we whispering?"

Hope smiles and sighs simultaneously. No dimples. Her eyes have the same "help me" expression that I saw in the couple crossing the lawn earlier. She escorts me past Mitch, who is trying to convince a woman that public schools are just as safe as private schools, and over to the stool. I sit down. Hope stands beside me. Mitch is telling the woman that he only recommends private schools to parents of troublemakers so that they can get the attention they deserve, but the woman has already dismissed him and is walking away.

Hope rocks briefly on her heals and steps over to Mitch. She lowers her voice and, from what I hear, tells him that he is not talking to people in a way that positively represents the public school system. He tries to interrupt, but she has more to say. He says, "You answer questions your way; I'll answer them my way." He sits in his chair. Hope gives him a smile that I hope she never has to give me. She gets out her phone, and Mitch shifts in his seat. Hope calls someone who assigned her here and explains the situation.

Hope relays a message to Mitch, "You can go."

Mitch throws a conniption and storms away, leaving a trail of pencils and brochures. Hope continues to talk on the phone, while I pick up loose brochures. A thin man asks about schools in his area. I take out a school district map and point out the local schools. A small family pulls in and asks what we've got. I offer pencils and brochures and bags – everyone gives bags – and magnetic schedules. They like the magnetic schedules. Word spreads about our magnetic school schedules. There is a stampede. Hope hangs up and helps out. She has everyone line-up, single file. Teachers like single file lines. There must be an introductory level course in educational lines that is mandatory for a degree in teaching. With few magnets left I stand on the stool and ask questions of the class to determine who wins the prize.

I ask them to identify the main symptom of the disease Gigglitis. A magnet is awarded.

I ask them to name the three types of Minnesota currency. A magnet is awarded.

I ask them to identify the special type of car that is being tested in Milltown on Sunday. A magnet is awarded.

The woman with the baby stroller and the wagon approaches. A magnet is awarded.

I ask them to sing a Melanie song. Several magnets are awarded.

I ask them to identify the name of the statue by Cameron Raymond that was installed in Wild Rice Park earlier this week. A magnet is awarded.

I ask them, "What's long and thin and has three feet?"

I wait. No one guesses a yardstick. No magnet is awarded.

Hope stands on a chair. It almost folds up beneath her. She joins in and alternates questions with me, until we clear out the magnets, half of the pencils, and a can of Cooler Cola that Mitch left behind. It's not about what you give, exactly... I guess I should say, it's not **just** about what you give. It is just as much about how you give it.

The crowd clears away, and Hope goes back to answering normal questions.

Sitting on the stool I look out at the crowd as they pass by. They look back at me. I think they're wondering what I am displaying. It couldn't be intelligence or education. I'm sitting to the side. Maybe I represent the opposing point of view. I can do that. I get off my high stool and rummage around in a box of supplies. Bending construction paper in the shape of a cone, I staple it in place. I cut a rubber band. I staple the ends of it to the diameter of the cone's circle. I write Dunce on it, using a Z instead of a C. I grab a sheet of scratch paper and two more rubber bands and climb back onto my stool. I untuck half my shirt and untie my shoes. I put on my dunce cap. Hope calls to me. I ignore her for the moment and focus on tearing off and rolling up little scraps of paper. I fold them in half like little Greater Than symbols. Hope gets in front of me.

"What are you doing?"

I look up toward my hat and down at the paper wads in my lap. "Providing a visual alternative to education."

"Okay."

Another male teacher has stopped by. Everything about him says teacher. Even his shorts say Teacher. He laughs and says, "Just as long as he doesn't do anything stupid."

I'd probably get in trouble if I shot a paper wad at Mr. Teacher. I'd have to buy him some cheese curds or something.

I start shooting paper wads at the curtain, while people in my booth, the booth across the aisle, and people passing by take notice. I think the booth across the aisle is in firing range. For some reason, it's filled with fragile things teetering on thin pedestals. Organizers of the fair and of conventions never put booths in any kind of order like the alphabet, not because of illiteracy but because there are more fundamental concerns, like separating rivals so that tensions don't escalate into booth wars. That's how the War Of 1812 got started.

I recognize a girl being dragged through by her parents. It's– It's– Don't tell me. It's Fingklukreb! Or else it's Molly or Carrie. Naturally, I shoot a paper wad at her. The paper wad hits her in the arm.

"**Hey!**" she says with major annoyance.

She looks for the culprit. Then she spots me.

There are four stages to recognition:

The Detective Stage – This is where they try to match your face or other distinguishing feature to their memories. In the jigsaw puzzle of their life, you are the missing pieces.

The Stage Of Denial – I don't actually believe there is a denial stage, but everyone says I'm wrong.

The Greeting Stage – I am so happy to see this stage again. How long has it been? Do you still do what you used to do when I last saw you? Yes, when you last saw me I was talking to you. Now, here I am, still talking to you. I can't believe you haven't noticed me talking to you for all this time, but here we are still talking to one another.

The Off Stage – Well, I better get back to my life. You know how living gets. You have the breathing and the heartbeating, plus all the eating and sleeping and monkeying around. I'm sure you have a life that you want to get back to also, so I won't keep you.

Fingklukreb saunters over like she is the hottest thing in junior high school. "Hi Milkshake!" she grins. "Are you in a witness protection program somewhere? I haven't seen you around." She looks at me then the booth and cocks her head, eying me in new light. She backs away. "You aren't a teacher are you?"

"No, that would go against my **principles**."

"You're a **principal?!?**"

"No, I'm dating a teacher."

"Almost as bad." Fingklukreb pokes me.

Hope comes over. "This is my girlfriend, Hope." Fingklukreb nods to Hope.

Fingklukreb cries out, "I suppose you're going to want your ring back!"

Everyone stares. People in Milltown stare. People at the Loon Lake Mental Health Center stare. People selling cheese statues in Wisconsin stare. Thankfully, Hope doesn't fall for the act. Fingklukreb tries to sit on the same stool as me, managing only to lean on my knee.

"Are you going to introduce me to your... friend?" Hope asks.

Here goes nothing. "Hope, this is Fingklukreb. Fingklukreb, this is Hope."

Fingklukreb's mouth hangs open. You could land a plane in there. You could even refuel it and do a full maintenance check. You could–

"**What** did you call me?!? Fingklukreb?!?" I nod with the pleasant smile of someone who knows he's wrong but doesn't have any bad intentions. She leans in to pressure me with her height, as if I'm the height of an average junior high schooler. "My name is not Fingklukreb. It's Freedonia."

"Like the country?"

"Yes." She stares at me for an automatic follow-up question. When I don't ask, she says, "Carrie said she saw you at Prospective Tower, handing out candles."

"I saw her too."

Freedonia's mother seizes her in a hug from behind, and she cringes. "Donia, who are your friends?" Tough for her to ignore her mother when being held like this, she battles the urge. She introduces us simply. The mother hardly notices. "We have to get going. The Minnesota Vowel Elongation demonstration is in half an hour."

Freedonia taps my leg. "In a minute."

"Now," her mother says, pulling her away.

"Bye," Freedonia whines.

"Say hi to Carrie and Molly for me."

"**What?!?** You remember their names but not my name?!?" Freedonia is enraged.

"I never clearly heard your name!"

Freedonia stomps off angrily. Before she disappears into the crowd, she blows me a kiss, accidentally slapping the guy behind her in the gut. Hope has her eye on me while talking about school fundamentals. Hope refers to a brochure, offers it, and asks me, "When did that rendezvous with the three girls happen?"

"The Monday night after we first met... no, after we second met."

"Where was this?"

"The Ice Cream Bar."

Hope nods and answers more questions about schools. Someone asks me where the bathrooms are. I could list them all, all that I know; instead, I list the closest ones. Someone else asks why math and other subjects are taught when computers can provide all the answers.

My response is, "Seven, 89, and 24. Math seems to be teaching things like multiplication and division and formulas and shapes and measurements, but behind all that, backstage, are the relationships of numbers. Math isn't subjective. That's our role. We decide how seven relates to 89 and 24. Are these good numbers or bad numbers? Computers can give us answers, but they don't give us proportions and relationships to what we're doing." Hope and a small crowd are listening in. "Your computer doesn't know you. It's objective. It knows the correct answers. You have to decide the right answers."

"So schools are teaching that any answer can be right?"

"No, I'm an engineer, not a teacher. What I'm telling you is that numbers quantify existence; we need to understand the fundamentals of numbers to qualify them. We produce charts and vector curves and shapes to visualize the information." His hand sails over his head to show that what I said sailed over his head. "Is seven better than 24? Are we talking about dollars or friends or feet of snow? What are the proportions of those numbers? Which number is good?"

He points around with his index finger, "So you're here to explain the practical side of education?"

"Yes, I am."

He nods, "Thank you."

A woman holds out her hand and introduces herself as Lenore Poe, "I've worked this booth before, but it was never like this. Such lively discussions! I got a call that you needed some help here. You're almost out of pencils."

"Right. Do you know how to inject graphite into used food sticks?"

She thinks about that, while Hope works her way back to the table to tell her that I'm just kidding. Another woman shows up to help, and we are excused. Hope grabs her things and takes a drink from her water bottle.

"Are we coming back?"

"Not until tomorrow."

Outside the Education Building, the long shadows have all been replaced with short ones. The fresh smell of cotton candy and corn dogs dominates the air. Heat up marshmallows and hotdogs in the same pan and stir them up. Maybe throw in a corn muffin. That's it. That's the smell.

As we walk, Hope tells me, "I didn't get to hear all of what you said about the value of math, but I liked what I heard of it. I would've liked to have heard it all."

"Right, measurements. Do you want to hear it again?" She nods. I go through it again for her. As I talk, I steer us toward vegetable kebabs, interrupting myself to tell her that I'm really hungry. I order two skewers full. Hope passes. "Do you know what you want for lunch?"

"Dessert." She glances at me. "I'd like a chocolate-covered banana."

"Then we will get you a chocolate-covered banana." A greasy haze rises up from the fairgrounds. We steer around the crowd and through the cloud. We find Hope's chocolate-covered banana on a stick and a stage with a juggling act. The guy has hushed the crowd to concentrate on having five plates of cheese curds spinning on five gigantic sticks. Until trumpets bring it all crashing down. I sulk away to answer my phone. It's Cy. "Hi Cy."

"What's up? Where's the Acapella's Pizza? With the special on cheese curd pizzas?"

"It's funny you should mention cheese curd pizza, because a guy was spinning five big plates of cheese curds until somebody's phone went off sending them all crashing down."

"You're kidding."

"No, I'm serious. I wonder if anyone sells state fair insurance?"

"Check the cheese curds menus. I think they sell limited term insurance policies."

"That makes sense. What's up?"

"You haven't checked your messages, have you?"

"I've been busy."

"You're at the fair."

"We were working a booth."

"Really? What booth?"

"Public schools. In the Education Building."

"We have to get you a real job."

"Don't worry about me. I'll be fine. Okay, so I'm reading through the messages and you're talking about meeting here at six o'clock."

"I thought I canceled that message. The new plan is to meet at your house at 6:30." It's weird her calling it my house. It's Hope's house. "Is that okay?"

"Yeah, that's fine."

"I just wanted to check with you. I'll try not to call you again. Bye."

"Bye, Cy."

I return to Hope and the juggling stage just in time for a calliope of crashing, thin ceramic plates. This time I had nothing to do with it. I just got here.

"**You!**" the juggler yells, pointing his finger at me. He tears off into the crowd, racing toward me, legs flailing in uncoordinated effort.

"Uh-oh!" I thrust my vegetable canoe at Hope to hold, and I run around the crowd and over an outstretched leg and onto the stage where he came from. I try to spin a plate on a stick without centering it. It spins off and shatters. He's yelling while trying to get back to me. A kid gets in his way. I try another plate. No luck. I throw another plate up at a 45 degree angle and hold out my arm like a rifle and I shoot at it like skeet. The juggler has returned to the stage. I run around it and across it and I hide behind a box. The juggler acts like he can't find me. I hear tons of kids yelling that I'm behind the box, the little rats. He finds me and drops a stack of plates behind me as if on top of me. He thanks his crowd and promises to have all the plates spinning in the next show, five hours from now. While he's talking, I examine a plate and find that it has a nick in the center of the underside, that would aid the balanced rotation of the plates. People clear out, and I remain hidden. The secret to hiding is to remain hidden. I once played Hide And Seek for weeks.

"Would you want to do this again tomorrow? Same time?" the plate spinner asks me from back stage. "If you could do it exactly like you did it, I'd give you 40 bucks." We swap phone numbers. And he tells me that the coast is clear.

I get up and the crowd has dispersed, except for a few scattered completionists, people who need to know that everything is all right, and Hope. There's always Hope. I brush myself off and hop off the stage and rejoin her. She's finished her banana and some of my vegetables. "Let me guess, you're still hungry." She's staring at me with bewilderment. "That was Cy on the phone. She wanted to know if we are okay meeting at our house," Hope smiles, "instead of here at six tonight." Hope nods. Maybe she lost her voice. She is still breathing. She must be really hungry and too weak for words. "You know what's great? The grilled corn on the cob. The corn on the cob that I made at Tom's cabin pales in comparison. Let's get you some corn on the cob. You can finish the veggies if you want." I take her arm, leading her to the corn.

The corn on the cob is so fresh, it's still growing. It is so yellow, it glows. It is so delicious, it's reason enough to come to the fair.

Each grilled cob is at least a foot long and dipped in melted butter. I buy over two feet worth and lead us to an undisclosed romantic spot, a quiet spot amidst the chaos. I take back my vegetables and hand her a corn on the cob.

Hope takes off her sunglasses. "Did you know the plate spinner?" I shake my head. "Did you know that was going to happen?" I shake my head. "Wow. It looked rehearsed. You came back at the perfect time." Mmmm, corn.

Eating corn on the cob is not romantic, any more than eating spaghetti is romantic. Food that makes you slurp or pick your teeth is not romantic. But I look at Hope, and it is. She makes it romantic.

I've known I'm in love. I didn't know how high I've fallen.

I study her muliebrity. I study her enough to want to make love to her, right here, in the middle of the state fair. This is a nice, romantic spot, but not that private. I need to think about other things.

Technically, the corn on the cob is not on a stick. It's on its stalk. The stalk is covered by the corn husks, pulled down from the ear but not off. The stalk and husk handle is wrapped in a napkin.

"What are you thinking about?" Hope asks.

"I'm analyzing this amazing corn."

"Would you like some help?"

"No, I think I've figured out how to make it drive to the store and back. What were you thinking about?"

"Mitch and Freedonia and the plate spinner." I start to nod my head and shift to shaking my head as I picture them in a group trying to do something... anything... involving engineering. We sit back and watch the fair crowd drift by booth signs that advertise their food without advertising name-brand products. There is a distinct lack of advertising at the fair.

"What would you like to do?" we ask each other simultaneously and laugh. I throw out our trash.

Hope leads me downhill through people crowded streets, past the slingshot, hurtling two victims 140 feet straight up, usually right after eating. She takes me to the cattle barn, which is more than any barn from a farm. It covers over 117,000 square feet with 560 cattle stalls. Right away when entering the barn, it's clear – these may be the finest cows in the state, but they aren't housebroken. Many of the cows have someone by them, young or old, grooming them and maintaining their stalls. "Look at the cows," Hope says. She's being cute.

I reply, "What cows?" A cow sticks its big cow head in my face, snoofs, analyzes my corn breath, and nods, appreciating the ambiance and aroma of my recent vintage of maize.

The building has bathrooms built in. That means they are trying to housebreak the cows. One cow is being hauled out of the women's room. Another big animal is being steered out of the men's room. We both go in to our appropriate rooms to show them how it's done. As we clear out of the barn I think about how it's been a month since we were in a barn together.

Hope says, "I think it's time to go, but even though it's not on our way, I'd like to stop by the Agriculture Building." I agree and find myself in one spoke of the round building, looking at a three feet wide by two feet tall image of the Savior of the Midway created with dyed rice and wheat grains. I think I'm going to be sick. Hope and I head back to her car. She tosses me her keys. I drive carefully over the rut riddled field. What happened to cause all of this? Oh yeah, Tuesday's storm. That must have been some picnic for everyone at the fair. Hope asks, "Have you always liked math?"

"It was something I could always count on." Hope laughs, but I'm serious.

"You have a lot of patience for answering questions," she says, adjusting her massage. "You should be a teacher, not Mitch. He isn't even from my school, but his reputation precedes him. Teachers transferred to get away from him. Teachers quit to get away from him. Most businesses have a Mitch, the guy that says the wrong things and does the wrong things and outlasts everyone else. The reason he was at the booth was to punish him. He punished us and the public more than he was punished."

47

A Snowflake On A Leash

We're in Tom's truck in the lead, followed by Jake's truck. Ruth's truck got stuck at some lights. "Just ahead on the sidewalk, do you see that?" Tom waves his arm out his window to signal Jake as we pull over. A guy is walking a small white dog, half the size of most cats.

"What's going on?" Hope asks.

I can't answer as I get out, and Tom, Todd, and Cy get out. From behind us, Jake and Erix get out to stare at the guy and his little dog. We observe them studiously and look at each other.

"Is that a real dog?" Tom asks. The guy nods, taken aback by all the attention. "Seriously. Aren't you worried about losing Snowball or Snowflake next winter?"

"No," he says, unprepared for this confrontation. Then he picks me and asks, "What kind of dog do you have?"

"I have a wolf."

"You have a domesticated wolf?!? I think–"

"No, I let it run free." I could tell him that on the North Shore of Lake Superior there's a highway sign that says I adopted a wolf. But this is about him. I don't want him to think that this is all about me.

We take one last look at the tiny dog and return to the trucks, shrugging at each other and shaking our heads.

"Poor guy," Tom says. "He doesn't understand."

Todd says, "I feel sorry for the dog. There isn't much time left before winter. Then, he's a goner." We climb back in and drive off. "Seriously," Becky says, "what was that all about?"

Tom replies, "Everyday tropical fish and birds–"

"And tropical plants," I interject.

"– and tropical plants, and desert plants, are pulled out of Mexico and Central America and hauled up here to die. Everyone knows something about that. Almost as bad are the people who buy little white dogs without a half a brain and little, stilt-like legs and expect them to survive the winter. If tiny dogs are kept in cages with other hamsters–"

"With the little wheel?"

"Right, with the little exercise wheel. That's one thing. But anyone who thinks it makes sense to take the half-rodents out for a walk, won't shell out the money for the complete cage system with the Sky-way-like connecting tubes."

"This is our cause."

"Exactly."

"What's the name of your cause?"

"Uh, Pets Without Snowshoes."

Tom says, "Six out of every seven pets in Minnesota are ill prepared for winter. Sad but true."

"You made that up," Hope says. "Didn't you?" No response. "How did this start?"

Long pause. Tom drives and sighs, "Joe was walking through the snow one day. He said that he stepped on something that didn't feel right. It felt like Indiana snow or Ohio snow, not Minnesota snow. When he looked at the sole of his boot, well... part of the snowbank had been wearing a tiny sweater. He hasn't been the same since."

"That's when his drinking problem started," Todd chimes in. Cy is holding her mouth. We drive in silence for a few miles, in memory of poor Snowflake or Snowball or whatever its name was.

I ask, "Whose turn is it to tell Joe that this happened to him?"

"I think it's your turn," Cy says. Hope doesn't know what to believe.

I get out my phone and send Joe a message. He messages right back asking where we are. I tell him we're in a caravan headed for the drive-in. "He says, 'Fenderberg Drill.'"

"Should we call the other cars? Calling all cars, Fenderberg Drill at the next stoplight." We jump out, circle the vehicles checking the wheel wells for fenderbergs. Not likely this time of year, but you never know. Al checks the tire pressure on his way by. We jump back in for the green light.

"There's the drive-in." We wave as we pass it.

Tom asks, "Should I take the next exit or tick off Jake?"

Cy responds, "We want to get spots all together. Besides, Jake has had a tough week. Go easy on him."

Ignoring Cy's response, I respond, "Both." I imagine the truck becoming invisible and turning off, while a satellite projection of the truck continues down the road. All it would take is–

"He's figuring out how to do it," Hope reports to the others. I look up, and Tom has already exited, so I throw away all my plans. Our three trucks get in line to wait for the drive-in to open. Tom and Todd set up a rug, card table, and chairs between his truck and Jake's. I sit down, but then I flinch when I see the cards and the poker chips.

"You know," Tom says, "a guy came to collect the deer."

"The buck?"

"Do you know who's snowman that is?"

"It's ours."

"Okay, I should be able to bring him by next Thursday."

"Bring him by sooner, he's got a busy schedule."

"I'll try. Oddly enough, there's been a gapers block on my block." Looking around, Tom taps the table, "This is District 4 Judicial Poker."

I offer my chair to Stephanie. Out of principle, she refuses. "I can't play."

"Why not?" Jake asks. "Oh, that's right. Seeing the futures. Very honest of you."

"No, it's not that. That doesn't work anymore." I stand up. "It's that I'm broke." Some of them eye Jake. It is kind of his fault that I don't already have a job. I try pushing Stephanie into the chair, and she lets me. I take a walk to the front of Tom's truck. The people in the car in front of us are all turned my way. The sun casts orange on my face.

Hope says, "You're not broke. What about the money that I just transferred to your account?"

"That doesn't count. I'm not going to gamble away your money."

"I don't recall putting any restrictions on it. It stopped being my money when it left my account." I disagree, but I don't know how to tell her. I shake my head. It rattles. "If you want to play poker with your friends, play poker with your friends."

I turn to her. Becky and Nicole are hanging around behind her trying not to invade our space but showing that they want to be around. "Hi." If anyone around here should be uncomfortable, it should be me.

"Wow, look at the ladies," someone says from the car in front of us, unaware that sound travels really easily through open windows. And he used a term other than "ladies."

Nicole whispers something, and Becky turns back to our group. Nicole steps up and asks,

"Remember my offer of helping you to find a job? I still want to help. I think I can help. I may not be able to find you a dream job, but I should be able to find you a compromise. That's what people do. They work at compromises. I never set out to be a receptionist, but I know my job, and I'm good at it. I can get you a job. Please let me help."

"Okay."

Nicole bounces up and down and hugs me. "Yea!" She hugs Hope. That car ahead is screaming in our direction.

I whisper to Nicole, "Just between us, I have a second interview a week from today. If that doesn't pan out, yes, I would like your help finding a job." Her lips retreat into her mouth, but she's still bouncing in place with barely contained excitement.

The card table and chairs are being folded up. The rug is being rolled up. The game barely had time to get off the ground. We climb back into our trucks. A gate has been opened, and the line is moving. Some kids try to hitch a ride in, but our drivers decline. The gravel driveway has blotches of upraised pavement breaking out here and there like acne. The old pavement helps tell where the old drive-in had been. That screen was tilted so the highway on the other side of the frontage road could get a glimpse of the screen, just enough to shock or offend or entice people to drive around the highway in circles. Now the screen has its back to the frontage road and the highway. Anyone wondering what life was like for the last remaining dinosaurs could just talk to drive-ins, the big, lumbering, last-of-its-kind outdoor movie theaters, that can't find a decent meal for half the year. Dinosaurs and drive-ins starved.

Tom pays for all of us in the three trucks. We thank him. Seagulls scatter from the field of gravel as we vie with other traffic for good middle, front spots – prime drive-in real estate to park three large trucks side by side. Hopefully anyone parking behind us brought lawn chairs to sit up front. The clouds turn pink. Cy and Becky pass around drinks from a cooler, and Todd tunes in the drive-in on the radio.

Hope says, "Hey Tom, I like your seat massager."

"I don't have a–" he turns and sees me giving her a back rub.

Cy is telling us all about what we're going to see before we see it. Why would anyone want to do that? Talk about what's going to happen before it happens? That's weird.

Jake reaches in and tags us. "Did you bring the Funnellator?" I shake my head. "Drop your drinks and come with me." He leads us toward the gigantic screen, carrying a football. Tom and Todd pick their teams. We start playing. Jake starts inventing rules, making up rules as we go. Weird rules. Odd rules. The whole thing is closer to Calvinball than football. Everyone is hopping on one leg and doing referee signals with their arms and catching fireflies and humming while chasing after Erix with the football. Spectators gather to watch. I call that Hope is on my team and has to kiss me. Jake calls she has to kiss him. Hope calls that Jake's rules don't count. She hops over and kisses me. After 20 minutes, we're exhausted and drag each other back to the trucks, which must have moved because they are way far away now. And the field has hillier furrows than it did before. Dusk signals the screen to light up with concession advertisements.

Local animation winners are announced and horns honk in appreciation. The winning animation is shown. It's about a gopher who leaves his burrow in winter and loses his identity – freezing off his tail, that sort of thing. He digs around the world to find someone like him and ends up talking on the web to his old burrow. It's a new cartoon but an old story.

The double feature is a pair of scary movies. Midway through the first one, my foot kicks my bag of flashlights. "I'm going to check on the others." Hope looks from me to the screen to me again, scared. "I'll be right back."

Tom's truck has Tom and Becky, Todd and Cy, and Hope. Jake's truck has Jake, Ruth, and Al. I offer them flashlights. Ruth's truck has Erix and Stephanie, alone, kissing. I would offer them flashlights, but they've already found each other. Al meets up with me and says, "Nadine and Nicole have been gone for a while." I tell Hope through the window that Al and I are going to take a walk. Stephanie calls us back to Ruth's truck and says that she thought she heard Nadine shouting and it came from that away. She points behind us. On the way, Al tells me, "She should rent out her ears."

I tell him, "You know she heard you."

He nods. For her benefit, he says, "Yes, I know."

Off to the side of the concession stands and bathrooms, a group of guys has gathered. I hand Al a high beamed flashlight, and I take one. We both shine them on the group while approaching. It's a hiccuping Nadine and Nicole in the middle. I say authoritatively, "The screen is over there." We shine our lights away from the girls and at the guys. I give Nicole and Nadine two club-like flashlights, and they return to the trucks with us. Nadine calls the guys knuckleheads. Nicole seems more annoyed at Nadine, and she joins Hope and me in Tom's truck, while a giant dinosaur stomps through the parked cars, stops, and sticks its nose out at us and snoofs. Nicole falls asleep.

A blizzard of popcorn is dumped on Tom's truck. The bucket drops too. The field mice will have a field day. Tom is annoyed because of the butter and because he just got the truck washed.

The next movie is billed as a Minnesota Mystery. You want mystery? There is no truer mystery than a Minnesota Mystery. You don't know if you are approaching a person or a polar bear until you see the parka. Polar bears don't wear parkas. Police investigations force cops to ask the people around them their gender and race. And the police are always wary because weapons the size of tubas could be concealed in most Minnesota coats. Breath breathes out steam like the smoke from an entire pack of cigarettes. People talk through clenched teeth like Bogart or Eastwood, or they mumble like Brando. Anywhere else this would be considered acting – acting of the finest caliber. Here, it's keeping your teeth from chattering and keeping your tongue from freeze-drying. Only idiots talk with freeze-dried tongues. Winds whip snow into swirls of white over gray over deeper gray, in this monochromatic winter world, this macabre emptiness of white on white on near white with hints of evergreen. Cinema Frosté.

Midway through this movie, everyone female in Minnesota has to go to the bathroom. Since I have the flashlights, I'm the state bodyguard. I escort them to the bathrooms where they must have captivating entertainment because I don't see anyone for 20 minutes. The women's room at the Field And Screen Drive-In is the place to be. Then they all want to swing on the swings, so I escort them all to the swings where we swing our way through the second movie. The third movie of the double feature is confusing, since it looks just like the first movie. It is the first movie. We go back to the trucks where everything is packed up and waiting for us, so that we can all go. On our way home we flash our flashlights at each other's trucks, while we talk about plans for the fair tomorrow.

Midway through the night, I wake up surrounded by Hope and Nicole. They're both awake. Nicole whispers, "How did you know that Nadine and I needed some help tonight? Can you see futures again?"

"Why are you whispering if we're all awake?" I check my alarm clock. It isn't asleep either. It's on edge. I push it back. "I got help from Al and Stephanie, but you didn't really need any help. You just needed some lights. Good night." I fall back asleep.

Hope wakes me back up. "Hey Sleepyhead, it's time to get up and go back to the fair."

"We just went. Can't we wait another year?"

"No, I have to go."

"How about I meet you there?"

Hope sighs, "Okay." I fall back asleep.

Ray wakes me, "Hey, Hope's been trying to call you." I look at my alarm clock. That's the saddest 11:30 I've ever seen. That's right, I shut off the trumpets. I'm glad today isn't tomorrow. I leap out of the room and dive into the shower, then I take off clothes. I get ready in record time, including stuffing my jacket with little rubber balls. The car starts right away... after 11 tries. I call her. "I'm on my way. I'm sorry. I overslept. And my phone ringer was still off from the plate spinning disaster."

"Rescue me," she says and hangs up.

About six miles from home, I approach an intersection that has people holding signs at two of the corners, a fuel station and a church. A sledgehammer-hitting-metal sound rips through the front end of my car. I've never heard that sound before. A red mist of hot anti-freeze sprays from the hood. The light turns red as my car goes mostly dead. I hit the brakes and turn on my hazard lights. Traffic works its way around me, staring and pointing at the obvious. My Pony Express is dead in the middle of the street, dark red antifreeze gushes out of it as it loses pressure. Girls in bikinis holding signs for a fuel station car wash try to shout something to me. I sit through two more red lights. Then when the coast is clear, I let my foot off the brake, coasting forward through the light, past the church at the other corner, and down into the first driveway of the church parking lot, just before a cemetery. The church is holding a car wash too, but they have no business. The girls look hopeful and then confused when I drift the car to the side instead of pulling in toward them. I pop the hood. It's reluctant to open up, like a puppy that doesn't want to give up its sock.

Bad puppy!

Two adults approach while I try not to burn my hands. They tell me about their unsuccessful Labor Day weekend car wash, while I call around to auto salvage places and outright junkyards. Asking questions, I find out that the fuel station across the street decided to take on the third annual church car wash by hiring a few models in bikinis to out-promote the little church car wash. Some of the church girls talked with the bikini models. I call another auto towing place. When I tell them about the car, they offer to remove all identifying marks from the vehicle. When I ask them if they're kidding, they hang up. In all fairness, the place sounded like it was related to Acapella's Pizza.

The guy standing with me calls someone, walks away talking to them, and returns to say, "A tow truck should be here in about a half an hour."

"How much will it cost me to get rid of the car?"

"Nothing. He's doing this as a favor to me."

"Thank you."

I call Hope. "My car is dead. I'm at a church, and luckily a cemetery is right here."

"I've been sitting here talking with Freedonia, wondering where you are."

"I'll call you when I know how I'm getting there. I'm sorry I didn't go with you this morning."

"Don't apologize. I'm sorry your car died."

"Well, I'll talk with you later. Bye."

"Bye."

I tell them, "I was supposed to meet my girlfriend at the fair." I hit the button to call Tom. "Hey Tom! Did you wash your truck yet?"

"No..."

"I'm at a church car wash. They'd really like to wash your truck."

"I'm not falling for it."

"It's no joke. My car died. I mean dead." I give him the address.

"But you're supposed to be at the fair?"

"I overslept." I give him the full story about the car wash. He asks me ridiculous questions and keeps me talking and talking, until he pulls in. The church kids, there are a few guys with them, wash, wax, and polish Tom's truck as if it were their own. We both call and send messages to everyone we know about the service here. I also send a message to the plate spinner – I know better than to call him – to let him know I won't be able to make the show. The tow truck comes and pulls up in front of the Pony Express. I pay the guy despite the fact that I was told that he was doing this for free. I sign over the title to the car. I cancel my car insurance.

One of the adults looks at my dead car and offers, "I could say a few words over it."

"That's not necessary."

Al is the next of my friends to show up. This is right up his alley. He loves his car. I should warn them that he loves his car and to treat it as a cherished memento, but he's already doing that by being right there with them every step of the way. I turn just in time to watch my silver and rust Pony Express being towed away. It leaves behind a light smear of red anti-freeze.

I've had that car so long. I'm carless.

Nicole pulls up in her cherry red convertible, wearing a shirt that reads, Moo. "I'll take you to the fair. Do we have time for a car wash?" I don't know. Hope's waiting, and I owe these people. I nod.

The crew calls in their people from the corner as three more cars show up. I look to see if I know them. One of the cars is Tom and Todd's dad. I go say hi and thank him for helping out the cause. Tom comes over and thanks me for telling him about this place. He tells his dad that he thought I was playing a practical joke on him. Mr. Pfuloree says, "I saw what you and your new girlfriend did to his yard. What's the car wash earning money for?"

"I'll find out."

"Are you going with Nicole to the fair?" Tom asks. I nod. "I'll probably see you there." Tom leaves. I step through the wash cycles and over to one of the adults, but I can't get their attention. I ask one of the kids.

She says, "We're raising money for our winter retreat to Harmony." I pass the word on to Mr. Pfuloree.

Nicole's express service has her car done before Al's. She has less car to wash. I say good-bye to all of them and give a donation to the church group. Nicole and I get into her convertible and go. "I know one of the girls across the street behind us." She says more but I don't hear the details. Basically she doesn't like the girl. I send Hope a message saying that we're on our way. It's too breezy to call. When we park near Lake Sarita at the southwest end, I call Hope again, and she meets. She says a great deal, but I don't understand a word of it. Nicole translates for me.

"Are you okay?" I ask.

"Are-you-okay?" Nicole quickly asks. Hope says something. Nicole says, "She's had eight chocolate bananas and two chocolate-covered cheesecakes on a stick. I've always wanted one of those. This place is model unfriendly. She's washed it down with four Double Bubbles. Someone named Freedonia was here and left. They talked and talked." Nicole and I hug Hope, who has the glazed look of the calories dimension. We take a red Skyride gondola up and through the greasy haze across the fairgrounds. They talk while I enjoy the view, wiping my eyes occasionally. My jacket is lumpy to sit on. My jacket has balls. We get off the Skyride and sit near the base of the Space Tower, a round donut-shaped room that rises up a tower and rotates for a view of the fairgrounds, the Midway area, Pigs Eye to the east, and Milltown to the west. Hope leans on me. She says something. I look to Nicole. "She says, 'I'm sorry about your car.'"

A group of people has stopped on the street in front of us, all carrying at least one balloon. They get organized and get their timing set. They launch their balloons. The balloons scatter as they rise up. Some drift up by the Space Tower as the observation deck comes down. Some balloons run into dense greasy mist, are overwhelmed and lose their color, and drop sickly down. Some balloons hover about. Some fly off, high up, dotting the sky.

"It's almost..." Jake sniffs, "beautiful." He parks his butt and leans on Nicole. "Hey losers. I hear your car died."

"I sent you the message. Did you read it or did someone read it for you?"

"I went to the car wash. Not your innocent high school girl car wash either. I went to the full service bikini car wash."

"You didn't," Nicole says, shifting out from under him.

"I did. Took the truck through. Looked it over. I found a nick. I raised holy hell. For a good 20 minutes. One of the bikinis went home crying. They shut down the car wash. I've called them twice so far. I'm about due for another call. You need to learn to be more efficient and look at the big picture," he says to me. He gets out his phone. "Channel your inner anger toward those that need it most." He laughs. "I've got them on speed dial. **Have you people figured out what body shop is going to fix my truck yet?!? I've talked to two more people who just got car washes and have damage! I don't care what your stupid sign says! Are you operating a shredder or a car wash?!?**" Several balloons get scared away. Jake disconnects. Everyone else unplugs their ears. He double-checks that he has the phone off and puts it away. He fluffs up Nicole and lays down on her. "That's how you handle things. You look at the big picture." Nicole shoves him off her. "Give me your jacket," he says leaning up. I toss it at him. He puts it under his head as a pillow. "What the fuck?" He gets off it and feels it and gives me a strange look. He sits up, examines it, and finds the hidden pockets. He's not an idiot, despite what everyone says or what you might read about him or the looks he gives you. He takes out a few little rubber balls. His eyebrows bounce up and down. He spots someone, and before I can stop him, he chucks a ball at them. He almost says something to me.

"What?"

"Forget it."

Tom steps up the little grassy knoll. "I just got pelted," he says, rubbing his shoulder. Jake cracks up. "What was it?" Jake holds up a rubber ball. "How did you get me with that?"

"I threw it." Jake takes a few more balls and tosses my jacket back at me. "Mr. Physics, explain to Tom here the principles of thrown objects, especially focusing on the factors of accuracy in relation to said objects."

"Where's Becky?"

"She's going to meet us."

"Where's Ruth?"

"She's right behind you. Erix is too." We look. They wave. "What's with Hope?" Becky joins Tom standing in front of us.

"Too much of a good thing. Eight chocolate bananas and two chocolate cheesecakes. I think she may have eaten the sticks too."

Jake says, "She's Hope Full. Get it?"

Becky sits down by Hope and says, "Don't eat the sticks." Hope says something. "Yeah, look at my nails," Becky replies.

Jake says, "Look at these people. It's that time of day. A lot of these people have had too much fair. That guy... That girl... Down in front, Tom." Tom sits, and we count the number of people passing by that have overdosed on the fair. A group of college students take offense at being counted, until they find out why they're being counted. They lie down by us and help us count people. A guy walks by with a leash without a dog. It would be more appropriate if he rode a saddle without a horse. Jake wonders, "What happened to the dog, you know, Snowflake? Probably getting deep fried..."

"**Jake!**" everyone screams.

"...on a stick."

"Jake!"

"What?!? You know you were thinking it."

Cy, Todd, and Gene find us. Todd tells Tom, "We should get our picture taken at the Department Of Redundancy Department booth."

"For the hundredth time, no."

"We should eat," I say. Hope winces. "Or not."

"What time is it?"

"Five," I say.

"It's 5:30," Cy says. "You're slipping."

"Thanks." That's weird.

"You're welcome."

"Kids," Jake says. "Don't make me pull over."

"Does anyone want anything?" Ruth offers. "I'll go get it."

"Right. We're going to make you run all over everywhere for our orders," Cy says. To Jake, she says, "We're not going to do that."

"I didn't say anything."

"You were going to," she predicts. Jake turns to me looking for confirmation but decides not to ask.

"No, they don't count. We already counted them."

"They're just messing with us, going by twice."

Behind us, Ruth has her camera ready, but she isn't taking any pictures. What's up? Al, Will, and Stephanie are here. Cy asks, "Is it time? It's time." Al hands her something. "Would you all please rise?" Rise? Oh, she means get up. Got it. "My friends, amidst this beautiful day we have experienced a loss. Ricky's Pony Express died today." Stephanie gasps dramatically. "Though it only left us a short time ago, the memory of the burning oil smell still lingers." It did not burn oil. Much. The college kids snicker. "It did not have an easy life. Road salt consumed it. Winter froze it. Summer fried it. It weathered the elements. Those of you that knew the Pony Express, those of you that rode in the Pony Express, will always remember it. Who can forget it? As we drive the roads of Pigs Eye and Milltown, we will remember that death trap of a vehicle. Because it left behind memories, memories and a trail of crumbling metal and spare parts." Is this a memorial or a roast?!? "We commend his car, a lamb amongst the flock, a vehicle amongst the traffic, to the... The..."

"Crash M Smash M Auto Salvage."

"...to Crash M Smash M Auto Salvage. And through their commendable and regulated commitment to recycling, it may drive again." Stephanie weeps dramatically. "Receive this vehicle at its final parking place. May it rest in pieces. Crashes to crashes and rust to rust." Cy holds up a small water bottle of blue liquid. "Just as windshield washer fluid blessed the windshield of the Pony Express at regular intervals, so too we are blessed for having survived it." Cy takes a drink and passes it.

Stephanie gets it, nearly drinks, and stops herself. "I can't," she sobs and passes the bottle.

Others fake like they are taking a drink and then pass it. After our group the college students take it. From them it continues to be passed across the fair.

Cy unwraps a car-shaped wooden plaque that has the Pony Express emblem mounted to it. How did they– Tom must have pried it off when I wasn't looking. She hands it to me. "Our deepest condolences." She hugs me and then shakes my shoulders. "Now, get a decent car." A receiving line forms.

"Sorry about your loss."

"My condolences on the death of your car."

"It was time."

"Can't believe you let your car die at a Methodist church!"

"That's the brakes, kid," one of the college kids tells me, while shaking my hand.

The memorial dinner is served on sticks. Hope drinks water and rests. Color is returning to her face. Jake is the last to leave us for this evening's concert in the Grandstand. He asks me if there was any correlation between pointed perception and AutoDrive. I say, no. He says he thinks that the common denominator is my concentration. "No matter what you do, you have intense, almost unbreakable concentration." And ultimately he leaves too, saying, "Seriously, I'm sorry about your car."

"Thanks." He disappears into the crowd. He comes back, frisks my jacket for a ball, takes one, and leaves again. "That man is an impostor. That was not the Jake I know. How are you feeling? Any better?" Hope nods. "Good enough to ride some Mighty Midway rides to wherever they take us?"

Hope says, "I feel good enough to walk and look at rides. Most of the rides. Some of the rides."

"I could get you a wheelchair."

Hope stands up. "I don't need a wheelchair." We take a Skyride across the fair. Twilight gives the horizon a hazy orange glow, and from above where there's more light, the fair is a magical mix of silhouette trees and lit buildings. It's like a picture perfect scale model. I go to guest services for a wheelchair. "Do not get a wheelchair." I compromise and get a baby carriage. "What are you going to do with that?" Hope asks.

"Where's baby?" Exhausted mothers leaving the fair with their last bit of energy turn to look with panic. "Baby!" I call out. When I've exhausted my search, I return the baby carriage.

The Mighty Midway is a mix of carnival games and carnival rides. The rides go by names like Wild Wheel, Flying Mosquitoes, Spinning Swings, Sky Whizzers, Silver Fish, Loose Change, Some Tsunami, Break Down, and Drop Out. They swing you, spin you, bounce you, drop you, launch you, splash you, shake you down, and take your money. An odd group of teenagers, each still holding a ticket stub, is walking purposefully into walls. At the Spinning Swings, which has 40 swings that spin in a circle, we read a sign that says, "Do not hold onto other swings or push off from other swings." What fun is that? The carnival games let you toss an overinflated basketball into an undersized hoop that's too high and too close. Or you can shoot a squirt gun with a scope aimed left and a barrel aimed right. Or knock down metal milk bottles from a table that has some magnets below it, or else they have lead weights. Or throw a dull dart at an underinflated balloon. We watch a few people holding padded mallets, trying to hit gophers that pop out of holes in a table. They are competing against each other so someone will win, unless that someone works here.

"Whack A Gopher is a great game for everyone except the gophers," I comment, turning to watch a strange figure go by. "Does that guy know he has a giant monkey on his back? I should tell him." Hope holds me back. We pass a sign featuring Fairchild the Gopher. He says you have to be this tall to ride the ride. "I'm too tall."

"That's funny," Hope says. "You have to be exactly that tall." We stop at bumper cars, where I first learned to drive. "Would you like to?" Hope asks. I escort her in. Hope climbs into my car.

"Don't you want a car of your own?"

"No, we have to share now," she says with a restraining loop across her breasts and resting her head on my shoulder. Uh-oh. Someone expects a smooth romantic ride. With Hope in the car with me, all the teenage boys are gunning for us. My foot is ready on the pedal and my route around traffic is preplanned. An announcement reminds us to stay in the cars at all times. A bell rings and electrical current hits the fence above us. I dodge three cars but someone behind us is bouncing off our butt. I can't get away fast enough. I turn away, half-expecting to see Jake, but it's someone I don't know. I decide on a zigzagged pattern. And we've almost gotten away when a kid slams into us and squeals with delight.

"Let's see your insurance," I call out. A tongue is stuck out in response. "Nice insurance."

A choir of angels interrupts the whizzing and bumping of cars. Hope answers, we're bumped, and she almost drops her phone. "Hello," she says. "Hi Mother, can I call you back, we're in bumper cars."

We get slammed again and hear more angels. "Hello," she answers. Just as I start to figure out a Plan F, another bell rings, signaling the end of the ride.

"Remain in your car until all cars come to a complete halt." That's us. Seconds later, we stop too. We take off our seat belt loops.

"Hi Nicole. What's up? I think we're about to leave. Yeah. Okay. See ya." Hope tells me, "I think I'd like to go home. How about you?"

"Sounds good." She sits down on a bench and calls her mom.

I think it's amazing that Hope never once asked me if I'd win her a stuffed animal, even a Smokey Four to keep Smokey Three company when they hibernate. Cy never understood the probabilities and the riggings that can be involved in carnival games, not necessarily this carnival, but at many carnivals.

Hope puts away her phone and takes my hand. She stops in her tracks when she sees the Flying Mosquitoes. She says, "I think I'd like to see you ride that." When I pull her along, she hits the brakes and says, "No, just you."

Why does she want me to ride this thing?

I get on. It's all lit up. The ride has six arms covered in lights that whip everyone around and then we all get swatted to the ground. Only a mosquito would come up with a ride like this. Lights flash by through the darkness. I'm spun around, disoriented, and slammed to the ground. Before I know it, the ride is over, but it takes another five minutes before I relearn how to walk a straight line. This explains all the teenagers walking into walls. We head across the fair.

I kiss Hope with fireworks bursting overhead. A herd of inflatable bison hide nearby. Inflatable animals run wild, being chased by street sweepers and garbage trucks, while I help Hope back to her car. She helps navigate. I help her walk. Hope falls asleep in the car. I drive her home and tuck her into bed. I set both my mental clock and my physical alarm clock for eight o'clock tomorrow morning. I kiss her good night.

48

AutoDrive

Hope shifts with me in her sleep to keep holding my shoulder. I move. She moves. It's weird. It's comforting. I may never be the same again. At two minutes to eight I wake up. My alarm clock goes off prematurely. I squint at it. It squints back at me.

"Good morning," Hope says. I doubt that, but I nod in acknowledgment. What should I call the naked woman in the bath? Beth? Beth it is. I shower and pray with Beth, shave, brush my teeth, and comb my hair. Beth smiles. Getting dressed in the bedroom, Hope exclaims, "Whoo-hoo, free show!" I empty my jacket of little rubber balls, replace my phone, add a big deflated beach ball, and earplugs. Let's get this show on the road. I give Hope a kiss and shoot down the hall when I remember that my parking spot behind the house doesn't have a car. I am car free. I need to get downtown.

How to get downtown:

I could wake Ray and get a ride on his motorcycle.

I could get a ride from Hope, but she would stick around. She can't get involved.

I could call a cab.

I could take a bus.

I could really use AutoDrive right now, so that I can deal with AutoDrive. AutoDrive would be the perfect car rental service, showing up where and when a car is needed.

Back in my bedroom, Hope is looking at the ceiling. "Hope, could I borrow your car to go downtown? I don't know how long I'll be gone."

"You have the keys."

"I do?" I left them on the floor by her purse. I pick them up.

"Good luck," she says.

"Wish me favorable probabilities."

"Okay, may you have favorable probabilities."

"So I can use–"

"Yes."

"Thanks." I run out, grab a banana, run back in, kiss her, and leave.

There are times when you must enter a bad situation, a battle of some kind, and no matter how many scenarios you imagine, none of them offer perfect solutions. It's a bad situation. You have a job to complete, a responsibility to fulfill. You tried talking. You tried reasoning with the people. Your adversaries are gated off from reasonable behavior and open, honest communication. That's what made them adversaries. You question if there is any way to just not participate in the situation. Right. If only it were that easy. It is a responsibility. So you're back looking at the options. None of them are great. You lower your expectations. You aren't going to be a hero on this one, but you'll do what you think is right and suffer the consequences. You do your best. You're trying to save people's lives. You're trying to prevent destruction. Sometimes that's all you can do. I will do my best.

I turn on the radio. It says, "This morning, downtown streets will be blocked off for a demonstration of a new type of car. This car drives itself. Created by a local company, Flight Control of Milltown, the test of 'Auto Drive' will block downtown traffic over the noon hour on Sunday. Hey, that's today."

There is almost no traffic. Welcome to the current world of AutoDrive. It isn't up for a real situation.

I take the long way around downtown and park in a parking garage. I'm blocks away. This is not how you test an unproven concept.

I didn't one day announce to the world, "Hey, I can see the futures," and then see if it's possible. Harry Houdini would not have tried to pick his first lock on stage. Carl and company should not be testing AutoDrive in front of the public and the media like this. It's their funeral. With any luck it will be a casket-less funeral.

I step down into Peavey Plaza on Nicollet Mall with pools of water and waterfalls and fountains and cement squares of different levels. I step through the pools and around the waterfalls. This park is a representation of Minnesota, water and land. That's its hook, slippery and steep portages between deep cold water. Except here, everything is squared off and urbanized, domesticated and shadowy. It's all about solid footings. From footings in the river 11 blocks away, a logger would take a long pole, a lever, with a cant hook, as in "I can't grab a hold of anything!" and a spike at the end. The Milltown loggers used the peaveys and concerted effort to clear log jams. The logs are gone now. A few trees still stand in the park, honey locusts and others, in raised planter boxes, as reminders of what once was. I wasn't here in 1975 when the park took shape, cement trucks pouring form after stepping stone form. This winter the water will take frozen forms as an ice skating rink and snow mounds, with little footprints that climb some snow mounds but leave others unexplored. I step through, reminded of all the steps I took to get here... all the steps it takes to do anything. I step up. Back at street level, the park is surrounded by a few monolithic buildings of blue mirrored glass, as if the whole city were made of sky reflecting water.

A pair of news vans pass by with all the rush of an orchestrated event. The vans advertise that they are on the scene when they're scheduled to be.

As a logger, I would be the sort of logger working, not from the edge of the log jam, but right in the middle, standing on the logs. Unfortunately I would also be the logger that is trying to lift the log he's standing on.

Watching the news vans stop several blocks away, I realize that once again, I forgot to bring my own satellite dish tower. I don't really need one.

I walk Mdewakanton Avenue to Third, bypassing the AutoDrive presentation stage. I push pedestrian Walk buttons the whole way to Forth. I heard something as I passed Millstone Street, and I'm still trying to figure out what it was. I think it was the memory of the Pony Express backfiring.

I am at peace with what I have to do. Peace is not motionless and quiet and without trouble. Peace is being in the middle of the action and the noise and the trouble and still being calm at heart.

A police officer is standing in the middle of the road, mouth agape, listening to his police radio, which is playing police songs. Blocking Forth Street, an officer is in his squad car opening up a sandwich. I wave. He gives me a funny look. Stopping in front of the Indulgence Hotel, I walk farther to stand in front of the Museum Of Questionable Inventions. I lean against the museum. Then I step back in front of the Indulgence Hotel. A September wind blows through the street. A newspaper page starts up the block from near the police car. I can't believe he littered! That reminds me. I take out my inflatable beach ball and blow it up. This had better work. All the old downtown beach ball stores closed up long ago. I only have this one. Holding the beach ball by its nozzle, I get out my phone and call 911.

If I look cool, it's only due to all my rehearsals.

"911 emergencies."

"A car, called AutoDrive, made by Flight Control, is about to crash into a police car at the corner of Forth and Third, downtown Milltown." There. Simple and succinct.

"Did you say, 'about to crash?'"

"That's right."

"How do you know that?"

"It's a self-driving car."

"Oh, right. A self-driving car."

This isn't going well. "Didn't you hear? They closed off much of the downtown traffic for this. It's call AutoDrive."

"Hold on a moment." Muttering, "There's this guy talking about downtown being closed off for something called AutoDrive? You said Flight Control? That's what he's talking about."

The driverless AutoDrive Pegasus Coup, with a smashed front right quarter-panel, turns recklessly onto Forth Street, hardly a right angle turn. It tries to correct and compensate, as fast as a fire through Swede Hollow. I throw out the beach ball. It comes back to me. My timing is off. The newspaper page hits me. I step on it. I throw out the ball again, underhand. It bounces picturesquely. AutoDrive **squeals** its brakes almost before the first bounce, hitting the ball repeatedly down the street, dragging some fencing from who knows where, before stopping inches from the squad car, popping the beach ball. I cringe for a crash that never happens.

Damn it. I liked that beach ball.

It worked.

I tell the 911 operator, "Never mind."

From beside me, Cooelle gasps.

AutoDrive practically predicted the ball before it could have seen it.

I suppose I should fetch the remains of my beach ball, so I don't get charged with littering. I walk leisurely over. The cop from the squad car has egg sandwich on his chin and his chest. His face is white, even though it didn't start out that way. The Pegasus Coup is still running. That means it is still in drive and has applied the brakes. I can't step in to retrieve the remains of the beach ball, without first turning off the ignition and removing the keys. The cop who was standing in the intersection on the other side of the squad car is coming around for a closer look. He's about to go between the cars.

"**Stop!**" I yell at the cop. He looks at me as if I've lost my mind. "Turn off the ignition first. This is dangerous."

"Who the hell are you?" I wait for the gears to click and register the danger. "Stay right there." He goes the long way around the squad car and opens the door to the Pegasus Coup and shuts off the engine. "Are these your keys?"

"No, I'd leave them on the seat." Wow, the car has bullet holes in it. There is even a boot print on the hood. Someone jumped on it?!? Good plan.

Tough car. They just had to use a Pegasus Coup, didn't they?

The officer comes back around the long way, and before I can retrieve the dead beach ball, we are mobbed by people. I hear talk that it ran through barricades, got shot at, hit a car, and now this car. I'm about to ask if there was someone in the other car, but then I figure, if this guy can't figure out that these two cars in front of us never touched each other, why am I going to trust any other information from him? A guy with a windshield as glasses is trying to tell anyone who will listen that the next test will be much better. Good plan.

"What's your connection to all of this?" the cop who'd been directing traffic asks.

I point to the car. "This? Nothing anymore. I just didn't want it to kill anyone that's all. The guy in charge is that guy over there," I point out a sweaty, red faced, fire-breathing Carl. I turn to go.

He stops me with a hand like I'm traffic. "What's your name?" He gets my name, address, and phone number. Will is waving to me from the other side of the crowd. "You used to be involved in this car company?" the cop asks.

"Yes, I worked for Flight Control until a month ago."

"And what did you just do?"

"I stopped it with a beach ball."

Reporters in the crowd stop talking and taking pictures. Maybe they didn't hear me. "You stopped it with a beach ball?!?" the cop asks. Thanks. The crowd crowds.

"Yes." I become the focus of the pictures.

"Could you explain that?"

"You really should talk with the owner of the company. I was just trying to save the life of Officer Egg Sandwich, that's all."

"But you didn't come down here knowing that Officer Egg Sand– I mean Officer Loring, was in danger, did you?" I open my mouth but say nothing. He nods and sketches a picture of me with my mouth open. Some of the reporters critique it. "A fine time to join the force," he comments, "right when they stop needing sketch artists, all together." Some of the reporters repeat him, while others try to pull me into their broadcasts.

Another cop and Carl and some people in suits are looking at the beach ball and looking at the damage to the Pegasus Coup and trying to figure it all out, figure out where they went wrong. I imagine myself raising my hand and jumping up and down, saying, "Oh, I know. Pick me. Pick me!" Trumpets sound and I excuse myself, and as I try to step around the corner to Third, Carl is right there. He's aged years in just weeks.

His coronary reddened face twists and contorts into a near approximation of a smile, "You want to fix this, don't you?"

I laugh, "That's your piñata. You smash it."

Destruction is easy. Creation is tough.

Many inventions happen by accident. Maybe this is one of them.

I answer the phone, "Hello Acapella's Pizza..." I can't think of a special. "How can I help you?"

"Hi Sweetie, you were on camera less than a minute ago," Hope says, as I walk away from the pandemonium behind me. "Are you all right? It looks like you did it."

"Yes, I did."

"They had some tight shots of you. The anchor people were guessing you were a bystander. We were loving it."

"Good." I think...

"Where are you? Are you still there?"

"I'm walking away."

"Darn. I wanted to see you more."

"Well, what if you saw me in person?"

"Sounds good." I can hear her dimples through the phone.

"Okay, I'll see you in a while."

"I love you. I'm so proud of you."

"I love you too." I disconnect and put away the phone. I leave my hands in my jacket pockets. Traffic has picked up and barricades are being taken down. I pay the parking attendant and drive out.

I stop by a cash machine. I give it my card and my PIN, and I tell it to access checking. It flashes a quick, resentful message that I ignore. It asks if I would like insect repellent. I haven't seen a bug in a while. I tell it, no. It spits out a mosquito. It asks me, are you sure? I say yes. It tells me it could get warmer. I push the button labeled Not Likely. It says Please Wait. It asks again, if I would like insect repellent. I say no. It asks about sidewalk salt. I say no. I left some sidewalk salt in my car that was towed away. This car is on loan. I need currency that's more portable. It says it understands and offers United States dollars. It says I could even have some extra. I tell it that's not necessary. It spits out the dollars. Then it makes a PSST sound. It says that the mechanical world domination will take place next week sometime. My finger hovers over the Not Likely button. I press the Okay button and drive away.

As I drive, I think about going to the Ice Cream Bar, but state law doesn't allow them to serve until after two on a Sunday. It's close now. What do I want to do? Go home. I'm tired. At home, I park Hope's car and stop by the empty spot where my car had been. I'm going to miss that car – AutoDrive and my car – both drove over the guardrail of life this weekend.

A checkmark formation of Canadian Geese flies straight south, honking as they go.

Hope, Ray, Becky, Nicole, and Faith are watching the news in the living room. They all say hi, encouraging me to sit and watch TV, specifically the news, news of something I already witnessed. The real News Break is the distance between what is and what is reported. The reports have truthiness; they sound true... "A driverless car goes on a rampage through Milltown, tearing downtown some new holes." ...but they aren't true. Based on that report, you'd expect to see parts of Milltown breaking into some of the caves below it. Everything is fine. Certain dreams are crushed, but that is hardly newsworthy.

"That's right Stan. From this spot at Nicollet and Forth, you can see a crowd of people. Just past that crowd is a car that just moments ago–"

"Almost an hour ago," I correct.

"–was careening its way through downtown."

Instead of truthiness, you could say verisimilitude, the appearance of truth, but a fake word is better than a real one to describe imagined news. What is reported are Shortest Stories.

"This man was almost killed after crossing a barricade. The lesson learned? Barricades are put up for a reason. When asked if he would do it again, the man said yes. The lesson learned? The lesson wasn't learned."

Hope pulls me in to the middle of the couch. "So what happened?"

"The news didn't tell you?" I ask. Faith shushes me.

"Fences and curbs, fire hydrants and chains, gunshots and police officers did not stop this car. What did? A beach ball. Here is a shot of the beach ball taken earlier. In answer to your earlier question, Stan, no, we don't know if the ball was inflated or not when it stopped the car."

"Yes, it was inflated," I tell the TV screen, instantly feeling idiotic for talking back to a one-way form of communication.

"How do you know?" Faith asks.

"I inflated it. It's my ball."

"And you used it to stop AutoDrive, right?" Hope asks.

"Right."

"Really? So, this is all about you? You should be there telling them what happened."

"Why?"

"So everyone knows."

"I'm tired. I'm going to bed."

"Wait. How did you use a beach ball to stop a car?"

"I bounced it out in front of it." In my room, I lie down. Then I get back up again, get out my phone, and find a place that custom makes shirts – If the Shirt Fits Wear It. I design and order some shirts. I turn off the ringer on my phone. I pull the curtains closed, check my clock, and fall asleep, comforted that AutoDrive or at least my part of AutoDrive, is done.

49

Train Of Thought

I wake up with uneasiness as if I left something cooking or forgot to turn off the Minnehaha Falls before I left or I forgot how to do something or I left my car somewhere or I forgot to tell someone something before they left or...

Hey. Everything is fine. Responsibility is gone. I haven't been free of Responsibility like this since life stole my childhood from me. There I was minding my own business devising a gear driven, rubber band catapulted car, when Responsibility knocked. I was busy, so Responsibility let itself in. Responsibility took the car and everything, even the rubber band. When I asked what I could play with, Responsibility handed me, The Inns And Outsides Of Being On Your Own, the children's edition. "Play with that," Responsibility said and sat down to make itself comfortable and looked at the toy car for safety hazards.

My room seems more empty without Responsibility.

I go out to the living room. My roommates are all still here, still watching TV, but with the curtains closed. Hope gets up, asking, "Did the door wake you?" I look at the door. It doesn't look like the type of door that would sneak off its hinges and wake me up. I shake my head. "Several news crews stopped by."

Faith says, "I had to hold Nicole down to keep her from flashing them."

"You did not."

"They probably have cameras, just so you know," I tell them, still not quite awake.

"That's so like them."

Hope hands me some notes and business cards. "So how did they find me?"

"The police had the information."

"Of course, the police! But they don't have a clue what is going on. When I left they were speculating if the beach ball had any relatives.

"They have a clue now," Becky says, switching the TV to a recording and reviewing back through it and stopping it on a picture of me, boxed in from an anchor person with eyes closed in a blink and mouth agape. The picture of me has me pointing, with the Museum Of Questionable Inventions sign behind me. The caption says my name and Inventor Stops Car.

"We thought it should say, 'Inventor Brakes B-R-A-K-E-S Car," Nicole says, spelling out brakes for me.

"Clever." I look at the notes. "So who should get the interview? Who's good?"

"Channel One is the best."

"What's the one with the guy with the permanent smile? No, really. I swear it's painted on," Faith says.

"He has no lips. Didn't you see the segment when he kissed the printing press?"

"You're kidding." Nicole laughs.

Hope's phone rings. "Hello. Hi– It's Cy. She's been trying to call you."

"Oops."

"We're talking about which station he should let interview him. What? I didn't know that. Okay. Switch to NOD."

"Huh?"

"Change the channel to News On Demand. We're national. Hey Cy, what if he did a press confer–Okay. Okay. No press conference." Now we're watching a Double Bubble commercial. I don't remember being in a Double Bubble commercial. "She wants to talk to you," Hope says.

"Hi Cy."

"You could've told us you were going to be on the news."

"I'm not on the news. They're still making it up."

"They have your picture."

"Yeah, but it doesn't talk."

"Right. Where's your phone?"

"In my room. With the ringer turned off. Under my jacket."

"Could you turn it back on again?"

"Yes."

"Thank you. Bye."

"Bye." I hand the phone back to Hope. "Do you want to get something to eat?"

"Are you thinking romantically or as a group?"

"Romantically. Technically Greek, not Roman."

"Where are you going?" Nicole asks.

"The Parthenon Greek Restaurant."

Nicole whispers, "Greek is better as a group. Greek is better as a group."

I shake my head, "Romance."

"Meet me in my room," Hope says and dashes upstairs.

Back in my room I reset my phone and try on a makeshift toga, which is Greek dressing. Looking in the mirror, I wonder what Hope would've thought if I'd been in a toga instead of the gorilla outfit. I change into jeans, a dress shirt, and a tie and run upstairs. Watching the news upstairs now, Becky tells me I wasn't fast enough; Hope got Nicole's help picking something to wear. "A guy with giant glasses was just talking for Flight Control."

"Did he know anything?"

"No."

"That would be Bailey. In baseball, he would be like a ninth inning relief pitcher." Hope comes in and all thoughts of baseball, bats, and balls go out. She shines in a silver blouse and skirt highlighted with the bracelet I gave her at First Street Station. "You're gorgeous!"

Hope blushes, "Thank you." She shows off shoes that are some sort of silver sandals that strap up her ankles and have little wings hanging off the heel. My eyebrows raise. Hope takes my hand and wishes her roommates good night. "Which way are we going?" she asks while driving, colored light dancing across the dashboard.

"Downtown Pigs Eye. Union Depot."

"Gotcha. How do you feel?"

"I feel good. I feel a burden has been mostly lifted."

"You say mostly..."

"Yes, I'm still living it. I'm still there. It's as if I poured so much concentration and adrenaline into that moment that I'm still recovering from it. I guess I feel a sense of accomplishment of having gotten this far. Anyone should. I've gotten to a stopping point with AutoDrive. It's not where I would have liked to have left it, but it's still good. It's still a completion of sorts."

Hope drives an indirect route, taking us slowly by Wild Rice Park and the still radiant Lactating Woman fountain before continuing toward Riverside Tower, to the Union Depot. This depot was the Pigs

Eye train station for almost 50 years, from 1923 to 1971. The Union Depot is a discount version of the Parthenon in Athens, with ten columns in front and that's all the columns it has, unless you take a second look. At second glance, four flattened column-like finishes are on either side of the ten columns, and then the flat columns are repeated on the sides, as if most of the columns had been run over by a train. The great hall or lobby of the Union Depot is large enough to be mistaken for an ornate hangar for airplanes. The ceiling is tall enough to have room for a cloud of smoke and steam from coal burning locomotives. Dwarfed by the vast room, the softly lit Parthenon Restaurant awaits us. I don't understand the menus they hand us at first. They quickly replace them with English menus. The main dinner items are: mousaka, pastitsio, tyropita, dolmathes, spanakopita, falafel, kebabs, and gyros, although they will make a cheeseburger if absolutely necessary.

"What's good?" Hope asks.

"It's all good, but I'm thinking about the spanakopita."

"What's spanakopita?"

Waiters and waitresses pop out from under tables and swing down from the balcony. "Spanakopita? Spanakopita? She asked him what is spanakopita?" Ompa, ompa, ompa, ompa. "First you take the spinach, you wad it with feta cheese, run it through some scallions, and add some dill to please." Ompa, ompa, ompa, ompa. "You roll it in some phyllo dough, it's like paper sleeves, pop it in the oven, and cook at 400 degrees!" The waiters and waitresses are pushed back to the balcony and disappear back under tables.

"You love the odd, train oriented restaurants, don't you?" Hope comments. "I have a few more questions about the menu." We hear a thunk from under a nearby table as someone gets ready to jump out again. "But I'm afraid to ask. I'd have the flaming saganaki appetizer, except I think it would remind me too much of cheese curds from the state fair."

"They're not exactly the same."

Our waiter takes our orders. Hope says, "I'll have the–" and then she silently mouths the word, spanakopita. She also orders a Greek salad and a Double Bubble. I order the vegetarian mousaka, a Greek salad, and a glass of Chippeau Valley Blanc Spirit. "What's the– Never mind," Hope says.

"The Minnesota explanation of mousaka," I tell her, "is eggplant hotdish."

She nods and gets out her phone. She pushes enough buttons to make it look like either she is doing a web search or playing a game. She shows me her phone, which has a picture of a car on it. "What do you think of this car?"

"It looks like a car."

"Read the description. Would you want it? I'd buy it for you."

What sort of car do I want? I want my old car. "I'm still mourning the loss of my car. I'm not ready to buy another car yet, but thank you." Our drinks arrive. "That reminds me. I have to call Channel One or NOD or whoever is going to interview me."

"Do you still have the information I gave you?"

"I left it in my room, but I remember the number to Channel One." Our salads arrive. My phone is full of messages. Channel One and NOD are both on the list of messages. I send a message to NOD about being available for an interview mid-day tomorrow. I copy in Channel One and tell them that they could interview me at the same time. Trumpets echo across the great hall of the depot until I turn the ringer off again. NOD sends me a message back that I show to Hope. It says that while Channel One in Milltown is not affiliated with NOD, they have a working agreement to share news stories that have been elevated to national prominence. At 11am they will interview me using either my home or the Channel One studios with the NOD anchors in Cleveland. If I don't have a suit, they can put me in a green outfit and superimpose a suit on me. Then the message draws a line. After the line is a legal notice. Cy taught me to read legal notices. It says that they reserve the right to ask me whatever questions they see fit. Questions of a personal or insulting or personally insulting nature should be expected. Interviews are exclusive and may not be repeated with competitor news organizations. Background checks will also be conducted. They reserve the right to edit any statements I make, even if the edits dramatically alter the content and context in which the statement was made. They reserve the right to use my likeness for any advertising or historical clip montages in perpetuity. Any reply to this message is considered an acceptance of these terms. "Did you read the legal notice?"

"No, I didn't see that."

"What I have to do is send a separate message to them, giving my legal terms."

"Are you going to do the interview at home or the studio?"

"The studio." I eat my salad and draft a reply that stipulates limitations on the interview and its content. If I do not receive a message in agreement in the next two hours, I will assume they don't agree and I will contact their competitors for an interview instead. I show the message to Hope. She asks if she can fix a few things. I nod. We send it off.

Hope's lightly tanned, flaky phyllo pastry spanakopita looks so good on her fork that I regret not ordering it myself. Who could have thought eating spinach could look so good? Hope likes it. My mousaka is delicious too. A waiter stops by to light our votive table candle. Hope's bracelet takes the light and reflects it colorfully across the vast decorative ceiling above us. "You light up the place," I tell her. I raise my glass, "To you, my love, with all my hopes and dreams." Our glasses clink.

She looks at the colored light on the white tablecloth and takes my hand. "I want to apologize for taking away your dreams. I really didn't intend them to stop. They're too amazing to stop. I don't want them to stop." I nod.

Guests at a nearby table are being served saganaki. The waitress lights the brandy covered cheese on fire and yells, "Opa!" The bluish flames rise two feet before being extinguished with lemon juice.

Across the restaurant, a mousaka song is sung. We're too far away to hear it. I would have liked to have heard what rhymes with eggplant. Our leftovers are boxed for us without needing the crate that the bison needed. Hope drives us to Como Park. We take a walk through the park and around the lake. We sit on a bench and talk about messages I've received and replies I should make. I turn the trumpets back on. NOD approves my terms for an interview. Tom, Dexter, and Ruth call. Hope has a message from her mother, saying that she was impressed that I wasn't talking to the press. Oops.

I'm still tired. We head home and to bed. We don't go to sleep right away.

Trumpets wake me. I answer the phone without waking up. I wake up and sit up when Avatrice Gaea says, "Hello Ricky, I was wondering if you would like to attend a ceremony of strong spirits at Wakan Teebe."

"Y-yes. When?"

"Today. At noon."

I look at my clock. It's looking at Hope. I turn it to look at me. It's nine. It turns to look at Hope again. "I will certainly be there. Thank you. My car broke down, but I will find a way."

"Do you need a ride?"

"No, that's not necessary. Thank you."

"I will see you there." She disconnects.

What just happened?

"Who was that?" Hope asks.

"Avatrice Gaea." Hope sits up. "She invited me to something happening at Wakan Teebe."

"I didn't think non-natives went into Wakan Teebe."

"I didn't think so either. Mostly just the Mdewakanton Dakota."

"So she's never done this before?"

"No."

"I wonder why she's doing it now? Maybe it has something to do with AutoDrive? But I can't see how that would matter. When do you need to be there?"

"Noon."

"What about the NOD interview?"

I laugh, "They can wait until tomorrow."

"Do you want a ride or to borrow my car? I might just have to buy a second car."

"I can't believe I'm going to Wakan Teebe." I flop back on the bed. Wakan Teebe.

"Did she say why you were invited?"

"No." Wakan Teebe is a cave. It is the cave. It is the dwelling of the Great Spirit. This is the place of God. It is simply the single most important spot in the Twin Cities, if not for all of Minnesota. We were not far from it when we were at the Union Depot last night. The cave is less than a mile east of there. What I visualize when I hear the name Wakan Teebe is the one petroglyph of a turtle and two snakes that they always show and reproduce. That's all I know. I'll probably pray. I should probably pray now. "I need to take a shower and start getting ready." I lick my arm, sniff it, evaluate it, and kiss Hope.

"I'll give you a ride," Hope says. "When do you want to leave?"

"Eleven. You know, I could be there for a while. It could be hours."

"I'll wait for you. This is a big deal."

In the shower, I greet Beth and just as I start to close my eyes, I feel confusion in my head. I tell my past, "I've been waiting for you. Never mind where you are. You are not wanted. Go back to your present." I tell myself some other things. My past says something stupid. I say, "You're wrong; your today does matter. Without today, there will be no tomorrow."

The confusion leaves my head, and I pray.

I get cleaned up and dressed. I wear a nice shirt and jeans. In a sense I should wear a suit because this is one of the most special things that has ever happened to me, but I also know that a suit is not appropriate. It just isn't. I change my shirt to be closer to the one that Cal was wearing at Mahpiyawicasta Tower two weeks ago.

Someone has set out the Major Munch cereal and two cereal bowls for me. They also set out a banana. Someone is very understanding. I eat the banana. I'm about to send a message to NOD postponing the interview until tomorrow, when Nicole and Becky tear down the stairs. Nicole's shirt says, Actual Size. "We heard where you've been invited."

"Please don't spread the word around. For all I know there's been some sort of mistake." They nod, but still smile at me. "Isn't today Monday?" I'm wondering why they aren't at work.

"Labor Day."

I nod. "Would you read this over to make sure it makes sense, before I send it?" I hand it to Nicole, but indicate that I'd like them both to read it.

"Doesn't this thing have a way to check the spelling?"

"I think it quit." They laugh for some reason and then suggest some changes. I make the changes, recheck with them, and send the message. They watch me eat my cereal for a while, expecting something spectacular. When spectacular doesn't happen in a reasonable amount of time, Becky pats me on the shoulder and wishes me luck, and Nicole hugs me and wishes me luck. They go back upstairs

I eat my cereal and ponder what could be expected of me. Pointed perception would come in handy right about now. I dream about being able to dream. Hope comes down, dressed very nicely. I don't know whether to offer her the majors or the munches, so I push both bowls toward her. She pushes them back, "No, thank you."

"Do you realize that I can't invite you to come with me into the cave? Almost anything else, anywhere else, I would just bring you with anyway."

"I know." I nod to the way she's dressed. "I just think this is really important. That's all. Now if I have to go, while I'm waiting for you, I will only be gone for ten minutes.

"Okay." I show her the message I sent NOD. She nods.

I make orange juice, which takes another 15 minutes. I drink some juice and go brush my teeth. Toothpaste and orange juice do not mix. Ray comes into the bathroom. "You done soon?"

"Yup. I made extra orange juice if you want some."

"Thanks."

"It's all yours." I grab my watch, jacket, and phone. I add two small flashlights and a few dozen feet of string to my jacket. Hope meets me in my room, just as I'm staring at my alarm clock. "It's still not quarter to 11, but I think I'd like us to go."

"I have never seen you this nervous before," Hope says.

"I just don't know what to expect." She nods understandingly. The sky is overcast gray with breaks of blue. Hope drives us back to downtown Pigs Eye and slightly past it to Dayton's Bluff, the bluff with the burial mounds, then looping down the bluff by way of Commercial Street. Dayton's Cave comes first. Wakan Teebe is east of here, right below where Short Street meets Mounds Boulevard. The oxidized, pale yellow limestone and white sandstone cliff face rises up 70 feet. We drive a little farther and pull over. There it is. Wakan Teebe. And no one's here. "No one's here."

"It's still early."

This is sacred ground. I'm not getting out until someone else is here first. Maybe several someones.

The cave entrance is about ten feet up from ground level, 60 yards from the Fargo-Ramsey-Ottawa-Minot Railroad tracks, another 30 feet from Warner Road, and another ten feet from the Mississippi River, at least from the perspective of the car.

"A minute has passed," I announce.

Hope flips her hair back as she turns dramatically to me. "I think this will be awhile." She gets out her phone. She passes her phone from her right hand to her left and back to her right hand. I hang on her every move. She checks her messages and pushes some more buttons. Trumpets sound. I answer my phone. "Hello." It's Hope. "You might want to turn your phone off."

"Good thinking. Two more minutes have passed."

"Have you thought about what you're going to do when you are in the cave?"

"No. I'll probably just do what everyone else is doing."

"You? What if they are all looking to you for inspiration?"

"They'll have to let me know then because this is the sort of thing where I just try to blend in and remain inconspicuous." I disconnect.

Hope laughs. "Oh, you were serious? I'm sorry." She's got the giggles. She tries to stifle them. Yes, she has an acute case of Gigglitis. Her dimples are playing peek-a-boo. Only time and plenty of rest will cure her Gigglitis. "Right," she says, "you are known for your blending."

"Two more minutes have–"

"Here's what you could do. Close your eyes and trust me. I will wake you when someone shows up or it's noon. The great thing about caves is that they don't have back doors. Close your eyes. Dream, if you still have dreams to dream." Hope tunes the car radio to the lullabies station and turns on my seat massager.

"I kind of want to be awake for this. I could wait outside, and you could go, if I'm being too much of a pain."

The lullabies station finishes a song and boldly announces that, "If you are driving and listening to this station and feeling tired, you need to wake up or pull over... not just for yourself and your responsibilities, but for all the other drivers on the road and the cleanup crews that have to pick up the pieces after you head the wrong way around a turn." It launches into the statistics of sleep deprivation related accidents. Then the announcer says, "If you're a baby in a crib, you can just relax. By the time you're old enough to drive, they may have figured out the driverless car, but based on yesterday's failed AutoDrive experiment, I doubt it." I smile faintly at Hope and turn off the radio. I turn off the massager too.

Hope says, "People know about AutoDrive now."

"Yeah, people know it as a failure."

"What do you think is going to happen to it?"

"That depends on Carl's leadership abilities. Anyone can manage routine situations. It takes a real leader to take on a bad situation with low or no expectations and turn it around into a success story. I don't know that he can do it. I don't think he has the health or the track record that would support an uphill battle. But anything can happen."

"What would you like to happen?"

"There is going to be a driverless car. It'll happen. The need exists. It would be a waste for the product to start over from scratch. Carl was once a friend, not a friend like Tom or Cy or even Jake, but still a friend. Friendships are important to me. They're all I have. I have high expectations of my friends, and I expect them to have the same expectations of me. I don't want anything bad to happen to Carl, and he's just a step away from a heart attack. It's as clear as the veins on his face. But I've finished my involvement. I've paid my bill. If someone had died or been seriously injured by AutoDrive, Carl would've torn himself apart, just as I would've, asking himself why he didn't do more to prevent such a thing from happening. There was no reason for a cop to be taking a break in his car, that is itself acting as a barricade for AutoDrive. No reason. And if I could've had some sort of open communication with Carl, that may have helped fix things. And maybe I could've given him some other tips, that may have turned the failure into something more positive. He lost the big picture. He lost his morals. He lost his ability to communicate. And I provided some unwanted assistance to put a finish to my end of the project. I'm done. It's up to other people to figure out what's going to happen. Did you ever have a kid in your class that was a pain in the butt all year long, but you fought and fought to make the kid work and learn and by the end of the year, when the kid graduated from fourth grade, you were sorry that you wouldn't be working with the kid again?"

"No," Hope laughs. "You don't–"

"Me too. This is freedom." I kiss Hope as she laughs. A car pulls ahead of ours. A guy gets out and walks toward Wakan Teebe.

"You know, maybe this has to do with the Chief of the Mdewakanton, Cal. Maybe that's why you're invited."

I shake my head. "I don't think so. He liked you better." Two men arrive together. "I guess this is it." I kiss her. "See ya."

50

Wakan Teebe

I climb the gradual slope to the area at the base of the entrance where the three others stand. I approach and stop. We acknowledge each other with our eyes or a slight nod. A grasshopper hops down the slope. We look at the ground and look out at the river, ignoring the traffic from Warner Road. Some leaves fall from a tree on the cliff whose leaves are already changing colors. That can happen to trees that don't have a decent water supply. A little crow calls from the tree. Nearer, a trio of black-capped chickadees calls to us from some bushes. They sing a medley of their hits, starting with a simple series of chirps – they're just getting warmed up, folks – then running through their song that sounds like they are whistling, "Spring's Here," which for much of the winter, teeters on the cusp of hilarious. Spring never comes and when winter is finally over, it's not spring, it's summer. At long last, the chickadees launch into a complex version of their theme song, their number one hit, Chickadee. One bird sings, "Chick-a-dee-dee-dee-dee." Another interrupts to sing the same thing. Then the third bird interrupts with its call. They end at once, take their bow, and leave. A truck rumbles by on Warner Road. I pick up a small feather that one of the chickadees dropped. A plane lands at the small airport across the river. A paddle boat, launched not far from here, steams slowly down the river. The feather is gray-white with a black tip. A breeze tries to take away my feather, rustling the seedpods of some bushes, making them sound like maracas. On the other side of the river past the airport are some more bluffs, bookending the river. This is a big river valley. Either a fierce battle took place here against the giant snake, Zuzehecedan, with thrashing and splashing that beat down the ground here but not up above here or way over there... or else this part of Minnesota used to be even wetter than it is today. This would've been a huge waterway. But now, looking out at the Mississippi, tucked away in a narrow part of the giant valley, it seems awfully small. A rabbit drops into its river warren. Most of the rows of lakes around here are remnants of buried river valleys. On the bluff above are surviving native burial mounds. Most mounds were destroyed to create the park that honors them. The mounds may have been made by the Hopewell, centered down river in Cahokia, Illinois. Or they were made by the Laurel of northern Minnesota. Or the Laurel may be offshoots of the Hopewell, from their mound building peak around the year 1050. I shuffle the clay dirt. I wonder what Hope is thinking right now. We're mostly in full view of her. It's good that she's not here right now, though. This is guy talk. I shuffle some dirt. One of the other guys responds with some dirt shuffling of his own. I suppose that with having so many brothers, Hope probably has a complete understanding of a group of guys milling about. A chipmunk darts by, stops, looks at me like I fit a description of someone in chipmunk mythology, shakes its furry head, and hightails it out of here along its little chipmunk trails under the bushes. Four more men and one couple join us. Many others arrive. The Chief of the Mdewakanton, Cal, mumbles an acknowledgment of me, calling me, "Sure Foot." He remembers me! We start to duck our way into Wakan Teebe. Avatrice Gaea blinks at me. I nod to her with a straight smile. I think of Hope and check my watch before stepping inside.

Hidden in the bluff, the mouth of the cave is like a mouth, more wide than tall. It's turned up at the corners. I wonder if it has eyes, somewhere on the bluff.

I spot a petroglyph in some moss on the wall, but it's not the turtle and two snakes. I don't know what it is. It looks almost like someone entering a white cave, head first, on their back. A wind blows through... from inside the cave. Another petroglyph, appearing faintly in the soot, looks like a bison feeding a tribe at Owamniyomni. Now I spot the turtle and two snakes. Someone was standing in front of it. It's not as bright and the lines aren't as complete as all the depictions I've seen of it. The child in me wants to go up to it and touch it. I resist. A coat of arms with a crown was carved by someone who was more of a carver than an artist.

The floor of the cave looks snow covered, but it's a fine white sand. Forty feet in from the entrance passageway, the cave opens up into an expanse of blackness. Lamps that look like fires and bark torches are switched on. The cave lights up around us. This great room is about 60 feet wide at its widest point. The uneven ceiling is 20 feet high at its tallest point. A darkly mirroring lake fills a third of the room but more toward the middle.

I've never been in a cave with a wind. It goes against all the rules of what is a cave. Caves don't have breezes; the air doesn't move. This wind is gusty; it's inconsistent. I casually drop a small feather at the next gust. The cave wind spirals it back through the crowd and, presumably, back out the entranceway. Several others notice my experiment, heads turn to follow the feather. I thought I was being subtle. I always think I'm being subtle.

In the bluffs across the river, the Wabasha Cave is damp and musty, like a typical cave. Wakan Teebe is alive. It's both silent and loud. I can hear the breathing of those around me. I can practically hear their heartbeats. This must be what it's like to be Stephanie. Someone's ears are ringing. I can hear that too.

I'm glad Hope helped me turn off my phone. The acoustics in here are incredible. I close my eyes, and I almost see something. My eyes open again. I think, No more AutoDrive. AutoDrive has been my role for so many 12 hour days and sleepless nights I can't imagine what's next. And I have a decent imagination. I pray.

The wind whips smoke from an incense burner into a blizzard of swirls over and through us in the Great Room. Words are whispered to the wind. Water trickles and gurgles a reply. Several of them turn to look at me. I pale in the attention. Whatever the water is saying about me isn't true. Well... of course it's true, but it was Jake's fault.

I'm glad Jake isn't here. He would be loudly messing with the acoustics. He's just the sort of person to invite to an avalanche party, to start things off.

The wind tugs at my sleeve. I turn my head, and nobody's there. A fine line of smoke spirals around me and reminds me that my clock needs to be wound.

A man nearby softly says, "Makoce nupa umanipi," and other things I wish I understood. We shift into a circle. I clasp my hands. Others imitate me. From right next to me, the man who started this says, "A spotted eagle flies from here and carries with it any anger we can't control. Leave your anger here." I'm not angry.

I'm not angry at Carl.

I'm not angry at my old neighbors or landlady at Whisper Willows.

I'm not angry at Jake.

The wind tugs my sleeve again. Okay, I'm a little angry at Jake. I do one final sweep of my mind and spot it tucked away in a mental cave. The anger is hiding something. I push the anger aside. It's my parents and Melanie. I'm angry at them? I'm mad at them for not listening to me and for dying on me. I'm mad at them for leaving me alone. "Leave something of yourself for the eagle. You delay it taking something else from you." Help yourself, Mister Eagle. Take whatever– And then I think of Hope. No. The eagle doesn't get Hope. How did I get so reliant on Hope? I would be hopeless without my love for Hope.

I love Hope. And her dimples.

The wind spins into our circle, pulls some sand a few inches off the ground like a little cyclone, and shoots through some of the others, pulling with it some smoke from incense burners.

One of the lights flickers out.

We stand in silence.

The wind sucks back in from outside, from the river. Then it blows back out.

Weird.

I close my eyes. The wind tugs on me here and there. After a time, I open my eyes again. I like it here. Several of the others are watching me. If I'm supposed to do something or say something, I don't know what it is. Our leader, standing by me, nods. He says something else I don't understand. We all nod and leave. The wind helps us out.

I step down the slope, past a lone sugar maple that is trying to decide when to change colors, to Hope's car. I climb in. "Hi Hope. I want to tell you how much I love you and how great it is that I am finally done with AutoDrive." Hope shakes her head, half smiling. "You **don't** love me?!?"

"I **do** love you. I just don't think you're as finished with AutoDrive as you think you are. This news radio station played your 911 call all the way through, with commentary. It was great! You're calling them, trying to tell them to do something about the car, then it brakes really loudly, and then there was silence for a moment until you said, 'Uh, never mind.'"

I don't think I said, uh. "What was newsworthy about playing that call?"

"I don't know if it was newsworthy, but I liked it. I could picture you talking, your brow wrinkling as you tried to communicate what was happening..."

I rub my forehead as Hope puts the car in drive. "My brow wrinkles?"

"Yes," she laughs. "It's nothing to worry about. So here I was waiting and wondering what was going on in the cave and then you were with me anyway, talking on the radio."

"So what was the commentary? Was it like Orson Welles and the War Of The Worlds? 'Ladies and gentlemen you have just heard from Mr. Wilmuth, owner of the farm where this thing has fallen!' Was it that sort of commentary?"

Hope giggles, "No, it was more like, 'How did this guy know it was going to crash?' and 'What did he expect the 911 operator to do about it?'" I look at her as she drives and think about telling her that it was her idea. It was, but I took the idea and did it so I really can't blame her. "They especially jumped on the operator who asked you how you knew it would crash, and you," Hope covers her mouth as she laughs, "you said–" Hope covers her mouth again. She's in hysterics.

"Remember to breathe. I can drive if you want."

Hope catches her breath, "You said, 'It's a self-driving car.' And the operator accepted that like, 'Oh well, that explains it.'" She cracks up again.

So when we were on our way to Chicago, she had suggested the 911 call purely for its entertainment value? Now I understand. I help her watch the road, while she wipes some tears from her eyes. "Are you sure you don't want me to drive?"

"Positive," she says, regaining her composure. I get out my phone, turn back on the ringer, and start reading through messages. "So tell me, what was it like?"

"It was cool. I'm glad I brought a jacket."

"**That's it?!?**"

"No, I was also glad you had me turn off my phone. It could've brought the whole bluff down. Thank you. We didn't talk much. It was as if we each brought our own issues in and took with us our own issues out."

"What did it look like?"

"It has a lake. This is Minnesota. Of course it has a lake. Even the lakes have their own lakes."

"Right. Lakes have islands, and the islands have lakes in the middle."

"It keeps going to the molecular level. Molecular lakes." I pause on a message. "NOD wants to know if they can do the interview later today."

"I have to get things ready for school tomorrow... But let's get home, have lunch – the leftover spaghetti is probably still good – and then see what you want to do." I nod. I tell her about Wakan Teebe the rest of the way home and through lunch. She likes the story of the feather. I tell her that the story isn't finished. For all I know, the feather is still floating around.

51

Pressed

Trumpets herald the call of an associate news producer. They don't just find the news; they produce it. She says she needs to interview me this afternoon. She says, "People are misunderstanding the purpose of your 911 call."

"What people?"

"People, people. Our viewers."

"Are they calling?"

"Mostly writing."

"Letters?"

"E-mail. And text messages."

"If you give me their addresses, I could write them back."

"That's confidential. Those are private communications."

"Wait. Wasn't my 911 call a private communication?"

"Uh, that's not in our control..."

"Unless I tell you that you can't air it."

"We've already aired it."

"I could tell you that you can't air it anymore."

"Look, this isn't going the way it should..."

"No, you lied. You don't need to do the interview. You want the interview. And you said that it's because you want to clear up misunderstandings that your viewers have, but if you want to clear up misunderstandings, you can just go on the air and clear up the misunderstandings. You really don't need me to do that, do you? But if you ask nicely if I would do an interview this afternoon, I would consider it."

Silence. I'll wait.

"Would you do an interview this afternoon?"

Silence. It's only fair. "Yes. Where?"

"At Channel One, EFN."

"What does EFN stand for?"

"I'm not going to get into that. Channel One is in Milltown on Mdewakanton at Broken Paddle. Can you get there at four?"

"Yes." She disconnects before I can say another word. I turn to Hope, "What does EFN stand for?"

"I've heard, but it can't be right." She checks the web. "This can't be right. Maybe you should ask when you're there."

"Can I get a ride to Channel One? I need to be there at four. It's at Mdewakanton and Broken Paddle."

"Yes, definitely." Hope stares at me. "Are you nervous?"

"For the interview? No. After Wakan Teebe, this is an everyday event." She's still staring at me, so I tell her, "Brave men run in my family." I help her to label folders with the names of her new students while she gets other supplies ready. Then I get cleaned up again and get my suit on. Hope has set the TVs in both the upstairs and downstairs living rooms to record NOD. On the way, I send a message to Cy and everyone else that I will be on NOD sometime after four. At Channel One, we are escorted from one lobby to another, where Hope is told she can wait and watch my segment when it comes on NOD. "She's coming with me," I tell them.

They put us in a room that looks like a barber shop and have me take a seat. A girl named Clarise puts a bib on my suit and puts makeup on my face. Hope laughs. When Clarise is finished, she leaves, and I put on another bib and wipe the paint off.

A college guy comes in, handing me a clipboard with a form to sign. It's fine print. I look at it under better light. "I need it now." I hand it back without signing it. "No, you've got to sign it."

"Then you have to wait for me to read it." I read it. Hope reads it too. I draw lines through everything I disagree with. I draw lines through some things I simply don't understand. I sign it and give it back to him.

We're escorted to a set that shows a picturesque lake scene. They obscure the view with a chair and me. A camera is pointed at me which films through a video of the anchors at NOD. It means that when I'm looking at the camera, from my perspective, I'm looking at them. Hope and my phone are escorted to a windowed booth on one side. They give me something to stick in my ear.

The NOD anchors have just finished an ambiguous news story and are asking someone other than their audience, "Don't we have a battle clip that we can use next time?"

"How about 503-127?" a voice from nowhere asks.

"That one? The guy that practically leaps on the land mine? That one has been done to death. Even the land mine manufacturers have complained about our overusing that clip."

"What piece is up?"

"You're leading with the driverless car. This is the guy that made it and stopped it," the voice says. We haven't even started and they're already getting it wrong. The voice in my ear tells me to look straight at the people in the camera. It tells me that the woman, Wilmette, will be interviewing me. When she welcomes me, that's my cue to say, "Hi Wilmette," or something like that.

Around the anchors, a Minnesota Inventions graphic swirls. There are graphics of softball called kittenball, grocery bags, adhesive tape, HMOs, staplers, water-skis, in-line skates, the Tilt A Whirl, Charlie Brown and Snoopy, frozen vegetables, Sears, Wheaties, Spam, and Little House on the Prairie. "Many inventions have come out of Minnesota," the graphics stop... they left out a whole lot, "but if you're waiting for the car that drives itself, you'll have to wait a little longer. We have with us the inventor of AutoDrive, which caused some property damage in Milltown on Sunday."

She introduces me. I say, "Hi Wilmette."

"What went wrong?"

"Everything. The product was rushed through development. I was fired a month ago, because I said it wasn't ready."

Wilmette asks, "What can we learn from this?"

"Learn? You mean what can people take away from this and apply to their everyday lives? Nothing. It's like your last segment. Did we learn anything? No. Are we going to investigate it further? No. You categorized two sides of an issue, boxed it up between commercials and moved on to the AutoDrive fiasco. If it helps anyone, maybe we learned that it's easier to smash around a half-created product than to explain delays to its sponsors. That placing schedules over safety in any transportation industry is a recipe for disaster. Planes, trains, NASA space vehicles... and AutoDrive. One day there will be a self-driving car; today is not that day. We learned that the road to hell is a series of shortcuts."

Wilmette says, "Let's listen to your 911 call."

"911 emergencies." "A car, called AutoDrive, made by Flight Control, is about to crash into a police car at the corner of–"

The voice in my ear interrupts to tell me, "Ease off. Just tell your story. We're not the bad guys. We didn't fire you. We just want to hear your story. It's an interesting story. Hey, I bet you don't get many bananas up there in Minnesota."

The 911 operator muttered, "That's what he's talking about." Tires **squealed** loudly with the sort of squeal that ends with a crash of glass, plastic, and metal. No crash this time. "Never mind."

Wilmette continues, "When you said, 'about to crash,' you sounded so confident that it was going to crash."

"Yes."

That wasn't the response she wanted. "Why were you so confident it would crash?"

"I saw it happen in a dream."

Wilmette's eyes shoot open wide, and she fumbles for her ear piece. "In a dream? That doesn't sound very scientific."

"It was about to crash."

"You stopped it by rolling a ball. How do we know you didn't rig it or program it or whatever to stop for a ball?"

"I did program it to stop for a ball."

"Then why bring up a dream? You knew how to stop it, and you stopped it. I don't see what a dream has to do with anything."

"I don't work for that company anymore. The dream told me that if I didn't stop the car, it would've seriously injured or killed two police officers who were in its path."

Wilmette asks, "Very quickly, why were you fired?"

"For stupidity... theirs not mine."

She chuckles, "You could write a book about your side of the story." I laugh. I laugh so hard I fall off my chair. I'm still laughing.

"We'll continue our interview with the creator of AutoDrive. Stay with us."

A man steps into the frame with Wilmette and says, "You covered that perfectly," while sneering at me through the camera. "Do you want to segue to the homeless piece or do you want to stick with Mr. Hilarity here."

"I can make this work," she says.

"Suit yourself." He steps out of frame. Pause.

"We are back talking with the creator of AutoDrive. He's still laughing at the idea of writing a book. AutoDrive is the car that chalked up property damage on its trip through Milltown on Sunday. Was a beach ball the only way to stop the car? That seems very shortsighted."

I catch my breath, "It was the only way I could think of to stop it. I called 911 just in case I was unsuccessful."

"But they didn't have any time. You called right before it happened. You didn't just dream it was going to happen did you?"

"No..."

"Then assuming you dreamt it at all, you should have called 911 soon enough for them to have done something with the information."

"You mean call before anything happened? They wouldn't have listened. They have no legal obligation to do anything. I was just covering the bases."

Wilmette nods at me as if listening to the imagined story of a child, "You didn't give them a chance. One last question, quickly, what is in your future?"

"Futures. I have many futures. Everyone does," I tell her.

Wilmette introduces me again as the "creator of AutoDrive, which failed this past Sunday. This is News On Demand."

Life is a do-over, I always say. When I say that, it isn't so much a statement as it's an argument. I want life to be a do-over. Reality has other things in mind. I wish I hadn't said anything about the futures.

Someone comes and pulls the ear piece from my ear.

Hope meets me at the door to her booth; her eyes are wide. "Is that the way you wanted that to go?" I shake my head. She hands me back my phone as we leave the studio. "I turned off the ringer," she says.

Outside I turn it on. Trumpets announce trumpets and more trumpets. I take my first call, "Hi! This is, Say The First Thing That Pops In Your Head, the show that requires no forethought. Go ahead, caller!"

"Hi," Cy says. "You didn't mean to say all that did you?"

"No, they put makeup on me. I tried to get it all off right away, but there must have been some sort of residual chemical that made me say the first thing I thought of."

"The makeup made you talk?"

"Yeah. What do you think?"

"I'm sorry I wasn't there to coach you. Listen, could you do me a favor? Stop talking to the press."

"That sounds like a good idea."

"Thanks for the message warning me. I had plenty of time to set up to record it."

"You're welcome."

"Are you going home now?"

"Are we going home now?" I ask my driver.

She nods and says, "Groceries."

"Groceries first, then home."

"Good plan. See ya," Cy says.

"Bye."

More trumpets. I answer as we get in the car, "Hey! This is, Say The First Thing That Pops In Your Head, the show that requires no forethought. Go ahead, caller!"

"**I saw your interview!**" Dan exclaims, I hold my phone next to the passenger window as Hope giggles. "**Are you okay?**"

"No, I don't think I'm okay. I'll probably be okay but not right now."

"**Hang in there! Take it easy!**"

"You too. Thanks." Dan disconnects.

More trumpets. "This is Say The First Thing That Pops In Your Head, the show with no forethought. Go ahead, caller!"

"I think you screwed that up," Stephanie says. "What do you think?"

"I think I screwed it up."

"As long as you know that, you'll be okay. I'll talk to you later."

"Bye." Stephanie disconnects.

Ray calls with similar questions, so I give him similar answers. I ask him what he wants from the grocery store. "You don't have to go to the grocery store."

"We're already there."

He lists off some things.

We pick up groceries while I take a call from Joe, who wants to know if I want to go out and get plastered. I think he means drunk, not to be made smooth with a paste-like mixture of lime, sand, and water. I pass but thank him for the offer.

A redeeming comfort is that people in the store haven't seen the interview, although for some reason, someone in line behind me recognizes my voice. We take our groceries home and put them away. Mica calls to say she liked my suit. Other news media want me to be candid for their news too. Hope makes me some soup. I eat it in bed and go to sleep.

Sometime in the night I'm visited by four women wearing night clothes, looking at me the way Lefty or Gene would look at an experiment that went awry.

52

Depressed

Hope kisses me awake. She's bent over me, dressed as a school teacher. I quickly realize that she's not just role playing; she really is a school teacher. Maybe I could still be the teacher's pet. I bolt up and offer to make her a lunch. She smiles and says she already has that in the car. I check my breath and kiss her. "I hope you have a great day and a class full of students eager to learn." She thanks me and from the doorway, waves at me. I check my alarm clock. It's puckering for a kiss. So I kiss it. It makes a yucky face. I fall back asleep.

Ray stomps into my room. His face is red. I check my clock. It says it's 10:25 and still has a yucky face. Its face must be stuck. "I just got off the phone with Disaster News! I told them off for some of the things they're calling you!"

Just some of the things? "Why? What are they calling me?"

"Crackpot. Crazy came up a lot."

"I can think of worse. They could have said that I'm not the brightest bulb on the tree, or I'm not the sharpest knife in the drawer, or that I'm not playing with a full deck, or I'm an assorted nut, or that all my pistons aren't firing in all my cylinders, that I'm counter intelligence, or that I'm a couple sandwiches short of a picnic, or the lights are on but nobody's home, the lowest common denominator–"

"I get the message."

"Thanks for calling." I check my messages, clean up, eat, and clean the house. I open up some windows. I always used to open up windows at the apartment. **Blam-blam-blam.** The noise from next door makes me close the windows again. I used to be used to noise.

Ray gives me regular reports on what is being said on TV. Taking out the trash, the construction crew next door applauds me, but I question their sincerity. Taking out the trash doesn't deserve applause. A package arrives in the mail.

Ray comes downstairs to the basement where I'm switching loads of laundry to tell me that, "Now one windbag is saying that you programmed the crash. That this is the hero complex. Your dream was a self-fulfilled prophecy." I stare into the dryer. "Someone else replied that you had been gone from the company for weeks. So he said, 'So?'"

"If he's such an expert at AutoDrive programs, maybe he should get a job at Flight Control. Seriously. They may be hiring. Carl could use someone saying 'So' to him."

I answer my phone like a normal person would. "What happened to Acapella's Pizza?" Ruth asks.

"Closed."

"How are you?"

"I've been better."

"What can I do?"

"I don't know."

"Try me. What do you need?"

"A job. A car. Parents."

"I might be able to find you a car."

I sigh. "Hope has first dibs. She already offered to buy me a car. I just haven't gotten over loosing the Pony Express."

"What if she got you another cruddy Pony Express? Would that make you happy?"

My face cracks. I nearly smile. "No."

"You know what I think? I think you should go back to dreaming. Gotta go." Ruth disconnects.

Maybe it is a little crazy to be missing my old car. I take a laundry basket upstairs. Folding and hanging up laundry, I think about what Ray was telling me. People think I'm crazy, a crackpot. I wonder how this might effect Belle and Sam at Common Communication. How can I show people I'm not crazy? I could take a lie detector test, but anyone who knows anything about lie detector tests knows how much of a sham they are. Besides, I know the Lavemore Methods for defeating lie detector tests, curling the toes, skewing the setup questions, working yourself into a mental frenzy for the simple questions... It's easy to defeat. Polygraphs are only used by scientists who still read their horoscopes. There is no perfect proof.

Recordings can be altered or forged. DNA tests can be skewed. Someone with a nosebleed drops a bloody tissue in a wastebasket. Someone else retrieves it. The blood is smeared at a crime scene. Or the crime scene samples are switched. No disrespect meant to Abe Lincoln, but it's gotten to the point that everybody thinks they are being fooled all the time. The only reliable thing is pudding. I don't understand how pudding relates, but I'm told that the proof is in the pudding.

Wilmette suggested that I write a book. I'm not going to write a book.

I need Lefty's help. I need to participate in the fMRI-Memmeograph STM experiment. I send him a message. Then I send another message mentioning that I no longer have pointed perception. I get a message back from Dr. Melvin Vagues asking me to meet him at room 41 of the Teska Building this Thursday at ten in the morning. He also says that he will do all that he can to prevent the loss of my short-term memories.

I'm finishing up my laundry when Ray tells me that someone is at the door for me.

Mani introduces himself as a representative of a group with special mental abilities.

This is what today needs. "So when you announce meetings you just say, 'You all know where and when to meet?!?'"

"No. Have you heard of us?"

"No, but my roommate is a comic book artist, so I've heard of superhero groups."

"We're not like that."

"You aren't... super-villains, are you?" I start to shut the door.

"No! We're not like that at all."

"How does seeing futures work for you?"

"I can't see the futures or even just one future. I have a sense of the obvious."

"A sense of the obvious?"

"Yeah. I see things very clearly. Well, not just see, but hear and smell, and to me, it's all totally obvious. But only when I spell everything out for people do they get it, and even then they're usually just humoring me. People rarely understand me."

"I understand."

"I'm just good at the semi-conscious recognition, retention, and retrieval of sensory input. It's one definition of the word phenomenal. It is phenomenal."

"That doesn't sound like ESP."

"It's not. What I have is excellent sensory perception, nothing extra. I'm not even sure that I believe in ESP."

"Then why are you–"

Mani interrupts, "Why represent a group with claims of special abilities? I want to believe. And I find it easier to believe people that aren't competing to prove themselves."

"Oh."

"Not that they don't have issues of their own. They use their supposed special abilities as excuses for not behaving normally. They can't talk normally. They are above it all. I'm the one who brings in plausibility. So what's it like for you?"

"It's just like everything else."

"Huh?"

"Today is yesterday's tomorrow. From the perspective of yesterday, you're in the future right now. But that doesn't make it freaky."

"So you're a precog?"

"I have no idea. I'm not like anything I've ever heard of before. Nothing in my life works like it seems to work for anyone else."

"Do you have fun?"

"I have lots of fun."

"Would you want to visit us?"

"No, thank you." Thinking for a moment about Scratch, I ask, "Do you want a cat?"

"No, thanks. It was nice meeting you." He turns to leave. He comes back and says, "There are a lot of parked cars on your street." I shrug. "There are a lot of parked cars on your block with people sitting in them." He leaves. He's right about the parked cars. I hadn't noticed.

Hope drives up and comes in. "You're famous," she says handing me some newspapers.

"If the article is as bad as that picture of me, I don't want to read it."

"No, I don't think you want to read it," she says, leaving me wonder why she's giving me the papers. "My mom called to check up on the crackpot." Hope smirks and turns to answer the door. "Yes, can I help you?"

She has a face that's out of place. I know I know her. "My name is Fran." My jaw drops. Just when I didn't think today could get any worse, it got worse.

Hope looks at me and at Fran and says, "Come in."

Fran stares at me and stares at me. I brace myself for the hit I have coming to me. She's still staring at me. I try smiling, but I don't really have it in me today. "Welcome to the crackpot club," she tells me. I exhale. "Now you know what it feels like. You're the latest in the crazy person spotlight. How does it feel?" I shake my head. "Right."

Hope asks, "Can I get you something?" Fran declines. "Would you like to sit down?" We sit down.

Fran says, "You made a fool out of me."

"I never meant to..."

"How's the French boy? The one with the broken heart?"

"There was no French boy," I admit.

Fran nods. "What were you doing on Prospective Tower?"

"I don't know. I'd had an odd day and had just eaten a bison." Fran turns to Hope for confirmation. Hope turns to me for confirmation. "Was that the same night?"

I ask, "Remember the fog when we were cooking it?"

"That's right. That was the same night." We turn back to Fran.

"Your clothes glowed."

"They didn't seem to glow when I was inside. I was trying them out to see if I should get rid of them."

Fran nods slightly. "Until I saw you on TV last night, I thought you were my guardian angel, like you said. I believed everything you told me. I believed I had been saved. I believed in a miracle."

I tell her, "I'm sorry. I wanted to save you. I wanted to give you a miracle. But I'm only a man."

Hope says, "You did save her. You did give her a miracle. I don't know how miracles usually work, but maybe they all work this way." She turns to Fran, "He said he doesn't know why he climbed Prospective Tower. When I was on the hill, I couldn't figure how he did it or how you did it." She turns back to me, "When was the last time you were up there?"

Now she's questioning me. "It was about five years ago."

"Had you ever been up there in the fog like that?"

"No."

"It was slippery, wasn't it?"

"Yes," Fran and I respond.

"Did you have a dream about it?" Hope ask.

"I don't know. I might have."

"I bet you did. I think you knew exactly what to do. You did something you normally wouldn't do, and I don't think you know why you did it. And you... thought it was a miracle. I still think it was."

Fran starts to shake. "Th-thank you for saving my life." She asks Hope for a glass of water. Fran still stares. I don't know what to say. Hope gets a glass of water for me too. "Something else is weird. There's a rumor going around that Melanie, as in Melanie Fields, has been asking around about the Savior of the Midway. That's got to be–"

Ray comes through and hits the brakes when he sees Fran. They both seem to recognize each other. God, I hope he's not the Felipe she mentioned. "Uh, Ray, this is Fran. Fran, this is Ray."

"Do I know you?"

Ray says, "I'm the sculptor of the Lactating Woman."

"No, do you have a different name?" Uh, oh.

"Yes. He calls me Ray. But my name is Cameron Raymond."

"The comic book artist?"

"Yes."

"I have a signed copy of Glory Girl! You signed it for me."

Ray gapes at her. "You're Fran! The woman that was saved at Prospective Tower! We used to live right near there! I had lost faith in miracles, until I heard about everything that happened that night!" We all exchange looks for what seems to be an hour. He shakes her hand.

"Do you still draw?"

"Yes. Do you want to see?" Hope and I follow them into Ray's studio, where he shows his latest work.

"You do it freehand?"

He nods. "Then I scan it and submit it."

"It's cool to see unfinished art. What's the next stage after this?"

"I ink over the pencil sketch. I could draw something for you. What would you like?"

"I can't afford–"

Ray waves her off. "I can't charge the woman the Savior of the Midway saved?!? What would you like?" They talk it over, and Fran agrees to come back next Tuesday. Ray exchanges phone numbers with her. "How do you know each other?"

We look at each other. Fran says, "I saw him on TV and wanted to talk with him."

Ray asks, "Even after all the things they've said about him? That's nice of you."

"They said nasty things about me too," she says.

"That just proves they don't know what they're talking about," Ray responds.

We escort Fran to the door. "See you next Tuesday," she says. We nod and say good-bye. Hope closes the door.

"Morton Gneiss died," Hope says. "I got the message a few hours ago."

"I heard about him on the news," Ray says. "Did you know him?"

Hope says, "He was a resident at the nursing home we've been visiting. I'm going upstairs to get changed and drop stuff off." Ray goes to answer his phone.

I'm stuck with television news.

"He's right here. Do you want me to ask him?" Ray asks his phone. "Cy wants to know if they can do a Restaurant Review here tomorrow night." I shrug. "He shrugged."

"It's a school night. And there would be plenty of meat stuff," I warn him.

"I already told her. I can handle that. As long as I don't actually have to handle it."

"Should I talk with her?"

"Do you want to talk with him? She says no."

Fine. I can just watch the news. Christie is on. She starts talking just as Hope comes back downstairs. Hope bounces onto the couch by me. I put my left leg over her right leg. Christie says, "You know? I don't care about cars that drive themselves. I'm sure they would take awhile to be available to poor people. And while I'm glad no one was injured last weekend, and while you have to know that this inventor is a friend of mine, I don't care if he's considered crazy or not. What people need to learn is that last part he said. Did you hear it? He said, 'Futures.' He said, 'I have many futures. Everyone does.' Futures. Plural. That's something. Everyone has choices. Everyone has opportunity. That's something everyone needs to hear. You have futures. Doesn't that make you want to sit back and think about your decisions and try to imagine where they will lead? Which of these futures do I want to choose to live? What path do I take? What road should I travel? That's what he did. He's said we're offered a choice of tomorrows."

"Technically," I tell Hope, "I never said that. I like the sound of it, but I never said it."

Slam! A door slams upstairs. **Bam!** I don't know what that was.

"I better go upstairs to check what's up." I free up her leg. The stairs thunder. Nicole comes in crying and piles on Hope and I. "What's the matter Nicky?" We hold her, but I don't understand a word she's saying. They look at me for a reaction. Hope interprets, "She tried to get you a job, but she ended up defending you all day."

I hug her. I can't imagine spending a day defending myself. That would be tough. To be someone else and defending me, that sounds impossible. "Thank you, Nicole. Thank you for trying and for being great to me." Hope and I hold Nicole tight across our laps and look at each other through Nicole's hair. "Cy just called Ray about having a Restaurant Review here tomorrow... night, I think he said."

Hope blows Nicole's hair out of her mouth, "What's a Restaurant Review?"

"That's where everyone orders takeout from restaurants that you'd normally eat in at or that normally don't do takeout and everyone brings it to one person's house. I think she called Ray to see if he would be okay with having meat around." I look around through Nicole's hair for Ray, but I don't see him.

"The self-inflicted limitations of who we are," Christie says, "is not who we have to be."

"That sounds interesting," Hope says.

"I sent a message to Lefty about the experiment." Nicole gets up with our help. Her shirt says Better Inside. "We set it up for Thursday morning at ten."

Hope nods and sighs. "You know how I feel, and I think I understand where you're coming from."

"There's something new added to everything else. If the experiment goes the way Lefty expects, it will be evidence that I'm not the crackpot the media claims I am."

"About that crackpot comment, that's one guy talking, and everyone knows he's a... a... jerk."

"Miss Hope Ranidae!" Nicole exclaims. "Such language!"

"It's true. He is. As a matter of fact, I was talking at school, and it was suggested that my class might like to hear you give a presentation about AutoDrive and cars and stuff."

"When?"

"Tomorrow?"

"How would I get there?"

"I'll drive you," Nicole says.

"Don't you have to work?"

"I'll take the day off."

"You don't have to do that."

"I want to."

"Okay. What time?"

"If you could be there at a quarter to ten, we would do it sometime before 11. And not too technical, remember this is the fourth grade, although one of my students is already doing programming for his parents or something." The television is advertising shirts. They show men wearing them. The shirts are green, at least originally. They ripen through repeat wearings to banana yellow or orange orange or apple red. Washing it reverts it back to green.

"What's for dinner?" Nicole asks. "And please, no more spaghetti."

I suggest, "Pizza?" Hope and Nicole agree. Ray pops in to request spinach pizza.

Hope asks, "What's the number to Acapella's Pizza?" She's kidding. She's ordering.

The news has switched to callers reacting to reactions of the reactions, which seems to be several steps removed from news, so I go into the kitchen where Ray is fixing, cutting, and washing celery. I take a stalk of celery. Hope calls, "Come back in here! It's Freedonia!"

The screen says Freedonia of Pigs Eye, Minnesota, as if some other state has a place named Pigs Eye. That's her voice all right. She is criticizing person after person; she's working off a list. The anchor interrupts to ask if her mother knows she uses such language. Freedonia says, "My mom's right here. Would you like to talk with her when you're done with me?"

"I think we're done with you, and only one caller per household. Those are our rules, most of the time. Go ahead, Cleveland."

Hope says, "She was something. She shredded all of them and some commentators from other channels too."

"Do you know her?" Nicole asks.

"Yeah, she hung out at the Ice Cream Bar."

Ray asks, "Is there anyone you don't know?" as he passes a plate of celery.

"I don't know." I munch on my celery. "I know good people."

A local commercial advertises that it's not too early to buy a new snowblower.

Faith comes and joins us for pizza, telling us that Becky is spending the night at Tom's.

While we eat our pizza, the fourth or fifth level of reactions wants to get back to something I said. "This guy said something important. He told us what we needed to know. Do you remember it? He said he's from Minnesota. Do you know why that's important? Global warming. Let me ask you. What is Minnesota known for?"

"Mosquitoes."

"Besides mosquitoes."

"Snow."

"What's on their license plates?"

"Smashed mosquitoes."

"Their license plates say 10,000 Lakes. What makes Lake Superior so superior? It is the largest freshwater lake, a deep giant natural reservoir. Minnesota is about the only place in the world that does not have to care about global warming. They have the water up there. They are the source of the Mississippi. They aren't on the coast. They won't be getting flooded, or hit with hurricanes or earthquakes. And if Minnesota gets warmer, it will only get better."

"You're nuts."

"Maybe, but I just bought a great deal of land up there in Minnesota because that's where the future is. Minnesota could use some global warming."

"That's it, I need to leave; I can't stand any more of this," I point at the TV. Nicole changes the channel, and my phone rings. "Hello, Acapella's Pizza. Tonight's special is pizza by the slice. We turned off the ovens. We aren't cooking any more."

"Hey, you know, you're all over the news," Will tells me.

"Yeah, I was meaning to ask someone. How long is this going to last? What's the shelf life of news?"

"Mid-twentieth century stories are still being discussed."

"That's not what I wanted to hear."

"I thought you should hear what happened today at Flight Control. Carl started the day by telling everyone to, 'Take an early lunch and don't bother returning.' He fired everyone. Everyone had been talking up the motto, 'Keep the ball rolling.' Wendy might have started that. I wanted her to call you, but she said she can't talk to you right now."

"That's funny. Keep the ball rolling."

"I need to go. I just wanted you to know about Flight Control."

"Thanks, Will." I put my phone away. I tell my roommates what Will told me. I go to my room. I come back out with a package. I hand out shirts to everyone. They say Hope's House on them. After some size swapping, we put them on and start watching a movie. The last thing I remember was something about a cold wind from Saskatchewan.

53

Impressed

I wake up in the middle of the night to go to the bathroom, only to find that I had fallen asleep with Hope and Nicole in the living room, and someone covered us up with a blanket. The question is, do I go back to sleep in my room or the living room? The living room is closer to the basement door. The basement has monsters. I climb back under the blanket in the living room. When I wake up again, Hope is saying good-bye. Nicole staggers zombie-like upstairs. I go into my room, set my alarm, and fall back asleep.

My alarm goes off, and I start thinking about what I need to say to Hope's class and I realize that I don't have everything I need. I run upstairs. Nicole isn't in her room. A shower is running. Well, I've seen her in the shower before. "Hey, Nicole," I knock.

"Yeah?"

"I realized that I need us to run by the Capitol on the way." No response. I run back downstairs and jump into the shower with Beth. I get cleaned up and ready and get out two bags of toys, and I meet Nicole at the stairs. "You look nice."

"Thank you. I like your race car tie. I thought about my Graded On A Curve shirt but decided that might send the wrong message. Besides it's very tight. What do you need from the Capitol?" she asks me on the way to her car.

"The Highway Department has copies of the Minnesota Rules of the Road." Nicole takes me there. The parking meter out front only takes Minnesota quarters. Nicole agrees to circle the block. I run in and ask for some copies. Someone is trying to get a driver's license for their seeing-eye dog.

"How many do you need?" Matilda asks.

"Fifty."

"Fifty? What's this for?"

"School."

"We mail copies every year to the high schools. If you haven't received yours yet, you will."

"This is for grade school. Fourth grade. We're starting them off early on lessons that will last them a lifetime."

Her eyes shoot open. "Will 50 be enough?"

"Yes." She gives me a box of a hundred.

Just as she starts to recognize me, I haul the box out, and Nicole's car crawls around the corner. "Good timing," Nicole says. We get to the school and park in a small lot full of education-related bumper stickers. The school office has been expecting me. Several teachers appear to greet me. My reputation precedes me positively. They didn't expect Nicole, but I'm quick to vouch for her. We're escorted to a classroom. All the windows have wires running through them like heated car windows. The door says, Miss Ranidae. It's the sweetest thing you can imagine on colored construction paper. I peer in the window and open the door.

Hope smiles with dimples that show she was meant to smile for her entire life. She is running three or four separate activities. It's an organized chaos. Hope seems aware of all things within these walls. I don't know how she does it. "Thank you for coming. Use your dictionary, Zoe. Two other teachers are interested in joining us, I hope that's okay. Mai, I will be with you in a minute. So we will use one of the main activity areas. Raphael, Nicole can give you a hug **after** you finish your assignment." I start thinking about my supplies. "Is that okay?"

"How many students?" Hope adds class sizes, subtracts absentees and special projects... "Roughly."

"Oh, roughly? 80." Hope helps Mai. Nicole and I find ourselves helping other groups. It's as if this is a school of fish and Hope is a drop of water and everyone is thirsty.

Two other teachers stick their heads in to Hope's classroom, while monitoring students in the hallway. Our three classes go to an activity area of chairs and carpeting. When eager faces ask what I'm carrying I disappoint them by saying, "Books." I try to reassure them by saying, "I have plenty of them for everyone."

"What kind of books?" I'm asked.

"Government books," I reassure them.

While the other two teachers monitor the group with arms crossed, Hope introduces me, telling them that I was just on the national news the past two days because on Sunday I stopped a car that didn't have anyone driving it. She avoids breaking any of their little hearts by not mentioning that I'm her boyfriend.

The one rule I have in talking to kids is not to talk down to them.

"Good morning."

"Good morning!" they yell back. Adults could learn from them.

"Sunday morning in downtown Milltown, all the roads were closed off to test a car that drives on its own, called AutoDrive. A car that drives on its own means that it has to see and hear and feel and know all the rules and know how to drive, to drive the way adults drive, or better. There are a lot of rules. This is the rule book for Minnesota. It tells drivers what all the signs mean and how to turn corners and everything." I hold it up. I pass a few out. I hand out stacks of them to the adults to pass out and to various kids to help hand out. "AutoDrive is a normal car with some unique sensors. And complex programming. One of the optical sensors, like a digital camera has, sees a red sign that says stop. Another sensor uses a laser to tell how far away the sign is. Other sensors check for other traffic at the intersection. AutoDrive's special computer tells the car what to do with this information, based on what it sees and hears and where it's trying to go. The car will wait for an ambulance to go by. The car will check to see if another vehicle isn't already stopped at the intersection. If the car has the right of way, it will go through the intersection. One of the first things I taught it was to be careful of a ball coming out into the street, because a ball can be a sign of danger, just like a stop sign. Does anyone know why a ball should be a sign of danger to drivers?"

A kid asks, "Because it could get in your way?"

"Good question, but no that's not it. Yes?"

"Someone could have been playing with it. And the ball got away. And the ball rolls into the road. And they say they want their ball."

"That's good. If someone playing with the ball runs after it without stopping and looking for traffic, there could be an accident. So kids need to watch for drivers, and drivers need to watch for kids. I worked for the company that was making AutoDrive, for five years. At first I was the only one designing it. But then I led a group of people figuring out all that it needed to know and teaching it. A month ago, the owner of the company said, 'We need to have AutoDrive ready in a month.' I said, 'It needs one or two more years.' He said, 'It needs to be ready in a month.' I said, 'It can't be.' So he fired me. That means I don't work there anymore. But I knew AutoDrive wasn't ready. It could hurt someone. I didn't want it to hurt anyone. I felt responsible. So on Sunday, AutoDrive was out of control. They tried stopping it with fences! They tried stopping it by jumping on the car! They tried shooting it! It was about to run into the side of a police car with a police officer in it!" I get out the bag of crashing cars, the ones that crumple their front ends, with nerve shattering, car crashing sounds. I show one to them. I show how to turn on the switch. I crash it into my hand. It crumples with a crashing sound. "I didn't want that to happen with real cars, injuring real people. So I blew up a big beach ball." I show them a little rubber ball. "The AutoDrive car is coming! I tossed out the ball. The breeze blew it right back to me. I tossed it out again. This time it bounced out right in front of the car. The car brake's squealed. **Skreeeeeech!** The car bounced the ball along in front of it. **Skreeech!** AutoDrive stopped just inches from the police car. Trapped between the two cars, the ball popped! That's how I stopped the car. Any questions?"

"Who's car is it?"

"It's owned by the company that made it, Flight Control."

"Did someone get arrested?"

"No. Because no one was driving the car. But the car caused a lot of damage that the owner of the company, or its insurance company, will have to pay."

"Did you know for sure positive that the ball would stop the car?"

"No. I thought it would. And I had a dream that it would."

"Could I have that car, when you're done with it?"

"AutoDrive? No, I don't own it."

"No, that car," he points to the toy car in my hand.

"Yes. Here."

Pandemonium.

I ask Hope to have everyone line-up to get a car and a ball. We wind up six cars short. We write down the names of fourth graders that need cars. Another class passes by. Friends ask friends what's going on, amidst the noisily crashing cars. A kid named Jake tries to get signed up for a second car. The teachers call for an end to the crashing sounds and slowly the crashes become just an ear ringing memory. Nicole and I are offered to join the classes for lunch.

"What're we having?" I ask.

Hotdogs, french fries, pudding, and half-pint cartons of milk.

"No, thank you."

Hope introduces me to the principal. Hope says that other teachers have already said that they'd like a similar presentation. She says it's entirely up to me. We get ready to go. Everyone thanks us and gives us hugs. Nicole takes me home by way of the toy shop, where I buy them out of crashing cars, again, and the sandwich shop for sandwiches. The wind of Nicole's convertible is actually kind of cool. Soon, people will be putting snow tires on their shopping carts and on their wheelchairs and start playing the perennial favorite game, What Have You Got On Under The Parka?

At home, Nicole and I eat and respond to messages, while watching Ray work on two new Kelly's, without the plumbing. Ray tells us that having people over tonight has encouraged him to get further on the new sculptures.

Lefty requests that I don't grant any more interviews, because he doesn't want any leaks about his experiment. I mention the 80 fourth graders. He calls me to ask if I'm kidding. I say, "No, but I didn't mention the experiment to them." He says he'll see me tonight.

People start arriving early. First it's Becky and Tom. They go up to her room. Joe arrives and takes out a lounge chair and starts critiquing the work of the construction crew. "Is this a remodeling or a rebuilding? At the rate you're going, you'll never get done in time for winter." What I hear of his comments are right on target. Minion joins him and gets specific about types of tools used, brands, and model numbers. Al joins them and corrects any errors made by the other two. I'm wondering if anyone actually worked today. Hope comes home and takes a pain reliever especially designed to handle headaches caused by noisy toys.

Nadine comes over early to borrow something of Nicole's to wear, but she doesn't know what. "Every time I see you, you're wearing the cutest things!" Nadine hiccups as they head upstairs.

Red comes in and shakes my hand and says, "I knew you could do it." He sets himself up on the couch, reading a book. I look over his shoulder. The book is normal, except it doesn't have any spaces.

Todd and Cy arrive with food. Stephanie and Erix arrive with food.

Sharon stops by soon after and asks me if I would have lunch with her sometime next week, "I want to show off that I know you." She talks with Cy and Hope and then goes, just as Ruth is pulling up.

Ruth takes some pictures of us and the construction crew next door. Then she hooks up a gadget to the TV and starts playing pictures, especially from the past few weeks.

Dexter and Mica arrive with their kids, Don and Bucca. Joe, Minion, and Al relay messages to the construction crew through Don and Bucca. Joe says, "Hey kid, go over to those people and tell them that winter's coming."

Bucca goes over to the construction crew and tells them, "Winter's coming."

Lefty asks for a drink and is almost bowled over by Nicole and Nadine trying to run outside to stop Bucca from getting in trouble. Mica, of all people, tells them to relax, saying, "Bucca is tough enough to handle all of them."

Gene comes in, showing us an electronic picture frame of pictures of a piglet with the beginnings of wings. It looks kind of gross. Right away, several people are in the hallway talking to Ray about becoming vegetarians. Faith comes home in time to see the piglet with wings. Faith looks ill. That's when a voice booms, "**Hey, there's a runaway car out here! Anyone know how to stop it?!?**" It's Dan! Jake is with the lounge chair group.

"Hey, have your shoulders gotten bigger?" Cy asks him.

Dan grins. We shake hands. "When did you get into town?"

Dan looks at his watch, "**Just an hour ago! Jakie picked me up at the airport! I had to show up, with the way you sounded on the phone!** Cathy had a cow! **Here's my carry-on bag!**" He hands it to me. "**Open it!**"

"Chicago Deep Dish Pizza!"

"**I just picked it up two hours ago! This is restaurant review, right?!? Let's get it baking!**" Al and I help him get the pizzas in the oven and set a timer.

Trumpets announce a call. Before I can grab it, Cy yells, "You still haven't changed the ring on your phone?!? You? Mr. Technology?!? I meant for that ring to be a one shot joke, not a long-term annoyance. Change it!"

"Hello, Acapella's Pizza. Today's special is deep dish pizza flown in from Chicago. How can I help you?"

"Hi, Ricky?"

"Yes?"

"This is Yolanda. I don't know if you remember me..."

"Of course I remember you. You were Valerie."

"I'm in the cities, and I was wondering if I might stop by? With a friend?"

"I have people over. You might recognize half of them from when we saw your play. I'll give you directions."

"I'm actually just up the street."

"Then come on over!" I'm putting away the phone as Cy ushers them inside.

I give Yolanda a hug. She says, "After we heard all the mean things they said about you, we had to come and tell you not to listen to them!" People voice their agreement. Yolanda says hi to Dan and says she remembers him. She introduces her friend, Paige Turner. Red blushes like a redhead. He and Paige start talking about books and stories. They might mix the two and talk about story books. Yolanda says she's in a new play, Crisis in the Middle East.

Jake comes in with Wendy and Will, as Dexter and Mica step outside arguing over whose turn it was to watch the kids. I approach Wendy and say, "Hi Wendy. I'm sorry about what happened to AutoDrive and what happened to Flight Control."

Wendy is about to say something when Dexter gets my attention, "Ricky boy, there's someone at the door for you."

I back away from Wendy. Everything is fine. Everything's... Jake? Jake turns white with shock. I turn.

It's Melanie. Melanie Fields is standing in the doorway. Stepping toward her, looking at her makeup, her outfit, and her big smile, I recognize her. She has the face of an angel but with a devilishness in her eyes. I mouth, A-Me-V, and pull her inside. I hug her with a thousand hugs in one. She breaks the hug and turns us side by side. She's nestled in my arm, holding it to her side, looking, grinning happily but tightly gripping my arm in fear. Ruth takes picture after picture.

Everyone is freaking out. Erix is. Jake could pass out at any moment. Drinks are dropped. Yolanda, Hope, Cy... everyone is stunned. Nadine loses her hiccups. "Everyone is freaked out," I tell her.

She looks up at me. "So you're the Savior of the Midway!"

Everyone freaks out again.

"What?!?"

I start to say, "Ixnay..."

"Of course he is. I don't know why you didn't see it. He's right in front of you, Lois," she tells Cy, with a hint of the Aimee attitude. Cy is busy freaking out, holding back her hair from her eyes. Aimee hands me an envelope. "Here's your security deposit from your apartment. I kind of freaked out your landlady too."

Tom comes downstairs with Becky, stops, looks, and says, "Hi Aimee!" Then he double-checks that it's her.

"Aimee?!?"

"Which way is your room?" Aimee asks. I lead her in. "I was so scared," she quickly tells me. She digs around in my closet, as Hope follows us in. "Your closet is like a theater's prop and costume department." She pulls out Melanie's guitar, and it looks so right on her. She takes it out into the living room and starts tuning it, in Melanie's odd ritualistic way. Aimee plays bits of several Melanie songs on Melanie's guitar. She stops and says to Cy, "I didn't think you ever cried. You didn't cry once at Melanie's funeral, but you're crying now... am I that bad?"

Cy says, "I've cried plenty of times since she died. I was still in a state of shock."

Erix comes lumbering toward Aimee. Aimee starts to shake. Erix says, "I didn't know what to do. You died, and I fell apart. I died too."

I ask him, "Do you remember little Aimee? This is little Aimee. She grew up. This isn't your sister. This isn't Melanie." Erix stands by me.

Aimee strums the guitar. "It's funny. I can't decide what to play. You know why she had so many different love songs? She was in love with each one of you." Cy nods. "She even had a song about Cy."

"You, you..."

"Brat?" Aimee asks. Cy always called her that.

"You're kidding," Cy says. Aimee looks at me. "Which one?"

"I don't remember. The clue was who she glanced at near the end of the song. But she didn't always do that, especially because you weren't all out front when she performed. Hey, is that the amazon?" Nadine waves. "You guys really haven't changed."

"Haven't we?"

"Nope. And you all still hang out together?" I start to nod. "Or do you all live here?" I switch to shaking my head.

"Hope, this is Aimee. Aimee, this is Hope. This is Hope's house. I live here. That guy does; that's Ray. She does; that's Becky. She does; that's Faith. And she does; that's Nicole. Oh, and she does; that's Savanna." I spot someone I don't recognize at the door. "I don't know who he is."

"I'm delivering dinners from First Street Station." Dexter pays the guy.

I introduce everyone else back to where I started with Hope. "Someone set us up together," Hope and I smile at each other, "but we haven't been able to pin down who it was."

"Ask Cy," Aimee says.

"Cy says she had nothing to do with it."

"Ask her again. Do you remember the night Melanie died?"

"What?!? Of course!"

"Remember when she sent you off for a drink for her?"

"Yes." I never got to say good-bye.

Cy yells, "Don't!" rushing, tripping, and diving head first into the floor.

"Smooth." Aimee taps me. "You don't know what she made Cy promise."

"You brat! Shut up!"

Aimee steps back from Cy's advances. "Melanie made Cy promise to take care of you, no matter what. She also said you were right. She said she should have listened to you. She said–"

Cy cries from the floor, "You bitch." Aimee kneels down by Cy. Cy swings her arm to slap Aimee, but Aimee catches it. Cy is crying again, her hair falls and covers her hands covering her face.

"You did it. You took care of him. I'm telling you, you don't have to watch over him anymore. Hope will take over."

"I hate you."

"No you don't. You've been a prisoner in your promise. I saw it before I left town. You broke up, but you still had the responsibility to Melanie... the responsibility to him... You had to be the parents he never had. You're free. He knows." Hope kneels down beside them. "Hope will take over." Hope nods. "You can get on with your life. Now, we can take care of you." Cy bawls.

"PIZZA'S READY!" Dan booms. Joe and Minion race in, hurtling Cy, and diving into the kitchen. Others follow. Todd sits down on the floor by Cy, holding her.

Salads arrive from Lettuce Feed You at the same time as Greek sampler platters from The Parthenon. While Gene pays for one of them, I announce out the open door, "Gene, don't deny that your successful cloning of Melanie wasn't a masterpiece." That'll give any surveillance people something interesting to chew on. I hug Cy and tell her, "Thank you for all that you've done for me."

"I swear, I wasn't involved until after you two met." Cy turns to look at Jake and then at Aimee.

Aimee has pulled over a chair to sit down with the guitar, while looking across to the TV screen at Ruth's pictures. Tom's rocket launches from our group at his cabin. Cy holds up the Pony Express logo during her service at the state fair. I hold up an egg in front of a group of upset emperor penguins. Avatrice Gaea has a picnic for us. The Double Bubble and deer crash in Wisconsin. The Pony Express has Minion as a hood ornament. We pick and wear blueberries. A group of us pose with artificially red hair. Most of us, with Savanna, pose with Kelly at her ceremony. Yolanda and I pose after Social Climbers at the Round

Lake Community College. Erix points at a nuthatch. Tom's house looking like winter. Cy sitting in Prairie Creek. A time-lapse montage shows us clearing out my old apartment and filling up the house with boxes. The Pig's mascot tries to grab Jake's beer while everyone else looks on at Met Stadium. I'm pointing at the AutoDrive car with the Museum Of Questionable Inventions sign behind me. I'm talking with Christie and Salome; Hope must have taken that picture. The my apartment refrigerator contents smile. Hope, Nicole, Erix, Becky, and I sit in the hay of Tom's barn and are blinded by Ruth's camera flash.

Cy explains some of the pictures to Aimee. Aimee plays a song. She sings:

> You wrote you loved me
> I didn't keep it
> cause you wrote it
> in the snow.

She changes her tune. Aimee sings:

> Well, it's snowing in Pigs Eye...

Tom joins in:

> There's snow showers in Milltown too...

I add:

> You can't get the liquid out of the state...

Aimee again:

> You can't go around without a canoe.

It goes drip, drip, drip, drip-drip-drip. (All of us. Others come in dripping.)
Drip, drip, drip, drip-drip-drip.

> The Mighty Miss starts as a drip. (During the verse, others keep dripping.)
> It starts here its long running drop.
> Through 'Sota it takes on more water...
> From here on it can't be stopped.

It goes drip, drip, drip, drip-drip-drip.
Drip, drip, drip, drip-drip-drip.

> Winter snow slips into summer's hot. (Others keep dripping.)
> Humidity keeps us swimming through air.
> That great big fish you thought you just caught...
> is just an angry wet polar bear.

It goes drip, drip, drip, drip-drip-drip.
Drip, drip, drip, drip-drip-drip.

Drip.
Drip.
Drop!

Applause. I tell Aimee, "You've been away, but you haven't forgotten The Minnesota Drip. Can I get you something?"

"Water," she gasps, and people laugh.

In the kitchen, I grab a bottle of water and a mixed plate of food for Aimee and one for Erix. Ray mutters, "So that's why Fran was here. She saw you on TV?" I nod and bring the plates out.

Jake is saying something about my not being crazy and that he knows me like the back of his hand. He looks at the back of his hand and says, "How did that get there?"

"Let's get back to the part about Ricky being the Savior of the Midway," Cy confronts Aimee and me. "How do you figure that?"

Aimee laughs, "What a difference a clue makes! Prospective Tower. It was Prospective Tower. Who was king and grand poobah champion of Prospective Tower? Sure Foot. Who lived within blocks of Prospective Tower? Who climbed it as though it were nothing and then would call down and tell us how great the view was? 'I can see five different sets of fireworks,' he'd say. Who climbed up with me hanging on his back and then climbed down it again? He has no fear of heights. He has no fear of Prospective Tower. He is always trying to save people: me, Melanie, AutoDrive and the cop..." Savanna holds up her hand. I never saved her. "You too? It's second nature to him. He doesn't even know he's doing it."

"What about the glowing? What about disappearing?"

Aimee shrugs, "Ask him."

Everyone turns to me, the Lake Weago community turns to me, Milltown, Pigs Eye, Minnesota, west-central Wisconsin... I shrug. "Some glow sticks might have burst open in my closet on some clothes I was thinking of pitching."

"What about disappearing?"

"It was foggy. I didn't disappear. I just walked away."

Many people including Don and Bucca sit on the floor, with their mouths gaping at us.

"So why did you want to hand out candles the next night?" Nicole accuses me. Steam hisses from her mouth and blows up the bangs of her hair.

"If you remember, I didn't really want to go. It was Becky's idea to go. I didn't know what it was all about. When I got there and realized, I left. You wanted to go back with Faith. Hope wanted candles, I had candles, so we handed out candles. If it had been a field it wouldn't have looked cool, but since it was a hillside off of University Avenue, the candlelight was cool looking and, I guess, inspirational. I wasn't trying–"

Aimee steps in front of me, between Nicole and I. "See? It's second nature to him."

"I wasn't trying to fool anyone, but I also wasn't trying to make a fool of anyone."

Hope intervenes, "Remember Nicky, when we kicked you out of his room at his apartment because he had something private to talk about? That's what he told me."

Ray goes to Nicole, "Hey I lived with him the entire time, and he never told me. Fran stopped by yesterday, because she recognized him, and they still didn't tell me."

"Tell me, who here doesn't have secrets?" I ask them. Yolanda and Erix hold up their hands. I apologize to them. "It's not something that I even fully understood. As Hope told me yesterday, I did something I normally wouldn't do. I hadn't climbed the Prospective Tower in a long time. And I'm not sure why I did it. I didn't mean to hurt you by not telling you, Nicole." I leave to get a plate of food.

I eat some things in the kitchen. I really didn't mean to hurt anyone. It's really strange that good actions and good intentions still can get you into trouble. I go back out. Some people have rearranged. Many have found seats. A cluster of people are talking to Jake. Erix is sitting between Stephanie and Nicole and tells Nicole that I didn't mean to hurt her. Dexter and Mica wave good-bye from the door.

I wave back and announce generally, "Anyone who has not eaten or is still hungry must eat. Ray is a vegetarian and would prefer not to have anything with meat leftover. That's a lot of food that will otherwise have to be shipped to India."

I make way for several people to go into the kitchen. Ruth says, "Food is your friend."

Jake tells me, "You know that crackpot stuff damaged some of your credibility."

"Credibility for what? I don't have any responsibilities." I can be unbelievable.

"I wouldn't say that–" Jake starts.

"The court of public opinion is mixed," Al says.

"It's not a court," I say. "That implies organization and authority. It's the traffic intersection of public opinion."

Jake says, "Cy is working on damage control. She'll be in charge of media relations."

"For what?"

Jake smiles. He grins. This can't be good. The last time he smiled like this was when he set up the Capture The Flag game. "I'm going to tell him now," he announces.

"Tell me what?"

"Flight Control. We're taking it over."

There is no more Flight Control, no more AutoDrive. Jake's lost his mind. In a swift counter-move, I take away his beer. "I know!" I tell him. "We'll gather our team together. We'll all wear black except Tom who forgot to do his laundry. Tom wears neon. We'll use our keen security system know-how that we just happened to teach ourselves to by-pass any security protocols in place at Flight Control. Or we'll just use my entry code which they will have forgotten to change. Inside we'll access the mainframe to download the AutoDrive programs to one convenient disk. All our other teammates will shout, 'Hurry' and 'They're coming' and 'Come on!' But! While grabbing a prototype, someone trips an alarm, and Carl and the guy with windshield glasses are already on their way over, carpooling in the middle of the night. They see us leave and immediately deduce what we've done and that they have to chase after us. They follow us with zero subtlety. We recklessly put the pedal to the metal, and the late night traffic is easy to swerve around without causing us to stop. Shots are fired! Windshield Glasses Guy is aiming a bumping, moving gun at a bumping, moving car. It turns out he is an expert marksman from vehicles, having grown up in North Dakota, shooting wobbly signs from pickup trucks, defying the laws of physics. Our chase is spotted by the police. They are a special kind of police with a radio that can only be used for making vague observations and snide quips. The radio cannot be used for coordinated efforts, contacting additional resources, or reporting specific identifying information. The special police are untrained and less than useless. They can't figure out how to slow their cars down or steer. The special police will give up without eliciting any sympathy. But not before... a whole fleet of AutoDrive prototypes converge on us and head our way. Cy and Wendy take credit for sending them along. Carl and Windshields will be stopped through their own actions, and for some reason, long drawn-out legal battles will not be considered." I take a breath. "Is that your plan?"

Jake says, "You make it sound so easy."

"We can't just take over Flight Control. What about Carl?"

"He has a facial twitch. Did you know that?" Wendy must have told him. "We've bought out the Dumas share for fractions of pennies on the dollar."

My face asks how, so my mouth doesn't have to formulate the word.

Jake moves toward his beer, so I put it behind me. "That Carl Dumas is one tough icicle. I needed someone tougher... more resilient to represent us."

My face asks who.

"Erix was our chief negotiator," Jake grins.

"Erix? You're–"

"He was a dream. He was in rare form. He was the big shot. Without him, we would've looked sane. We bought him a suit. He owned it. He went in there, shook hands, and took over Carl's seat. Erix sat. He listened. When a question was addressed to him, he would ponder and stare Carl down. Only when Carl's expression changed, would Erix nod and turn to me, and I would take over. It was art. It was a dream. I thought we had a fifty-fifty chance of pulling it off. We really couldn't have done it without him. He bullied the whole room without a word. Two of them were probably scrambling to investigate him while we were talking. I don't think they could find anything on him. We owe him. We've consolidated most of the outlying interests, most came cheap. We even used the crackpot angle once or twice. Almost everyone was happy to bail from all the bad publicity." Jake holds out his hand. "My beer, please."

Erix nods, unknowingly.

"Not so fast." His voice isn't slurred. He isn't leaning. His skin isn't blotchy or discolored or moving like an alien has taken control of him. You have to watch for these things.

"Here's the breakdown. Carl has already contacted us wanting to renig. That was when we were packing up the bulk of the equipment and all those toy cars. Wendy has also been beneficial, but we made it seem like we were picking her at random. I also received a call on my personal Flight Control phone from an anonymous party wanting to buy Flight Control with a nine percent profit. They went to 13 while I still said no. For the few remaining investors we have taken back our offers. We're playing hardball. If we don't get them, we aren't worried. But we will be trying to reel them in before Lefty's experiment. Wendy is ready to go back to work. So are Scott, Clarence, Barbara, Harvey, and Robin. So am I. We are all ready to work for you. Al would like to join us."

"I'm not going to be involved in Flight Control unless it is done my way."

"Agreed. Welcome aboard." Jake shakes my hand.

What just happened? "Wait. How did you keep this secret from me?"

"We made a pact not to tell you until we agreed otherwise. We just broke that pact."

"Oh. We should get Cameron from Owatonna Opticals."

If I do this, I need to keep perspective in my work and establish the same level of responsibility for the company. I need to make sure that what we do doesn't go against my principles and could not be used in a way that would go against my principles. That's the way to keep morality current with technology; don't let technology be created in an imaginary world that has no consequences. I had lost sight of that concept. Or else I never really had it. Now it will be a key consideration of the work.

Structural integrity sensors would be nice. It wouldn't be tough to add a few simple circuits to safeguard the occupants of a compromised vehicle. A higher order of redundant sensory input would be good too. People don't rely on one level of sensory information, why should AutoDrive?

I want to get it right.

They're all staring at me again.

Hope tells Jake, "If he's in, I'd like a piece of this." They shake hands.

Jake says, "Everyone needs something they believe in, a true challenge. We just want to snowpack onto yours."

Once AutoDrive is completed, then work can start on the flying car.

Aimee plays the guitar and bangs the back of it to simulate big fireworks. Erix joins in for the background fireworks sound effects, as he did originally.

Boom

Pop

Boom

Poppity-pop-pop

Boom
Pop
Boom
Fizzle-fizzle-fizzle
(repeats)

Aimee sings and shouts:
Mint chocolate chip
ice cream drip
rolls from the roof
s'where we lay

Sticky-wicky fingers
firework burst lingers
smartest stupid goof
you keep away
Hopes and dreams

Rockets drizzle
unfazable and proper
we should nuzzle
us invincible teens
Hopes and dreams

Booms boom around
moon the moon
Next day redeems
drive vroom-vroom
Hopes and dreams

Nearer to thee
tomorrow redeems
snow body knows
all my dreams
Hopes and dreams
Us invincible teens?
Hopes and dreams

Aimee says to me, "You know, that one was yours."
"My what?"
"Your song."
"What do you mean?"
"Who the F did you think? Unfazable and proper."
"Wait. We should nuzzle?!? Smartest stupid goof?!?"

"Right."

"She was seeing Tom."

"He asked her out. I told you, she loved all of you." I look at Tom. Cy brings out a lit cupcake for Ruth. We sing our own version of a happy birthday song for her, hoping that this time it's actually her birthday. Ruth blows out the candle and helps Cy distribute cupcakes to everyone.

That reminds me. I go into my room and put six crashing cars in a bag for Hope. I come back out and hand it to her. She looks in the bag and rubs the side of her head. She says, "We'll give these to the kids on their way out of school tomorrow. What would you think of Savanna down here in the living room and Aimee upstairs in the living room? I don't think Savanna could take the stairs in her condition."

"I can stay at a motel," Aimee says. Hope and I stare at her. "Okay, here is fine! I'm sorry! I'll be in Ricky's room. We'll flip to see who gets the bed." She runs out and runs back in with her bag.

"That was fast."

"I left it in the bushes."

"Dan? Do you have a place to stay?"

"Jake's!"

Yolanda and Paige, do you have a place to stay?"

"Paige's dorm room."

"Please bring back some food with you."

Jake offers Aimee blueberries. "I don't still do that."

"What?"

"Orgasm to the sweet succulent taste of blueberries."

"Oh."

"Now it's just Blue Razzles." Jake returns to the kitchen. "He's such a goof," Aimee observes.

Lefty shakes my hand, "I will see you tomorrow morning."

"Good night."

"What's up?" Todd asks.

"I'm taking part in Lefty's experiment tomorrow," I tell him.

"What experiment?" Aimee asks.

"Lefty is using a functional MRI and special equipment to read people's short-term memories and record and transcribe what they see."

"All of your short-term memories?"

"Yes."

"How far back does this go?"

"For me, weeks."

"So everything that happened tonight, today, the AutoDrive stuff..." I nod.

"Everything?" Cy asks. I nod. "What about your account numbers and PIN numbers and phone numbers?"

"I talked with them about all that. None of that will get published. None of the technical details of AutoDrive–"

"Published?!?" Becky says. "How about sex?"

"No thanks Becky, I'm seeing Hope right now."

"No. I mean–"

"They told me that health and medical issues will be left out, which wasn't a concern. I have the strength of ten men." Stephanie snickers. "I'm just not as strong as Stephanie."

"What about all our names?" Cy asks.

"You can still use them."

"No, will they be in the transcript?"

"If I remember your name, yes, it will be in the transcript."

"I don't think it should. I think our names should be changed."

Todd laughs, "Tom has already changed his name."

"No, I haven't."

"Yes, you have." The twins battle. "Tom changed the pronunciation of his our name."

"Pfuloree is pronounced with a short U," Tom says.

"No, it's a long U," Todd says.

I get out my phone. "I'm calling your parents."

"Don't bother," Todd says. "They agree with the rest of us. It's a long U."

They continue to argue while I ask Cy, "Would you like to have a different name?"

"Is that possible?"

"Yes, all I have to do is remember a different name."

"Can you do that?"

"Hey Ray, what's your name?"

"Cameron."

"See? I can do it."

Several people want their names changed. Will says he likes the name Davis from the movie Twelve Angry Men. I tell him that's not a name. I mean, that's not a first name. Besides Davis sounds made up. They turn to books for ideas. Todd reads that, "Minnesota has 90,000 miles of shoreline... more than California, Florida, and Hawaii combined!"

Tom replies, "That's such a meaningless statistic. It's like asking which has more edges a jar or a sponge?"

I check my watch. It's getting late.

Jake asks me, "You don't have any Blue Razzles, do you?" I shake my head. He nods. "I'm going to take Dan home. Is that your name? He has an early flight out."

I say, "I don't care what anybody says about you, Jake. You're a good man."

People clarify their names with me before leaving. I'm sure this sort of thing happens to everyone. Todd grabs my ears and says, "Boeggity-boeggity-boeggity." Ruth thanks me for the party, although I'm not certain I know how it happened. Red tells Hope everything will be all right. Aimee borrows my race car pajamas. Faith, Hope, and Nicole set up a bed for Savanna in the living room. Savanna tells me, "I'm trying to remember all the names that people mentioned. Some of them were pretty good."

Aimee comes out in my pajamas and tells me, "An acorn is growing in your bathroom." She says good night. I say good night as well.

I follow Aimee into my room. Nicole follows me into my room.

I get out a quarter. Right. Now, I've got a Minnesota quarter. I tell Aimee to call it.

Aimee shakes her head with a smirk. She does a flip. "Okay, your turn."

"The bed is all yours," I tell her. Aimee jumps in with my teddy bear from Melanie and gives my alarm clock a funny look.

I turn to Nicole. She asks, "For Lefty's experiment, what do you do?"

"I remember everything." I get out the toy MRI and set it on my dresser.

Nicole sternly asks, "What's so special about that?" Hope comes in and listens.

"Not everyone remembers everything."

"No. Why do you have to go someplace special to remember everything?"

"Because they're recording what I remember."

"Oh, they have a recording device. I have one upstairs. You have one on your phone."

"No. This one reads thoughts, memories in short-term memory."

"I don't have one of those. I'll have to get one. But what's the difference?"

"You can't lie in your thoughts."

She thinks about that, "Are you sure? I know people who lie to themselves all the time."

"I never thought of that."

"Some people don't know the difference between lies and truths."

"I guess at least in my thoughts there's an impression of how others see me."

"Through your eyes. That's not real either."

"But it's as real as anything I know."

"So I haven't talked you out of this?"

"Not even close."

Nicole hugs me. She has the strangest look on her face. She leaves.

I get out my sleeping bag, a sheet, and a blanket. I wad up a sweatshirt as a pillow.

Hope asks, "How are you going to get to Lefty's experiment?"

Aimee says, "I can drive him."

"It could last all day."

"I don't have anything else going on."

Hope kisses me good night. She seems to be blushing as she leaves.

"Do you know how good you've got it?" Aimee asks me, while reaching for the light. I shake my head. "I didn't think so." She turns off the light.

"We missed you, America."

Hope comes back in. "Dream. Dream like you have never dreamt before." She kisses me. I fall asleep.

54
Lab Rat

My dreams are as intense as a cold wind blowing in from Saskatchewan. Hope wakes me up, kissing me with every lip on her face. She takes my hand and pulls me up. Aimee whistles from my bed, and I notice what little Hope is wearing.

"Where are we going?" I ask.

Hope grunts, "Upstairs." Oh. Hope pulls me upstairs. Dawn shows its first signs of cracking. "Nicole and I talked all night. We decided that you need a way to remember me."

"Hope, I'm not going to forget you."

"We'll make sure of it." Hope takes me into her room and makes certain I will always remember her. How could I not?

I kiss Hope good-bye using every lip on my face. I grab some clothes from my room and jump in the shower. Back in my room, Aimee tells me that Nicole left a note. It says, "If you don't come back, I'll leave lights for you." ♥

Aimee says, "You aren't going to actually wear that, are you?" I look at what I have on. "Make you a deal. I'll pick something out for you. And you make me some coffee."

"We don't drink coffee."

"None of you?"

"Ray and I don't."

"What about upstairs?"

"I don't know. And I've never raided their kitchen before."

Aimee gets up, sets my bear aside, scratches my race car pajamas, and looks at my clothes. "These don't even fit you." She looks at my closet. She goes through my closet.

"I can't wear anything with metal on it."

"Why?"

"The MRI."

"Oh. Okay, I'm going to check with Ray." I hear Aimee knock on Ray's door. I hear her tell him something about "he doesn't have any clothes." She brings back a shirt. "Try this on." I take off my shirt and try on Ray's shirt. "Much better," Aimee says. "Now if we can get me a coffee and a California Muffin, we'll be okay."

"What's a California Muffin?" I ask as she leaves. She stops in her tracks and comes back. "We have bakeries. They have muffins..."

"There is no muffin in a California Muffin. Where is this experiment?"

"The university."

"They should have something close. I'm surprised how long you've survived in the wilderness." She pads off to the shower. Twenty seconds later I hear a scream. Ray and I dash to the bathroom. Aimee is catching her breath and points with her thumb over her shoulder, "Whose chick?"

"That's Beth."

"Beth?" Ray asks.

"You know, Beth, bath... She came from Tom."

"Remind me to kick his butt. Better yet, we'll get him back."

"It's his turn."

Aimee shakes her head, "It's **my** turn." She shuts the door. When it's my turn, my inflatable elephant and helium tank could get a rise out of his neighborhood.

Ray says, "She doesn't mind being naked, does she?"

"Which one, Aimee or Beth?" Ray goes back into his room without answering.

In my room, I change my phone ringer to an engine revving, and I use the phone to try to find California Muffins in the Twin Cities. No luck. Maybe she'd like Minnesota Muffins. I don't think she's in that sort of mood. I take off my watch and bag up some clothes. I squeeze some oranges for juice and have some Major Munch separated into distinct cereal categories.

I offer Aimee a glass of orange juice. She almost spits it out pointing at my cereal bowls. "I can't believe you still do that! How old are you?"

I shrug and clean up my stuff. "Are you ready?"

She chugs the freshly squeezed orange juice and nods.

Ray answers the door. "You got a package from India." I wasn't expecting anything. Wait a minute... I look at it. I'll deal with this when I get back. I throw on the lab coat I got at Southedge.

Her car is full of luggage and boxes. My mouth drops. "Do you need a place to stay?"

"No," she lies.

I grab a couple boxes, reminding myself of my strength, and take them inside. "Hey Ray. Could I get your help moving Aimee in?" Ray smiles and comes out. We move her stuff in. We drive off. "This your car?"

She rolls her eyes, "Rental. How do we get there?" I navigate. A sign at the end of the block reminds everyone of this evening's Art Trade. That's right, it is the first Thursday of the month, isn't it? I call Ray and suggest that he get involved. The time is right to stir up the Lake Weago art community. "What happened to your car?"

"It died last weekend."

"What of?"

"Exhaustion."

She wildly drives across town to the university, stops in the middle of traffic, and runs into a coffee shop. Los Angeles driving in Minnesota. Traffic works its way around her car, glaring at me. She runs back out. I navigate her into a parking ramp. We take the elevator into the tunnels where we quickly get lost. The tunnels wind and twist like caves that turn three times in two steps. We could be under here for eons. I take a few more turns. The dinosaurs aren't extinct. They're just lost in the tunnels under the university. We follow a pterodactyl for a while on the theory that it will head for the light of day, but actually it is trying to lead us to its nest to feed its young. It is tearing down signs and eating them as it goes, but it leaves a piece of a sign with an arrow for the Teska tooth mark fMRI Unit. We turn off, head up a ramp through a cream colored cinder block corridor, grab a student newspaper by the pop machine, and turn a corner for room 41.

We turn on the lights. I borrow a pen and paper from her. I write her a note explaining that the mirror is a one-way window. I pace. I read the newspaper. It has an editorial cartoon with me tossing a beach ball titled Ideas in front of an AutoDrive car. The caption reads, Throwing Out Ideas. I don't get it. I pace. I pick up a piece of paper. It says that goldfish have a three second memory span; how did they test that?!? Aimee is reading my Safari Of The Mind book. I go over to the mirror. I look at myself. I stick out my tongue. I make faces. On my fifth face, Aimee whistles me back to my chair and hands me a surfer magazine. Technically it's Go Away, a travel magazine, but this issue is dedicated to surfing.

It says that if you like to surf, you could go to California or Hawaii, but you might as well look for a wave in Minnesota. Ha. Seriously, Australia is the place for surfing. There are three hazards to surfing. The jellyfish and the sharks are supposed to be the dangers to surfers, but the real danger is what you bring with you, the surfboard. When you wipe out, and you will wipe out, you and your surfboard will get separated. You'll get as far apart as the line attached to your ankle will allow. Then your surfboard will boomerang right back at you. You might think you can swim away from it, but listen mate, it's tied to your ankle. You're not going to get away from it. You might think, I'll just duck under it, but that's what that little fin is for on the underside of the board. It'll part your hair if you try to clear it from below. And if you really do manage to clear it and head down, now you've got a torpedo headed right after you. Here's what you've got to do. Let the surfboard come after you. Here it comes. It's just about to hit you. Now dash to one side, hop on, and go back for another ride.

Several miles off the east coast of Australia in the Tasman Sea, stretching from Wollongong in the south, up past Sydney and Bondi Beach and following the coastline all the way up to Surfer's Paradise is the Not So Great Barrier Reef. The Not So Great Barrier Reef is composed of all the surfboards that were carried out to sea since about the 1950s. Marine biologists have discovered that the lowermost layers are mostly wooden surfboards. The nearer and upper layers are plastic and fiberglass boards, all twisted up in old brown kelp and ropes and old fishing nets. The real danger is the instability of the Not So Great Barrier Reef. Some future storm could destroy the Not So Great Barrier Reef, sending thousands of surfboards hurtling back at the beaches.

Avatrice Gaea knocks on the door, comes in, and hugs Aimee. "I heard you were in town. Welcome home. How are you?"

"I'm good. I'm staying at their house for now."

Avatrice holds onto Aimee and turns to me, "Were you glad you went to Wakan Teebe?"

"Yes, thank you for inviting me. I wondered why you invited me."

"It was the right thing to do. Are you and Hope still doing well?"

"Definitely." We sit and stare at each other for a moment. "Did you... Were you the one who brought us together?" Her eyes sparkle. I smile. "You did, didn't you?" And that's when Lefty, Lena, Sven, and Dr. Forrester enter the room. They all take a moment to drool over my lab coat, feeling its fine weave and its meticulous craftsmanship. While the others greet Avatrice, Sven takes me down the hall, asking me how I'm feeling. He has me provide a urine sample. I once knew a guy who collected outmoded phones, so I give him a sample for his collection. I change into my extra pair of race car pajamas.

Lefty is saying, "The vagus is the tenth and longest of the cranial nerves." He's getting on my nerves now. Avatrice wishes Lefty luck. I guess she knows I don't believe in luck. Or else she doesn't believe this has anything to do with me. Aimee wishes me luck anyway.

It's time to play lab rat again for the first time.

"Lie still," Lena tells me as I'm being slid into the giant coffee maker. I stop her and wiggle my body frantically, then I give her the okay sign.

"How far back can you remember vividly?" Lefty asks from the other side of a window.

"The weekend I first met Hope, dressing up in the gorilla suit for Tom's."

This is clean plastic, like shiny white silk or a plastic blanket of snow. I can almost see myself. The arm restraints keep me from running my fingers through my hair. The coffee maker hums a familiar tune. That's my ATM's hum!

"Ricky?"

"Yeah?"

"What are you doing?"

"Nothing."

"Quit shifting around, please."

"Yes, sir. This is really some setup. As long as Paul Bunyan doesn't come looking for his coffee maker, this should turn out well. I'm really looking forward to–"

"Ricky. Ricky! We're ready to begin. What is your earliest short-term memory?"

"Unbuckling my seatbelt and putting on my head at Tom's house."

"Your head?"

"The gorilla head."

"Right. Okay, hang on a minute."

Speaking of having your head on straight, I'm not sure if they have their heads on straight. And since they may wind up listening in, I mean that while I trust them, they certainly are explorers in unchartered territory. How's that for covering my tracks?

"Ricky? You were describing your earliest short-term memories. Think it through from that moment to now. Hang on."

I'm glad I'm not claustrophobic. I might be in here for a while.

"Anytime you're ready."

I sit on the front steps of a house that isn't mine. I'm watching for guests. It is a quarter past dusk. The light above the front door floods the steps in light, making it difficult for me to see much more than silhouettes, and the fur of my mask does not help me to distinguish the guests from the passersby or the swaying bushes. Not that I'm complaining about the dimming light, because I really don't have to see at all to direct people verbally, and I like what evening breeze I feel.

Up the sidewalk a silhouette moves more than a few yards, and I decide it probably isn't a bush. Footsteps. The silhouette comes closer, and I decide definitely that it is not a bush because the silhouette is walking a silhouette dog. Bushes can't do this, I've checked. The silhouette is leading by a couple feet over the silhouette dog, but neither are any threat to the sound barrier, let alone any Olympic records. I'm doubting whether either will turn up this house's walkway due to what seems to be an overabundance of maturity.

They pass me, apparently not noticing a person wearing a gorilla outfit and sitting on the front steps of a house. Or perhaps considering the house, it's just par for the course. Two moments go by. A car pulls up. The inside light of the car shows this to be a woman I don't know but certainly young enough not to be weighed down by much maturity baggage at all...

Afterword

As the preceding document indicates, the fMRI-Memmeograph STM experiment was a success. News of the experiment's success spread, as the patient might say, "like a fire through Swede Hollow." Neither the university nor the researchers involved were prepared to immediately release the results of this experiment nor its conclusions and practical applications. However external pressures have caused the advanced publication of the recorded portion of the experiment, the preceding document. A subsequent publication in a scientific journal will contain conclusions and comprehensive descriptions of this and the other fMRI-Memmeograph STM experiments.

In response to a veritable plethora of requests, this office must assure the reader that the technology described within is not currently available for use and probably never will be available to help find the keys your spouse or other family member lost.

In looking at the results of the transcription, Dr. Vagues disagrees with Ricky's perspective on several of the events and requested edits to the transcription. Conversations led to an agreement to include the following statement here: "The events transcribed here are from the perspective of one individual. Other individuals involved may have different interpretations of the events. If there is a doubt regarding the characters and actions within, please refer to the indicia at the front of the text."

Technical details regarding the creation of AutoDrive and the fMRI-Memmeograph STM experiment were removed from this text to protect their continued development.

Lena
Minnesota University

Glossary

bushwhacked - an unprovoked attack.

cachinnates - laughs noisily.

Calvinball - game where the rules are made up as you go along. From Calvin and Hobbes by Bill Watterson.

chipmunkese - chattering, storytelling language of chipmunks and other fast talkers.

deus ex machina - (Greek) god from a machine; a plot device in Greek plays where a god or long dead hero appears to solve everything in the end.

effluerage - a gentle stroking or caressing technique used in massage.

fenderberg drills - checking the vehicle for wheel well ice blocks. Out of season Fenderberg Drills are dangerous and illegal if not executed by trained professionals. Trained professionals must watch out for rookies.

funnellator - a water balloon slingshot.

Gigglitis - contagious giggling disease often overwhelming young people.

gongoozler - someone who stares for hours.

holm - an island in a river.

jobation - a long tedious scolding; a lengthy reprimand; a tirade.

Hahawakpa - (Ha Ha Wakpa, Dakota) the Mississippi River.

histoplasmosis - a respiratory illness caused by inhaling festering bat droppings.

hotdish - casserole.

Kaposia - (Dakota) White Rock village of the Kapoja, lightning fast lacrosse players.

kryptonite - the weakness of Superman.

lagniappe - an unexpected gift or benefit.

lutefisk - whitefish prepared in lye.

Mahpiyawicasta - (Ma-hpi-ya-wi-ca-sta, Dakota) Man-of-the-Sky. Reyataotonwe (Inland Village) Chief in the 1830s.

Makoce nupa umanipi - (Dakota) "We're walking in two worlds."

mammiferous - having breasts.

Mde Maka Ska - (Dakota) White Earth Lake. Large round lake on Milltown's west side.

Mde Unma - (Dakota) Other Lake. The other big round lake.

Mdewakanton - (Dakota) Spirit Lake Village. Band (subtribe) of the Dakota.

Memmeograph - device that interprets and records fMRI data from short-term memory areas of the brain (the subiculum, the anterior cingulate, and the hippocampus).

muliebrity - state of being a woman; qualities or characteristics of women.

mumblese - the language of mumbling people. Fluency is shown through conversation.

newel - a post supporting a handrail at the bottom of a stairs.

nomenclator - one who assigns names as in scientific classification.

non-maleficence - ethical duty to not injure others.

Glossary - continued

Owamniyomni - (Dakota) the whirlpool, also known as St. Anthony Falls.

pharos - lighthouse.

Pigs Eye - the city of Pigs Eye was named after Pierre Pigs Eye Parrant the French-Canadian whiskey trader and scoundrel, who led squatters to Kaposia at White Rock. Pigs Eye is the capital of Minnesota. With Milltown, it is known as the Twin Cities.

rutilant - bright red in color.

SETI - Search for Extra Terrestrial Intelligence.

skyways - second or third floor corridors that connect buildings over streets.

snowcone - finely crushed ice packed in a paper cone and rounded on top, flavored with grape, cherry and other artificially flavored syrups. Never eat yellow snowcones.

snowpack - to join up or team up.

squamous - scale covered.

sudorific - sweat causing.

tricyclists - kids on tricycles.

wacipi - (Dakota) powwow.

wahumapa wasna - (Dakota) corn balls.

Wakan Teebe - (Dakota) dwelling of the Great Spirit; the cave in Pigs Eye.

Wanagi Wita - (Dakota) Spirit Island, holm in the Mississippi River below the falls.

wojapi - (Dakota) frybread.